Elizabeth Mary (Smee) Odling

**Memoir of the Late Alfred Smee, F. R. S.**

Elizabeth Mary (Smee) Odling

**Memoir of the Late Alfred Smee, F. R. S.**

ISBN/EAN: 9783337094201

Printed in Europe, USA, Canada, Australia, Japan

Cover: Foto ©Raphael Reischuk / pixelio.de

More available books at **www.hansebooks.com**

# MEMOIR

OF THE LATE

# ALFRED SMEE, F.R.S.

# MEMOIR

OF THE LATE

# ALFRED SMEE, F.R.S.

BY

## HIS DAUGHTER.

WITH A SELECTION FROM HIS

## MISCELLANEOUS WRITINGS.

LONDON:
GEORGE BELL AND SONS, YORK STREET,
COVENT GARDEN.
1878.

LONDON:
PRINTED BY WILLIAM CLOWES AND SONS,
STAMFORD STREET AND CHARING CROSS.

# PREFACE.

It is with much diffidence that I submit this Memoir to the public. It was undertaken partly as a duty to the memory of my father, partly in the belief that it would not be unacceptable to the many readers of his different works. His pursuits, indeed, were so earnest and various, and his writings extended over such a wide range of subjects, that some account, however imperfect, of his doings, and some selection, however incomplete, from his writings, could not, I felt, be without interest to the general reader.

I was further desirous to bring under public notice a record of my father's inventions and researches, especially in that branch of science to which he first gave the name of Electro-Metallurgy. His treatise on this subject, which went through several editions, has long been out of print. From it has been taken the introductory chapter on the history of Electro-Metallurgy, included in the present selection.

I have devoted considerable space, also, to the enunciation and discussion of my father's views on Mental Philosophy, and have extracted several passages from 'The Mind of Man,' his last work on this his favourite subject, and the last published work of his life.

The numerous scientific papers, lectures, pamphlets, anonymous and other writings of my father have also furnished contributions to the present volume. Artists will find something to interest them in his remarks on binocular vision, and on the methods resorted to by various eminent painters to produce effects whereby the results of binocular perspective are more or less successfully imitated.

In connection with the potato disease, the views put forth by the subject of this Memoir in 1845-47 receive fresh interest from the confirmation afforded them by the recent researches of Mr. Worthington Smith.

My father's knowledge of gardening and love for natural history in all its branches meet with frequent illustration. Some account more especially is given of the experimental garden which he formed at Wallington, in Surrey, now, indeed, become almost of celebrity through his well-known book entitled 'My Garden.' It may interest many to know that this garden is still kept up, in tribute to its founder's memory, by my brother, Mr. Alfred Hutchison Smee.

E. M. O.

# CONTENTS.

## CHAPTER I.

### AGE - TO 16—1818 TO 1834.

## CHAPTER II.

### AGE 16 TO 21—1834 TO 1839.

## CHAPTER III.

### AGE 22 TO 24—1840 TO 1842.

## CHAPTER IV.

### AGE 25 TO 29—1843 TO 1847.

## CHAPTER V.

### AGE 30 TO 31—1848 TO 1849.

## CHAPTER VI.

### Age 31 to 36—1849 to 1854.

## CHAPTER VII.

### Age 36 to 40—1854 to 1858.

## CHAPTER VIII.

### Age 41 to 48—1859 to 1866.

## CHAPTER IX.

### AGE 46 TO 52—1864 TO 1870.

## CHAPTER X.

### AGE 52 TO 57—1870 TO 1875.

## CHAPTER XI.

### 57TH YEAR OF HIS AGE—1875.

## CHAPTER XII.

### AGE 57 TO 58—1876 TO 1877.

# APPENDIX.

## LIST OF ILLUSTRATIONS.

---

## LIST OF BOOKS BY ALFRED SMEE.

# MEMOIR OF ALFRED SMEE.

## CHAPTER I.

### 1818 TO 1834.

Alfred Smee born June 18th, 1818—Family—Infancy—Love for fruit—Goes to
St. Paul's School—His natural power of observation displayed as a boy—
Fights a bully—Other traits in his character as a boy—An adept in climbing
trees—Ignorant of all games—Love of animals shown—Dislikes cruelty to
dumb creatures.

ALFRED SMEE, the subject of this biography, was born on the
anniversary of the battle of Waterloo, the 18th of June, 1818.
He was the second son of William Smee, who held the position of
Accountant-General to the Bank of England. The Smee family
is derived from an ancient English stock. From the time of
Charles I. the family was to be found in the county of Suffolk;
previously to the turbulent times of the Civil Wars, they crossed
the country from the north. Many curious traditions exist in
the family; but as I am not writing the history of the Smees,
but of one of its members only, there is no need here to narrate
them. It suffices therefore here to say that my father's great-
grandfather was a man of considerable influence and wealth in
the county of Suffolk, and was, like the rest of the family, a
staunch Tory; his high character and integrity were known to
all around him. He was, as I have heard, on intimate terms with
Sir Hans Sloane and with Lord North, and he knew also the
renowned Wedgwood. On the tombstone of this ancestor of ours
are the significant and laconic words: " An honest man."

Alfred Smee's father, William Smee, was being educated at
St. John's College, Cambridge, when family misfortunes obliged
him to leave the University to seek his own livelihood. I have
heard my grandfather say how he wept on the bridge at
Cambridge at the thought of being obliged to leave that aca-
demical town. Had Lord North not been dismissed from office,

my grandfather would have had a good government appointment given to him; however, that was not to be, and so William Smee entered the service of the Bank of England. He, like his grandfather, bore a high character for integrity; and that, coupled with uncommon talents and an iron will, made him respected and esteemed throughout the mercantile community of the City of London. On his death a long resolution was passed at the Court of Directors of the Bank of England, testifying to the "high integrity of his character and his indefatigable exertions" in the discharge of his duties, and to the high esteem in which he was held by all who knew him. Some years previously the directors wished him to become a member of their body, but my grandfather declined this honour; and when the time for the election drew near, he disqualified himself from becoming a director by withdrawing certain sums of money from the Bank stock, and so remained in his old position. Whether he acted in this case wisely may, I think, be considered an open question. When William Smee was between thirty and forty years of age, he married a young Suffolk lady of the name of Ray, and she was ever to him a wise, frugal, and an intelligent companion. For several years they resided in a house of their own at Camberwell, and it was here, amidst fields and trees and orchards (for Camberwell fifty-eight years ago was very different to the Camberwell of the present day), that Alfred Smee was born, and spent the first few years of his life.

As a child, Alfred Smee was singularly precocious, and, like many precocious children, gave, as my grandmother used to say, a great deal of trouble to his nurse; indeed, that unfortunate attendant must have had a very hard time of it, if the various anecdotes that my grandmother was wont to tell about this madcap boy are to be credited. From his earliest years Alfred Smee had an inordinate love for fruit, to obtain which he would but too frequently rise with the sun, and, eluding the vigilance of the servants, stroll into the garden, climb the trees, and satisfy himself to his heart's content. One day, as my grandfather was walking in his garden, his attention was attracted to a peach-tree full of fruit, which was just ripe. To his dismay a small piece was bitten out of every peach, and all the fruit bore unmistakable signs of a child's teeth. Little Alfred, who was by his side at the time, and who was then about four years old, could not forbear inquiring into the fact whether snails have teeth. Besides an excessive love for fruit, which remained with him till the last, my father ever had from infancy a great love of natural history in all its branches. When he was four years old, through running and over-heating himself on a hot day in June, in a hay-field, after a favourite rabbit that had escaped from its hutch, he became ill with what was then supposed to be a kind of croup, but which proved to be the first attack of hay-fever, a complaint of rare occurrence at that time; but from that summer to a late period of his life he was always a great sufferer from that disagreeable disorder.

In my grandfather's account-book for June 18th, 1823, is the following entry, which shows the far-seeing character of the former in the estimation of his second son's abilities, this son being at the time five years old.

This day I have transferred £10 Imperial £3 per Cent. Annuity into the names of William Smee, of the Bank, Gentleman, and Alfred Smee, of Camberwell, Gentleman. I have been much gratified with the good conduct and zeal displayed by my dear Alfred in his studies, and I hope the Almighty will continue such dispositions, which I confidently think will lead to a brilliant result.

After my grandfather had left Camberwell to reside at the Bank of England, my father went, as did his elder brother, to St. Paul's School. At that school, which prides itself on having educated Milton, Marlborough, and many distinguished men, Alfred Smee did not shine as a scholar; but notwithstanding his want of book learning, he left a mark, and at St. Paul's School his name is held in respect. As a schoolboy his powers for natural observation were a strong feature in his character. One of my father's schoolfellows (afterwards one of our judges) amused him one day by telling him that, on first coming to school, Alfred Smee's first words to him were, "What a long back you have got!" The other boys were questioning him on his name, age, parentage, &c., but only Alfred Smee noticed this peculiarity of his. "I have often," added the judge, "laughed over this observation of yours."

While he was a small boy at school, his prowess was shown by thrashing a "big bully" some years older than himself; and though Alfred Smee was not a fighting boy, and small and unskilful in the art, yet his temper could not brook the imperious tones of a bully. The unfortunate boy who had incurred his ire was wofully "mauled," to the delight of the rest of the school. Another trait of his character we see in the following anecdote. At the time he was at St. Paul's, the schoolroom clock was fast, consequently the boys got into trouble for coming late. The clockmaker was made aware of the fact, but several mornings passed, and the clock was not set right. In my father's class the master was very strict, and, quite ignoring that the fault lay in the clock, caned the unfortunate boys for being late. This was more than young Smee could submit to—it was an injustice; he accordingly hit upon the following expedient to set right such a dismal order of affairs. He persuaded the classes under his master to march up Cheapside in single file to the clockmaker's at the Royal Exchange. Then every boy in turn, according to his age, was to enter the shop, and taking off his cap, say, "Please, sir, master's compliments, and will you put the schoolroom clock right?" At first the man was very civil, but as naturally may be supposed, after about the tenth boy had appeared with the same message, he became excessively irate. Young Smee entered the shop, saw the fury the man was in, made a wry face at him, did not wait to say anything, but rushed out of the shop. "What did he say?" was the eager inquiry. "Oh, nothing," replied young Smee. In went the next boy (a very stupid boy I have heard, who turned out badly in life), but it was too late : the man, exasperated beyond all endurance, caught him and thrashed him. Off went then the boys round the Exchange, running in and out of the legs of the sober merchants, and finished their amusement, much to the discomfiture of that respectable body of citizens. It is almost needless to add that the schoolroom clock was speedily set right, and though the clockmaker made a complaint to the master, yet the latter was too much amused with the story to chastise the boys for their audacious expedient. After this adventure it was a long time before St. Paul's schoolroom clock went again in advance of Greenwich time.

About the same time a very favourite amusement of Alfred Smee's was to climb trees. In this accomplishment he excelled. He would climb the highest trees where no other boy would venture, and, to use his own expression, weave in and out the branches, swaying the while like a bird, and ascending, and ascending, until he reached the topmost branch ; when, waving his cap to his schoolfellows below, it was duly acknowledged by that august assembly that he had done "their dads." One poor boy, however, tried to emulate him, but not being so skilful, fell into a pond of water beneath, from the effects of which he died ; and so young Smee remained undisputed master of the trees.

With cricket or other amusements of schoolboys my father never meddled. In after-life he never entered into such recreation as billiards, backgammon, or whist, or any other game. Strange though it may seem, yet he was ignorant of any of the games belonging to cards, and not only did he not know their names, but he was also totally ignorant of the names of the cards themselves.

While he was a schoolboy, as at other periods of his life, he was extremely fond of animals and birds. Not many days before my father's death, an old schoolfellow of his came to see him, and he talked with him about the innumerable rabbits in hutches—simple contrivances, all made by young Alfred Smee—that he used to go and see in a court of the Bank, between the hours of school. Here it should be stated, that from early boyhood my father showed a great aptitude for carpentry. A few old boxes, and a few pieces of wood, nails, a saw, gimlet, hammer, and a few of the like common implements, were sufficient for him to make many ingenious contrivances. We have still an old table that had a fractured leg, which was bound up and mended by him when he was but a boy of eight years old, and I think even an indifferent person would admit that a grown-up man, or even a carpenter, could scarcely have done the job better.

Besides keeping innumerable rabbits at the Bank, he used also to keep some pigeons. In one of the anecdotes in 'Instinct and Reason,' he relates how he once, on leaving London for some days, left the birds in charge of a servant. Upon returning, the first question naturally asked was, as to the health of the favourite birds.

But (says he) I received the startling answer, " Lor', indeed, sir, I never once thought of them." Their fate seemed inevitable; and up I ran to the dovecot, to confirm, as I thought, my worst fears. To my astonishment, however, all the birds were in good health. The young ones looked fat, and the old ones had built new nests, although not a particle of food nor a drop of water was to be found. As the birds had done so long without food and water, I thought they could not hurt by waiting a little longer, and therefore I determined to see what they did. After a little time the birds became uneasy, and, after pluming their feathers, they all flew off. I watched them as far as the eye could reach, and I could trace them beyond Shoreditch Church; and after an hour and a half they came back. There is no doubt that they had flown off to the fields for food, and thus were not the least the worse for the servant's inattention.

Besides pigeons and rabbits, young Smee had, when a boy, other pets. One of these was a magpie, who used to be allowed his liberty in the room where Alfred Smee and his elder brother were having their early breakfast, before the rest of the family, previous to their setting off to St. Paul's School, where the boys had to be, at those times, by 8 o'clock. This magpie was, like his young master, partial to buttered toast, and he would hop about the table, making a good breakfast. When Mr. Mag had partaken of as much toast as was consistent with his comfort, he would betake himself to tease the dog, who was basking before the fire, by hopping up to the poor beast and awakening him by a violent tug at his tail. At first the drowsy dog would just raise his head, give a growl, and would go to sleep again, upon which Mr. Mag would repeat the same disagreeable operation. When, after several repetitions of the like affront, the poor dog would be fairly roused from his slumbers, then the magpie used to hop round the room in a state of exultation, crying, "Mag, mag, mag!"

But this dog was not always doomed to be made miserable, for my father and his brother were fond of taking him to bed with them, although it was strictly forbidden them to do so. As this anecdote is forcibly given in 'Instinct and Reason' as an example of reason in animals, I will quote the rest from that work.

The mamma was determined to stop the practice, went at night into the room, and turned the dog out, and he was compelled to sneak down stairs with tail between his legs. On the next night, however, the boys put the dog into one of the drawers and shut him up, so that, when the mamma came, no dog was found, and the boys afterwards took him to bed. The dog seemed fully to appreciate the boys' movements, and used perfectly to fall in with their plans. Some nights, indeed, the dog was discovered, but generally he was hid up in such an ingenious manner that he was not discovered. If the dog was called or whistled he took no notice, but used to lie perfectly quiet till the boys took him out of his hiding-place.

My father always retained his love for animals, and inculcated that love in his own children. I suppose few other children (if any) have been brought up from infancy with so many kinds of birds, animals, reptiles, and fishes. We had pets in thrushes, blackbirds, canaries, goldfinches, bullfinches, and even nightingales; we had pets in pigeons, pheasants, godwits, magpies, sea-gulls, owls, and hawks. We kept, at different times of our infancy, pet dogs, cats, guinea-pigs, and, amongst many other animals too numerous to enumerate here, was a domesticated wild rabbit. This rabbit used to be allowed to come out at dessert-time, when it would immediately jump up on the table, and glide so dexterously in and out among the glass, that it never broke one or even knocked a wine-glass down, but would stop at the plate of each person present until it received a piece of fruit, after eating which it would continue its walk around the table, allowing everyone to pet and caress it.

This rabbit was specially fond of my father, and he of it, and great was the grief in the family when Bunny at last died of old age. He kept pet hedgehogs and tortoises, and a pet Guernsey lizard, which would partake as a *bonne bouche* of a dish of black beetles for breakfast. He had also at one time a pet toad, which was caught by my father during one of his walks in the wood which formerly existed on the spot where the Crystal Palace now stands. This toad was quite a baby when he first became possessed of it, but it throve so thoroughly upon black beetles, that in due course of time it became a full-grown toad, and lived many years. My father took a great liking to this toad, and was wont, whenever a friend dined with him, to show, as soon as the cloth was removed, to the astonished guest the wonderful powers which this creature possessed of seeing, and its rapidity and unerring seizure of its prey. The unfortunate toad at last met with an untimely death, through a quarrel arising with the Guernsey lizard over one delicious black beetle. The toad received a blow on the head from the lizard which paralysed it. It lingered some time, but ultimately died from its effects. He kept besides pet mice and even a pet rat. The latter's favourite place was in a person's pocket, where he would remain for a long while quite still and comfortable. When he was tired of that locality, he would walk out and sit upon the shoulder, and nestle to a person's neck. In this manner this rat used to frequently perform little journeys through the streets of London; but I am bound to say my father never took him out. The very goldfish knew my father's voice, and when he whistled to them would come up from amongst the various water-plants which were kept in a large tank in the greenhouse at the end of the garden of Finsbury Circus, and take the food from his fingers. Others might whistle to them, but the goldfish took no notice (though it might even be at feeding time) of any other voice but that of my father.

Mr. Smee ever abhorred cruelty to animals, especially when it was occasioned through wanton wilfulness. But, on the other hand, he considered that there are times when animals must suffer for the weal of man; then morbid sentimentality ought not to be permitted to step in to stop experiments which are needful to be made, in order to obtain knowledge by which the sufferings of the human race may be relieved; at the same time those experiments should be conducted in such a manner as to cause as little suffering to the poor beast as it is practicable. The best plan to prevent wanton cruelty to animals is to bring up children from their tender years to love all the lower creatures, and to teach them that God has made them all, and has implanted into them feelings, curious instincts, and to a certain extent reason.

When a boy my father made a fair collection of insects, and a collection of birds' eggs, both of which still exist. He also made a collection of what fossils his limited resources could procure. These are dispersed, but by the catalogue of them, which he neatly wrote in a book, there seem to have been some interesting specimens among them. In this book the names are given, the stratum each specimen was found in, the locality, and whether found by himself, or how otherwise procured.

# CHAPTER II.

## 1834 TO 1839.

Leaves St. Paul's School, age sixteen, and enters as a medical student at King's College, London—Distinguishes himself at King's College; age seventeen —Takes more prizes; age nineteen—Alfred Smee reads his first paper; age twenty—His second paper—Leaves King's College and goes to St. Bartholomew's Hospital—Takes more prizes in 1838—Invents a splint; age twenty-one — Experiment-book — Account-book — Laboratory—Life at the Bank of England—His love of music.

In midsummer 1834, Alfred Smee left St. Paul's School, and in October of the same year he commenced his studies for the medical profession, and became a medical student of King's College, London. Up to this time we have seen him as a boy endowed with strong feelings, possessing a strong will, keen susceptibilities, and an innate love for natural history; a sharp pair of eyes which nothing passed unheeded, a keen sense for fun, an open and very generous disposition, and a kind heart towards his fellow-creatures and the lower animals.

But up to this period of his life he had not shown any disposition for book lore. His literature when a young boy was limited, and it consisted principally of a few works on natural history. For Gilbert White's 'History of Selborne' he ever entertained an unbounded admiration, as he did also for the immortal works of Shakspeare. By this it will be seen that Alfred Smee was not what is termed a "reading man." Of the plays of Shakspeare the 'Tempest,' supposed to be the last written by the poet, was his favourite. Perhaps it may not be out of place here to mention that my father, to the last year of his life, never ceased to speak of the marvellous and unrivalled manner in which Shakspeare's plays were put on the stage by Macready in 1839–40.*

---

\* For a full account of the exquisite pains which Macready gave himself in putting on the stage the plays of Shakspeare, I refer the reader to the interesting diary of that tragedian, edited by Sir Frederick Pollock.

But to return to my subject. As a medical student, Alfred Smee became studious. Indeed, from the moment he became one he never ceased from the most laborious work. At the time my father began his professional career, medical students, as a rule, were not all that could be desired. But too many of them were addicted to idleness, drinking, and other vices; and, indeed, they had the character of being but too frequently very rough members of society. Young Smee, however, though full of fun and of buoyant spirits, was noted for his unexceptionable good conduct, steadiness, and sobriety, and was besides a most hard-working young man.*

Alfred Smee had not been more than two years at King's College before he carried off the silver medal, the prize for Chemistry; Professor Daniell, so well known to the scientific world as the inventor of a battery which bears his name, being professor at King's College at the time. The following year, in 1837, Smee took the silver medal for Anatomy, Partridge being professor; and he also took the silver medal for Physiology, Todd being professor. For the latter he used to prepare the experiments for the lectures which that distinguished physician delivered. In 1837 young Smee also contended for the theological prize at King's College. He lost it by one mark only, and it appeared that his answers on the one hand, and those of the winner of the prize on the other, were so even, that there were thoughts of giving two prizes, as the examiner, the Bishop of London's chaplain, said that the answers in divinity were so excellent as to entitle Alfred Smee to take orders for ordination. I mention this fact particularly, as it shows how, at a very early period, my father's mind was imbued with religious thoughts, which hereafter proved a very remarkable feature in his character.

On the 4th of April, 1838, Alfred Smee's first paper was read before the Geological Society; it was 'On the State in which Animal Matter is usually found in Fossils,' and it was communicated by Professor Royle of King's College. The paper will be found in the Appendix, No. I., of this work.

In the following month, on the 26th of May, 1838, appeared in the 'London Medical Gazette' the second paper from his pen.

---

* In all the testimonials which Alfred Smee received from his masters and professors, his extreme steadiness and good conduct, and the great talent which he displayed in his various professional attainments, are made a great point of.

This was entitled 'On the Chemical Nature of the External Envelope of the Frog's Spawn.' For this see the Appendix, No. II.

The same year Smee left King's College and entered his name on the books at St. Bartholomew's Hospital. King's College Hospital was not then erected, and therefore it was essential for the aspirant to medical fame to gain practical knowledge elsewhere. He became dresser to the eminent surgeon Lawrence, and held the dressership a whole year. Alfred Smee was not long at St. Bartholomew's before he carried off the surgical prize, which consisted of three volumes of books by Lawrence. As at King's College, so did young Smee distinguish himself at St. Bartholomew's by his good conduct, his steadiness, and by his untiring industry. When he was only eighteen years of age, he became engaged to a young lady, whom he married shortly after he had finished his medical education.

In 1839, besides giving much attention to surgery, he also employed himself upon chemistry, and some of his numerous experiments were given to the public the following year. Through an explosion which ensued in conducting one of these varied experiments he met with an accident to one of his eyes, which at the time it was feared would cost him the sight of it. Through the skilful treatment of Sir William Lawrence, the eye was saved, although that eminent surgeon had for two or three days almost despaired of it.

Besides these experiments, Alfred Smee about this time invented a form of splint for fractures, and wrote a paper on it, which appeared in the 'London Medical Gazette' of the 9th of February, 1839. It was published also in the 'Lancet,' and it was also translated into French and into German. The title of the paper was, 'On the Formation of Moulding Tablets for Fractures.' The splint was tried in every hospital in the metropolis, and was used at St. Bartholomew's, as well as in other hospitals. Some years later (in 1846), after gutta-percha had come into use, he invented a modification of the above tablets, and the article on 'Gutta Percha Splints' was also published in the 'London Medical Gazette.' Both these papers will be found in the Appendix, No. III., of this work. Following these two papers will also be found a very curious paper on 'Photogenic Drawing,' which he wrote in 1839, in the 'Literary Gazette.' See the Appendix, No. IV.

During the year 1839 the 'Experiment Book' of Alfred Smee shows that his mind was employed upon other subjects

besides splints and surgery and photogenic drawings. He was
at work on the 'Contractility of Tissues,' which was intended to
be exemplified by many hundred experiments. He was at work
on 'Melanosis,' which was designed for a paper, but which was
abandoned before its completion for other more weighty subjects.
He was experimenting on inks. He was experimenting on a
waterproofing liquid. He was besides making his researches on
his important paper on the 'Ferrosesquicyanuret of Potassium;'
he was devising his "battery," and was besides carrying on other
experiments relating to electro-metallurgy.

By the account-book of Alfred Smee, we find that up to the
time he left school, when he was sixteen years old, he only
received ninepence a week for pocket-money. This money
he carefully husbanded, and expended on retorts and other necessaries for chemical experiments. Even after he became a
medical student he had not more than £30 a year, which had
to suffice for the expenses of his wardrobe, for obtaining objects
for dissecting, and for the various other objects required to
carry on his numerous researches. I have heard my father say
how pinched he was in early life for money, and what a benefit
it would have been to him throughout his life had he, at the
commencement of his career, had more money at his disposal.
But he made the most of his small means. His microscope was
given to him, but it was a very inferior one. With a five-
pound note, given to him by his father on gaining one of the
prizes, he procured for himself a $\frac{1}{8}$-inch lens, which he had long
coveted to possess. I must here exonerate my grandfather's
memory from the supposition that he was either a mean man, or
an unnatural father. On the contrary, he was very fond of his
children, and particularly proud of his son Alfred. But my grandfather had been brought up in the school of adversity. He had
seen his father's fortune go from him; he had lived in turbulent
times, when the revolution of France had filled men's minds with
horror; he had, as a young man, lived in the society of French
noble refugees, amongst whom was an archbishop who had
escaped to this country for protection against the oppressions
of their own countrymen: thus my grandfather having from his
youth witnessed the instability of fortune, it had thereby caused
him to become in middle age more prudent, more cautious in
money matters than it was his natural disposition to be.

The room in which he carried on his numerous experiments
—where all the experiments for 'Electro-Metallurgy' were worked

out, where "Smee's Battery" was devised—was one having a
stone floor which led out of one of the drawing-rooms at the
house my grandfather occupied at the Bank of England. This
room, which produced such great works, was not worthy of the
appellation of laboratory.

Through the kindness of my mother, I am enabled to give
a picture of this room. It was etched on copper by her brother,
the late Mr. William Hutchison. The lines which appear below

FIG. 1.

*My working room
in the Bank of England
Alfred Smee*

the etching were written by my father on a copy belonging to
my friend Miss Fooks, which she kindly placed at my disposal.
In this room my father worked ; he had no assistant to help him ;
every single experiment for 'Electro-Metallurgy,' &c., had to be
carried out by his own hands ; and his pecuniary means were, as
already observed, small to a degree. Think of this, young men
of talent, and turn your abilities to as good an account as Alfred
Smee did his, and with such a pittance!

The home life at the Bank was a singularly simple one.

According to the rules of the Bank of England, its gates were locked and barred at 10 o'clock at night (a few years later than the time I am now writing about, the gates were not closed till 11 o'clock); consequently balls and evening parties were interdicted to the members of the Smee family, for to have the Bank gates opened after they were closed for the night was attended by so much formality, such as ringing up the chief cashier, and having the names of the party entered in a book, that practically it never was done unless in a case of urgent necessity. Thus in a great measure society was a sealed book for the young people, and they were obliged to seek their amusements in themselves. After dinner, which was always precisely at 5 o'clock, the family generally used to devote themselves to music. Some played the piano, another the violin, and another the violoncello, and the daughter of the house sang; and thus by delightful duets, trios, and even quartetts and songs, the long evenings were beguiled. My grand-father was a skilful amateur performer on the piano; he had been a pupil of Battershill, the well-known pupil of Handel. My grand-father had, besides, a thorough knowledge of musical composition. He would read off musical compositions as he would an ordinary reading book. It is not, therefore, surprising to find that a talent for music was inherited by the children, though in various degrees. My father was generally too much engaged with his numerous researches to be able to take a prominent part in these musical soirées. He, however, was very fond of music, and played a little on the violoncello. He had an infallible ear for rhythm, and it was painful to him to have to listen to performers (however skilful they might otherwise be in their playing) if they did not give the precise accentuation: the slightest fault his ear detected. His favourite musical works were those by Mozart, more especially the music of 'Don Juan' and the 'Zäuberflöte;' those by Meyerbeer, the music from 'Roberto' being the favourite; and the music of 'Der Freischütz,' by Weber. He liked, too, classical chamber music, although he used to say he found that class of music too fatiguing to listen to after a long hard day's work. He was especially fond of sacred pieces, such as the 'Messiah' by Handel, the 'Elijah' by Mendelssohn, the 'Creation' by Haydn, and other oratorios. For some years he regularly took two stalls at Exeter Hall, and there weekly he and his family enjoyed by turns the magnificent rendering of the various oratorios by the great masters. Besides oratorios, my father liked chorals and hymns, Pergolesi's 'Hymn of Praise' being among his favourites.

At his house on a Sunday he would not permit other than sacred music to be performed. He was also particularly skilful in analysing the musical works of the great composers, in which he could detect the particular phrase or subject upon which the work—be it a sonata, an oratorio, or an opera—was framed; and he would come home from an opera, for instance, humming the subject upon which the opera was based. He was very fond of a good opera, and had stalls at one of the opera houses for several years, and he was very fond of a good ballet. He was no dancer himself, but it afforded him pleasure to see others dance, and he liked dance music for the rhythm's sake. His ear was not, however, acute for tune; for whether the instrument were somewhat flat or sharp made but little difference to him, provided the rhythm or the accentuation of the playing was strictly correct.

In speaking of the home life of the Bank, I should not omit to mention that Alfred Smee was much attached to his father, towards whom he ever behaved in the most filial and respectful manner, and he was devoted to his mother and to his only sister. His sister seems to have possessed much of my father's zealous and active disposition; but she died young, leaving behind her not a few traces of uncommon talent, and the memory of a sweet disposition which was treasured by those who knew her.

After Alfred Smee had completed his medical education at King's College and at St. Bartholomew's, he became for a short time (a month or two) an articled apprentice of a general practitioner, and later, in 1840, he became member of the Royal College of Surgeons, after which he set up in Finsbury Circus as a consulting surgeon.

# CHAPTER III.

## 1840 TO 1842.

Twenty-second year of his age—"Smee's Battery"—Marriage of Alfred Smee, June 2nd, 1840—'Ferrosesquicyanuret of Potassium' paper—'Electro-Metallurgy' published December 1840; age, twenty-two—Alfred Smee's researches in electro-metallurgy—Base coinage—Delivers a lecture at the Royal Institution, February 1841; age twenty-three—His specimens in electro-metallurgy shown to the Prince Consort—Surgeon to the Bank of England—Elected Fellow of the Royal Society—Makes a durable ink—Elected Surgeon to the Royal General Dispensary, Aldersgate Street—Paper on the 'Reduction of Metals'—Lecture at the Royal Institution on 'Reduction of Metals'—Paper on 'Inhalation of Ammonia'—Other scientific papers, &c.

THE year 1840 was, perhaps, the most momentous one in my father's life, for in this year many of his inventions and discoveries were given to the public. On the 29th of February his paper was read before the Royal Society, 'On the Galvanic Properties of the Principal Elementary Bodies, with a Description of a new Chemico-Mechanical Battery'—now of world-wide repute, and known by the name of the "Smee Battery." The same subject was made a paper, which was read at the Society of Arts, June 1st, 1840. For the latter paper, the Gold Isis Medal, which he received from the hands of the Duke of Sussex, was bestowed upon him. Millais, the celebrated artist, also received a medal on the same day.

"Smee's Battery" was devised through conducting a series of experiments on the ferrocyanuret of potassium, which gave frequent occasion for the use of a galvanic battery.

I found (Mr. Smee adds in 'Electro-Metallurgy'*) that although the batteries of Daniell and of Grove were admirably-contrived instruments, yet it was very desirable to possess one that could be set in action at a moment's notice, and with comparatively little trouble. It became

---

* Page 23.

thenceforth my endeavour to construct one that should require little or no labour in its employment, and this was followed by devising the Chemico-mechanical battery.

This battery, after I had minutely investigated every property which belongs to the metals of which batteries are constructed, was made upon noticing the property which rough surfaces possess of evolving the hydrogen, and smooth surfaces of favouring its adhesion.

The value of the battery process, Smee's battery (he writes in his 'History of Electro-Metallurgy'[*]), over all others, is its applicability to all cases; moreover, when we use a single cell of the battery, the quantity of zinc dissolved to do any amount of work is the same, or even less, than attends the use of the other apparatus, because the local action in a battery of this construction is less than in the single-cell apparatus, and lastly, the quality of the precipitated metal can be regulated with the utmost nicety.

The platinized silver battery is peculiarly suitable for the operator, for when it is in action it communicates to him the degree of work that it is doing; in fact, it completely talks to its possessor. If the current is very feeble, a faint murmur is heard; if a little stronger, the battery whispers; if a moderate current is passing, it hisses; but if a violent one, it roars. At this present moment I have nineteen batteries at work in the same room where I am writing, and they are each telling me the work they are performing. This very instant the fall of a heavy ledger in a neighbouring office has jarred two wires into contact, and the roar of that one battery has immediately informed me of the fact, notwithstanding the action of the eighteen others; I have separated the wires, and the universal singing communicates to me that all are now working satisfactorily. Any local action on zinc in the same manner is immediately notified by its different and peculiar voice, and I have been surprised how quickly the experimenter catches the characteristic peculiarity of each noise, which is learnt more readily than the sound of different bells in a strange house.

As soon as this new battery was made known it created a great sensation throughout the country. The great manufacturers entertained so high an opinion of it, that before the year had closed some thousands of them, or about £2000 worth, were sold to the country. Thirty-six years have now passed since its invention, and yet it is still in use.

As with most, if not with all inventions, there are always to be found a few persons to endeavour to cry down any important novelty, so it may be supposed that "Smee's Battery" did not escape the ire of the jealous few; but in this case, as in all other cases where merit exists, it only brought its worth more into view, and thus it became the one employed by the great manufacturers of this country. Soon its fame reached other countries, where it was likewise employed.

* P. 23.

† This was written at the time when he lived at his father's house at the Bank of England.

In the Appendix, No. V., a description of this battery will be found, illustrated by woodcuts, with a very full account for the working of the same.

The day following that on which Alfred Smee received the gold medal from the Society of Arts for his battery, he was married to Miss Hutchison, a young lady of Irish descent, to whom he had been engaged at the early age of seventeen. The marriage took place at 8 o'clock on the morning of the 2nd of June, 1840 (before the Bank of England was opened to the public), at St. Margaret's, Lothbury, the venerable Archdeacon Hollingsworth officiating, in the presence of six members only of the two families. This privacy was occasioned through my grandfather's official position at the Bank; and as my mother was an orphan, and Mr. and Mrs. Smee were her guardians, she and her brother lived with them. Alfred Smee was ever a most devoted husband, and his great affection for his wife is shown in the dedication to her of 'My Garden.'

In April 1840, he wrote a paper on electrotypes, which I have inserted in its place in the Appendix, No. VI.

The next paper of Alfred Smee's was a very important one: it was the one through conducting the experiments for which he had invented his battery, namely, 'On the Ferrosesquicyanuret of Potassium.' It was read before the Royal Society on his birthday, the 18th of June, 1840, only sixteen days after his marriage, and it was printed in the 'London and Edinburgh Philosophical Magazine:' see Appendix, No. VII. Although in this paper he pointed out, before Schönbein's discovery of ozone, that electrolytic oxygen converted the ferro- into the ferri-cyanide of potassium, yet for some reason or other, best known to that learned body, or to the set or clique which at that time governed it, this highly important paper was, like its predecessor on the battery, ordered to be deposited in the archives of the Society; that is to say, it was not allowed to be published in the Royal Society's 'Proceedings' or 'Transactions.' In consequence of this treatment Alfred Smee did not for some time send any more papers to the Royal Society, but published them elsewhere.

'Electro-Metallurgy,' the first great work of Alfred Smee, was published on the 1st of December, 1840.

Although most of the subjects contained in that book are now generally known to the public, yet few only are aware that the greater part, and indeed a very important part, of the science of electro-metallurgy was the creation of his brain, and that at the time this work was written, now thirty-seven years ago, it was the only important contribution and the only complete exposition of the subject embraced therein. The very name of the science, electro-metallurgy, owes its name to him. The late Prince Consort graciously allowed the book to be dedicated to him. In the Appendix, No. VIII., will be found the history of this science, as it is given in every edition of 'Electro-Metallurgy,' as well as a brief view of the various subjects treated of in the work itself. It suffices, therefore, here to enumerate some of the more important researches which Mr. Smee made in the science of electro-metallurgy. The important ones, therefore, were :—

1. "The laws regulating the reduction of all metals in different states." By these laws, gold, silver, platinum, palladium, copper, iron, and almost every other metal, can be thrown down in three states ; namely, as a black powder, as a crystalline deposit, or as a flexible plate.

It is these laws (he says) which raise the isolated facts hitherto known as the electrotype into a science. The hundreds of experiments (he adds), I may even say the thousands, that have been tried to elucidate these laws, could never have been executed had I not first discovered my galvanic battery ; for its simplicity alone enabled me, without any assistance, to undergo the laborious undertaking.

2. The processes for platinating and palladiating, until described in his 'Electro-Metallurgy,' were facts altogether unknown to science ; for the reduction of those metals into any other state than that of the black powder had hitherto been always considered impossible. By these processes, reliefs and intaglios in gold and nearly every other metal were enabled to be executed.

3. To Mr. Smee we are also indebted for being the first to discover the means by which perfect reverses of plaster could be obtained : for it may seem singular that although every writer on the subject had previously given directions for making moulds of plaster casts in metal, yet before Smee's investigations no perfect reverse of plaster had been obtained. He soon found out that the reason of the failures lay in the extreme porosity of the plaster, and he removed the difficulty by rendering the plaster non-absorbent. In speaking of this matter he says :—

The success of this department of my experiments has amply repaid me for my labours and expense ; for there is not a town in England that I have happened to visit, and scarcely a street of this metropolis, where prepared plasters are not exposed to view for the purpose of alluring persons to follow the delightful recreation by the practice of electro-metallurgy.

4. He also extended the use of white wax, bees'-wax, and resin.

5. Amongst the many other novel facts first brought forward in this work, 'Elements of Electro-Metallurgy,' a work which naturally created a great sensation at the time, is the novel application for the coating of fruit, ferns, leaves, &c., with copper. As this would afford a pleasant recreation for ladies, I have transcribed the directions for coating these natural objects in the author's own words (see the Appendix, No. VIII.)

Besides being well reviewed, from the moment 'Electro-Metallurgy' was published, numerous were the letters which poured in to my father about some matter or other appertaining to the subject, not only from most of the manufacturers of this country, but also from those of other countries. Indeed, up to the time of his death, he never ceased receiving letters or seeing persons engaged in the application of electro-metallurgy, all seeking for information respecting either Smee's battery or some matter connected with the process. As my father always gave his advice gratuitously, his family have often been surprised and pleased by receiving some small token made by the above kind of battery as a recognition of some service, in the form of advice, given by my father. As may be expected, there were not wanting forgers of base coin to take advantage of the process of electro-metallurgy for counterfeiting the coins of the realm. In the prosecution of such cases my father was frequently called as a witness.

I have dwelt long upon Smee's 'Electro-Metallurgy,' because that work is now out of print, and it has been my desire to show exactly to what extent Alfred Smee contributed to this science, for other works are now appearing on that subject, in which his name is more or less being ignored. I have also given many details of Smee's battery, so as to serve as useful hints to those employing the same ; for now the inventor is dead, his advice concerning its management can be heard no more.

On the 4th of January, 1841, the distinguished chemist, Brande, wrote from the Royal Mint to Mr. Smee, thus :—

MY DEAR SIR,—Mr. Palmer has been good enough to send me a copy of your valuable essay on Electro-Metallurgy, and as it will shortly fall to my lot to give an evening at the Royal Institution, I am inclined to take up that subject, provided you will lend me your aid. I was in hope Faraday would have done it, but he is not well enough to take an active part at present. Pray give me a line to tell me your feelings upon the subject, and whether you will allow me to talk the matter over with you in a day or two.          Yours faithfully,
                                        W. T. BRANDE.

Ten days later the same wrote : —

> Should you happen to be this way on Monday forenoon next and would look in, you will find me at work on electrotypes, and might perhaps be able to give me a little practical advice.

The lecture was delivered at the Royal Institution on Friday evening, January 22nd; and on the following month, Friday evening, February 26th, 1841, one was delivered by Alfred Smee 'On the Laws regulating the Voltaic Precipitation of Metals.' The theatre was densely crowded on both occasions, and from letters from members of the Royal Institution and from other sources, it would seem that Mr. Smee's lecture was a great success, as was that of Brande. Previously to this, Mr. Smee had also given a very successful one before the Numismatic Society, on the 21st of January, 1841.

In April of the same year my father showed his various specimens of electro-metallurgy to the late Prince Consort, at Buckingham Palace. The Prince was greatly interested with them. A cucumber that my father had coated with copper was shown to her Majesty, and she became so interested with the subject that she broke the casting with her finger, to see if really the cucumber was inside. This coppered cucumber with the hole is still in existence, as well as some of the other first specimens in electro-metallurgy that were made by Alfred Smee. These specimens were also frequently shown at the various great soirées of London.

Besides the works already described, Alfred Smee had other occupations to engross his time and attention. We find that on the first Thursday in January, 1841, he was elected Surgeon to the Bank of England. This appointment was specially created for him, and for it he was mainly indebted to that eminent surgeon, Sir Astley Cooper. Sir Astley had taken a great interest in the young man, and came several times to the Bank to see his various experiments. Being a friend of the Governor of the Bank, Sir John Ray Reed, Sir Astley Cooper told him to be sure "not to let Mr. Alfred Smee leave the Bank," for, said he, —

> You don't know what a treasure you have got in that young man; he has shown signs of working out problems for himself which will be sure to be useful some time or another.

I give this conversation as I have been told it by one (not the person interested) who heard it. Evidently Sir Astley Cooper thought that " It is not the place honours the man, but the man the place." *   Besides being surgeon to the Bank of England, my father held other public offices : he was also in private practice, and was considered eminent as an oculist.

How he got through his various avocations is a marvel, but the truth is, he was never idle.   His mind was ever employed upon some matter or other, and it resulted in his mind wearing out his body while he was only in middle age.

On the 10th of June, 1841, before he was twenty-three years old, he was elected Fellow of the Royal Society.   There was some opposition got up from a quarter least expected; but on the eminent mathematician and actuary (B. Gompert) and some others taking the matter up warmly, and on that gentleman, on the day of the election, entering the room where it was to take place, and signifying his intention of noting down the name of every Fellow that voted, and how he voted, with a view of publishing it to the world, those who led the opposition ended by voting for Mr. Smee, who was duly elected.

The close of 1841 saw Mr. Smee the father of a son, an only one.

In 1842 Mr. Smee succeeded in making a writing ink for the Bank of England.   Various specimens of writing made with his ink about this time, thirty-six years ago, now exist, the letters of which are as black as jet.   Other specimens of writing made by some of the manufacturers of ink at that time are more or less faded, in some cases so much so that the writing is scarcely legible.   As the receipt for making this ink is no secret, it may interest some of my readers to know what its ingredients are, and how it is manufactured.   I have, therefore, endeavoured to satisfy them by giving the receipt in the Appendix, No. IX.

While I am on the subject of inks it will not be out of place here to add that my father, to use his own words, made at various times " almost innumerable examinations of different inks."   In Rush's case,† all the inks found in Rush's house were sent to my father's house for examination, together with the paper thrown into Stanfield Hall, with the inks from a large portion of the county of Norfolk, to compare with that with which the document was written.   Another time his chemical analysis of some ink was the means of showing that a gentleman who had been accused of carelessness had been the victim of fraud, and thereby he had the

---

* See Talmud.                     † A celebrated murder case in 1847.

gratification not only of sustaining his reputation, but of saving him from the payment of £1000.

In February of 1842 Mr. Smee was elected surgeon to the Royal General Dispensary, Aldersgate Street. The " success " to this election " is much enhanced," writes Lord Carington, " by the handsome majority."

During this year a paper of Mr. Smee's appeared in the twenty-first number of the 'Philosophical Magazine,' and also in the second volume of the 'Archives de l'Électricité.' It was entitled ' On the New Definition of the Voltaic Circuit, with Formulæ for ascertaining its Power under different Circumstances.' This paper was afterwards incorporated in the second edition of ' Electro-Metallurgy,' on which Mr. Smee was this year hard at work. During this same year he wrote a few medical papers, among which may be mentioned, ' On Glossites producing Suppuration,' to be found in the ' London Medical Journal ' of March 10th ; ' On the Treatment of Syphilis,' and an account of 'Violent Hysteria in a Man.'

On the 9th of March, 1843, Mr. Smee read before the Royal Society his paper, ' On the Cause of the Reduction of Metals when Solutions of their Salts are subjected to the Galvanic Current.' This paper was also incorporated in the second edition of ' Electro-Metallurgy.' The paper itself will be found in the Appendix, No. X.* The following evening he delivered a lecture on the subject at the Royal Institution, which appears to have been very successful.

Previously his attention had, with others, been directed to a plan for conducting a Medical Association for Clerks, in connection with the Provident Clerks' Benefit Association and Benevolent Fund. It is a long draft, and the MS., which is in his handwriting, consists of several sheets of paper. The gist of the plan was to ensure for those gentlemen who are occupied as clerks in the city of London the benefits of being attended by the highest medical skill, and for procuring for them the best medicines and all the various comforts applicable in cases of sickness at a rate commensurate with the pecuniary means of such seeking benefit therefrom. The institution was to be in a central position, and was to have baths, drugs, and a dispensing department. Medical

* This paper was published in the fourth volume of the 'Archives de l'Électricité,' in 1844 ; in Majocchi, ' Ann. Fis. Chim.' vol. xv. 1844 ; in the 'Philosophical Magazine,' vol. xxv. 1844 ; in the 'Proceedings of the Royal Society ;' and in the 'Poggend. Annal.' No. lxv. 1845.

men were to be on the spot to attend to patients. There are long rules and numerous regulations, which show that the most minute detail was fully considered for the management of this institution. I believe the scheme fell through for want of funds.

The 'London Medical Gazette' for April 3rd, 1843, contains a paper by his pen, 'On the Inhalation of Ammonia Gas as a Remedial Agent.' See the Appendix, No. XI.

This year his only daughter was born to him.

# CHAPTER IV.

## 1843 TO 1847.

'Sources of Physics,' second book, 1843-1844—Lectures on 'Detection of Needles'—1845—Paper, 'Application of Electricity to Surgery'—Carmine injections—Potato disease—1846—Third book on the 'Potato Plant' —*Aphis vastator*, nomenclature of—1847—Rancorous animosity and skits on A. S.—Famine Food soirée—Skeleton of lecture—Lecture—Ventilation —Smee's ether inhaler.

THE same year appeared Alfred Smee's book on 'The Sources of Physical Science,' which was specially written as an introduction to the 'Study of Physiology through Physics,' and which comprises the connection of the several departments of physical science, their dependence on the same laws, and the relation of the material to the immaterial. This work was published on the 1st of September, 1843. It is divided into seven chapters, thus :—

CHAP. I.—*The Fundamental Sciences.*—Matter—Arithmetic—Attraction.
    ,,    II.—*On the Sciences of Matter under Attraction.*— Chemistry— Crystallography—Geometry—Trigonometry—Gravity—Magnetism.
    ,,    III.—*On the Sciences of the Disturbance of Attraction.*—Electricity— Mechanics—Hydrostatics—Pneumatics.
    ,,    IV.—*The Sciences of Actions and Reactions.*—Time—Heat—Light— Sound—Odour.
    ,,    V.—*On the Performance of Human Operations.*
    ,,    VI.—*On the Complex Sciences.*
    ,,    VII.—*On the Relation of the Material to the Immaterial.*

He had originally intended to draw up a slight sketch of physical science to form an introductory chapter to his great work, 'Electro-Biology,' which appeared about six years later ; but finding that he was unable to compress the matter of the intended chapter within three hundred pages, he resolved to publish the work as a separate treatise.

At the commencement of my physiological inquiries (he writes) I had no idea of dedicating a separate volume to the Sources of Physical

Science, nor should I have published it if I could have referred to any sufficiently condensed work on these subjects. But having felt the want of a work considering the subjects of the sciences, and showing their relative position, I conceived that my own attempts to forward these inquiries might not be unacceptable to many lovers of scientific knowledge. If I shall hereafter find that my labours have been useful to society, or have induced others to produce a more perfect treatise, I shall feel most amply rewarded.*

From these words we learn that Alfred Smee was the first who published a condensed yet exhaustive view of the physical sciences.

Although since this work was written, now thirty-four years ago, great strides, nay, colossal strides, have been made in physical science, yet it must be borne in mind that 'Sources of Physics' was the forerunner of all the numerous treatises which have since been issued in this branch of knowledge, and it was therefore at the time of its publication a most original work.

In this work he impresses the reader with the importance of studying physics as a whole, not in divisions.

For (says he) by the investigation of the phenomena of one science we become more acquainted with its details; but when we are desirous of contemplating the real nature of the phenomena, and the cause of their production, we must study the effects as a whole, to prevent erroneous conclusions and vain creations of imponderables.†

The tendency of the present day is to take up one branch of knowledge only—nay, to divide one branch of knowledge into various subdivisions, and to investigate only the details of one of these subdivisions, thereby narrowing the mind; for as the sight of man is injured by viewing objects only through the microscope, so in a similar manner is the mind narrowed by only using it for the investigation of mere matters of detail.

In another place ‡ my father advocates for different classes more freely to interchange ideas.

The tendency of the period (says he) is for society to group together in classes; even the Royal Society for the Promotion of Natural Knowledge is most exclusive to all but actual followers of natural science. The clergy separate themselves, the doctors congregate together, but a continual intercourse in a right spirit has a tendency to perfect the mind of all; and whether they work in the upper, lower, or middle departments of their minds, all should accord.

---

* See 'Sources of Physics,' Preface, p. vii.          † Idem, p. 254.
‡ See 'Mind of Man,' p. 106.

My father also always held that the older a person grew the more he should cultivate the acquaintance of young people; for by these means mutual benefit is derived. A young person brings the new facts and feelings of the age added to a freshness and vigour of mind, and thus prevents the older from growing old in intellect.

To return to 'Sources of Physics,' a full analysis of that work will be found in the Appendix, No. XII., together with the two concluding chapters, which, as they treat on the relation of the material to the immaterial, are there given in entirety, as they not only strongly bear upon subjects in his mental philosophy,* but further they fully demonstrate how Alfred Smee's mind was, as a young man as in middle-age, ever dwelling upon that which is infinite; and how he was ever demonstrating that that which is infinite must not be limited, neither must time be confounded with eternity, matter with space, the body with the soul, or material actions with God.

Mr. Smee had for some time previously been elected lecturer to the Aldersgate School of Medicine. In the Appendix, No. XIII., is the Introductory Lecture delivered the 5th of October, 1844, and in the same place at No. XIV. is part of another lecture delivered before the same audience on the 9th of December in the same year. The latter was embodied in a paper entitled 'The Detection of Needles impacted in the Human Frame.' During this year he received pressing letters from the Royal Institution authorities to lecture before that scientific body, but I am not aware that he did so.

His lectures were clearly delivered, and as it has been remarked of him, "he possessed great perspicuity of language," and "his manner was pleasing;" but unfortunately he did not possess a good voice. He suffered as a young man much from affection of the throat, which often deprived him in a great measure of the use of his voice, and rendered him for a considerable time afterwards husky and hoarse. He used to deplore his not possessing a melodious voice, which was indeed a great drawback in his lecturing and in his speaking before public meetings, which he did frequently throughout his life.

A paper on the 'New Application of Electricity to Surgery' was published in the 26th volume of the 'Philosophical Magazine.' The same year he was elected Vice-president of the Medical Society at King's College. I should not omit to mention that

* See 'Electro-Biology,' and 'The Mind of Man.'

when he was a student of King's College, he belonged to their Debating Society, and it was there he learned to speak in public. He would speak on any question that was before the meeting in order to acquire a fluency of language—a custom from which, he observed in later life, he had derived considerable benefit.

In March 1845, he wrote a paper for the Microscopical Society, 'On Vessels in Fat smaller than the Capillaries.' Curiously enough the paper was lost by that society, which caused him considerable irritation and annoyance : * for this paper contained the description of the process he adopted in the preparation of his beautiful carmine injections of the brain and spinal cord. These injections were exceedingly difficult to prepare : they were made by using a solution of carmine in ammonia mixed with size. The preparations were then dried and placed in balsam, so that they are permanent, and, being transparent, constitute the most lovely microscopical specimens which can possibly be perceived. These carmine injections will bear a very high magnifying power. They were the very first that were made. Over a period of more than thirty years these beautiful microscopic preparations have been constantly shown at the various great soirées of London, and up to the present day never are they exhibited without filling the mind of the spectator with wonder and admiration.†

Early in the summer (June 1845), my father and mother, with her brother, went to Switzerland for a month. Since the time of his marriage, this was the first holiday he had been enabled to take. It was the first time he had seen the snow mountains, and from his intense love of Nature we may well imagine his feelings of delight on beholding the Alps, where—

> " The palaces of nature . . . . . .
> Have pinnacled in clouds their snowy scalps,
> And throned eternity in icy walls
> Of cold sublimity."—Byron, *Childe Harold.*

In the summer of the same year a disease appeared in Europe among potato plants, which caused the tubers to decay. The first communication of the fact was in the 'Gardeners' Chronicle,' on the 16th of August, 1845, by Dr. Bell Salter. No sooner had this letter appeared than other communications were sent to that journal, stating that the disease had existed to a large extent the previous season, although such an important state-

---

* It was supposed to have been stolen.
† See 'Mind of Man,' p. 233.

ment had not previously been chronicled. The disease was at
first considered a totally new malady, but Mr. Smee found, on
inquiry, that in Germany, in 1830, Martius wrote on the subject,
and that he attributed its effect to a fungus. Berkeley, the great
fungologist—who, though differing in opinion from Mr. Smee,
always carried on the controversy in the most courteous
manner, and whom my father held in great respect and esteem
—considered the fungus called the Botrytis to be the cause.
My father became interested in the subject, and began making
his own researches. He concluded that the first cause of the
disease was occasioned by an aphis which punctured the leaf,
sucked the sap, and destroyed the relation between the leaf and
the root, thus causing the leaf or some other part of the plant to
become gangrenous, and die. After the attack of the aphis, fungi
grew, which "growth," he writes, "is probably in many cases
materially assisted by the prior attack of the aphis." The results
of Mr. Smee's inquiries and researches on aphides, and their
relation to the potato and other plants, became so numerous, that
he was led, in 1846, into embodying his views on the subject in a
treatise containing 170 pages, which is well known by the title
of the ' Potato Plant, its Uses and Properties, together with the
Cause of the Present Malady.' *  In this book, which is dedicated
to the late Prince Consort, the properties and growth of the
potato plant are set forth, as is also its individuality, and the
chemistry and use of that plant, &c.; its gangrene, or present
disease, and the chemistry of the disease; the relation of the
disease to internal and external causes; the effect of temperature,
light, electricity, upon the disease; the relation of the disease
to soils and manures, to fungi; the relations of gangrene to
animal parasites. The various aphides are then described. The
insect that attacked the potato plant he considered to be an aphis,
which, when fully grown, is about a tenth of an inch long, and
its colour, either white, olive-green, brown, or inclined to red.
This aphis, the destroyer of the potato, he found was identically
the same which had been previously known to infest the turnip,
and which is called by Curtis on that account the *Aphis
rapæ*. On the great confusion attending such a nomenclature,
Mr. Smee determined, for the sake of perspicuity, to call it
the *Aphis vastator*, or destroyer of our best provisions: for
the *Aphis vastator* destroys, in a similar manner as it does the

* This book is still in print, and is published by Messrs. Longman and Co.,
Paternoster Row.

potato, the turnip, the swede, the beetroot, the cabbage, the broccoli, the radish, the horse-radish, the various wild Solani, some kinds of henbane, the Stramonium, the Belladonna, the clover, the groundsel, the Euphorbia, some sorts of Murex, the mallow, the shepherd's purse, the holy thistle, some kinds of grass, and even wheat, the Jerusalem artichoke and the sweet potato, and perhaps other plants.

There are many other kinds of aphides, besides the *Aphis vastator*, which destroy other plants, and even trees, and we had, about five years ago, some large willow-trees totally destroyed by their ravages at " my garden" at Wallington.* Many of these different sorts of aphides and injuries caused by them are also delineated in this work on the potato disease. He also shows the relation of the Vastator and other aphides to fungi ; and he then gives the natural and artificial remedies for the present diseases among plants. The work is illustrated by ten lithographs of potato plants in health and in disease, of diseased carrots and turnips, parsnips, and mangold-wurzel, of the *Aphis vastator* and of other aphides, and of various fungi.

Mr. Curtis, the distinguished entomologist, blamed Mr. Smee for having violated the established custom, in not having used the prior name of the aphis. " But it appears," says my father, " that Mr. Curtis named this self-same creature *rapæ*, when it had the former name, *dianthi*, assigned to it, as Mr. Walker has informed me." Thus we have *Aphis vastator* (the destroyer) alias *rapæ*, alias *dianthi*. How many more aliases will this dire scourge to mankind receive ?

The moment this book on the potato plant was published, it was assailed in the most extraordinary way. The writers did not attempt to attack his facts or his reasoning, but they misrepresented his views, and indeed but too frequently made my father say the very reverse of what he did say, and then they wrote their own fabulous versions of his writings.†

The controversy which ensued during this potato pestilence, and the violence of various parties, were truly a reproach to science. At last, as my father has said,‡—

Foolish people used to amuse me by sending threatening letters by nearly every post (many of these have been collected together), cautioning me that I should be amply punished if I dared to continue to write upon

---

* See 'My Garden,' second edition, p. 477.
† See 'Instinct and Reason,' p. 263.                ‡ Idem, p. 265.

the subject (his life was even threatened). Notwithstanding all this, it was very curious to notice how kindly the public used to supply me with facts for my guidance; and I received valuable communications, some of them of great length, though, when the controversy was at its height, they were sent anonymously. By the middle of summer nearly every agriculturist was made acquainted with my investigations despite this rancorous animosity.

I can just remember the time of the potato disease. Our drawing-rooms were ornamented with innumerable specimens of diseased potatoes. Potatoes were on the mantelpieces; potatoes were on the tables; potatoes innumerable were on the floor. I am by no means sure that the chairs were not occupied by potatoes! Wherever the eye glanced, diseased potatoes met the view.

In the Appendix, No. XV.B., will be found a selection from the voluminous correspondence which Alfred Smee carried on in various newspapers on the potato disease during the years 1845, 1846, and 1847.

In the 'Annual Register' for 1805 it is stated in an article upon the aphis, "In some years the aphides are so numerous as to cause almost a total failure of the hop and *potato plantations*; in other years the peas are equally injured, while exotics, raised in stoves and greenhouses, are frequently destroyed by their depredations." In the Linnæan Transactions Mr. W. Curtis states, "To *potatoes*, and even to corn, we have known the aphides to prove highly detrimental, and no less so to melons." Mr. Curtis further states that "the aphis is the grand cause of blights in plants, and that erroneous notions are entertained, not only by the vulgar and illiterate, but even by persons of education, that aphides attack none but sickly plants, with other notions as altogether false in fact as unphilosophical in principle."*

Besides the rancorous animosity of the ignorant and of the bigoted, Mr. Smee was subjected to be taken off in humorous skits. Mr. Punch, of course, was not behindhand.

In the pantomime at Drury Lane appeared :—

*Scene, a Village Fair with Shows, &c. &c.*
*Little Boy looking at a peep-show.*

*Showman.*　This is the *Aphis vastator*, as you may see,
　　　　　Very much magnified by Mr. Smee.
*Boy.*　　Please, sir, which is the aphis and which is the tater?
*Showman.*　Whichever you like, my young investigator.
　　　　　　　　　　　*The Knight and the Wood Demon;*
　　　　　　　　　　　　　*or, One o'clock.*

---

* 'Instinct and Reason,' p. 263.

In one of the newspapers appeared the following humorous lines :—

*Lines on reading Mr. Smee's Account of the Aphis vastator, supposed by*
*him to cause the Potato Blight.*

> Well! this confounded *tater* blight
>   Is now clear'd up by Smee;
> And for a cure all people must
>   To fumigation flee.
>
> Let all peruse his handsome book
>   About the wondrous fly,
> Which is the cause of all the ill—
>   So says his theory.
>
> On reading first the title-page
>   (I say it in no joke),
> From seeing F.R.S., I thought
>   The thing must end in smoke.
>
> That some large bugs have been the cause
>   We've had some keen debaters;
> But none till now thought little flies
>   Could turn out such vast (e)aters.
>
> That this vast-eating insect thrives
>   On its new kind of food,
> There is no doubt, for milliards are
>   Born daily to the brood :
>
> Which shows potatoes 'mongst all plants
>   Still hold the foremost place,
> In making insects breed in swarms,
>   As well's the human race.
>
> Alas! how many other crops
>   This aphis now will finish !
> And though we may have *gammon* left,
>   We'll have no more of spinach.
>
> On turnips, carrots, and on beets,
>   They jump about in flocks;
> Even dandelions are not free,
>   Nor nettles, grass, nor docks.
>
> Let some strong dose be now devised
>   By chemic speculators,
> To massacre, this very year,
>   These terrible vastators.

Other lines appeared elsewhere, such as—

> "The butcher, the baker, the candlestick-maker,
>   All jump'd out of Alfred Smee's rotten potato"—

and others I might enumerate had I space so to do.

But in the midst of the investigations, in the midst of the bitter controversies and the humorous skits on the subject, the disease still went rapidly on, till the scourge became so great that a famine ensued in the land, and in Ireland the people were dying of starvation. Then, in the midst of their distress, the people bethought them of turning to Heaven for assistance; and accordingly we find that, on the 11th of October, 1846, prayers to the Almighty were offered up in all the churches and chapels in England and Wales, for relief from the dearth and scarcity then existing in parts of the United Kingdom. A few months later, on Wednesday, the 24th of March, 1847, a form of prayer was used in all churches and chapels throughout England and Ireland, that being the day appointed by proclamation for a general fast and humiliation.

Meanwhile, my father was trying various experiments to ascertain how far other kinds of food might be employed for the relief of the poor starved population of these realms. On Saturday, the 6th of February, 1847, he held a large soirée at his residence in Finsbury Circus, expressly to exhibit his famine food, at which between 200 and 300 of the most distinguished professional and literary men of the metropolis were present. The account of the various kinds of bread constituting the famine food is given in the Appendix, No. XV.A.

The company tasted all the samples prepared, and pronounced Mr. Smee to have succeeded beyond expectation in his attempt. Though a mere child at the time, I have a distinct recollection of the nauseous taste of the Iceland moss bread; but the hay bread and the hay biscuit I remember having found very sweet and palatable. It should here be added that my father did not himself believe that any of these breads, excepting the cereal breads, could compete with wheat in nutritive power or price, so that, besides being inferior in quality, they could never be brought into use from their additional cost.[*]

On the 10th of March of the same year Mr. Smee delivered a lecture at the London Institution on aphides being the cause of the potato disease. Whenever he delivered a lecture or wrote a book, he always drew up on a card, or on one sheet of paper, the plan of the lecture or of the book. This he called the "skeleton." And in lecturing he only employed such brief notes as were contained in his "skeleton." I will here subjoin the skeleton of the lecture he delivered on the cause of the potato

[*] See 'Instinct and Reason,' p. 106.

disease, as it is a very good example of all of them. The lecture clothed in its proper form will be found in the Appendix, No. XV.ʙ.

Insect Plagues.   800,000, St. Augustine.          Barnes, 2000 miles
                                                   covered by them.

Aphides.
Demonstration :
      1. Live plants.
      2. Healthy.
      3. Sucks juices.
      4. Impairs qualities.
      5. Alters properties.
      6. Bad sap not nourish.
      7. Imperfect tissue dies.
      8. Death local, remote.
      9. Remote death entirely kill the plant.
     10. Wild plants resist better than cultivated.
     11. Cultivated plants ill resist.
     12. Deposition of fibre.
     13. Propagation of diseased fibre.
     14. Injury to plants hastens transformation.
     15. Growth of fungi.

Destroyers of aphides—ladybirds, gauze-wings, synphidæ, ichneumons, Chalcididæ, birds.

    Great fleas and little fleas have smaller fleas to bite 'em ;
    These smaller fleas have lesser fleas, so on *ad infinitum*.

        Aphides live on all plants.
        Vastator potato no novelty.
           Gangrene.
Vastator, name, leaf, root, history, anatomy, chemistry.
          Subsistence.
Tendrils.          Oxyhydrogen.          Microscope.
      Future prospects, transitions.

"I will rebuke the devourer for your sake, and it shall not destroy the fruits of the ground."

Whenever my father found a plant infested by an aphis, he used to secure some specimens, put them in a pill-box, and in the evening place them in Canada balsam so as to carefully examine them. In this way he preserved all his evidences upon this point for future reference, and the name of the plant on which the insect fed was immediately scratched on the glass with a diamond, so that no source of error could possibly arise. The mode of fixing the insect in Canada balsam was very simple : a slip of glass was warmed over a candle, and a drop of the balsam was then placed upon it; the insect, whilst yet alive, was then placed on the balsam, and the glass was again very gently warmed in order to kill the insect; another piece of the glass was then heated over a candle and placed on the insect, when the creature was hermetically sealed up for ever.

It is necessary (he says) that the insect should be dry when it is mounted, and we must take especial care not to apply too much heat, which will corrugate the antennæ and destroy the form of the insect. I strongly recommend to all entomologists this mode of preserving small insects; and having once properly secured them, they will last for an indefinite period, and can be handled without the slightest risk of injury.*

Mr. Smee mounted many hundreds of these microscopic preparations of the *Aphis vastator*, and of slices of diseased potatoes; and these slides have, after the lapse of nearly thirty years, been the means by which this great controversy on the potato disease has probably at last been settled. For in the winter of 1876, when Mr. Worthington Smith was investigating the subject of diseased potatoes, my father placed in his hands for examination 360 slides of diseased potatoes and of aphides, all of which the latter had himself mounted during the great potato murrain of 1846–1847. On placing these slides under a powerful microscope, Mr. Smith discovered that some of the aphides were completely filled with the fungus internally and covered with it externally, and that gentleman has further demonstrated that this insect punctures the potato, and inserts in it the fungus. A full account of these recent observations of Mr. Smith, together with two drawings which that gentleman has kindly made for me from my father's mounted specimens of the *Aphis vastator*, and of a diseased potato showing the resting spore of the fungus within the aphis, will be found in the Appendix, No. XV.c. By this it would appear that the primary cause of the potato murrain of 1846–1847 was the aphis, and the secondary cause the fungus.

The following question, which my father addressed to a well-known actuary, is transcribed for the amusement of those who may be fond of figures:—

An aphis arrived on my cucumber, January 1, 1861. It had ten young ones at the end of ten days, ten more in ten days' time, and every succeeding ten days. Every young one had ten young ten days after birth,

---

* See 'Potato Plant,' p. 14.

and again every other ten days, till December 31st, 1861. How many aphides in all, if the mother aphis and her whole progeny were alive on the 31st of December?

Every aphis weighed $\frac{1}{10}$ grain. What was the total weight of the aphides so produced?—ALFRED SMEE.

Answer.

Let $a$ = total number of generations from the mother aphis = 36.

Let $b$ = the number at each birth = 10.

The formula will be $1 + ab + (a - 1) b^2 + (a - 2) b^3 +$ etc.....
$(a - 35) b^{36}$.

The answer to the first question, *i.e.* what number of aphides in all, is—

1,234,567,901,234,567,901,234,567,901,234,567,861 aphides, or nearly 1¼ sextillions of aphides.

The answer to the second question is—

78,728,820,231,496,422,293,148,463 tons weight, or nearly 78¾ quadrillions of tons weight.

Besides interesting himself with aphides, we find him occupied on other subjects; for in 1846, in conjunction with one of the managers, he was engaged on the ventilation of the theatre of the London Institution. To draw comparisons is odious: yet we cannot but wish that all public rooms were as well ventilated as is the theatre of the London Institution. During different periods of his life he was employed on the ventilation of various large buildings, and the Grand Hotel at Brighton owed its proper ventilation to him.

During 1846 he was invited to take part in a discussion at the Civil Engineers' on the explosion of boilers, as he was known to have turned his attention to the subject.

In 1847 he invented an ether-inhaler, which was exhibited at his soirée. The first one was made by Messrs. Maw, of Aldersgate Street. The 'Illustrated London News' * says—

In a former number (245) we called attention to the important medical discovery, whereby a state of the body could be produced by the inhalation of ether, which renders the patient insensible to the pain of the most severe operations. Since the discovery has been promulgated, medical men have been actively engaged throughout the country in prosecuting their inquiries upon the subject, and numerous forms of apparatus have been devised for conducting the inhalation.

It is found by experience that the more rapidly the effect is produced

---

* January 30th, 1847.

on the body the better is the result for the patient. It is upon this idea that an inhaler has been contrived by Mr. Alfred Smee, surgeon to the Bank of England, whereby the evaporization of ether is promoted by warmth given to the apparatus from a little chamber of hot water.

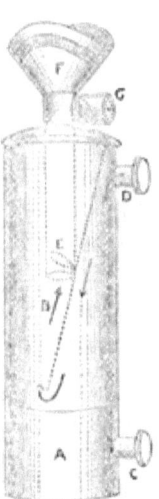

Fig. 2.
Smee's Ether-Inhaler.

Mr. Smee's inhaler, which is here figured, was made by Mr. Ferguson, of Smithfield; and consists of a tin vessel, either circular or oval, about eight inches long and three wide, divided into two compartments—one smaller (A), to contain hot water; the other larger (B), to contain the ether. The larger compartment is divided into two by a diaphragm, and has another opening to admit the ether and the entrance of the air (D). Into this larger compartment a tube is fixed, which has a valve at the extremity (E), for inspiration, and another valve (G) near the mouth-piece, for expiration. The mouth-piece (F) has an india-rubber covering, to adapt itself to different mouths.

When this instrument is to be used, the smaller chamber is filled with hot water (C), and a little ether, an ounce for instance, is placed in the larger compartment, which has sponge placed in it, to prevent its moving about. On inhalation, the current of air passes in the direction of the arrows, and is said to produce far more rapid effects than when any other instrument is employed.

This instrument, with other ingenious arrangements for the inhalation of ether, have been submitted to us by the proprietor of the celebrated Depôt for Inventions, 201, Strand.

## CHAPTER V.

### 1848 TO 1849.

'The Eye,' fourth book—Smee's optometer—Smee's horizontal fish-tail burners
—Sheet of Accidents and Emergencies—Royal Society : on its reducing its
number of Fellows—Personal appearance of Alfred Smee—Love of his family
—His powers of abstraction—His untidiness—Indifference to dress—His
walk—Jingling keys—Quick temper—Quick in action—Sensitive to a slight
—Not jealous — Impatient of opposition — Disliked arguments — Expected
others to have the same quickness of apprehension as himself—Works for
others — Disposition — Never feared responsibility — His dislike of routine
work—His charity—His genial and social disposition—Loved society, but
disliked the London season being in summer—His favourite authors.

ON the 16th and 23rd of March, 1848, Alfred Smee gave a course
of two lectures on Vision at the London Institution ; he also gave
other lectures at the Central London Ophthalmic Hospital, which
were afterwards incorporated in a book, and published under the
title of 'The Eye in Health and Disease.'   The book had an
extensive sale and was translated into French.   In it there is an
account of one of his clever contrivances for the adaptation of
glasses for impaired, aged, or defective sight.   The optometer—for

Fig. 3.  Optometer.

such is the name of the instrument—is most simple in its construction, yet most useful, and it should invariably be employed
by the optician before spectacles are sold to the applicant.   The
instrument consists of a convex lens to which a graduated scale
is affixed of such a length, that convergent, parallel, and diver-
gent rays may be brought within a reasonable scope, and thus
the eye may be tested by it.   In this book is also an account of
a novel kind of photometer, which he designed to judge of the

amount of light; but I shall have to speak of this instrument
when I give an account of its being used at the eclipse of the
sun in 1858, so that there is no need of further describing it
here.   There is also a description of his ingenious contrivance
for the better lighting of rooms by horizontal fish-tail gas-
burners.

It occurred to me (he writes) that the light should be placed at about
an angle of forty-five degrees if placed about the centre of the room, or if
near the ceiling, almost horizontal.
In my own library (and in his dining-
room, too), I am using a star with
three fish-tail burners, so arranged
that the gas passes out horizontally,
a direction which causes the flame to
assume a curve eminently calculated
to illuminate the table.   An enormous

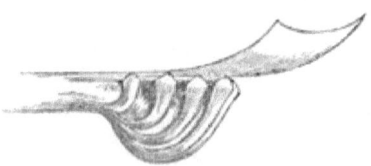

Fig. 4.  Gas-burner and jet.

increase of light is obtained by these means.   From the very great
superiority of the illuminating power obtained by this very simple
arrangement, I feel but little doubt that it will be at last generally
adopted.

He lived to see it universally adopted, although few if any
beyond his intimate circle of friends know to whom they are
indebted for originating this perfect manner of illumination.

The treatise contains also fifty short rules for the preservation
of sight, and for the choice of spectacles.

It may suffice here to add that the eye was my father's
speciality, and that over a series of years he was largely consulted on that subject by a high class of patients.   It is to me a
source of regret that other inducements caused him to abandon
in a great measure this part of his profession, in which he was,
to use the words of Sir David Brewster, " so distinguished."

In 1848 he also brought out a sheet of Directions for Accidents
and Emergencies to be used before the arrival of medical aid.
This sheet was specially designed for the poor.   For the title of
the sheet, which was made ornamental so that the poor should
hang it up in their cottages, an engraving after a painting
by Sir Joshua Reynolds, in the Dulwich Gallery, was selected.
In this painting the idea of life is represented by an angel,
death is depicted by another figure, and disease in the form of
a child.

A few other short papers also appeared from his pen during
this year, amongst which may be mentioned one in the 'Illustrated London News' for December 2nd, 1848, 'On Electric
Light and Gas Companies.'

This year he was elected member of the Hunterian Society.

During the same year (1848), Mr. Smee's mind seems also to have been bent on setting the Council of the Royal Society to rights, for the 'Athenæum' on the 25th of November contains two anonymous letters from his pen. Here it should be mentioned that he was always adverse to the Royal Society curtailing its number of Fellows, whereby he considered the strength of the Society was proportionately reduced. If the Institute of France be taken as an example, then certainly his suppositions relative to the Royal Society would give some grounds for apprehension. He was also opposed to the system by which the publication and rejection of learned papers are determined. In speaking of the rejection of a valuable paper by Mr. Spencer, we find in his history of Electro-Metallurgy these remarkable words :—

It is improper to throw the whole blame of the rejection of that paper upon Dr. Lardner, for this is by no means the only essay of importance which has been consigned to oblivion. The rejection of valuable papers is a fault of the system, not of the man. At all the learned societies a paper submitted to the society is referred to persons to report upon its merits, and upon that report the committees act with regard to its publication or suppression, which, in some cases, is facetiously termed a careful deposition in the archives of the society, which expression literally means, that it is placed in some large box from which it will be excluded from the cheering influence of the sun's rays for ever. The examination into the merits of any particular paper is, however, a most unthankful, disagreeable, and troublesome office. And it is not, therefore, surprising that the referees should sometimes exercise their characters as men, in supporting their own or the opinions of their friends and those to whom they are under obligations, and occasionally forget their situation as judges. Their services being gratuitous, entitle the referees to the heartiest thanks of the public; but an important office like that they occupy, in which the prosperity of the whole country is interested, should decidedly not be held without remuneration, and when remunerated the officers should be held responsible for their decisions. One never can tell to what great end a single new fact or application, though in an ill-drawn-up paper, may not ultimately tend.*

These remarks, it will be seen, are also applicable to other societies.

Perhaps before this I should have given an account of my father's outward appearance. He was short, not exceeding 5 feet 8 inches in height. As a young man he was very slim; became, however, in the prime of his life corpulent; but the last eight years again became very thin, and indeed emaciated. Although

* See 'Electro-Metallurgy,' p. xix.

short, he would have been taken for a tall man when seen sitting in a chair. There appears to have been an arrest of growth between his hip and his knee; otherwise, as his family frequently heard him remark, he ought to have been a man nearly six feet high. He always sat bolt upright, and disliked lounging chairs. His face was singularly handsome, and he possessed delicate yet well-defined features. He was very dark, and had a clear complexion, his cheeks being slightly tinged with colour. Through intense mental work his hair became grey at the early age of eighteen. When I first remembered him, his hair was of an iron grey and very short and curly. When a boy, he had, as I have heard, beautiful long ringlets which fell over his shoulders, and all who saw him called him the "beautiful boy." In the prime of life his curly locks used to glisten like silver in the sun. If, however, he were not quite well, his hair would assume a leaden tint; but no sooner was he again better in health, than his hair resumed its usual silvery beauty. His forehead was broad and prominent, and singularly square. His mouth was small, his lips thin and firmly set, and his face was set off by a pretty dimple in his chin, which, when he was animated in conversation or when he smiled, enhanced the beauty of his countenance. Later in life he wore a beard which robbed him of a part of his good looks. He had also small ears, a well-formed nose, small hands—singularly handy in manipulation—and small feet. But perhaps the most striking feature of his appearance were his eyes, which were truly wonderful. All who saw him in former days can testify to this. When a young man, they would flash fire. I have myself seen many instances of the marvellous power of a glance of his eye on persons trying to conceal any matter or to prevaricate. It was terrible to such persons!

Here I must remark that my brother and myself from early childhood were constantly with my father. We were always with him at his breakfast and frequently during his dinner, for my father, unless conducting his experiments or seeing patients, was never thoroughly happy unless he had his family around him. In the morning he used to write at the breakfast-table —whether his books or his pamphlets, or his papers, or his reports or letters—whilst my brother and myself were supposed to be playing about the room. But too often our play was stopped to make observations upon him. Yet at other times we were quite noisy, and would have, as we used to say, a bear-fight between ourselves, when down we would go on the floor on our hands and knees and pretend to be two bears fighting. Nothing of our play or conversation escaped my father, busy and seemingly absorbed as he was with his writings. Afterwards I have heard him observe, that during those breakfast hours he obtained a greater insight into our separate characters than he would have done had he seen us only when we were fully aware that he was watching us, for we as children looked upon him as an extraordinary man, who was so absent that we might do what we liked, and he would not notice it. How differently perhaps should we have behaved had we known that his eyes too were upon us!

In this way we heard and saw much of great interest, for he had the remarkable faculty of being able to write on the most abstruse questions with people talking around him in the same room, so great were his powers of abstraction and concentration. It was his custom to write books, as it were, in the mind, as he moved about in any ordinary avocations of life. When composed in the mind, it frequently became, as he has written,

a mere question of mechanical labour to transmit to paper those ideas when thought out; and so mechanical is the act of writing, that I frequently find myself using the pen on important matters whilst conversing with those around me on the ordinary trivial subjects of the day.*

Sometimes his mind could attend to two matters at one time, as instanced above, and sometimes even three operations of the brain would occur to him simultaneously, besides many slighter matters which the mind apprehended, such as the "ticking of a watch or the passage of a figure before the eye," &c. However, in laughing with him over his doing three things at one time, so contrary to the adage, he would own that he "generally made a hash of that." But duality of mental action or thought was an ordinary habit with him. He has written concerning this—

With me it is so constant, that it is my custom to read or even to write upon one subject when my family are conversing upon another. Most of my published treatises have been written, after having been thought out, when I have been talking with my family and friends upon the ordinary subjects which are discussed at a family gathering on a winter's evening.†

---

* See 'Mind of Man,' p. 13.          † Idem.

But against this there were times when the mind required to isolate itself, as it were, from the external world, and concentrate thought upon the subject to be worked out.

The ear must not hear nor the eye see. Many times I have been so thoroughly absorbed in developing a general scheme, that whilst walking the public streets I have found myself standing still to grasp, as it were, the relation of one part of the complicated details of the subject to another; and one day when it poured with rain I was amused on passing a friend to find that I had said, "A fine day," so entirely was my mind engrossed by the consideration of the matter before me.

This was by no means an uncommon case; for on similar mistakes arising from his absorption of mind, I might quote many laughable occurrences and sources of merriment to his family. His powers of memory were truly remarkable.

He was once at an important meeting where no reporter was present, and it was considered desirable for a report to appear. Upon application two or three days afterwards, he wrote out such of the speeches as were required, in such a manner that the substance was so correctly given that no person found out that his very words had not been taken down in the room by a shorthand-writer. Those proceedings happened to interest the public, and have been copied from paper to paper, and from newspapers to standard works.*

After this it may seem a paradox to state that he could never learn anything by rote: to commit Homer or Virgil to memory would have been to him an impossibility. Yet he could quote numerous favourite passages from the immortal Shakspeare's works. When at King's College, he used to write the lectures that he there attended *verbatim* after he came home. He did not take notes during the lectures, but afterwards, for his memory was so perfect that he could often write them out as they were delivered. It has been told him that he could learn from a book by heart if he only chose, to which assertion he always gave an unequivocal denial. Yet any image that had once been registered on his brain he never forgot. As an instance of this, he would remember thirty years after where he had placed a most trivial object, which ordinary individuals speedily forgot; yet he did not take any trouble to remember, but did remember nevertheless. I must confess that his family would not have regretted the absence of such a power of memory, for he was particularly untidy and careless; and as he used every room in the house as his study, and as he never dreamt of sorting or

* 'Instinct and Reason,' p. 52.

arranging his numerous papers and letters (and I think few houses had so many letters and various papers sent to them as his had), it followed that the house was one huge writing room and waste-paper basket, the intricacy of which no one knew but himself; and as he quite ignored that there were such creatures as house-maids in the world, he had but too frequently to suffer for his determined forgetfulness of that necessary appendage to society. Then, if some cherished scrap of paper or some letter requiring instant answering (the moment my father had an idea in his head it must be done that very instant), or whatever object it might be that was required, were not instantly forthcoming, then ruesome were the faces in our household! Whoever could hold his ground, now was the time! "If you please, mum, master won't have his papers touched; how am I to clear the breakfast table?" was the incessant question from the servants. At last I tried to keep his multifarious papers in somewhat like order. He would ask, "Where is that paper or letter which came on such a subject, three or four years ago? I want it immediately;" and matters had to be arranged so that what was required could be found in the twinkling of an eye. All was well so long as I remained at home; but if by chance I left home for two or three days on a visit (I never left home for more than ten days together, and then never more than three times in my life), then everything went wrong with the papers. On one of these occa-sions I received the following letter from my father :—

My dear Mary,—The head magpie has so badly taught the other magpies that all think themselves quite competent to take the place of the head magpie, and nothing left out for a moment is thrust under the pillows, or behind the sofa, so that the house is so magpied that every-thing is unfindable. It is a great dispensation of Providence that I am so heavy that they cannot hide me, or I should be hid in an old shoe, or perhaps in the key-hole, and never be able to find myself again.

My father was also extremely indifferent about his dress. So long as they were baggy and he could slip quickly into his clothes, that was all he required. Unless it was very cold weather, gloves he would never wear, excepting sometimes in the evening, and then he insisted upon having them about two sizes too large for him, that he might put them easily on, his fingers not being inserted more than half-way in them. But they were too frequently never put on; yet from the peculiar twistings and contortions they had undergone during the evening, they were invariably quite unfit to appear on any future occasion.

To show his utter indifference to dress, he was going one evening to a large dinner-party, at which he wished to appear at his best. His dress-clothes were duly put out for him (he never looked to such things himself) in his dressing-room; by ill luck, an old worn-out garden coat was lying near: my father, thinking of utterly different things from what he should be at that moment, slipped into his old rusty worn-out garden coat, and went off to the dinner-party; when to his discomfort, whilst sitting at the table next to the hostess, he suddenly discovered the mistake. Speaking of evening dress, it should be observed that my father ever had a great partiality for tail coats, and for many years of his life nothing could induce him to wear any other form of coat.

Besides this peculiarity in his dress, my father had also a peculiarity in his walk—if walk we may call it, for he usually used to run along, taking very short steps; but what with his short steps and his peculiar run, it was no easy matter to keep up with him. He usually had a large bunch of keys in one hand, which he jingled all the time he was running or walking. Oh, those keys! I cannot think of them without a horror. What have my nerves suffered through ye, O keys? If he was thinking, jingle went the keys; if he was writing, again jingle went the keys: whenever an opportunity was afforded him to jingle those precious keys they were jingled. I have often wondered he did not jingle them in his sleep: if they had been near him, I am sure he would have done so. In later life he gave up this dreadful habit, to the satisfaction of his family.

My father's temper was quick, as indeed was everything he did. When once his mind was made up for any given action, he seldom paused, but acted immediately, and it is thus he got through such an immense amount of work. Whilst others considered he acted. To a supposed slight he was particularly sensitive: this unfortunately caused him at times to take offence when none was intended. He had not the slightest tinge of jealousy, and he was always willing to give, and did continually give, a helping hand to any who required it. As a young man he had suffered considerably from the jealousy of others, his elders, and it made him have a feeling heart for others in a similar position. Opposition, however, my father could not brook. What he saw distinctly, that he expected others also to see. This made him an impatient teacher. He always expected his hearers to meet him more than half-way in understanding a subject, forgetting, or rather ignoring, that they might not be even cognizant of the facts on which his conclusions were based. Arguments he detested. To his mind a proposition was either right or wrong; and if one person took one side of a question, and another person took another, no amount of argument, he contended, would alter the opinion of either party, but would make both sides more pertinacious in their respective views. So my father would never permit an argument to be carried on by his family in his presence, which was often vexatious to them, the younger members being of an argumentative and contradictory turn of mind. As it has been just above observed he was extremely quick in his own seizing the points of a question, or in deciding on any course of action. This made him intolerant of slowness of comprehension in others; and once having determined upon any course of action nothing would irritate him more than for others to begin to talk or discuss upon that which as his quick mind had already perceived allowed of only one course of action. Woe betide that unfortunate individual, for Alfred Smee would invariably cut short his "twaddle." But in this it must be admitted he committed a grievous mistake, for this quickness of character is not born in everyone, and most persons *amour propre* would be wounded on being told in forcible language that their talk was not worth listening to. This, I must admit, was the worst feature in my father's character. Though impetuous to a degree, never had a man a kinder heart than had Alfred Smee. What labour would he not give himself for the good of others entirely without the domestic circle! His family, not possessing perhaps a sufficiently philanthropic spirit, have often said to him, "Why do you work so hard for so-and-so? You will never be thanked for it—or, So-and-so will not appreciate your kindness towards him." "You are only killing yourself," the writer of these lines used invariably to add "for others who do not deserve it." This was but too often the case:—he has often overworked himself for several who have proved ungrateful. Upon these remarks his family were always censured, and reminded that it was not right to do good only when we were sure of our reward, but that it was our duty to be always trying to do good to others. Alfred Smee was also most kind-hearted, and would never willingly inflict pain by word or look or by action, to any person or creature, unless indeed his ire was roused by being thwarted, molested, or personally abused either by words or writing. It so was a homely yet a favourite expression of his if

anyone "trod on his toes;" then he spared not his foe, but with
his pen he cut deep until he made his adversary writhe again.

My father never feared responsibility, neither did he fear
asserting that which he considered to be the truth. Where others
shrunk, he ventured; where others wavered, he decided: he was
essentially a man of action. He trusted his own powers and
acted up to them. He had a great idea of persons forming themselves decided opinions upon a subject and acting up to them.
He writes to his son from abroad, on a question in dispute. "You
must come to the front and form a clear, decided opinion, and
contend for a very definite course of action upon the best opinion
that can be formed."

With my father's love for action, and with his restless disposition, it is a wonder that he did not take the management of
his house into his hands; for that, however, he ever showed an
indifference quite remarkable. He had his own peculiar ways
of managing his own money matters. So much a year he put
by for house expenditure and for his family, and so much he
allowed himself for pocket-money. What he allowed for himself
was mostly spent on treats and presents to the different members
of his family, or for charity. So long as no more money was
required for the house, or for the necessities appertaining to
the family's social condition, well and good; he then troubled
himself but little, if indeed at all, how the money was expended.
Especially did the evil grow upon him in later life of a dislike
of routine work. He detested attending to any matters of
detail, and liked instead to soar in the regions above, and pro-
pound those noble generalizations of physical force and mental
phenomena, which it has been more especially the object of
this work to show.

In charity he gave not a little, and from what his family have
learnt from persons who have proved grateful for his bounty, it
seems that in the bestowing of his charity he let not his left
hand know what his right hand did. But although he was very
beneficent, yet he was wise in his acts of charity; for he liked to
assist persons by procuring for them some occupation befitting
them, that they might thereby become independent workers of
their own livelihood instead of living upon the charity of others.
This little trait is seen in the following anecdote. For some
years a poor woman sat on the steps of a house situated at the
corner of a street which he daily passed, and solicited alms of
the passers-by. One day it struck my father, Why should not

this woman get her own livelihood? He accordingly accosted her, and asked her, Why did she always sit there doing nothing? Why did she not sell newspapers to the passers-by, and thereby earn something instead of begging. It was a good position for that purpose, for the house was a corner one, in a busy and frequented part of the city of London. "Alas," replied the poor woman, "I have no money to get the newspapers, and nobody will give me credit." "If that is all," said my father, "take this sovereign, and get some newspapers, and let me see you to-morrow selling them." The woman did so, and for many years she might have been observed at the same corner, selling her stock of papers, and looking much happier than when she solicited alms of the passers-by. She is now dead—having died of old age. I doubt not that sovereign given her in that manner enabled her to end her days in more comfort, and certainly with greater happiness. For her little business throve every year more and more; indeed, it must have become a capital speculation, for after her death another old woman appeared carrying on the same business.

Many instances similar to the above might be enumerated to show my father's beneficence. After his death, how many of the poor came to tell his family that they, too, mourned his loss— that they, too, had indeed lost a true friend!

From Alfred Smee's genial and social disposition it may be inferred that he loved society, and shone in it. Much as my father liked being in society, yet never could he tolerate the London season being in the spring and summer months, when the country was looking its best. For no sooner did the flowers begin to bloom, the trees to push forward their buds, and the birds to warble their melodious songs, than his soul panted to be amidst such scenes, rather than in hot ill-ventilated rooms during the lovely months of May, June, and July. Why the season could not be in winter, when people would more enjoy social intercourse in warm rooms than they could in hot weather, he never could understand. He was not a fox-hunter himself, and perhaps had not sufficient sympathy with the par-takers of that sport, and, therefore, he could not appreciate the motives for persons preferring the country in the winter to the summer.

My father's mode of reading was cursory. He had a peculiar facility in seizing at once what was valuable in any book without perusing it from beginning to end. He would read philosophic works or books on travels, but novels he never could be induced to read, and always declared, and indeed boasted, he had never read a novel through in his life. If he saw anybody about him with a novel, he would contrive to get hold of it, and would then amuse himself by holding it up to ridicule by picking out in an instant one of the weaker parts of it, and, reading aloud the passage, would then, to the discomfort of the reader, laughingly inquire, " What pleasure could be derived by reading such stuff?" He disliked books where truth and fiction were so interwoven that the one could not be distinguished from the other. But books of fiction, such as fairy tales, and other works of imagination or satire, he liked. And so those wonderful conceptions from the vivid imagination of Shakspeare were to my father the most delightful specimens of the kind. My father's keen sense of imagination and of fun enabled him to enjoy farces, comedies, and pantomimes, and I doubt whether any child had more delight in the transformation scenes of a pantomime than had my father. He therefore delighted in taking children to see them. On a friend's not allowing his children to see a pantomime until he considered them old enough to go behind the scenes and see how delusive everything was, my father expressed his utter disapprobation of such a course, and remarked that children should be brought up to know that no one is exempt from being taken in by his senses. Those children, my father asserted, who were brought up without imagination, and who never saw tricks played before them without having them all explained, were sure to be the ones who would be the most likely to be deceived in after-life, and to become the victims of designing men.

# CHAPTER VI.

## 1849 TO 1854.

Fifth book, 'Electro-Biology'—Lecture on Electro-Biology—'Principles of the Human Mind'—Cholera—Cholera medicine given away—'Instinct and Reason' written to illustrate Electro-Biology—Sketch of the general plan of the work—Smee's hot and cold detector—Third edition of 'Electro-Metallurgy' brought out—'Process of Thought' written—Long articles in the 'Illustrated London News'—Plants that can be grown in London—Lecture at Newbury—Writes a memoir of Wyon—Lectures to the clerks of the Bank of England on 'Instinct and Reason'—First visit to Paris—Alfred Smee an angler—A regular attendant at St. Paul's Cathedral—Power of prayer.

ALFRED SMEE's great work, 'The Elements of Electro-Biology,' which embraces his 'Natural System of Mental Philosophy,' appeared in February 1849. On this work he had been engaged at intervals for the last ten years. The important researches detailed in this work cost him an immense amount of time, labour, and thought, and they were nearly all worked out at his residence in Finsbury Circus, " unaided," as he has sadly written, " by the advantages which public laboratories afford to their fortunate occupiers." Indeed, he had not even an assistant to aid him, if we except the services at times of a young lad in his teens, who was only too pleased to run and search for cats, or perform other little services for my father.* At one time the dearth of cats occasioned by these electro-biological researches was so great, that friends used to shut up their pussies to prevent them falling into the hands of the enemy. The anxiety among the ladies became at last so distressing, that one young lady, a personal friend, wrote the following amusing letter :—

MY DEAR SIR,—Having been apprised by my brother of the instructions which you have given to your page to obtain violent possession of the

---

* This lad was bright and intelligent, and he learnt a good deal from my father. He has since done well in life.

sacred person of my only and beloved child, I beg to say, that if such instructions are not countermanded, I shall be obliged to put personal restraint on the actions of my darling; in consequence of that restraint he will pine away and sink into an early grave, leaving a tender mother and a doting grandmother to bewail his loss. Mr. Smee, you are a father, and to your feelings as a father I appeal. I need say no more, I am sure. Be generous, and my thanks, my warmest and most unbounded gratitude, shall be yours.

The carrying out of the numerous experiments required for this great work was laborious, and his private practice and his official duties taking up the best part of the day, he was obliged to steal those hours that are by most persons devoted to rest and sleep. The physical experiments relating to the laws of voltaic electricity are to be found in ' Electro-Metallurgy,' and we have seen that ' Sources of Physics ' was expressly written as an introduction to the ' Elements of Electro-Biology.' There is such a lucid plan of this book in ' Chambers's Edinburgh Journal ' that I have transcribed it among my father's writings, at No. XVI. of the Appendix. I do not know by whom the account was written.

In April of the same year Mr. Smee delivered a lecture at the London Institution on Electro-Biology before a crowded audience. At this lecture Mr. Smee's injections of the brain were exhibited, which elicited these words from one of the daily papers, "These injections were of surpassing beauty, and well illustrated the exclamation of the inspired Psalmist, 'How fearfully and wonderfully are we made!'"

The lecture was afterwards printed, and published with the ' Principles of the Human Mind,' written as a sequel to ' Electro-Biology.' This—as the learned Dr. Pereira wrote, "Your lectures on Electro-Biology and the Principles of the Human Mind are very briefly but clearly drawn up, and will aid much in reading your longer copy"—I have transcribed in the Appendix, No. XVII. Besides this lecture, Mr. Smee gave others on the same subject elsewhere. Throughout the country he was repeatedly asked to deliver lectures, but he had not time at his disposal so to do.

This year also he wrote (the 3rd of March, 1849) in the ' Morning Chronicle ' a short article on Gutta-percha and its Uses.

The summer of 1849, it may be remembered, was a sad one for numbers of persons; for that direful scourge, pestilence, in the form of cholera, had made its ravages felt throughout the

length and breadth of the land.   My father was himself attacked
by it towards the close of the summer : happily he recovered, yet
I believe he permanently suffered from its effects.   In September
we find him investigating into the cause of this direful malady,
and the results of his inquiry are incorporated in a paper
which appeared in the 'Lancet.' (See Appendix, No. XVIII.)   It
should here be observed that whenever an epidemic of cholera
ensued, he had large quantities of cholera medicine (his own
prescription) made up and largely distributed.   No one who came
to the house and asked for cholera medicine, whether for himself
or for friends, was refused.   Numbers of persons flocked to the
house and availed themselves of this privilege.

The close of this year was to bring a heavy affliction to Alfred
Smee, in the loss of his mother, to whom he was devotedly
attached, and for whom he held the highest respect and esteem.
He felt this loss most acutely, and his mind seemed for a time
quite unable to throw off its sorrow and pursue further scientific
investigations.   At length Dr. Roupell, the senior physician to
St. Bartholomew's, persuaded him to write an illustration or key
to 'Electro-Biology,' whereby the abstract principles of that
important work could be illustrated by facts, so that it might be
more readily comprehended by a larger portion of mankind.   No
sooner did my father commence this new work than his wonted
energy was roused, and he entered with such heart and soul into
'Instinct and Reason' (for that was the name of the book) that it
was published in April 1850.

He did not even commence to write the book till the beginning of that year, and it is a matter of surprise how such a work,
full of coloured plates and of various woodcuts, could have been
got out in such a marvellously short period.

In the first chapter of 'Instinct and Reason' he treats of the
relation of Mind to Life, in which he makes the comparison
between man, animals, plants, stones, and pieces of mechanism.
For an example of animal existence he gives the dog, and shows
how the volitions of animals are regulated by experience, to prove
which he gives numerous facts ; and, indeed, I may here observe
that the great charm of this treatise consists in the most abstruse
laws of mental action being all made palpably clear to the mind
by various facts set forth in the form of interesting anecdotes,
nearly all of which were facts that had come under the range
of his own observation and experience.   After showing how the

mind is dependent upon the brain and nervous system, he passes on to consider the Organs of Sensation in man and in animals. Then pleasure and pain are fully described; pain being proved by abundant illustrations to be absolutely necessary to our welfare, and its absence impossible in a material world. The fourth chapter is devoted to Memory in Man and Animals. Without memory all that ennobles man is destroyed, and he is lowered almost to the condition of a plant. Reason in Man and, Animals is then exemplified. Up to this part of the treatise, it has been shown that man, in respect to the powers of mind which he possesses, is similar to animals; and yet we know that man far exceeds all living creatures in the faculties of the mind. If mankind possessed no further faculties than what have been already enumerated, he would be no whit better than the beast; therefore, in the chapter following that on Reason, those other faculties which entitle man to hold the first place in the scale of Creation are considered, and so the greatest works of man are here set forth as illustrations to prove his superiority over the brute beast. Passing from the operations of man, he next treats of Instinct. Accordingly, the works of animals, birds, and other creatures occupy the greater part of the seventh chapter. Instinct is also shown to exist in childhood. This chapter is particularly interesting to those possessed of the taste for natural history. Beautiful coloured plates illustrating the various and curious specimens of bird-nests, wasp-nests, spider-webs, ant-nests, bee-hives, and nests of other creatures, form a valuable adjunct to this chapter. Then he proceeds to define Intuitive Ideas, and shows their influence on mankind. Thence he proceeds to show that man has the faculty of expressing his ideas by sounds or marks. From words and language he proceeds to compare the works of man with the works of Nature, and shows that there is a limitation of the works of man. He then passes on to the Theory of Instinct and Reason, devotes a chapter to Reason and Faith, and another to Perverted Reason. Then he gives a chapter to the various Families of Man, and shows that even the savages and the lowest types of man possess faculties which give to him a superiority over all animals. A great gulf divides the mental powers of the lowest type of man from that of animals, which can never, he declares, be bridged over. The natural Classification of Mankind ends this highly original and interesting work on Instinct and Reason. The illustrations to this book are very beautiful: it has ten large coloured plates, and is, besides,

interspersed with numerous woodcuts.* Although the work itself
is based on such an abstruse subject as mental philosophy is
generally considered to be, yet it is so interwoven with anecdotes, most of which had come under his own observation, on
natural history and other subjects, that not only does the book
afford a forcible illustration to 'Electro-Biology' and 'The Mind
of Man,' but it is also admirably suited to be placed in the hands
of the young; for by interesting the reader in the investigation
of Nature, he is led on to discipline the mind, and thereby able
to seek a knowledge of the laws of God, obey the divine will, and
act rightly to his fellows. I know of no better book for a prize
at school than is 'Instinct and Reason.' Unfortunately at the
present moment the work is out of print; but I hope that a new
edition may appear, as it would afford a lucid illustration to that
work which has been based on 'Electro-Biology,' namely, 'The
Mind of Man.'†

In 'Instinct and Reason' is a description of one of Mr. Smee's
clever little contrivances, which he called the Hot and Cold

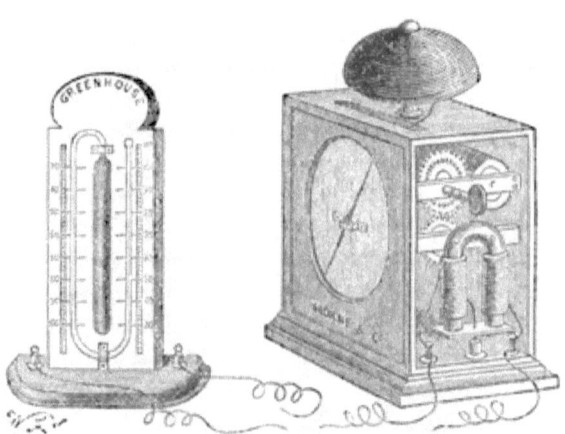

Fig. 5.  Hot and Cold Detector.

Detector; "a trifle" which he conceived in order to inform him
of the temperature of a small hot-house behind his house.‡

* The illustrations for 'Instinct and Reason,' such as the various bird-nests
and birds, wasp-nests, fossils, minerals, the South Sea Islanders' various implements, &c., were arranged in a long case which formed one complete side of
our drawing-room at Finsbury Circus.

† 'The Mind of Man' was published in 1875, and was written as another
edition of 'Electro-Biology.'

‡ See 'Instinct and Reason,' p. 97.

Now my plants (he writes) would be injured if the heat fell below 50° or rose above 90°, and I therefore wished to have some contrivance which should inform me in my own study whether the temperature were remaining or not within these limits.   For this purpose a thermometer was made for me into which two platinum wires were inserted, which came in contact respectively with the mercury at those two points (fig. 5).   By this contrivance, when the heat either fell below or rose above these two points, the mercury and platinum were not in contact, and a voltaic current could not be maintained.   Telegraphic communications were laid down from these two platinum wires to my dwelling-house, and a large pair of zinc and copper plates were sunk into the ground for a battery.   By attaching the wires to a galvanometer we can always ask how the temperature is; and, by attaching an alarum, a gardener might be warned of any accident at any time of the night.   I must say, that had I the care of so valuable a collection of plants as that of Kew, I should never be easy till I had such an apparatus in my bed-room to tell me if any of my plants were under unfavourable circumstances.

This hot and cold detector was also modified and used under other circumstances than telling the temperature of a hot-house. Many years ago Mr. Smee's father had a cottage at Clapton, on the banks of the river Lea.   The garden abounded with fruit, which the boys in the neighbourhood were only too glad to avail themselves of—generally choosing the time for their thefts when the family were at dinner.   Now one day my father attached fine thread to the wires of the battery, in such a manner that as soon as the boys were fairly in the garden they must insensibly move one of these threads.   Immediately down went the alarum in the house, out ran my father, followed by his brothers and by his brother-in-law.   The boys, surprised in the very act of taking the fruit, were soundly thrashed, and one of them having a squint was marched off into the house by my father, and then and there had to submit to the operation of having it cut.   I am afraid that boy's ideas of right and wrong must have been from henceforth rather confusing. He had done wrong, for the effect of which he immediately derived benefit, which he would not have derived had he done what was right and had kept out of the garden.   Let us hope, however, that he possessed a contented mind, and that he went not forth again to steal fruit, in order to derive further benefits therefrom.

The beginning of 1851 found Mr. Smee re-writing and bringing out in an enlarged form a third edition of 'Electro-Metallurgy.'   This was followed in the month of March by a short treatise from his pen on 'Process of Thought,' which contains a lengthy description of the Relational and Differential Machines.*

* Woodcuts and explanations of the relational and differential machines are to be found in the 'Mind of Man,' pp. 91, 100.

As this treatise has since been incorporated in his last work,
'The Mind of Man,' I refer the reader to that book for further
information on the subject.

In May he became one of the jurors to that most interesting
of all exhibitions—the one held in Hyde Park.

Between the months of May and of September he wrote
several long and interesting articles for the 'Illustrated London
News,' on various articles exhibited in the Exhibition.  Amongst
these may be mentioned 'On the Origin of the Forces which
have been employed in the Manufacture of the Articles exhibited,'
which appeared in that journal on the 10th of May, 1851, as well
as another article, 'On the Application of Electricity.'  On the
17th of May that journal contained the following articles from
his pen :—'Light and its Applications;' 'Electricity' (Supple-
mental Notice); 'Dumas's Expanding Model of a Man.'  On
May 24th, 'Heat and its Application.'  On June 7th, 'Mechanical
Force.'  On June 14th, 'The Food of Man.'  On June 21st,
'Ibbetson's Castings.'  On July 5th, 'Chemitypy, Stylegraphy,
and Galvanography;' 'Microscopical Preparations;' 'Food of
Man' (No. 2); 'Philosophical Instruments.'  On July 19th,
'Food of Man' (No. 3).  On August 2nd, 'Wardian Cases.'  On
August 9th, 'Surgical Instruments.'

Besides these long articles in the 'Illustrated London News,'
there are long articles on 'Electricity,' 'Electro-Metallurgy,' and
other matters, in the 'Morning Chronicle' for the 15th and 31st
of May.

The following extracts from the article in the 'Illustrated
London News' on Wardian Cases is here quoted, as it may
interest those who are fond of plants, and who are obliged to
dwell in a smoky town, to know which can be grown under such
adverse circumstances.

In London (says he) but very few plants will thrive.  The Oriental plane
rears its head in the heart of the city, in Cheapside, and forms a stately tree.
Russell Square and Guildford Street exhibit also noble specimens of this
beautiful tree; yet by coming into leaf late, and shedding its foliage early,
it is not so susceptible of those influences which injure other plants.  The
lime-tree will also partially flourish ; and in the very centre of the Bank
two noble and ancient limes shade the parlour from the scorching sun of
summer, and yearly cast forth delicious perfume from abundant flowers.
With these exceptions, flowers and vegetable structures can scarce be
cultivated in London, except with the aid of a Ward's case.  Residing in
the very centre of the metropolis, we now write with two beautiful Ward's
cases before us, which exhibit the most luxuriant foliage.  In these cases
we have at this moment the beautiful wax-plant, or *Hoya carnosa*, in

abundant flower. We have recently introduced the newly-imported and lovely *Hoya bella*, which is also now in flower; and the odoriferous *Francisca Hopeana* is always ready to refresh us by its scent on opening the door of the case. We have five species of Lycopodia, which gratify the eye by their luxuriant green; and no less than fifteen or sixteen species of exotic ferns gladden the eye by their charming forms, their verdant foliage, and luxuriant appearance. The leaves of the *Maranta bicolor*, never soiled by wet, are of surpassing beauty; and several species of Achomenes are rapidly growing, to display their brilliant colours in the latter part of summer. Many of our plants have been in their present situation for ten years, and so the delight which we have had in the observation and cultivation of them in the Wardian case makes us look with increased interest upon those first examples of construction which Mr. Ward has contributed to the Exhibition.

We take this opportunity of calling attention to the Wardian cases, because, much as their use has increased, still they are not nearly so much employed in large towns as they ought to be. The cultivation of plants is an occupation delightful in itself, and one that is calculated to afford intense pleasure to those who follow the amusement. In that gloomy prison of Pentonville, where the inmates are not allowed from their cell to see a passing cloud, it is recorded that the only pleasure which a prisoner could find was to watch from day to day the growth and flowering of a few pieces of grass, shepherd's purse, chickweed, and groundsel, when he took his daily airing in the little space allotted to his walk. Every London child should have his Wardian case, if on ever so small a scale. The love of the cultivation of plants would grow with the knowledge of their perfection, and the mind would be led insensibly by the true and natural process of thought from a study of Nature's works to the contemplation of Nature's God.

And the following account taken from 'Instinct and Reason' will further show my father's observation on this question.

In this vast metropolis so much poisonous gas and smoke is exhaled from the chimneys of the thousands of houses and manufactories here accumulated together, that the sulphurous acid poisons the plants, and the absence of light is fatal. Under such circumstances, horticulture seems futile; and yet, when I say that, despite these difficulties, I have now, in the middle of January, lilacs, azaleas, an oncidium, and an epidendrum, in full bloom, it must be acknowledged that even here plants may be grown not altogether in vain, although in less perfection than in the horticultural gardens surrounding London.

As far as appertains to the foul sulphurous acid and smoke, Ward has taught us that by simply covering the plants with a glass shade, they may be effectually grown. In my dining-room I have had two of these cases for nine years; and the plants which I first purchased from Loddige's are still alive. In fact, the luxuriance of their growth is so great, that I am periodically compelled to remove large quantities of the plants. Besides ferns, I attempt the growth of a few flowering plants. I commence with crocuses; I go on with hyacinths, and an occasional tulip or narcissus. Later in the year the common cereus is generally covered with flowers, affording a gorgeous display. However, this plant generally blooms itself to death.  In July, my *Hoya carnosa*, or wax-plant, gives rise to a dozen or a dozen and a half of fine flowers ; and I am now venturing to try the charming *Stephanotis floribunda*.  During the fall of the year I obtain a fine display of Achomenes, and my ferns and Lycopodiums form an elegant green covering all the year.[*]

Now, from observation and experiment, I think I can communicate a great secret as to the plants which will do well in a London atmosphere ; for I find that the tropical plants, as a general rule, flourish nearly as well as in the country.  We read that the lights of tropical countries are apt to be yellow, like the dismal yellow lights of London.  Palms, bananas, and many plants of this description will thrive.

Some orchids, although they do not like the sun, require much light, and they do not thrive, though others may be grown satisfactorily.

I have lately constructed a portable hot-house which can be heated by a candle, oil, or coal-gas.  The one which I have is like a Ward's case, but has a compartment to hold water at the bottom, through which is inserted a copper tube, to carry the heated air and warm the water. I hope to be enabled, by this contrivance, to obtain the more beautiful orchids and tropical plants in ordinary dwelling-rooms ; and I question, if I can fully succeed, whether the largest conservatory in the most extensive orchideous house, when cultivated by the hired gardener, can give half as much pleasure as this little portable hot-house.

My father also, assisted only by a lad, constructed a green-house at the bottom of a narrow strip of ground at the back of his residence in Finsbury Circus.  This house he heated by pipes, and in it he grew many varieties of tropical plants.  The sugar-cane here throve.  Besides, he had a tank in it with hot-house water-plants, and which also contained gold-fish. These gold-fish knew their master, and it was most amusing to see them come to the water's surface when he whistled, and take the morsels of bread from his hand.  In 'Instinct and Reason' he gives an interesting account of the breeding of gold-fish in this tank in the hot-house at the bottom of his garden.  He afterwards converted the hot-house into a green-house, where all the British ferns were to be found growing in the greatest luxuriance.  Amidst my father's numerous avocations he always found time to attend to his beloved green-house, and even to paint it whenever it was required.  How well do I remember the times of painting the green-house, what fun it was, and what trouble

---

[*] See 'Instinct and Reason,' p. 131.  In the obituary notice of Alfred Smee in the 'Gardeners' Chronicle,' January 27th, 1877, we read—

"Many years ago the fern-cases in his dwelling-house in Finsbury Circus were as remarkable, and attracted almost as much attention, as those of the late N. B. Ward.  The writer of these lines well remembers the time when he was in the habit of passing and repassing the windows in Finsbury Circus, with the sole object of ascertaining what were the species that throve under such disadvantageous circumstances."

we children got into afterwards with the higher powers of the nursery!

On the 11th of September, 1851, Mr. Smee gave the opening lecture of the session at the Newbury Literary Institution, 'On the Results of the Great Exhibition;' and later on, the 8th of November, he had the melancholy satisfaction of writing in the 'Illustrated London News' the memoir of his much-lamented friend William Wyon, R.A., the chief engraver to the Mint, whose numerous medals of high artistic worth have given the name of Wyon a wide celebrity.

On the 25th of November Mr. Smee delivered a lecture before the Bank of England Literary Association, on Instinct and Reason.

During the early part of the summer of 1851 there was a *réunion* of English savants at Paris, under the auspices of Napoleon III., then President. This occasion was the first visit of my father and mother to Paris, and it was the first holiday of more than a day's duration that my father had since 1845. He used, however, to take at times a day's holiday, and spend a few hours at a favourite pastime—fishing: for my father was a keen fisherman, and as his love of and skill in angling were well known among many, he had always abundant orders and invitations to fish in some choice spot or other. Jack-fishing was a favourite sport of his, and in his dining-room was a very noble specimen of that ferocious fish. Its form is perfect; it weighed twenty-two pounds, and was killed by a small hook. To hear my father describe the landing of this fish, one could fancy one was listening to a page of Izaak Walton. But my father did not disdain other kinds of fishing. He would sit in a punt on the river for hours, angling for any fish that would come to his hook.

In such times the scenery of the river, the singing of the birds, afforded him ample enjoyment, and his overworked brain found rest and solace in the charms of Nature. He knew the note of almost every bird, and loved to teach the different songs of the songsters to his children. In trout-fishing he was an adept. During the summer months my grandfather used to take a house for himself and for us in the country, at such a distance from London that he and my father could daily attend their businesses in London, and thence return in the cool of the evening and enjoy the quiet solitude of a country life. Somehow or other our country

house was generally situated near a river, and so my father in the
cool summer evenings had frequent opportunities of exercising
his skill in fishing.  At these times he was generally surrounded
by his family.  My grandfather, too, frequently mingled in our
sports; and when the latter caught a fish, how speedily did the
length of the fish increase until it grew to a wonderful size!
But in fishing, as in other things, my father generally won the
laurels: but what fun it was for the domestic circle each to
contend for our places as skilful fishermen, none can appreciate
but those who have tried their hand in the art!  The distinguished
chemist and investigator Professor Graham (former Master of the
Mint) had similar tastes to my father.  How amusing it was
to spectators to hear them intermingling their conversations on
abstruse chemical and philosophical theories with their theories
on the art of fishing!

On Sundays my father used with his family to be a regular
attendant at the morning service at St. Paul's Cathedral.  In
various parts of this work it has been shown that one of the
great *peculiarities* of Alfred Smee's mind was that it belonged
to that class (Pneuma-Noemic) which is particularly capable
of appreciating spiritual qualities.  He was ever labouring to
demonstrate that religion and reason were not discordant.
After my father had fulfilled the duties of attending a service
at a place of worship, he would then with his family betake
himself into the country, and there investigate Nature, and,
contemplating the Author of all things, would rejoice in the
works of the Almighty, and sing in his heart, Glory be to God
most High!

Although the following anecdote is perhaps unconnected
with my present subject, yet it is so typical of the minds of
the two men—Faraday and Alfred Smee, both electricians, and
both possessing a fervent and deep-rooted religion, though each
of his own kind—that it may not be out of place to mention
it here.  It was on one Sunday morning, now many years ago,
as my father and myself were going to attend the 10 o'clock
morning service at St. Paul's Cathedral, that we met Faraday
close to the General Post Office.  He was hurrying to the San-
demanian Chapel, not far from St. Martin's-le-Grand, where he
was wont to preach.  He stopped us, and after a few words of
conversation suddenly inquired where we were going to at that
early hour in the morning.  "To St. Paul's," was the reply.

"Is there anything particular going on there, then?" exclaimed Faraday, in a hurried manner. "Nothing particular," said my father, "only the ordinary morning service." "Ah!" replied Faraday, "we are then all three bound for the one great object." The fervent manner in which he uttered the last few words made a great impression upon us. I never hear the name of Faraday mentioned without seeing him as I saw him then, his fine intelligent face lit up with reverence and devotion.

Alfred Smee was a firm believer of the power of prayer, as we find in the following lines:—

Some men learned in many sciences have called in question the efficacy of prayer to alter the natural course of events. These men argue that, because God governs the world by immutable laws, He heeds not prayer. Experience shows that the direct course of the affairs of the universe is not interrupted by prayer: the sun never reversed its course in consequence of prayer; nor did any person rise, contrary to gravity, from one floor to another by praying. But a study of the human mind indicates that in all human actions prayers have great effect in governing men's actions, and leading to results. When a man prays with earnestness and sincerity, it affects his whole mind, and all his actions are directed to obtain the result for which he prays. When many men pray for one object, the purpose of many persons is directed to one end, and all continue in heart and will to obtain the desired object.

The influence of prayer on human actions, if tested by experience, will be found to be immense. In producing resignation, and in confirming action, its power is great, although its influence to control the laws of the universe is void, and of no effect.[*]

In 'Instinct and Reason' is the following illustration, showing the power of prayer over the actions of man, during the great trial of the year 1849:—

During the prevalence of cholera in the infected districts, neither writing, nor talking, nor preaching, could cause the inhabitants to rouse themselves and prepare to endeavour to ward off death from their habitations. At length, however, when Death had extensively accomplished his work, men were afraid, and in some parishes they even sacrificed a weekday's profit to pray that the malady might be stayed. To their prayers and supplications they added all their endeavours to stop the pestilence: they subscribed for the poor; they provided attendance, remedies, and visitations; and immediately the effect was felt, and the disease was lessened. The people saw the necessity of acting vigorously and decidedly according to the laws of the attack of the malady, which were, in fact, the laws of God; thus their prayers were instantaneously followed by more or less beneficial results.[†]

[*] See 'Mind of Man,' p. 128.          [†] See 'Instinct and Reason,' p. 226.

The following prayer was written by himself when he was a young man :—

Most gracious God, the beneficent Author of every good thing, we bless Thee for all Thy mercies bestowed upon us. We magnify Thee for our creation, preservation, and existence. We truly thank Thee for Thy goodness in granting us senses, intellect, and inclination to love and enjoy Thy noble works. We render Thee our sacrifice of praise for food, clothing, and habitation. We worship Thee for warding off dangers and averting afflictions. We glorify Thee for the peace and happiness conferred upon us. We heartily adore Thee for averting death and promising us everlasting life through our Saviour Jesus Christ; and finally, we acknowledge Thee the only true God, Father Almighty, to whom all blessing, praise, love, worship, and adoration are due from everlasting to everlasting.

# CHAPTER VII.

## 1854 TO 1858.

Second edition of 'The Eye'—Binocular Perspective—Soirée at which ladies were first present—Lecture on Education at London Institution—Originator of educational lectures at the London Institution—Alfred Smee originates and establishes a new form of printing the Bank of England notes—Decimal coinage—Lecture on Monogenesis of Physical Forces—Visit to Paris—Eclipse of the sun; experiments at Blisworth—Loses his father.

In the beginning of 1854 Alfred Smee brought out another edition of 'The Eye.' This edition contained a long account of his investigations on Binocular Perspective, which will be found in the Appendix, No. XIX. It will be sufficient, therefore, to notice here that Mr. Smee possessed several paintings executed purposely for him in this Binocular Perspective system, by the late Mr. Price of the Bank of England. Mr. Smee had also many photographs taken for him by the moving camera. These photographs were shown by my father to the late lamented Prince Consort, who was considerably interested in the system, and compared these delicately shaded photographs to the soft tones of Rembrandt. In June of the same year these paintings and photographs, illustrating the system of Binocular Perspective, were shown at a large soirée held at Mr. Smee's residence in Finsbury Circus. I believe this was the first time that ladies were present at a réunion hitherto only resorted to by distinguished members of the sterner sex.

Mr. Smee further devoted much attention to the system of education, which he not only considered to be in a deficient state, but too frequently based on a wrong principle. He contended that in youth the observation and registration of facts should be carefully cultivated and practised, and upheld the system in Germany, " where the youths are taken out in the country to be shown the flowers and plants, the rocks and stones and soils, so

as to acquire rudimentary botanical knowledge, as well as a
knowledge of mineralogy and geology. Accurate 'Syndramic'
knowledge is a department of education which requires cultivation in England."*    Mr. Smee was ever from the first a consistent and strong opponent of the present system of "cramming,"
and of competitive examination, both of which he contended
materially injured the functions of the brain, and thereby lessened the mental faculties of man.    In the Appendix, No. XX.,
is a long letter on education from Mr. Smee's pen addressed to
the Committee of Industrial Instruction in London.    For his
further views on education I must refer the reader to the chapter
on that subject in ' The Mind of Man.'

So firmly was Alfred Smee's mind bent upon endeavouring to
improve the education of the youths of the city of London, that
through his means he induced his co-managers of the London
Institution to allow educational lectures to be given two afternoons every week in the lecture-room, on astronomy, botany,
chemistry, geology, and zoology.    They were delivered by
eminent professors.    At first his brother managers tried to laugh
my father out of the idea.    I remember one of them saying in my
presence, " Smee, whatever are you thinking of now ? Just as if a
parcel of children could understand or care about lectures."    One
of the parcel of children that heard this remark was considerably
offended, I remember, and it was a long time before the writer of
this entertained friendly feelings towards that gentleman.

But my father pressed the matter, and the managers con-
sented to try the experiment.    The first lecture of the first course
of educational lectures at the London Institution was delivered
by Alfred Smee on the afternoon of Saturday, October the 14th,
1854.    The object of this lecture was to set forth the objects and
advantages of educational lectures, and it was based on his
" natural system of mental philosophy."    The lecture-table and
space around was covered with apparatus for experiments.    The
children were delighted and learnt much ; the adults were
delighted, and also found that they had much to learn.    The
success of the various educational lectures was greater than
even my father had anticipated.    For myself, I shall never
cease to think of those years during which I regularly attended
those lectures without grateful feelings for the units of knowledge which I thereby acquired, and regret only that I was not
more diligent in taking advantage of such golden opportunities.

* See chapter v. on Education, in ' Mind of Man,' p. 34.

The lecture is to be found in its place in the Appendix, No. XXI.

For some time past a considerable part of Alfred Smee's time had been devoted to arranging a new mode of printing the Bank of England notes, which he at last succeeded in effecting with the assistance of Mr. Hensman, the engineer to the Bank of England, and Mr. Coe, the superintendent of the printing department to that establishment, after enormous labour, and after having to surmount innumerable difficulties.    A full description of the process will be found in the Appendix, No. XXII., in a paper ' On the New Bank of England Note and the Substitution of Surface Printing and Electrotypes for Copper-plate Printing,' which was read before the Society of Arts on the 22nd of December, 1854.

Previously to the establishment of this new form of printing the bank-notes by Alfred Smee, the Bank authorities had been thrown into a state of alarm by discovering that some ingenious persons had succeeded in splitting the old form of note—so that two notes were obtained in the place of one.    The matter was brought before Alfred Smee, and he soon found that, with a little practice, it was by no means so difficult a process as at first would appear.    By the new form of Bank of England note this "splitting" of it could not be effected.

There was some talk in 1856 about introducing into this country the decimal coinage, and the two following letters will show the interest Mr. Smee took in the subject.

### PRACTICAL APPLICATION OF THE DECIMAL COINAGE.

#### To the Editor of the Society of Arts' Journal.

Sir,—Permit me to occupy a short space in the Journal to detail a practical plan for introducing decimal coins into our monetary system.

The difficulty which has to be encountered arises from our penny, which, as the $\frac{1}{240}$ part of a pound, cannot be converted into a decimal fraction; and unless some system be adopted, by which our present coins shall bear a definite relation to decimal coins, decimals must remain a bugbear to the million, and their use be unpopular if not almost impossible in practice.

The thought which has occurred to my mind is, to construct our decimal and present systems in definite relations, which shall be evident to the mind through the medium of the senses, so that, on throwing two masses of coins upon the table, they may be either sorted into the decimal or ordinary systems, and one may be rendered exactly equal to the other.

The decimal coinage might consist of the Pound, the Florin, the Decat, and the Mil.

The penny, however, cannot possibly bear any relation to decimal coinage, and we cannot afford to neglect the consideration of this coin, as probably more than 2000 tons, and possibly as much as 6000 tons of copper, are in circulation over the country.

To meet this difficulty a set of small copper coins should be issued, called the mite, half-mite, and quarter-mite, the mite bearing the value of the $\frac{1}{5}$ of a mil. A penny would be equal to four mils and one mite, the halfpenny to two mils and half a mite, and the farthing to one mil and a quarter-mite.

By the conversion of our present money into mites, the untaught could always tangibly satisfy themselves of their mutual relations, and they would find that, by dividing the number of mites by six, the result would represent decimal coins.

This mode of dealing with the question, which is applicable to weights and measures, as well as money, has been forced upon my mind upon psychological grounds, based upon the properties of matter on the one hand, and on the powers of the mind on the other. In support of it, I would refer to the statement of Mr. Bidder, the great mental calculator, who tells us that he satisfied himself of the properties of numbers through the medium of the senses, as he made the multiplication table for himself, by grouping sets of objects and counting them, thus demonstrating to his own mind, that the multiplication table was an absolute fact of universal application.          I remain, Sir,

Your obedient servant,

7, Finsbury Circus,                          ALFRED SMEE.
June 10th, 1856.

## Relation between Decimal Coins and Weights and Measures.

Sir,—The serious objections which exist against the adaptation of decimal coins to our currency again must be pleaded as a reason for my addressing the Journal, to point out the practical manner by which they may be probably introduced with least injury, and be rendered sufficiently attractive for the mass of people to desire their adoption.

In my last letter I recommended for practical use the additional issue of the $\frac{1}{10}$ of a florin, and the $\frac{1}{100}$ of a florin, with the superaddition, for adjustment, of little coins of the value of the $\frac{1}{5}$ of the $\frac{1}{100}$ of a florin, the $\frac{1}{12}$ and the $\frac{1}{24}$ of the same, to be called respectively mites, half-mites, and quarter-mites.

Without unnecessarily occupying space in your Journal with abstract views on this question, which I have fully considered in my 'Sources of Physical Science,' I have here to propose that the new coins be brought into relation with our weights and measures, so that, tens of centuries hence, upon the discovery of these coins, a near approximation may be obtained of the standards of value, length, weight, and capacity used in our times.

The decat or $\frac{1}{10}$ of a florin might represent also the $\frac{1}{10}$ of a pound of avoirdupois, the $\frac{1}{10}$ of a foot, the $\frac{1}{10}$ of the $\frac{1}{10}$ of the weight of an imperial gallon of water, and the $\frac{1}{10}$ of the $\frac{1}{10}$ of the bulk of an imperial pint.

To accomplish this object the decat must weigh 700 grains, be the $\frac{1}{10}$ of a foot in diameter, and the metal must either have a specific gravity of 8·75, or, if copper, have its rim raised to compensate the excess of specific gravity. which is from 8·8 to 8·9.

The mil might represent the $\frac{1}{10}$ of the $\frac{1}{100}$ of a pound avoirdupois, and be ¼ inch diameter.

The mite should weigh 10 grains, the half-mite 6 grains, and the quarter-mite 1 grain, which would be useful weights for chemists and other dealers in small quantities of matter, and thus coins would be brought into relation with apothecaries' and troy weights.

As this letter is merely suggestive, I do not think it necessary to enter minutely into all the practical results which would be attained by the above system.   It is manifest, however, that it would give a basis of a decimal division of value, weight, length, and bulk, and at the same time afford a material relation between the decimal division and the other modes of division now in use.

If the principle be adopted, the nomenclature would have to be carefully reconsidered; and it appears to me, whether we consider value, breadth, surface, weight, or capacity, from five to ten of the decimal divisions should have definite words assigned to them.   At first we should have both systems in operation at once, but by degrees, hereafter, all divisions not found to be practically convenient might be gradually withdrawn.                      I remain, Sir,

Your obedient servant,

BANK OF ENGLAND,                                    ALFRED SMEE.
June 28th, 1856.

A very interesting lecture was delivered by Mr. Smee on the 18th of February, 1857, at the London Institution, on the Monogenesis of Physical Forces.   This lecture is a connecting link between 'Electro-Metallurgy,' 'Sources of Physics,' 'Electro-Biology,' and later 'The Mind of Man.'   The lecture itself will be found in the Appendix, No. XXIII.

In the autumn of this year my brother fell ill, and an entire change of air and scene was considered necessary for him.   We were taken to Paris.   It was our first visit to the Continent. During our stay there my father had the greatest possible delight in taking my brother and myself to see all the sights of Paris: he never wearied.   One of our favourite amusements used to be to go into the Tuileries Gardens and take part of our breakfast roll and feed the wild pigeons who used to eat out of our hands, and the sparrows who used to hover about in the air before us and catch the morsels of bread we threw up to them.

The following spring there was a total eclipse of the sun. The astronomical savants flocked, on the 17th of March, 1858, to Blisworth in Buckinghamshire, that being considered the best spot to observe the phenomenon.   We—that is to say, my father and mother, my brother and myself—also betook ourselves thither, for my father had a great desire to try the effects of his photometer.*    We were located for the day in a stiff clay ploughed field—rendered extra stiff and disagreeable for quick locomotion by some continued rains previously.    There was a hut hard by at which the savants and the ladies of their party retired to warm themselves and refresh the inner man, when their presence was not required for observing the great natural phenomenon.    There were some amusing accounts of these savants and of the eclipse sight-seers in some of the journals of the time, especially in the local papers.

It came on to rain, and at the end of the day we all left that ploughed clay field, thankful that we could get out of it : yet most, if not all, felt that they had thoroughly enjoyed themselves, and had lived a day to be remembered always with delight.    The results of my father's experiments with his photometer were published in the 'Times,' the 'Morning Chronicle,' and some other papers.    For his letter to the 'Morning Chronicle,' with the drawing and description of the photometer, see the Appendix, No. XXIV.

A brilliant comet followed this total eclipse of the sun, and later, in the middle of November, my grandfather died, just nine years and one day after the death of his wife.    As 1849, so did 1858—both eventful years in physical phenomena—close in sorrow to Alfred Smee.

---

* See p. 39.

# CHAPTER VIII.

## 1859 TO 1863.

THE oration of the Hunterian Society was delivered on the 9th of February, 1859, by Alfred Smee, one of the fellows of that society. The subject chosen by him was 'Debility and Defective Nutrition: their Causes, Consequences, and Treatment.' The oration was published in a small volume consisting of about ninety pages, which are divided into six chapters. In the first chapter his views on the structure of man, and the proper nutrition required for the use of the body, are detailed. In the second the varieties and symptoms of debility are given. He shows that debility is often mistaken for disease or incubation of disease, and he dwells on capricious appetite, by which a person in affluence may, amidst the greatest delicacies which a skilful cook can prepare, yet not take sufficient food to sustain nature. He then shows the various causes of debility. He also treats of excess in drink, and shows how the frame of the drunkard is debilitated throughout, until he is prematurely cut off by one or other of the maladies attendant on debility. "If the career of a drunkard be watched, it is astonishing how soon he passes away, as if the voice of Nature exclaimed, 'Cut it down; why cumbers it the ground?'"

My father was always an extremely sober man, and had a great horror of, and indeed disgust for, spirit-drinkers. He never took spirits himself, and even within a few days of his death would constantly refuse even small quantities of brandy. Whenever he saw an inclination in any person to spirits, he would warn them in the most solemn manner of the danger they were thereby incurring. He considered spirits ought to be used only as a medicine, and then only when ordered by the doctor.

In speaking of Alfred Smee being a sober man, I may here add that he never took wine excepting at dinner, and sometimes at his luncheon. He considered the taking of a glass of wine, with or without a biscuit, as being most destructive to the digestive organs.

Opium-eating, smoking, and other causes for debility are also examined in the above treatise. The fourth chapter is devoted to the consequences of debility, the fifth to its treatment, and the relation of debility to different periods is given in the sixth and last chapter.

There is an interesting appendix to this little work, in which is given the chemical composition of various substances of food, &c., as well as a table showing the solid constituents in one gallon of water supplied to towns, which was compiled for him by Professor Attfield, F.C.S., Chemist to the Pharmaceutical Society. This little book has had a good sale—a second edition was issued in 1862—and it is a serviceable little book for families to possess, for much practical and useful information concerning one's every-day life may be obtained from it.

In August 1859, my father went with his wife and his two children to Switzerland, and enjoyed for a month the grand and sublime scenery which that country affords. A dreadful accident, attended by loss of life, had occurred at Zermatt the day previous to our arrival there, which occasioned some letters to the 'Times' on the bad organization of the guides at that place. Among these letters is an anonymous one on the 16th of September, 1859, from the pen of Alfred Smee. Before leaving this subject I will here merely add that, during this visit to Switzerland, my father amused himself by taking many observations with his photometer, the description of which will be found in his letter on the Eclipse of the Sun in 1858, No. XXIV. of the Appendix.

During this visit the natural flower-garden of the valley of Zermatt was robbed of many of its choicest specimens, to be transferred to that garden near London which has now become of worldwide repute.

The trout-fishery of the Wandle was what first attracted

my father's attention to Wallington. Already, in 1858, he had rented that fishery, and a little later obtained a narrow strip of land, where he grew a few peas, beans, &c. At that time what is now "my garden" was a barren field, which it was impossible to walk across without sinking above your knees in water. A few willows divided the field almost midway, and along the side of the road it was skirted by tall elms, and a little thicket of trees in Beddington Park enclosed it on another side. This field, this waste land, the soil of which was singularly devoid of vegetative qualities, Alfred Smee converted into an experimental garden where there is grown the largest collection of fruit-trees and other species of plants of any private collection in Europe, for the description of which I must refer the reader to his great work, 'My Garden.' The forming of this garden, and the experiments he there carried on for the cultivation of various plants, were ever the recreation of my father from his multifarious mental labours and anxieties of life. The objects of this garden are seen in my father's dedication—"In Lucem, Lucrum, Ludum." The dedication of a garden is new in England, yet in Italy it frequently occurs, and it was from the latter country that my father borrowed the idea. From the year 1859, most of the Saturdays were spent in this garden, among his beloved plants, and here he would throw off all cares, and show in a remarkable way how his genius was not to be confined in one path. In the memoir of him in the 'Gardeners' Chronicle,'[*] we read that this garden

contains something of everything. Though the surface is flat, landscape effects and artistic surprises are numerous. The visitor passes in a moment from a bold bit of lake scenery to a tiny fern-clad ravine, through which meanders a crystal stream, laving as it goes a host of lovely bog-plants. A turn, and the visitor is in a rose-garden, or admiring a choice collection of alpines. Now long shady walks invite attention; now the treasures of the herbaceous border attract notice. Nor is the more utilitarian part of gardening omitted: on the contrary, it is in places somewhat too obtrusively prominent. Be this as it may, the collection of vegetables, and specially of fruit-trees, is very remarkable. No mere amateur's collection within our experience rivals this one in extent and variety. As to the houses and garden structures, they are numerous and efficient. They have no architectural pretensions; indeed, one object of the proprietor was to show how, at a comparatively very slight expense, men of very moderate means might enjoy the pleasures and luxuries of a green-house, a fernery, a stove, or a vinery. Mr. Smee's "poor man's houses"

---

[*] See 'Gardeners' Chronicle,' January 27th, 1877.

exactly realize this ideal. They are sufficient to give profit, pleasure, nay, luxury, to the mere labourer. Of course it is not to be expected that the keeping or the condition of the houses, or of the plants in them, would satisfy a head-gardener on a ducal estate; but from the point of view of the proprietor they are all that could be desired or expected, and relatively to the outlay we should not be surprised if the produce were larger, as the pleasure to the proprietor was certainly greater, than in establishments of greater pretensions. Insects, fishes, birds, fossils, nothing came amiss to the hospitable proprietor of this garden. How keen his interest, how great his delight in these matters, is evidenced in his work, ' My Garden,' reviewed in these pages at the time of publication.

What happy days were those to us—those which were bestowed on the laying out of that garden ! From a narrow strip of land came a little more under cultivation, then a little more, until the whole plot of ground consisted of nearly eight acres of land and water. Well shall I ever remember how we looked forward to the Saturdays, on which days my brother and myself had always a holiday, and when we two with my father betook ourselves to Wallington, my mother joining us in the afternoon. Well shall I ever remember the excitement of the Friday evenings, fearing lest we might not awake betimes on the morrow, and thereby miss getting to the embryo garden by the dawn of day. And the planting of trees, the forming of the bowers, the walks, the constructing of the glass houses, the bridges and other works of the like kind, which must necessarily interest children who had from their earliest years imbibed a love of Nature !—for who could live with Alfred Smee without becoming a votary to her shrine ? The entertainments which my father and mother gave during the summer months, commencing on the 1st of May, the first day of trout-fishing, at " my garden " at Wallington, will long be remembered by the hundreds who not only enjoyed their hospitality, but who were benefited by the botanical knowledge obtained therein, whereby many had awakened in them a keener appreciation of Nature's works. The ' Gardeners' Magazine ' for the 4th of July, 1868, contains an interesting description of one of these Saturday *réunions*. Many friends have told us how from year to year they have looked forward to spend some Saturdays with Mr. Smee in his garden.

In an anonymous little pamphlet in which one of the members of the B's* amused himself by portraying in verses some of the

* The B's is a club composed of some of the leading chemists of the day. They call themselves B's because the department for chemistry was grouped in B section at the Great Exhibition of 1851.

leading characters of his chemical brothers, my father is hit off
in these few witty lines :—

> " Smee, the vivacious, who, as chance may wish,
>   Invents a battery, or hooks a fish,
>   Famous in both exploits as well can be
>   (An old inhabitant of Finsbury)—
>   The welkin rings with his ecstatic shout
>   When from the stream he lands the spotted trout :
>   Now wrapt in science, then a thought will strike
>   His varied mind, and straight he trolls for pike ;
>   Or, at that pleasant spot in Surrey, shares
>   A market-gardener's spoils without his cares—
>   Grapes, nectarines, peaches, figs, bright apples, plums, and pears."

But my father was not long destined to enjoy his fishery and
his garden without molestation, for the Croydon Board of Health
carried all the sewage into the river which passed through
Beddington Park to his garden, and as he said, " the effluvium
was noxious ; the fish died, and foul mud was deposited at the
bottom of the river." It became a question whether he should
abandon the fishery and the garden. Fortunately he determined
otherwise, and commenced instead an agitation, which, with
intervals, lasted two years, to stop the pollution of rivers.*
" Communications were made to the Privy Council ; a series of
bills in Chancery were filed nearly simultaneously by three
separate landowners ; and injunctions were obtained restraining
the Board of Health from polluting the stream. The Croydon
Board resisted the law till a committal was signed to commit the
members of the Board to prison." Indeed, the members of the
Croydon Local Board were very near being incarcerated on one
Christmas Day ; and if I remember rightly they have to thank my
father that such a misfortune did not overtake them, though I
must admit that I thought at the time, and think so now, that
they would have richly deserved the punishment for the unfair
manner of their proceedings. Through them the ratepayers were
involved in great costs ; but in the end the law proved too strong
even for a Board of Health, and so my father was again permitted
to enjoy his garden in peace. The correspondence between the Local
Board of Health of Croydon and my father is curious and highly
instructive, especially to those interested in the manner in which
Local Boards of Health sometimes conduct their proceedings.

The cholera which devastated the East of London in 1866
resulted in many warm discussions on the quality of water

* See 'My Garden,' p. 32.

supplied to the metropolis; for it may be remembered that the cholera in that part of London was attributed to the drinking of impure water. Into this question Mr. Smee entered with his usual enthusiastic temperament, and spoke at various meetings on the subject. Moreover, some of the daily newspapers contained several letters from his pen. For his opinions on the subject see the Appendix, No. XXV.

During five years, from 1860 to 1865, we were greatly dismayed at finding Finsbury Circus was threatened to be taken away from us by a railway. Headed by Alfred Smee, the inhabitants determined to resist this encroachment. The fight commenced by resolutions passed by the inhabitants on the 12th of December, 1860, who viewed

with surprise and dismay the proposed demolition of Finsbury Circus, which comprises by far the most beautiful open space in the city of London. Whilst affording a choice spot for exercise and recreation, both to the poor of the district and also to the higher class of residents in the City, it is used by the professional and mercantile men compelled to live within the precincts of the City, as one of the few places where houses available for residence are left. This meeting pledges itself to use its utmost influence to preserve it in its present state, and to oppose any attempts to encroach upon it by railroads.—That the directors of the Circus be requested to prepare a memorial in accordance with the foregoing resolution, to be presented to the Aldermen and Common Council, to her Majesty's Government, to the members for the city of London, and to both Houses of Parliament.

This was followed by the accompanying letter from Mr. Smee, which appeared in the 'Times,' Christmas Day, 1860, as well as in the 'City Press.' For this letter, in which all the beauties of Finsbury Circus Gardens are highly coloured, he was greatly bantered by his friends. Everybody read the letter; and everybody who knew my father and the Circus, smiled. In one of the journals of the day (the 'Athenæum') Finsbury Circus was termed Mr. Smee's "Paradise," and this term ever clung to him. But he said he intended to highly colour the beauties of the garden, and he certainly did so. It was this letter, followed by energetic action, which has saved Finsbury Circus from being converted into a huge, unsightly railway station.

### THE PROPOSED DEMOLITION OF FINSBURY CIRCUS.

#### *To the Editor of the City Press.*

SIR,—I trust that the importance of the subject will excuse the occupation of your space with this letter, to call public attention to the proposed demolition of Finsbury Circus, the most important spot of the city of London.

As an open area it is of priceless value to the citizens, for all experience shows that open spaces are of paramount consequence to secure the health of the inhabitants of the City. The area of this open space is so arranged that it forms a complete semicircle, with a south aspect on one side, which is protected against all cold winds, and on which every ray from the sun can in the cold spring months fall.

At that period of the year hundreds of the young and tender, of the old and infirm, of the sick and weak, resort to this delightful sheltered spot to enjoy the air and genial breezes.

The centre constitutes a circle planted with exquisite taste with the choicest trees, and forms a *tout-ensemble* which might be admired in any part of the world. It challenges for beauty the garden of any square in London, and it is the admiration and astonishment of foreigners as an affair of private enterprise, and not a creation of the State.

A return made by the gardener states that it contains three trees 60 feet high, and 180 feet in the circle of the head; 20 trees between 45 and 55 feet high; 34 trees between 35 and 45 feet high; 60 trees between 25 and 35 feet high; and 107 trees between 15 and 30 feet high; besides upwards of 700 fine shrubs and several beautiful weeping trees, all of more than half a century of growth. The effect of trees in the centre of towns cannot be too much appreciated. They carry up large quantities of water into the over-dried atmosphere, and this little forest of trees must play an important and beneficial part to the neighbourhood.

At the present time the City is too crowded, and contains by far too few open spaces and trees. There are (it is true) two trees in the Bank of England, and one in Cheapside, two or three smaller ones in St. Paul's-churchyard, and a few others scattered about, but where are the trees which we possess in Finsbury Circus?

Nevertheless, regardless of beauty, healthfulness, or of any consideration but gain, a speculative terminus has been projected to utterly annihilate Finsbury Circus, with its beautiful gardens and excellent residences; but, as such a garden could never be formed in our time, it behoves all who reside in the City to be up and stirring to avert a calamity which cannot be remedied during the days the present generation may reasonably expect to live. Half a century has passed away while these trees have made their growth. Half a century would be required for a second Finsbury Circus, even could a suitable space be found.

As long as London stands professional men must live within its precincts. Finsbury Circus is in one of the few spots adapted for their purpose, and many of its residents are in dismay, asking each other where they can find a suitable habitation. The Bank of England, the banking-houses, the large mercantile firms, must have residents to protect the wealth therein deposited, and where can the daily constitutional walk be so well taken as in Finsbury Circus?

If a great central railroad terminus is to be made to bring persons from everywhere and take them everywhere, let those who live in London exact that by its construction an additional lung be created for the City, that disease may be lessened and the value of life increased.—I am, &c.,

ALFRED SMEE,
A Director of Finsbury Circus.

7, FINSBURY CIRCUS,
Dec. 24th, 1860.

In 1869, the unfortunate Circus was threatened by no less than three railways, as is shown by the following resolutions :—

That the inhabitants of Finsbury Circus regard with surprise and regret, after the determination of the Legislature to protect the gardens of the squares of the metropolis, that no less than three railroads, including the Metropolitan, are projected, which involve the reckless spoliation of the gardens of Finsbury Circus.

That a committee of the House of Lords having carefully framed rules for the guidance of railroad projectors in the formation of lines throughout London, it is the opinion of this meeting that the wilful neglect of these rules is not only disrespectful to the Legislature, but a wanton disregard of private rights; and that the repeated parliamentary notices which year by year have harassed the inhabitants of Finsbury Circus, inflict great and unnecessary injury upon them.

That the inhabitants request the Committee of Management to oppose the Metropolitan and other railway lines seeking to spoliate the garden, and in conformity with the above views to present petitions to both Houses of Parliament, the Board of Trade, the Board of Works, and to petition that the railroad projectors who seek parliamentary powers to construct lines, in contravention of principles laid down by the Legislature, may be made amenable for any injury inflicted upon individuals by loss of trade and deterioration of property caused by their act.

The fight between the inhabitants of Finsbury Circus and the promoters of the railways waxed yearly more fierce. It was proposed in 1864 that one of the railways should contribute £12 annually for the maintenance of the gardens. In consequence of this paltry sum being offered, the following handbill was immediately sent round to all interested in the matter.

### FINSBURY CIRCUS SPOLIATION.

The committee of the House of Commons yesterday declared the preamble to the Metropolitan Extension Bill proven.

They recommended clauses for the protection of the garden, and a sum to be paid of £12 annually for its maintenance.

The practical effect of this decision is to give to the Metropolitan Railroad land worth many thousand pounds for the paltry pittance of £12 a year, and to destroy the garden, which is so attractive to the neighbourhood.

The City of London, who engaged to defend the garden, neglected to call more than three witnesses; but it is hoped that so great a violation of private rights, and so great a public injury, may not receive the sanction of the House of Lords.

                                                    ALFRED SMEE.

July 6th, 1864.

Various petitions against these railways were presented from the owners, lessees, and occupiers of house property in Finsbury

Circus, from the Corporation of the London Institution, from the Ophthalmic Hospital, from the inhabitants of the district who use and frequent Finsbury Circus, &c. &c., to both Houses of Parliament. There were numerous deputations also against the railways to the Board of Trade—to the First Commissioner of Office of Works, &c. Voluminous, too, was the correspondence between my father and the late Lord Derby, Sir William Tite, Sir Joseph Paxton, and many others, on the subject. But I think the railway promoters wished Alfred Smee had lived in any other part of London than in Finsbury Circus.

The result of this fight was that the railways were all worsted with the exception of the Metropolitan, which only carried the bill by the insertion of a clause that it was only to tunnel underneath the garden, and not to destroy any of the houses or the garden, and was to pay £100 for the annual keeping up of the latter. Here again we find that my father's energetic character carried all before him. I must here plead guilty, as having done my best to fan the flame of opposition to the railways, for even those who had no unfriendly spirit towards them were like *chaff driven before the wind*, and found themselves opposing that which they would otherwise have let go unheeded.

That Mr. Smee did not cease to take an interest in Finsbury Circus Gardens after the termination of this fight, is shown by the following letter. He also greatly assisted and promoted the holding of Horticultural Shows in the Gardens. We thus see that even in small matters he was as enthusiastic and as energetic as he was in more weighty matters. So far as he himself was concerned, he was perfectly indifferent whether Finsbury Circus was or was not converted into a railway station. Still, in so crowded a place as the city of London, it must be a matter of gratification to the citizens that one open space is reserved for them.

### FINSBURY CIRCUS GARDENS.

According to promise, I have made an inspection of Finsbury Circus Gardens.

The contractors were willing to meet the views of the inhabitants, inasmuch as they undertook to provide any reasonable quantity of earth to improve the design of the parts of the garden injured by the railway works; and it was hoped that this London garden might in some manner have partaken of the picturesque features of Paris gardens.

However, the general curves and contour lines, which were exceedingly well laid in the former garden, are now arranged in such an extraordinary manner as to be offensive to the eye, and from the upper windows of the houses present a comical appearance, as in its general effect the garden, besides a general bad design, is divided into two unequal and unsymmetrical portions.

A rare opportunity for the improvement of the garden has been lost, which is much to be regretted, as the error cannot now to any great extent be rectified.

The grass-plot is not level, which will be detrimental to the game of croquet, for which lawns are used in many of the other London square-gardens.

The garden as a whole, excepting the trees and grass, which always have an agreeable appearance, is little more than a dreary waste, which has been arranged in effect, if not in intention, to require the minimum of labour. Should the inhabitants think fit, the gardens may be kept up in their present condition by a labourer employed on an average one or two days a week, as there is really no occupation for a gardener. In bygone years there used to be abundance of flowers, and the atmosphere of the City is better now than it was at that time.

As Finsbury Circus possesses a scientific institution, with its Professor of Botany, there is no reason why the garden should not be rendered instructive as well as ornamental, and there is now a good opportunity for this to be done, as our accomplished Treasurer is well versed in botanical knowledge. Such a plan will only require the vigilance of a competent gardener, as, from the influence of many of the inhabitants, the plants could be obtained gratuitously for an educational object, and the natural families of plants might be illustrated by interesting growing plants.

By raising the character of the garden, order and decorum can be more rigidly maintained than it has been of late years.

It was particularly desired that the playground should be so enclosed by a sufficiently raised border that it should not be seen by the factory boys who frequent the road, who are apt to throw stones: this has been neglected. The interior of the playground has been lined by a wall of loose brickbats, which is actually a source of danger to the children, as its materials are well known to be liable to move and crush the limbs or bodies of children, who will and now do climb to the top of it. This rough wall should be immediately removed, to prevent destruction of limb or life, and perhaps legal liability to the inhabitants.

In the rough manner in which the swings, &c., are used by full-grown men and women, some serious accident may, and in all probability will, arise; to prevent which the gardener ought to exercise a supervision at those times when the playground is frequented by children, and be held responsible for a proper use of the apparatus.

The earth which has been selected for the flower-beds is perhaps the very worst which could have been obtained from any source. It is the old moor earth of the ancient Moorfields, and contains the leaves of moor plants and the shells of water snails. At the present time it is utterly unfit for horticultural purposes, and can only be made so by much expense and skill.

The few recently-planted trees, which are important for the general effect, should at once be taken up and replanted in topspit fibrous soil, such as has been used for the trees on the Thames Embankment.

Where flowers and plants are to be grown, a similar soil should have been employed as is now being used in the Temple Gardens; and, to show the importance of using this soil, I may mention that about forty years ago the circle of lime-trees in the Circus showed signs of decay, and some actually perished. At that time every tree at much cost had its roots laid bare and topspit loam placed against it, since which time the trees have grown to their present size.

The contractor is in my judgment bound to supply a reasonable quantity of topspit fibrous mould, and more especially as the inhabitants have facilitated the operations of the railroad.

The gravel in the playground and elsewhere (if it is finished) is bad, and the loose stones should have been removed by the gardener.

The new shrubs and trees have been planted in defiance of all horticultural principles. The kinds of trees appear to have been selected without judgment, and many of them have been planted so deeply that they can hardly be expected to live, even if the earth had been suitable for their growth.

The planting of all the evergreens at one spot looks singular, and the whole of the newly-planted trees should be inspected by some person who understands planting, and many should at once be replanted.

Many of the roots of the old trees have been covered so deeply with earth that it may be anticipated that the roots will perish and become the nidus of fungi, which sooner or later will kill the trees. This effect occurs with different rapidity in varying circumstances, but there is no doubt that many will be killed by the depth to which they have been covered.

It is a remarkable fact that no part of the restoration of the garden exhibits the slightest gardening talent or merits approbation, whilst so much which has been done necessitates severe condemnation, inasmuch as grave errors might have been avoided by a minimum of knowledge and attention.

That my father was an advocate for having trees in a town is also seen from the following extracts from a letter in which he pleaded for a row of trees to be planted along the whole line of the Thames Embankment.

The effect of trees planted along the edge of the pavement (he writes) is well seen in Paris, where not only on the Boulevards but along the line of the Seine the trees are tended with the utmost care. Plane-trees would probably be best adapted to the situation, as the noble plane in Cheapside and in our squares shows how well they grow in London. Limes might also succeed, as the two beautiful trees in the Bank of England testify.

He then goes on to show how in

no other city in Europe are there so few trees as in London, where they are so much required. Should the Board of Works consent to adopt these suggestions, now would be the time to begin to select the trees suitable for the situation, so that they may be planted in October or the beginning of November, and become well rooted before next year.

My father was fond of late years of rising with the sun, and, when he could, of going to bed with the same orb.  One summer's evening (Sunday, June 30th, 1861), he was going upstairs to bed about a quarter before nine o'clock, when on the staircase he suddenly espied a comet in the heavens. This was too interesting and too novel a spectacle, so, to the surprise of all of us, down he came again into the drawing-room, sent for his telescope, and the result was the following letter, which appeared in the 'Times' the next morning.

Sir,—It may interest your readers to hear that an enormous comet has this moment appeared in the north, having been suddenly discovered by the passage of a large cloud.

Its nucleus is of great dimensions, much larger and brighter than a star of the first dimensions; and its tail, which extends many degrees in the heavens, is of the same form, and will probably equal in extent the comet which visited this country in 1858.  At the moment I write it is not so bright as the comet of 1858 in its brightest periods, but it is only second to that in relation to any comet which has appeared within my memory, and therefore everyone should witness this object when it again becomes visible this evening.

At twenty minutes past 11 o'clock it is twelve degrees east of north, by a magnetic needle, and about ten degrees above the horizon; but these measurements are only rough estimates, as I have not accurate instruments at my command.

I remain, Sir,

7, Finsbury Circus,         Your obedient servant,

Sunday Evening, half-past 11 o'clock.     Alfred Smee.

Alfred Smee was the first to discover this comet in England. The President of the Astronomical Society—an old friend of my father's—was greatly surprised on his going to town on the Monday morning to read in the 'Times' the discovery of a new comet, he having, like other astronomers, missed seeing the phenomenon.

Alfred Smee was the first to introduce the French system of pisciculture into England.  He introduced it into this country in the beginning of 1860, and on the 24th of April of the same spring he wrote the following letter to the 'Times :'—

Sir,—The great interest which is now taken in pisciculture induces me to call more particular attention to the French system devised by Professor Coste of the College of France in Paris, and practised on a large scale at Huninguen.  I learnt the system at Paris in 1859, and brought it at once to England, but even now it is not as sufficiently known or appreciated as it deserves.  The plan consists in placing the ova on a grid-iron of glass, where they remain with a jet of water passing over them till the young fish are hatched.  Coste's system is absolutely perfect, and leaves nothing to be desired, provided excess of light is excluded.  Any number of fish may be hatched at a cost and trouble almost nominal, for I do not think that I lost 5 per cent. this year of good eggs subjected to the process. Much however has still to be learnt with respect to the treatment of the young fry, for it is still a debatable question whether we should place them in small streams full of weeds and animalculæ, their natural food, or cram them, as the French recommend, with the flesh of frogs or powdered bullock's liver. I adopt the former plan, but am not so confident as to its superiority to consider it the sole good treatment of these delicate juveniles. The great liberality and kindness of the French Government in gratuitously aiding English pisciculturists is beyond all praise, but the time has surely arrived when all English society might imitate the works of the French State and stock our rivers with salmon, trout, and grayling. The breeding boxes which I have had made in England far surpass in excellence those sold in France, and had M. Coumer's unqualified approbation on his visit to England last summer. One of these may now be seen at the 'Field' office in the Strand; and until a piscicultural society on a large scale is formed, I shall be happy to hatch and distribute to the Thames any number of thousands of salmon ova which our northern proprietors may send me.

I remain, Sir,

7, Finsbury Circus,                    Your obedient servant,
   April 24th.                         Alfred Smee.

The first fish he hatched according to this system were young salmon. In 1861 he sent salmon ova to Hampton to Mr. Ponder, chairman of the Sub-committee on Pisciculture. My father was continually being asked for information on this subject, not only from various persons in this country, but also from America. And he was constantly sending ova or young fish to stock different rivers. His own fish-breeding house, which he conducted on a large scale at his garden at Wallington, was highly interesting, and during the early spring months many came there specially to see it. For a fuller account of pisciculture, see 'My Garden,' page 497.

My father was not only a complete angler and lover of pisciculture, but was also during parts of his life fond of shooting. From 1863 to 1866 he rented with a select party some pheasant-shooting of considerable extent in Hertfordshire, where he used to spend one day a week, and from which he always returned in raptures with the beautiful woods and the country. In 1867 he held with others some shooting at Tunbridge Wells, but this he did not enjoy so much as his Hertfordshire shooting. He had, besides, many pleasant days of sport at different times with friends on their estates and at their shooting-boxes. After 1867, with the exception of a few hours on the moors at Whitby, he shot no more.

Besides being a sportsman, he was very fond of yachting,

and would delight in a sail at the mouth of the Thames in his son's yacht, the *Snowfleck*.* Often on these yachting excursions he would betake himself to his old and favourite pastime, fishing, and obtained not a little experience in sea-fishing. At other times, when not engaged in catching fish, he would station himself by the helm, and would employ himself in, to use his own words, "looking out for dangers." This, his family would jokingly tell him, was to him a source of great amusement. He did not, however, seem to appreciate such levity, and was, I believe, thoroughly convinced that he was thereby the means of preventing sundry dire accidents, such as collisions with steamboats or sailing boats, or being shipwrecked by running on sandbanks, wrecks, &c. But his being on the look-out for accidents generally ended by his going to sleep, to the no small satisfaction of the crew. After all these "outings," whether he had been yachting, fishing, shooting, or gardening, he returned home, his mind invigorated and refreshed, and would work with redoubled energy.

London was much alarmed in 1862 by its houses being broken into in the dead of night by burglars, and by its sober-minded and respectable citizens being garrotted in the streets. Some of the sentimental part of the community held that burglars and garrotters ought not to be severely dealt with; whilst others, again, viewed with horror the spreading of this pestilence to society, by which it had become unsafe for persons to be out of doors after sunset, or to sleep with safety of a night, and these urged strong measures for the suppression of such crimes. Whilst these two conflicting opinions were running high, the following anonymous pamphlet appeared from Alfred Smee's pen. Shortly after its appearance (it was widely circulated) a Bill was passed for the flogging of garrotters, and soon after the Bill was put into force the citizens of London were left unmolested by these ruffians. In 'The Mind of Man,' at page 63, the best manner for dealing with our criminal classes is given in the chapter on the government of mankind. "Our present system," he says, "is as useless as it is unphilosophical, as the professed thief goes to prison to come out and repeat his career as before."

It is curious that this anonymous pamphlet on garrotters was entirely thought out one Sunday, while one of our eminent preachers was giving a long sermon at Westminster Abbey. My father was observed at the time to be seemingly listening with great

* The yachting commenced in 1867, when a friend kindly lent us his yacht for the season. Afterwards my brother built himself a yacht.

attention to the sermon.  On being asked after the service by a friend, one of the clergymen of the Abbey, his opinion of the sermon, my father replied, " Oh ! I liked it very well."  " Liked it very well ? " exclaimed his friend ; " I am surprised to hear you say so, for I have often heard you denounce similar sermons to that which you heard to-day."  My father, finding he was thus driven into a corner, confessed he had not heard one word of it.  This still more perplexed his friend the clergyman, for Mr. Smee had appeared to be paying marked attention to it.  " Well," said my father, " I must tell you the truth.  I have been mentally writing an anonymous pamphlet the whole time —— has been preaching ; and so intent have I been upon my subject, that I have not heard a single word of the sermon."  And he added, " I will send you the result of my work, providing I have your promise not to divulge from whom it came."

The pamphlet was written out within twenty-four hours, and it was published within a week.  It was sent to the clergyman, who, I believe, was never after thoroughly convinced that Mr. Smee ever listened to any sermon, however intent he might appear to be.  And I am afraid that but too frequently he was correct in such conjectures ; for as soon as the preacher ascended the pulpit, then was that quiet time when he could think out his various projects.  The following is the aforesaid pamphlet.

## PHILOSOPHICAL REASONS FOR NOT HANGING GARROTTERS AND BURGLARS.

### BY A MEMBER OF THE SOCIETY OF FRIENDS!!!

*Preface.*

DEAR FRIENDS,—Stirring times have come upon us, when it behoves us all to be up and moving, or all our devices for centuries past will be undone, and all the schemes which we have successfully promulgated for comforting the assassin, the burglar, and the garrotter, will be swept away at one fell swoop.

It is by our care that a goodly race has arisen, which is not without its proper influence on society.  Persons are now nightly stopped, and are either eased of " the root of all evil," or, by suffering bodily injury, are deprived of " the incentives to personal vanity."

A panic has, however, all at once seized the people ; and unless the Society of Friends wake up, and use all the instruments under their control, as sure as Friends are meek and humble and wear broad-brimmed hats, an Act of Parliament will be passed to hang every man caught committing an act of burglary, or garrotting.

To prevent this interference with the scheme of creation, which has formed Quakers or good people, and burglars or evil people, I write earnestly that thou mayest be primed with arguments to resist the invention of the enemy, and retain those whom worldly-minded men call felons, to balance the order of creation.

Remember, it is only by a strong pull, a long pull, and a pull altogether, that it is possible, with the present morbid temper of the public, to preserve to society the burglar and garrotter; but with great exertions they may be retained for the blessed operations of a second Elizabeth Fry.

I remain,

MEETING HOUSE,                         Thy affectionate Teacher,
    November 18th, 1862.                         AN ELDER.

### Arguments.

1. The first great argument for not hanging burglars and garrotters is the terrible example which would be set to others, as the capture and execution of a few would have such an effect upon the remainder, that there would be speedily none left, and at once an important section of the community would disappear. In my young days a burglary or highway robbery was never heard of, but it is only since the human mind has been more enlightened, and the beautiful model of Thugs has been exposed to view in the British Museum, that the taste for burglary and garrotting has been developed; but to stop suddenly the progression of the thinking mind, would be to fly in the face of Providence, who has created both bad and good. So, we Friends and thinking people must stop so terrible an exigence, and preserve the garrotter and burglar to the world.

### Police Argument.

2. If we regard the consequences of the burglar and garrotter, we find that the guardians of the peace, frightened out of all propriety, have doubled the police force, and thus we see how beautifully evil produces good, for winter is coming on, many honest men will have employment in the police, and be kept by an over-fattened public simply to look after them. It is quite clear that this additional force will cause the garrotter and burglar to take sufficient exercise before they obtain their end. And it may be likened to the wise dispensation in natural history, which causes the tiger to prowl for a long time before it finds its victim, and to seize it with more relish from the keen appetite it has obtained in its pursuit.

As long as burglars are not hung they do not care now very much about the inconvenience of being caught; and whilst they take all reasonable care to overcome or escape the police, they constantly get away, and, in fact, are so rarely taken, that their chase causes them to experience the same pleasing excitement which the Indian feels in hunting the tiger.

### Fire-arms Argument.

3. Lancashire is now weeping from lack of employment, owing to the dearth of cotton, but Birmingham thrives by reason of the burglar

and garrotter. What a powerful evidence of design to fill the stomach
of the infant and mother is here to be traced to the presence of the
burglar and garrotter! The public, strong in their own conceit, say they
will not be robbed, they will not have their houses invaded at night.
For resistance they are now arming themselves with guns, pistols, and
swords, to enter into combat with their opponents. As a Friend, I
naturally make acquaintance with these people, and my acquaintances
tell me that "they go for plunder, not for bullets and bayonet wounds."
For this object they parade in twos and threes, and their system is to
half-kill their victim before he knows he is attacked. One man said,
"Would he not like to poke a man's weapon into his own torso?"—a sentiment worthy of classical times. That man told me that "the gun and
pistol dodge would soon come to an end, for they would be shooting
the wrong man, and what a lark it would be to make one victim shoot
another, a circumstance which would frighten the public, and render the
garrotter safer than ever."

Besides, said he, "our noble judges are so good that they never allow
the hair of a garrotter to be ruffled." He must be taken by the police, that
is, if they can catch him at all, as tenderly as a lover handles his sweet-
heart. Our considerate law administrators sometimes have men more
severely punished for resistance than they have the robber. Nobody can
doubt but the burglar simply desires to possess something the other man
has. Would it not be a proper Christian act to give at once what is desired,
when the possessor might dispense with fire-arms, and be spared the chance
of an attack?

### Hope and Anxiety Argument.

4. Untrained minds indulge continually in the lower feelings. How
grovelling was that picture at the International Exhibition of a young
mother with an infant in her arms drawing aside the blind to look after
the lost husband, the prop and support of the home. What an untrained
mind does the mother show to be anxious! For the father is either
alive or dead: if he is alive, she ought to exhibit hope, not anxiety; and
if he has been proved to have been garrotted and past all hope, then she
ought to exhibit resignation. To my female friends say I, Train thou thy
mind, and when thy husband is proved to be garrotted, then exert thy-
self and get another. What a blessed instrument in mind-training might
the burglar and garrotter become, and how great ought to be our exertions
to prevent their being hung!

### The Fog Argument.

5. During the severe fogs of November persons are now fearful of leaving their homes because fog gives to the garrotter an easy chance of carrying
out his plans. This is surely a most unreasonable accusation against
garrotters, because, in this instance, they do a positive benefit by keeping
people out of the influence of a fog, which is known to be extremely bad
for their constitutions. Such, however, is the perverse character of the
human mind that they would use the liability of being maimed or killed by
robbers during the prevalence of a fog, as an argument for hanging them,
as a terror to other evil-doers. During great fogs in London gentlemen
are watched from their clubs, when there are scamps who think it great

fun to seize suddenly their hats and bolt with them without fear of pursuit. This fooling pastime and small robbery is checked by the garrotter, for many who do not care for the mere chance of losing a hat, are kept at home when they fear to lose their lives, and then their wives and children know where they are.

### The Over-Population Argument.

6. Nobody doubts that the country has plenty of people to take any place which may become vacant, when its present occupants are killed. A great fuss was made last year, because an M.P. was strangled in Pall Mall, when returning from his parliamentary duties. What could it have mattered if he had been so far garrotted as to have lost his life? There would be still too many in Parliament to transact its business properly. and not only too many, but a hundred applicants for every vacant place. What is true of a Member of Parliament is true of any other occupation : for there is not a clergyman in the country who would not delight to take the office of a bishop, if one should unfortunately be garrotted, though, as Friends, we must consider that bishops are altogether superfluous. Under the present system there is not a person in the kingdom who may not be destroyed by the burglar or garrotter; and should one be so destroyed, there would be plenty delighted to take his place. Now, Friend, I would ask thee this question, Why should we hang a garrotter or burglar who may, in pursuing his usual avocation, give delight to any person in this over-populous country?

### Timidity Argument.

7. When a burglar enters a house at the dead of night, and kills the inmates, such as was done at the celebrated Frimly murder, it is a vulgar fashion for other people, neither killed nor attacked, to take on great fear. In secluded houses the inmates remain sleepless all the livelong nights, fearing each noise, and listening to every rustle of the leaves, and spending their lives in terror and trembling. Other persons witnessing these results, revile the burglar and wish him to be hanged, that their friends may enjoy their homes in peace and comfort. Now, in these cases, as members of the advanced thinking community to which we belong, we should like to put the burden on the right shoulder, and, instead of punishing the burglar, would severely reprimand the nervous sufferers, and command them to sleep soundly, even when they are conscious that burglars have broken in the front door.

### Assurance Argument.

8. Assurance Companies are frightened out of all propriety by gar-rotters and burglars, because they say that lives are lost, and claims arise therefrom. It is quite clear, however, that there would be no assurances if there were no deaths ; and, surely, Accidental Death Assurance Companies must derive business from the knowledge which the public possesses, that no person can tell whether he will be attacked on any given day, and maimed. Nothing can more completely show that the complaints of the Assurance Companies are quite groundless, and not to be entertained for a moment, when the great social problem of petting great criminals is at stake.

### Injury Argument.

9. If we believe the doctors, who are always dogmatical, we shall hear that cases of personal violence leave traces for life. Dr. Forbes Winslow may say that insanity is often traced to blows on the head inflicted years before. The brain doctors tell us that epilepsy, apoplexy, and with females, the most severe and terrible hysteria, are brought on by a shock to the brain. We hear oculists declare that vision is often impaired. Aurists tell us that persons are rendered deaf. Some persons are deprived of smell, others of taste, and innumerable cases of stiff joints and lameness are produced by personal violence arising from resistance to the demands of the garrotter for his victim to give up his personal property, or to the burglar from entering his house. It is, thereupon, argued that garrotters and burglars are so savage and relentless in their course, that death by the gallows should be their doom. Can anything be more foolish? for a damaged man is a patient for life, a certain annuity to the doctor. Under these circumstances, medical men have no cause for grumbling; but, on the contrary, ought rather to rejoice that the garrotte and house-breaking have so deep a hold upon our social system.

### The Expense Argument.

10. Mean hardhearted citizens consider that, as they work for their living, they have no right to keep hundreds in idleness and greater luxury than their own workpeople. Nothing can be more futile than this argument, although it must be confessed that it is very hard to drive it out of their heads, that it is not right to give a garrotter meat when the workmen live on bread and cheese. He argues, naturally enough for a mere counting-house man, that the criminal should not be better off than the honest workman. The more comprehensive mind will discover that the criminal is the pet of pets of a certain section of the thinking community, and the honest man may go to the wall.

### Outbreak Argument.

11. All experience shows that it is no easy matter to keep a number of burglars and garrotters, used to every kind of cruelty and violence, in due subjection. With the greatest care caged murderers will do violence to the gaoler. Used to every brutality, they stand very badly the slight restraint imposed upon them by a prison life. What can be greater proof of the folly of catching them, when, by convicting them of a murder, you induce them to commit two or three more? As a matter of fact, wouldst thou like a house-breaker or murderer to live in thy family? and if thou wouldst not like him in thy house, is it fair and equitable to expose the warders to his influence?

### The War Argument.

12. In warfare how many brave men sacrifice themselves simply as a matter of duty to their country, or a sense of manly feeling to protect their wives and families. When in battle we see thousands of the good and just fall in a single day, unthinking people inquire why should millions of Englishmen be kept in terror by one or two score of worthless, degraded reprobates. But the fact is that neither the garrotter nor burglar is a brave

or just man.  He is an arrant coward.  It never entered his head to be
killed or even to be hurt, and he maims or kills his opponent as an act of
cowardice for his own protection.  Under these circumstances the fate of
the brave man who is killed in war, and fears not his doom for the sake of
duty, is not to be compared with the cowardly miscreant who is fearful and
cruel.  For this reason the entire population had better be kept in continual terror than that the garrotter or burglar shall receive the doom
which he never contemplated.

### The Food Treatment.

13. It is now very difficult to catch a burglar or imprison a garrotter.
This might all be obviated by properly regulated prisons.  If there was no
restraint, and they could go where they liked, they would undoubtedly
come into prison of their own accord; that is, if they had sufficient inducement for so doing.  Now, bread and water continuously is no inducement
for anybody; but a well-ordered prison with parks, pleasure-grounds,
winter-gardens, fish and game preserves, with a proper supply of such fare
as turkey and plum-pudding for Christmas, and of the various delicacies
at the earliest possible moment they respectively come into season, would
soften the garrotter's heart, and, instead of assaulting the police as they do
at present, they would freely admit their own guilt, save all the expenses
of prosecution, and come into gaol when they felt they had had enough of
their adventures.  What a beautiful sight it would be to see troops of
garrotters and burglars coming to repent every morning of their wickedness
done in the night !

### The Bump Treatment.

14. No member of the Society of Friends nor thinking individual can
doubt but that the cruelty of the burglar and garrotter is due to certain
bumps of the head which are too prominent.  The first process in the
treatment would be effectually to gauge the head.  Possibly an humble
petition numerously signed by Friends and Unitarians would secure for
that object the services of Dr. Carpenter, whom some people consider to be
as great in his physiology as sound in his religion.  Under his instruction
gentle young ladies might be employed to manupress the cruelty bumps
and draw forth with an exhausting tube the benevolent ones.  Who knows,
when the heads of garrotters are rubbed into models of benevolence and
kindness, how many cases of affection may spring up between the garrotter
and bump-represser, which would give to the young robber-changer a most
amiable partner for life ?  The process is so efficacious that gorillas can, by
the manipulation of their bumps, be turned into perfect men.  How many
gorillas have been so changed nobody can tell, unless it be the Bishop of
Oxford, who at the British Association appeared to have some special
knowledge of these creatures.  What more powerful reason can be given
for stopping the stupid Legislature from hanging garrotters than the
possibility of their being rubbed into judges, bishops, or members of
Parliament?

### African Project.

15. In looking at the question of dealing with great criminals we must
not overlook the proposition to send burglars and garrotters to Sierra

Leone, or West Coast of Africa, for the purpose of performing the labour necessary for an experimental growth of cotton, sugar-cane, or other tropical productions. As Friends we must not tolerate such a proposition, which might cause criminals to live no longer than honest, virtuous men. Upon the whole, the question may be safely left to competent statisticians, and no doubt such an able man as Mr. Newmarch would settle the duration of life to the thirty-ninth place of decimals, and would rather the globe itself on which he lives should dissolve than allow a criminal to have no longer a duration of life than an upright, honest working man.

### The Whipping Project.

16. Not a few persons are to be found who commend whipping for brutalized criminals; and when a citizen has been severely maimed by a person of this class, the evil passions of his neighbours naturally desire to see the criminal well flogged. It is difficult to meet the argument; but if whipping is allowed, the Friends' trust must be in the doctor, who should receive orders to discontinue the process the moment the pulse rises one beat, or any emotion can be detected. The arguments against whipping are very awkward to be applied, as flogging has proved to be an admirable remedy against attacks upon her Majesty, or in cases of wanton destruction of works of art. Nevertheless, thou hadst better ask those who recommend its application, how far they would like the cat-o'-nine-tails themselves; and if they would dislike it, why apply it to the garrotter?

### Conclusion.

17. Those who read the arguments against hanging garrotters and burglars must perceive that, although the reasons are strong, it will require the greatest possible exertion to prevent the gallows from rearing again its lofty head. London is nightly patrolled by garrotters; England has a nest of cruel, cowardly assassins, who terrify the peaceable and well-disposed. Men and women have such an antipathy to robbery with violence, that they instinctively desire to shoot their dastardly maimers, or hand the man to a terrible justice. In this great emergency it behoves all Quakers, and other thinking men, to bestir themselves vehemently, and the more fear is exhibited by the public of being killed, robbed, or permanently maimed, the more will be our merit to protect the ill-doers. When people are killed, or paralysed, or maimed by law-breakers, in the eyes of mankind the robber is thought to be a great criminal; and the greater the criminal, the greater pet should we make of him. A vulgar public will treat a felon, brutalized by every vice, and degraded by every cruelty and passion, as they would a mad dog, or a venomous snake. A thinking man, however, would supply him with every comfort, and give him food, clothes, habitation, and luxuries, beyond the means of honest working men.

Friend, there is one thing, in conclusion, that I would have thee never forget, and that is, when a burglar and garrotter is hung, he is never able to rob or kill again, and others are deterred by his example. Remember, when criminals cease, sentiment is done, and Quakerdom and cant must fall.

In July 1863, commenced the celebrated fight between Alfred Smee and the Jesuits. My mother's brother had joined one of their confraternities, and had during this month died, leaving the whole of his property inherited from his father to the Principal of the Brompton Oratorians. For many years before my father had wished to have a passage of arms with the Jesuits, and would have done so had not my mother been fearful lest they should send her brother to some monastery on the Continent where she could never see him again, and she ever indulged in the hope that her brother might one day be rescued from the clutches of the Oratorians. This hope, however, was not realized, for he died in the forty-first year of his age; though I think that had he recovered from his last illness he would have been induced to leave the Oratorians, and live under the roof of his sister and her husband, both of whom he had, previous to joining the Romish Church, ever held in great affection. After my uncle's death the fight commenced: there was a lengthy correspondence in the press during the summer and latter part of 1862, and the beginning of 1863, to which I must refer the reader. The will was contested, and it was not until it was brought into court that any information could be obtained. However, the case was lost: there was not sufficient legal evidence—which we were not surprised at. But it was as well the will was put into court, for it thereby showed to the world the manner in which the wills of the members of the Brompton Oratory are made. It awakened against them a feeling of disgust among those who love the liberty of Protestant England. Already, long before his death, my uncle was a poor man: the bulk of his property had gone. Where? My father also contested the right of religious communities to have private and secret burial-grounds. Here, again, the correspondence was lengthy, but the gist of it is that my father complained, "1st, That the Oratory has a private and secret burial-ground, without public access or boundary walls, which has no public register of burials, and where the names on the tombstones are changed; 2nd, That this private and secret burial-ground, and the means of concealment you have in your houses, are used to obtain money from converts under religious intimidation."

During this summer a party wishing to see the grave were refused, as they had no private order from the Oratorians with them. This private and secret burial-ground is in the garden attached to a house they have at Sydenham. Great interest was felt in the Brompton Oratorian case throughout the country. It was referred to several times in the House of Commons.

In the Appendix, No. XXVI., is the rejoinder to the manifesto of Dr. Dalgairns, Principal of the Oratory, entitled 'The Private and Secret Burial-Ground of the Oratory,' together with a correspondence with Sir George Grey, and a petition to the House of Commons.

My father was always a consistent opponent of religious houses such as monasteries and nunneries, and in 1871 he gave evidence against them in the Committee Room of the House of Commons.

The pamphlet 'On the Practical Remedy for Extortion and Intimidation practised by the aid of the Superior Law Courts' was written by my father in 1863. This pamphlet had the desired effect of drawing the attention of the Legislature to the abuses there alluded to. Such extortion can now be no longer practised, for by an Act passed in 1867 it was provided that any person against whom an action for malicious prosecution, illegal arrest, illegal distress, assault, false imprisonment, libel, slander, or other action of tort, may be brought, may make an affidavit that the plaintiff has no visible means of paying the costs of the defendant; and thereupon a judge of the court in which the action is brought is empowered to stay the proceedings, unless full security for the defendant's costs is given. See Appendix, No. XXVII.

## CHAPTER IX.

### 1865 TO 1870.

Contests Rochester—Alfred Smee a Freemason and an Oddfellow—London Institution saved from becoming a clerks' school—Aquarium at Paris—Accident Sheet—Professional life of Alfred Smee—Illness—Visit to Whitby —Posting up storm telegrams at Whitby—Contests Rochester a second time—Speeches—Visits Italy—Anonymous writings on the Unseaworthiness of Ships, on Chancery Reform, &c.

At the General Election of 1865, Alfred Smee contested Rochester, and there brought forward political views under a new phase, which he termed "Conservative Progress." Although enthusiastically received at that city, he was unsuccessful. He was surrounded by his family during the contest, and I still always look back to that general election as a very agreeable phase of my existence. The year after he wrote two political skits, the one termed 'The Puppet Parliament,' and the other 'The Final Reform Bill.' Neither of the pamphlets bore his name. See the Appendix, Nos. XXVIII. and XXIX.

In that entitled 'The Final Reform Bill,' he says :—

There are four great diseases before Parliament this year : 1. The rinderpest, or death of cattle ; 2. The cholera pest, or death of mankind— both bodily diseases, to be treated after an exact study of Nature's works : 3. The nigger pest, white murder by blacks ; 4. The Fenian pest—the annihilation of social order and religion—both mental epidemics, to be treated after an earnest study of God's moral laws.

Who shall legislate upon these serious maladies ? Shall they who have bought their parliamentary seats by money, and pandered to the follies of their age ? Or shall they who represent independent, thoughtful voters, and who have studied Nature's works and followed moral laws ?

In 1865 Mr. Smee was made a Freemason at Gundulph's Lodge at Rochester, and he was about the same time also elected a member of the Oddfellows in the same city. On the 22nd of February, 1867, he was elected a member of Jerusalem Lodge, in London, one of the oldest lodges. Although he took a warm interest in Freemasonry, yet he was too idle to learn the symbols, and never attained the rank of Master. Many of his Freemason brethren had determined to make him at last a Master, and I doubt not that in course of time, had he lived, they would have cajoled him into learning the requisites necessary to attain that office. He always declared he never could learn by heart; but as it has been seen that his memory was so excellent that he was able to take down on one occasion some important speeches two days after they were delivered, and as he used always to take down the lectures delivered at King's College *verbatim* on his return home in the evening, it would seem that, had he so willed it, he could also have learnt by rote. However, he did not do so; but whether he could not, as he said, or would not, is very doubtful. He had several decorations and orders in Freemasonry, and he was present at the installation of His Royal Highness the Prince of Wales as Grand Master at Albert Hall. I mention this because it was extremely difficult to obtain an invitation to that installation, and I suppose he was the only one present who had not ranked as a Master. He was extremely pleased at being present at that ceremony, which interested him much, and thoroughly appreciated the kindness of the donor of the invitation.

In 1868 he was admitted, on the 7th of February, among the first five hundred of the City Carlton Club, a Conservative club in the City. He was also admitted among the first hundred members of St. Stephen's Club. He had previously, it should be added, belonged to the Reform Club, but had to leave it on his contesting Rochester. He had not joined the Reform Club for political motives, for until he contested Rochester in the Conservative cause he had never previously taken a leading interest in party questions, and, indeed, had not troubled himself to use his vote at political elections. He had several friends at the Reform Club, and it had other attractions in possessing a good library, and better still a good *cuisine*, for Francatelli was at that time the *chef*.

In 1866 there was a movement for a clerks' school (the City of London College) to be associated with the London Institution. By this project the London Institution was to keep the building of the college in repair, the students of the college were to have access to the educational lectures, the life shares of the London Institution were to be given as prizes to the students, and the students were to have access to the library, besides sharing in other emoluments. It may seem surprising, but nevertheless true, that one of the managers tried his utmost to bring about this arrangement. Mr. Smee wrote to him as follows:—

My dear Sir,—I have read with very great care your proposal to annihilate the London Institution.

It does seem to me to be a most highly objectionable project, and one which I hope there will be but little chance of carrying out.

It is a total change of purpose to convert a literary and scientific institution into a mere boys' school, but one step better than that of a charity school.

You have fixed the meeting at a time when I am afraid I cannot possibly attend, next Wednesday, which I extremely regret, as I fear that I shall feel it my duty to oppose it with all my might.

My doctrine would be to improve what we possess, not to radically destroy.

Mr. Smee went to the meeting, which was attended by the proprietors and managers, and in a long speech denounced the movement as being most pernicious to the London Institution. When he finished his speech, the proprietors rose *en masse*, and cheered and cheered him again and again. The scheme was upset, my father victorious, and the London Institution saved.

While my father and myself were on a short visit to Paris in the autumn of 1866, we visited a splendidly fitted-up aquarium, which had recently been established, and which, before the Brighton Aquarium was made, was a master one of its kind. This aquarium in Paris fired my father's imagination, and forthwith he considered that it was a grievous pity that an equally good if not a better one should not be immediately established at the Zoological Gardens in London. Accordingly, the next morning, when I came down to breakfast, before 9 o'clock, I found he had written off to the late much lamented and distinguished naturalist, Dr. Gray, of the British Museum, on the subject, and I found afterwards the aforesaid letter published in the 'Annals of Natural History,' 3rd series, vol. xix.*

### The "Monde de la Mer."

My dear Sir,—I have just returned from a visit to the "Monde de la Mer," a noble aquarium opened to the public at a charge of two francs per head within the last week, on the Boulevard Montmartre. It is arranged as a large grotto, with cement stalactites, and the light almost entirely comes through the glass front of the aquarium. There are no less than thirteen aquaria, with glass fronts, about 15 feet long and 4 feet deep;

---

* The Brighton Aquarium was not in existence when this letter was written.

and there are glass facings to brick and cement tanks, 5 or 6 feet wide. These thirteen are for salt water alone; but there are others for fresh water, and two little ponds 10 or 12 feet across. The aquaria are lit by gas-lights placed above, which light up in the most efficient manner the interior, and show every fish most perfectly. There appears to be no confervoid growth; and doubtless the gas-light is unfavourable to such vegetation, but gives an illumination more resembling the natural condition in deep water. A gas-engine is employed to change the water, which continually runs to a tank below, and is pumped back, the jet being thrown with such force as to carry down a great quantity of air in very minute division—so much, in fact, that I thought it was done by an air-pump, until the attendant obliged me by allowing me to go behind the scenes and inspect the contrivance. The "Monde de la Mer" in these tanks were truly wonderful: large fish a yard long, soles and skates of ample proportions, with lobster, crayfish, and numerous species of fish of brilliant colours from the Mediterranean. Hundreds of anemones made a sort of flower-garden; and the effect was so interesting and so beautiful that it has to be seen to be believed and appreciated.

The aquarium at the Zoological Gardens, which formerly attracted so much attention, was a mere baby to it, and gave no idea of the behaviour of the great-grandfather fish which are here contained.

It occurred to me, that if I was a child and fell in love with this beautiful exhibition, there must be hundreds and thousands of grown-up children who would also like to be introduced to the "Monde de la Mer." Then why not get up a bigger "Mer," and a more distinguished "Monde" at the Zoological Gardens?

The place would be the bank sloping to the canal, looking towards the north: for fish have a decided natural objection to be cooked by a southern sun. And the moment I arrive in England I shall rush to the Zoo to see if perfidious Albion has copied the idea and out-Mer'd and out-Monde'd the "Monde de la Mer" of Paris.

I remain, my dear Sir,<br>Yours faithfully,

HÔTEL MEURICE, Paris,                              ALFRED SMEE.
   Nov. 19th, 1866.

In 1866, it will be remembered, a great monetary panic occurred in the city of London, when many families lost large fortunes, and when, to add to the misfortune, the discount house of Overend and Gurney stopped payment. To endeavour to stop the stagnation which was occasioned by large sums of money which were not lost, but not get-at-able, in fact " locked up " for a considerable space of time, an ingenious remedy was suggested by Alfred Smee, which will be found in the Appendix, No. XXX. This panic was succeeded by hardships which had to be endured by unfortunate shareholders of public companies in liquidation, and which elicited some anonymous letters from Mr. Smee's pen. These letters follow those on 'Locked-up Money,' in the Appendix, No. XXXI.

In 1867, Mr. Smee brought out another form of Accident Sheet somewhat similar to, though in a more complete form than, the one he published in 1847.*

Up to the present time very little notice has been taken of my father's professional career, beyond his being a surgeon of no mean repute, and of his being more especially eminent as an oculist. That part of his work which has hitherto been given was performed mostly in his leisure, and was chiefly the intellectual pastime of his prolific brain, but the greater part of his time was taken up by his medical profession, and by various companies, to some of which he was medical officer, whilst of others he was a director.

It has already been mentioned that the office of Surgeon to the Bank of England was specially created for him when he was only twenty-two years old. He was also elected at an early age, and almost immediately on entering his profession, Surgeon to the Royal General Dispensary, in Aldersgate Street, to the Central London Ophthalmic Hospital, and was besides surgeon to several other important institutions. He was medical officer to several Life Assurance Companies, amongst the more important of which may be mentioned the Accident Company and the Gresham, of both of which he was one of the founders. But the latter company was materially assisted by my grandfather, Mr. William Smee, Accountant-General of the Bank of England, who was also one of the trustees of the Gresham, in conjunction with the Chief Cashier of the Bank, Mr. Matthew Marshall, and the banker Mr. Oldham. Without my grandfather's assistance the Gresham would not have existed. As it was, it was born in the dining-room of 7, Finsbury Circus, during the autumn of 1847.

One of the companies to which he belonged caused, for a space of time stretching over several years, my father a great deal of anxiety, and added many cares to his life. Fortunately these anxieties came to a satisfactory termination. Through the indomitable courage and high principle of Alfred Smee many were saved from pressing cares and losses; but, unhappily, the intense mental excitement and labour attending it, left an indelible mark upon his bodily powers, and sowed the seed of the disease which he succumbed to at the early age of fifty-eight.

---

* This Accident Sheet can be either obtained in the form of a sheet or in a small book, at the printers', Messrs. Collingridge, Long Lane, or at the office of the Accident Company, 37, Old Jewry, E.C., for the small sum of one penny.

From the huge packet of MS. papers, of printed speeches, various reports, written and spoken by Alfred Smee for the benefit of sundry companies to which he belonged (which I had the curiosity to collect and preserve), it would seem that he must have been the moving spirit in them, and in losing him they must indeed have lost a friend and a strong supporter.

In the summer of 1868 my father had a serious illness, which at the time was supposed to be a severe form of colic, but which would appear to have been rather the beginning of the disease which proved fatal to him at the beginning of last year: for from that moment he lost his stoutness, and became year by year thinner and thinner. From that moment, too, he cannot be said to have enjoyed robust health. Through the kind attention of his old friend Dr. Jones, he rallied from this illness, and when convalescent he went to Whitby, where he thoroughly enjoyed himself, sometimes in fishing, sometimes on the moors, sometimes amidst the rocks, searching for fossils embedded in the lias or oolitic strata, and sometimes in the beautiful woods in the vicinity, searching for ferns for his beloved garden at Wallington, which, when absent from it, was never forgotten by him. At such times we would return to Whitby with the carriage so filled with oak ferns, beech ferns, and other sorts of ferns, that our heads only would just be visible above the mass of lovely foliage, much to the amusement of the good folks of that seaport, who thereupon styled my father the "Professor of Ferns." Besides these innocent amusements, which tended to restore his health, he took steps to promote the interests of the fishermen of Whitby, as will be seen from the following letter, which he wrote immediately on his return to London, to the late Mr. Gassiot, F.R.S.

MY DEAR SIR,—I have been at Whitby during the last equinox, and took great interest in the storm signals on that dangerous coast, and I write the general result for you to lay before the committee for their information.

1. The barometer was of the highest importance to the fishermen. Every morning they walked up the pier to examine it, and their decision was most materially guided by its rising and falling.

2. The storm signal seemed to be of secondary importance to the indication of the barometer, though of great use taken in conjunction with it, and the reason for its being hoisted. Upon this matter I have a suggestion to make. I found that whenever the drum was hoisted, every sailor knew the reason of its being hoisted from the Preventive Service men, and they would tell me that there was a great storm raging in the Channel, a high wind on the coast of Scotland, and one day that there was a storm so near as Yarmouth.

Now, I recommend that the reasons for the hoisting of the drum be always posted up in writing, as I am quite confident that these men are thinking of the bearing of the question all day long, and gradually they will use the drum in conjunction with the barometer, and obtain for each place much closer results than can be obtained by any other method.

Practically my recommendation is to give the fishermen facts for them to apply. I think then great results will ensue, and they will be able to bring the foretelling of the weather for a few hours to as near a certainty as possible.

It was resolved by the Meteorological Committee of the Royal Society that Mr. Scott be instructed to take steps to promote the posting up of the weather telegrams at Whitby. The following summer, on our second visit to Whitby, my father took much interest in the working of the same.

In 1868 there was another election at Rochester. His address to the electors was issued from Whitby, where he was staying on account of illness, and he was on that account obliged to postpone appearing among his friends and supporters for several weeks. He, however, wrote many addresses to them, and amused himself with drawing up rules and regulations for the organization of the Conservative party in that city; and before he was quite recovered from his indisposition he, against the advice of his medical adviser, Dr. Jones, and of his friends, threw himself heart and soul into the contest, quite regardless of his own health. He went to the poll, but again met with unsuccess. That he had good grounds for expecting success will be fully seen from the following letters sent to his wife and others during the heat of the contest, and by the speech he made at the complimentary dinner which was given to him by his supporters in the city of Rochester on the 17th of December, 1868. His family have heard since, from information obtained from the Radical side, that Mr. Smee was so beloved at Rochester, that had he but paid a select number at the rate of a day's wages he would have been elected. But bribery he would not allow to be resorted to. Not very long after this election a great many men emigrated from Rochester. Their last act on leaving Chatham for their ships was to give three cheers for Mr. Smee. "Had we returned him as our member for Rochester," they exclaimed, "we should not have been obliged to leave Rochester and emigrate." My father was not a little pleased when he heard of this demonstration of affection and esteem for him.

MY DEAR ELIZABETH,—We have had a most extraordinary meeting at Rochester: 20,000 people out, all the road lined. The moment I arrived

at the station. tremendous cheering, a great procession of torches, with red
fire, with a boy dressed in pink. typifying Conservatism, with a band preceding.  We marched through the town, all the people calling out, "There
he is. he has come at last," till we got to the King's Head, where the
crowd was so great that policemen had to keep order, and the pressure so
tremendous that the windows were broken.  I gave my speech, a pretty
violent one.

I told the people that they must do the work, as I could not, and read
my parody on Longfellow.  It is reported that Kinglake has resigned on
the strength of it, but that is improbable.  I must see ———— on Monday,
and am to see Elliot to-morrow.  Mary would have enjoyed the fun.

KING'S HEAD HOTEL, Rochester,
          October 29th, 1868.

MY DEAR ELIZABETH,—Great meeting this evening "to protest
against recent attempts to stir up class feelings in the city."  The whole
meeting called for Smee, and I was sent for, and entered the room amidst
the most uproarious cheering. I got up on the platform, and shook Martin
warmly by the hand (with such a scene as you never saw), but after waiting
for two hours neither of us could be heard, so we agreed to leave the
meeting quietly, when the police rushed in and cleared the hall.  I was
enthusiastically cheered, and all is now quiet, the Blue magistrates being
furious.  Promises pour in to me, and we have a good chance.

KING'S HEAD HOTEL, Rochester,
          November 13th, 1868, 10 o'clock.

Overwhelming show of hands in favour of Smee; all going on
gloriously.

ROCHESTER, November 17th, 1868.

This telegram was sent to us after the nomination, and the
day before the poll.

In a letter he wrote after the election he says :—

SIR,—I have lately contested Rochester in the Conservative interest
and although not successful, from special reasons appertaining to that
city, yet I think that I have found the key to obtain the enthusiastic
support of the masses for the Conservative cause from the following
principles :—

1. Conservatives desire a step by step progression from that which is
good to that which is better; in fact Conservatism is a continual growth
and improvement.

This doctrine always flashed in the people's minds, and when illustrated
by natural phenomena, always delighted and enchanted them.

2. The interests of the working men have a natural affinity with those
of the gentry and aristocracy, and both should act together.

This always stirred up marked enthusiasm.

3. The Church belongs to the people, the clergy having ever de-
fended the people against oppression, and is the source of England's
freedom.

This carried conviction, but I did not find it desirable to say too much
upon Church questions.

4. The liberal doctrines of Bright, Mill, and Co. really amount to the lowest pay for the largest amount of labour, and the least quantity of the necessaries of life for the largest amount of money.

This was almost too exciting for the masses. It completely carried them away, and completely turned the tables against the employers of labour and the small shopkeepers, the enemies of the Conservative cause.

5. Labour and capital equally suffer from disagreement, and members of Parliament should be their mediators.

6. The Conservative Reform Bill has given the power to the people, but at present the people are not freemen, as their masters compel them to vote as they please, to their own injury.

This doctrine was generally met with shouts of the names of the Government contractors at Rochester, who command the electors, and frequently with suggestions for the ballot.

7. Violent political struggles are inimical to the interests of the people: hence Gladstone had done great injury by stirring up the Church question.

By this line of argument I showed that the aristocracy, gentry, and clergy constitute the Conservative party, with the working men, but that the Liberal party were composed of the employers of labour and the small shopkeepers.

The Liberal party were furious at the enthusiasm produced by these doctrines, and called an indignation meeting, but the multitude completely foiled the attempt.

At Rochester I carried the clergy, the gentry, and the working men with me, and I have no doubt that we have the key to the future Conservative government of the country. A large majority of working men were compelled to vote as their masters dictated.

And again, at the complimentary dinner given to him at Rochester on the 17th of December, 1868 :—

It is with a great deal of diffidence that I rise to express the thanks which I feel for the honour you have done me this day in asking me to come amongst you after the defeat we have experienced at the late election. We have unmistakably had a great defeat in Rochester, a defeat which we did not expect. The moment I entered the city I received numerous promises of support; those promises came rolling in day by day till 10 o'clock each night; they amounted at last to 1024 on the day before the nomination. After the nomination, at which, as you know, we gained the show of hands, that same evening no more promises came in, but promises began to fall off; withdrawal began to be made, which showed the city must be under the power of certain persons in it (sensation); and on the next day these 1024 promises degenerated into 702 performances (shame). Accustomed as I am to numbers, I sat ticking off the votes at the Guildhall as they came in, and I soon saw that there was something wrong. I sent word to my committee, "Why don't the voters come up?" No answer came. I wrote again: "Tell me, why don't the voters come up?" A slip of paper then came with £ s. d. upon it (sensation). I understood at once the meaning. Now there must be some very potent reason which prevented 1024 promises from realizing more than 702 votes. In the first place I think many good Conservatives were victims to despair. I found they worshipped success, and the moment they saw we were not likely to be at the head of the poll, they stayed at home and did not vote (shame).

In speaking before public meetings Mr. Smee varied not a little. Generally his speeches were fluently delivered, and were at times most brilliant; at other times his speeches would fall flat, and then he would search for the words to use. When he got up, no one could predict whether he was in the humour and would give one of his brilliant speeches, or whether it would be painful to listen to him. Two sentences were, however sufficient for those who knew him well to tell whether the speech would be a success or not. His facts he would generally, not always, get up beforehand, but the manner in which they were to be arranged was always left till the time of speaking. But perhaps the most brilliant and most effective of his speeches were those which he took no trouble about, when he rose on the spur of the moment and delivered them off-hand.

In the spring of 1870 my mother and I accompanied my father to Italy, and there enjoyed all the beauties which that classic land can yield. How much the charming scenery of the Riviera delighted him, and Florence—that lovely city where

> " Sculpture with her rainbow sister vies ! "

> " Girt by her theatre of hills, she reaps
>    Her corn, and wine, and oil, and Plenty leaps
>    To laughing Life with her redundant horn."

From Florence we went to Naples, which city and its neighbourhood afforded Mr. Smee, as may be supposed, fresh novelties of intense interest. He was greatly surprised to find the Ceterach fern thriving almost at the summit of Mount Vesuvius, and the Maidenhair fern luxuriating in all its glory in the ruined amphitheatre at Pozzuoli near Naples.

Some of the fronds (he writes) were eighteen or more inches in length, and the earthen walls were covered with sheets of this lovely fern, standing out at right angles from the wall, or hanging down from the roof. I must confess that, when I beheld this great and glorious sight, I was more impressed with it than with the thought that I was present on a spot where dramas of blood were enacted centuries before. I speedily collected a number of plants, to the no small disgust of the cicerone, who could not do the amphitheatre at his usual gallop, and who shrugged his shoulders at my utter want of taste in gathering useless weeds. Some of these plants now grow at my garden in the fern cave.

My father, wherever he went, found something new or tempting for his garden.   His portmanteau was but too frequently converted into a flower-garden before he reached England again, and which not a little surprised the Customs' officers, when they inspected his luggage.   Plants were the primary consideration, clothes secondary, if they could claim any consideration at all. At Pompeii he found more Maidenhair ferns growing on the walls of that ruined town, to which he paid repeated visits.   At Rome he was much impressed with the grand buildings and ruins. He went daily to St. Peter's, the Coliseum, and was much struck with the noble proportions of the Pantheon.   The pictures and sculptures afforded him much pleasure, and it was during this visit that he made those curious notes on Binocular Perspective which are alluded to in the Appendix, No. XIX.   My father gained much recreation and enjoyment, and would have returned, I doubt not, a stronger man, had he not, unhappily, been obliged by untoward circumstances to stop, and not only doctor, but also help with my mother to nurse, severe cases of illness.   He was urgently required in London, and he could not leave, and the worry and anxiety attending this delay greatly marred the enjoyment of this visit, and prevented that benefit to his health which his family had hoped to see.   What a keen interest he took in the new forms of vegetation he met with in beautiful Italy, the following extracts from letters to my brother, who was in England acting as his deputy, will show :—

*March 16th*, 1870, Florence.—To compare with Carshalton.
Almonds now in flower; some peach-trees and pear-trees swelling their buds; anemones in flower; sloe-trees in full flower.

*April 6th*, 1870, Florence.—I forgot to tell you that swallows appeared at Naples on March 28th, and I saw them here on March 31st.

*April 12th*, 1870.—The country is really very beautiful with wild tulips, wild flowers, and all the fruit-trees in flower, and the mountains look lovely.
M. is still very weak.   I do not know how I am to get home; I shall be so thankful to write and state that we are on the move.

*April 23rd*, 1870.—I heard the nightingales last night, April 22nd; compare with Carshalton, for I believe the birds distribute well over Europe on the same day.   Inquire at Carshalton, and make a note of it.

*April 24th*, 1870.—Nightingales in quantities.   I heard yesterday also the cuckoo the first time.

*April 25th*, 1870.—People must clearly know that illness is the cause of my absence. Poor Carshalton has not seen me this spring. I hope everything is properly attended to.

Lilies are now in flower. The May is just coming into flower. Pear-trees are beginning to go off. Plum-trees are mostly gone off. Peach-trees are generally off. The vines are beginning in warm situations to sprout (not in the vineyards). The spotted orchis is in flower.

*April 25th*, 1870.—The swallows are building. The buttercups and tulips, all over the fields, red and yellow, are in flower. The white mulberry is just breaking. The first leaf of spring is coming over the poplars and elms. The underwood has much leaf.

Before Mr. Plimsoll, to whom great praise is due, had the courage to bring forward his Merchant Shipping Bill to the notice of Parliament, there had appeared numerous anonymous letters in the ' Insurance Times,' besides some pamphlets circulated elsewhere, in which was shown in a very strong light the unseaworthiness of ships that were (according to these writings) " sent to sea at the peril of men's lives." These letters and pamphlets caused a good deal of excitement at the time among persons interested, among owners of ships, underwriters, and marine companies. Frequently half-a-dozen short pithy letters would appear in the same paper on one day, followed up for some weeks by others equally short and telling. Many of these letters were from the pen of Alfred Smee. There was a great grievance, he conceived, to be remedied only by strong measures. In many of his anonymous writings he writes as if he were himself a sufferer ; but that form, it will be speedily seen, was merely used as a figure of speech, so as to bring more forcibly forward the grievance which he was endeavouring by agitation to redress. The following spring Mr. Plimsoll brought forward his Merchant Shipping Act, which my father thought erred only by being "too lenient;" and the remarks that gentleman uttered in the House of Commons on the unseaworthiness of ships sent to sea came, I have heard my father say, "far within the mark:" yet the virtuous indignation with which Mr. Plimsoll was assailed may still be remembered. But although the Bill was lost that Session, the storm was fairly roused, and the sailors were in a body with Plimsoll, and in 1876 the Government deemed it expedient to pass an Act to stop unseaworthy ships being sent to sea. A selection from the various anonymous letters from Alfred Smee's pen on the above subject is placed in the Appendix, No. XXXII. It must be remembered that these letters are not to be looked upon as specimens of logic or of literature; they were purely intended for one end, and that was to bring forward in a prominent way before the public the above subject.

Mr. Smee was throughout his life frequently writing various papers or pamphlets to which he did not affix his name: amongst the most important of these anonymous writings are those on Chancery Reform. Although the papers were not written during the years treated of in this chapter, yet as this and the preceding one contain most of the anonymous writings of Mr. Smee, it may not be out of place to mention them here. These papers were printed separately, and were from time to time distributed by post among the leading members of the legal profession, and more especially among the members of the Chancery bar. The perusal of these papers will suffice to show their extreme importance to the public. They are placed in the Appendix, No. XXXIII.

# CHAPTER X.

## 1870 to 1875.

'The Widow and the Rabbits'—Letters to the 'Times'—'My Garden,' seventh book — Impromptu lecture — The marriage of his daughter — Attends an International Botanical Congress — Letters to his daughter from abroad — Address at Rochester — Letter to the Council of the Royal College of Surgeons, England.

It would occupy too much space to insert all the anonymous writings of Alfred Smee, for they were voluminous. I cannot, however, refrain from giving a few extracts from one more of his little works, to which he did not attach his name, more especially as it forms a link to show his vivid imagination, his unwearying energy, and how numerous and various were his publications. This was written in the autumn of 1871, when he, myself, and my mother went for a short trip to Scotland. We were hospitably entertained for a while at a friend's house, after which we travelled over the wildest and most beautiful parts of Scotland :—

> "So wondrous wild, the whole might seem
> The scenery of a fairy dream."
> Scott's *Lady of the Lake*.

My father was an early riser, and was generally up before the rest of the family. For two or three mornings before breakfast he amused himself by writing 'The Widow and the Rabbits.' This fairy legend by a Ferret, which is really a humorous skit, as the following dedication shows, is very prettily illustrated.*

* Published by Messrs. Rixon and Arnold, 29, Poultry, London.

## THE WIDOW AND THE RABBITS.

To Elizabeth Mary, who has visited many Happy Valleys and observed the ill Effects of excessive Rabbit Preservation, this Story is dedicated by her Father.

The story opens thus:—

In the North of Scotland there is a very beautiful valley. A foaming river runs through it, where abundance of trout disport themselves in the sun and rise to every little fly which settles upon the water. When rain falls, the river swells and overflows its banks; but amidst the roar of the water, the salmon rush up the torrent from the sea, and thus a delicious food is afforded to the fishermen. These catch them with an artificial fly, and not only supply the people of the district with fish, but exchange them for other luxuries with the inhabitants of Edinburgh and London, who have neither trout nor salmon in their rivers. The whole valley was formerly filled with villages, the people of which tended their flocks and herds, and cultivated their fields. The inhabitants were good and kind to each other, and aimed at promoting the happiness of all. As the land was good, and Providence was bountiful in bestowing the fruits of the earth, everyone was thankful for the gifts he received, and rejoiced in the lovely scenes which he daily saw, from the time the sun rose in the morning till it gave forth its heat in mid-day, and set in the west in the evening; when the villagers, after they had uttered their praises for the blessings already received, and had prayed for a continuance of their joys in the future, retired to rest.

The valley is surrounded by high hills to the west, so that no man has ever been able to pass. It has rugged hills to the north, which almost constitute a wall, and to the south there are also hills, leaving only one narrow entrance for foreigners to come in, or for the inhabitants to go out. It was, therefore, always called "The Happy and Secluded Valley of the North."

About 1000 years ago, more or less,—for the learned have never been able to decide the exact time; some say it was in the year 770, others in 790; but the most reliable, from documents existing in the great library of Kamskatka, consider that it was in the year 772,—a foreigner named Lord Gryndum came with numerous retainers, and took possession of this happy valley, and built himself a great castle. The villagers, always happy and living in peace with each other, were never accustomed to resist; and, in fact, they never had either an army or policeman to protect them, and so the villagers suffered the foreign Laird to take possession of their valley and charge them rents for their lands. Not contented with this, he soon after took their hunting-grounds from them, where they were wont to kill game, especially deer, white hares, and grouse for their winter's use; and the Laird liking himself to kill fish (as he had nothing else to do but fish, shoot, and hunt) ordered his retainers to drive the villagers from the river, and prevent them catching a single salmon, or even killing a trout. He was not even satisfied then, and his aggressive disposition caused him to bring some rabbits from England, which he forbade to be killed under the pain of a severe fine, or even of imprisonment. The better to carry out his wicked device, he made interest with the king, by bribing the attendants with haunches of venison and with salmon, to make him a magistrate, by which he had power to cruelly ill-treat his tenants, and to punish the peasantry for the slightest offence.

The rabbits multiplied exceedingly, and the whole valley became a vast rabbit warren, from which the creatures sallied forth by armies at night and devoured all the grass in the fields; and when they had finished the grass, they ate the turnips; and when they had eaten the turnips, they attacked the corn; and when they could get neither grass nor corn, nor turnips, they set to work and destroyed the young trees by eating the bark and young shrubs.

The poor people in vain encircled their garden plots with close palings, for wire fencing was not invented at that time. The rabbits either scrambled over them, or burrowed underneath. Sometimes it is recorded that they actually ate their way through the wooden palings, and, when under the pressure of hunger, they smelt the poor men's cabbages; they have been seen to jump over the fence, when, in a short time, the vegetables were eaten and disappeared. It was particularly noticed that they always took the choicest and sweetest vegetables in the garden. What they did not eat they spoilt, so that nothing was left for use in the winter.

\*　　　\*　　　\*　　　\*　　　\*　　　\*

In ten short years the rabbits so changed the Happy Valley of the North, that all the population were wretched, and it became known in more southern countries as "The Valley of Misery and Woe."

At this time there was a poor widow named Mary Suffermuch, whose family had lived in the village more than five hundred years. She had lost her husband by the fall of an ash-tree which overhung the road, and which was blown down in a high wind, after the rabbits had undermined the tree by cutting the roots with their sharp teeth, which are formed like chisels.

\*　　　\*　　　\*　　　\*　　　\*　　　\*

But on the 10th of November, which in that year 780 fell on a Monday, the poor widow looked at her prospects, and she found that the rabbits had so far destroyed her crops that she had no turnips left for her cow, as the interior of every one was eaten out, and merely the outside shell was left. The ground was covered with snow, as winter had set in early that year. She had only porridge for two days more. The barley had all been sold, and the money expended for shoes for the children. The poor widow, when she realized her position, was miserable indeed, and cried most bitterly.

\*　　　\*　　　\*　　　\*　　　\*　　　\*

The widow then goes off to a relation for assistance in her misery, but finds him as destitute as herself. On her way thither she admires the beauty of the country. Dispirited and disheartened with her fruitless errand (all this is most pathetically told), she sets off to return home.

To rest herself she sat down on a bench in a beautiful wood, where the waters of the river ran alongside, roaring among the rocks and large stones; there, too, the bright mid-day sun shone upon the white barks of the birch-trees, and on the deep-coloured branches of the ever green Scotch pines. She cried very much when she thought of her past happiness and present misery, till she was quite exhausted and fell sound asleep.

A fairy here suddenly appears before her, coming "with a rush of wind." After a long colloquy between the fairy and the widow,

the lovely fairy, who was quite distressed at such grievous misery, gazed with the tenderest compassion upon the face of the sorrow-stricken widow. In a tone of authority, the fairy said, with earnestness but sweetness: "Homeward go, Mary! Rabbits shall no more trouble thee! This day I have full power over the rabbits in this valley." And then with a clear, shrill, musical voice the fairy cried, "Change, bunnies, change." The sound in the dead stillness echoed through the woods from rock to rock, and from tree to tree, "Change, change, change," and died away in the extreme distance, echoing "Change, change, change," till the last murmuring was scarcely audible to the most delicate ear. In an instant the snow was torn up like a whirlwind, and, with a rushing sound, the fairy passed away in the cloud of snow the wind had raised. . . . .

On her way home the widow saw, to her surprise,

a large black cat rush out of a rabbit hole and prowl about, seeking for food; presently she saw many other cats, some black, some black and white, but there was not a tabby amongst them. The words "Change, bunnies, change," came to her mind, and she perceived that the rabbits had been changed, and that their tails had grown long, and their ears had become short, and that it was perfectly clear the rabbits had been changed into cats.

As she slowly continued her journey homeward, she noticed the rooks wheeling in circles to the south, and then fly away in the direction of the next valley. After that, a long zigzag line appeared in the sky, which she knew to be a flock of wild ducks. Later an immense pack of grouse, screaming wildly, flew out of the valley towards the highest hill of the east. Then the linnets and warbling tribes of small birds, which she could not exactly distinguish, formed a great flock, and darted about like flies in the air, and then flew out of sight. Even the owls, although it was only two o'clock in the afternoon, were on the wing, screaming in B flat. The herons, with their immense wings, flew away to distant places.

The widow sat to rest herself on a large granite stone by the side of the river, and she was surprised to see that the salmon were jumping over the stones and swimming down to the sea as fast as they could. She then plainly understood that all living creatures were leaving the valley for fear of the number of black and black and white cats which were prowling about.

The quaint and cunning description of the "Rabbit Protectors" here follows, and should be read to be appreciated, but is too long for these pages.

A stone, long since decayed, was placed over the grave, with the inscription: "To the Perpetual Memory of the thirty-four Rabbit Protectors, of the Valley of Misery." Two of the keepers ran down the road to England, one of whom escaped across the sea in a trading vessel to Holland, where he was heard of many years afterwards. Seven went to the South, and were never heard of again; but as they had to cross a river, it was surmised they were all drowned, and that their bodies were carried out to sea. Two quarrelled over a piece of cold venison; and one had his leg broken by a kick by his companion, and perished in the snow. His companion was tried and executed at Edinburgh. One got into a deep snowdrift directly he started, and perished; but the remaining nine were sheltered by a compassionate old woman at the north of the village, and returned after two weeks' time, and became good labourers, declaring they never would be Rabbit Protectors again. In this way the whole forty-seven were exactly accounted for. With regard to those who crossed the river, it is stated by the great historian Findout, that several bodies were washed ashore one November, at the parish of Seaside, not seven miles from the mouth of the river; but Mr. Exact, in his popular account of the district, points out that the year is not mentioned, or the number of bodies stated, nor was the identity ever proved; so whether they were the bodies of the keepers, or of sailors from the wreck of some ship, can never be discovered.

Thursday came, and the cats, from exposure to the intense frost of the preceding night, were very hungry, and were prowling about in all directions for food. It was particularly mentioned that, although the birds flew over the valley that day, none settled when they saw the terrible army of cats ready to devour them.

In the evening the Laird was in a state of wild passion at not having his grouse for dinner, and went to bed half stupefied, after having drunk a bottle of brandy. The cats, in the desperation of famine, attacked the house by myriads, and tried to get in; but the windows and doors were securely bolted. As the Laird heard the shrieks and cries of the cats, he shivered with fright in his bed; when of a sudden the Fairy appeared in a sheet of fire, standing on a table before his bed. "Who are you, and whence do you come?" cried he; "how did you enter when all the doors were locked and the windows barred? Tell me quick." The Fairy, unmoved by his violent gestures, sweetly replied, "I am the Fairy Dogood: I am flesh and blood like you, but not so gross. I dwell where I like; where all is peace; but generally at the mountain top, to overlook the valley. Sometimes I lie in the scarlet flower of a lichen; sometimes I nestle amidst the pollen of Linnæus' flower: when I go abroad, I flit on the wings of a blue butterfly to survey the flowers, or I soar in the air between the wings of a gnat to enjoy the evening breeze. I practise gymnastics on the delicate thread of a spider's web, and dance on the top of a thorn of the gorse; I feed upon the odour of the sweet gale; I drink the invisible water of the air, and eat the blue bloom which covers the fruit of the dewberry; I bathe in the particles of the mist as it rises over the mountain top, and I swim in the dewdrops which hang on the flowers; I slide on the snow-flakes as they drift in the air, and I skate on the hailstones as they drop from the sky. When I suspect wrong, I leave the mountain top; and I have dwelt in the key-hole of your bedroom to see what you have been about. When I see injustice, I ride upon the whirlwind and gallop in the flames. I have come to visit you through a crack in a pane of glass in your bedroom window, which, although you can scarcely see, is quite wide enough for me to pass through."

At these words, the Laird shook and shook again, as well he might, and covered his face with the bedclothes; but he saw the Fairy nevertheless, and could not hide her from his view. In a stentorian voice which shook the very walls of the house, the Fairy continued: "I have answered thy questions fully, and perhaps more fully than you expected; now answer mine. Will you compensate the villagers for the damage the rabbits have caused?" "I will," he quickly cried, "but spare me, O Fairy Dogood." "Will you promise never to keep Rabbit Protectors again?" "I will," he wildly shrieked, more dead than alive with fear; "but, O dear Fairy Dogood, keep the cats from devouring me." The Fairy with a voice like thunder exclaimed, "Don't call me dear, but keep thy promise; for if ever thou breakest it, the proprietorship of the lands of the valley shall never descend in the direct line in thy family; and mark, if thou art ever guilty of further extortions, the lands you have acquired by conquest will be taken from you, and given back to the people from whom, in plain truth, you have stolen them. Power has only been given to me by Queen Mab over rabbits, but not over cats," said the Fairy; "I cannot help you, and would not if I could." And then in a flame which lit up for a minute the whole valley, and was seen by many persons hundreds of miles around, the Fairy instantly disappeared through the same crack she had entered, saying with a voice like thunder, "Keep thy promise." A great scientific man, Mr. Factfinder, who carefully examined the pane of glass with a lens, is reported to have been of opinion that the flames fused the two sides of the crack which the fairy passed through, as he could not find any reflection on the surfaces; though he clearly perceived the direction of the cut by a slight irregularity in the glass.

In the celebrated collection of Baron Oldfinder, a window was mentioned in the catalogue one pane of which showed signs of having been cracked. A minute investigation showed a central part of the disturbance of the substance of the glass, from which irregular curved lines radiated. It is possible that this might have been the very pane of glass which Fairy Dogood went through. It is impossible, however, to clear up the mystery, as the heir of the seventh Baron Breakeverything Larky, when a boy, and not knowing the priceless value of this antiquity, used it as a target to fire at, and literally smashed it to atoms. He ever regretted the circumstance, and used to say, in after-years, that any object which could throw light on the important legend of the Widow and the Rabbits was of great interest to the whole civilized world, and he deeply deplored that he had inadvertently destroyed this important link of the evidence.

After the flames, which occurred three minutes past midnight, and are recorded in all good astronomical books of a subsequent period, the air became very still and cold, in fact colder than ever has been known before or since. How cold it was, never can be known, for no thermometer has ever been made to register such extreme cold as prevailed that still night. The cats, exhausted by hunger and fatigue, succumbed to the frost, and lay dead in all directions. The next day, when the villagers looked out of the windows, the white snow was literally strewn with dead cats; the black cats were very distinctly visible on the white ground, though the white ones were not visible, as they could hardly be distinguished from the snow.

In the course of Thursday, the Laird, who was still afraid, and very ill from the effects of the brandy which he had drunk and from the fright he had received, sent his trusty forester, Mr. Treecarer, to the village, to say, that he would compensate all those who had suffered injury from the rabbits, and he begged them at once to make out their accounts that he might discharge them. When the villagers heard this, their joy was unbounded, and they cried: "Away with misery and woe; now come back happiness and joy." One old man, however, said, "Do not waste your time in merry-making too soon: we should not be wasteful, if we were rich; but now we are poor, we should waste nothing. Remember that a good cat-skin is worth fourpence, so skin the cats and sell the skins." All the villagers thought this good advice, and started off at once with a hurrah, and up to Saturday night got as many skins as realized £2,500 exactly, at fourpence each.    Thus it is proved that 150,000 rabbits existed before they were turned into cats; and as the valley contained 15,000 acres, it is proved that there were 10 rabbits to every acre of land.    But this is not quite exact, for rain set in on the Sunday, which spoilt the skins of many of the black cats, and many of the white cats had been passed over, as they could not be seen in the white snow.    It is possible that the total amount of rabbits which lived in the valley were 15 per acre, or 225,000 in the whole. After much consultation and consideration the villagers were compensated by a return of five years' rents, which actuaries consider fair under the circumstances; because the rabbits had been brought to the valley ten years back.    At first there were very few rabbits, and they did but little harm; gradually they increased, by a geometric progression, till the above enormous quantity was bred.    By accepting five years' rents as compensation, a fair average was struck, and a very difficult discussion avoided.    The lawyers indeed wanted to go into fractions, because in some years the rabbits multiplied more than in others, and hence the progression was not uniform. One lawyer, Mr. Stirupstrife, desired to file amicable Bills in Chancery as to the appropriation of the money; but the villagers were too sensible by far to listen to this proposition, although Mr. Barrister Helplawyer strongly advised that course.    All legal difficulties were surmounted: and the lawyers were prevented from eating up the funds, which they very much wanted to do, by each payment of the Laird being a free gift, subject to the terms and conditions of the giver, which were equitable in each particular case where the money had to be divided amongst the children who had lost their parents.

On Thursday the birds, seeing that the cats were dead, returned to their own haunts; and on Sunday a rapid thaw took place, which caused a great flood, and on Monday morning the salmon returned by shoals to the river; and all was again prosperity and peace.

The villagers, out of the proceeds of the sale of the cats-skins, bought the poor widow a new house, with a farm of thirty-five acres of arable and grass land, and seven roods of wood. She also had ample compensation for the damage done by the rabbits. The remainder of the money was spent in building a new church—which was badly wanted—the round arches of which exist to this day. Unfortunately the builder, who came from a town called Cheatem, took the villagers in, or they would have been able to construct a bridge over the river. To this day, 1,000 years afterwards, the river has to be crossed by a ford, to the great peril of the inhabitants; and when I went to the ford, had I attempted to pass, I should certainly have been drowned, showing how long the effects of roguery may be felt.

The Laird carried out honestly his compensation to the peasants and his promises to the Fairy; and was always happy and contented afterwards. All the villagers ever since have protected his partridges, grouse, and deer, and reserved to him three miles of river, containing five fine salmon pools, for his own private use. He lived to the ripe old age of 91, and on his tombstone he ordered to be engraved, after his name, date of birth, and age at death—

Beware of Rabbits!!

The previous year the two following letters were published in the 'Times:'—

It was known all over London that the venerable church of St. Saviour's was this morning struck by lightning, when the majestic peal of thunder rolled throughout the metropolis at about half-past eight, and this afternoon I examined the course of the electric force in its destructive career.

The church has a noble central tower, with four stone turrets, one at each angle, and each turret is surmounted with a large copper vane, over which is placed a copper ball. The south-east turret has been struck by lightning; and as a result, the stones of which it was composed were thrown off in all directions, exactly as the bark of a tree is thrown off when that is struck by lightning. The force with which the stones composing the turret were scattered may be appreciated when it is stated that one stone was thrown at least fifty yards to the western extremity of the churchyard, where it broke two iron rails and then injured a house. Other stones were thrown on the roofs of the houses near London Bridge. Some were thrown on the roof of the church, breaking through to the pavement below, and all the surrounding houses bear more or less the marks of violence with which large stones were thrown from the turret at the top of the tower.

An inmate of one of the almshouses below told me that what with the lightning, the roar of the thunder, the pelting rain, the falling stones, and the breaking in of the roofs, she really thought the end of the world had arrived. The copper ball at the top of the vane bore the marks of the lightning discharge. The turret itself being composed of stone, and therefore a bad conductor of electricity, offered a resistance to the transmission of the electric force, and was consequently disintegrated and its component parts thrown outwards. The electric force then passed to the flat lead roof at the top of the tower, and was thence conveyed by a water-pipe to the lead-gutters on the roof of the southern aisle of the nave. From this roof it passed down two other water-pipes to the churchyard. On the most easterly of these pipes, or the nearest to the tower, the pipe showed a curious lateral discharge, forming a funnel-shaped hole, and on the more westerly water-pipe a dilation existed, but without the aperture. From the examination which I made, it is demonstrated that, had there been a conductor from the vane to the water-pipes, at a cost of two or three pounds, the present damage, which is roughly estimated at £500, would have been spared; and the moral may be learnt, never to have two surfaces of metal in so high and exposed a situation without a lightning-conductor. I have lived in a house struck by lightning where the lightning-conductors, from being badly constructed, were really lightning attractors, but in this case the mischief is due entirely to the parsimony of the parish authorities. Thunder and lightning is in no part of Europe, not even excepting the high Alps, so terrifically grand as in the centre of the city of London; and when to this marvellous natural phenomenon is superadded its power of destruction of the more beautiful works of man, the interest attending its operation is materially increased.

July 26th, 1870.

Another magnificent display of the aurora borealis occurred last night. I was driving from Carshalton to London when I noticed that it suddenly became very chilly, and that the sky exhibited much the same appearance as when a beautiful aurora occurred at Oxford about five weeks since. The remark had hardly been made when the first light appeared in the south-east. Within two or three minutes a grand display of red light appeared overhead, with streamers stretching down to the northern horizon. A few minutes afterwards the light showed itself towards the west, with streamers of light stretching to the western horizon. The glorious scene was ever changing, when a vast mass of red light appeared in the north-east. This resembled the light of a large London fire, and was in the greatest perfection whilst we were on Clapham Common, about a quarter to 6 o'clock. It continued, however, till we arrived in London, and ceased about 7 o'clock. These great displays of northern lights so early in the season are unprecedented in my recollection.

Oct. 26th, 1870.

On January 24th, 1872, a violent gale passed over the metropolis, which occasioned a letter to the 'Standard' on the 25th, on barometric pressure, and which called for the invention of cheap barometers for the use of our fishermen, so that they might thereby be enabled to prognosticate a coming gale.

The violent gale which passed last night over the metropolis was accompanied by corresponding changes in the barometer. Yesterday the barometer stood at 29·03, but in consequence of the violence of the gale which raged this morning I examined the barometer at half-past 4 and found that it had fallen to 28·35, and that at 5 o'clock it had receded to 28·34. The flint glass barometer of the London Institution, which is a duplicate of the famous instrument made for the Royal Society, with a platinum ring in the tube, recorded at 6 A.M. 28·37 inches of pressure, and at 6 P.M. 28·87, showing a rise of half an inch in twelve hours. I kept my mountain aneroid barometer, specially constructed for me by Messrs. Horne and Thornthwaite, under observation the entire day. By 9 o'clock it had risen to 28·6; by 10 to 28·65; by 11 to 28·7; at noon it stood at 28·74. Then a storm of wind and rain ensued, when by 1 o'clock it had fallen to 28·73. By 2 o'clock the mercury rose again to 28·76; by 3 o'clock to 28·84; by 4 to 28·86; by 5 to 28·87, when it remained stationary till half-past 9, when it reached 28·9. At 11 o'clock P.M. it stood at 28·93, when the observations

I

were discontinued, as the mercury had returned to nearly its former position. The mercury in the large tube in the barometer of the Bank of England was at noon in a state of visible motion from the rapidity of the variation of the atmospheric pressure. It is important to call the particular attention of our mariners to the occurrence of great gales, with rapid changes in barometric pressure; and he who can invent a cheap, delicate, and practical instrument for the use of our fishermen and seamen, to enable them to prognosticate a coming storm, will be the greatest philanthropist of the age, by tending to the protection of life from the perils of the winds and waves.

On July 25th, 1872, a letter was written to the 'Times' on the incident of Brixton Church having been struck by lightning in the storm.

The intensity and violence of the storms throughout Europe this summer naturally attract general attention. On Thursday, July 11, so frequent were the electrical discharges that I counted in one hour 394 flashes of lightning. The storm over London on Tuesday was severe, but singularly enough at Carshalton, although the roars of the peals of thunder came from every side, and the repeated flashes of lightning were dazzling and terrific, scarcely a drop of rain fell. Between Carshalton and London the full force of the storm was experienced, and the steeple of Brixton Church was struck by lightning. I was curious to examine the injury, and to trace the course of the electric force. I found the steeple was built of stone, and had a stone ornament at the summit, with a stone cross. All this was supported by stone columns, and there was no good electric conductor between the stone cross and the earth. The electrical discharge shivered the stone ornament, breaking it into fragments, which were dispersed in all directions. Some fell upon the roof of the church, breaking the slates and even the rafters, but many of the pieces of broken stone were thrown to the churchyard beneath. In this particular instance the electrical discharge did not appear to have passed between the clouds and the earth by any water-pipe, gas-pipe, or other electric conductor connected with the part of the steeple struck, but probably was carried by the down-pouring rain, which is itself an efficient conductor of electricity. I remember this steeple to have been struck by lightning about thirty years ago, and this second injury indicates that even a stone steeple in an exposed situation is not safe without an efficient metallic lightning-conductor.

These letters on storms show the great interest which Mr. Smee evinced in such phenomena. Indeed it was seldom that he heard of a building or tree in the metropolis or its vicinity being struck by lightning, but he would hasten to the scene to take observations on the occurrence.

'My Garden' was the next published work from Alfred Smee's pen. It was written in every spare moment as a solace to his mind. The work, now so well known, details the geology of the

district. The Celtic, Roman, and Anglo-Saxon periods of its
history are exemplified, as are also the mediæval. The principles of gardening are given, and the very tools that are necessary for that operation fully described. The construction of glass
houses, with their ventilation, and the curious and novel modes
for heating them, are also explained. The arrangements for the
propagation of plants, the management of garden vegetables,
of the fruit garden, the general flower garden, the special flower
garden (comprising the roses, orchids, climbing plants, Alpine
flowers, ornamental grasses); weeds and wild plants; the algæ,
mosses, lichens, liverworts, fungi; the ferns, lycopods, &c., are
all fully set forth. Forest trees and shrubs are duly noticed
(this chapter was written during the three weeks he was in Scotland, in the autumn of 1871, when he also wrote 'The Widow and
the Rabbits'); and the animal kingdom, from the animalcules
in the river Wandle and insects of the garden to the larger
animals. The birds and the fish and the reptiles hold an important part in the work. The climate and spring frosts are
recorded; and the work ends with a calendar of plants in flower
under glass and out of doors, of fruit, of vegetables, of garden
operations, and of the natural history, during every week for the
year 1871. 'My Garden' is illustrated by 1300 engravings,
nearly all taken from nature; it is not only a work of reference,
but it is fitted, from the beauty of its illustrations, for the
drawing-room table. This book has been compared to White's
'Natural History of Selborne.' To those who are lovers of
gardening this book is indeed a prize!*

Not many months before 'My Garden' was issued to the
public, Professor Huxley, who was giving a course of lectures
at the London Institution, fell suddenly ill. The audience were
already assembling in the theatre of the London Institution.
What was to be done? Some one rushed off to our house, a
few doors off, and fortunately my father came in at that very
moment. "It is a pity," he said, "that so many should come,
some a long distance, and should go away disappointed. Suppose
I give them a lecture?" "Yes, do!" was the eager exclamation.
Then my father said he would give them a lecture, a gossip about
gardening. So, without any preparation, he walked into the
theatre, crowded with people who had come to hear Professor
Huxley on Biology, but who remained to hear what Mr. Smee

---

* 'My Garden' is published by Messrs. Bell, York Street, Covent Garden.

had to say about gardening. Without any notes or premeditation he commenced. On another occasion, within a few months, my father delivered another lecture on the same subject at an equally short notice, but this is the only one which has been preserved, through the kindness of Mr. Shadbolt, a proprietor, who took shorthand notes of it, and which was afterwards printed in the Journal of the London Institution, February 5th, 1872. (See Appendix, No. XXXIV.)   My father's family are naturally proud of this fresh demonstration of his genius.

A few weeks after the publication of 'My Garden,' he gave in August 1872 a fête in his garden, on the marriage of his daughter. On this occasion he invited the children of the neighbourhood to exhibit wild flowers, so as to "develope in them intelligence, observation, emulation, and the sense of the beautiful." He gave rewards in useful books to those who exhibited the most beautiful collection of wild flowers, of which the species were the most varied or which were arranged with the best taste. The exhibition took place and was a great success, and contributed to the interest of the fête.

My father was an active supporter of flower-shows being held in the city of London. Of late years, flower-shows, or rather exhibitions of window-plants grown within the City, have been held in Finsbury Circus, and he gave prizes for wild flowers at these little horticultural displays. He gave two prizes in 1875, three in 1876, and in 1877 he had intended to give no less than six prizes for wild flowers, which were to be collected by any resident in the city of London coming within the limits of the society.

The first prize will be for the best collection of wild flowers, correctly named.
2nd. Second best collection, correctly named.
3rd. The best collection of wild flowers, unnamed.
4th. Second best collection, unnamed.
5th. The best collection of wild flowers tastefully arranged.
6th. The second best tastefully arranged.
The judges are empowered to withhold any prize if in their opinion a sufficient standard of excellence is not attained.

ALFRED SMEE.

These prizes were distributed last summer by my mother, according to the wishes of her husband. These shows have been very successful, and they have already realized the hopes of the most ardent of their supporters.

My father laid out our garden at Oxford and stocked it
with the choicest kinds of the fruits and outdoor plants which
were grown in his own garden, and he always looked upon the
former as a miniature Carshalton garden. After my marriage
rarely a day passed, if ever, without his writing to me
one, and sometimes two letters, in nearly all of which some
advice or information is given appertaining to the little garden
formed by his skill. These letters, perhaps more than anything
else, show the energy and extreme activity of his character, as
well as his love for Nature, which was with him a veritable
passion.

I shall not come down till Thursday, and then will stop till Tuesday.
Go and hurry on the workmen to-day (Wednesday) to finish the green-
house, to get it painted inside, and to have the ends ready that I may
plant on Saturday, to save Sunday. To be precise:
Have the greenhouse painted twice inside and glazed (glazed first).
Get the end glazed and fixed if not time to paint.
Get the ventilators up.
Make B. get the vine borders ready.
I hope that all the vines will be growing by Saturday.

In another letter he says :—

There is a cart-load of things waiting to come to you, and cart-load
after cart-load will follow. Drive them on. You would make a bad nigger
driver. You do not fluster them half enough.

Got home all right.
We tumbled into the work yesterday pretty well; but there is a lot
to do.
Tell your husband he was right about the axis of the croquet lawn; it
was out about 15 inches. I adjusted roughly, but it will require the most
minute adjustment at the finish.
I do not like the south part of the walk near the park. It is like a
hedge and looks vulgar.
Give B. the enclosed drawing, and tell him to get out the earth as in
the enclosed drawing, beginning right down at the path, and carrying it
back somewhat in the enclosed form to the very verge of the croquet
ground, &c.

Whenever my father came down, he always found the work
done wrong. I was only too glad his instructions were not
properly carried out in his absence, for by that means I got him
down oftener than I otherwise should have done. My father
took great interest in our garden, and I was always having
letters about it, and I was well lectured if I did not give that
amount of attention to it which his enthusiastic spirit wished.

An immense hamper of plants will be sent from Carshalton, and I have made arrangements for Saxifrages, Sempervivums, and Sedums to be sent, as well as a stock of bedding plants.

The hampers had better be sent back to Carshalton.

I have ordered my largest Wistaria to be taken up and sent to cover your verandah.

I have ordered some lavender and the various herbs to be sent. I think that they had better be planted under the peach-trees near the road, but perhaps they had better wait till I come down.

Drive on the men! Get in the earth. Get me lots of stones, and give B. the enclosed plan for him to finish the park side. You must worry them three times a day at least, for you will gain a year by working hard this month and getting in your crops.

I shall bring some seed-peas with me and other seeds to be planted at once, and the rest will follow.

Let me know every day what is done.

I have made inquiries about some peat, for I must contrive that you have a few American plants if I can manage it.

I have ordered your Azaleas and Camellias to be sent directly, also some Alpine plants. I have also sent a hamper full of bulbs, so necessary to make your garden beautiful in spring. The Hyacinths and Narcissi are to be planted in pots for the greenhouse; the Scillas on the mound.

Then follows a drawing how the bulbs should be arranged.

We have just come back from Carshalton. The garden is most lovely; all our Cacti are planted out. Many of the little ones are in flower; most interesting. Our Cacti have only been watered once this winter.

I am quite afraid your man will seriously damage yours, so plant them all out forthwith, but label them first. I should have gone to bed straight, but I did not like you to spoil your plants, &c.

There is an anemone on the mound, with a white flower somewhere in this position (here follows a drawing). I think you had better either eradicate or curtail it to a very little bit. It is a most aggressive rascal. Mine has eaten up nearly twenty species, and has almost driven me wild.

Whit Monday, 10.20.

For some years previously he had been a member of the Council of the Royal Horticultural Society; he was chairman of the fruit committee, as well as a member of the scientific committee, of the same society. Just before his death he was elected vice-president of the scientific committee. He ever took an active part in these committees, and was rarely absent from them.

In May 1874, an International Botanical Congress was held at Florence, and Alfred Smee was sent there as representative of the Royal Horticultural Society of England. He read a paper at that congress on 'The best Varieties of Fruits cultivated in England,' with a view of advancing horticulture by communicating from one country to another the experience which has been obtained of the cultivation of flowers and fruit under varieties of soils and differences of climate. He received a few months later a silver medal from the King of Italy.

Whilst abroad I received many letters from him; two or three of which are here transcribed.

You have passed the Semmering, and you remember how we turned round to ascend the pass. Well, we left Vienna and slept here, stopping at the station at the turn round at the eleventh station. (Here follows a diagram.)

*Semmering.*—The place is most beautiful, with a face of rock of astounding grandeur behind the hotel. This morning we started about 8 o'clock and drove up the gorge, which is perhaps the finest in Europe. The first mile or two was flat, and we saw the waterworks for Vienna, which come out of limestone rocks, as the water comes from the ground at Carshalton. After a time the valley narrows to a gorge, only sufficient room for the river and the wood. At one place the road is carried on planks over the course of the river thus (here is a drawing). The whole road had abundance of wild flowers; amongst the most remarkable were Sempervivums, Sedums, Saxifrages, the blue Hepatica, the Cyclamen, the grape Hyacinth, the beautiful Gentian Verna. Several plants I never saw before—the wild Auricula, the Trolleus Europæus, the green-stalked Spleenwort, all of which I sent many specimens, of which you shall come in for your fair share. I was quite tired grubbing up the plants, and got a large quantity. On our return many of the party saw a number of chamois, seven of which rushed up the mountain, sending down the stones and mightily delighting the observers.

From the cold and wet we have had lately, the tips of all the mountains, which are about 5000 feet high, are covered with snow; and the *Cupicah* of snow-clad mountains, pine-clad sides, the clear, sparkling river, and the cumulous clouds casting their shadows over each and towards the mountain-tops, produced a scene which was truly delightful in itself, and caused us all to think that the day was one never to be forgotten. You must never go to Vienna without visiting this mountain gorge, which is superior to anything which I have ever seen before. It is much larger and finer than the Hellerthal of the Black Mountains; it is wider and finer than the gorge which you saw in Switzerland; and it is much larger, and the mountains higher, than the gorge of the baths of Pfeffers, which you have so often laughed at me for so much admiring.

We are all well, and your mother is behaving like a brick, getting up at seven in the morning. She is now drying some flowers.

To-morrow we go to Trieste, thence to Venice, Hôtel Europe; but it will be no use sending any more letters till we arrive at Florence, where we hope to be on May 10th, in the evening.

SEMMERING, May 3, 1874.

We came yesterday (Monday) to Trieste, arriving at ten at night. As you have done the road, I need not describe it. It is a very fine journey, the Semmering being covered with the lovely Gentian Verna. The Edelweiss was sold by rugged boys at the stations. I bought you a little bouquet of flowers. I wanted to have got a lot of roots, but somehow or other Herr B. did not act with sufficient energy, and I only bought two plants of the gardener at English prices, one for you and one for myself.

We did our journey amidst cloud and rain, which made the effects in the mountains very fine and beautiful. To get from here to Venice we go either by water or by rail. Some want one way and some another, whereupon an argument arises.

I shall remain calm upon the point, as I do not care one hair's breadth which way we go.

I have been much pleased to watch the progress of the trees, for although we are so much south, we are still much in the same state as you are in England: for example, the apple-trees are in the beginning of flower; the horse-chestnuts in the same state. The vines have barely started, so that when they begin they will go on at a terrible rate, to make up in summer for the lost time in winter and spring.

Keep your house moist. Give water to the atmosphere by watering the floor and walls every day, and, above all things, do not permit cold blasts of air.

Yesterday I despatched a box of alpines to England of my own getting, but really, when you are out for the whole day, there is very little time for plant-hunting, which is tiring and wearisome.

I am writing this letter, looking over the Adriatic, with its ships and port.

Write and tell me how your little man is (his grandson) . . . . I must bring him home a little plant, as we must make him love fruit and flowers, &c. &c.

Yesterday we had the most lovely day at Trieste; one of those grand sunshines which Italy only can offer. We drove along the bay to the house of Maximilian, one of the most beautiful houses which I ever saw. It was faultless in design, fitted up with the most exquisite taste. The gardens were delightful, and for the first time the nightingales sung their delicious tunes. All was lovely, whether within or without. But where were the proprietors? The lady in a mad-house; the master dead from the ruthless bullets of foreign barbarians! Avoid too much ambition. Do not desire to have the baby grow as high as St. Paul's, or write poetry like Homer before he can speak.

> " Who pants for glory, finds but short repose;
> A breath revives him, or a breath o'erthrows."—POPE.

At Trieste we found the Maidenhair fern, and got a pretty good handful. If you show due obedience, and speak very prettily, I will give some to you.

The Wistarias were in full blossom, and all Nature is putting forth its spring attire.

Poor Venice looks more decayed than when you were here; but we will let you know further when we have seen more, &c. &c.

Here we are, and asked for a letter from you, but, alas! no letter to hand. Are you weary? are you dreary? or are you too cheery to write?

Perhaps little Georgey attracts all attention, and poor —— is forgotten.

The setting sun fades, the rising grows higher and brighter; so grandpapa grows less, grandson bigger. You may be able to telegraph to me till Saturday if you think of coming to us in Switzerland. [There was some talk of myself and my husband joining them abroad, but it fell through.]

I am writing to you with a thunderstorm raging over the Apennines. It is warmer here than before.

The king opens the Horticultural Exhibition to-morrow at half-past eleven. We are all well. As you have seen Florence, I need not describe it. There is an absence of swifts which is remarkable, as there was a great number which used to skim by the windows when we were last here.

In January 1874, the Conservative candidate for Rochester having withdrawn at the last moment, Alfred Smee suddenly stepped into a train and found himself at Rochester the day only before the nomination, causing a great fright among the Radicals, who thought they were going this time to walk the course. Notwithstanding such a short notice, he telegraphed to Rochester to say he would address them that same evening. The room was crowded so as to cause great inconvenience, even the road outside the house being blocked up; and what was most peculiar was, that the meeting was almost entirely of working men. He polled 835 votes,* and for his pluck in coming forward like this at the last hour he received from the working men of Rochester a very handsome testimonial, consisting of a silver claret jug, cups and salver, accompanied by an illuminated scroll, containing the signatures of 600 subscribers. On the claret jug is the following inscription :—

" Presented to Alfred Smee, F.R.S., by the Conservative freemen and electors of the city of Rochester, in recognition of his spirited conduct in contesting the city on constitutional principles, April 2nd, 1874."

The presentation was made the occasion of a very imposing demonstration. One of the papers recording the speeches says,—

Mr. Smee and some London friends arrived at the South Eastern Railway Station at Strood about 7 o'clock in the evening, and was met by a large and enthusiastic gathering of his followers, accompanied by a strong band and by bearers carrying flags and banners. A carriage and pair had been provided for Mr. Smee, and several of his followers were also in carriages. Immediately on Mr. Smee's arrival a procession was formed, headed by the band, and the principal streets of the borough were paraded

---

* Mr. Smee polled upwards of 200 more votes than were ever before recorded for a Conservative candidate for Rochester.

by the imposing gathering. Red lights were burned all along the route, and gave a romantic touch to the procession. Crowds of persons watched the progress of the demonstration through the streets, windows were thrown open, handkerchiefs were waved, and the cheering was immense. The Corn Exchange was entered at about half-past eight, and was soon entirely filled with Mr. Smee's warm-hearted supporters. The silver articles forming the presentation lay upon a table on the platform. Mr. G. Watson, jun., hon. secretary to the presentation fund (a true, zealous, and steadfast supporter of Mr. Smee), read some letters from various gentlemen who signified their gratification at Mr. Smee having a presentation. Major McCory was in the chair, and after an excellent speech Mr. C. J. Carter, a working man, in appropriate terms presented the testimonial. Mr. Smee then rose to reply.

A full report of his speech, as reported in the 'Rochester Journal,' is in the Appendix, No. XXXV.

Previous to this and immediately after the election, I received this letter from my father :—

MY DEAR MARY,—The Rochester affair is quite a romance, and too long to tell you. I went down and had only half-an-hour to sign the preliminary forms.

I found that the party was so split up that I determined to return to London; but having called a meeting at about three hours' notice, when the hotel was full and the whole street was full, I felt bound to address them. I was received with extraordinary enthusiasm, and my voice being much more than usual obedient to my will, I made a *most elegant and eloquent* speech, which fetched the whole audience.

At the end I told them that the party were not sufficiently organized, and that I should go back to London.

There was the greatest uproar you ever heard, and I believe, if I had, some of the Conservative leaders would have been lynched. The whole room called upon me to stand, but I replied that the money came out of my pocket, and I could not, in justice to my family, permit it.

I required half-an-hour for consideration, and the chairman was taken by me from the working men. They appointed four delegates to wait upon me, who said they wanted neither money nor beer, but wanted me to be their member, whereupon a solemn compact was formed between us that I should pay nothing for organization, that they would do all the work for nothing, and I, on my part, should stand and pay the Act of Parliament expenses.

The most enthusiastic and exciting affair took place, and they kept their word. They brought up eight hundred and thirty-five people, and we had only thirty-six hours' notice. Carts and waggons and—more remarkable than all—a donkey-cart decked out in pink ribbons stood before the King's Head all day in case they should be required.

Not one drop of beer or wine was given away, and not one shilling passed.

The election would have been secured by the distribution of a few half-crowns among the very poor.

We had two enormous meetings on the day before the poll, at one of which the Admiral came from Chatham and spoke strongly in my favour.

The city was perfectly quiet. The present members received me with every courtesy. Martin spoke of the rows of former times, and said what a fright he was in. He spoke of it with laughter, and said if I did not get in he hoped I would write another book, as he had bought ' My Garden,' and was very much pleased with it. Mr. Goldsmith was purposely courteous, to show there was no ill feeling. I spoke to Foord and Aveling and the town clerk and Steele, the chairman of the other side. He roared when I told him that I offered a man a sovereign at the last election to cover his house with my bills, to give him a hint as to how he should vote; but I told him he was afraid of the Bench. We had also a good laugh with the mayor and town council in solemn conclave assembled. There was a question whether I might or might not stop in the council chamber, when I told them perhaps I had better stop, or they would form a committee to oppose my return, which caused the member and some of the council who saw the joke to roar with laughter; but some of the Blues did look blue indeed at having their dignity trifled with. The result of the election is looked upon as a gain for Conservatism, by the manner I have worked the industrial classes; but I have lost, and there is an end of it.

Perhaps it may not be out of place here to insert the kind terms in which Mr. Martin, the Liberal member for Rochester, referred to Mr. Smee in a speech delivered to his constituents shortly after my father's death, for it shows so well the generous nature of Mr. Martin and the entire absence of ill feeling between them.

Mr. Martin, on rising to address the meeting, was received with a round of applause. He said, before proceeding to the topics of his speech he would do what he felt was only English and manly to do, and that was to refer to one who had just departed this life. The person he meant did not belong to their side, but he had known him many years and had four times contested that city with him. He referred to the late Mr. Alfred Smee. (Applause.) He was a man of great good humour, of pleasant manners, and an able man in his profession. He was affectionate and pleasant in his private life, and although they had fought he hoped they had never interrupted their friendship. (Applause.) Although an opponent, Mr. Smee used to send him a copy of all his new books, and he (Mr. M.) must acknowledge that he was a most formidable opponent. At the last election, by his plucky manner and great good humour, he not only got the votes of nearly every Conservative in the city, but he also got more neutral votes than any other man could have got, and he (Mr. M.) deeply regretted that he had been removed from amongst them. (Loud applause.)

In 1875, he put forth the hypothesis that the Council for the Royal College of Surgeons in England should be elected from Fellows by seniority of their membership, and not of their Fellowship; and on that principle he offered himself as a candidate for a seat on the Council.  For this purpose the following circulars or letters were published :—

GENTLEMEN,—I beg to return my thanks to the numerous Fellows who have answered my last circular, asking their opinion whether seniority should be determined by the date of membership or Fellowship.

The Fellows, in the proportion of nearly twelve to one, have expressed an opinion that seniority should rank from the date of membership.

One of our most distinguished army surgeons adds these significant words: "Just as in the army, medical service time for progressive increase of pay counts from the date of the first and lowest commission."

It has been suggested to me that there is a combination of medical schools to return their own men, which, if true, would practically amount to a disenfranchisement of the Fellows, as no individual candidate can stand against a combination of interests, and thus the creation of the Fellowship for independent election is absolutely frustrated.

To the minority who desire seniority to rank from the date of Fellowship, I would point out that, as in the past the members were deprived of their just seniority by the institution of the Fellowship, so in the future there is nothing to prevent the Fellows from being deprived of their present seniority by the creation of a new class, such for instance as the institution of doctors of surgery, from whom the Council might be chosen, to the exclusion of the remainder of the Fellows.

It now clearly appears, that the Fellows who approve the principle of seniority from membership cannot come to the College to vote without the almost prohibitory inconvenience of a journey to London.

It must not be forgotten that, from the peculiar properties of members in connection with election matters, it will be necessary (particularly if combination exists) that plumpers and only plumpers be recorded, in order that the election may be secured.

For that reason, as this is a contest of principle, and not, as far as I am concerned, a fight between rival competitors, I earnestly beg all those Fellows who desire that a seniority once obtained should never be taken away by any subsequent legislation, to vote for myself, without any respect to personal consideration, but solely as the representative of the principle of seniority by membership.

SIR,—The last election at the Royal College of Surgeons has revealed a wide-spread discontent among the Fellows.  It is assumed that the members of Council are elected by the Fellows at large; but the election takes place at the College in London, whilst the majority of the electors reside in the country, hundreds of miles distant, so that it is not possible that any election can represent the opinions of the general body.

It is a mere mockery of justice to bestow a franchise on Fellows which in many cases they cannot possibly use, because they are unable to leave their duties and incur the cost, the loss of time, and fatigue of the journey, simply to enable them to drop a voting-paper into a ballot-box. Every man entrusted with a vote is bound to have a *bonâ fide* opportunity of recording it; for if he have not, he is virtually disfranchised.  For this reason, Parliament has wisely decreed that the members of Univer sities, who are in a similar position with respect to residence to the

Fellows of the Royal College of Surgeons, can vote by papers without the necessity of a journey.

By the Act 24 & 25 Vict. cap. 53, the members of the Universities of Oxford, Cambridge, and Dublin are empowered to employ voting-papers. This privilege was extended to members of the London University by 30 & 31 Vict. cap. 102; and the details of election were further simplified by 31 & 32 Vict. cap. 65. The College of Surgeons having been shown the way, has only to take advantage of the precedent by procuring an Act, of a few lines in length, rehearsing the University Election Acts, and applying their provisions to the particular case of the College of Surgeons before the next election takes place. The question has only to be raised for its propriety to be admitted; for where is the surgeon who would not rather watch a serious case, when life or death may depend, than neglect his patient, that he may formally hand over a printed paper to the recognized official of the College of Surgeons? To obtain the desired end, proper means must be taken. The body of country Fellows must ask before their request can be granted; and I shall be glad to receive the names of every Fellow desirous of voting by papers, that we may at once take steps to obtain the Act of Parliament necessary to give us our just due.                           (Signed)    ALFRED SMEE.

P.S.—Only fifty-seven country Fellows voted at the last election.

## CHAPTER XI.

### 1875.

In the spring of 1875, 'The Mind of Man, a Natural System of Mental Philosophy,' was published. This was the last printed book from Alfred Smee's pen, and was based on his earlier work, 'Electro-Biology.'

In 'The Mind of Man' we find that mankind is primarily divided into five great classes or groups, according as man exhibits more or less of each particular quality of mental power. These classes or groups are again subdivided into lesser divisions. Thus:

1st Class. Aisthenic ideas, from $\alpha \check{\iota} \sigma \theta \eta \sigma \iota \varsigma$, meaning "sensation."

2nd Class. Syndramic, from $\sigma \upsilon \nu \delta \rho \alpha \mu \epsilon \hat{\iota} \nu$, "to combine." It means the possession of ideas, and is the result of all the actions on the ultimate fibrils at any one instant of time.

3rd Class. Noemic, from $\nu o \hat{\upsilon} \varsigma$, "mind," is the faculty of inducing laws and acting upon them, and evinces the higher powers of mind.

4th Class. Pneuma-Noemic, from $\pi \nu \epsilon \hat{\upsilon} \mu \alpha$, "spirit," as it appertains to the appreciation of spiritual qualities, where the qualities of the mind are regulated by the consideration of the soul, of eternity, of heaven, and of hell.

5th Class. Dynamic, from $\delta \acute{\upsilon} \nu \alpha \mu \iota \varsigma$, "force." Individuals may be comprised in this class who evince great activity either from an external stimulus upon their organs of sensation, or from the internal stimulus of their own thoughts. All active men therefore belong to this class. Activity may have its origin at various parts of the nervous system.

Each of these groups or classes admits of subdivisions: thus the *Aisthenic group* admits of six subdivisions, five of which represent the mental power derived from the respective organs of sensation and one from knowledge derived from bodily feeling, as—

Eye sensations or Opsaisthenics.
Ear　　　,,　　,, Ousaisthenics.
Taste　　,,　　,, Gumaisthenics.
Odour　　,,　　,, Rhinaisthenics.
Feeling (bodily) ,, Cœnaisthenics.
Feeling (mental) ,, Somaisthenics.

Each of these divisions may be again subdivided: thus a man may have a powerful vision for small objects, a great range of adjustment, a power for the appreciation of colours, or a quickness in the perception of objects.

Every other organ of sensation may be likewise subdivided.

The *Syndramic group* comprises not only all those qualities of the mind which appertain to the first or Aisthenic group, but also superadds to them the faculty of receiving information from the words and writings of others: and this second quality again presents many varieties, from the classes of knowledge which the mind of any particular man is competent to receive. Again, all the above varieties of mind are also doubled by the consideration that the same impression may variously affect different men: for instance, "the same amount of light, though a delight to one man, is a pain to another."

"As there may be three qualities in each subdivision of this group, it follows, therefore, that no less than eighteen divisions of this class may be noted."

The *Noemic group* are likewise also governed by all the lower subdivisions, but have also characteristics superadded, so that this group may also be considerably subdivided. We read that, under Noemic reason, "There is a gap in the powers of mind between the human reason and the reason of brutes. The mind deals with its various ideas, and forms abstract conceptions. It forms the notion of mankind apart from any particular man: the notion of heat apart from hot things; of light apart from illuminated bodies. The capability of using these higher abstractions confers upon all men powers not possessed by the lower animals. Mankind alone of all the animal creation uses words and language for the communication of ideas; employs fire to cook food; lamps to illuminate rooms; electricity to convey intel-

ligence, or tools by which mechanical force is regulated.   No
animal but man has the power of abstraction or of using abstract
ideas."   For further illustrations of the great difference there is
in the mind of animals and the mind of man, I refer the reader
to 'The Mind of Man,' as well as to 'Instinct and Reason.'

*The Pneuma-Noemic group.*—Where the faculties of dwelling
upon that which is infinite—such as the Deity, the soul, eternity,
heaven, hell—"bear a proper relation to the other faculties comprised within the former classes, the man is greatly dignified and
raised above his fellows.   In cases where these properties of the
mind are shown, to the exclusion of the other faculties, the man
degenerates to the degraded position of the wild fanatic and
devotee."

We must (he adds, in 'Instinct and Reason') not mistake cases of perverted reason for instances where these faculties are fully developed.   For
instance, the Hindoo priests induce the widow to sacrifice herself on the
funeral pile only by an intense excitement of her nervous system; so also
the Popish priests ensnare their victims for nunneries and convents in a
similar manner.   In like manner the fanatical enthusiasts of America are
so over-stimulated that it is recorded that they not only injure their bodily
frame, but occasionally damage permanently their mental powers.   All
these cases do not come under this class; but the sufferers exhibit the
natural degradation of perverted reason under the false guidance of a
heartless priesthood.

*The Dynamic group.*—There are also many varieties or subdivisions of this group.

Some persons are quick of action, others indolent; some act by
aisthenic impressions, others direct their actions by thought.   Some are
governed by religious impressions; others act solely from the immediate
impressions of pleasure or pain.

Throughout all these subdivisions the human mind is modified
by memory or forgetfulness.

All these states of the mind, too, are governed by the age of the individual.   The boy exhibits properties in the various departments of the mind
different from those of the child, the youth from the boy, the adult from
the youth, advanced life from the adult, and senility from advanced life.

This is beautifully shown in the diagram accompanying the
fifth chapter on 'The Mind of Man,' in which he speaks of education,
and how it should be conducted, so that *no one department of the
mind should be brought into play to the exclusion of the rest.*   In
'Instinct and Reason' is a pretty illustration of the difference in

the mental faculties that is required according to the profession or calling of the individual. Thus he shows how the lawyer requires the second and third class of faculties (Syndramic and Noemic) more especially to be brought into play. The doctor has a more extensive range, and requires for his profession the first three classes of faculties to be fully developed (Aisthenic, Syndramic, and Noemic). The engineer requires faculties in almost all respects similar to those which the doctor must possess for the successful exercise of his profession, and the clergyman *should* have a full development of the faculties of the second, third, and fourth classes (Syndramic, Noemic, and Pneuma-Noemic).

Besides dividing the mental faculties into the above-named classes or groups, he further proves that the nervous system is a voltaic circuit.

All batteries (says he) in animal bodies are compound batteries, one battery being in the body, the other in the brain; and, moreover, it is not only a compound battery, but is also one in which its fibres interlace in a wonderfully complex manner.

This he most fully sets forth and further illustrates by maps, diagrams, and various woodcuts. In two diagrams at page 213, the theoretical nervous combination of lower animals and that of man are demonstrated. It suffices here to mention that these two diagrams show a marked difference between the nervous combination of lower animals and that of man. In the diagram showing the nervous combination of man, we find that the Aisthenic occupies the lower department of the mind; higher in the mind we come to the Syndramic department; then higher still the Noemic, until we reach the Pneuma-Noemic, which is the highest department of all of the mind.

Such is the rough sketch of the general plan on which the 'Mind of Man' and earlier 'Electro-Biology' are based. Upon this model were all Alfred Smee's writings and speeches constructed. His whole course of life was modelled upon this his cherished metaphysical and moral structure.

This work treats extensively of the supposed discordance of religion and science: for to show, and indeed to prove, that for the welfare of mankind religion and science must go hand in hand, was ever the favourite task of his life. In this work he has fully proved where the fallacy lies; how it is to be remedied, so as to prevent idolatry, ignorance, and matter-worship on the

K

one hand, and conceit, infidelity, and ignorance on the other.
We read—

There are two modes by which the human mind may be affected, and
all our actions regulated to a common purpose : one by the impression of
the nervous system by induction from below upwards,—that is, from the
action on the nerves of sensation through the mind to general laws; and
the other from the effect of general laws, which act downwards by deduction to the particular instance.

The one by induction is the ordinary result of the natural mind as
detailed in this work. The one by deduction is by the reception of the
laws of God as given us by religion.

Are religion and reason discordant? No! One affects from above
downward, the other from below upward; and if both are right, they must
agree, they cannot possibly differ. The doctrines of religion would be vain
unless they are the laws of God and the word of God. In like manner it
must be remembered that the inductions of the human mind, if made in
sincerity and truth, are equally the result of the mechanism created by God.

Man should therefore accept as a fact that the results of the true
reason of man are identical with the laws of God, and the one originating
inductively from the human mind should accord deductively with the
results which are obtained by the ordinances of religion.

Mentally, if both are right, there can be no disagreement ; for whether
we examine the question from above downwards or from below upwards, no
difference can possibly exist, inasmuch as the mind is one whole. Then why
should there be, therefore, these continual differences between the teachers
of religion and the teachers of science? At the present time it is difficult
to enter a church without hearing the name of science being held from the
pulpit to disrespect; and it is equally difficult to enter the chambers of
science without hearing the pastor of religion in a like manner spoken of
with dissatisfaction. And why? The pastors of religion are, as a rule,
profoundly ignorant of the physical laws which govern the universe, and
the teachers of science are equally ignorant of the moral laws which govern
the actions of mankind.

Then a little further on we read—

The fault of the present day is the education of teachers of religion
at one school, where physical science is not only discarded but ignored,
and the education of teachers of science at another school, where the laws
of religion are almost as equally ignored.

The remedy for this gigantic evil would be to teach all men to a
certain extent knowledge in common, so that when they diverge afterwards
into their special studies, science shall not be without religion, nor religion
without knowledge. . . . . .

The priest trained to the study of the external world, and of the
natural operations of the human mind, is a totally different man from the
priest who ignores knowledge and the effect of reason. The one sees
Nature and God as they are, the other only by his own unenlightened mind,
which leads many to inconstancy, idolatry, and man-worship. . . . .

Wherever religion and science do not exactly accord, the discrepancy
marks error. It is then worth any labour to make them agree, by the con-

joined operations of the labourers in religion and science, that truth may prevail.

For the last five-and-forty years I have been a regular attendant at St. Paul's Cathedral, and consequently have heard most of the preachers of mark in the metropolis of this century. It is clear to any rational mind there is error in the pulpit: one affirms, another denies, whilst it is the property of truth ever to remain unchanged, and to stand the test of fair inquiry.

### And further on we read—

Those who love their church, and view it as an inestimable blessing to mankind, most earnestly wish that the pastors should so discipline their own minds by knowledge that they might appeal to the minds of their hearers from the general law to the particular instance, and from the particular instance to the general law, for the teachings of religion and science must be identical when both are true. It is a lamentable fact, but nevertheless one which admits of no contradiction, that religion, as frequently taught in the pulpit, is not the religion of the mass of the congregation of ordinary knowledge and intelligence. Religion is often brought forward in a form positively distasteful to the minds of many. The omnipotence of God, and the importance of His almighty laws, are neglected for human traditions and mediæval superstitions. This very serious position cannot long remain without danger to the community, for reason and religion are one, and cannot be divided; and, above all things, it is of paramount importance that religious teachings, involving as they do the laws of God, should be in every minute particular based on absolute purity and unswerving truth.

### And in another part—

Every good follower of religion must admit that the time which ought to be spent in the elucidation of the moral laws of God to regulate actions, is frequently spent in discussions of the propriety of frivolous garments, or the vain conduct of idle ceremonies, and on the discourse on vain superstitions, till those who pretend to be teachers show that they ought to be taught, as they bring the doctrines of religion into contempt.

### On Darwinism, or the gradual development of the higher animals from the lower, he writes :—

There appear to be some persons who imagine that every conceivable form of organic being is produced by chance, or a fortuitous concurrence of atoms; and of these all which are not suitable for surrounding circumstances perish, and only those which are suitable for the circumstances live.

When we regard the intricate complexity of many parts of organic beings, to say nothing of the requisite relation of one organic being to another, as for instance an insect to a flower, it requires a much stronger exercise of faith than such persons themselves would like to admit, when they adopt a theory of chance where infinite contrivance and wisdom seem so clearly to manifest themselves.

I have lingered long over this last and important work of Alfred Smee, because it embraces his great system of Mental Philosophy, which should be studied by every intelligent youth, that he may conduct on a sure basis the discipline of his own mind, and his relations with his fellow-men. Of all the books Alfred Smee wrote this was unquestionably his favourite. The frontispiece contains an admirable likeness of him drawn by Mr. H. R. Robertson, which was most delicately and finely engraved for this work by the celebrated engraver Mr. C. H. Jeens. The picture was expressly taken for the above work, and was the gift to my mother from one of the public companies to which my father belonged, as a kind token of grateful recognition for some great services he had done it. There are besides fifty-eight woodcuts, and the book, like 'My Garden,' is beautifully got up, and published by Messrs. Bell.

In the summer of 1873 there was an outburst of typhoid fever in the West-end of London, in the close vicinity of Cavendish Square. The question was raised that this pestilence was caused by the milk from cows fed upon sewage grass, and a controversy ensued whether or no sewage grounds were hurtful to health. For some years Alfred Smee had been investigating the question of sewage; and his son, Alfred Hutchison Smee, who kept a small herd of cows at Wallington, had also been making various experiments on the feeding of cows, the results of which the latter gentleman has embodied in a valuable little treatise full of important statistics, which is entitled 'Milk in Health and Disease.' * No sooner did this controversy on sewage begin in the daily papers than my father wrote his own experience. The correspondence of Alfred Smee on 'Milk, Typhoid Fever, and Sewage,' will be found in the Appendix, No. XXXVI.A., as also the paper he read before the Health Section of the Social Science Congress at Norwich, October 3rd, 1873, on 'Sewage, Sewage Produce, and Disease.' (See Appendix, No. XXXVI.B.) Later, on December 3rd, 1875, Alfred Smee read a paper before the Society of Arts, on 'Proposed Heads of Legislation for the Regulation of Sewage Grounds.' (See Appendix, No. XXXVI.c.) The discussion on this paper was adjourned to January 19th, 1876. To this discussion Alfred Smee replied, and that evening was the last time I heard my father speak before a public meeting. Little did I think that evening that exactly in a year and

* This little book is published by Messrs. Newman, Devonshire Street, Bishopsgate Street. (1875.)

three days we should have laid him in his grave.  Happy it is for us that we cannot read the future !

One of the members of the Croydon Board of Health made an eloquent speech on this occasion, in which he several times reproached Mr. Smee with the absurdity of wishing to draw a *concord* round the farm at Beddington.  The absurdity was evident to other persons besides the speaker, for as he sat down amid general cheering, the following epigram was handed to Mr. Smee :—

> " To think a man the Croydon Board on
>   Should take a *concord* for a *cordon !* "

## CHAPTER XII.

### 1876 TO 1877.

Book on Fishing—Hand-working—Letters from abroad—Letters to the 'Times,'
'Standard,' and the 'Gardeners' Chronicle'—His death, January 11, 1877,
aged fifty-eight—Buried at St. Mary's, Beddington, within sight of the
garden, January 16, 1877.

In the beginning of the year 1876 we have seen Mr. Smee discussing
the heads of legislation which he had drawn up for the regulation
of sewage grounds; this was immediately followed by his taking
a great interest in the fresh facts relating to the potato disease
(see p. 35, also the Appendix, No. XV.c.). He was also interesting
himself in the Colorado beetle, and was carrying on a correspondence in America and Germany, finding out all that was known
of the devastation and habits of the insect. He had himself
obtained a dead Colorado beetle from a friend, and had had a
woodcut made of it. Besides this, in the midst of his other
business, he was, in spare moments before breakfast and after a
late dinner, busy writing a new book on Fishing. Much was
written; still the finishing touches of the master hand were required for those chapters which were otherwise completed. This
book was to have been copiously illustrated; and from some of
the woodcuts which have come under my notice, and from fragments of the manuscript which my father read to me from time to
time, I should say that this work on Fishing bade fair to rival
its sister book, 'My Garden.' But this work was not to be completed; and as Longfellow tells us:

> "Labour with what zeal we will,
>     Something still remains undone.
> Something uncompleted still
>     Waits the rising of the sun."

My brother has kindly offered me one of the illustrations for this
work. It is a woodcut taken from a water-colour drawing, of

FIG. 6. ALFRED SMEE, WITH HIS SON, FISHING IN THE THAMES.

Page 155.

my father and my brother in the latter's boat on the Thames. The one is fishing and the other rowing.

In May, Mr. Smee went abroad on business connected with one of the companies to which he belonged. That he contrived on this journey to see some of his favourite haunts, will be perceived in the following letters he sent to his daughter. He had intended to go in March; but as he writes to her—

The weather indeed has been awful: terrible snow-storms; horrible gales and tempests; excessive rain; darkness; floods; eruptions of Vesuvius.

I intended to have gone abroad, but did not like the aspect of things.

The poor children must suffer from this detestable weather. Tell Georgey I really love him very much and should like to see him, and I hope nice warm weather will come, and then his pretty flowers will grow and grow, &c.

Here I should perhaps give a passing allusion to an extraordinary attachment (if I may so call it) which had sprung up between himself and his little grandson; for no one who had not been a witness to it could appreciate this attachment to its full extent. Upon the child what pains would not the grandfather bestow! He would never tire of explaining to him the different plants, and would take him frequently to the Zoological Gardens to teach him not only the names of the animals, but the habits of the various creatures that are there kept. So often did they go that the keepers knew my father and his little charge, and were only too eager to show the child the peculiarities of the different animals committed to their care. Even in the midst of business hours this grandson was still often in his grandfather's thoughts, and he would at those times go and search for books or toys, or send him letters which, although written with the simplicity of a child, yet at the same time always contained some knowledge worthy of a great and good man.

On sending a lock of his little grandson's hair, his daughter received the following letter:—

Many thanks for your kind wishes and handsome donation, which you only could have sent. This gift of gifts deserves a crystal box to preserve it, and perhaps after I have attained my hundredth year, and I return to the earth of which I am made, and your kind present returns to you, this little token of affection will be looked upon by you, himself, and peradventure his descendant, with rare and curious interest, and your thoughts will be carried back to time about persons past and with hopes for time and persons to come.

From Zurich, May 13th, 1876, he writes :—

We have been to Brussels, from thence to Frankfort, thence to Passau, from Passau to Lintz down the Danube, and then from Lintz to Vienna by the Danube.

We then went to Ansteller, from thence to Salzthal across to Innspruck, by the most wonderful road that you could imagine.

It was a single line which ran through gorges over mountains by bad curves, by terrible inclines, across mountain torrents, altogether a remarkable ride through mountains, for hour after hour, till the eye became weary. Acres of lovely violets covered the ground. Masses of marsh marigolds lit up the fields; the lovely gentians gladdened the eyes; and literally acres of violets or rather pansies, yellow and tricoloured, formed a natural flower garden gorgeous to behold. The skirts of the woods were Nature's own landscape-gardening, with curved lines of woods and shrubs on the sward of emerald green grass mixed with flowers. Then the mountains were snow-covered and cloud-capped, and different views were opened out at every turn of the road.

Every now and then an eagle or huge hawk traversed the valleys.

Any traveller must go right through, for the accommodation is queer, as you may judge when I tell you that we took our meals at a restaurant at a station, and slept in a cottage.

I sent the boy (his grandson) a letter. Tell your mother how he liked it, and she can tell me when she writes.

I suppose your husband will be off before this arrives; if not, give my love, and tell him I wish him a happy and prosperous voyage.

The weather has been very bad—cold, dark, and cloudy; in fact we have not seen the sun for fourteen days.

The Tyrol Pass was not altogether free from danger. We saw a railroad carriage which had been smashed to atoms in a mountain torrent below, and we did not go more than three to ten miles an hour. We could not go over the Madler Pass or up the Engadine, because there was so much snow; in fact some patches of snow were lying at below 3000 feet.

The snow mixed with the black pines and bright green foliage was very striking. We shall move from here to Lucerne; thence to Vevey; thence to Lyons, Toulouse, Nantes, and home : altogether 3000 miles. Kiss the boy and girl.

In another letter he writes thus :—

I wrote a letter to the dear boy (his grandson) which I thought would do for the *dear girl*—that is, you also; but I have not heard how your little daughter progresses.

We have had an extraordinary journey : we went down the Danube from Passau to Lintz, from Lintz to Vienna, which I much enjoyed. It was so bitterly cold that we were compelled to keep in the cabin, where the views were as good as out of doors.

We then crossed the Tyrol by a new route to Inuspruck, the worst travellers' route which ever was seen. The way lay south of Salzburg.

Then he speaks of the flowers he saw, which have been already alluded to in the former letter, and continues :—

From Innspruck we took a drive up the Bremer and crossed the Lake Constance, and came to Zurich. From Zurich we came to Lucerne. From Lucerne we went up the railway to the Rigi: there was so much snow that we could not get to the top, but only one-third the way up.

The mountains about here are covered deeply with snow. Pilatus is snow a long way down. All the mountains up the lake are well covered, which makes the views intensely beautiful. We went up the lake to Fluelen, and have returned to table d'hôte. The lake never looked so lovely, and, what is best of all, we are not troubled with numerous tourists. We are still like the premature swallows. I enjoy my rest excessively; and as I have nothing to do, not even to settle accounts or railway tickets, it is a thorough rest to me, which I feel I want.* We have been at least 1600 miles in fourteen days, which is more than 110 miles a day.

I hope the tall boy (the gardener) does his work in the garden, for soon all the succulent plants must take a promenade. Write to me to Hôtel de France, Bordeaux. I have seen a glorious sunset over Pilatus, also a sunrise. We have had a fish in the lakes of Zurich and Lucerne, without being troubled with any weight of fish to carry afterwards. With best love to boy and girl.

During this visit my father visited Clermont in France, and was interested with the geological formation of that place. One of the mountains at Clermont is an extinct volcano, and from there he brought home a Roman coin. This Roman coin was "found," he writes, "in digging the foundation of an observatory on the top of the Domo, about 5000 feet high, the centre of a huge series of extinct volcanoes at Clermont, in the centre of France." My brother has kindly allowed me to take a woodcut of the coin, which is here given.

Fig. 6a.   Roman Coin found at Clermont.

On the 17th of August he wrote the following letter to the 'Times' on "A Homicidal River."

The river Lea was as famous for its annual deaths half a century ago as it is now. For several summers I resided on its banks, and on

---

* When they came to sundry towns, it should be observed he had to attend to weighty matters of business; but, although he was travelling at the rate of 110 miles a day, even this was a rest compared to his mental work in London.

no year did we escape witnessing terrible calamities. On one day about twenty-two were drowned by a boat casualty. Continually there were deaths from swimming misadventures, notwithstanding that an almost fabulous number of lives were saved by a skilled boatman named Solomons.

The bed of the river Lea is unequal. At every curve there is a deep and dangerous hole, with under back currents, and there are deep shelves in many parts of the banks. Hence the ordinary apparatus used by the Royal Humane Society for dragging the river is comparatively useless, and the boat hook has to be relied upon.

I have been present when bodies have been raised. The exact position to a foot has been known. The body could be felt by the hook and even turned over, and yet could not be raised till repeated trials had been made. All this caused so much delay that the last spark of life had fled before the body could be recovered; and well do I remember the terrible scenes of grief which were witnessed among the surviving relatives at so sudden a bereavement.

No person ought to venture to swim in the river Lea unless an expert swimmer, and then only when thoroughly conversant with the peculiarities of the river, and the boats ought to have police surveillance to see that they are sound in structure, and that they are not let to an undue number of persons.

There was always a popular idea that the water of the Lea was particularly deadly, but at that time the water was clear and pure. Probably its deadly character is to be ascribed to its sluggishness, its great depth, to its undercurrents, and to the difficulty of reclaiming bodies from the dangerous shelves at the bottom.

---

> " This is true glory and renown; when God,
> Looking on the earth, with approbation marks
> The just man, and divulges him through heaven
> To all His angels, who with true applause
> Recount his praises!"
>
> MILTON, *Paradise Regained.*

His health now broke down. Being anxious to see his daughter, who was ill at the time, he came down to Oxford with the intention of staying two or three days. I was shocked at the change in his appearance since I last saw him, about three weeks previously. He said he was tired, and had been examining medically about a dozen persons. He stayed between four and five weeks with us at Oxford, and then returned to his house in London, and at our urgent solicitations he promised to give his whole attention to his own health, and to put himself under the care of Dr. Moxon, one of the senior physicians of Guy's Hospital, whose skill in medical knowledge is only equalled by the extreme thoughtfulness and kindness of his disposition. Dr. Moxon was ever a great favourite, they having many sympathies in common, and both being lovers of Nature's works. But my father was beyond human skill, and the eyes of his family were rudely opened to the shock that nothing could save him. His lungs were too far gone; and he was also suffering from that seemingly incurable complaint, diabetes. But his family owe a debt of gratitude to Dr. Moxon for the untiring zeal and kindness he displayed in lessening and soothing his patient's sufferings.

Throughout his illness my father's vigour of mind never forsook him: to the last he retained the full use of his faculties. At first he took delight in reading, in looking through and properly arranging his carmine injections; and when he became too weak to write himself, he dictated to others. The following letter from his pen, on the "Distribution of Seeds by Panthers," appeared in the 'Standard' on October 17th, 1876 :—

An interesting fact in natural history was revealed during the recent visit of his Royal Highness the Prince of Wales to India. In one of the hunting excursions in the neighbourhood of Baroda a panther was shot, and numerous seeds were found to be attached to the skin. The seeds had two perfect hooks, manifestly designed to attach themselves to foreign bodies. As the panther moved about it collected the seeds on the skin and carried them about wherever it went, but when it rubbed against the shrubs it of necessity brushed some off, and thus distributed them. These seeds were taken from the skin by an officer who was one of the hunting party, and several came into the possession of Mrs. Horne of Staines, a great lover of horticulture, who did me the favour of sending me specimens. I was so struck with the incident and the remarkable character of the seed, that, after accurately figuring it, I desired it to be sown at " My Garden," when it rapidly grew into a handsome plant, and produced beautiful clusters of tubular flowers. It was immediately recognized to belong to the genus Martynia, and on examination both Professor Oliver, of the Royal Gardens, Kew, and Dr. Masters agree that it is *Martynia diandra*, a plant which, although introduced into this country as far back as 1731, has scarcely ever been cultivated for many years. I have placed my specimen in the hands of Mr. Sowerby, the secretary of the Royal Botanic Society, Regent's Park; and the plant, with one of the seeds taken from the panther's skin, are now exhibited in the great conservatory.

Later, in November, he dictated the following little letter, which was sent to the 'Gardeners' Chronicle,' and was copied into many papers :—

### BIRD-CATCHING EXTRAORDINARY.

In " My Garden" a somewhat large collection of ericas is grown, and many of their beautiful flowers are coated with a layer of sticky and viscid material, the use of which is by no means apparent. It is somewhat similar to the viscid material which is found on the so-called carnivorous plants. During this summer a little bird, probably one of the hedge-warblers with which the garden abounds, entered the greenhouse in which the plants were located, alighted upon the heath, when the feathers adhered so tightly to the plant that the bird was retained a prisoner. When the gardener came, he could only set free the bird by detaching a number of the feathers. Of course it is not to be supposed that the erica is a carnivorous plant, and that it eats up little birds! This remarkable event has been twice noticed this year at " My Garden."

Throughout his illness he took pleasure in seeing his friends, and was vexed when any were denied him ; for so many would come every afternoon to see him, that his family were sometimes fearful lest he should be over-tired. In the mornings he would drive with my mother, myself, and his dearly loved little grandson along the Thames Embankment.

Throughout his last illness Alfred Smee showed himself a true philosopher, and was most thoughtful and solicitous for the comfort and welfare of others. He was soon to reap the reward of his labours, for about 5 o'clock on the morning of Thursday, the 11th of January, 1877, amidst the wild storm of a raging wind, he gently passed away without a sigh. The problem of his life was now solved ; but how solved, he was unable to impart to us. Many who mourned his loss came once again to see him, and these, though parting in sadness, yet went away in a firm and steadfast belief that to a righteous man death has no terrors.

A few days later, on Tuesday, the 16th of January, 1877, a sad procession left 7, Finsbury Circus, and passed on its way the Bank of England, Kennington, Clapham Common, Mitcham, along the road which skirts that beautiful garden at Wallington, which is delineated in the book ' My Garden,' and stopped before the schools of St. Mary's, Beddington. Thence the mortal remains of Alfred Smee were borne to the church by the gardeners and by the men of my brother's yacht. Though the family wished the funeral to be strictly private, yet so many testified their respect to Alfred Smee that St. Mary's Church was full of persons,— that church which but four years before had been

Fig. 7. VIEW OF ST. MARY'S RESIDENCE, FROM THE GARDEN.

Page 141.

filled with friends who had thither repaired to show their sympathy with him on the occasion of his much-loved daughter's marriage,—that church which received his dear grandson as a member of the Church of England, and to which his own eyes had so often turned with pleasure during the happy hours spent in his garden. It is thus he speaks of it in his book: "The church with its churchyard is one of the most picturesque near London. It has been supplied with a melodious peal of bells, which record the sorrow and declare the joy of the inhabitants. The tower of the church is seen through a vista of trees from my garden, and then reflected from the transparent waters of the lake, as though Nature ordained that so good an object should be twice seen."

The service was choral, and the lessons were most impressively read by the much esteemed rector, the Reverend A. H. Bridges; and after the beautiful and touching hymn which commences—

> "Christ will gather in His own
>   To the place where He is gone,
>   Where their heart and treasure lie,
>   Where our life is hid on high " *—

the sad procession wended its way to the little cemetery in Beddington Park; and there, after the most solemn yet most exquisite singing by the choir, of Dr. Dyce's hymn—

> "Days and moments quickly flying
>   Blend the living with the dead;
>   Soon will you and I be lying
>   Each within his narrow bed " †—

there, amidst the sobs of the multitude of high and low estate, we laid in his grave all that was mortal of Alfred Smee. In his lifetime flowers he loved: we covered him with flowers in his grave, and left him, the investigator of Nature,—he whose thoughts were ever contemplating the Author of all things,—in that little cemetery seen from his garden, amidst the scenes which he in his lifetime had so much loved.

The numbers of persons who came, many from long distances, to pay their last respects to Alfred Smee, and the sobs of the multitude, showed how much he was beloved, and how much his

---

* From a German chorale.  See 'Hymns Ancient and Modern,' No. 400.
† 'Hymns Ancient and Modern,' No. 289.

loss was deplored.   The poor said: " We have indeed lost a good
and kind friend; we shall never have one like him again."

" Let your light so shine before men, that they may see your
good works, and glorify your Father which is in heaven."

" Blessed are the dead which die in the Lord; for they rest
from their labours, and their works do follow them."

Fig. 7a.  The Grave, with large Trees in Beddington Park in the background.

Page 142.

On the base of the cross, which is of white marble, is the following inscription:—

Alfred Smee, F.R.S.
Born June 18, 1818.
Died January 11, 1877.
"He rests from his labours."

# APPENDIX.

No. I.

ON THE STATE IN WHICH ANIMAL MATTER IS USUALLY FOUND IN FOSSILS. By Mr. Alfred Smee, Student of King's College, London, and communicated by Prof. Royle, M.D., F.G.S. (Proceedings of the Geological Society of London, No. 57. 1838.)

The author first describes briefly the composition of those parts of recent animals capable of being preserved in a fossil state; and then proceeds to detail his investigations into the composition of fossil organic remains.

For the sake of arrangement, he divides fossils into two great classes, one in which animal matter is present in various states, the other in which it has been removed. The first class he further subdivides into three cases: 1. Comprehending those fossils in which animal matter retains its original condition. 2. Those in which it has been partially changed. 3. Those in which only the carbon of the animal matter remains.

1. The following examples were given of the first case.

Small portions of the tooth of a horse, of an ox, and a stag, from the chalk rubble at Brighton, were submitted to the action of diluted muriatic acid; and after the earthy portions had been removed, the animal matter retained the shape of the bone, was white, and of the consistence of cartilage. Fragments of a tooth of a mammoth from Norfolk, and of a rib of a mastodon from Big-bone-lick in Ohio, when similarly treated, gave the same results. A thin slice of the rib exhibited under the microscope the structure of recent bone. Fragments of a stag's rib and horn, of an ox's head, and the tusk of a boar, found near the Bank of England, associated with Roman implements, retained their animal matter unaltered. Small portions of a Terebratula and of two species of Productæ, from the Silurian rocks of Malvern, were placed in very diluted muriatic acid; and when the earthy portions had been removed, small flocculi of animal matter, resembling the recent membrane of a shell, floated in the solution. A minute fragment of *Asaphus caudatus* yielded little shreds of animal matter. The experiments on the shells were repeated several times with the same results. Under the microscope these fossils exhibited also the structure of recent shells.

2. The second case in which animal matter has been partially changed was illustrated by the following experiments:—Portions of a stag's jaw

from the Brighton chalk rubble, of a fish-bone, and a shark's tooth from the London clay, when dissolved in diluted muriatic acid, gave only a brown powder; and the animal matter of a fragment of the humerus of a mastodon from Big-bone-lick exhibited but little flexibility, and was easily torn, particularly in the longitudinal direction. It was found impossible to make sections of the jaw-bone of the stag or the humerus of the mastodon for microscopic observation. Part of a human parietal bone found upon the site of the cathedral of Old Sarum, and human bones obtained from the churchyard of St. Christophe le Stocks, on part of which the Bank of England stands, were ascertained to have had their animal matter reduced to the same state as that of the stag's jaw. A fossil oyster from the Isle of Wight, when placed under the microscope, showed black spots over its surface, and the structure of the shell was apparently destroyed. A fragment of a Pecten from the lias also exhibited opaque spots. Part of an ammonite when dissolved left a substance resembling sepia.

3. The third case, where only the carbon of the animal matter remains, was explained by two series of experiments, one of which proved it to be associated with bitumen, and the other that it existed by itself. The scales of *Dapedium politum* and other fishes from Lyme Regis, when acted upon by acid, left carbon undissolved; and when heated under a test-tube gave a considerable quantity of bitumen.

Portions of the bones of the Ichthyosaurus and Plesiosaurus from the lias yielded a black residuum, which deflagrated with red-hot nitre, and the resulting mass gave a precipitate with chloride of calcium. To prove that the carbon was a portion of the bone and not an adventitious ingredient, a section was made, and the greatest quantity of carbon was found in the thickest part; and an analysis showed that the proportion of carbon was about the same as in the animal matter of a similar mass of recent bone. A still further proof was adduced, in no gelatine having been detected after thirty-six hours' boiling of a fragment of the fossil. A section of recent bone displayed, when carbonized by heat and charged with crystals of alum or a composition of whiting, a similar appearance in the arrangement of the carbon as in the fossil bone. No bitumen was given off, when fragments of these bones were acted upon by heat under a test-tube.

With respect to the second great class in which the animal matter has been removed, the following cases were mentioned:—Portion of the external and internal parts of a mammoth tusk from Siberia did not blacken by heat, and dissolved completely in muriatic acid. The internal part of a tusk from Ohio gave the same results, but the external part was found to contain a considerable proportion of animal matter. In bones from the crag, the animal matter had been abstracted. Human bones which had been long buried were found to be in the same state.

The paper concluded with the following remarks:—As the different states in which animal matter is found in fossils pass insensibly into each other, and as many of the changes occur in churchyard and other bones, it follows that no extraordinary circumstances are requisite to produce these alterations, but that they may be effected by the ordinary processes of putrefaction. Even the carbonization of animal matter may be accomplished by similar processes without the aid of heat, as bones become black by being macerated too long. It is also to be observed that the parts of animals preserved in the fossil state are those which longest resist putrefaction. It having been likewise shown that the degree of change does not depend upon the age of the bed in which the fossil occurs, it is a curious subject of inquiry for the geologist to ascertain how far the conditions necessary to putrefactive air, a certain temperature and moisture, were present in those strata in which the change has been great; how far they were absent in those in which the change has been small.

## No. II.

### ON THE CHEMICAL NATURE OF THE EXTERNAL ENVELOPE OF THE FROG'S SPAWN. By ALFRED SMEE, Student of King's College. ('London Medical Gazette,' May 26, 1838.)

THE nature of the envelope of the spawn of the frog does not seem to have been investigated chemically, some authors stating generally that it is of an albuminous, others that it is of a gelatinous nature. To me, however, it appears to be neither of the above substances, but rather a form of mucus, as the following observations show:—

1. When the envelope is separated from the ova, it gradually sinks in water.

2. It is not soluble either in hot or cold water, but swells considerably when first placed in it, after which it may be dried without losing any of its former properties, for on the addition of water it will again swell to its former size and appearance.*

3. When portions of the external covering were boiled in water, it was not dissolved, nor was there any coagulation.

4. When the spawn was treated with nitric acid, there was no coagulation, but after a short period the external covering was dissolved, leaving the ova.

5. Sulphuric acid had the same action on the spawn as the nitric.

6. Muriatic acid, like the preceding acids, did not coagulate, but dissolved the envelope.

7. Acetic acid, even when pretty strong, produced little or no effect on the spawn.

8. The action of the oxalic acid was found to be the same as the acetic acid.

9. The envelope was then treated with a solution of caustic potash, when it was dissolved.

10. Ammonia produced apparently no effect on the envelope.

11. When the ova were treated with alcohol, no coagulation ensued, nor was the envelope dissolved.

12. Tincture of galls was also found to produce no effect on the envelope.

* It does not appear, after a long time, to be dissolved, as after five or six weeks; but probably here decomposition may, in some manner, alter its nature.

13. When the ova were placed in a solution of prussiate of potash, no coagulation or other change ensued.

14. When the envelope was placed in a strong solution of corrosive sublimate in alcohol, no change took place.

15. Solutions of muriate of ammonia and common salt produced no change.

16. The solution of the envelope in nitric acid was treated with ammonia when it was not again re-precipitated.

17. The solution was then treated with potash, when the result was the same as before.

18. A solution of tannic acid gave a white precipitate with the acid solution.

19. A solution of gallic acid failed to give a precipitate with the solution.

20. When the acid solution was neutralized and treated with ferrocyanates of potassa, no change ensued.

21. The acid solution was found to give no precipitate with acetate of lead.

22. The gelatinous, or rather the mucous envelope, was found to be neutral, neither changing the colour of litmus-paper to red, nor restoring reddened litmus-paper, and it was also found to have no action on turmeric paper.

From these experiments it is decidedly proved that this covering is neither albuminous nor gelatinous : for had it been the former, many of the above tests would have coagulated it ; and had it been the latter, water would have dissolved, and tincture of galls had a sensible effect on it, &c. The nearest animal product then, which it approaches in its general characters, is mucus, which is known to differ in different situations of its secretion.

This mucous envelope is found to be a product exclusively of the oviduct, for the ova at no period of their existence in any way possess it, the proof of which is obtained from killing a frog just before spawning is expected, when the ova in the ovaries will be found to have no covering, and when placed in water do not swell out. Those ova, however, which have found their way into the oviduct possess the mucous covering, and when placed in water do swell out. The oviducts do not form the mucus suddenly when the ova are about to be discharged, but keep forming it for a considerable period, as I have found the oviducts to be distended with it six months at least previous to the period of spawning, and even immediately after the ova have been discharged are not entirely free from it, though they are much contracted in size. That the substance contained in the oviducts and the envelope of the ova after their discharge is identical, is proved by the following experiments :—

1. When a portion of the oviduct was placed in water, it swelled as the envelope when first excreted ; and if a frog before spawning be killed and cut open, and then placed in water, the contents of the oviducts will swell to an almost incredible size.

2. When the contents of the oviducts were placed in acid, they dissolved, and did not coagulate.

## No. III.

ON THE FORMATION OF MOULDING TABLETS FOR FRAC-
TURES.  By Alfred Smee, Dresser at St. Bartholomew's Hospital.
('London Medical Gazette,' February 9, 1839.)

The importance of a substance that can be moulded accurately to any
part of the body at a moment's notice, must be admitted by every member
of the medical profession, yet many difficulties attend the formation of a
composition which shall at the period of its application be so yielding and
soft that it may take an accurate cast of any part, and when dry shall still
retain the form given it, and become sufficiently hard to resist external
impressions, and at the same time shall be tough, elastic, and devoid of
brittleness and much flexibility; and further difficulties present themselves, where the capability of its being quickly dried is required.  The
advantage of lightness and cheapness is also a great desideratum.

As I had frequently noticed that the composition of gum-arabic and
whiting, when dry, possessed great hardness and toughness, and yet was
so free from brittleness that it could scarcely be pounded in a mortar,
I was determined to ascertain how far it would answer to make tablets
which might be used to form extemporaneous splints.

For this purpose a piece of coarse sheeting was copiously brushed
over on one surface with a thick solution of gum, after which it was
covered with a composition made by rubbing whiting with mucilage, continually adding the powder until the whole was of the consistence of a
thick paste; a second piece of sheeting was now rubbed over on one
side with the solution of gum, and the moistened side applied upon the
composition with which the piece of sheeting had been covered, and we
thus had two thicknesses of sheeting, with an intervening layer of the
composition of mucilage and whiting, the thickness of which may be
increased or diminished as strength or lightness is desired.  The whole
was then dried, and formed a tablet about the thickness of slight
pasteboard.

This experiment succeeded beyond my most sanguine expectations;
for whilst the tablet remained dry it was exceedingly hard, and, when
sponged over with a little warm water, became so yielding that, by moulding it with the fingers, a cast could be taken of any part of the body.  The
hand and knuckles were defined with great accuracy, and I succeeded by a
little management in taking a cast of the greater part of the face.  It is
sometimes advisable not to allow the substance to dry upon the part on
which it is moulded; but after the depressions and elevations have been
traced with the fingers, it should be carefully removed and partially dried
before the fire, and as soon as the texture is sufficiently dry to retain its
shape it may be placed near a stove, or even on the hob of a grate, without
fear of corrugating or becoming otherwise deformed.  In most cases,
however, this drying is quite unnecessary, it being requisite only to
envelope the moist tablet with a bandage.  A cast thus taken is extremely
hard and tenacious, so that when not much thicker than a wafer, it may be
struck violently and repeatedly against any hard substance and not be
destroyed.  It possesses but slight flexibility, and after being bent returns

L 2

to its previous form, showing considerable elasticity. It is neither liable to be torn nor broken; and, lastly, it possesses the advantage of lightness combined with durability. Whilst in search of a moulding substance, I thought it advisable to try various compositions in order that the best might be selected, but none appeared so excellent as that last described.

[Several paragraphs here follow of other ways for making these tablets, which I omit here.]

Of all these preparations, and many others that were tried, few were applicable, and none in all respects equal to the composition of gum and whiting, both of which substances are always easily obtained, and have the additional advantage of cheapness. The solution of gum which was found most adapted contained 10 or 12 ounces of gum to the pint of water. As far as regards the nature and texture of the cloth it is to be remarked that linen is stronger than cotton, and less liable to be torn, and therefore to be preferred. Of the various kinds of linen, none moulds so perfectly as moderately coarse old sheeting; for when the tablets were made of finer Irish, they were inferior in this respect. The application of these tablets is rather extensive; they may be used with great advantage for all fractures of the metacarpal bones, also for those of the forearm, or even for the humerus. When the humerus is fractured, the method which has been adopted is to cut a piece of paper somewhat into the shape of the required splint. It should cover a portion of the pectoralis major, and extend as high as the bend of the neck, and include the whole of the scapula. From this broad plate a piece descends to the bend of the elbow, and should be sufficiently wide to cover about two-thirds of the outer part of the arm. The paper is then placed on one of the prepared tablets, which is cut to a similar shape. The piece thus prepared is moistened until it becomes perfectly soft, and it is then moulded on the arm and neck. From the general shape of these parts, there will be found a superfluity of substance about the deltoid, which must be pinched up and turned down so as to form a fold over the other part. The splint then may be in a degree dried, and its inner surface lined with lint. The whole is to be enveloped in a starched roller.*

This mode of proceeding may appear tedious, but it is a source of much comfort to the patient; for whilst the upper arm is enveloped in this hard case, so that it is quite immovable, the forearm and hand may be let loose, and the patient may in some degree enjoy the use of them. The benefit of this mode of treating fractures is not confined to the patient only; it lessens also the labour of the surgeon: for when the injured limb is once put up in this manner, it requires no further attention for days, weeks, or even till the cure is accomplished. Its application to chronic diseases of the joints will be found particularly useful. In these cases two lateral splints are to be formed, and enveloped in a starch roller. It is hardly necessary to add that in fractures of the lower jaw it must prove a valuable auxiliary. Great, however, as these advantages may be, perhaps they are trifling in comparison with the importance of its application to simple fractures of the leg. The mode of treating these fractures at

---

* The roller is merely soaked in boiled starch and wound up in the usual manner before it is applied.

St. Bartholomew's Hospital has been for some months the method first adopted by Mr. John Lawrence, of Brighton. His plan was to form two strong splints on either side of the injured leg by successive layers of pieces of bandage, united together by white of egg and flour. Now, as far as this method is concerned, it requires no improvement, as durability, strength, and an accurate cast are obtained by this mode of proceeding, and the numerous cases which have been treated by it at the hospital show its complete success. By using the tablets formed of gum and whiting, upon the same plan as that of Mr. John Lawrence, a great saving of the surgeon's time is effected, and equal firmness and durability obtained. The mode in which I have made splints for the leg is first to obtain the exact shape by drawing a piece of sheeting or paper round the limb, and marking the part which corresponds to the tibia for the whole length of the leg, and continuing the line on the foot to the extent that it may be considered necessary to cover.* By this means, it is apparent that the exact size of the limb is obtained; but as the leg is to be enclosed by two splints, it becomes necessary to divide the cloth into two, which will give the exact pattern of either splint. These splints are to be moistened and moulded; and after being first lined with lint or leather, the whole is to be enveloped by a roller soaked in boiled starch. This composition of gum and whiting has answered perfectly in all the cases in which it has been tried, and splints made with it are perhaps superior to the splints made with flour and white of egg, because, when dry, they preserve accurately the shape of the limb, and do not at all corrugate, which all compositions of flour are liable at times to do.

Fractures of the patella are treated in a similar way, a splint being placed on either side of the knee, extending from about the centre of the thigh to about the centre of the leg. The patella is not to be covered with these splints, but a gap left corresponding to its shape, and the two pieces or splints are not to meet accurately at any part, but an interval is to be left of about three-fourths of an inch, or an inch, throughout their whole extent.

In enveloping these splints for fractures, they are not to be applied when there is much inflammation or swelling, but the part should be allowed first to get into a perfectly quiet state. Leeches, cold water, or poultices should be applied, if necessary, to effect this object. In general, a delay of a week, ten days, or even sometimes three weeks, is required, but in some favourable cases there is no occasion to wait, and the splints may be applied with safety and advantage on the second or third day after the accident. This mode has also been adopted in favourable cases of compound fracture, but most surgeons are agreed never to cover these wounds with concealing bandages.

It is not for me to expatiate upon the advantages with which this method of treating fractures is attended, for that belongs rather to Mr. John Lawrence as the first adapter of the principle; but the fixing of the bones more firmly and securely than can be accomplished by any other method, the prevention of loss of health by enabling the patients to walk on the

---

* Either splint should overlap the heel and under-surface of the foot in cases where they are used immediately after the accident, but where this application is delayed this is of no importance.

fourth or fifth day after receiving the accident. and permitting them to be moved to a situation more healthy and airy. The prevention of stiff joints, and more speedy and final uniting of the bone, are advantages too great to be passed over unmentioned. These benefits are likely to be enjoyed by a greater number when the time required for the first application of the splints is diminished, and the objection is removed of allowing the limb to remain without bandages during the time required for drying the splints. The tablets which I have described possess these additional advantages. and with them superior cheapness is also subjoined.

---

[Some years later (in 1846), after gutta-percha had come into use, he invented a modification of the above tablets for fractures, and the following article " On Gutta Percha Splints " was published in the London ' Medical Gazette,' the same paper in which his first invention had been made known to the world.]

At the introductory address to the Medical Society of King's College. I called attention to a novel surgical application of the new material called gutta-percha.  I have employed this substance, when rolled out into tablets, for the formation of splints. similar to those which I described as being made from the moulding tablets in the ' Medical Gazette ' and ' Lancet ' for the year 1839.  It has advantages over the moulding tablets which I then described, inasmuch as tablets of this material, rolled to the required thickness, are more easily moulded into the required form when soaked in water.

It has moreover advantages in its being impervious to and uninjured by water, alcohol, ether, acid, and alkaline solutions, and therefore especially applicable to interrupted splints where an aperture is required to be left for the application of these substances.  It is not so good however as the moulding tablet, inasmuch as it retains the perspiration, whilst the moulding tablet transmits it.  This difficulty may be overcome by puncturing numerous holes in the gutta-percha, or by lining it with a piece of thin lint, which allows the perspiration to escape.  If the perspiration is retained, it irritates and excoriates the skin.  I have employed this substance for fractured limbs and diseased joints.  I have also found it of great value after the division of tendons for contractions, and in cases where pressure and counter-pressure are to be employed, as the force may be then distributed over a large extent of the body.  The moulding tablets for fracture are, in my opinion, not so much employed as they deserve to be; solely, I believe, because surgeons do not like the trouble of their preparation.  Under these circumstances, I hope that gutta-percha tablets will lead to a far more extensive adoption of this form of splint.

---

## No. III.A.

## ON THE STRUCTURE OF NORMAL AND ADVENTITIOUS BONE.

*To the Editor of the 'Medical Gazette.'*

Sir,—The enclosed paper contains the results of observations on the structure of bone, made at various times during the last three years. It was read before the Royal Society last winter, and I have now added here and there new matter from my physiological note-book.

I remain, Sir,

Bank of England,　　　　　　　　Your obedient servant,
　Oct. 27th, 1840.　　　　　　　　　　　Alfred Smee.

The intimate or microscopic structure of bone has been the subject of much investigation both in this country and abroad, yet there still appears to be much scope for further discoveries. To the uninitiated the structure of bone under the microscope is one of the most splendid sights possible. To the initiated, though he may often have participated in the pleasure of examining it, yet the beautiful arrangement never ceases to afford the greatest delight.

The best mode of preparing the sections of bone is to cut portions, of a convenient thickness, with a saw, and then to rub one surface quite smooth on a hone, and afterwards to polish it upon a piece of leather; a slip of glass is then to be obtained, and one or two drops of balsam of Canada are to be placed on one surface: the polished side of the bone is to be put on the balsam, the glass is to be heated, which melts the balsam, and causes it, when cool, to fix the section firmly on the glass. The next operation is to polish the opposite side of the bone, and render it sufficiently thin to be translucent, which is to be effected either by grinding it upon a hone, or, if the section is very thick in the first instance, by filing the bone down to the required thinness; lastly, the specimen is to be polished as before. Occasionally the structure is best seen by scraping down the bone, but this is a tedious operation and seldom required.

The sections by these processes are made extremely thin, and are now fit for examination by the microscope. The canals of Havers are seen conspicuously when the bone is moderately magnified. They are irregular canals running for the most part in the direction of the long axis of the bone, and frequently anastomosing with each other. They are frequently seen to arise either from the external or internal margin of the bone.

Around these canals are small irregular bodies, arranged in circles, and having the surfaces parallel to the long diameter, looking towards their several canals. Apart from these series of corpuscules, attached to the Haversian canals is a row running round both the exterior edge of the bone and the edge of the medullary cavity. These run round every filament of the cellular tissue of bone, which, unless any portion happens to be very thick, has more of the Haversian canals.

A junction is effected between the corpuscules and the Haversian canals, and also between the corpuscules and the margins of the bone, by numerous little fine lines which communicate in every direction with the neighbouring corpuscules. These fine lines also connect the corpuscules of the extreme circles round each Haversian canal with the corresponding corpuscules of the neighbouring canal. Between the system of corpuscules surrounding the Haversian canal there is no row taking the general direction of the bone, as some have asserted.

If the Haversian canals are examined in a recent subject, where the capillaries are well filled with blood, they are observed to contain vascular tubes, and the blood can be distinctly recognized in them. To ascertain this fact it is better that the bone be scraped, and no heat applied to fix the bone to the glass.

The corpuscules are arranged around the Haversian canals in a series of rows proportionate to the size of the canals: thus a small canal has one, two, or three rows round it, while a large canal has five or six rows. It is to be noticed that the rows around the medullary canal and external edge of the bone seldom exceed two or three series.

An opinion is very prevalent amongst physiologists that these little bodies are solid; and many consider that they consist of the phosphate of lime and earthy matter of bone; but this opinion appears to be incorrect, from viewing sections of bone under different circumstances.

A similar opinion has been entertained of the fine lines running from the corpuscules, which have been termed the calcigerous tubes, but I would suggest the name of corpuscular lines or tubes, as the truth of this will be shown presently.

When a section of fresh bone is examined, these bodies appear opaque as well as their lines; but when a section from the same bone is thoroughly boiled in balsam of Canada, the balsam enters the canals of Havers, the corpuscular lines disappear, with few exceptions, and some of the corpuscules become transparent and nearly invisible, and others partially transparent. The same effect has been produced by our forefathers in their process of embalming; for in the tibia of a mummy which I possess, the corpuscules are transparent, and most of them are decidedly filled with a yellow matter similar to that which exists in the blood-vessels. The corpuscular lines are so translucent as to be scarcely visible. In this case the canals of Havers were also filled with yellow matter.

When the section of recent bone is ground down to the utmost possible limit, the corpuscules either appear as a transparent irregular oval ring, or they have the appearance of containing some shrivelled matter in their interior. In these cases the section of bone is only a portion of corpuscule in thickness.

The corpuscules with the lines are exceedingly opaque when a section of bone is examined in which the canals of Havers are filled apparently with adipocere, which occasionally happens after maceration.

If a thin section of bone is thoroughly calcined, then soaked in oil, and afterwards carefully ground down extremely thin, the canals of Havers, the corpuscules, and corpuscular canals will be quite visible in the substance of the bone.*

---

* The labour and care required to make these specimens are very great. It is better to calcine a thin section in a crucible, over a hot fire, then to place it in oil, and keep it there for a very long period, when it may be fixed to the glass with balsam of Canada. No heat should be applied, but it must be allowed to remain till it spontaneously dries, when its thickness may be further reduced and gently polished.

When the earthy matter is removed from calcined bone, the corpuscular lines disappear, but the corpuscules themselves, though transparent, are still visible.

In these instances the examination has been made by transmitted light; but differences, according to circumstances, are seen when the object is viewed by light thrown on the surface. The corpuscules with the lines appear white when a thin section is examined with a dark ground underneath it; but a thick polished piece of bone, or a section of bone with a portion of white paper underneath it, does not present these appearances. The reflection of light from the deeper corpuscules is the reason why the corpuscules are not apparent in a thick section, nor when white paper is placed underneath one of greater tenuity. Those corpuscules which present a transparent ring by transmitted light still appear white when viewed by reflected light, for some are seen as white rings on a black ground, and others as rings having a little irregular white matter in the centre. The whiteness of the corpuscules is owing to the reflection of light from the surface of the corpuscules, whilst between them it passes to the back, and is absorbed. The same effect is produced when a piece of black cloth or scratched glass is viewed under similar circumstances, in which cases the elevations on the one and the depressions in the other appear white.

If, however, the piece of mummy-bone before mentioned be examined by reflected light, the transparency of the corpuscules allows the light, in some degree, to pass, and that part which is reflected appears of the same yellow colour as when the section is viewed by transmitted light.

Such are the principal circumstances which modify the appearances of the corpuscules, and which may be thus summed up : first, that the earthy matter is associated with the animal matter, and pervades every part of the bone, which is shown in the section of burnt bone; secondly, that the corpuscules may exist without any earthy matter being there, as in the cartilage of the shark, or the animal matter of bone which is left after maceration; thirdly, that the corpuscular canals communicate with the Haversian canal, as the specimens boiled in Canada balsam prove; fourthly, that the corpuscules present themselves under two circumstances, for they are either opaque, as in recent and adipocere bone, or transparent, as in those boiled in balsam of Canada, as are also those of the mummy-bones.

All these facts show that the corpuscules and corpuscular lines are themselves cavities into which the various substances enter. We have already mentioned that, in the bones of mummies, a yellow matter is found in the corpuscules similar in appearance to that filling up the Haversian canals. That they are cavities is farther proved by the corpuscules appearing as rings when the section is reduced to extreme tenuity.

Attempts were made to fill the cavities with a coloured substance by various methods, such as had been effected in the bones of the mummy, but watery solutions penetrated only for a short distance into the Haversian canals, so that double decomposition of ferrocyanate of potass and sulphate of iron were found to be useless.

Balsam of Canada and dragon's blood were melted together, and pieces of bone were then boiled in the mixture. On the examination of thin sections of this, the Haversian canals were found filled with the compound, but whether it entered farther I could not so satisfactorily make up my mind as to enable me to state the fact positively; but, upon the whole, after numerous examinations of various specimens prepared in this manner, it may be stated that there was an appearance in those corpuscules immediately surrounding the canals, of its having penetrated the cavities; but, perhaps, the facts already adduced require no confirmation.

Having proved by the results of direct observation that the corpuscules are cells, and therefore ill named corpuscules, but better cellules, their use is the next point which demands our notice; but this will probably be for ever theoretical. Perhaps they act the same part to compact tissue of the bones as cells do to the cellular; namely, that of giving lightness without materially diminishing their strength.

What the particular structure of the bone is between the corpuscular lines and corpuscules there appears to be no means of ascertaining; for the highest power in the thinnest section only exhibits a transparent homogeneous texture.

Whether the corpuscular tubes contain blood perhaps we may also for ever be ignorant, but, considering that they communicate with decided blood-vessels, this opinion is far from improbable. It is certain they are much too small to carry the globules, but the opinion of their being blood-vessels may receive additional weight from the fact that in bone there are no canals smaller than the Haversian.

The size of the corpuscules or cellules is about equal to two or three globules of blood; they appear for the most part broader when viewed in a section parallel to the Haversian canals, than when seen in a section perpendicular to them: if it is really the depth which is seen in the longitudinal section of bone, it follows that these little bodies are deeper than they are broad, and we have already noticed that their length is much greater than their breadth. I conceive that the form of the corpuscules may be exactly given by taking a piece of wood twice as deep as it is broad, and twice or three times as long as it is deep, and then rounding off all its angles. Sections in different planes through this would present every form which is observed in the corpuscules.

Thus we have seen that the structure of bone is extremely simplified, as there is a medullary cavity from which spring the corpuscular tubes, and three or four layers of corpuscules or cellules around it. The same is seen with regard to the exterior part of the bone. Between these two layers run tubes for blood, irregular as to size, frequently anastomosing with their neighbours, and having the general direction of the bony tissue in which they are imbedded.

Radiatory lines are spoken of by some as existing round the Haversian canals, but they have no real existence, and are only the corpuscular canals or lines seen deep in the section, and out of focus; and they are only to be seen when these lines are opaque, and the section thick.

The cellular tissue of bone has no Haversian canals; for there the cells have the same relation to the bony structure of each cell as the Haversian canal has to the bone immediately surrounding it.

With regard to the laminæ of bone which have been described by other authors, they appear to me to exist only as the result of the ingenuity of the anatomist, for we see that the shaft of a long bone consists of a large medullary cavity, with a series of corpuscules and corpuscular lines, and a number of Haversian canals containing blood, with their series of corpuscules around them. Now, if a bone has long undergone putrefaction, it can be torn precisely in this manner. It will, in fact, tear to shreds, and a transverse section of each of these shreds shows the Haversian canal in the centre, and the corpuscules around it.

The corpuscules are to be seen in every true bone of the body, and form a good criterion to distinguish bone from other tissues. It is worthy of remark that but little difference exists between the structure of different bones, and even the intense hardness of the temporal bone immediately surrounding the semicircular canals presents no microscopic difference to account for that peculiarity.

The changes which bones undergo in the interior of the earth are very interesting. They may have their animal matter entire; they may have the animal matter removed; they may have the earthy matter partly removed; or, lastly, the animal matter may be carbonized.

The bones which exhibit the animal matter entire are those which have lain in certain situations not exposed to the air. I find them in this state from Beg Bone Lick, in Kentucky; and I have sections of the bones of the mastodon from thence, showing the structure in the most beautiful manner. Some bones found in making a sewer behind the Bank of England, together with Roman sacrificial utensils, were in a similar state. In both these instances, as well as in others, the Haversian canals appeared to be full of black matter.

The relation which the proportion of animal matter bears to the earthy, I have examined by calcination in twenty different species. The bones were all well macerated, and not greasy. The proportion in these varies but little one way or another, and that more from the state of the bone than anything else; for the average is as near as possible 60 per cent. of earthy material.

When the animal matter is removed, we may always venture an opinion that the bone has been imbedded in a sandy or gravelly stratum. In every churchyard with this soil that I have examined, bones have been found with the smallest trace of animal matter, and others not so far advanced in decomposition have been noticed. Many fossil bones possess their phosphate of lime, with so little animal matter as scarcely to be coloured by heat. None of the bones without animal matter can by any contrivance whatever be made to show the corpuscular structure, although the Haversian canals are distinct to the naked eye, and the general appearance of the bone is not materially altered, except perhaps being white, and of a somewhat mineral aspect.

The next division is that in which the animal matter is too abundant, part of the earthy matter having been removed. This condition is rare, and in these cases the bone will tear into shreds, each containing its Haversian canal and series of corpuscules. I do not know under what conditions this takes place.

The last change is the conversion of animal matter into bitumen or carbon. This change is common to the blue clay and blue lias, as here the bones retain their usual quantity of phosphate of lime, but their animal matter is converted into coal. This alteration appears quite unconnected with heat, and takes place as a spontaneous change in a moist situation, to which no air has access. I have seen different bones in every transition of this change from different situations; they mostly show not only the Haversian canals, but even the corpuscules.

We have next to examine adventitious bone; which may be arranged under the heads—reproduction of bone, growths from bone, and ossifications of other tissues. Of the former a piece of callus from a simple fracture was examined, and was not found to differ in any respect from true bone; it had the cellules with their lines, and the Haversian canals, precisely as normal bone. The same thing was noticed in a section of callus from a compound fracture. The new bone after necrosis, or even the necrosed portion, exhibited no diversity from this structure. The reproduction of bone is particularly interesting, as the new deposit is precisely the same as normal bone, with almost all the tissues; the reproduced part widely differs from the normal tissue.

Of the different growths from bone, a piece was examined which had been thrown out from two anchylosed vertebræ for additional strength, and this presented the appearance of true bone.

Hard bony exostoses were examined with exactly the same result.

Ossifications may be divided into two classes—bone of cartilages, and bone of other tissues. Ossifications of the thyroid and corncoid cartilage in the human subject were examined, and both presented the cellules, and the former the Haversian canals not at all different from recent bones.

The human trachea is not in general sufficiently ossified to show the corpuscules of the natural size, for in partial ossifications large cells are seen, but a section of a small part showed these cellules of the size natural to bone. The trachea of the macaw, and the inferior larynx of the widgeon, which are naturally bones, also present no difference from the general appearance of bone.

Examinations of the structures of the costal cartilages when ossified were attended with like results.

The ossification in the thyroid ligament was examined, which showed here and there the cellules.

The fibrous membranes when ossified do not generally exhibit this structure; in fact, we may say never, unless they be connected with bone. A portion of ossified tendon attached to bone was examined, which had these cellules differing in no respect from bone.

A section of a fibrous tumour of the uterus was examined. This had the fibres running in the osseous matter, but no cellules nor anything like cellules could be discovered.

Of the serous membranes, the pleura is sometimes ossified, but that appears to be only a deposit of irregular granules, and no structure could be detected.

The arterial tissue is frequently ossified, and then its appearance is similar to that of the pleura; it displays a granular mass and no cellules.

Thus we may state that ossifications are of two kinds: first, that of true bone, which, in a word, always exists when any enlargement of bone in any way takes place, either as an ossification of the neighbouring tissues, or in any other way. Secondly, ossification of the tissues not at all related to bone, which presents nothing but a mass of granules.

The structure of bone from a very old person was examined, which, after six weeks, had made no effort at reparation, but no difference could be detected.

A section of a femur was examined, in which the head of the bone was affected by scrofula, but no change could be detected in the cellules.

A transverse section of enlarged femur had the cellules in the enlarged part, but in this case the canals of Havers did not run in the direction of the long axis of the bone, but ran from the exterior edge.

The structure of bone and that of the cellules have been examined in numerous specimens of recent bone from different parts of the body. The long, the round, the flat, the sesamoid bones, have all received their share of attention, and these, with macerated bones, mummies' bones, bones altered by chemical agents, diseased bones, and ossifications connected with cartilage or bone, possess these cellules.

The bones of animals and of birds which have been examined also possess them. The bones of some fish, as the sturgeon and porpoise, and the ossific plates or the skin on the former, agree in possessing these cellules. Even the cartilaginous fishes are not destitute of them.

The structure of bone is not only such at the present moment, but has been the same from the earliest period, for the mighty ichthyosaurus, the tyrant of the water in former ages, and the vast mastodon, the giant of the land, possessed these cellules. Although six thousand years had elapsed before the microscopic structure of bone was made known to the anatomist, yet in every age, in every country, geological and antiquarian researches have revealed that the same structure has existed. The imperfection of our instruments has been the cause of our previous ignorance, and doubtless there is now ten times more to be learned than is already known.

In every case where the corpuscules or cellules exist, they can be distinctly perceived to be hollow. Let, therefore, the universality of this fact be the only apology for its communication.

For the following measurements I am indebted to the kindness of Mr. Bowerbank :—

### Haversian canals.

Small.
$\frac{1}{303}$

Large.
$\frac{1}{800}$ in diameter.

### Corpuscules or cellules seen in a transverse section.

One of the largest.
Diameter $\frac{1}{1695}$. Length $\frac{1}{1153}$.

One of the smallest.
Diameter $\frac{1}{9310}$. Length $\frac{1}{9353}$.

### Longitudinal section.

One of the largest.
Diameter $\frac{1}{2021}$. Length $\frac{1}{727}$.

One of the smallest.
Diameter $\frac{1}{1166}$. Length $\frac{1}{837}$.

---

## No. IV.

### PHOTOGENIC DRAWING. ('Literary Gazette,' May 18, 1839.)

VARIOUS have been the methods detailed for the preparation of paper which can be acted upon with facility by the powerful agency of the light from the sun; yet, notwithstanding all that has been written on this interesting subject, the practical student in this art finds that great difficulties occur in every department of photogenic drawing.

In the first place, he finds that the paper which he has prepared the preceding evening is by no means equal in its qualities, as sometimes he may have two or three sheets very excellent, so that, when they are exposed to the light, they become in every part of a uniform dark colour; sometimes, on the contrary, he finds that the paper, after it has been similarly acted upon by the solar rays, becomes black over the greater part of its surface, yet numerous white spots occur throughout which detract much from the beauty and effect of drawings made with it; and, lastly, it occasionally happens that some sheets are not affected by the most powerful light, except, perhaps, at a few points.

Indeed, should the paper be good, and the drawings made, yet, without the greatest care in the fixing of them, they may be found to have a ground of an irregular tint, or they may be imperfectly stopped, and even the colour may be altogether removed.

To surmount with certainty these various difficulties, numerous experiments have been performed in every department of the manufacture of photographs, which we shall now describe; first as regards the chemical substances, then the paper, and, lastly, the most efficient stopping solution.

The various compounds of silver have been long known to be acted upon powerfully by the solar rays: this property is possessed by far the greater number of the preparations of that metal, yet not by all; and upon the former, the effect of light differs materially in its degree of sensitiveness.

The two soluble salts of silver with which we are most acquainted are the nitrate and sulphate, both of which communicate to organic textures and substances made from them a black stain when exposed to light; but these, neither on paper nor in combination with albumen, gelatin, gums, or glutea, have sufficient delicacy to be applicable for the manufacture of photogenic drawings.

The ammonia-nitrate of silver will be found considerably more delicate than either the nitrate or sulphate, and may be used where rapidity of action is not required, particularly as it lessens the trouble, by the application of only one solution to the paper.

The chloride of silver is the substance to which we principally look for the ready action of the solar rays, and the modes of its application to the paper are numerous. It is by itself very insoluble in water, and, on the contrary, easily dissolved by ammonia; but, unfortunately, the ammonia-chloride of silver cannot with good effect be used for the preparation of this paper, and thus we are compelled to form a chloride upon it by a more circuitous process. This object may be effected by the application of either chlorine, chloride of an oxide, chloride of metal, or hydrochloric acid, first to the paper, and afterwards a solution of nitrate of silver.

When a nearly saturated solution of chlorine is used, it should be applied lightly with a sponge to the paper, taking care that every part is moistened by the liquid: the paper should then be allowed to dry, and the solution of nitrate of silver applied also with a sponge, in a similar way.

This form of chloride is not quite so delicate as some others, and requires a long time to become quite black. It has its advantages from enabling the most highly-glazed papers to be prepared with great facility and certainty, and it becomes of a beautiful brown, which is but slightly altered by the stopping agents.

The chlorides of oxides, such as the chlorides of soda and of lime, may be advantageously applied in some cases where the chlorine is useful. . . . . The chloride of soda, however, must not be used for absorbent papers, such as those used in printing; but with the glazed papers it becomes very delicate and sensitive to light, whether it be applied before or after the solution of silver. The strength which was found most useful was that usually employed for medical purposes.

The solution of chloride of lime was made by adding twelve grains of chloride of lime to an ounce of water, and allowing any insoluble part to subside. This is found applicable both to printing and to glazed papers, but is more certain when used prior to the nitrate of silver.

The chlorides of metals, as common salt, require more care in their proportions than the foregoing substances; and an experiment which was tried, shows the absolute necessity of using an excess of nitrate of silver.

A weak solution of nitrate of silver (twenty grains to the ounce) was treated with excess of chloride of sodium, when an insoluble chloride was precipitated: this was exposed to the direct rays of the sun, without the slightest change; the supernatant liquor was then poured off, and the precipitate well washed two or three times with distilled water, to remove any superfluous salt which might perchance be present: the chloride of silver was again exposed to the light for many hours, when only a slight brown tint was produced. On the contrary, when the nitrate of silver was treated with such small quantities of salt that part of the solution of silver remained in excess, the light speedily blackened the chloride exposed to its action. . . . . Similar experiments were tried with chlorine, chloride of lime, and chloride of soda, when excess did not prevent the blackening; but when muriatic acid was used, the same phenomenon was observed. . . . . Without endeavouring to explain the difference of the action of light under these different circumstances, an important practical inference is to be drawn from them; for if any circumstance prevents the nitrate of silver being in excess, no action will be produced.

The proportions given by Mr. Golding Bird are evidently so designed, that an equivalent proportion of each substance should be used; for although he employs only a 20-grain solution of nitrate of silver to the ounce, with a 12-grain solution of salt, yet, by using the silver twice, it becomes equal to the single application of a 40-grain solution. To insure success, the ratio of the chloride of sodium to the nitrate of silver should be about one to five. As the relative proportions of these two substances are of importance, great care must be taken in the application of the salt in the first place to the paper. A 10-grain solution of salt should be sponged over one surface of the paper, and all superfluous moisture carefully removed by the sponge wrung dry; the paper ought then to be allowed to dry, but taking care that the salt does not settle in any part, and thereby cause an excess; when the paper is dry, the solution of nitrate of silver is to be applied in a similar way. An advantageous mixture can be made of the chlorides of oxides and chlorides of metals: thus, a very excellent paper may be made by a solution containing ten grains of salt and twelve of chloride of lime to the ounce of water.

Dilute muriatic acid may also be used for the manufacture of the photogenic paper, in the proportion of about twenty-four drops of the distilled acid, sp. gr. 1·12, to an ounce of water. It may be used either on the glazed or absorbent papers, but for the latter it should not exceed half the strength. The same observations apply to any excess of muriatic acid as were noticed to apply to the fluoride of sodium. This forms a delicate paper, and becomes of a very even colour.

A more sensitive paper may be prepared by using the bromide of silver instead of the chloride; but the expense of bromine and its compounds is an objection.

A solution of bromine in water cannot be used in a way similar to a solution of chlorine with any good result, and recourse must be had to the bromide of potassium, of which twelve grains to the ounce, applied in the way described when treating of the chloride of silver, and afterwards conjoined with a solution of nitrate of silver (fifty grains to the ounce), will be found a suitable proportion.

Other salts may be used besides the chloride and bromide, such as the phosphates, chlorates, &c., but have the disadvantage of not being so sensitive to light. A benefit, however, attends the use of the phosphates, &c.; for while any excess of the chlorides must be carefully avoided, an undue proportion of the latter salts is attended with no inconvenience.

The expense of the nitrate of silver renders it desirable to reduce the quantity used; but if a dark ground is wanted, a smaller quantity than fifty grains to the ounce cannot well be employed.

Having considered the chemical substances which may be used for the photogenic paper, the different kinds of paper, and those suited to each particular preparation of silver, next demand attention.

Papers may be divided into three classes—the bibulous, the absorbent, and the highly-glazed papers. Of the bibulous papers, blotting-paper and tissue papers are examples; but none of them will be found at all applicable to the purposes of the photogenic art. These papers are made from rags, but there are papers made from other substances, such as old sacking, &c., which possess great strength, as well after they have been moistened as before.

The finest paper of this sort is called "double small ends." That which I employed, when sponged over, seemed to be equally moistened in every part, and was found well adapted for the intended purpose, as there was not, after being prepared with the solutions, a single spot that resisted the action of light in any one of the sheets. There are, however, disadvantages attending the use of this paper, for it is not so smooth as others more highly glazed, and therefore not so well adapted for every description of photographs.

The absorbent papers, or the papers used in printing, possess a finer texture than that last described; and when they can be obtained good, they answer very well for photogenic purposes.

Of the various papers which have been tried of this description, a thin paper used for printing newspapers, called "double copy," was found the best; for the thicker papers, that have much plaster of Paris added to increase their substance and weight, do not answer so well, as they are apt to absorb the solutions unequally. These papers are fittest when the common salt and nitrate of silver are used.

The highly-glazed papers, or writing papers, require no particular observation, for if either chlorine, chloride of lime, or chloride of soda be used, the colour will be found uniform; and the finer and more highly glazed the paper is, the better will it suit the intended purpose. These will be found advantageous, not only from possessing a smooth and uniform colour, but also from a smaller quantity of the solution of nitrate of silver being used in their preparation, as it is applied only on the surface, and does not penetrate any distance into the texture. For this latter property, paper such as the satin post may be prepared on both surfaces, should that be deemed advisable.

The modes of applying the chemical substances to the paper have been already noticed, and the sponge was mentioned as being the agent employed.

The extent to which the paper should be moistened is, that such a quantity of solution should be used, that it may, as artists term it, "bear out" in every part of the surface; that is, that a slight layer of moisture should appear at every point after the usual absorption has taken place, and that all superfluous moisture is to be carefully removed by a pressed sponge.

After the paper has been prepared, it will be hardly necessary to state that it must be kept carefully from the action of the light.

The mode of making the drawings has been sufficiently detailed in various publications. When prints are to be copied, the printed side must be pressed by a piece of flat glass close to the prepared paper, and exposed to the light of the sun. When drawings of feathers or other irregular bodies are desired, a piece of the photogenic paper is to be laid upon any yielding substance, as folded linen, flannel, or, what is perhaps better, a layer of sand or bran; the object is then to be covered with a square of flat glass, and, if necessary, pressed down by weights, and is to be finally exposed to the light of the sun.

The paper will be found to be most rapidly acted upon by the direct rays of the sun, but this is by no means indispensable, as a clear sky is very effectual, and even on a very cloudy day a delineation is produced, only it requires a longer time. The circumstances which appear most to retard the photogenic properties of the solar beam, are those dense collections of smoke which hover over the metropolis when the wind has not sufficient power to disperse the deleterious particles of which they are composed.

Most of the modes of preparing the paper which have been described, are applicable to the camera obscura with a short focus; and those prepared with the chloride of soda, chloride of lime, and bromide of potassium, do extremely well. Its use in this department will for ever be limited, for a portion of an object only can be represented accurately, as, for every distance, the camera requires a different adjustment of its focus; so that to take a landscape a hundred different foci would scarce suffice. For this reason, it certainly appears that the results of M. Daguerre's experiments must be exaggerated.

The fixing of the drawings after they have been made is completely a chemical action, and requires as much care as the preparation of the paper. The substances that may be employed for this purpose are dilute muriatic acid, chloride of sodium, hydriodic acid, hydriodate of potash. iodic acid, hyposulphites, and sulphocyanate of potash. Before using any of these substances, the drawing ought to be soaked in common water for a few minutes, to remove any excess of the salt of silver; the stopping solution is then to be applied with a sponge to every part of the surface equally.

No particular advantage attends the use of the muriatic acid, but it will be found to stop pretty well when in the proportion of about twenty-four drops of the distilled acid to an ounce of water, but it is not quite permanent. The chloride of sodium, or common salt, is very effectual in stopping any further action of the light, as drawings fixed by this agent have not undergone the slightest alteration from many hours' exposure to the brightest sunshine. When the impressions are very dark, they do not change colour, but lighter drawings become altered to a yellowish brown : the addition of a little sesquichloride of iron corrects this, and gives a pink tinge to them. The solution recommended by Mr. Bird answers very well; it contains two ounces of salt, and one ounce of the sesquichloride of iron, to the pint of water. The hydriodic acid, and the hydriodate of potash, are also very effective in preventing any further action of the solar rays; they turn the white parts to a pale yellow, and are very apt. if the solution be too strong, to remove the colour of the dark ground. especially if the drawing has been exposed to the light for only a short time : for this reason, the solution of hydriodate of potash ought not to exceed ten grains to the ounce of water. A solution of iodic acid, fifteen or twenty grains to the ounce, is very excellent for stopping photogenic drawings; it is particularly applicable to delicate drawings of feathers. when it is desirable not to allow them to remain long in the light; and at the same time the contrast of black and white heightens the effect. Care must be taken not to apply too strong a solution, for that is apt to whiten the dark ground, but it never turns it to any other tint.

The hyposulphates of potash and soda have been much used for the fixing of drawings, but, if exposed to the sun, they do not appear quite so effective as the common salt, or hydriodate of potash; they have the advantage, however, of stopping them a darker colour. The sulphocyanate of potassa is also found to stop these drawings; it changes the colour of the ground to a brown, and has no particular advantage.

The different effects of these several fixing-solutions can be turned to good account by suiting the colour of the drawings to the fancy of the artist, or the nature of the subject ; and a still greater alteration of tint may be produced by varying the duration of time which the light is allowed to act upon the paper.

Many other chemical substances have been tried for fixing the drawings, but none attended with success. The following are the principal :— Chlorine, chloride of soda, chloride of lime, tincture sesquichloride of iron, chloride of manganese, chloride of tin, chlorate of potassa, solution of iodine in water and in alcohol, carbonate of potash, hydrocyanic acid, dichromate of potash, biborate of soda, oxalate of ammonia, fluate of ammonia, benzoate of ammonia, succinate of ammonia, phosphate of soda, gallic acid, arsenite of ammonia, and sulphite of soda.

Should it from any cause be thought desirable to remove from the paper the colour which it acquired by light, this may be performed either by a strong solution of corrosive sublimate, which will render the paper quite white, or by a strong solution of hydriodate of potash, which gives it a yellow tint. If to the saturated solution of corrosive sublimate a little gum be added, it may be used with a quill pen, either to prevent the action of light, or to make white lines or marks after the action of the solar rays. Drawings may be made with great effect in this way, on paper previously exposed to the sun; and this is by far the best mode of proceeding, when naturalists or others are desirous of circulating a few copies of any delineation among their own friends; for, as the white parts are exceedingly diaphanous, and the black impervious to light, the drawings made by this means are much more distinct than those made by the ordinary described processes. This mode will be found exceedingly valuable where a few copies of any drawing of machinery are suddenly wanted for estimates of prices or other causes; and the strongest light will never affect the original drawing.

By the common method of making photogenic drawings, should any be imperfect or otherwise damaged, it will be better to expose them freely to the action of the sun; by which means a uniform black ground will be produced, which will be suitable for the use of the corrosive sublimate: and thus any waste will be prevented. A thin paper, which should be slightly moistened before use, is most applicable to this mode of drawing. The photogenic paper may be blackened either by a dilute solution of protosulphate of iron, or by hydrosulphate of ammonia.

The principal points in every department of the photogenic art have now been described; and if the minutiæ which have been detailed are strictly followed, and the preparation of silver suited to the kind of paper as here laid down, the student in this interesting and new field of science will be enabled not only to prepare his paper, but also to make and fix his drawings with ease and certainty.

An omission was made in the paper on Photogenic Drawing, which was inserted in the last Number of the *Literary Gazette*; for, whilst treating of the ammonio-nitrate of silver, I forgot to mention the proportions which were found most suitable: this may seem unimportant in a paper which is not very sensitive, but, as the ease and certainty of its preparation, as well as its cheapness, exceed all other described papers, it possesses a particular claim on our notice. Twenty grains of nitrate of silver are to be dissolved in an ounce of water; then a few drops of ammonia are to be added, which at first throws down a considerable precipitate; this, by a further addition of ammonia, redissolves, and the solution becomes quite clear, when it will be ready to be applied by a sponge to the paper. The most suitable paper for this preparation of silver is the "double copy." The whole cost of photogenic paper does not exceed, by this process, one penny for a sheet equal in size to large foolscap, which, if bought of vendors, would cost between one shilling and fourpence and four shillings. The cost of all other papers does not exceed twopence-halfpenny the sheet, except that prepared with the bromide of potassium; which, for the same quantity, would be about one penny more expensive. The preparation of paper suitable for the use of the corrosive sublimate is still more simple, for here it is only necessary to sponge over a very thin paper with a 20-grain solution of nitrate of silver, and expose it to the action of the light of the sun. Drawings made in this way have analogy with etchings executed on glass, covered with black varnish, but are more easily made; the white parts of the paper are, however, not so transparent as the glass. An error requiring notice has also crept into my paper; for the hyposulphates, instead of the hyposulphites, are there mentioned as stopping agents.

----

No. V.

## THE PRINCIPLE, CONSTRUCTION, AND USE OF SMEE'S BATTERY; ITS VARIOUS FORMS, WITH FULL DIRECTIONS FOR ITS MANIPULATION, MORE ESPECIALLY IN THE PROCESSES OF ELECTRO-METALLURGY. (Transcribed from Paper read at the Society of Arts, June 1st, 1840, and from Smee's 'Elements of Electro-Metallurgy,' &c.)

THE most valuable instrument which chemists employ for their analytical experiments is, no doubt, the galvanic battery; but so much trouble attends its use, that, except in the laboratory of the professed chemist, it is not employed to any considerable extent. Experiencing this inconvenience in the experiments which I conducted on the red ferrocyanate of potash, it became a matter of the greatest importance to ascertain how far a battery could be constructed, that at once should possess a capability of being used at a moment's notice, and have besides considerable power united with cheapness of action, and, at the same time, without the necessity of much laborious cleaning after its employment.

After experimenting with the batteries before known to the public, I became convinced that it was of the highest importance to supersede the necessity of diaphragms, attended as they are with continual trouble and expense; and as the power of the battery seems to depend upon the facility offered to the evolution of the hydrogen and preventing its adhesion to the negative metal, whereby it is coated as with a varnish, and the action almost entirely destroyed, all my experiments were directed to this object. I first perceived that the gas was not evolved equally from every part of the surface of a smooth piece of platinum, but chiefly from the corners, edges, and points. Following this hint, I roughened the metal with sand-paper and found the evolution of the gas to be increased; and when the surface of other metals, as silver or iron, was roughened by some acid, I found the gas also to'be much increased. Moreover, zinc shavings, which present the singular anomaly of having one surface extremely bright and the other of a delicate frosted appearance, show this property well, gas being freely given off from the rough, but adhering firmly to the bright surface. The same differences are also observed when rough and polished steel are employed. These experiments induced the idea that spongy platinum, which may be considered as a mass of metallic points, would be very efficient in forming a galvanic circuit; and on trying

the experiment, the quantity of hydrogen evolved from a minute portion of
this substance, when touched with a piece of zinc, was truly astonishing.
The mass in this state was so fragile that the hydrogen disintegrated it
almost instantaneously, showing that in this form it could not be used for
a voltaic battery.

My next experiments were to coat other metals with this finely-divided
platinum; and I found that platinum, palladium, or silver, answered
admirably for the reception of it, and similar help was afforded to the
evolution of the hydrogen, as the contrast between the gas given off from
the smooth metal and rough metal forms a most striking experiment.
Other metals received the platinum with advantage; as plated copper or
iron, and even charcoal, was benefited to a similar extent.*

The metals thus roughened by platinum have, in addition to their
power, some properties which are very interesting: thus, when a piece of
the prepared metal is placed in dilute sulphuric acid and touched with a
small rod of zinc, gas is not given off from its whole extent, but only from
the space of a small circle; and when contact is completed with a smooth
piece of platinum, the gas will not be given off from the latter, but will
travel principally to the rough portion, there to be evolved. This curious
experiment affords a marked difference from those cases where the hydrogen is absorbed, as when a piece of silver is touched with a rod of zinc in
dilute sulphate of copper, for in this case an immense circle of copper will
be thrown down.

A difficulty now arose in this stage of the proceeding, for the finely-
divided platinum was so easily rubbed off that it could not be practically
used with advantage. However, when the silver or other metal was first
roughened by the removal of the surface by an acid, then the adhesion was
so great that a piece of platinum thus prepared was sent accidentally to
the instrument-maker, where the workman mistook the finely-divided
platinum for dirt, and could only remove it with sand-paper.

It now became desirable to ascertain the power of metal thus prepared
relatively with the other batteries, and also with metals uncovered with
the finely-divided platinum; and to make this comparison, I perceived that
considerable difficulty occurred, for as this preparation of the metals increases the quantity, but does not interfere with the intensity, a fair comparison cannot be made where there is any impediment or difficulty to
be overcome, unless that difficulty be superseded by increasing the number
of cells of the battery: and therefore, had I at first taken the decomposition of water as the test for my numerous experiments, they would have
been attended with an immense expense; had I taken the heating of wire
as my test, that would also have been uncertain, according as the heating
of large or small wires was estimated, but I considered that a close relative estimate of power could be ascertained by the magnetical effect; for
by using large wires round the temporary magnet, but little impediment
was offered to the current, and thus the quantity, independent of the intensity, could be accurately ascertained; and in repeating my experiments,
at different times, on the same magnet and with the same surface of like

---

* Charcoal and plumbago might be considered to afford points enough for
the escape of the hydrogen, but to these there is great adhesion of the gas.

metals, I found that they coincided with remarkable accuracy, and only
one cell was required for the experiment. Though the weight, which was
supported even by a small magnet with *large wires*, was inconveniently
great, I determined to ascertain the distance at which a small but lesser
weight was attracted.

The following are the results of like surface of metal with the same
metal :—

|  | Layers of paper. |
|---|---|
| Smooth silver, supported keeper through . | 2 |
| Smooth copper . . . . . . . . . . . | 1 |
| Silver heated, quenched in acid . . . . | 9 |
| „ surface removed by nitric acid . . | 9 |
| Iron rough . . . . . . . . . | 8 |
| Daniell's battery . . . . . . . . | 6 |
| Platinized silver . . . . . . . . . | 20 |
| „ iron, two or three varieties . . | 20 |
| „ platinum . . . . . . . | 18 |
| Grove's battery . . . . . . . . | 26 |
| „ platinized platinum . . . . . | 30 |
| Plain platinum heated, quenched in acid . . | 12 |

By these experiments we see the great advantage of the rough metals
and those covered with platinum over the smooth metals and Daniell's
arrangement.

The only metal which may take the place of finely-divided platinum is
palladium, but probably rhodium, iridium, and osmium would have the
same property, as they are precipitated in a fine black powder by zinc.
The cause of this black colour is not at all evident; and the form of the
black deposit has eluded not only my own but the observation of others,
although aided by the microscope. Probably, however, the colour is owing
to the particles being too small to reflect the light, as is said to be the case
with a specimen of quartz in the cabinet of the Duchess of Gordon, but
this is merely hypothetical.

We have now seen that platinum, palladium, silver, plated copper, or
iron, are suitable for the finely-divided metal, and these are to be first
roughened, the two former with sand-paper, and the three latter with a
little nitric acid, which is to be again cleaned off by washing. The metals
are then to be placed in any convenient vessel with a little dilute sulphuric
acid, to which a small quantity of nitro-muriate of platinum has been
added; a porous tube or paper bag, containing a piece of zinc, with more
dilute sulphuric acid, is also to be placed in the vessel, when, as soon
as the circuit is completed, the platinum is precipitated on the metal
placed for its reception. The cost of this process will be best understood by mentioning that the assayers sell one ounce of the prepared
silver for one shilling above the price which is charged for the silver
alone.

The zinc which is used for the battery should be the best thick rolled
zinc, as this is far preferable to the cast zinc, and it is to be amalgamated
with mercury aided by dilute sulphuric acid; for the application of this
process to the zinc of my battery will be found, unlike other batteries, not
to require repeating.

The form which is most suitable for the battery appears to me a matter of fancy rather than of importance—one circumstance alone being requisite; that is, if we are desirous of obtaining the greatest power with the utmost economy of silver, it is requisite that every portion of silver should be opposed to a piece of zinc, but the size of the latter, within moderate limits, is but of little consequence.* Thus, if we use the many-celled porcelain trough, it is better to surround the silver by zinc in the same way as the copper surrounds the zinc in the old Woollaston battery. If the circular form be adopted, a piece of zinc should be placed in the interior as well as the exterior of the cylinder, as by that means both surfaces of the silver are brought into action; if the Cruikshanks be adopted, one surface is necessarily lost, but in this case plated copper answers sufficiently well, as the edges are sunk into the cement which, if exposed as in the other forms, are apt to have a portion of the copper dissolved, which is again deposited on the silver, and is liable to become oxidized and be detrimental to the power of the battery. The closer the zinc can conveniently be brought to the other metal, the more favourable will it be.

Whichsoever form is adopted, the power will depend on the series and size of the plates. For decomposition of water and most other purposes, it is better to have twelve pairs of plates and then to increase their size. The battery having twelve 5-inch plates, which was exhibited to the Committee of the Society of Arts, gave off fifteen cubic inches of mixed gas in the first minute, and showed great calorific power by immediately burning stout steel music wire.

The duration of the action of the battery will depend, like a fire, upon the quantity of fuel supplied to it in the first instance, for, as there is no local action, it follows that the solution of the zinc will be exactly proportionate to the power produced; and for this reason, when the battery is required to continue in operation for a long period, as in the method which I detailed elsewhere for the production of electrotypes, a larger receptacle for acid should be employed, or a contrivance can easily be adopted to carry off gradually, by means of syphon tubes, the saturated solution of sulphate of zinc, whilst at the same time dilute acid is supplied from another tube.

A galvanic battery thus constructed owes its increase of power to the mechanical evolution of the gas; and as the experiments of Faraday have shown that the source of power in any voltaic pile is chemical action, I have ventured to call my form of apparatus the "Chemico-Mechanical Battery."

To those versed in electrical science it may be needless to mention that, this form of battery simply increasing the quantity of electricity, it is most important that large communications and large wires should be used in its construction, or else the whole of the additional power might be lost.†

The advantages of the Chemico-Mechanical Battery are, the cheap-

---

* It is of great disadvantage to employ the zinc too small, as a simple rod to a large cylinder of silver. A certain quantity of zinc seems absolutely necessary to elicit the full power of this arrangement.

† This I have actually known to be the case; the power of the battery being almost destroyed by the use of small wires and small connexions.

ness in its employment, and its requiring not only less manipulation
than any other battery, but also less cleaning. It can be put into action
at a moment's notice, and, after having been used, can be as readily laid
by. When in the fluid, it will be quiet till communications are made, and
will then possess considerable power. It neither gives off poisonous fumes
nor requires the aid of strong acids, and but one fluid is employed; and,
lastly, the amalgamation of the zinc does not require to be renewed. Such
are the principal advantages of this battery, and they appear to be sufficient to entitle it to the very extensive application which it has met with;
but, in conclusion, I wish to be clearly understood that it does not possess
the absolute constancy of Daniell's, or the intensity of Grove's battery.

--------

Smee's Battery was invented through noticing the property which
rough surfaces possess of evolving the hydrogen, and smooth surfaces of
favouring its adhesion.

"Thus, whatever metal we use for our negative plate, we take care
that it be roughened, either by a corrosive acid, as iron by sulphuric acid,
copper and silver by nitric acid, or mechanically, by rubbing the surface
with sand-paper. Even by these means the metals are rendered much
more efficient; but, to take advantage of this principle to the fullest
extent, I cover platinum with finely-divided black powder of platinum by
galvanic means; that is, I place the platinum as the copper is placed in a
Daniell's battery, but, instead of employing sulphate of copper in the
outer vessel, I use a small quantity of nitro-muriate of platinum, so that
the finely-divided metal is thrown down on the sheet platinum previously
roughened by sand-paper. In this way it was also placed on palladium,
silver (roughened by nitric acid), plated copper, iron of every sort, and on
charcoal, with the same good result; but no other metal was found to
answer for its reception. The metal generally employed is silver, because
of its cheapness and its not undergoing any alteration. But whatever
metal be used, the principle is the same, viz. the affording a surface to
which the hydrogen shall not adhere, but from which it shall be evolved;
and the infinity of the points which are presented by such a surface as
above described, appears to be the cause of this excellent result. The preparation of the silver is now made a separate branch of a trade, and perhaps
it is the first application of the decomposing power of the galvanic battery
which was publicly sold. The platinized metal can now be bought ready
for use; but for those who desire to perform this operation a brief description is here added.

"The metal to be prepared should be of a thickness sufficient to carry
the current of electricity, and should be roughened, either by sand-paper,
as in the case of platinum or palladium, or, when silver is employed, by
brushing it over with a little strong nitric acid, so that a frosted appearance is obtained. The silver is then washed, and placed in a vessel with
dilute sulphuric acid, to which a few drops of nitro-muriate of platinum
are added. A porous tube is then placed in this vessel, with a few drops
of diluted sulphuric acid; into this the zinc is put. Contact being made,
the platinum will in a few seconds be thrown down upon the surface of the
silver, as a black metallic powder. The operation is now completed, and
the platinized metal ready for use. However, iron when thus prepared is

as effectual as silver, and may be sometimes employed with advantage. With this metal all that is required is to rub a little nitro-muriate of platinum over it, and an immediate deposit of the black powder takes place. Palladium and iridium are found nearly as effectual as platinum to coat other metals with, and the platinized silver of commerce usually possesses a considerable quantity of this latter metal. Within the last few months an idea has prevailed in the minds of some, that wire-gauze might be used with advantage; but it is difficult to conceive where the benefit would lie, for the cost of the material would be greater, the surface for the same weight of metal would be less, and neither space nor power gained by its adoption.

"The liquid generally adopted to excite this battery is a mixture of one part by measure of sulphuric acid, and seven of water, which will be found amply strong for all purposes. When we desire greater intensity, we can obtain it by the addition of a few drops of nitric acid; but if too much be used, it might attack the silver. When, however, platinized platina is employed, the nitric acid may be used with impunity. The electro-metallurgist will frequently find it advisable to use dilute sulphuric

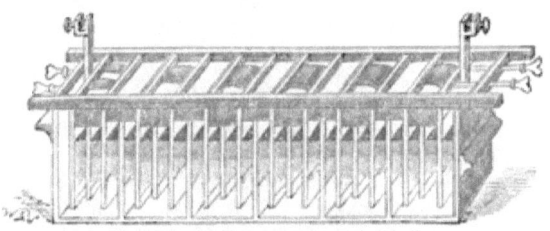

Fig. 8. Smee's Battery, compound six cells.

acid, only containing from $\frac{1}{15}$ to the $\frac{1}{18}$ of the pure acid, and adding some acid when the first is exhausted; taking care, however, that the quantity of acid never exceeds $\frac{1}{8}$ of the original water, for any excess above that quantity will be useless, as the liquid will then become saturated with the sulphate of zinc. The zinc, acid, and water being severally required to excite the battery, it is possible to regulate them that they should all be exhausted at once, so that the zinc should neutralize the acid, and the resulting sulphate of zinc exactly saturate the water. This, however, may be very interesting in principle, but practically it would be impossible to act with such precision; yet we must never forget this fact whenever we charge our batteries.

"Numerous inquiries have been made as to what arrangement is best suited for this battery; but this must depend upon the purpose for which it is employed. For the student's laboratory the porcelain trough of many cells appears to be best adapted; and it is some-times so constructed, that any number of cells can be employed, independently of the others, as they may be required. The silver being the most expensive metal, the zinc should completely surround it, so that the whole of the silver may be brought into action. Where a battery is required to continue in action for a very long time, as for days or even weeks, a larger vessel, to contain more dilute acid, must be used: for electro-metallurgical purposes it has been hitherto found most economical to use a vessel of a size sufficient to hold liquid to last for seven or ten days.

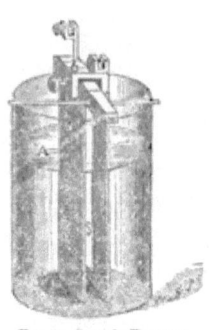

The form of battery now most universally employed for these purposes consists of a piece of silver (s), on the top of which is fixed a beam of wood (w), to prevent contact with the silver. A binding screw is soldered on to the silver to connect it to any required object. A strip of zinc (z), varying at the fancy of the operator from one-half to the entire width of the silver, is placed on each side of the wood, and both are held in their place by a binding screw (b), sufficiently wide to embrace the zincs and wood. These batteries vary from the size of a tumbler to a 10- or 12-gallon vessel. In the very extensive application of this battery to the arts, the little pieces of zinc which remain undissolved in the battery form an important consideration to the

Fig. 9. Smee's Battery, for Electrotype.

manufacturer. Some distil the mercury from them, others sell them to the zinc works, whilst others have never turned them to any account at all, waiting patiently in the hope that some more beneficial application of them might be discovered. These latter have hundredweights of odds and ends in hand which they are desirous to employ. After considering the matter carefully, I have to propose the following use for them; in fact, I make them the positive pole of a battery, by placing them at the bottom of a vessel and covering them with mercury. A silver wire is then placed down a glass tube into the quicksilver, so that the wire may nowhere touch the dilute sulphuric acid with which the vessel is filled, but simply make a good metallic communication with the mercury. At the other end of the wire a binding screw may be attached, for the convenience of the operator. The platinized silver plate (s) is then to be immersed in the fluid, and placed as near to the mercury as possible, without actually being in contact, whilst no part of it should be more than three inches from it, as a considerable reduction of power would then ensue. This form of battery may be fairly called the Odds-and-Ends Battery; and though not so philosophical an instrument in its construction as the form last described, yet no manufacturer should

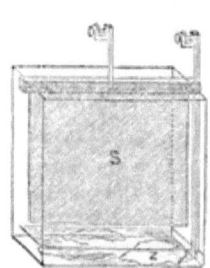

be without one to use up the scraps from his other batteries; and I must say this instrument requires less trouble in its manipulation than any other form I have ever seen. An odds-and-ends compound battery, which will only require a binding screw at each end, may be made by placing the mercury and zinc at the bottom of a many-celled porcelain trough; the platinized silver should be cut into suitable squares, leaving a narrow slip to connect it with the next cell. The strip must be placed in a glass tube, or covered with any non-conducting substance, leaving the end only to dip in the mercury of the next cell. A series of little

Fig. 10. Smee's Odds-and-Ends Battery.

glasses may be used instead of the many-celled trough for some purposes. The only objection which I have found in this form of compound battery is the possibility of the zinc in one cell being completely exhausted, when the silver wire will begin to dissolve; in all other respects it is a delightful instrument when you do not care about obtaining the maximum of power, and you can obtain the galvanic principle by this means at a lower cost than by any other way. The odds-and-ends battery is admirably adapted for gilding and plating, or it may be employed for any operation that requires much time for its performance. The charge for this battery might contain one-third by measure of strong sulphuric acid, as the local action is very trifling; but it is found more advisable not to employ the solution so strong, as, when nearly exhausted, the sulphate of zinc will sometimes envelope the zinc and mercury, and prevent further action before the top part of the liquid is fully saturated. An advantage of this instrument is, that spelter, or raw zinc, may be used instead of manufactured zinc, and that no mercury is wasted, as the whole is left after the solution of the zinc.

" When we desire to employ a battery for manufacturing purposes, it might be as well in some cases to remove the sulphate of zinc as soon as formed, by means of a syphon tube passing to the bottom of the vessel, while fresh acid is continually supplied at the top; but this is not generally necessary. For these purposes the battery should be so constructed, that any of the zinc plates, when worn out, can be readily replaced. There are many other forms which may be adopted, as the circular with the zinc outside; or it may be used as a tumbler battery.

" The characteristic of this battery is the great quantity of electricity produced, and its simplicity; moreover, it requires but very little trouble in its manipulation. The zinc seldom demands but one amalgamation, as that will generally last till the metal is all dissolved. It is very important to use for batteries zinc as pure as possible, for by that means the chance of local action is materially lessened. The manufacturers of zinc plates have a trick which is very fatal to this metal, for they buy up the refuse or waste pieces which frequently contain solder, a composition of lead and tin, and melt them with the raw zinc. This mixture always tells its tale during the action of the battery, as a light spongy flocculent precipitate rises to the top of the liquid, which is metallic tin, and when any particle touches the zinc a little local battery is formed, which causes great waste of metal.

" In using this battery it is important that no salt of copper, lead, or other base metal be dropped into the exciting fluid, as by that means the silver would become coated therewith; the plain consequence being, that a surface of copper, instead of that of the finely-divided platinum, is presented to the fluid. From a want of knowledge of this fact, in some who have used the battery, I have seen the negative metal covered with copper, which, finally becoming oxidated, rendered the platinum useless. When this takes place, it is best removed by immersing the plate in dilute sulphuric acid, to which a few drops of nitro-muriate of platinum should be previously added; by this process the baser metals are dissolved and metallic platinum thrown down. Some manufacturers prefer dipping the silver into a solution of this sort every week. In this battery the zinc is never reduced upon the negative metal, from the sulphate of zinc formed during the action of the battery, so long as the exciting fluid contains any acid at all. Other interesting matter connected with this subject will be detailed when treating of the reduction of zinc."

After explaining the difference between his battery and the two other batteries, he finishes thus :—

"Professor Daniell's excellent invention being distinguished by its constancy; Mr. Grove's powerful battery, by its intensity; and my own, by the cheapness with which the quantity of electricity may be developed, and by its simplicity. By some it (Smee's battery) has been too much extolled, by others too much blamed. Notwithstanding the mis-statements on both sides, it has fully stood the test of time, and has been employed by the public in a manner which I had not even hoped. The reason they prefer it for general and especially for manufacturing purposes, appears to be, that it does not require the use of porous tubes or of the strong acids, and that it does not give off poisonous fumes. It usually continues in active operation for six, eight, ten, or more days, when a sufficiency of acid is supplied to it. The zinc frequently demands but one amalgamation; and the time required either for setting it in action, or for maintaining its operation, is comparatively not worth a thought; and, lastly, the expense of working it is reduced to the lowest possible amount, being exactly proportionate to the power obtained.

"Although theoretically it is not absolutely constant, yet practically, for the purposes of the electro-metallurgist, its constancy remains for two or three days, or, in other words, until the battery is nearly exhausted; and then, to replenish the solution of zinc with a fresh supply of dilute acid will not occupy more than half a minute. In recording my own experience of its practical, though not of its absolute constancy, I can at the same time conjoin the testimony of some of the most extensive manufacturers in this country. By the practical manufacturer this instrument is re-charged with acid, at intervals varying from three days to a fortnight, according to the size of the vessel containing the acid. Whilst upon the use of the battery, I may state that the platinum, with proper care, never wears off the silver, and that the platinized silver never undergoes the slightest change, or is affected by the slightest local action.

"Perhaps I may be expected to give an approximation to the relative cost of working the three batteries. In mine it is the cost of the zinc dissolved by the acid: zinc + acid + a local action. In Daniell's battery, it is zinc + acid + sulphate of copper + much local action. Each cell of this, to do any given amount of work, would cost about twice as much as mine. In Grove's battery it is zinc + acid + nitric acid reduced by the hydrogen + nitric acid combined with ammonia formed during the action of the battery + extensive waste of the zinc = about three times as much as mine."

---

## VI.

**ON THE PRODUCTION OF ELECTROTYPES.** By ALFRED SMEE, Esq., Surgeon. ('London and Edinburgh Philosophical Magazine and Journal of Science,' April 21st, 1840.)

THE mode of taking copies of medals by the galvanic current is deservedly occupying much of public attention, and each is striving to add his mite to the perfection of this elegant and useful process. There are two or three points to which I am desirous of drawing the attention of your readers, as they appear to open a new and important field for investigation for which I have not the time at present. With regard to the precipitation of the copper, I beg leave to submit a modification of a plan first proposed by Mr. Mason, but I believe also contemporaneously used by other persons, that of making copper form the oxygen side of the battery, which being dissolved is again thrown down at the platina or hydrogen end upon the medal or cast put for its reception.

The mode which I adopt is, first to obtain a long dish or trough, and then to place a wire in the inside along its bottom, which is connected to the zinc of one of the cells of my battery along the opposite side of the vessel; a large piece of copper is placed in connection with the silver of the battery, and a solution of sulphate of copper is then added. By this arrangement the current is generated at the zinc, passes to the medal, reduces the copper whilst the oxygen and acid are transferred to the refuse copper, and dissolves a corresponding quantity of copper, and by this means the solution is always kept saturated with the metal.

When medals are to be copied, they are singly placed in contact with the wire in connection with the zinc of the battery, and in this way many may be done in the same vessel, and either may be taken out and examined without the slightest interruption to the others. The rapidity of the process may be increased without detriment by the use of two to six or even more cells of the battery, as the copper will still be extremely tough. It will be found that my battery will require not the slightest alteration, except once a day, when the liquid should be changed. I have tried other solutions of copper, such as the nitrate: but although the process is hastened, the metal is apt to be brittle, or have other imperfections.

When engraved plates are to be copied, the first copy is in basso-rilievo, and therefore a second is required to be made which is in "intaglio," and then ready for printing. Copies may even be taken of non-conducting substances, as woodcuts, &c., by brushing them over with black-lead, taking care that the copper wire is in good contact with the plumbago.

The great advantages of this mode of proceeding above all others are: first, the quality of the copper is far better than when reduced in the usual way as described by Messrs. Spencer and Solly—this advantage is owing to the use of the copper at the oxygen end as suggested by Mr. Mason; secondly, all the plates or medals, for there is no limit to the number, are in the same vessel; thirdly, the process may be hurried or retarded, according as the number of plates of the battery are increased or diminished; fourthly, the plates will not require to be interfered with till the precipitation is completely finished, and there are even many other more trifling advantages which it would be tedious to enumerate.

The mode of proceeding here detailed differs but little from others which have been described; but these trifling differences are so important in practice, that this mode will probably supersede every other. In fact, I have had the pleasure of seeing many most valuable copper-plates subjected to this process, and the specimen which accompanies this paper I believe is the first which has ever undergone the ordeal of having the large number of impressions, required for any publication, printed from it. Of course it is a perfect facsimile, and therefore this method would be of the greatest importance to bankers for their notes, and is far superior to Mr. Perkins's apparatus for the multiplication of plates, because in that case they almost invariably require to be touched up afterwards, and therefore absolute identity is destroyed. The cost of their manufacture would be trifling, being merely the value of the zinc * dissolved in the battery, and a pound of zinc of the value of sixpence would produce a copper-plate weighing about two pounds; and I trust that copper will again, from its beauty, take the place of steel engravings.

So much for the precipitation of the copper: and the next thing to which I have to direct your attention, is a mode of making copper-plate engraving without an engraving in the first instance. This is done by drawing upon a smooth piece of copper (such as a plate used for engraving) with any thick varnish or pigment insoluble in water, and then exposing the plate in the usual way to the influence of the current, when first copper will be thrown down upon the uncovered parts and will gradually grow over the drawing, and the electrotype when removed will be ready for printing. A practical difficulty arises in the application of this for the arts, as unless very thick oil paint is used, sufficient depth is not obtained to hold the ink. However, judging from the sharpness of the edges of the lines, I have but little doubt that this difficulty may be overcome by those who are accustomed to drawing; and it possesses, as an additional advantage to its cheapness, the valuable property of not requiring the artist to reverse the design. An opposite effect to this may be produced by placing a piece of copper similarly drawn upon at the oxygen end of the battery, when the metal will be acted upon, leaving a drawing in basso-rilievo.

## No. VII.

### ON THE FERROSESQUICYANURET OF POTASSIUM. By ALFRED SMEE, Esq., Surgeon. (' London and Edinburgh Philosophical Magazine and Journal of Science,' September 1840.)

THE action of chlorine upon the ferrocyanuret of potassium is a subject of much interest to the chemist, and has not been examined to any extent in this country. It therefore has been my endeavour to investigate this action carefully, and to see under what circumstances the change from the ferrocyanate into the ferrosesquicyanuret takes place; and the methods which are here detailed to obtain this latter salt uncontaminated with impurities, will be found free from the difficulties and uncertainties attending on the present mode of preparing it.

When a current of chlorine is passed through a solution of ferrocyanate of potassa, or an aqueous solution of that gas is added to it in certain quantities, the persalts of iron are not precipitated. This solution has no

---

* The zinc in the fluid might be precipitated as a carbonate, for which there is great demand in the arts, and thereby the expense of the electrotype would be further diminished.

smell of chlorine, and is changed from a yellow colour to a dark red, and deposits on evaporation red crystals. A similar change takes place when bromine is added to the ferrocyanate, and in both cases the weight of the entire red mass is equal to that of the yellow ferrocyanate, plus the weight of the chlorine or bromine used, but minus the quantity of water which the yellow crystals are known to contain. This indicates, first, that the red crystals are anhydrous; and, secondly, that the chlorine or bromine is actually absorbed by the salt. The former fact is confirmed by heating the red precipitate in a test tube, when no water is given off; and the latter fact is also proved by the evolution of chlorine or bromine, on the addition of two or three drops of strong heated sulphuric acid to a few grains of red salt.

When heated alcohol is added to this red mass, a small portion is dissolved, which is again deposited when the spirit is evaporated. This salt by its characters is known to be either the bromide or the chloride of potassium. By this method the red ferrocyanate of potassa, which is insoluble in alcohol, becomes purified: but this is a troublesome and expensive process, as the bromide or chloride is but little soluble in the spirit, and therefore a large quantity must be used.

About half an equivalent of chlorine or bromine is required to effect this change, and great care must be employed to prevent excess of these substances, as they are apt to react upon a portion of the salt. The liquid in this case contains Prussian blue dissolved, which materially discolours the salts, and it can only be precipitated from the solution by the addition of neutral salts, as sulphate of soda, which renders the red ferrocyanate impure. In a similar manner, chloride of soda, as might be expected, forms the red ferrocyanate of potassa.

From the foregoing details a knowledge is obtained of the action of chlorine and bromine upon the ferrocyanate, for we have seen that chloride and bromide of potassium is formed, and that one-half an equivalent of these substances is necessary for this change. Now it is manifest that half an equivalent of potassium is removed from the ferrocyanate, so that the new salt, instead of consisting of iron one equivalent, potassium two equivalents, cyanogen three equivalents, contains iron one equivalent, potassium one and a-half equivalent, cyanogen three equivalents; and therefore it is rightly named the ferrosesquicyanuret of potassium: that half an equivalent of potassium has been removed from the salt, two or three experiments have verified.

The acids as a class will not effect a similar change, because as they combine not with potassium but with potassa, water must be decomposed, the oxygen uniting with the metal, and the hydrogen passing to the ferrocyanate, forming hydroferrocyanic acid.

A question naturally arises whether the potassium may not be removed from the ferrocyanuret by other processes, and we are led to try the action of the anions, and of these I attempted to add oxygen to the salts by the use of nitric acid. This acid, when added in small quantities to the yellow ferrocyanate, acts as the other acids by liberating hydroferrocyanic acid, which is speedily decomposed into a pale bluish cyanuret of iron. When, however, further additions of this acid are made, the potassium takes oxygen, forms potassa, deutoxide of nitrogen is evolved, and the solution becomes dark-coloured. This liquor, when neutralized with potassa, is found to give no precipitate with the persalts of iron, but forms Prussian blue with the protosalts of that metal. The rapidity of this change depends upon the heat of the solution, for when warm the effect takes place immediately, whilst, on the contrary, two or three days are required at a low temperature. When evaporated, a large quantity of nitrate of potassa is deposited; and, lastly, some red crystals are formed. When acid is more used, the ferrocyanate is totally decomposed; the black mass which is the result has at first a sweet, but afterwards leaves a dis-agreeable metallic taste upon the palate. This process can never be used advantageously to form the ferrosesquicyanuret, from the quantity of acid which is required, the degree of nicety which must be employed to effect the change, and the impurity of the salt when obtained.

The next highly-oxygenated acid which we have to examine is the iodic: this when added to ferrocyanate of potash becomes decomposed, the oxygen passes to the potassium to form potassa, free iodine is evolved, and the potassa passes to another portion of iodic acid, and is precipitated as the iodate of potassa. The free iodine can be readily removed by agita-tion with a little ether, and in this way a tolerably pure ferrosesquicy-anuret of potassium can be extemporaneously obtained, for the solution contains but little iodate of potassa from its insolubility.*

Chloric acid operates in the same way as iodic acid, but is more diffi-cult of decomposition, and it requires the action of heat before the smell of chlorine is exhaled and the red ferrocyanate formed.

If chlorate of potassa be added to the ferrocyanate, and dilute sul-phuric acid be dropped into the solution, red ferrocyanate of potash will also be formed.

Bromic acid will not act upon the ferrocyanate with the production of the ferrosesquicyanuret, but acts as other acids in forming Prussian blue.

A great variety of other oxyacids have been tried, but none were found to part with their oxygen.

When a large quantity of peroxide of manganese in fine powder is added to a solution of the ferrocyanate of potash, and the mixture digested for a considerable time, the ferrocyanate becomes converted into the ferrosesquicyanuret, and on evaporation crystals of the most beautiful ruby red are obtained. The salt thus procured appears to be very pure.

If a little dilute sulphuric acid be added to the solution in conjunction with the peroxide of manganese, the action takes place more quickly, but sulphate of potassa is formed, which is a great disadvantage.

The last process in which nascent oxygen contributes to the formation of ferrosesquicyanuret of potassium, is, perhaps, one of the most elegant, efficient, and simple processes in the whole range of chemistry. This mode I was induced to follow from the consideration, that as nascent oxygen effects a change of the yellow to the red ferrocyanate of potassa, a similar change must be produced by its being subjected to a galvanic current. Accordingly some solution of the salt was placed in a tube bent

---

* This elegant process can be employed with advantage when a small quantity of the salt is suddenly wanted, as it scarcely requires a minute to effect.

like a syphon, and at the bottom a piece of tow was thrust, in order that a separation might so far be effected, that the solution on one side could not readily pass to the solution on the other. Having thus completed the arrangement, a galvanic circuit was passed through the fluid; when at the cathode, hydrogen was evolved, and at the anode no oxygen, on the contrary, was given off, but the solution became of a dark colour. The dark solution was found to precipitate only the protosalts of iron, and on evaporation deposited red crystals of the ferrosesquicyanuret, but at the cathode potash was discovered. The *rationale* of this change may be deduced from circumstances attending slight alterations of arrangement: for if on the zinc side of the bent tube a saturated solution of the ferrocyanate be placed, and on the platinum side distilled water, and then the galvanic circuit be completed, potash will appear at the platinode, and red ferrocyanate at the zincode. On the contrary, if the distilled water is placed at the zinc side and the ferrocyanate at the platinum side, potash is left at the platinode, whilst at the zincode no red ferrocyanate is found, but a substance which does not redden litmus-paper, and which speedily decomposes into Prussian blue: this is probably ferrocyanogen. Thus it appears that one equivalent of the yellow ferrocyanate is decomposed, the free potash travelling one way and the hydroferrocyanic acid the other; the oxygen unites with the hydrogen of the acid and sets ferrocyanogen at liberty; this again unites with an equivalent of ferrocyanuret of potassium to form the ferrosesquicyanuret.

Various other attempts were made to form the red ferrocyanate by oxygen, such as heating it with nitrate of potassa, but the mixture exploded at a temperature below redness.

When a mixture of powdered ferrocyanate and peroxide of manganese was heated together, no ferrosesquicyanuret was formed. Several other oxides, as those of mercury, silver, tin, iron, &c. &c., were digested with ferrocyanate of potassa, but none that were tried, except the peroxide of manganese, formed the red ferrocyanate; many of them were converted into cyanurets.

A current of oxygen gas passed through the solution of the salt produces no alteration, showing that the gas must be in a nascent state to cause the change.

The next substance we have to examine is phosphorus, and its action is somewhat remarkable; for little or no change is effected by the addition of an alcoholic or etherial solution of phosphorus. When a piece of phosphorus is also placed in a solution of the ferrocyanate, or when phosphorus is heated with powdered ferrocyanate, the sesquicyanuret is not produced; but if a stick of phosphorus is placed in a bottle containing a solution of the salt, and only a portion of it is covered with the liquor, the phosphorus gradually burns away, the solution becomes sour and red, and ceases to precipitate the persalts of iron. This change takes place with a rapidity exactly proportionate to the wasting of the phosphorus; for if the temperature is below 45°, but little action takes place, but above 60° the reddening is very speedily produced. The red solution is not to be tested with the salt of iron whilst it is acid, for in that case a copious greenish-white precipitate is produced of phosphate of iron; but after it has been neutralized with potassa, a solution of baryta is to be added, to throw down the phosphate, and a drop of dilute sulphuric acid may then be added to remove any excess of baryta.

The solution will now be found not to precipitate persalts of iron, but, on the contrary, a large quantity of Prussian blue is produced with the protosalts. The actual combustion of the phosphorus seems essential to this change; for if the water in which phosphorus has been allowed to burn be added to the solution of the ferrocyanate, a similar change will not be produced. The cause of this change appears paradoxical, for phosphorus has in other instances a deoxidizing agency, so that a piece placed in a solution of either gold, silver, platinum, or copper, has the metal precipitated upon it. Perhaps it depends upon decomposition of water and the formation of phosphuretted hydrogen; for a narrow bottle, to which air has but limited access, is more favourable to the change than a wide vessel. If this explanation is correct, the action of phosphorus must be classed with the other oxygenating substances, for oxygen, and not phosphorus, removes the potassium.*

No mode of abstracting the half equivalent of potassium by sulphur is known; for if half an equivalent of sulphur be heated with powdered ferrocyanuret, the ferrosesquicyanuret is not produced, and the alcoholic or terebinthine solution of sulphur, added to a solution of the ferrocyanuret, also failed to produce this change. Even nascent sulphur arising from the decomposition of sulphuret of potash by an acid did not produce any effect.†

A current of cyanogen gas passed through a solution of the salt is gradually absorbed, and it becomes of a very dark colour, but red ferrocyanate is not formed.

Doubtless many may be surprised that the action of iodine has not been adverted to before, and more especially that it should not have been mentioned with chlorine and bromine, as to these it has a striking analogy in most of its properties; but in reality little resemblance exists between the action of iodine on the ferrocyanate of potassa, and that of chlorine and bromine, as we shall immediately see. If iodine is added to a solution of the salt, it speedily becomes dissolved, the solution turning to a dark red, and gives a blue precipitate with salts of either oxide of iron. One equivalent of ferrocyanate of potash dissolves about one equivalent of iodine, which remains in great part uncombined in solution. If the solution is allowed spontaneously to evaporate, the free iodine passes off, and a whitish uncrystallized mass is obtained which has no free iodine, but hydriodate of potassa in its composition. This gives a precipitate with both oxides of iron. Now there is a ready method of ascertaining how much iodine the ferrocyanate will not only dissolve, but combine with, and for this purpose a definite quantity of the salt is to be dissolved in a small quantity of water, and then placed in a phial. Upon the solution ether is to be poured, then the iodine is to be added gradually, when as soon as the ether is discoloured the saturation is known to be effected. Brisk and continued agitation must follow each addition of the

* No change takes place if the phosphorus is completely under the solution of the salt.

† It is foreign to this paper to describe the sulphocyanuret of potassium.

iodine, in order that the ether may part with any iodine previously to the point of saturation. When evaporated to dryness, more of the iodine is evolved, but still hydriodate of potash may be abstracted from the mass by alcohol. When all the iodine is removed from the mass, a result which is known by its not discolouring starch upon the addition of nitric acid, it still retains its power of forming Prussian blue with salts of either oxide of iron, and still presents the same indisposition to crystallize, for it neither shows itself as the yellow nor the red ferrocyanate of potash, but as a compound having properties intermediate with both.

When iodide of potassium is added to the ferrosesquicyanuret, iodine is evolved, the solution loses its red colour, and the salt possesses the characters similar to the mass obtained by the action of iodine on the ferrocyanate of potash. Thus it is evident that if a solution of persulphate of iron be treated with the red ferrocyanate whilst an iodide is present, Prussian blue will be formed.

Whether this is really a mixture of the ferrocyanuret and ferrosesquicyanuret or a distinct compound, it is difficult to determine, but the latter is rendered probable from its generally presenting itself as an amorphous mass; yet, however, when the purified mixture is dissolved two or three times in water, a dark mass is deposited, and at last crystals of the yellow salt are formed.

Every method which has been discovered of converting the ferrocyanate of potassa into the ferrosesquicyanuret has now been detailed, and we have seen that they may each be referred to the class of anions, for of the cathions the powerful agency of potassium was unable to effect this change.

Upon the first formation of the ferrosesquicyanuret the colour will occasionally be a very dark red, but this is an adventitious, not a necessary property; for when prepared by peroxide of manganese or chloride of soda, it does not possess this dark colour. If the red crystals be carefully picked and re-dissolved, in no instance is this seen, and in every case where the dark red exists it yields to liquor ammoniæ or potassæ, with the production of a small quantity of the ferrocyanate.

The ferrosesquicyanuret, however prepared, has the same peculiar properties. It has been already mentioned that the protosalts are precipitated blue, whilst the persalts are not effected by this agent; however, the solution in the latter case is always much darkened, and after a time a small quantity of dark-coloured substance is deposited. The mode of preparation of the ferrosesquicyanuret does not influence this result.

With almost every acid, especially if heat be applied, Prussian blue is formed and hydrocyanic acid is given off; and thus upon testing for minute quantities of metal, care must be taken to prevent any excess of acid, as in that case the chemist would find iron in everything he examines. With excess of alkali, on the contrary, no precipitate of Prussian blue is produced; and therefore if search be made for that most useful of all metals, the experiment would declare that iron had no real existence: but if the golden mean be employed, or the solution be but very slightly acid, the ferrosesquicyanuret, as well as the ferrocyanuret, become most valuable and delicate tests, the one for the peroxide, the other for the protoxide of that metal.

The change by chlorine and bromine has been shown to result from the abstraction of the half equivalent of potassium by the formation of chloride or bromide of that metal, and therefore the ferrosesquicyanuret is impure till that is removed by alcohol. We have seen also that the change may be effected by the iodic, nitric, and chloric acids, but by these methods the salt is also contaminated to a great extent by the nitrate of potash, but to a much less extent with the chlorate, and scarcely at all with the iodate; with phosphorus the salt in a very impure state may still be made. With peroxide of manganese, however, and the galvanic current, it may be made of absolute purity.

This last mode will probably supersede entirely every other mode of preparation, as with a galvanic battery a large quantity can be readily made. The battery which I have used for these experiments is the platinized silver, which from its simplicity is so well adapted for general purposes, and suitable for long-continued action.

### TABLE OF DECOMPOSITIONS.

#### *By Chlorine and Bromine.*

$$
\left. \begin{array}{l} \text{1 eq. ferrocyanate} \\ \text{of potassa} \end{array} \right\} = \left\{ \begin{array}{l} \text{Iron 1} \\ \text{Cyanogen 3} \\ \text{Potassa 2} \end{array} \right. \left\{ \begin{array}{l} = \text{1 eq. red ferro-} \\ \quad \text{cyanate} \end{array} \right. \left\{ \begin{array}{l} \text{Iron 1.} \\ \text{Cyanogen 3.} \\ \text{Potassium 1.} \end{array} \right.
$$

$\frac{1}{2}$ eq. of chlorine $\qquad\qquad\qquad\qquad\qquad\qquad$ $\frac{1}{2}$ eq. chloride of potassium.

Bromine acts in the same way.

#### *By the Galvanic Current.*

$$
\left. \begin{array}{l} \text{1 eq. ferrocyanate} \\ \text{of potassa} \end{array} \right\} = \left\{ \begin{array}{l} \text{Iron 1} \\ \text{Cyanogen 3} \\ \text{Potassium 2} \end{array} \right. \left\{ \begin{array}{l} = \text{1 eq. red ferro-} \\ \quad \text{cyanate} \end{array} \right. \left\{ \begin{array}{l} \text{Iron 1.} \\ \text{Cyanogen 3.} \\ \text{Potassium 1}\frac{1}{2}. \end{array} \right.
$$

$\frac{1}{2}$ eq. of oxygen. $\qquad\qquad\qquad\qquad\qquad\qquad$ $\frac{1}{2}$ eq. of potassa.
$\frac{1}{2}$ eq. of hydrogen from decomposition $\qquad$ $\frac{1}{2}$ eq. of hydrogen evolved.
$\qquad\qquad$ of water.

The action of the acids, &c., has been already sufficiently adverted to.

### TABLE OF PRECIPITATES WITH THE IODO-FERROCYANATE OF POTASSA PURE.

| | |
|---|---|
| Gold . . . . . . | solution red, no precipitate. |
| Platinum . . . . | a little white deposit. |
| Mercury, bichloride | white, becoming green. |
| Lead . . . . . . | white, abundant. |
| Silver . . . . . | white, with a little reddish tinge. |
| Bismuth . . . . | white, afterwards yellow. |
| Zinc . . . . . . | white. |
| Copper . . . . . | dark brown. |
| Iron protosalts . . | Prussian blue. |
| Iron persalts . . . | Prussian blue. |

### TABLE OF PRECIPITATES WITH THE RED FERROCYANATE OF POTASSA.

| | | |
|---|---|---|
| Gold | chloride | solution darker, no precipitate. |
| Platina | chloride | solution darker, small crystals deposited. |
| Palladium | nitrate | red-brown precipitate. |
| Silver | nitrate. sulphate. acetate. | deep orange. |
| Nickel | nitrate | red brown. |
| Copper | sulphate | yellow brown. |
| | ammoniuret | deep-greenish brown. |
| Mercury | protonitrate | at first yellow brown, then white, then green. |
| | bichloride | none. |
| Bismuth | nitrate | pale yellow brown. |
| Tin | protochloride | white, gelatinous. |
| Iron | protosulphate | Prussian blue. |
| | persulphate | none, with iodide, potassium, Prussian blue. |
| Antimony | potassio-tartrate | none. |
| Manganese | chloride | sepia. |
| Cobalt | chloride | chocolate brown. |
| Zinc | sulphate | buff. |
| Cadmium | sulphate | pale yellow. |
| Curanium | nitrate | deep red brown. |
| Lead | acetate | solution brownish, none. |
| Alumina | acetate | none. |
| Baryta | muriate nitrate | none. |
| Strontia | nitrate | none. |
| Lime | muriate | none. |

---

### No. VIII.

### ELEMENTS OF ELECTRO-METALLURGY. By ALFRED SMEE.

THE 'Elements of Electro-Metallurgy' was first issued to the public on the 26th December, 1840. The first edition was speedily sold off, and the second edition appeared at first in parts, thus: the first forty pages appeared on the 1st April, 1842; forty pages more were ready on the 1st May; the third forty on the 1st July; the succeeding forty on the 1st August; the fifth part, containing forty-four pages, was published 1st September; the sixth part, to the 236th page, on the 1st October; the next forty pages on the 1st November, and the remainder on the 1st of December, when all the parts were published in one volume.

During these two years (1840 to 1842) Alfred Smee had prosecuted his labours in this branch of knowledge to such an extent that the second edition of the 'Elements of Electro-Metallurgy' bore rather the feature of a new treatise than of a second edition; for the work had been doubled in bulk and partly re-written.

The book commences with a brief but lucid exposition of galvanism, and then proceeds to describe the most approved batteries, concluding with a general view of the one invented by himself, which has been employed by him in all the processes of electro-metallurgy. The second part of Electro-Metallurgy treats of the apparatus to be employed for the reduction of the metals; of the substances capable of receiving the metallic deposit; and of the laws regulating the reduction of the metals.

Although the laws which regulate the deposit of every metal appear to be the same, and although they are very simple, yet they cost Mr. Smee much labour for their development. He states them as follows:—

Law 1.—The metals are invariably thrown down as a black powder, when the current of electricity is so strong in relation to the strength of the solution, that hydrogen is evolved from the negative plate of the decomposition cell.

Law 2.—Every metal is thrown down in a crystalline state, when there is no evolution of gas from the negative plate, or no tendency thereto.

Law 3.—Metals are reduced in the reguline state when the quantity of electricity in relation to the strength of the solution is insufficient to cause the production of hydrogen on the negative plate in the decomposition trough, and yet the quantity of electricity very nearly suffices to induce that phenomenon. For further information on the reduction of metals I refer the reader to the paper read before the Royal Society, 9th of March, 1843, at page 188.

The third part of Electro-Metallurgy treats of electro-gilding, electro-plating, &c.; of coppering non-metallic substances, medallions, fruit, vegetables, baskets, earthenware, &c.

In the fourth part we learn the various applications of the reduction of metals by galvanism: as the multiplication of coins and medals; of copying seals; of plaster casts, &c.; of the multiplication of brasses; of making dies from embossed surfaces; of the manufacture of moulds from fruits, vegetables, &c.; of the application of electro-metallurgy to sculpture and other purposes.

Part the fifth treats of the electrotype: as the multiplication of type; of plain copper-plates; of copying engraved copper-plates; of the multiplication of steel plates; of woodcuts; of the daguerreotype.

The sixth and last part of this work treats of galvanic etching.

Such is the plan of Smee's 'Elements of Electro-Metallurgy.' In order to show more thoroughly how and to what extent the author of this work contributed towards the discoveries which led to the application of this science not only in this country but throughout the civilized world, I here transcribe its history as it is given in every edition of Smee's 'Elements of Electro-Metallurgy.'

" We have not," he says, " to extend our inquiry into remote periods to trace the history of the arts of working in metals by the galvanic fluid, for truly it may be said that this art belongs to our own time, and is a characteristic of the present age. Whilst, however, we pursue our investigations into the history of this subject, we find that it has had by no means a sudden origin: for, at different periods, various persons have, by degrees, worked out one fact after another, till the comprehensive science has been developed. Electro-Metallurgy may be said to have had its origin in the discovery of the constant battery by Professor Daniell, for in that instrument the copper is continually reduced upon the negative plate. In his first experiment, this distinguished author observed, on removing a piece of the reduced copper from a platina electrode, that scratches on the latter were copied with accuracy on the copper. In this experiment we have the electrotype; but the author, in the first paper detailing his experiments, had devoted all his attention and centred all his energies to the construction of the battery itself, and this valuable fact attracted but little of his notice.

"It was but a short time after the discovery of this battery that Mr. De la Rue experimented on its properties. In a paper printed in the 'Philosophical Magazine' for 1836, after describing a peculiar form of battery which he adopts, the following remarkable passage is found:— 'The copper-plate is also covered with a coating of metallic copper, which is continually being deposited; and so perfect is the sheet of copper thus formed, that, being stripped off, it has the counterfeit of every scratch of the plate on which it is deposited!' This paper seems to have attracted very little attention; and, what seems still more singular, the author, although well qualified, from his scientific attainments, to have applied these facts, never thought of any practical benefit to which this experiment might lead.

"In this state the subject remained till October 1838, when Professor Jacobi first announced that he could employ the reduction of copper, by galvanic agency, for the purposes of the arts. His process was called galvano-plastic. Immediately upon his discovery being announced in this country, in 1839, Mr. Spencer stated that he had executed some medals in copper, to which the public afterwards gave the name of electrotypes or voltatypes, or, what is better, electro-medallions." The exact value of these primary discoveries "is simply the idea of the application of these facts; but that idea has been everything for Electro-Metallurgy. The only apparatus which Mr. Spencer employed was, in fact, a simple Daniell's battery. He employed various metals for the reception of the precipitated metal, which, however, was nothing new; but he does not seem to have succeeded with any non-conducting substances. He executed medals, and perhaps duplicate copper-plates; but he does not give any details as to the different methods for the reduction of the copper in different states, neither did he succeed with the reduction of any other metal. However, to Mr. Spencer the British public are principally indebted for the idea of the electrotype; and perhaps the idea, as far as relates to its application in Great Britain, originated entirely with himself. I may further notice, in order to confirm what I have already stated, that the galvano-plastics of Jacobi, and the electrotype of Spencer, are not inventions the result of inductive reasoning and laborious research, like Professor Wheatstone's electro-telegraph, or certain elaborate machines, but merely an application of a fact formerly known to Daniell, recorded particularly by De la Rue, and observed by hundreds of others; that both Spencer and Jacobi could work only in copper, and in no other metal; whilst, had they prosecuted their subject as a science, they would have seen that the same laws regulate the reduction of all the metals.

"Electro-Metallurgy, as first made known to the world by Jacobi and Spencer, was the simplest of all inventions—the application of a fact known and recorded previously; and it forms another instance of an invention of the greatest magnitude and utility to mankind, arising from the most simple beginnings.

"The next discovery, which is fully equal in value to the idea of the electrotype itself, was made by Mr. Murray. He found out that non-conducting substances might have metallic copper thrown down upon them by previously applying black lead. Mr. Murray's process is extremely simple and absolutely perfect. The first application of this invention was made in January 1840; but it is to be lamented that he did not further extend its application and publish his researches, for his method was communicated orally, in the conversaziones of the Royal Institution, and not by any paper. I lay particular stress upon the value and perfection of plumbago, because some have denied its applicability; and the reader will find, throughout the whole of the work, that I have extended the use of the substance, to the benefit of the public and to the fame of the inventor. I have made very extensive inquiries in order to ascertain who really first used plumbago for this purpose, and I have the testimony of several authorities that it was Mr. Murray, whose claim, therefore, to this invention is rendered quite indisputable. . . . .

"Up to April 1840, the single-cell apparatus was invariably used, but then Mr. Mason very ingeniously devised another mode by which the reduction might be effected. He used the single-cell apparatus as a Daniell's battery, which he connected with another cell to reduce another metal. In the second cell he used a copper positive electrode, which was dissolved during the action. By this means he made two metals by one pound of zinc, or, in other words, obtained two equivalents of copper for one of zinc.

"In the 'London Journal' for April 1840, as far as I know, is contained the first specimen of printing from an electrotype, by Newton. It is a small rough sketch, but as the first of the kind is peculiarly interesting.

"The laws regulating the reduction of all metals in different states were first given in this work, as the result of my own discoveries. By these we can throw down gold, silver, platinum, palladium, copper, iron, and almost all other metals in three states; namely, as a black powder, as a crystalline deposit, or as a flexible plate. These laws appear to me at once to raise the isolated facts known as the electrotype into a science, and to add electro-metallurgy as an auxiliary to the noble arts of this country.

"The regulation of the power of the battery to the strength of the metallic solution also required an investigation of the principles which regulated the diffusion of the newly-formed salt, which is of great importance to the operator. In this work I have also appended data whereby the manufacturer may calculate the expense of particular processes before he adopts them. The formulæ for ascertaining the work that would be performed by a galvanic battery, under different circumstances, cannot fail to be of great utility to the workman, if he rightly employ them; and the intimate *rationale* of the motion of electricity in the battery must be a subject, at least, of great interest to all. The principle regulating the adhesion of the reduced metal is also one of paramount importance in all cases where it has to be removed from the plates on which it is deposited.

" The hundreds of experiments, I may even say the thousands, that have been tried to elucidate these laws (for this book is not a detail of experiments, but rather a digest of them), could never have been executed had I not first discovered my galvanic battery; for its simplicity alone enabled me, without any assistance, to undergo the laborious undertaking. I am fully aware that some may disagree with me as to the superiority of my battery over all others for experimental and manufacturing purposes. I shall not flinch on this account from stating its advantages, especially as they appear to me likely to contribute to general benefit.

" The value of the battery process over all others is its applicability to all cases; moreover, when we use a single cell of the battery, the quantity of the zinc dissolved to do any amount of work is the same, or even less, than attends the use of the other apparatus, because the local action in a battery of this construction is less than in the single-cell apparatus; and, lastly, the quality of the precipitated metal can be regulated with the utmost nicety; and I have no hesitation in stating that the battery process is the only one that ever can be employed by the manufacturer with advantage. . . . .

" The departments of electro-metallurgy comprising electro-gilding and plating, received great impulses from Elkington; some of his processes being most admirable. As far as gilding is concerned, he was anticipated by Brugnatelli nearly forty years ago, for which see letter of Brugnatelli to Van Mons, in the 'Phil. Mag.' for 1805, also 'Archives of Philosophical Knowledge.' The process by Brugnatelli differs in nothing from the one now employed, and doubtless ought to be considered as the introduction of electro-metallurgy, being the first instance in which any metal was ever reduced by galvanism for the purposes of the arts.

" The processes for platinating, palladiating, &c., rest upon the authority of this work; for hitherto the reduction of these metals, in any other state than that of the black powder, has been always considered impossible. The electro-metallurgist will be enabled, by the processes which he will find here fully described, to execute reliefs and intaglios in gold, and, in fact, in nearly every other metal; facts altogether new in science. The working of all other metals, as zinc, silver, &c. &c., except copper, is also due to the discovery of the laws regulating the precipitation of the metals.

" Every author has given directions for making moulds on plaster casts in metal; but it is singular that by no process hitherto known can a perfect reverse plaster be obtained. In investigating the cause of this, I soon discovered that the extreme porosity of the plaster was the block over which they had all stumbled, and the difficulty was overcome by rendering the plaster non-absorbent. In this work the reader will find that the copying of reliefs in plaster is brought to the utmost possible perfection, and by very simple means.

" The success of this department of my experiments has amply repaid me for my labours and expense; for there is not a town in England that I have happened to visit, and scarcely a street of this metropolis, where prepared plasters are not exposed to view for the purpose of alluring persons to follow the delightful recreation afforded by the practice of electro-metallurgy.

" The extended use of white-wax, bees'-wax, rosin, &c., for the electro-

metallurgist, I trust, will be found acceptable.   Their manipulation I have
given as the result of my own experience, and therefore, doubtless, those
who make a trade of working these substances will find the account not so
full as might have been expected or wished; yet I believe practice alone is
required to make the operator perfect in these arts.

" The application of electro-metallurgy to the copying of leaves, fruit,
&c., is for the first time described in this work.

" The new mode of etching here detailed, I confidently trust, will be
also found a valuable adjunct to the knowledge of the engraver.   The
principle which regulates the adhesion and non-adhesion of the plates will
enable the operator to conduct his operations with certainty — a circumstance of no small importance to the engraver, ignorance on this score
having already produced untoward results.  . . . .

" The laws which I have given in this work, and the universality of
their application, will doubtless influence importantly the attainment of
the grand object of using the galvanic fluid commonly among our manufacturers; and having thus, as I believe, raised the isolated facts called
the Electrotype into a vast and comprehensive science, a new name is
required which may be suitable to its importance, and embrace its various
applications.   The term which I have ventured to apply to the science is
Electro-Metallurgy, which comprises the principles regulating all the arts
of working in metals by the galvanic force; and the value of the new
nomenclature is evident when we consider that it takes in every mode by
which it is possible to work metals, either by dissolving or precipitating
them, by the agency of the voltaic current."  . . . .

*Directions for coppering fruit, vegetables, leaves, seeds, &c. from Smee's
 'Elements of Electro-Metallurgy,' page 221.*

" A pretty application of the art of coppering is suitable to horticulturists, as by its means fruit, vegetables, leaves, seeds, and various other
specimens may be coated with copper, either for ornament or for the
purpose of illustrating the size, form, and other peculiarities of the object.
Apples and pears may be very readily coppered; they are to be brushed
over with black-lead, and then a small pin is to be thrust in at the stalk :
to this a wire should be attached, which is connected with the zinc of the
battery.   It may then be placed in the solution, and the whole arrangement
completed by the insertion of a piece of copper, which is to be connected
with the silver of the battery.   In a similar manner cucumbers, gourds,
potatoes, carrots, and a hundred other vegetables, seeds, and roots can be
covered.   The form, after the process, is characteristic, and marks so
strongly the individual character of each variety, that the horticulturist
is at no loss to distinguish the specimens at once.   The condition in which
the copper is thrown down can, of course, be varied according to the laws
set forth in the last chapter.   For ornamental purposes the crystalline
copper is the most beautiful; but for a specimen intended to illustrate
the form of the object, the smooth copper is best adapted.   After the
objects are completely covered, the pin is to be withdrawn, which will
leave a little hole, and that enables the evaporating juices of the vegetable
to pass freely out, and thus promotes the complete drying of the encased
object.   A cucumber which I coated during the past summer appears now

to contain scarcely anything inside the copper, and the pears, apples, &c., consist of little else but the metallic coat. The botanist will readily perceive in what way this process may be employed for his advantage.

" The beauty of electro-coppered leaves, branches, and similar objects is surprising. I have a case of these specimens placed on a black ground, which no one would take to be productions of art. In the same room with them are a couple of those cases in which Ward has taught us to grow in this smoky metropolis some of the most interesting botanical specimens. In these cases are contained varieties of fairy-formed adiantums, verdant lycopodiums, brilliant orchideæ, rigid cacti, and creeping lygodiums, all growing in their natural luxuriance. The electro-coppered leaves, however, are beautiful when placed by the side of the productions of this miniature paradise; and when I state that the numerous hairs covering the leaves of a melostoma, and even the delicate hairs of the salvia, are all perfectly covered, the botanist must at once admit that these specimens have rather the minuteness of nature than the imperfections of art." He also shows how a beautiful effect of metallic surfaces may be obtained by the deposition of crystallized metal on baskets which, " filled with metallic fruit, leaves, insects, &c., might be used as ornaments for the drawing-room, and would greatly exceed in interest the usual appendages."

---

## No. IX.

### RECEIPT OF A WRITING INK made by ALFRED SMEE.

56 NUT-GALLS to 50 gallons of water; specific gravity 22.

15 lbs. copperas to 5 gallons of water.

15 lbs. of gum to 5 gallons of water.

1 gallon of pyroligneous acid.

¼ lb. corrosive sublimate.

Hot water to be poured on the gall-nuts, and this is to be allowed to stand about twenty-four hours.

The infusion of galls is then to be poured off, and the gum (previously mixed with the five gallons of water) to be first added; then the copperas, which also has been previously mixed with five gallons of water, the pyroligneous acid, and the corrosive sublimate are all to be mixed together. The whole to stand till the ink is dark enough for writing, when bottle off.

The specific gravity of ink, when made, to be 35–37.

The ink should be run through sieves four or five, or even six times, to make it clear.

## No. X.

## ON THE CAUSE OF THE REDUCTION OF METALS WHEN SOLUTIONS OF THEIR SALTS ARE SUBJECTED TO THE GALVANIC CURRENT. By Alfred Smee, Esq., F.R.S., Surgeon to the Bank of England, &c.* ('London, Edinburgh, and Dublin Philosophical Magazine, and Journal of Science,' December 1844.)

1. At the present time, when the new science of electro-metallurgy is improving and multiplying the arts of this already extensive manufacturing empire, there cannot be a subject more fit for the consideration of the Fellows of the Royal Society than the cause of metals being reduced when solutions of their salts are subjected to the voltaic circuit.

2. The opinions of philosophers upon this point, from the period when electricity first lent its mighty aid to chemists, are various. Some have supposed that hydrogen evolved by the decomposition of water reduces the metals, others that the poles directly attract the metals to their surfaces, and lately a paper has been printed in the Transactions of this Society whereby a new constitution of the salts is inferred; the acid and oxygen being supposed by electrolysis to pass in one direction, the metal in the other. The first opinion was put forward by Hisinger and Berzelius, and may be found in the 'Annales de Chimie,' vol. li. p. 174: "Il résulte de tous ces faits, que l'on a une idée fausse de la réduction opérée par l'électricité, puis qu'on l'attribue au dégagement de l'hydrogène, comment expliqueroit-on la réduction du fer et du zinc, qui ont la propriété de décomposer l'eau sans l'électricité."

A similar opinion has been advocated by Faraday in the 'Philosophical Transactions,' and he applied a new name to this kind of action, giving it the term electro-chemical action. The second hypothesis was promulgated by Sir Humphry Davy, who states, "that hydrogen, the alkaline substances, the metals, and certain metallic oxides are attracted by negatively electrified metallic surfaces, and repelled by positively electrified metallic surfaces; and contrariwise, that oxygen and acid substances are attracted by positively electrified metallic surfaces, and these attractive and repulsive forces are sufficiently energetic to destroy or suspend the usual operation of chemical affinity." (Phil. Trans. 1807, p. 28.)

3. The hypothesis of the direct electrolysis of metallic salts has been advanced by Prof. Daniell in consequence of some ingenious experiments which have been detailed before this Society, and in which it is supposed that he directly stopped the metal in its passage to the negative pole. The mode in which the experiments were performed is as follows:—A solution of the metallic salt is placed on the positive side of a diaphragm apparatus and a solution of potassa on the other side, when, on the circuit being com-

---

* Communicated by the Author; having been read before the Royal Society, March 9, 1843, as recorded in Phil. Mag. S. 3, vol. xxiii. p. 51. This paper was also published in the 4th vol. of the 'Archives de l'Électr.' in 1844; in Majocchi, 'Ann. Fis. Chim.' vol. xv. 1844; in the 'Philosophical Magazine,' vol. xxv. 1844; in the 'Proceedings of the Royal Society,' vol. iv.; in the 'Poggend. Annal.' lxv. 1845.

pleted by a powerful battery, the metal is deposited on the diaphragm. From this experiment it has been conceived that the acid and oxygen are in combination, forming a proximate principle, which in sulphate of copper is called oxysulphion; and the salt of copper is believed to be an oxysulphion of copper. When this salt is subjected to the voltaic circuit, he believes it to be directly electrolysed, the oxysulphion passing one way and the copper the other.

4. This experiment is so much at variance with the electro-chemical doctrine of Dr. Faraday and the inference to be drawn from my cinder experiment, that on rewriting my 'Elements of Electro-Metallurgy,' I felt it to be my duty to examine carefully this hypothesis before I adopted or rejected such an important doctrine. For this purpose his experiments were repeated and varied in different ways; and with alkalies on the negative side I readily and immediately obtained the metal on the diaphragm, but failed when neutral salts were used on the negative side, or when solutions of gold and platinum were employed on the positive. A series of experiments were then instituted on the polarity of solid substances interposed between two platinum poles. I placed a series of copper wires in all directions and situations between the poles, in a solution of sulphate of copper, and found that one part of each wire became positive and was dissolved, and another part of the same wire became negative and reduced the metal from the solution; so that all the wires were, at different parts, either dissolving or increasing. I next extended my examination as to the capabilities of platinum wires to become polar, and found that a much greater resistance was effected in this case than when other metals were employed; still, however, by particular management they were readily made to give off abundance of gas ('Elements of Electro-Metallurgy,' p. 53, 2nd edit.).

5. The polarity of interposed conducting substances having been fully proved, I endeavoured to ascertain how far non-conducting bodies would take on a similar condition, but could not obtain very satisfactory proof on this matter. Sufficient evidence not being obtained to prove the possibility of interposed non-conducting substances to become polar, I determined not to rely on the investigation for the cause of the reduction of the metals on these experiments, but seek proofs from other causes.

6. I repeated the experiments made in 1839, and communicated to the 'Philosophical Magazine' in 1840, from which I discovered that porous coke or charcoal, when arranged as the negative pole in dilute sulphuric acid, absorbed a large quantity of hydrogen. The mode in which I repeated these experiments was as follows:—A piece of well-burnt charcoal or cinder was removed red-hot from the fire and quenched in dilute sulphuric acid, so that all chance of the presence of oxygen in its texture might be precluded. In this state it had no effect on metallic solutions. It was then arranged as the negative pole in dilute sulphuric acid by connecting it with the voltaic battery, when it became charged with hydrogen, which was ascertained by the circuit being completed some time before gas was evolved from its surface. Pieces of coke thus charged with hydrogen were dipped into various metallic solutions, when the metal was instantly deposited as a brilliant coating on the coke. The deposit of copper affords the most beautiful example, though the deposit of other metals, as of silver and gold, is also striking. Coke charged with hydrogen retains the property of reducing metals many days after its first saturation.

7. The repetition of these experiments deeply impressed my mind that hydrogen evolved from the decomposition of water is really the cause of the reduction of the metals, and I pursued my experiments to test this idea, the first promulgated on the subject, and the one supported by our eminent galvanist, Dr. Faraday.

8. The next stage of investigation consisted in inquiring as to whether the transfer of the metal took place uniformly and synchronously with this reduction. It is apparent that such a transfer is absolutely necessary to the theory of the direct electrolysis of the metallic salt, but let us see what is the result. I prepared a uniform solution of sulphate of copper, and placed at the bottom of a tall vessel containing it a positive copper pole, and at the upper part a negative pole of the same metal, forming a circuit by means of one or two cells of my galvanic battery. On the action of the voltaic force bright reguline copper at first appeared at the negative pole; this was followed by a brittle, this by a sandy, this by a spongy deposit, this by black powder, and finally hydrogen was evolved.

9. This most important experiment was repeated in a variety of ways and with various metallic salts, with the details of which there is no need to trouble the Society, because the experiment just described as an example points out in the most positive manner that the transfer of metal is not proportionate to the metal reduced. The positive pole indicates the same fact, for it became coated with metallic salt, showing beyond all source of fallacy that the metallic salt was directly formed at one pole and the metal directly reduced from another portion of the metallic solution at the other. In a neutral solution of any metallic salt, as that of copper, the acid is no more equally transferred to the positive pole than the metal is to the negative; and we find in its decomposition that the positive pole is frequently coated with oxide of copper of considerable thickness, and from the liberation of an equivalent of sulphuric acid from the sulphate the solution speedily becomes acid.

10. Not only in the above-described experiments have I observed this fact, but in the experiments of the decomposition of above one hundred different salts, including those of twenty distinct metals, which I performed for my work on 'Electro-Metallurgy,' did the results show themselves more or less evidently; and I may state that no electro-metallurgical process can be conducted without the production of these phenomena; and one of the greatest, if not the very greatest difficulty which the electro-metallurgist has practically to contend with, is the variation in the strength of the metallic salts subjected to decomposition.*

---

* *Nov.* 20, 1844.—I happened to call yesterday upon that excellent practical electro-metallurgist, Mr. Horne, of Newgate Street, and found that he was making an electro statue of Sir John Crosby, in a mould prepared by the sculptor, Mr. Samuel Nixon, from the original model also executed by him. Mr. Horne was engaged about the leg, and he stated that he was much troubled by the non-uniform diffusion of the metallic salt through the solution. The mode in which he overcame the difficulty was very simple: he introduced a glass tube every now and then to the bottom of the leg and blew through it, which caused a proper mixture of the exhausted and saturated solutions. The fact was a pretty practical example of the opinions which I have been endeavouring to enforce; it shows that the theorist may in vain attempt to bolster up

11. In what way are the metals reduced if they are not transferred from pole to pole? A careful investigation of a solution depositing its metal will at once explain the phenomenon, for from the negative surface a colourless lighter fluid is seen to rise, which in some cases will destroy the electro-metallurgist's hopes, by causing grooves on the reduced metal, sometimes even to the extent of an inch or more in depth, and the same fluid at other times will cause a sandy or spongy deposit. From these facts it is evident that water is formed at the negative surface, and that hydrogen probably reduces the metallic salt.

12. We have now as arguments in favour of the reduction of the metals by hydrogen gas liberated by decomposition of the water, first, the results obtained by the cinder experiment; secondly, the non-transference of the metal; thirdly, the imperfect transference of the acid; fourthly, the rise of a light aqueous fluid from the negative pole of a metallic solution. We have, fifthly, besides these cases, the analogy of the reduction of nitrous acid in Grove's battery by hydrogen, for the removal of the gas by the acid gives to it its intensity; and in this case no other mode can even be supposed by which the decomposition of the acid is effected, save and except its decomposition by hydrogen. The further alteration of the persalts of metals into protosalts favours strongly, by analogy, the same opinion. Such evidence is amply sufficient, but I have now to detail some direct experiments in which hydrogen alone reduces metals from various salts.

13. The mode in which this satisfactory result is obtained is very simple. The metallic solution to be examined is placed in a glass, a test tube filled with the same solution is then procured, into which a slip of platinum, platinized as for the construction of my battery, is then placed. The whole is then placed within a glass of metallic solution, and a current of hydrogen introduced sufficient to extend half-way up the platinized platinum. It will be seen that the arrangement is similar to that of one of the tubes of Professor Grove's elegant gas battery, and the various results obtained by this mode of examination it will be my duty immediately to explain.

14. If the solution employed be chloride of platinum, the hydrogen disappears gradually, and the black powder of platinum is coated here and there by a beautiful bright layer of reguline metal.

15. With a solution of chloride of gold the same result is seen, the platinum being gilt with a beautiful deposit of metal. With this salt the action is immediate.

16. With nitrate of palladium the hydrogen is rapidly absorbed and bright palladium deposited.

17. With nitric acid and platinized platinum the hydrogen is gradually absorbed and the acid decomposed.

18. A solution of sulphate of copper under similar examination yields a plentiful crop of small crystals of copper in a short period.

19. A solution of persulphate of iron yields rapidly its oxygen and becomes converted into the protosulphate.

crude notions, for the practical man must, to be successful, not only adopt, but act upon the true *rationale* of the phenomena. Societies may determine that the metals are directly electrolysed, but the practical man will find that their edicts will have but very little effect upon his processes.—A. S.

20. A solution of nitrate of silver yields slowly small crystals of silver, but the action with this metal is not so rapid.

21. The hydrogen was slowly absorbed when exposed to a solution of muriate of tin in contact with platinized platinum.

22. Nickel was slowly deposited from the chloride, when exposed under similar circumstances, as a white deposit.

23. Hydrogen, contrary to my expectations, did not appear to reduce iodine from iodic acid.

24. From the solution of protosalts of iron I could not determine that the metal was reduced.

25. I next subjected to experiment the extraordinary compounds of cyanogen forming the metallo-cyanides. From the aurocyanide of potassium I obtained metallic gold.

26. The argento-cyanide of potassium, in a similar way, yielded slowly silver, the hydrogen becoming at the same time lessened.

27. These last two results are interesting to the chemist, for it appears to open a path for investigation on the nature of these very curious and now highly important combinations.

28. Such were my results with platinized platinum and hydrogen: the hydrogen becoming absorbed and the metals being reduced. It was found that chloride of platinum, chloride of palladium, persalts of iron, chloride of gold, and nitric acid yielded the oxygen most rapidly. It next became my endeavour to ascertain how far other metals, or different conditions of the same metal, might be used; and smooth platinum was next the subject of experiment. With sulphate of copper or persalts of iron no absorption, however, took place.

29. Palladinized platinum was made the subject of experiment; and when employed with hydrogen in a manner similar to platinized platinum in sulphate of copper, it caused that metal to be reduced.

30. The effects of silver were then examined, and for that purpose a piece, carefully cleaned by nitric acid, was immersed in a solution of copper in contact with the hydrogen, but no change occurred even after many days.

31. No better result attended the employment of silver sponge used for the same purpose.

32. Nor did the black deposit of silver answer better to effect the absorption of the hydrogen, and the reduction of the metal from a solution of sulphate of copper did not occur.

33. Copper, both in its bright and spongy states, was next examined; in its bright state, cleansed by nitric acid, no change occurred.

34. In the spongy state it appeared to be of no greater efficacy to cause the reduction of the metal.

35. Considering the interest attached to carbon in the cinder experiment, detailed in a former part of this paper, a piece of carbon was exposed to the action of hydrogen and a solution of copper, but, singular to state, no deposit of copper took place, nor was any hydrogen absorbed. In fact I have no mechanical method of charging coke with hydrogen, by which it can be made to cause the reduction of the metals.

36. The last set of experiments which I instituted upon the reduction of the metals by hydrogen was the value of bibulous paper to effect that object. In dilute chloride of gold apparently no action after two or three days took place.

37. In a solution of sulphate of copper, after many days, no action apparently occurred with paper and hydrogen.

38. In a solution of nitrate of silver the same negative result with paper occurred.*

39. The persulphate of iron was not changed into the protosalt by the action of that gas in contact with paper.

40. As a summary of results obtained on the direct reduction of the metals from their solutions by hydrogen, it may be stated generally, that platinized and palladinized platinum alone were found to be competent to promote that change, negative results being obtained with smooth platinum, smooth silver, black powder of silver, bright copper, spongy copper, cinder or paper. These negative results are by no means to be taken as a proof that under these circumstances hydrogen might not reduce the metals, for it is possible under certain conditions that many other substances, like finely-divided platinum, might possibly take on the power of assisting in this mysterious way the absorption of the gas.

41. These various direct experiments of the deoxidizing agency of hydrogen gas are valuable to the electrician, as they point out the cause of some of the most interesting galvanic phenomena. To the electro-metallurgist they assume a much higher importance, for they point out to him, that in the decomposition of the metallic fluid the uniform strength will not be preserved by the changes taking place by virtue of the voltaic current. He must therefore remember in all cases to bring into play the attraction of gravity, not only to cause the diffusion of the newly-formed salt, from which the metal is to be deposited, but the acid to dissolve the oxide formed at the positive pole. The mode in which the metals are reduced may appear quite immaterial to the practical man, but he will find that the non-uniform diffusion of the metallic salt arising from the particular manner in which the reduction takes place, is the cause nearly of all his troubles.

42. From all these experiments we have an overwhelming body of evidence, of different kinds, to support the notion of the reduction of metals from their solution by hydrogen. The direct reduction in the cinder experiment, the non-transference of the metal, the imperfect transference of the acid, the rise of a light aqueous fluid from the negative pole, the analogous case of the decomposition of nitric acid and persalts of iron, and finally the direct experiments of the reduction of gold, silver, platinum, palladium, nickel, copper, tin, and the decomposition of the persalts of iron and nitric acid enclosed within a tube, appear to set the question to rest, and to point out in the clearest manner that

* After some time the paper exhibited a black deposition of silver; the surface of the glass tube became encrusted with a brilliant layer of metallic silver. The importance of this experiment is manifest, for it shows that hydrogen and siliceous matter may at any time reduce metals from their solutions, a power doubtless in frequent operation in the bowels of the earth. How far metallic veins are thus deposited remains to be proved by future investigations. The decomposition of organic matter will always yield hydrogen, and hydrogen, under certain circumstances, will always reduce metals from the solutions of their salts. ·

hydrogen is the cause of the reduction of the metals. All the experiments which I have detailed only add confirmation to the valuable researches of Faraday on Electro-Chemical Decomposition, published in the 'Philosophical Transactions.' To the inquiring mind a question naturally arises as to whether the hydrogen reduces the metal directly from the metallic solution, or whether it reduces its oxide. The former opinion, from the above experiments, appears to be most worthy of credit, though should other facts be discovered to elucidate that action, they will form subjects hereafter of a separate communication to this Society. It follows from these interesting experiments, that when a solution of metallic salt is subjected to the voltaic influence, the water is decomposed, oxygen passing one way and hydrogen the other; and that this hydrogen at the moment of decomposition on the negative plate performs the same part to sulphate of copper and other metallic salts that a piece of iron or zinc would to the same solutions.

---

## No. XI.

## ON THE INHALATION OF AMMONIA GAS AS A REMEDIAL AGENT. By Alfred Smee, F.R.S. (From the 'London Medical Gazette,' April 7th, 1843.)

Of all the physical states in which bodies are known to exist, substances in the form of vapour or gas are most readily absorbed by animal membranes, producing rapid and powerful effects from very small quantities. As a mass, we are but little acquainted with the properties of gases upon the animal economy, and the little we do know is principally due to the persevering inquiries of Sir Humphry Davy. The rapidly deleterious effects of minute quantities of the vapours of hydrocyanic acid, of bromine, of sulphuretted hydrogen, and even of many other gases, exemplify well their powerful action on the animal economy. At present gases are almost entirely discarded as remedial agents, but doubtless there are numerous cases where substances may be advantageously employed as remedial agents in their gaseous or aëriform state. Without wasting time upon general remarks, let me at once call the attention of the profession to a simple remedy of this nature; namely, the value of diluted ammonia gas for stimulating the mucous membrane of the mouth, fauces, trachea, and bronchi. By its local administration it may exercise its power over the whole system, as this gas may either be made to have a topical or general influence, according to the extent of its application.

The inhalation of so stimulating a gas as ammonia is well known to be, at first sight, perfectly startling to those who have never either tried it on their own persons or never seen it applied by others, but it is really, in many cases, with proper management, a simple and one of the most delightful remedies that can be employed. If a bottle, containing a solution of the gas, as the common liquor ammoniæ or hartshorn, be opened, part of the gas escapes. If this comes in contact with the conjunctiva, it stimulates it and causes much fluid to be poured from its secreting surface, and its influence on the delicate lining membrane of the nasal cavities is not less powerful. In fact, this vapour appears immediately to cause a secretion of fluid from the parts with which it comes in contact.

When this gas is absorbed by the mouth in far larger quantities, it appears to cause in a similar manner an increase of the watery part of the secretion, usually passing from all the several parts with which it there can come in contact. A priori it might be expected the glottis would resist the intrusion of the gas, but this is by no means found to be the case when in a diluted state, as it apparently readily passes into the innermost recesses of the lungs, and, instead of producing disagreeable effects, causes sensations which are extremely grateful and agreeable. The gaseous nature of ammonia allows it to come in contact with every chink of the air-passages, and even the upper and back parts of the pharynx, which from its peculiar construction resists the application of other topical remedies.

The immediate effect of the inhalation of this gas is to cause the fauces and pharynx, before dry, and perhaps covered with inspissated adherent mucus, to force out a watery fluid to lubricate and relieve the membrane; the phlegm will then separate and come away, and a more or less instantaneous relief is frequently felt. We all know the expectorant qualities of ammonia, and the value of its sesquicarbonate, whenever the system will bear its administration, as a general remedy, but its qualities, when used as a local agent, seem to be more active in this respect than when used as a general remedy.

The most convenient mode of administering the ammoniacal gas is to use the vapour that spontaneously exhales from solutions of ammonia. Of these it is preferable not to employ a solution stronger than the liquor ammoniæ of the shops, or weaker than the same diluted to twenty or thirty times its quantity of water. For general purposes, perhaps, the usual liquor may be employed diluted with ten times its bulk of water; but the strength of the ammonia must be regulated by the medical practitioner according to the nature of the case, and the susceptibility of the patient, and even according to the strength of the original liquor.

The liquor ammoniæ, diluted according to the discretion of the medical attendant, may be placed in a common phial, and as much should be inserted as to occupy about the two lower inches of the bottle. The patient has only to apply his lips to the mouth of this homely contrivance, and draw in his breath, when he will inhale a certain quantity of the ammonia. Before the application of the mouth to the bottle the patient should take care that none of the liquid adheres to the aperture, which on coming in contact with his lips would cause them to smart, and, being no part of the cure, the pain would be perfectly useless. The number of inspirations to be taken at one time may be determined by the strength of the water and the effect of the remedy. Two, three, or four inspirations will in general be sufficient at one time, but this must be repeated three or four times during the day.

A more convenient apparatus than the simple one last described may be readily made and advantageously employed. A bottle may be selected, and a cork procured, bored with two holes. Into one a piece of bent glass tube may be inserted, having the other end dilated for the convenience of applying the lips. Into the second hole of the cork a tube should be thrust, within half an inch of the liquid, so that when the patient inhales, the ammonia passing from the liquid tube, is taken into the chest, and this is perhaps to be preferred to drawing the breath itself through the solution of ammonia.

Though the last apparatus will answer the purpose more or less efficiently, I have yet to describe a far more elegant device to be employed as an inhaling apparatus. A two-necked bottle is procured; into one mouth a tube is adapted, to serve as a mouth-piece. This tube is ground to fit the neck, and when not used is removed for the insertion of a common stopper, that the strength of the ammonia may be preserved. Into the neck another tube is ground, into the inside of which another stopper is fixed. When the inhaler is in operation, this stopper is withdrawn to allow the air to pass into the bottle, but when not wanted it serves to close the apparatus. This inhaler is most admirably adapted for the desired purpose, and perhaps for gaseous inhalations cannot well be surpassed. The diluted liquor ammoniæ is seen at the bottom of the vessel, extending to within half an inch of the tube.

The vapour inhaled from the liquor ammoniæ does not seem to pass away immediately, but may be distinctly tasted for some minutes afterwards, even subsequently to the commencement of its beneficial action. The value of the local application of this gas is seen in cases of what is called dryness of the throat, which appears to arise from a deficiency of the secretion of the liquid which normally lubricates the mucous membrane. The mucus from that cause becomes dry, and causes much uneasiness to the individual. The common and popular remedy of applying hartshorn and oil to the throat for various affections is probably in great part owing to the inhalation of the vapour of the ammonia, which necessarily at the same time occurs, as it is impossible that this external application can be effected without a large quantity being imbibed at the same time.

Ammonia gas is also beneficial in chronic hoarseness, especially in that which is often left as a sequela of influenza. This gas affords great relief and comfort to the relaxed, swollen, and apparently semi-œdematous state of the mucous membrane, which supervenes from remaining in crowded, overheated, and ill-ventilated rooms, where every person not only inhales his own breath over and over again, but is under the infliction of breathing his neighbour's also. In cases of incipient cynanche tonsillaris it appears to be of much value if used at the very commencement of the attack; the slight impediment to deglutition, which is generally the first premonitory sign, is sometimes removed by one or two inhalations.

There are occasionally cases of syphilitic ulceration of the throat witnessed, where the patient suffers from such debility that the practitioner is afraid of applying any remedy capable of depressing the system, where the inhalation of the gas might probably be of great service, but as such a case has not occurred in my own practice for a long period I am unable to speak practically upon the matter.*

In old-standing cases of asthma, especially in those in which the medical man considers that the internal use of the sesquicarbonate of ammonia is indispensable, in which the extremities are cold, the pulse feeble, and the general vital powers depressed, the local application of ammonia is particularly grateful, the patients feeling, as they describe it, a glow after its exhibition, and the warmth first imparted to the lungs extending by degrees over their whole system.

In cases where the patient feels a peculiar sense of contraction upon passing into cold atmospheres, as though the lungs resisted the intrusion of so unpleasant an agent, the inhalation of ammonia seems to quiet the spasmodic action, relieve the breathing, and give a comfort to the whole chest, which is delightful to the feelings of the sufferer.

Perhaps it is almost needless to notice that this remedy would be deleterious when either special organs or the general system are attacked with acute inflammation, for there is but little doubt that the ammoniacal vapour is a decided stimulus, first locally in those parts with which it comes in contact, and, secondly, on the system in general, by its absorption into the circulation. As a stimulating agent it must obey the laws of stimulants generally. It should not, therefore, be employed when the part with which it comes in contact is inflamed, nor when a dry parched tongue, a full pulse, and a dry skin, denote a feverish system. In all chronic cases, or even occasionally with acute cases, with a feeble circulation,—in fact, whenever the system is depressed, and stimulants are advisable,—the inhalation of ammonia may be used with the greatest advantage and comfort to the patient.

I have made inquiries of those who have to deal with large quantities of ammonia, and are necessarily exposed to the inconvenience of a large escape of gas, but cannot find that even with extensive exposure it ever exercises poisonous or deleterious effects, nor does Ramazzini, in his curious little treatise on tradesmen's diseases, notice its action.

Not alone to the relief and cure of diseases is ammonia capable of lending its aid as a remedial agent, for it is an invaluable and effectual antidote to certain direct and powerful poisons. One of these poisons, the effects of which it thus counteracts, is bromine. This volatile fluid is perhaps one of the most deadly poisons with which we are acquainted. It lowers the circulation with great rapidity, and makes the action of the heart irregular, and unfortunately, from its volatile nature, cannot well be used without considerable escape. Its hurtful action on the animal economy is instantly counteracted by the vapour of ammonia, for when the two gases meet, dense white fumes are produced, when bromine probably ceases to exert its baneful influence, or at any rate only to a much

---

* The inhalation of ammonia might, perhaps, also perform the same good offices to syphilitic ulceration of the throat as cinnabar fumigation is known usually to effect. The use of the cinnabar, however, may be so much dispensed with by the antimonial and antimonio-ferruginous treatment which I have recorded ('Med. Gaz.'), that the ammonia has not been used in any of these cases; but should further information be obtained upon this point, it will be the subject of a future communication.

less extent.* I have known persons nearly poisoned by incautiously using this substance, and who have been quite at a loss to know how to proceed to neutralize its action. Those who have to deal with bromine would do well to have an open vessel of the liquor ammoniæ by their side, which is in general quite sufficient to prevent any unpleasant consequence, by combining with any bromine which may pass off in vapour.

Ammonia is also useful when prussic acid is floating in the atmosphere of a room, as in this case it not only neutralizes the acid, but its stimulating properties are directly opposite to the depressing action of the acid.

As all bodies in burning give off ammonia, a consideration arises as to whether some of the effects of smoking may not be attributed to that agent independently of the active principles that substances used for smoking are known to contain. The possibility of such a thing has been suggested to me, but it is quite certain that only a small portion of the effects of smoking can be attributed to the ammonia. The presence of ammonia in a burning cigar may be shown by collecting its vapour in a bottle containing a few drops of muriatic acid, when abundance of fumes arise. If liquor potassæ be added, the ammonia is again set free, and will again exhibit the white fumes if brought near muriatic acid.

There is an interesting physiological fact connected with the inhalation of ammonia, for in determining the lungs to increase their aqueous exhalation, it frequently at the same time causes a similar action on the skin by the exhalation of moisture from its entire surface. For the last two or three years I have occasionally been in the habit of inhaling ammonia as a luxury during the prevalence of the easterly winds, which by their action so dreadfully dry up and parch all living creatures.

The application of ammoniacal vapour, in the manner which has been already pointed out, is rather an agent of comfort, removing slight ailments and troublesome affections, than a remedy which is capable of saving life from violent diseases, except indeed when used as an antidote to certain poisons. Still, however, there is no complaint, however trifling, no system, however unimportant (if attended with discomfort and inconvenience to mankind), that it is not the duty of the medical man to endeavour to relieve or remove.

---

* The production of these white fumes by the admixture of these two gases is interesting, and, so far as I know, has not been noticed by chemists, though I have myself long been in the habit of applying ammonia to distinguish between the fumes of bromine, iodine, and chlorine, the two latter elements having apparently not the same influence when brought into conjunction with ammonia. These white fumes are liable to be confounded with muriate of ammonia, if muriatic acid is present.

## No. XII.

ANALYSIS OF ALFRED SMEE'S SECOND BOOK, 'THE SOURCES OF PHYSICAL SCIENCE; OR, AN INTRODUCTION TO THE STUDY OF PHYSIOLOGY THROUGH PHYSICS, COMPRISING THE CONNECTION OF THE SEVERAL DEPARTMENTS OF PHYSICAL SCIENCE, THEIR DEPENDENCIES ON THE SAME LAWS,' &c.  From a Review. Together with the two concluding chapters of 'The Sources of Physical Science,' which treat of the " Relation of the Material to the Immaterial."

MR. SMEE tells us in his preface that it had long been "a favourite subject with him to endeavour to investigate the physical structure of man, and to endeavour to unravel the mysterious means by which all physical forces, when acting on the human frame, are converted into nervous impressions.  To conduct such an inquiry, it became necessary to examine the sources from which the several departments of research, constituting physical science, have their origin."

For this purpose he intended to draw up a sketch of physical science, which might be prefixed to his physiological inquiries, in the form of an introductory chapter; but the length to which this chapter extended induced him to publish it as a separate volume.

The work, then, contains a condensed view of the physical sciences, exhibiting the nature and mutual relations of the various divisions of those sciences, and attempting to show the real nature of those forces, such as electricity, magnetism, &c., by which matter is commonly said to be acted upon, and which have often been treated as so many independent existences by various philosophers.

The first chapter treats of matter, number, and attraction; and first, what is matter?—how is it comprehended?

" Man," says Mr. Smee, " being composed of the material and the immaterial, of body and soul, can have no distinct idea of anything not partaking of his own constitution.  He can form no conception of matter without that which gives it properties, nor can he understand that which gives it properties without the matter. . . . . That which men call matter is known by its properties; so that the term matter is given to anything which exerts these peculiar properties. . . . . All the properties or influences of matter are dependent on an ultimate property, which confers a power whereby two particles or portions of matter are drawn towards each other by a force exerted in a particular direction."

But it may be said that it is necessary to prove that matter really exists—that what we call the effects and properties of matter are something more than the results of a visionary *dynamis*.

" Ingenious persons," says our author, "speculating upon the properties of matter independently of the thing itself, have persuaded themselves, with some show of reason, that matter has no existence.  Their minds have, however, been led astray by their mode of arriving at their conclusions.  They have not commenced with a sound definition of what we designate matter.  *Defining matter to be that which attracts*, and allowing attraction to be its test, obviates all difficulty."—P. 3.

Having next spoken of the origin, meaning, and right use of those terms which denote the abstract properties of matter, and having treated of the nature of matter, with a glance at the question whether it comprises one element only under a diversity of forms, or whether there really are as many elements as there are bodies yet undecompounded by the skill of the chemist, he then treats of number,—that is to say, the abstract idea of a series of particles; and thus, in the first chapter, he has considered the three points which he assumes as fundamentals—that is to say, matter, attraction, and number—from which all physical forces and conditions of existence are derived.

In the second chapter Mr. Smee treats of the " science of matter under attraction," and he proceeds to show that the *power of attraction* (which has been described as the primitive property of matter and the test of its existence) *being exerted with various degrees of energy upon various numbers of atoms, and in various directions, gives to masses of matter all the properties which they apparently possess.* We may observe, *en passant*, that Mr. Smee gives no credence to the existence of any of the so-called *imponderable* substances. He treats the idea of the separate existence of heat, light, electricity, magnetism, &c., as a palpable absurdity, and contends that each of these terms merely refers to one class of actions or effects produced by the attraction of matter exerted in various manners.

In discussing the science of matter under attraction, one of the first points to be noticed is the manner of estimating the force with which any two particles of matter are attracted together, and of comparing that with the force of other attractions. On this point, observes our author—

" As we have not the power of appreciating the units, or atoms of matter, we have not the means of obtaining a perfect unit of the force of attraction. The only absolute unit of this power would be the force of attraction exerted between two ultimate particles of matter, a unit which we can never hope to obtain.

" As we have not the power of using the primitive atoms of matter, we take a given mass, and assume that to be a unit. The force exerted between this mass and the whole bulk of the earth at the level of the sea is then obtained. This is assumed as a unit of force which is called a unit of weight, and to which all other weights are referred."—P. 22.

" In our artificial standards of weight the unit is the grain, which is the force of attraction of a cubic inch of water to the earth at the temperature 62, barometer 30, divided by 252·5. . . . . It has been recommended, and perhaps is preferable, to take any piece of matter and assume its weight as an arbitrary standard, for philosophers disagree as to the true weight of a cubic inch of water, or indeed of any other body. The utmost limit to human ingenuity in weighing is about 1·10000th part of our comparative unit of weight, or grain; but in this quantity so many circumstances lead to error as to render the result very unsatisfactory. The finger held over a scale, which by its warmth causes currents which exert a force contrary to that of the earth, will materially influence the result in very small weights. I have tried this experiment with an excellent pair of scales, made for the Bank of England by Mr. Bate, and found a most sensible disturbance of the equilibrium of the balance when the finger was held half an inch above one of the scale-pans."—P. 24.

The next point which Mr. Smee adverts to is the fact that the force of attraction is always exerted in a peculiar direction, a series of which attractions constitutes polarity; and "this peculiarity in the direction of the force, whereby attraction is exerted, is of fundamental importance, for it enables us to oppose one attraction by another. This opposition of attraction enables us to effect decomposition, disintegration, and to give rise to the phenomena of heat, light, sound, &c., at will."

The author now proceeds to examine *seriatim* the various properties of matter, and to show how they are derived from simple attraction; and the first of those which he touches upon is what is called *impenetrability*, which literally means that two bodies cannot occupy the same space at the same time. This he explains thus :—

"The reason why impenetrability is conferred on matter by the act of attraction is perfectly evident, if the mode of the generation of attraction be carefully examined. The attraction being exerted in a certain direction, one particle of matter, although capable of being attracted so as to adhere firmly to a second portion, would, if the second passed into the first, instantly be destroyed, because the direction of attraction exerted in one atom would oppose, neutralize, or counterbalance the attraction in the other. The attraction, therefore, between two atoms is most violent at contact, but ceases upon one having a tendency to pass into the other. The above observations will be rendered perfectly intelligible by the following notation :—

NP　　　NP
O　　O

"If the two O O represent the two atoms, and the NP NP the ends of the forces with which they are held together, then the very moment one atom had a tendency to pass into the other, the two 'N' or the two 'P' would oppose each other; upon that account the two particles would be firmly attracted till they came in contact, but no further."—P. 26.

Having briefly alluded to *shape*, he next comes to the *volume* of bodies, which he shows to be far from an inherent fixed property, but merely to depend on the energy with which attraction is exerted. "We have no proof that matter possesses any absolute volume, for, under different circumstances, the same number of particles exhibits very various volumes."

"Volume, from the above consideration, seems rather a negative than a positive quality. It is the absence, or the comparative absence, of attraction; for as the force increases, the volume diminishes. The advantages of thus viewing the nature of volume are multifold. It does not require the creation of 'repulsion' to separate particles attracted together, and it overcomes numerous difficulties which arise from the assumption of a certain size to the ultimate particles of matter. From this view, which is forced upon us from multitudinous evidence, one atom of matter, if alone, and unacted upon by any other atom, would fill the universe."—P. 28.

He next speaks of the science by which size and measure are estimated. The following observations, on the impossibility of finding a standard unit of measure, are interesting enough :—

"But as our organs of sense cannot appreciate the ultimate particles of matter, we never can arrive at, or obtain, an absolute standard of size; on this account we are compelled to take a certain piece of matter under definite conditions of attraction as unity, and by multiplying or sub-multiplying it we obtain all other measures proportionate to that unit. The Legislature formerly thought fit to take three barleycorns from the middle of the ear, from which they formed a measure called an inch. Of course a unit derived from anything so uncertain as three barleycorns is most unsatisfactory, for every measure thus made would doubtless vary.

" The greatest anxiety has been felt by all nations to find some unit of length to which at any time posterity might be enabled to refer all future measures, but we have already seen that philosophers have been attempting an impossibility. The French have taken that quadrant of the meridian which passes through Fontenara and Greenwich, the middle of which is in the 45th degree of latitude. This measure they have divided into ten million parts, each part of which they constitute a comparative unit. In assuming this measure, it is perfectly impossible exactly to obtain the greater measure to divide, and even, in fact, we do not know whether the earth, in a series of ages, may not slightly alter in form. The English have assumed the length of the pendulum vibrating seconds in a particular latitude as a unit of measure, but that assumption is highly objectionable, because it infers the existence of something absolute in time, which is not the fact. It, moreover, first requires us to ascertain or determine the duration of a second, which will be as difficult for posterity as the determination of a measure for length. The length of the pendulum vibrating seconds appears to vary not only in the same latitude, but even slightly, from some unknown causes, in nearly the same spot; and, moreover, no two pendulums, of as nearly the same length as human ingenuity can form them, will vibrate in exactly the same time. The best mode of making and maintaining a new standard of measure for this country has lately occupied the attention of the Government and philosophers, in consequence of the former standards having been destroyed by fire in the Houses of Parliament. Although three or four sets of these standards were then made with the utmost human skill, philosophers cannot determine that these duplicates are exactly similar to those destroyed. This forms an excellent practical proof, not only of the impossibility of possessing an absolute standard, but also the impracticability of using it if we obtained it; because, as we are unable to weigh below 1-10000th of a grain, so we are incompetent to measure below a certain amount. Probably, in measuring, we can obtain rough results to the 1-1000000th of an inch; but as the measures decrease in length, so the errors increase, as all measurements must only be regarded as rough comparative approximations to truth.

" Under these circumstances, we find that our standards are purely arbitrary, and, therefore, the best mode that can be adopted is, to take any arbitrary length, which should be as near the inch now adopted as possible. This measure we should constitute our arbitrary unit, or inch, to which all other measures should be referred. Several copies, that is, as near as human ingenuity and skill can make copies, should then be formed, and deposited in various places of security for reference. This artificial unit, moreover, should be compared by different observers, and by different instruments, with all the most fixed things in the material world, so that if, by any accident, the primitive artificial standard was lost, posterity might be enabled to compare their measures with ours; and though, doubtless, they would never be able to obtain the exact relative size of our standard, yet they would be able, for all practical purposes, to have ample knowledge of our measures. All other measures would be obtained either by multiplying the inch, or expressing the relation in fractional parts of it."—P. 34.

Referring to the same point, he observes further on:—

"Our standard inch is no longer of the same length, and therefore not an inch if the temperature varies ever so little from that point at which the standard was assumed; but let the temperature vary ever so much, the number of particles cannot be multiplied or diminished, it is only the size that varies. In conducting the ordnance survey of England, the measures were obliged to be most carefully adjusted for temperature or variation in the thermometer. So also in adjusting the standard bushel, the difficulty was found to be extreme, for it was found that the heat caused by a human body coming near so large a bulk caused a sensible alteration in its exact size."—P. 39.

Having then spoken of the abstract ideas of length, breadth, cube, and other geometrical properties of matter, he passes on to *cohesion*—a state in which a number of particles of the same kind of matter are attracted together into a mass.

"Bodies," he observes, "in a state of cohesion resist the action of other bodies presented to them to an extent proportionate to that cohesion. Lead, in an extremely divided state, burns vividly upon simple exposure to atmospheric air, whilst the same metal in a state of cohesion, or in a rolled malleable state, undergoes but little change from long exposure. Spongy platinum, and other metals in a finely-divided state, also have very different properties from the same metals in a state of cohesion. There is no more curious instance of the effects of cohesion than in the varieties of coke; for when tinder, the slightest spark will inflame it; when soft coke, it readily burns; when hard coke, it can scarcely be made to ignite; but when a diamond, it requires a skilful chemist to inflame."—P. 44.

The threefold state in which bodies may exist—solid, liquid, or gaseous; the various properties depending on the degree of attraction—such as hardness, softness, &c., are next spoken of in order; and the author having brought before our notice that attraction exerted between particles of dissimilar matter known as *chemical affinity*, the remainder of the chapter is occupied with the subjects of atomic weight, heterogeneous and capillary adhesion, endosmosis, the attractions of gravitation and magnetism—all of which topics are set forth in an equally novel, clear, and simple manner. But we must hasten onwards from these to the third chapter, on the *sciences of the disturbance of attraction*—including electricity, mechanics, hydrostatics, and pneumatics.

"We have shown the mode in which attraction gives quality by chemical affinity; quantity, by the union of many atoms; form, by the mode in which the particles are united; size, by the intensity of the attractive force; and, lastly, position of masses by gravitation."—P. 70.

And we now have to see how these attractions may be disturbed or destroyed by other attractions, acting in an opposite direction.

In the study of the disturbance of attractions, he begins with considering the effects produced on a compound consisting of two elements, when a third body is presented to it, which abstracts and combines with one element, setting the other free.

Such a circle of atoms is called a *voltaic circuit*, and the apparatus in which the action is performed, a *voltaic battery*.

The decomposable substance, which forms the basis of the battery, is called an *electrolyte*; and the substance which decomposes it, by exerting a strong attraction on one of its elements, is called the *positive element* of the battery. The simplest idea of a voltaic circuit is presented by a particle of water and a particle of zinc; in which the zinc presenting an attraction for oxygen in the reverse direction to that of the hydrogen, the former unites with the metal, the latter is given off. But—

"Had we no means of increasing the length of the interval between the abstraction of one element of the electrolyte, by the new attraction exerted between it and the positive pole and the evolution of the second element, voltaic batteries would be but of little advantage. But we have the power of increasing this interval indefinitely; sometimes miles intervene between those two points.

"The mode in which we increase this interval depends upon the power of the new attraction exerted between the zinc and oxygen of the water, to propagate the tendency to the destruction of the old attractions of hydrogen and oxygen through a series of particles of fluid. A second point is then placed, at which the hydrogen, or second element, may be evolved. This second point is the negative element."—P. 75.

We thus see that the *positive* pole or element is the source of all the phenomena manifested in the voltaic circuit. The degree of their energy is the degree of chemical attraction exerted between that positive pole and one element of the electrolyte. Whatever can be an obstacle to chemical affinity can also be an obstacle to voltaic action.

These obstacles may be briefly stated thus :—

First, there is the previous attraction existing between the two elements of the electrolyte to be overcome. The best way of countervailing this seems to be (supposing water the electrolyte as it generally is), to place at the negative pole some substance, holding oxygen in a loose state of combination, with which the hydrogen may combine at the moment of its liberation; so that the hydrogen, finding a new affinity exerted towards it, may be more ready to relinquish its oxygen to the zinc. This is the theory of Professor Daniell's battery, in which sulphate of copper is placed at the negative pole, and is reduced by the nascent hydrogen, and of Mr. Grove's, in which the same purpose is effected by nitric acid.

A second and third obstacle are offered by the force with which the particles of fluid are kept in their situation, and by the force with which the particles of metal cohere.

A fourth is frequently presented by the formation of a new compound at the positive pole (sulphate of zinc), which prevents the zinc from coming into contact with the electrolyte.

Hence it is evident that the measure of the intensity of the voltaic circuit is equal to the excess of the attraction of the positive pole for one element of the electrolyte, over the force exerted by these impediments.

Mr. Since next speaks of the compound voltaic battery—disposes very summarily of that theory which attributes the production of electrical effects to the contact of metals, and mentions the mode in which the voltaic force effects the decomposition of binary compounds in a state of solution; and then treats at some length of *tension*, that is to say, "a desire for action ungratified"—a force contending with obstacles, ready to act, but not actually in action.

The effects of tension may arise from a variety of causes, since it is always produced when a new attraction is offered, which is counteracted by a previously existing one. The *electrical machine* is the instrument by which the greatest amount of tension is procurable.

"The electrical tension generated by the machine arises from friction. Friction, we shall hereafter show, is the result of force—force of some new attractions. Friction, therefore, being derived primarily from attraction, may counterbalance other attractions. In the electrifying machine and all its analogues, where friction is exerted, there must be more or less tendency to the destruction of the attractions. This tendency may be called the desire for action, which is opposed by the attraction of cohesion; this desire for action is the tension."—P. 20.

The theory of the electrical machine, and the phenomena commonly said to arise from *induction* of electricity, having been disposed of, our author passes to a stupendous chain of phenomena, depending on the same principle, of which we extract his explanation at some length :—

"Having considered galvanic tension and frictional tension, we have next to describe lightning tension. The tension in this case is evidenced between the surface of the earth on the one hand, and a cloud on the other, the air being the imperfect conductor, at the surfaces of which the ends of the tension are manifested; that is, one surface is positive, and the other negative. The attraction which is the source of the tension, perhaps present facts have hardly sufficiently proved. Still, when we perceive that a rapid formation of clouds, of rain, and even hail, always accompanies the phenomena, we shall not probably much err in attributing the effects to the sudden attraction of aqueous vapour into cloud, rain, or hail. This new attraction, acting upon the air as a non-conductor, causes a polarity of that air, which is communicated between the surface of the cloud on the one hand, and that of the earth on the other. Such a mode of the formation of a thunder-cloud agrees well with the natural phenomena. It is apparent, from such a cause, that the entire surface of the cloud on the one hand, and the surface of the earth opposed to it on the other, would be in a state of high tension—a result which is in perfect accordance with the fact.

"The electrical power capable of being exerted between the cloud and the earth is enormous. The intensity is so great, that it is capable of passing through a thousand feet, or more, of air during the discharge. The quantity is equally vast; for the cloud and tension may be exerted over very many square miles, occasionally even for 100 square miles. The electrical effects being equal to the intensity (1000 feet of air) multiplied by the quantity (100 square miles), will produce a result which, when compared with the power of an enormous Leyden jar, the intensity of which (half-inch air) is multiplied by 100 square feet, shows so wide a difference that a comparison can scarcely be made. This difference, while it shows to the presumptuous philosopher the vanity and impossibility of attempting to produce this great phenomenon of nature, yet it amply demonstrates to those who undervalue scientific investigation how, by paying attention to minute experiments in the laboratory, the operations of nature may be explained and comprehended. The lightning-cloud almost invariably appears when rain follows long-continued easterly winds, which render the air and earth exceedingly dry; but occasionally the lightning-cloud is formed when the surface of the earth is saturated with wet, and the air highly hygrometric. In this latter case, a dense cloud is generally seen to form in the atmosphere without any apparent cause; with the utmost rapidity, and within a few minutes, and sometimes within a few seconds of its appearance, hail, rain, and lightning follow.

"The lightning-cloud sometimes expands itself nearly at the place where it is first formed; and in this case, perhaps, the cloud and earth are in an uniformly opposite state, which would have the effect, by virtue of the attraction of oppositely electrified surfaces, of causing the cloud to be retained in its position. Sometimes, however, without any wind, the cloud takes a rapid travelling fit, crossing England in a few minutes, and paying our French neighbours a visit, as we find by the account in the papers the next day, striking and carrying devastation in its progress. Sometimes the cloud will travel away for two or three hours, and then travel back; sometimes it will take a circular motion, and, in fact, the freaks which a travelling cloud will pay are innumerable. The travelling cloud may possibly owe its properties to an unequal tension at different parts; for if one end of the cloud, or the entire cloud, had an attraction to the earth under this end, and in advance of it, the cloud would be drawn towards that part; but as there is a force which resists its direct downward attraction to the earth, it moves in the diagonal of the force tending to raise the cloud, and the force drawing all the cloud to one point, when a motion more or less rapid must be the result. In this case we must suppose that the earth under one end of the cloud as it advances immediately assumes a violent tension."—P. 102.

The subjects next considered are the effects of the tensive electricity exhibited by the thermo-electric and magneto-electric apparatus, and by the hydro-electric apparatus, in which the force is generated apparently by the friction of steam, a gigantic specimen of which is exhibited at the Royal Polytechnic Institution. The remainder of the chapter is devoted to dynamics—force, its origin, and various modes of adaptation to the wants of mankind. But this we pass over, in order to arrive at Chapter IV., on the *sciences of actions and reactions*.

Action is the exertion of new attractions; reaction, the tendency to the maintenance of old ones. When these two forces are nearly balanced, *vibrations* ensue. Here let us show our author's idea of the nature of *time*, and its essential dependence on matter. He observes, first of all, how fortunate it is for the economy of the world that attractions meet with opposition.

"Former attractions act as an impediment to the exertions of the new ones; the energy of the desire for combustion, of carbon for oxygen in our fires, is held at bay by the former attraction of the particles of coal, which is gradually and progressively overcome. Our fires, therefore, burn regularly and steadily, our candles with slowness and precision, and all other actions, even to the railway engine, take place with an energy proportionate to the resistance of the new action which causes the effect.

"The energy with which a new attraction overcomes an old one is called the time of its performance; and, conversely, the energy of the resistance to a new action by an old one is called the time at the attempt of performance. Time, therefore, is the abstract idea of the energy of an action and reaction. Time is, therefore, a strictly material property. Without matter we could not have time, and even with matter the phenomenon of time requires for its manifestation some new attraction to overcome an old one. The tendency of the action of the new attraction to overcome the old one is called the commencement of a unit of time; the actual performance of the new attraction, after the destruction of the old one, or the actual resistance of the new attraction by the old one, is called the termination of a unit of time. The absolute performance or resistance of a new action—that is, its commencement and termination—constitutes an event, and, according to the energy of this event, it is said to be of shorter or longer duration."—P. 161.

Having thus shown time to be a material property, its abstract idea to be that of resistance to an action, and having treated of the instruments for its measurement, he next reviews the effects produced by matter when under the influence of conflicting forces.

" Having seen the conditions of matter in a quiet state, we have next to examine its properties when in commotion; and the sciences of commotion, or rather of actions and reactions, which now fall under our notice, are respectively those of heat, light, sound, and scent. All these terms are abstract ideas of material actions and reactions, and there is no imponderable or essence in either heat, light, sound, or scent, to which matter owes its power of being hot, illuminated, noisy, or odoriferous." —P. 172.

The first of these sciences is that of *heat*, which he believes to consist in a peculiar vibrating condition of bodies, caused by the conflict of new attractions seeking to overcome former ones.

" We find, if we take a review of all sources of heat, the phenomenon is owing to some new attraction acting on a body, the particles of which are held together by former attractions. A hot body is, therefore, a body whose attractions are interfered with by other attractions, and heat is the abstract term of this disturbance of attractions in a particular manner."— P. 173.

The *sources of heat* next come under consideration: and, firstly, those of the heat exhibited during electrical phenomena; then a much more familiar and important source.

" The next source of heat after that derived from new attractions producing electrical forces, is that derived from the attraction of chemical affinity. The phenomenon of heat is not manifested by the chemical union of any two bodies, if the combination takes place without being impeded by the other attractions, or if the other attractions are quietly destroyed. If the combination takes place with great energy, however, the rapid tendency to the destruction of attractions, reacting against the desire for maintaining them, gives rise again to the phenomenon called heat. In the combustion of coals, the rapid desire for the particles of coal to unite with the oxygen of the air, acting upon the desire of the particles to maintain their old attraction of cohesion, causes that heat to be manifested which so comforts and cheers us in our dreary winter's night."—P. 176.

After describing the other sources of heat, and treating of its properties and conduction, &c., which are clearly and minutely detailed, he passes to light and sound, which, like heat, depend on certain classes of vibrations, perceptible by certain of our organs of sense. Odour he supposes (but does not actually affirm) to depend, in all probability, on a like cause, rather than on an emission of corporeal particles.

He shows that an infinite number of these interesting, sense-affecting actions may be going on in the universe continually, which our organs are not fitted to recognize. We cannot discern the sights and smells which are at once perceptible to the dog or hawk; and no doubt there is an unseen world, of countless sights and sounds, hidden from us, but revealed to higher intelligences. Thus the teaching of philosophy is that also of religion.

Thus we can understand how the seer, "falling into a trance, and having his eyes opened," could discern the horses and chariots of fire encamped about the tents of the righteous; how the harmonious movements of the universe may be attended with music, inaudible to mortal ears, since the time when the foundations of the earth were laid; "when the morning stars sang together, and all the sons of God shouted for joy."

If we may recapitulate, we may observe that he commences with three fundamentals—*matter*—*attraction*, the test of matter—and *number*;—particles of matter being *attracted together* give rise to form, volume, cohesion, adhesion, position;—peculiarity in the *direction of attraction* causes crystallization, polarity, magnetism; attraction acting on attracted matter causes *tension* and *force*;—force, by *destroying attractions*, causes decomposition and the phenomena of electricity:—the effects of force, counteracted by the *resistance of existing attractions*, produce time, and vibrations; whose results are heat, light, sound, and perhaps odour.

## The concluding Chapters of 'The Sources of Physical Science.'

### On the Relation of the Material to the Immaterial.

Having now traced the manner in which the material universe is composed of atoms, or ultimate particles, to which we give the name "matter," and that the term "matter" is given to whatever attracts, the mind of man is naturally led to consider how and from what cause matter attracts, and by that attraction produces all the varied phenomena observed in the physical world.

The first question that naturally suggests itself to the mind that attempts this investigation is the probability which is given to the attachment of some imponderable or essence to matter, by virtue of which attachment the power to attract is bestowed on material particles. Such a question appears to be answered without much depth or profundity of reasoning, for if matter exerted attraction by virtue of some principle, essence, or imponderable attached to it, then would that principle exert attraction without matter, or at least we cannot perceive why it should not exert that property.

From the general views that are forced upon us by our present mode of studying physical phenomena, we must assume that attraction was first exerted before new attractions would produce the effects of electricity, galvanism, heat, light, sound, &c. As attraction must have preceded the greater number of physical phenomena, we may also presume, or in fact we must admit, that attraction itself had a commencement. And time itself, we have already shown, is derived from an old attraction resisting a new one acting upon it. Each event, consequently, must have a commencement and a termination. To increase the number of these events will not assist us, for, how far soever we carry back the events, still their character is immutable; there must have been one event which was prior to all others, and that first event must have had a beginning.

The beginning of the first event affecting matter was the primary attraction, which the subsequent attraction sought to disturb; and the great question which the human mind desires to speculate upon, is the cause of this first exertion of attraction.

The first exertion of attraction, probably, does not arise from any principle attached to matter; but still, even if it owed its power of attraction to an imponderable, the cause of the imponderable attaching itself to matter would be the obscure point on which the human mind delights to contemplate; for the first exertion of attraction, however arising, would alone give to matter its material properties, or, in fact, there would not have been matter (according as we define matter) without the capacity of its particles to set up attraction.

This power of matter to generate attraction in the first instance would never have arisen from anything inherent: we, therefore, are compelled to admit that from something extraneous it derived its power. If we look at the means necessary to endow matter with the property of attraction, we are instantly astonished at the unbounded magnitude, magnipotence, and magnipresence of that power; for we have evidence to show that that power was evinced over enormous masses of matter separated by hundreds of thousands of millions of miles. If that power is continually being exerted, the Author necessarily appears as the Governor of material phenomena; but if the government of the world is continually being affected, we discover that no variation has taken place in the general properties evinced by matter since the world began: the earth still continues to run its daily and yearly course; matter continues to be hot, illuminated, and capable of causing sound when acted on in a peculiar manner; and, as far as we can learn, not the slightest alteration has occurred since the earliest human event was recorded.

Whether that power was in the first instance implanted for once and for ever, or whether, by a continuance of the exertion of that power, matter continues to attract, are subjects for contemplation far beyond the capacity of human intellect to deduce from physical phenomena. We can only admit that the same power which first caused matter to attract, may also cause, at any given moment, that phenomenon to cease.

To the source of that immensity of power, which we see either has been exerted once or which continues to be exerted, we attach the name of the Creator or Almighty.

The attributes of the Creator of all material particles naturally form a subject of the most sublime contemplation for all beings endowed with reason sufficient for that purpose. But here again we must refer to our incapacity to enter into a subject so much beyond human understanding, for man can only appreciate things which are material, and which, by virtue of their properties, communicate impressions through material organs to the human mind. We find that we cannot determine the absolute attributes of the Deity from physical science, but only infer certain attributes by not attributing to His divinity the properties of matter, which solely derives its properties through the exertion of His power. In fact, nothing is more erroneous than the comparison of perfections in God with natural qualities in man. Out of this have arisen incalculable mistakes.

If we review the properties of matter, we find that its first property is number; that the juxtaposition of units forms addition and multiplication, and the mass of matter so formed is susceptible of diminution and division. The material character of number forbids us to attach that property to the attributes of the Almighty, for His attributes are clearly immaterial, having no connection with the properties which His mighty power caused matter to evince. Natural philosophy, therefore, teaches us that the Almighty has no relation to number; that, consequently, He is indivisible and incapable of addition. For ages the greatest disputes have arisen, and schisms and heresies sprung up throughout Christian communities, by attributing the properties of number to the Deity, and conferring material virtues on the Almighty. It is equally incorrect to attach unity as plurality to His indivisibility, for unity infers a possibility of plurality, and, therefore, a possibility of being amenable to number, which property matter solely derives from the will of the Creator.

As we must discard the very idea of number as being an attribute of God, so must we also deny the possibility of any attribute arising from attracted number. We cannot, therefore, give to His majesty form or size, for these are properties of His created matter. His presence, moreover, cannot be limited to one spot, for position is a material effect. He must extend over space, and consequently omnipresence must be a characteristic attribute of His greatness.

His omnipresence cannot be interfered with by the presence, in certain positions, of created matter. Impenetrability is a property of matter, perhaps by virtue of attraction, and therefore cannot interfere with the Immaterial. The omnipresence of the Deity will not be prevented by attracted matter: but He must be present in the structure of the hardest stones, the most massy rocks; in fact, throughout the matter of this great globe, and even throughout the matter existing over the universe.

The phenomena of electricity, of galvanism, of motion, are in similar manner material actions, which alone have their existence by virtue of attraction. The immaterial character of the Almighty forbids these phenomena to be attached to His attributes; indeed, we scarcely imagine how the Deity, whose attribute is omnipresence, can have the property of motion.

As the material character of the preceding properties forbids their assumption as an attribute of the Creator, so are we compelled to deny the possibility of time, with its dependencies, to be a phenomenon to which the Author of that time should be amenable. The Almighty consequently could have no beginning, no end. Eternity is His distinguishing attribute; and time can have none, no, not even the feeblest quality of eternity. Time, however exaggeratedly it may be increased, never becomes eternity; for time is made up of a series of events, each having a beginning and an end. Eternity is not made up of events, and has therefore no beginning, no end.

The actions called heat, light, and sound, are similarly material, appertaining to particles of matter alone. The Maker of all things cannot, therefore, be supposed to be subject to phenomena which exist by His almighty fiat.

We have thus seen, that whilst all the properties of matter are strictly material, so the attributes of the Immaterial are purely immaterial. Science, therefore, directs us to attach materiality to the material, immateriality to the Immaterial; and by no means at any time, under any circumstance, to confound the properties of matter with the attributes of the Immaterial, or the attributes of the Immaterial with the properties of matter.

It is, then, the property of matter to attract, and by virtue of that attraction to yield number, size, form, duration. It is the attribute of the Immaterial not to yield number, to be omnipresent and eternal. Matter attracts by virtue of power conferred upon it by the Immaterial. Matter is matter by the volition of the Creator.

The power which conferred attraction on matter is present not only where matter is, but even where matter is not, inasmuch as position is a material phenomenon. In consequence of that omnipresence, we may infer that He is cognizant of every alteration of each respective particle of matter, which omnicognizance is called the omniscience of the Deity. Our material bodies allow certain expressions to be carried to the mind through certain material organs called the senses, and therefore we only appreciate those impressions which act upon those senses. His omnipresence must know every single change, without respect to any material conditions. His omniscience cannot be interfered with by darkness, quiescence, or temperature. Darkness is no darkness with Him; the stillness of an action cannot cause it to be hid from His observation. His omniscience is derived from omnipresence, not from the properties of matter from which man derives his knowledge.

We, therefore, are compelled to admit and believe that matter owes its properties to a power conferred upon it by the omnipresent, omnipotent, omniscient, eternal Creator, who first by His Almighty fiat commanded matter to attract, and who, by the same Almighty fiat, may at any instant will attraction to cease, when worlds would end, when time would be no more. As far as regards all material properties, He must have absolute power. At any moment He may dissolve the earth, the sun, the moon, the stars, and as instantaneously summon their particles to assume new shapes, to occupy new positions. This infinite power or omnipotence is of a totally different character from our power, which is derived from the properties of matter. Man's boasted power is derived from availing himself of attraction. The Deity can control that property, and from that we infer the attribute of omnipotence.

It is useless to conceal that these great and glorious perfections are quite incomprehensible to our senses: we can only appreciate material impressions; all else is quite incomprehensible to our mind. To say that God has no relation to number is as unintelligible as His omnipresence, His omniscience, or His eternity. We cannot conceive the nature of such attributes, though we are compelled to believe them because we cannot conceive that such attributes should not exist.

What other attributes belong to the Almighty we are incapable of ascertaining by physical science; and even the contemplation of these, we must admit, will suffice to fill our minds with an amazement productive of reverence, submission, and humility. . . . .

*Conclusion.*—We live in a material world, and can only converse with matter; everything we treat of is material. We can only use material properties to effect material phenomena; and our very existence here depends upon a series of material events taking place in our own bodies, for if these events do not take place, other actions ensue which end in decomposition. An event of definite energy we call a unit of time, and the total of events, taking place in our own bodies in our present condition, we term the period of life. Time itself, therefore, is a material phenomenon, depending solely on material properties.

But whilst man can only clearly understand material phenomena, and use matter to give rise to material effects, and thus conduct his affairs, yet he has the power, by virtue of an immateriality in his own constitution, to perceive indistinctly through a veil the existence of an Immaterial to whom matter and all material phenomena owe existence. The attributes of the Creator of matter are, indeed, in this world quite beyond the comprehension of man's faculties; and the attributes which man is compelled to attach to the Almighty are but positive expressions for the absence of the properties of matter, which are solely derived from His Almighty will.

Having completed our inquiries into the sources of physical science, we have found that man has no conception of matter without the existence of a Supreme Being, who endowed it with properties, *i.e.* caused it to be matter. We have seen that no imponderable attached to matter gives it its properties, but that they are evolved simply from the will of the Almighty. That which gives to matter properties is the will of God, and we have before mentioned that man can have no conception of matter without that to which it owes its property.

As we can form no idea of matter apart from its Creator, so in our present state, living in a material world, and being ourselves partly immaterial, partly matter, we cannot form any clear conception of the Almighty totally apart from His works. From natural science, man only knows God as being the Creator and Maker of all material things; but hereafter, when man shall rise again and assume a higher condition, he shall understand these glorious mysteries apart from all created matter.

We have seen that all physical subjects depend on the existence of the Supreme Being, the Creator of matter, from whose will matter is. We have seen that matter is that which attracts; that particles of matter under attraction give to masses of matter their properties; and that this attracted matter, being acted upon by new attractions, produces all physical effects.

Physical science depends on matter, and its property, attraction; and the great problem for man to solve, when he desires to perform his various operations, is comprised in the effect which attraction produces on attracted matter. The object of this volume has been to contribute to the solution of this problem, and to condense the foundations of human knowledge into so small a compass, that the reader from its perusal, by simply having attraction and attracted matter, may be able, at will, to give rise to all physical phenomena.

As a summary of the sources of physical science, I have drawn up the accompanying table to show at one view how physical phenomena may be produced, and how the entire range of physical studies constitutes physical science.

Matter is matter, and solely exists by the will of God. Matter is made up of finite particles or atoms; a series constituting number, and the study of number arithmetic.

| | |
|---|---|
| Particles of matter *attracted together* give rise to . . . . . . . | Form, Volume, Composition, Cohesion, Adhesion, Position. |
| Peculiarity in the *direction* of attractions produces . . . . . | Crystallization, Polarity, Magnetism. |
| Attraction *acting on* attracted matter causes . . . . . . . | Tension, a tendency for action. Force, a capacity for action. |
| Force, by *destroying* the attractions of attracted matter, exhibits . . | Galvanic phenomena, Electric phenomena, Electro-magnetic phenomena, Motion, Disintegration, Decomposition. |
| The results of force, in consequence of the *resistance* of old or previously existing attractions, produce the phenomena called . . . . . | Time, Heat, Light, Sound, Odour (?). |
| These latter, being the *result* of force, exhibit . . . . . . . | The effects of force generally; and, therefore, capacity for the destruction of attractions. |

---

## No. XIII.

INTRODUCTORY LECTURE DELIVERED AT THE ALDERSGATE SCHOOL OF MEDICINE. By ALFRED SMEE, F.R.S., Lecturer on Surgery at the Aldersgate School, Surgeon to the Royal General Dispensary, to the Central London Ophthalmic Institution, to the Bank of England, to the Provident Clerks' Mutual Benefit Association, &c. &c. (From the 'Medical Times,' October 5, 1844.)

GENTLEMEN,—The solemn occasion for which we are this day collected together, is to inquire into the nature of the studies necessary for the education of a gentleman, to enable him to practise medical science. You will doubtless consider that it will suffice for me simply to enumerate the views of those associations of great men who, in different countries, preside over the members of the medical profession; but, unfortunately, on a more careful examination into their proceedings, we perceive that the

Faculty of Medicine of Paris refused leave to Ambrose Paré to print his work on the application of ligatures to arteries after operation. This invention, I have no hesitation in asserting, is the most important practical application of science for the purposes of the surgeon which has ever been submitted to the world, and yet, instead of being fostered by the distinguished men of the age, it was opposed, and never would have communicated its benefits to the unhappy victims of amputation, had not private interest been made with the king to allow the work to be printed, and thus confer its blessings on mankind. Nor is this a solitary instance. Did not the College of Physicians of London oppose the Royal Medico-Chirurgical Society—an association of the medical practitioners of this country, unrivalled for the extent of information that it has disseminated amongst those who devote their time to practise the healing art? The College of Surgeons, moreover, have looked with a jealous eye on that great University of London, which promises, by the talent which it has fostered, to effect great results for the improvement of our profession. These extraordinary instances of ill-directed authority, by men of the highest reputation in their day, show that we must receive with care their edicts, and, instead of taking for granted that the medical education they require is that best suited to make a practitioner of medicine, we must examine for ourselves a subject of such fundamental importance to the whole community.

Disregarding, then, the orders of human councils, we must take Nature for our guide, and, as a preliminary inquiry, we must study the relation of man to the external world. Now, on a most cursory view of those objects which are presented for our examination, we perceive that bodies divide themselves into two great divisions—one set in which no changes are taking place, and another in which continual alterations are occurring. These two sets of bodies we call respectively things with life, or organic things; things without life, or inorganic things.

Let us take as a type of a lifeless thing this piece of ice, and consider its qualities. We know that it is a compound of oxygen and hydrogen, in fact an oxide of hydrogen, the two elements being held together by the force of attraction. No change is taking place between these elements, but it possesses its individual characteristic by virtue of that attraction. As long as that attraction exists, it is still oxide of hydrogen, but a destruction of that attraction, or a supervention of a new one, would cause it to be no longer an oxide of hydrogen, but some other body. I may act upon this compound by external forces, and cause it to assume either the liquid or gaseous state, but it is still an oxide of hydrogen; and unless I destroy the attraction existing between the oxygen and hydrogen, it remains the same body. I can in the same way make this body hot, luminous, electrical, or vibrating, without any alteration in its composition. I might divide it to its finite particle, or increase its bulk indefinitely, but still its characteristic as an oxide of hydrogen would not be impaired.

An inorganic body, then, possesses matter and force; the force being only exerted between its own particles. Other matter indeed may act upon this matter, though it would not contribute in any way to produce its individual existence. To express these facts in the fewest words and most comprehensive manner, we may state that an inorganic body is a body which exists by means of forces exerted between the particles of matter of which the mass is made up.

Proceeding onwards in our investigation, we perceive another class of bodies said to be organic, the particles of which are continually undergoing some change of arrangement. The most simple division of this class of bodies is to be found in vegetables or plants, samples of which I now present to your notice in the India-rubber tree, the black-tea plant, and the beautiful filmy fern. We find that the material has tenacity and form, from a certain amount of the particles of which they are composed being held together by internal forces similar to those of inorganic bodies. In this respect stones and plants are identical; both having matter and internal forces. In the latter, however, we have continual changes occurring, and the mechanism of this change gives to the vegetable its characteristic property. In every plant we find that it is essential to vitality that it should contain not only a solid portion, but also a fluid: hence a plant is in two physical states, solid and fluid; in other words, it consists of stem and sap. Neither part alone exhibits any signs of life; a combination of both being required for that object. But the stem and sap, as a whole, will not exhibit change by means of forces generated alone within its own structure, for we find it to be essential for these results that external forces should act upon the whole plant to enable these alterations in the arrangement of its particles to ensue. The absolute necessity for the exertion of these external forces may be learnt from the fact, that if I either increase or diminish the amount requisite for each plant, the actions immediately cease; and if they cease but for one instant, the matter becomes inorganic, and no human power can ever make it take on the changes occurring in the vegetable or plant. If either this India-rubber tree or tea-plant were frozen, its action would cease for ever; and in the same way, if this delicate filmy fern, or even the other plants, were either to be over-heated or stimulated too highly by light, electricity or force, they would certainly perish. We thus find that a plant is a body held together by internal forces in two physical states, solid and fluid, undergoing certain changes by means of the action of external forces. As a consequence of this arrangement, a plant cannot be indefinitely divided; for to possess the characteristics of a plant it must retain all these essentials, and we cannot divide it if we desire to preserve its individuality beyond a single cell. As a short expression for the difference between plants and stones, we may state that a plant is a body whose particles are undergoing change from the action of forces from without. This property, I shall hereafter show you, is common to all organic bodies, so that definition can only be used to ascertain whether a body is a mineral or a vegetable. This expression harmonizes with the phenomena observed in all the numerous forms of plants habitating the globe; one plant differing from another not by its possessing some new attribute, but from a difference in the nature of the matter which composes its structure, the degree of force holding that matter together, the ease with which its particles assume new combinations, and the amount of external force required to effect that change. Every species of plant of necessity requires a peculiar amount of external force. If the filmy fern which inhabits the cracks and crannies of the rocks at Tunbridge Wells were exposed to the light which this tea-plant requires, it would speedily be killed, and this tea-plant would very ill bear the shade absolutely required by this little fern.

Having thus given you a rapid and cursory sketch of the properties of plants, I must now direct your attention to another division of organized bodies, which we term animals. In the diagrams which cover these walls, every form of animal known to Cuvier is delineated, and I have selected as an illustration of a living animal, this interesting little creature, the English dormouse. Here we again perceive the integral or component matter to be held together by internal forces, as we have before noticed in plants and vegetables. We observe, also, changes taking place in the arrangement of the particles, through the agency of external forces, as was before exemplified in the examination of the vegetable kingdom. We not only observe these things, but we notice that external forces acting upon the body of an animal make an impression which is not transitory, but is retained to influence the result of subsequent impressions. This registration of impressions gives rise to the effect of memory, which influences, in an important manner, the proceedings of the animal: for when external forces act upon the body, the effect of these forces is modified by antecedent impressions. The choice of action between present and past impressions we call volition, which is to be observed throughout the entire range of animal bodies; you may even observe it in the *Hydra viridis*, a polyp common in the neighbourhood of London; but an animal whose structure is so simple, that it has been described as a mere fleshy bag.

I will no longer occupy your time by narrating instances of actions from past impressions, in the animal kingdom, but will simply state, as a short expression of these facts, that the animal kingdom is peculiar in acting, not only from present, but from registered or past impressions: this property is common, not only to animals, but to man, and therefore can only serve as a mark to distinguish the animal from the plant or mineral.

I have now arrived at the more important part of my subject—the study of man himself—and there is as much difference to be observed between man and animals as between animals and plants, or even between plants and minerals. On examining his structure we find a material frame, the particles being aggregated together, and exhibiting form and volume; these properties are due entirely to the particles of matter being held together by internal forces, as in animals, plants, or stones. We find that the matter composing his body is in two physical states, the solid and fluid, at the same time, and that changes are continually taking place, by reason of the influence of external forces, as we have already observed, in plants and animals. Man, moreover, we notice to act upon registered or past impressions, as animals are known to do. Man, however, exhibits higher powers, and to these powers I have now to call your attention. If I take this piece of potassium and throw it into a basin of water, you perceive that it inflames, which inflammation is caused by its exerting a powerful attraction upon the oxygen of the water, and setting free gaseous hydrogen. In this experiment I am using the power of attraction, and using it to overcome other attractions. Now the employment of this power is far beyond the sphere of any animal, and can only be exerted by man. (Applause.) I could give you other instances of the application of attraction, as the use of a weight to set in motion a clock, but one instance of the exertion of a power will amply suffice for my purpose; I can employ light to give rise to certain actions. On the table before you lie daguerreotypes, calotypes, cyanotypes, chrysotees, enargyotypes, photographs, produced by the action of light. Man alone can use light, and in the instances before you it even required such men as Daguerre, Herschel, Fox Talbot, and Hunt, to turn the force to account. (Applause.) We all of us use heat; in fact, no meal is prepared without its agency. From the manufacture of the homely bread to the preparation of the most costly viands, this force is equally requisite for man; and yet what animal can or does employ this force of matter? I will show you a somewhat mysterious application of heat, if you will please observe the head of the worthy god which was placed by the builder in this theatre for ornament. You will perceive that an explosion will occur. The explanation of this explosion is simple—a wire was previous to the lecture placed around this theatre, and when I requested your attention to the image I completed a galvanic circuit, and the force generated in this battery was transmitted through the wires, and produced heat where I wanted it, namely, at the top of that figure. There, before lecture, I had placed some gunpowder, which exploded on the application of the heat.

Nor are these forces alone obedient to the power of man. I will show you how we can use the power of electricity; I will connect this electro-magnetic machine with the battery, and you will see the result. The rapidity with which it turns is enormous, and it affords a practical application of the power of man to use electricity. You can hardly view that beautiful bas-relief without admiring the sculptor's design; but when I tell you that specimen, the largest yet executed, was deposited, atom by atom, by means of the galvanic force, you will admit the power of man to use electricity. Other examples are on the table; those beautiful solid electro-silver and electro-silver-gilt waiters, made from the natural vine-leaf, show the power of man to employ this force.

We daily use ordinary force. The model of the locomotive engine on the table is brought here to impress that fact on your mind; but, as you must all be practically conversant with railway engines, I have not thought it necessary to set the model in action.

Man can also employ the force of sound,—of which a musical snuff-box is an instance;—but perhaps the use of the porter's bell, to signify the commencement of this lecture, suffices for an illustration of man's power to employ this force.

I have thus demonstrated that man can employ attraction, heat, light, electricity, force, and sound, to act upon matter; but, doubtless, you will tell me the electric eel kills his prey by electricity, the glow-worm lights its lamp, animals in their own bodies generate heat, and the merry cricket gives rise to cheerful notes. All these creatures, however, only employ the forces which arise from peculiar structures in their bodies—man gives rise to these forces. The electric eel uses the electricity generated in the organ, which I now exhibit to you, called the battery; the glow-worm furnishes light by the peculiar organization of the last two segments of the body. Man, however, makes the battery—man makes the candle, so that man causes matter to produce light, heat, and the various other forces which I have enumerated—a power which no animal possesses. (Applause.)

Nor is man's power limited to the application of these forces upon inorganic matter alone, but he can use them also to influence vegetation. Regard these little wild crabs, and see how cultivation has converted the same fruit into this large apple. Look also at these common hedge-nuts, changed by cultivation into the delicious filbert. I need hardly say that this power is only possessed by man.

Animals are as much under the power of man as plants are; he can improve their breed, and reduce them to subjection. The common use of horses is an example of that nature. One animal, however, cannot employ another animal. Who, for instance, ever saw an elephant drawn by camel-leopards? (Applause.) And yet, we might readily forget that the subjection of animals belongs to man alone.

We have now shown that man can employ heat, light, attraction, electricity, sound, the vegetable and animal bodies. Now, what is the nature of these powers which he uses? Attraction is an abstraction of a material property; heat is the same; so is electricity, sound, force, &c. The powers of animals and vegetables are in like manner the results of matter. We may, therefore, class all these powers together by stating, that man can employ matter to act upon other matter; man is not confined to the use of any particular piece of matter to produce these results, but any piece of matter will equally suit his purpose. We therefore find that man takes a higher stand, for he employs abstractions arising from the properties of matter.

To recapitulate the leading phenomena exhibited by man, we find that he is composed of integral matter, held together by internal forces; that the matter is in two physical states, solid and fluid; that actions are continually taking place by reason of external forces; that he acts not only upon immediate but upon bygone or antecedent impressions. In all these conditions, however, he is similar to animals; but the human being has the power of acting upon an arrangement and combination of simple material impressions, or, in other words, he acts upon their abstractions. To separate man from all other material bodies, we may define him to be a being acting upon the abstractions of material impressions.

In all human operations, matter must be employed, but man can only use the properties with which matter is endowed; he can neither add a new property, nor subtract an old one. Man's power, then, is confined to the use of the properties of matter; but though he cannot control matter, he perceives there must be a Supreme Power which in the first instance caused matter to have properties, and who, by the exertion of the same power, may will these properties to cease, or new ones to supervene. The contemplation of the Great Controller of the powers of matter forms the limit of the investigations of medical science, for at that point medical science ends and natural theology begins.

We are now in a condition to determine the means which are in our hands to act upon the human body. We can act upon it directly, by matter, through its power of attraction. We can act upon it also by heat, light, electricity, force, sound, as in the case of animal, vegetable, or mineral bodies. We have, however, another power by which we can act upon man—we may act upon his mind by abstractions. The influences of mental impressions may be inferred from deaths occurring from joy, fear, or other strong emotions. Let me, however, warn you and entreat you never to employ a false mental impression, as the effects of employing false mental impressions are most dangerous. Here is a charm which is supposed effectually to ward off all ill, physical or moral, from a child so protected. It consists of the berries of the mountain-ash, tied round with red thread, with the following couplet :—

> " Rowan tree, and red thread,
> Drives the witches at their sped."

Here are amulets used for a similar purpose. I show you also an Abraxas, a power presiding over 365 others, which is supposed to have wonderful efficacy. Here are the casts of all the royal-touch pieces known at the British Museum ; and I am enabled to exhibit to you an original coin from the museum of the great London antiquary, Mr. Charles Roach Smith : this, although as recent as the reign of Queen Anne, has been so much worn, to ward off the dreadful scourge of scrofula, that the impression is quite abraded. Here is a cast of a touch-piece of the Pretender, who, thinking that he had right to the English crown, had also equal right to confer the royal cure by touch. Do not think that spells, charms, or superstitions are at an end. In your professional career you will frequently be astonished at their use. I hold in my hand an engine of that character, called an Homœopathic Medicine Chest (applause), which has already produced so many cures, according to the statement of its owner, that their enumeration would occupy me till to-morrow. In an examination of the chest this morning, I perceived the bottle labelled camphor had no odour ; that of musk had lost, in a similar manner, its physical properties—a single grain of musk will fill a large room with odour for twenty years, and yet here was not the slightest scent to be discovered. The idea flashed across my mind, that these little globules were all made alike, and I transferred over to the laboratory about 100 globules, containing two or three substances which were not likely to have become injured by keeping, and the presence of which could most readily be detected. The united skill of two or three chemists failed to demonstrate by ordinary means the smallest trace of the assumed substances. (Much applause and laughter.) The evidence on this point is negative ; but yet it appears to me improbable, that 100 globules should contain a substance easy of detection, and yet not give immediate indication to chemical tests.

I do not doubt that the owner really effected cures with this chest ; nor do I doubt that the amulets, abraxas, and royal touch-pieces, produced, in some cases, a similar effect ; but I do most earnestly warn you never to lend yourself to produce a false mental impression, for the human mind has been in the bondage of astrology and witchcraft, and may again return to its former degraded position. Look, I pray you, at this book ; see how accurately it gives the position of the stars for good and evil, when to apply medicine, to stop a flux, or to cause a purge, and let that be sufficient to warn you from the horrible effects of superstition, and deter you from ever using charms, amulets, homœopathic globules, the combination of stars, or any other mental abominations.

Man is composed of integral matter, held together by internal forces, so that the first investigation that we must undertake is, to inquire into the nature of the matter, and the character of the forces. This study constitutes chemistry, a class at this school under the care of Mr. Makins; and let me urge upon you the necessity of chemical knowledge. I speak as one who has been considered by medical practitioners to have devoted too much time to this science; but I must say that on no subject do I now feel my ignorance so much as on this. Chemistry is not only of paramount importance to medical practice, but is an ornament in every rank of life. The manner in which this matter is actually arranged constitutes general anatomy, a subject which is in the hands of Dr. Goodfellow, whose acquirements in this department are too well known to require any comments from me. The surgical anatomy, another department of the study of the matter of the human body, is taught by Mr. Holthouse and Mr. Chance; and the study of the actions taking place in man, or physiology, is under Mr. Holthouse, with whom you are already personally acquainted. You would naturally expect that, man's characteristic being mind, the study of mind would occupy our especial attention; but perhaps you will not be astonished, when I state that neither the opponents of Paré's discovery, nor those of the Medico-Chirurgical Society, have considered that the study of the human mind is in the slightest degree requisite. The practical effect of their determination is, that madness is of no consequence, its treatment of no importance. Do not believe them: regard the ordinances of nature, not those of man; and make yourselves thoroughly acquainted with the properties of the mind, in health and disease. The agents which we employ to affect the human body are called Materia Medica, comprising matter, forces, and mental impressions. This department we have entrusted to Dr. Garrod, a gentleman who has obtained the highest honours in the prosecution of his studies, and whom we may also believe will receive corresponding success in carrying them out. The practice of physic, or the exact application of medical agents to particular diseases, is, as heretofore, still under the care of Dr. Aldis and Dr. Grant; and now you will have ample opportunities of observing the actual practice of these gentlemen at their respective institutions. The surgery, gentlemen, has been confided by my colleagues to my charge; and when I consider that in this theatre almost every distinguished man in London, of this century, has lectured, I feel deeply impressed with the importance of the duties which I have to perform, but I promise in sincerity and truth, that to the utmost of my abilities I will endeavour to discharge my duties, to your instruction and benefit. There are certain collateral branches, as botany and comparative anatomy, which are under the care of Dr. Brown, and I may state the latter course is gratuitous. Forensic medicine, or that part of medical science which is especially connected with the courts of law, is in the hands of Dr. Sewell, a gentleman whom, you doubtless are aware, has, in the prosecution of his studies, received the highest rewards for his industry and talents, and whom we consider a valuable adjunct to our staff. The last class, or that of obstetric medicine, one of the utmost importance to the general practitioner, will be undertaken by Mr. Druitt, known to the world as the author of the 'Surgeon's Vade Mecum.'

Gentlemen, the study of our profession divides itself into two departments, science and practice. Science leads to the honours of the profession, practice to the emolument; but the really great man must combine science with practice. The lecturers of this school have been extremely anxious to afford you every opportunity of observing disease, and to further that object they have determined to throw open, without additional charge, the practice of the several institutions to which they are respectively attached. We have opened to you a chest infirmary, an eye institution, and portions of the practice of seven dispensaries. At these institutions, eleven clinical clerks will be appointed from this school. At these charities, you will see diseases as you will have to treat them in after-life; you will see them under the same circumstances of position and state, and you will have most ample opportunities of making yourselves acquainted with diseases in all their multifarious forms.

I trust you will excuse me if I say a few words upon the relation which we are desirous should exist between the teachers and pupils. We are one and all desirous that free intercourse and communication should continually take place between us. We wish you to regard us as students further advanced in that knowledge, the end of which we can never attain. Whatever you would ask of a friend, ask of us, as your teachers, and nothing will please us so much as continually to contribute to your welfare.

You are about to enter, gentlemen, upon the study of the most exalted profession. Every moment of your life will be spent in the study and observation of nature. The most intimate structure of the human body will be exposed to your view, and the innermost recesses of the human mind will be revealed to you. Every moment of your life will be spent in doing good, and contributing to the happiness and welfare of your fellow-creatures; day by day you will receive the praises and heart-felt thanks of gratitude for your aid in the time of danger and disease. Let me not deceive you, gentlemen; do not think you will attain eminence without the most incessant labour and the most unremitting attention; and you will find, with all your exertion, your utter inability to master the subject you have taken in hand. Delighted with every step you make, you will, in the language of the Psalmist, exclaim, "Such knowledge is too wonderful and excellent for me, I cannot attain unto it."

[NOTE.—The lecture throughout was profusely illustrated with specimens of the power of man, and the room presented generally an imposing appearance, from a display of beautiful examples of the novelties of science.]

---

## No. XIV.

### ON THE DETECTION OF NEEDLES, ETC., IN THE HUMAN BODY. Lecture delivered at the Aldersgate School of Medicine, December 9th, 1844.

WHEN the foreign body, retained in the wound, is either iron or steel, we have means by which we may readily and effectually determine its presence. Portions of steel are particularly liable to be introduced into the body, in the shape of needles, or as parts of cutting instruments; and, especially in the former case, cause irremediable injury. Some time since, I had a case under my care, where a small portion of a needle was introduced into one of the joints of the finger, but of which no indication existed beyond the effects which might have been expected from the presence of a foreign body. The exact spot of its insertion was unknown; and indeed it was equally uncertain whether it was inserted or not. Subsequently the joint swelled, suppurated, and discharged, and a small piece of needle was found firmly impacted in the bone. Now, a very small piece of foreign matter is capable of producing these disastrous results; and, on having weighed the piece discharged in this case, I found that it scarcely amounted to the ⅓ of a grain. To this case I shall again draw your attention, when I come to my lectures on the diseases of the joints, because it showed accidentally, on the human subject, the course of the inflammation and suppuration of the part, the subsequent ulceration of the cartilages and osseous tissue, and, finally, the course of the reparative process, by the termination of the inflammation by anchylosis. On reference to my note-book, for the purpose of studying this case, it occurred to my mind that, had I known that the needle was actually present, and could have demonstrated its exact spot, I might possibly have averted the present inconvenience of a stiff joint to the unfortunate sufferer; and, after having carefully considered the matter, a plan suggested itself to my mind for the detection of needles in future cases. You are all acquainted with the curious condition which steel assumes under certain circumstances, whereby it evinces properties which are called magnetic; you know, moreover, that like magnetic poles repel, and opposite attract each other. You have, therefore, but to render a piece of enclosed steel a magnet, and you will be able not only to ascertain its presence, but to determine by its polarity its general direction; and, by the amount of magnetism it evinces, you may even infer its probable bulk.

When you suspect the presence of a piece of needle, or other steel instrument, you must subject the suspected part to a treatment calculated to render the needle magnetic; and there are two principal methods by which this object may be effected: the first, by transmitting a galvanic current, at right angles, to the suspected part; the second, by placing a large magnet near the part affected, so that the object may be magnetized by induction. You may accomplish the first end by taking a copper wire, covered with cotton, or still better with silk (in fact, you may employ the covered wire as generally used for the formation of electro-magnets), and

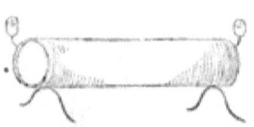

Fig. 11. Covered Wire, as generally used for the formation of Electro-Magnets.

wind it round the parts suspected to contain steel, several times, so that the same current may act at right angles, many times, upon the piece of steel; you may then take a galvanic battery (one of my little tumbler batteries will amply suffice), and connect one end of the wire to the zinc, the other to the platinized silver. The adjoining cut, fig. 11, shows the general arrangement which may be adopted to effect this object. The current might be continued for half an hour, or more, when the steel would become magnetized, and thereby give strong indications of its presence.

For my own part, I should use the second plan, or the plan of magnetizing by induction, to render the needle magnetic. For this purpose, I have employed a temporary electro-magnet, which I magnetized by the voltaic battery; and you will find that, by keeping the part affected as close as possible to the instrument, for about half an hour, you will sufficiently obtain the desired object.

The electro-magnet might be made of the horse-shoe form, if we knew the direction of the object; but, in that case, we should not require its use at all, as the proof of the existence of the needle is our only aim. I have used the horse-shoe magnet, but should prefer in most cases an electro-magnet like this (fig. 12), made for me by Messrs. Horne, of Newgate Street, which is made of a simple straight bar of soft iron, wound round with wire. You will perceive by the diagram that the iron has a plate of brass (B) fixed on both ends to retain the wire (w) *in situ*; and you may also perceive that the two ends of the wire are attached to binding screws (s).

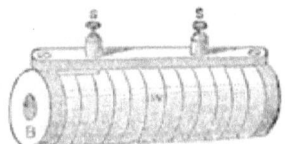

Fig. 12.   Electro-Magnet.

Your chemical lecturer has, doubtlessly, made you aware that the magnetic effect, *cæteris paribus*, is proportionate to the power of the battery; accordingly, you must select a voltaic combination suitable for the desired object. You might use a Cruikshanks' battery, made of alternate pieces of wire and copper soldered together. You might use one of the old Woollaston batteries, made of a plate of copper, surrounding a plate of zinc. You might employ one or more Daniell's batteries, which consist of an outer copper cylinder with a solution of sulphate of copper, and an inner porous vessel containing zinc and dilute acid. You might employ the battery invented by Mr. Grove: he uses for his negative platinum, and in the inner porous cell he puts strong nitric acid, and in the outer vessel with the zinc dilute sulphuric or muriatic acid. It really is of no consequence whether you select the one or the other battery for this particular purpose. I believe, however, that mine is far more commonly used for the ordinary purposes of life. Of my batteries you may use the triple or pot battery, which consists of a piece of platinized silver, in the top of which is fixed a piece of wood to prevent contact between the silver and the zinc. To the silver a binding screw is fixed to connect it with any desired object; a strip of zinc is placed on each side of the wood, and both are held in their place by a binding screw, sufficiently wide to embrace the wires and wood. You may use the odds-and-ends form, which consists of a plate of platinized silver for the negative pole, suspended in a vessel of acid, and fragments of zinc and mercury, placed at the bottom of the vessel for the positive pole. When you require considerable power, you will find the compound trough battery very convenient for this purpose, formed of two plates of zinc, one on each side the silver. The liquid generally adopted to excite the platinized silver battery is a mixture of one part by measure of sulphuric acid, and seven of water. The compound battery will magnetize a needle, in conjunction with the electro-magnet at the distance of an inch, in the space of two or three minutes.

A powerful permanent magnet would answer as well as the temporary magnet; but permanent magnets are expensive, and not so constantly at hand. When soft iron is impacted in any part of the body, we do not require either the electro- or permanent magnet, for on this substance we are unable to confer magnetic properties.

We should never think of taking the trouble of magnetizing a part suspected to contain steel, or iron, unless we could get no indication of its presence without; for, perchance, the object might be sufficiently large to give indication without being magnetized, or it may have been magnetized before its introduction.

Almost all my steel instruments, in common use, are more or less magnetic, from their having been exposed to electricity whilst performing my electrical experiments; and, therefore, should I have the misfortune to introduce them into my body, they would be indicated without any process to render them further magnetic. Although foreign to a course of lectures on surgery, I may state that, when handling powerful magnets, you should always put aside your watch, for my own has many a time played me most troublesome pranks from its springs having become magnetic.

To test the existence of a magnet within the body, we may take a magnetized sewing-needle, and suspend it by a piece of silkworm's silk, when it will exhibit certain phenomena upon the approach of the suspected part, provided it contain a piece of magnetized steel. Although this simple contrivance will amply suffice, I myself possess a needle which was made for me by Messrs. Willats, of Cheapside, and which is well adapted for the purpose.

It consists, as you perceive, of a delicate needle, about six inches long, centred upon a small agate cup, resting upon a steel point, so that the smallest possible amount of resistance is offered to its free play, fig. 13.

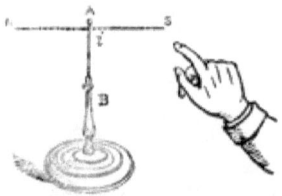

FIG. 13.   Magnetized Needle, for discovering needles within the body.

When a part, containing magnetic steel, is brought near the needle, it may be either attracted or repelled; it may move upwards or downwards; or it may exhibit disquietude according to the position in which the new magnet is held. We may detect the position of the foreign body, when it is of any size, by ascertaining where its north and south poles lie; and these are determined by their repelling and attracting the opposite poles of the magnetic needle. The disquietude, or motion upwards and downwards, merely indicates magnetism, but not the direction of the magnet.

You will doubtless be surprised when I tell you that, in this manner, I have detected a piece of needle impacted in the finger of a young woman, although it weighed but the seventh of a grain. This gave such marked indications, that I found out tolerably well the position of its north and south poles, though I could not ascertain the presence of a foreign body in any other way. I tried experiments on smaller pieces, at short distances, such as half an inch to an inch, and I found that a piece of needle, weighing $\frac{1}{35}$ of a grain, gave decided indications after having been magnetized, and, perhaps, even a still smaller amount of steel might in some cases be detected.[*]

The batteries, electro-magnets, and magnetic needle, you may procure of Messrs. Horne, of Newgate Street; or of Messrs. Willats, of Cheapside; or, by order, of any other instrument-maker: but if you, or any of your friends, meet with doubtful cases of this character, my own apparatus is at your service, and I shall esteem it as a favour if you would allow me to be present at the examination, in order that I may see the varieties which different cases present.

A centred magnetic needle should always accompany the ordinary electro-magnets used for medical purposes; as the medical practitioner, having that machine, might, with this addition alone, always determine the presence of steel particles.

Of medical electrical machines the primary coil machine may be employed; as the bundle of wires, when magnetized, will serve to magnetize the needle. The platinum spring machine may be employed in a similar manner, and the bundle of wires in the rack machine may also be used to effect the same object. In all these cases you must be careful to continue the voltaic current in the same direction; for, if you reversed the current but one instant, it would tend to undo what has already been done.

I have now satisfactorily demonstrated to you, that magnetism may be used for the detection of steel particles, impacted within the body, with absolute success; and, though but a very trifling application of natural philosophy to the practice of surgery, I have no doubt that, had it been adopted before, many joints would have been saved; and I confidently anticipate that it will be the means, in future, of frequently saving these parts from destruction.

---

## No. XV.a.

## AN ACCOUNT OF THE VARIOUS BREADS EXHIBITED UNDER THE TITLE OF " FAMINE FOOD," at Mr. Smee's residence in Finsbury Circus in February 1847. Taken from sundry newspapers.

The 'Morning Herald' states: " A very interesting collection of bread in fourteen varieties was exhibited under the title of 'Famine Food.' The rye, barley, and Indian corn breads require no comment, from their want of novelty. The root breads were respectively made of half of the root previously boiled and reduced to a fine pulp, with half its weight of wheaten flour. The yam bread was good, and much resembled potato

---

[*] These weights are the nearest fractions, but we ascertained the exact weight of these fragments by the standard balance belonging to the Bank of England: these two portions amounted respectively to the $\frac{155}{1000}$ and the $\frac{17}{1000}$ of a grain; the exact weight of the portion alluded to in the former part of the paper was the $\frac{152}{1000}$ of a grain.

bread. It is a mere scientific curiosity in this country, though we are informed that it is employed in the West Indies. The turnip bread had a very agreeable flavour, but the loaf was very small. The relative price was not stated, but we should think it would not be an economic food. It might, perhaps, be used as a luxury. Bread made with the sugar-beet was good and palatable, so was also that made with mangold-wurzel. There was a good sample manufactured from the red beet by Mr. Farnes, which had the colour removed by repeated boilings. Parsnip bread was one of the best breads shown, and was moreover a large loaf. Bread made with the white carrot in the same manner had no peculiar flavour, which of course is a great advantage for food which is to be used constantly. Artichoke bread has the flavour of that root; it makes a good bread. Perhaps the root breads can hardly be called famine food, because the materials of which they are formed are articles of food under any circumstances, and they will be just as available for human food when cooked in the usual manner as when made into bread. There were, however, two decided novelties exhibited, namely Iceland moss bread and hay bread, which will strictly bear the name of famine bread. Half Iceland moss and half wheaten flour make a dark-coloured bread of great weight and probably highly nutritious. It, however, possesses a peculiar bitter flavour, agreeable to those who like bitters, and disagreeable to those who dislike that taste. The hay food attracted great attention; it was shown in two forms—as hay bread and hay biscuits. The colour was very dark and repulsive, but the odour was agreeable. In taste it was sweet and high-flavoured, somewhat resembling that of strong and high-flavoured tea. The greater part of the company agreed as to its palatable character; some even thought it delicious, though others thought it disagreeable. To prepare it the hay was ground into an impalpable powder and mixed with half flour, to hold the particles together. The hay food is probably highly nutritious, and might form a valuable famine food; but, being quite a novelty, experience is wanted upon the subject."

The 'Sun' states that "the hay bread was a sweet-smelling and not unpalatable food. The Iceland moss bread alone was nauseous: all the other varieties were well tasted, and presented the appearance of an ordinary loaf, and indicating by the smell the vegetable from which it was prepared."

The 'Morning Post' states: "The most interesting objects, and those which excited the greatest attention, were specimens of famine food. About a dozen different kinds were submitted for examination, consisting of rye, barley, Indian meal, parsnip, yam, beet-root, artichoke, carrot, Iceland moss, and hay. With the exception of the two last, these breads seem to be well adapted for use, not only in times of scarcity, but also when no such dire exigency exists. The Iceland moss and hay breads are black, and fit only to be used as human food when terrors similar to those described by Josephus of the last siege of Jerusalem shall fall upon us."

The 'Morning Advertiser' observes that "foremost among the series of illustrations exhibited we have to notice those which are immediately connected with the progress of the potato disease, and with the inventions to which that great calamity has given birth, in the formation of substitutes both for the potato and for bread, from the most available natural pro-

ducts. In the former part of this subject Mr. Smee, who has given it great
attention, has procured specimens of diseased bulbs in almost every stage
of the blight: from these he has obtained sections passing through the
seat or origin of the disease, and, by a proper arrangement of the sections,
he has succeeded in exhibiting its progress at one comprehensive glance.
He has also obtained several specimens of the *Aphis vastator*, or destructive insect, to the agency of which the ruin of the potato, and indeed of
other plants, has been attributed. Mr. Smee placed them under the
lenses of powerful microscopes, twelve of which were adjusted at one table.
Amongst the specimens of potatoes sent up were some from the estate of
the Right Hon. the Speaker of the House of Commons, in Hampshire.
They were also accompanied by some large plants, and by leaves of the
mangold-wurzel destroyed by the *Aphis vastator*, which in some instances
was found upon the plant itself. Other diseased specimens of the forthcoming crop have been received by Mr. Smee from various other parts of
the country. Amongst the substitution for potatoes and bread Mr. Smee
exhibited fourteen loaves made from as many different materials. Amongst
them might be mentioned those of hay, sweet beet-root, turnips, carrots,
parsnips, mangold-wurzel, Iceland moss, and hay biscuits. Many of these
are unquestionably very palatable and nutritious, as, for instance, the
bread from turnips, carrots, and beet-root. The hay biscuits and bread
are most singular compounds. They are of a deep brown colour approaching almost to black, possess all the fragrance of hay, and are nutritious in
a high degree. Of their nutritious powers, indeed, there seems to be no
question; the grand point to be ascertained is their susceptibility of
yielding to the action of the digestive organs. Most of the other breads
mentioned above are of the same colours as wheaten and maize."

---

## No. XV.B.

### ON THE POTATO DISEASE, 1845–46–47.
### By ALFRED SMEE, F.R.S.

#### THE APHIDES AND THE APHIS VASTATOR.

*As reported by* ED. LATHAM, *Royal General Dispensary, Aldersgate Street.*
On Wednesday evening, March 10th, 1847, A. Smee, Esq., F.R.S., Surgeon
to the Bank of England, &c., delivered at the London Institution a
lecture on aphides and on the *Aphis vastator* as being the cause of the
potato disease, &c. The following is the substance of Mr. Smee's
lecture:—

I feel deep responsibility in coming before the public to consider the
subject of the present scarcity of food. My observation has proved to me
that the cause of this scarcity is a plague of insects, resulting from a preternatural abundance of those insects, and their settling, feeding on, and
destroying various kinds of plants. History records numerous devas-
tating plagues of insects analogous to the present; immense and almost
incredible swarms of locusts, which destroyed every green thing, are

spoken of by Orosius, St. Augustine, Barrow, and others; but the first
account of such plagues is handed down to us in the 8th and 10th chapters
of Exodus. Another example is furnished by the cockchafer of this
country, which increased so excessively some years ago as to destroy every
plant and blade of grass existing in various districts. Other insects have
also at various times been most destructive; but I may refer you to the
delightful work of Kirby and Spence on Entomology for most interesting
information on these subjects. My observations and researches touching
last year's scarcity have proved to me that its cause was attributable to a
preternatural increase of an insect of the family of the aphides, a tribe so
small that they may be passed unseen and unnoticed, though assembled in
vast nations on the plants around, subsisting on and destroying an
important item of the food of man. This insect, so insignificant in
appearance, has thus given rise to considerations of high importance: it
has produced famine in Ireland and Scotland, scarcity of the means of
subsistence in England, and the effects of its ravages have disturbed the
political relations of the whole habitable globe. My previous observations
and the facts I had collected on this subject are before the public, which
amount to testimony the accuracy of which cannot be disputed. I am not
here to-night to enunciate any new thing, but simply to draw your careful
attention to such facts as the present season affords, in order that you
may consider what may be the best means of averting future ravages, with
their consequent scarcity and distress. Aphides, as I have stated, are very
small creatures, but frightfully prolific. On a moderate calculation, one
aphis may be the progenitor of ten, and each future one of ten more; so
that, increasing in geometrical ratio, the first aphis may become the
ancestor of a quintillion at the end of the season; arriving at an amount
so vast that it almost overcomes the understanding. Ten generations of
aphides increasing in this ratio, each one producing ten, if placed the
head of each at the tail of another, would form a circle extending round
our globe: indeed, their fecundity is most enormous. Aphides will exist
in all parts and through all seasons. They are very tenacious of life, and
are connected with all scarcities, not only the present, but no doubt with
many that are past.

In investigating the nature and character of these insects, it becomes necessary to ascertain the quality of their food, which must consist
of organic matter, animal or vegetable, and also must be either dead
or living animal or vegetable matter. As an illustration of such inquiry,
the leaves of the strawberry-plant before me were found covered with
black spots similar to those observed on the leaves of the diseased
potato, &c. I had this strawberry-plant placed in a pinery where no
aphides existed, but in due time these black spots on its leaves were
further developed, and became insects, each of which passed through the
various stages of its insect life, from the larva to the pupa, and from the
pupa became the imago or perfect winged aphis. In these conditions
it was found living and feeding on the leaves of the plant; therefore
its proper food is demonstrated to be vegetable, and living vegetable,
matter.

The next inquiry, and one which has been controverted, is whether the
vegetable matter on which the aphis subsists be healthy or diseased. This
strawberry-plant, when first placed in the pinery, was healthy-looking and

flourishing, but so soon as the insects were developed, and preyed upon its juices, it became deteriorated, and manifested unequivocal symptoms of disease. To-day I placed some living aphides upon the leaves of the healthy potato-plant on the table, upon which they are actively feeding, and, if means are not adopted to stop their ravages on this plant, it will become diseased and die in consequence. Then from these examples we may infer that aphides appear first on healthy plants, and, therefore, live on healthy vegetable matter.

In the next place, in order to understand the process of this disease, we should know the part of the plant that aphides exist on, and which must be either solid or fluid. To determine this point an examination of their apparatus for feeding becomes necessary. This is extremely delicate. Situated on the under-side of the head is the rostrum, which is about one-fourth as long as the whole body, and contains a fine instrument for piercing the leaf and the walls of its cells: this is found to consist of three fine setæ or delicate piercers, one of which answers to the tongue and the others to the jaws of the insect. These are very beautiful objects for examination with the microscope. If an aphis be examined by means of a magnifying-glass, whilst attached, it will be seen to have a sort of proboscis applied to the leaf, and if touched it will be found to adhere pretty firmly by this, which constitutes its suctorial apparatus, and it requires some seconds to disengage itself from its position. This apparatus, by which it is so closely attached, is that by which it is enabled to pierce the leaf, break up its cells, and suck the vital fluid as it passes through the leaf to be rendered fit for the nourishment of the plant.

From these facts, then, we deduce that aphides suck the juices of plants, which is analogous to the blood of animals. and, therefore, the sap is impaired in its qualities in that vital organ—the leaf, whence its power of fulfilling its various functions is either weakened or destroyed. If the sap is taken away, its functions cannot be performed ; and if its nutritive properties are weakened, it cannot properly nourish the plant, which in consequence becomes debilitated, and an imperfect vegetable tissue is formed, that is in itself very prone to die, of which I have had numerous examples in large tulips, crocuses, mangold-wurzel, potatoes, &c. Death of a plant may be either local, i.e. confined to the spot where the aphis penetrates the leaf or leaflet, as is shown by the spots seen on the various kinds of leaf upon the table, as of the turnip, potato, horse-radish, &c. ; or one single leaf, or a certain number of leaves or leaflets, may die without the disease passing further into the plant. One portion of the stem may perish and cut off the supply of nutriment from other leaflets, which will die from this secondary cause, or the whole of the stem may be cut down, and thus the due supply of properly elaborated sap being prevented, the plant must perish. The plant may also begin to perish at the extreme ends of the rootlets, the ascent of crude sap for elaboration being rendered impossible. Any portion of the stem may also first manifest the disease ; but most frequently the malady first shows itself at the part which is technically and vulgarly called "the collar" of the plant (being the intermediate part between the ascending and descending axes). This is very frequent, especially in the potato and turnip. Then we find that partial death following the attacks of aphides may be only local at the part where the insect makes its puncture, and breaks up the cellular tissue, or the death may be remote from the part first attacked; and remote death resulting from the attacks of the aphides invariably kills the plant, because the supply of nourishment becomes cut off from its upper part. Death produced in this remote way often causes the potato-plants which appear in a green, succulent condition to wither up in a few hours, the communication between the stem and root being cut off by the action of disease; so that the total death of the plant may arise from the death of a part necessary to the whole. Plants resist the attacks of aphides better under some conditions than others. All wild plants resist better than cultivated ones. A wild turnip in a field will flourish amid the ravages of aphides when all the cultivated ones are destroyed; and the same is true in reference to the wild potato, and indeed all wild plants. The potato-plant, as we cultivate it, is in an unnatural condition, differing from the wild or natural plant in having great excess of tuber (an excess of cellular tissue over fibre) and great deficiency of leaves. Wild plants, or plants in a condition well calculated to develop fibre, well resist the attacks of aphides, when highly-cultivated plants, or plants not under circumstances favourable to the formation of fibre, resist them badly. There is a particular period in the growth of the potato-plant (as well as others) when the solid material formed or elaborated in the leaf is most wanted. At that period the plant becomes most liable to die from any injurious causes. In the potato, the most critical time in its growth is when the supply of nourishment contained or stored up in the old potato, or set, at its base is consumed; then, if the organization of the leaf has been injured, its functions are impaired, and when called on for that purpose it cannot give the necessary healthy vital fluid for the nutriment of the plant and the deposit of solid fibre, and it dies in consequence; or it exists in a debilitated condition, forming imperfect tissue; therefore it may be stated that plants are most injured by aphides at that period of their growth when they are required to deposit most fibre. When from such causes the tissue of the plant has once been rendered imperfect or diseased, all future growths have a tendency to continue the diseased action and to form unsound tissue. You all know familiarly the hereditary tendency to disease that exists in families, which may pass from generation to generation, and thus the faults and imperfections of one are transmitted downward to another. Apple-trees, rose-trees, &c., when once debilitated, have been noticed to exhibit a return of such condition in all future growths emanating from them, and it is so in the potato, &c. This, then, leads us to deduce a law, that plants having their tissue damaged from aphides propagate diseased tissue in all their future growths. Generally, if a plant begins to perish it is soon cut down, indeed in a very few days, and the influence of the hot sun often causes it to perish very greatly in a single day.

The death of the plant exercises also an important influence on the aphis. When its supply of subsistence becomes diminished, it does not remain to perish amid the famine itself has made, but the pupa of the aphis casts its coat, and becomes the winged insect, prepared to fly away and commit similar ravages elsewhere. Vast clouds of them rise together from fields that have perished, often forming quite a mist in the atmosphere. I have accounts of these vast clouds of insects being seen in nearly all parts of England. After migrating to a new locality, they will settle down perpendicularly in a mass upon the fields to recommence their work of destruction. Last summer I was informed that travellers in the neighbourhood of Norwich were very much inconvenienced by the clouds of aphides flying about and almost blinding them. From these manifestations of the insect, then, we find that the injury to plants hastens the transformation of the aphides. After the attacks of aphides and damage to the tissue of the plant, we find upon examining the decaying tubers, &c., that they become covered with parasitic fungi, of which there are thirty or forty varieties. These grow and flourish in the decaying vegetable matter, and are, in fact, the scavengers provided by nature to remove the decomposing substance and to prevent contamination of the atmosphere by putrid and poisonous exhalations. These fungi are in most cases observed on the diseased potato. As they grow they eat up, as it were, the soft and decaying parts as fast as they rot; and thus is inorganic matter converted into organic—thus is death converted into life. These fungi have been considered to be the source and cause of the disease; and Martius, who was the first investigator of this subject, traces many fungi, and attributes the disease to them; but, in fact, they never make their appearance until the potato-plant has been previously damaged, and until some portion of it is already dead. I have tried many experiments to produce the disease by inoculating sound potatoes, but the result has been a failure. I conclude, then, that it is a necessary law that the attacks of aphides are almost invariably followed by the growth of fungi.

We have now spoken of the effects of the attacks of aphides on plants, and the conditions or laws of those effects. We have also noticed the excessive numbers that can be produced from a single aphis; and that, assembled in vast swarms, they cause immense and serious mischief. Aphides, which we have shown to be so destructive by their excessive numbers, are themselves the natural prey of numerous creatures; and their increase, therefore, may lead us to believe that the natural balance of creation has been disturbed, and that their natural destroyers have been diminished. Ladybirds are enemies to and destroyers of aphides, and being more conspicuous often lead us to the discovery of the latter. Last year it is believed that ladybirds were scarce, though in many seasons, particularly that of 1805, these creatures have been noticed in great abundance on the cliffs at Dover, and other places on the coast. The hop aphis often produces great havoc in the crop, and ladybirds are always much welcomed in the hop-grounds. The gauzewing, too, feeds on aphides with equal voracity, as also do various dypterous insects of the genus sylphidæ. It would be well if we could breed these creatures by millions. Various hymenopterous insects are great destroyers of aphides, one genus of which, called ichneumons, deposit their egg in the body of the aphis: the egg becomes a maggot that feeds upon the aphis, which swells, assumes a globular form, and at length dies, remaining adherent to the leaf. After the death of the aphis the enclosed creature eats a hole through the case which contains it, and comes out a winged insect. I have watched this process, and seen the ichneumon escape from aphides in my own possession. Nature, amid all her wonders, goes a step further than this, for another genus of hymenoptera, the chalcididæ, deposit their egg within the maggot of the already punctured aphis; and thus we have an aphis with a maggot within its body, eating it up, and lastly a maggot within this maggot devouring that also; in part verification of the lines :—

> " Great fleas and little fleas have smaller fleas to bite 'em,
> The smaller fleas have lesser fleas, so on *ad infinitum*."

Aphides live on all plants; and therefore, if not kept in check, are competent to destroy all human food. They are materially checked by a variety of birds as well as the different insects, such as the swallow, the robin, &c., and also ducks: these destroy them in great numbers; and consider how many aphides it must take to make a meal for a single bird. When a schoolboy I formed the idea of examining the crops of birds, and have found them to contain innumerable insects, and, no doubt, aphides. It must be recommended, then, to protect such birds during the inclemency of winter, and they will amply repay the trouble in summer. Almost every plant has one particular aphis belonging to it, which it has been usual to name according to the plant it infested; but the aphis which comes more especially under our consideration as being the cause of the potato disease feeds also on a great variety of other plants, both wild and cultivated, many of which are necessary to man for food or medicine, as the wheat, Indian corn, artichoke, turnip, parsnip, shepherd's-purse, mustard, spinach, nightshade, henbane, stramonium, carrot, pasture-grass, couch-grass, spurge, groundsel, celery, &c. &c.; and every day I am adding to a much longer list fresh specimens attacked by this particular aphis. A distinguished naturalist asked me the other day how I managed to breed aphides. My answer was that I could not help breeding them, for where I do not want them the creatures get upon my sound plants, which they would destroy if not removed.

The potato disease and failure in crop is no novelty. We can trace the same disease through a series of years, sometimes occurring here, sometimes there; and the only difference between these visitations and the present one is, that this is more general, affecting all localities. Hollins describes a similar disease as occurring about the beginning of the eighteenth century, and states that the Society of Arts awarded a premium for the best remedy. When Martius wrote in the year 1830, the same disease existed and spread rapidly in Germany. This disease is in the potato itself without any difference of opinion; and it is essentially gangrene or death, gangrene of the leaf, of the stem, or different parts of the stem, the underground stem, tuber-bearing stems, and of the different tubers. There are two forms of mortification or gangrene, and they present themselves as the *gangrene humide* or moist gangrene, and the *gangrene sicca* or dry gangrene. In the moist gangrene the potato-tuber, &c., becomes disorganized by rotting, and is wet and offensive. In the dry gangrene the tuber shrinks up and becomes quite hard and desiccated; and in certain cases it becomes as hard and dry as a bit of wood, and will even bear a polish. Both kinds of gangrene are accompanied by fungi, but especially the moist; and all gangrenous tissue is deficient in starch, as may be seen in my preparations under the microscope; and examples of the empty condition of the starch cells were figured by Martius when he wrote. Chemical analysis also proves that the diseased tubers are deficient in starch, and starch-makers cannot obtain from them more than half the usual quantity.

Examining this question physiologically, then, we find on the plant a certain insect, and that on a part of the plant, viz. the leaf, which is destined to elaborate solid matter for the growth of the whole. Anatomy and physiology also show that the insect, by its conformation, is calculated to take away and feed upon the sap or vital fluid of the plant, which was destined to form solid and healthy vegetable matter. The microscope demonstrates that a due and healthy proportion of solid material does not exist in the diseased tissue; and chemical analysis also fully confirms the fact. So that the cause, the progress, and the ultimate effects of this vegetable malady are clearly and satisfactorily explained by the conjoint evidence of observation, physiology, anatomy, and chemistry. This aphis produces the same results in all plants, its operations on which I have watched one after the other, and I am now watching others go through the same progress. Some strong plants are not easily affected by the attacks of the aphis; for example, a large beet-root vigorously resists the ravages of these creatures, and requires, at least, ten thousand of them to destroy it. As there have been many different plants attacked and destroyed by aphides, these creatures have accordingly received different names, usually with reference to the plant on which they subsist; and I am told there is a book in the British Museum in which all these are recapitulated. It appeared to me, however, that the aphis giving rise to the potato disease also commits great or equal ravages on many other plants good for the food of man, or otherwise useful to him; but, not being able to find that any characteristic name was applied to it, I carefully consulted with Mr. Thompson, the intelligent librarian of this institution, and, after unsuccessfully ransacking the library for some applicable cognomen to give this individual, we agreed to give it a name characteristic of its depredations, and called it the *vastator*, or destroyer.

When a scarcity of food exists, or future plenty is doubtful; or when famine seems impending; and when, at the same time, we have authentic accounts of numbers of our destitute fellow-creatures starving through lack of food, it becomes an imperative duty to exercise our utmost ingenuity to adopt any substitutes for the natural food of man that can be proved available, and several such have been suggested. Mr. Hamp, an intelligent gardener, has proposed a root, called the *Apios tuberosa*, to be used as a substitute for potatoes, and I have no doubt it would answer the intention remarkably well. I have tried experiments in the manufacture of various kinds of bread, such as carrot bread, turnip, mangold-wurzel, rice, and parsnip bread, &c. The vegetable is boiled up with an equal quantity of flour, and is afterwards baked in the usual way. Some of these kinds of bread are most delicious, several of which are on the table before me. But by using such articles we secured no gain to the available stock of human food, and I, therefore, tried what hay would do if manufactured into bread. You all know its nutritive properties to various animals, and I have no doubt that, both from the result and from analogy, it contains much nutritive matter that would be serviceable and acceptable to man in a time of famine. Hay made into biscuits is preferable to hay bread. The hay is ground into an impalpable powder, and, when mixed with an equal quantity of flour, is to be made up and baked in the usual way. Iceland

moss, too, is considered to be very nutritive, as given to consumptive and
debilitated persons; therefore I had some bread made from Iceland moss,
but it turns out to be a complete failure, for it is so intensely bitter that it
cannot be eaten; indeed, it is quite as bitter as either quinine or Peruvian
bark. These investigations in reference to the scarcity of food have
occupied much time when my other engagements have been numerous and
pressing, and several other subjects have had their consideration necessarily postponed by them, but I have always received the utmost kindness
from all quarters in carrying out my inquiries.

At this moment the room was darkened, when Mr. Smee gave an
interesting description of numerous preparations of aphides in their
different stages of existence, of the various insects which prey upon them,
and of a number of specimens of diseased potatoes, and other plants, with
various fungi, and also of living aphides, &c. &c., all of which were
exhibited by means of a powerful oxyhydrogen microscope, manufactured
by Messrs. Horne and Thornthwaite, of Newgate Street. This part
was most highly applauded, and the whole produced considerable sensation.

*Objects shown under the microscope :—*

Eggs of aphides; larva; pupa; and perfect *Aphis vastator*.

*Aphis lanigera*, which infests apple-trees. Sir Joseph Banks has
given a description of this, and states that it has damaged one orchard to
the amount of £50 per year.

Couch-grass aphis, fox-tailed.

Aphis, called the black collier, taken from the beet-root.

An ordinary green-fly, having long legs, &c., and being very different
from the vastator.

Rose aphis.

Pea aphis is very destructive to peas, which were destroyed partly by
this insect, and partly by the dry summer, last year.

Barley aphis, with its wings in repose.

Grass aphis, by which whole tracts of grass were destroyed last
year.

Willow aphis, which is one of the largest of the family.

Wheat aphis is two or three times as big as the vastator, which, however, also lives on the wheat.

The nut-bush aphis is very small.

(?) Hyemal aphis; the large black spots which are a fungus on the
leaf probably follow this aphis.

Cabbage aphis; the cabbages brought to market last year were covered
by this white downy aphis.

Many aphides secrete sugar, and in honeydews this is very obvious.

Ichneumons, or hymenopterous insects, from the swollen aphis.

Another ichneumon with a round body.

Various others found about potato-fields.

Red acarus, about the size of a large spider, and which eats aphides
very voraciously.

Minute acarus.

Lancets of the gad-fly, showing the difference between them and the delicate piercers of the aphis.

Lancets of the tobanis, which are large and coarse.

Lancets of the blow-fly.

Leaf of the potato, with numerous aphides incarcerated in balsam, whilst in the act of feeding.

Leaf of diseased potato.

Section of a healthy potato-tube with its minute cells filled with starch.

Section of a diseased tuber, with marks of the injury of the disease, &c.

Another piece of diseased potato with brown and black spots.

Little quantities of starch after all other parts have been eaten up.

Section of a stem of wild potato with granules of starch seen in it.

A stem of potato with a beautiful specimen of a black fungi.

Blood-red fungus.

Another fungus with round heads like peas, which are covered by sporules.

Celery-leaf with fungi.

Couch-grass with aphis and eggs.

Horseradish-leaf.

*Acarus farnæ*, which run about putrefying potatoes, destroying offensive matter. One may compare this creature to a rhinoceros trotting about in the jungles.

Living aphides in a very active state.

As yet the future prospects of the disease are doubtful, and I have shown the destructive appetency of aphides. It is evident that the balance of nature is disturbed, and that these insects are preternaturally and immensely in excess. The human species has frequently been threatened with total destruction by these plagues; but, though ten thousands of mankind may have perished, we find by experience that the insects have ceased and men lived. No doubt this calamity will eventually pass away, though, indeed, it may not yet have reached its maximum. Up to the present time we have only known the disease as increasing. It has been worse last year than it was the year before; but the ensuing season, we may hope, will be healthy. No doubt many growers of potatoes will be deterred from planting; but I should say, do not give up cultivating, but cultivate in all cases, under the most favourable circumstances. I believe few have yet been planted this year; therefore, at all events, the crop will be scarce. Yet it is not too late to plant, though those potatoes which are placed earliest in the ground will have the best chance of succeeding, because they have an opportunity to deposit more fibre before the time that the aphides appear to commence their attacks. The cost of potato sets per acre last year, from the scarcity of good ones, is reported to have been about eighteen or twenty pounds, which becomes a serious outlay to small farmers, and will, therefore, greatly hinder their plans. If the insects do appear this season, from experiments that I have tried in my own house,

and which appear to succeed, I have no doubt means may be applied to
cut them down at once; and the first opportunity I have I shall try my
experiments on a larger scale, when I think I may be able immediately
to put a stop to the disease. The balance of nature must be restored; and
this year we may not see the disease. Science and history show that the
calamity will be transitory; and, further, we have a higher promise, for it
is said, "I will rebuke the destroyer for your sake, and he shall not
destroy the fruits of your ground."

---

MONTHLY REPORTS AND CORRESPONDENCE IN VARIOUS NEWSPAPERS
ON APHIDES. By ALFRED SMEE.

### MONTHLY REPORT OF APHIDES FOR JANUARY 1847.

Aphides having appeared to such excess that vegetation has been
damaged and famine produced, it requires that continual observations
should be made to ascertain the exact position and numerical strength of
this vast army of insects, that we may be better enabled, when spring
advances, to fight with success the formidable battle. It is now a question
whether men or aphides are to live; for, if aphides continue in the same
ratio to increase for the next two or three years, millions of human beings
must inevitably perish; but, if we can but extirpate this overwhelming
troop, food will again abound and famine will cease.

The vastator is our great enemy, and from the number and importance
of the plants which it kills, it deserves our fullest attention. As this is
my first monthly report, I shall commence by recapitulating those plants
the death of which I have actually myself traced to the action of the
vastator.

#### PLANTS TOTALLY DESTROYED BY THE VASTATOR.

| *Wild Plants.* | | *Cultivated Plants.* | |
|---|---|---|---|
| Shepherd's-purse | over large tracts. | Beet | rarely. |
| Groundsel | abundantly. | Spinach | whole crops. |
| Wild turnip | numerous. | Turnip | abundantly. |
| „ mustard | ditto. | Carrot | plenty. |
| Solanum nigrum | plenty. | Parsnip | more rare. |
| „ dulcamara | more scarce. | | |
| Violet | plenty. | | |
| Clover | ditto. | | |
| Pasture grass | ditto. | | |
| Nettle | occasionally. | | |
| Spurge | abundantly. | | |
| Geranium molle | rarely. | | |

There are, however, many plants which I have not yet noticed to be
utterly destroyed by its ravages, but are only partially or locally affected;
and all plants which are sometimes killed, are at other times but partially
or locally damaged.

### PLANTS PARTIALLY DESTROYED BY THE VASTATOR.

| *Wild Plants.* | *Cultivated Plants.* |
|---|---|
| Plants before enumerated. | Plants before enumerated. |
| Belladonna. | Potato.* |
| Stramonium. | Tomato. |
| Hyoscyamus. | Sweet potato. |
| Plantain. | Jerusalem artichoke. |
| Heartsease. | Garden artichoke (?). |
| Mallow. | Wheat. |
| Chickweed. | Indian corn. |
| Thistles. | Cabbages, swedes. |
| Docks. | Horse-radish. |
| Elder. | Celery. |
| | Parsley. |
| | Strawberry (Walker). |
| | Major convolvulus. |
| | Marigolds. |
| | Balsams. |
| | Tulips. |
| | Crocuses. |
| | Cinerarias. |
| | Verbenas. |
| | Many Solani. |
| | Peach and nectarine. |
| | Numerous other greenhouse plants. |

This list of itself is sufficiently formidable, but we must also fear the aphis of the hop, the cabbage, the pea, the bean, the corn aphis, the grass aphides, the black collier, and the aphis of the apple-trees. It is upon the recurrence of aphides, especially of the vastator, upon which future food or famine depends. We only know that aphides are continually increasing, and, if we do not destroy them, they will infallibly destroy us. All aphides are alike in sucking the juices of the plant and causing it to die locally at the puncture, or generally throughout the system. All live upon the vital fluid, and all induce the fatal gangrene, which the potato has abundantly shown.

The past month has been unfavourable to animated beings. Alternate freezings and thawings have been sufficient to destroy almost everything which has life, and even the deaths amongst men have been much above the average. Notwithstanding this inclemency, there are plenty of the vastators alive upon the plants out of doors. I found it upon the turnip, shepherd's-purse, docks, and mallows, and I have no doubt, had not business and the bad weather prevented me, I should have found it in abundance upon many plants. It is not yet living upon the wheat, nor can I find any other species upon this plant. In greenhouses it exists in profusion on young potato plants, cinerarias, verbenas, crocuses, and

---

* The potato plant is very rarely utterly destroyed. Generally speaking, there is some portion of a whole plant, some round eye, remaining amongst all the tubers, to continue the growth of the plant.

tulips, in some cases even so as to render them loathsome to the eye rather than an ornament.

I have just received from Mr. Walker, the distinguished entomologist, who is writing a work upon Aphides, a note, wherein he states that the eggs of the vastator, together with the larvæ, are abundant in his garden under the strawberry leaves, and he has kindly furnished me with samples. This demonstrates that, even if every vastator were killed, the species would be amply maintained.

Confining ourselves to the facts of the case, I am certain that there is abundance to furnish a stock to destroy our crops next year. According to Professor Owen, one single aphis may give rise to a quintillion during one year, a number which we may write, spell, or pronounce, but which we cannot comprehend. Perhaps we may form a faint notion of a quintillion of aphides when I state that they would form an army which would extend round the globe, and be thirty millions of miles in breadth. This is perhaps an exaggerated account of the rate of increase, yet, under a greatly diminished estimate, it will show that there is plenty left for the next year's brood.

By the very lowest increase the quantity which might be produced by one aphis is ten billions, and that is certainly much too low, as this number is formed upon the supposition that each aphis only brings forth one litter in ten, whereas I believe that they bring forth many litters. Upon this calculation one aphis now living might give rise to a progeny which would form an army, if there were nothing to destroy them, which would extend completely round the globe, and be a furlong in breadth.

In greenhouses the green-fly, the *Aphis rosæ*, the aphis of cinerarias, and some other species, are to be found; but out of doors I have not met with other species this January.

During the last month the effects of the vastator of last year have more fully manifested themselves by the rottings of the bulbs of infected turnips, and the extensive rotting of carrots down their central portions.

With respect to the operations for February, I must refer to my letter of January the first, and to the farmer I would say—Remember that a potato plant, once diseased, is like human beings in its tendency to propagate disease, without the further action of external causes. A tuber from a former diseased plant, though apparently sound, may show the malady without a new attack of the vastator.

Sets from plants which have never been diseased, and absence of the vastator, will secure to the husbandman abundant crop for the future; but, above all things, let everybody who requires food to eat, be taught the necessity of destroying the vastator.

----

## Probable Failure of the Strawberry Crop.

In my report for January, I stated, upon the authority of Mr. Walker, that the eggs of the vastator were upon the strawberry leaves. Since that report was written, I find that the leaves of that plant have great abundance of eggs everywhere; and I learn, upon inquiry, that the strawberry plants were affected like the potato last autumn.

Upon examining the plants in hothouses, live aphides in the larva state are now feeding; but, after a minute microscopical view, I have noticed some anatomical differences which lead me to infer that this aphis is possibly not the vastator, although a species very nearly allied to it. Under these circumstances, I must defer passing a decided opinion until I have observed it in the final or winged state.

It is really of but little consequence to the husbandman to know the particular aphis which causes injury to any particular plant, for every aphis is equally destructive, and wherever there are abundance of aphides, there does the death of the plant occur. From this view of the question, I now caution gardeners to watch the aphides which attack the strawberry plants, and destroy them, together with their eggs, as far as possible, otherwise they must not be surprised to find their strawberry plants destroyed, or rendered unfruitful through their agency.

Let every farmer, gardener, and naturalist now record their observations upon aphides, that the talent of the country may be concentrated upon their eradication.

1847.

---

## REPORT OF APHIDES FOR FEBRUARY 1847.

During the past month we have had both cold and warm weather, for the season of the year. At the commencement the temperature was as low as ever observed in this country, and subsequently the weather has been so mild that a great stimulus has been given to vegetation, and the buds have put forth as though spring had commenced in real earnest. Such weather has been unfavourable to insect life, and consequently but few facts have come under our notice. Our great enemy, at the present time, the vastator, has been extensively destroyed in the open air, and since the frost, I have not myself observed a single specimen living in that situation.

I have received, during the month, Jerusalem artichokes, on the roots of which a large aphis was feeding.

Aphides, as a general rule, bear frost well, for I took a crocus covered with vastators, and froze them with ice and salt, but, on being brought into a warm room, they resumed their activity, and again fed upon the plants.

In greenhouses the vastators are now feeding on various plants. Several of my crocuses, on which they were allowed to feed undisturbed, are now completely killed, and numerous others are on the high road to destruction. It appears that crocuses, like the potato plants, suffer most when the leaf is required to deposit the solid matter for the bulb of the next year. In my peregrinations round London, I have observed a few vastators upon nearly all the plants exposed for sale, which doubtless, during the next month, will multiply at their ordinary rate of production, and thus form a stock amply sufficient to destroy our crops alone. The tulips have, in most instances, some of the destroying creatures upon their leaves, though they may escape notice by fixing themselves on that part of the leaf which is sheltered from rain or wind. During the last month some of my tulips have been entirely killed by them. The creatures prefer some varieties of

the same plant to others, and hence I have observed that some kinds of
crocuses and tulips are more injured than others.  The vastators are
attacking, pretty constantly, the verbenas, and many have materially
suffered from their ravages.  The same creature is also to be met with
upon numerous other plants.  I have observed them to be feeding upon
the sweet potato of Shakspeare, a plant which they much admire.

The grower of strawberries may have the worst apprehension for his
crops this season, for there is scarcely a leaf in any district which has not
from three to twenty little black eggs upon it.  Plants which have been
placed in stoves for forcing, have had the eggs upon their leaves hatched,
and large broods of aphides have already appeared: I fear, next month,
that I shall have to record the injury or death of the forced plants
from this cause.  To avert the probable injury to the outdoor crop, I
should advise all the old leaves which have the eggs upon them to be
collected by hand, and burnt.  Not having, as yet, seen the final state
of the strawberry aphis, I must defer passing a positive opinion; I
do not think that it is the vastator, although, in all probability, equally
destructive.

At my residence I have an extensive colony of vastators, feeding upon
tulips and crocuses; but I have also two Ward's cases, into which I had
strictly forbidden their entrance.  The creature has, however, found its
way into my little London garden, and threatens to destroy my plants,
unless I can first destroy it, and thus prevent the mischief.

From accounts which I have received, I find that the vastator is now
attacking, in many situations, the potato plants; and when this occurs, the
plant is hurried into premature decay.  In other cases, the potato plant is
again showing the disease which has been imparted to its structure from
the injury inflicted on plants by aphides, during the last three or more
years, without a fresh attack of the insect.

The potato malady is no novelty; it may be traced over a great series
of years; at one time showing itself here, at another there, but at the
present time it unfortunately has manifested itself everywhere.  In all
former instances temporary inconvenience has resulted, but after a period
the disease lessened, or disappeared for a time, and abundance succeeded
the scarcity.  As a peculiar feature in the present scarcity, however, we
find that the farmer has not been taught to consider the malady transitory,
but the awful mistake has been made by some leading journals, to
recommend this crop to be abandoned, because the disease is permanent.
From this alarming advice, given by men who were in a position to have
made observations for themselves, which would have led to an opposite
conclusion, scarcity in the potato crop next year is inevitable.  A sufficient
amount has not been, and probably cannot now be, planted to suffice for
use next season.  The best kinds of potatoes for planting are those which
ripen early, because aphides most abound in July and August.  The Early
Shaw is one of the best varieties, but so valuable are they at the present
moment, that to crop one acre of land, an expense of fifteen or eighteen
pounds would be entailed.  Nevertheless, as scarcity next year is inevitable,
those who plant immediately, even at that price, will reap an abundant and
profitable harvest.  It is important for the farmer to know that, although
it is now discovered that the vastator is the cause of the potato disease, we
are utterly ignorant of the cause of its preternatural appearance at the

present time; and, whilst we are ignorant of this ultimate cause, it is manifest that no person can state whether the disease will recur.

During the last month I have ascertained that tubers from former healthy plants grow without showing the least signs of disease, even under the unfavourable conditions of the vitiated atmosphere in the forcing house, proving this year, as last, that there is no other cause for the potato disease but the vastator, and that, if the vastator does not recur, tubers from former healthy plants will produce crops free from disease. As an article of food, no root can compete with the potato; but as an article of luxury, numerous vegetables can be substituted where we only desire an adjunct to animal food; but these latter would not be expected to nourish the body by themselves. Wheat, oats, and perhaps rye, can alone, in this country, successfully compete with the potato, and therefore, where food is required, one of them must be selected. Of vegetables, to be used with animal food, the following may be employed:—Scarlet beans, French beans, turnip v., carrot v., parsnip v.a., Jerusalem artichokes a.v., leeks a., onions a., cabbages v., savoy v., greens v., cauliflower v., broccoli v., spinach v., mustard v., lettuce a., beet v. Those marked with v. are liable to be destroyed with the vastator; those marked a. by other aphides. The poor man would perhaps do well to make the following selection:— Scarlet beans, parsnips, carrots, Jerusalem artichokes, onions, cabbages, savoys.

Those who have not already planted their potatoes should do so forthwith; there is not a day to spare, for the sooner they are in the ground the greater chance of success will be afforded. Should the vastator again appear in our fields, and threaten to produce a continuance of the famine, I have great pleasure in being enabled to announce, that from experiments which I have lately conducted, there is strong reason for believing that a cheap and effectual plan may be employed for their total eradication, even for the most extensive potato-grounds.

----

### Food or Famine.

#### *To the Editor of the ' Morning Herald.'*

Sir,—We have throughout these realms met this day to acknowledge that the famine of the past year is beyond human control; and the deep reverence with which it has been kept indicates the universal belief that in Providence lies our only hope for its alleviation.

Insect plagues have formed, from the earliest times, the immediate cause of the destruction of vegetable food, and the consequent production of famine. In this respect our present failure differs not from antecedent periods of scarcity; and that which has been due to the locust, cockchafer, and caterpillar, is now to be attributed to the vastator and other species of aphides.

As far as my observations extend, no vastator is now living out of doors, and no mortal can tell whether this plague has passed away, or is again about to recur. Fear of the disease must not, then, make us abandon ourselves to despair, and leave our land uncultivated; as that which is unsown cannot be reaped, that which is not planted cannot afford fruit.

Famine now exists; its subsequent pestilence is beginning to appear; it is now then high time not only to regard the present scarcity, but to look to the probability of future want. Our land is untilled in many parts of the country, seeds cannot be procured in others, and the potato crop, the great resource of Ireland, is abandoned, as though it were to fail for ever.

There is no evidence to show that the potato, rather than the wheat, turnip, carrot, or any other plant, will perish this year; and from the great produce which the potato affords, and the poverty of land which suffices for its culture, it forms a highly eligible crop to be planted to the ordinary extent.

Potato tubers are now scarce, and high in price. Any attempt to buy them for seed would double or treble their cost unless those who still use this vegetable will cease to employ it for food. It becomes now, therefore, highly desirable that all who use potatoes should, for this season, at once abandon them. By ceasing to use potatoes, they would preserve that which should afford food and prevent famine next year. And by eating them, they are tending to aggravate the scarcity, and cause the death of numbers, by destroying their food.

Let every householder at once substitute other food for the potato, this year, for if there are none to buy, there can be none to sell; and there is now a sufficient abundance of good tubers for planting, if no more be used.

Their present application for food should be prohibited, if not by an Order of Council or by Act of Parliament, by that which is more powerful than law—universal public opinion. The preservation of the lives of our fellow-creatures is at stake, and I feel confident that all those will abstain from potatoes who hear that such abstinence is eminently calculated at this season to prevent the poor from perishing from want next year.

Having stopped their employment as a luxury at this time, they should be sent directly to Ireland, and freely distributed amongst the poor for planting, and the sets now to be met with in the London market are far superior to those heretofore cultivated by these unhappy people, and are far better adapted to resist the ravages of the vastator, should it unfortunately again appear.

Sets from former healthy plants which I have cultivated this year in my friends' greenhouses, are now perfectly healthy, showing that healthy sets and absence of the vastator will ensure the usual abundant produce.

In the event of the reappearance of the destroying insect, I trust and believe that, under the blessing of Providence, I shall be enabled to give a simple and effectual plan for its complete eradication.

March 24, 1847.

During the past month I have been unable to add materially to our knowledge of the ravages committed by these pests to the vegetable kingdom. My former observations have caused gardeners to attend more attentively to their existence, and I find that, in greenhouses and hot-houses, so much more care is taken of their annihilation than formerly, that scarce any exist.

I have found no vastator living out of doors, though other aphides have, in some places, commenced their plant-killing labours. The peach is, in some instances, affected, a fact to which Mr. Hurst (p. 196) has called attention; but this aphis is not the vastator. The peach-trees which I have examined have been perfectly free. My infected tulips and crocuses are nearly all dead; as they perish, it is curious to observe the myriads of winged ones which leave: they collected the other day in such swarms on my passage window that, in one corner of a pane of glass, at least a pill-box full were congregated together. On examining the mangold-wurzels, they are found in many places to rot; and, notwithstanding that they have been packed in clamps throughout the winter, a few vastators may be found on the young leaves, interspersed here and there, showing that the cause of the rotting had been really present. I have heard that the vastator is on the wheat in Ireland, but have been unable to authenticate the fact. I beg that the corn crops may be continually examined, and should feel greatly obliged for communications upon this matter. The strawberry plants which have the eggs of aphides on their leaves have much suffered this winter.

With regard to the potato plant, I have some Russian varieties in perfect health in a greenhouse, showing that there is no atmospheric or other cause but the vastator which is likely to produce the disease. These Russian potatoes were a little damaged in their passage, nevertheless are healthy in structure. I have yet in my possession about one hundred tubers, and it will afford me great pleasure to give one to any applicant, that the seed may be extensively circulated. Those who receive a tuber will perhaps do me the favour to furnish a short account of the produce, and their power of resisting the disease, at the end of the season.

In my last report, I called attention to the probability of scarcity of food, from the certainty of deficiency in the produce of potatoes next season, and urged agriculturists to plant, for it is impossible to foresee whether the insect will recur this year. Experience shows that a certain and large crop can only be obtained from whole tubers, or considerable pieces of tubers; therefore such sets are to be preferred. Nevertheless, the produce from a single tuber may be increased by planting very wide apart, and layering, or by taking shoots off, as they sprout from the potato, and planting them.

" I should be inclined to try the experiment of using but small portions of the potatoes for sets—such as scooped eyes or potato-peelings—although Marshall has ascertained that, under ordinary circumstances, the crop is thereby materially lessened. These means would only be serviceable to restore the health of a diseased plant, not to arrest the malady at its commencement.

" Perhaps it might be advisable to allow the stalk to grow from the tuber two or three inches high, and then to detach it and use it as a set. By this plan we should throw the potato-plant for its resources upon the leaves, and not upon the original set; and doubtless, by attending to other circumstances influencing the result, we should thus place the plant in a good condition for regenerating its fibre.

" One potato-tuber upon this plan would send forth numerous shoots, and thus a great saving would be effected in the amount of potatoes used for seed. We may expect, from the experiments of Marshall, that this course would lessen the produce, and therefore this method would only appertain to the regeneration of the potato plant, with the view of obtaining again healthy seed, from which to propagate our plants."— *Potato Plant*, §§ 487, 491, 492.

In London we are supplied with the very best potatoes which exist, and therefore we are literally eating, as a luxury, that which should serve as food for the poor man next year. If thoughtless persons will eat the seed potatoes, and others cannot be bought, surely the good of the community, or even their own good, requires that public measures should be taken to prevent the mischief.

Heretofore, when the crop failed, its culture was not abandoned; and, indeed, as every vegetable used by man for food occasionally fails, we might have been left utterly without food had such a foolish course been adopted. The absurd dogma of the wearing out of the plant, and its being no longer capable of being trusted, has produced all the mischief which will continue the scarcity next year.

---

### REPORT ON APHIDES FOR APRIL 1847.

During the last month the weather has been still cold, and the spring has been so extremely backward that but little vegetable matter is to be found suitable for animal life. The backward spring has kept back the aphides, and comparatively few species are yet to be found. At present I have seen no vastator abroad, except in greenhouses. The vastator feeds eagerly upon the orange-tree, tuberous nasturtium, and many other greenhouse plants, showing its omnivorous character. I have it now feeding upon endogenous and exogenous plants. The aphis of the rose has appeared sparingly, in warm situations; so has also the aphis of the apple-tree, cherry, plum, blackberry, fir, and perhaps of other plants. The aphis of the currant has appeared in many situations in great abundance; on both black and red currants it may be readily found by looking on the underside of the leaf, and the discoloration of the leaf will indicate its position. From an examination of several strawberry grounds, I have been greatly astonished at the extent of mischief which has been effected in some places by the aphis last year. The presence of the eggs indicates that the aphis lived upon the plant; and where eggs are found on the leaves, there may be observed great patches of dead, withered stalks. In these cases, doubtless, the damage inflicted upon the plant by the aphis last year caused it to be so debilitated, that it ill resisted the severity of the weather during the past winter. The ladybirds are exceedingly numerous, an occurrence which should be hailed with delight, as they destroy the aphides by thousands. The early potatoes are generally looking perfectly healthy, although I have seen a few which are badly diseased. The next month will probably indicate pretty well the extent of damage which we are likely to experience from aphides this season; and here I may observe, that if the weather be uninterruptedly hot, in all probability the creatures will multiply to a great extent, and do great damage. Under any circumstance, I urge every gardener and farmer closely to watch his plants, that as soon as aphides extensively occur, we may commence our war of extermination. It is very curious to watch a field of potatoes; to see the destructive cloud of insects hovering over, settling, and then distributing themselves over whole fields; to observe how they first attack the larger leaves; to notice the death of the leaves, and finally of the entire haulm; and then to perceive the troop acquire wings and fly away. After all these have occurred, the farmer may then study the fungi which come to eat up the damaged plant; and, lastly, he will have unfortunately to separate the sound from the unsound, the healthy from the diseased. I return my best thanks for the kind information transmitted to me, and beg to offer my sincere apologies for not having directly answered my correspondents.

### REPORT ON APHIDES FOR MAY 1847.

In my previous reports, I have had to record but few facts of the progress of these creatures, in consequence of the lateness of the spring. May, however, has been remarkable for the great heat which has existed, and with this heat a numerous host of these destructive creatures has appeared. On the lime-tree, the beautiful spotted aphis, peculiar to that tree, may now be found in the larva and winged state. On the sycamore, two species now exist—one which feeds upon the larger leaves, the other on the top shoots. The oak has also its aphis, on the under-surface of the leaf. The large aphis on the thistle is now feeding abundantly in some places. In one instance I observed the ivy to be literally covered with countless numbers of aphides; the leaves at the same time having a great abundance of honeydew on their surface. The currant-tree has a profusion of its aphis, causing the leaves to be corrugated and discoloured. The nut-tree aphis may also be detected; and the willow, in some instances, has thousands of aphides on its young shoots. The *Aphis lanigera* may be noticed on the apple-trees; and an aphis may also be found on the larch and fir.

All these are but of trifling importance when compared to the vastator. I regret to state that this pest has reappeared; but from whence it has come, or how the species has been continued, I am unable to state: for although I have abundance of eggs of other species, none have been found of this insect; and, since February, I have been unable to discover any living specimen till this week. It first appeared on warm walls, on the peach, nectarine, and apricot trees, to such an extent, in some places, that the young shoots are blighted, become withered and dried up, crumbling under the slightest pressure : from these trees the creature has flown into various other plants in their neighbourhood. On the turnip, it may be found on the under-surface of the leaf; it has also made its appearance on the potato plant. The first vastator which I observed on the potato in open situations was found on May 24th, since which time I have found it sparingly in every district round London ; at present they are scarce. In answer to an attempt which has made to show that my observations last year were made upon a small tract of ground, I beg to state that the plants were narrowly watched over an extent of country of not less than 400 or 500 square miles, and I obtained insects and specimens from various other parts of the country ; my observations during the last week have not been less extensive. With respect to this crop, the leaves look exceedingly well, although below ground ; in most situations there is extensive decay in the stalks. Several practical men think but little of this decay, but there appears to me no question of its importance. I have noticed little tubers, hardly so big as a pea, to be separated from the parent stalk by the destruction of the stem. In a former report I mentioned that I had Russian tubers perfectly healthy, though much damaged in their transit by salt water. It is very curious that the greater number which were left have become thoroughly rotten, and many which grew have since exhibited the gangrene, at the underground stems.

At the present time there is not much to be done. With regard to the renewed attack on the potato plant, I should be inclined to be passive, because any attempt to remove the very few aphides which now exist might injure the plants rather than benefit them : the gardener should destroy the insect by any of the methods he already well knows.

Besides the vastator, there are still other aphides committing their ravages. On the melon and cucumber may be found thousands of a very minute aphis, feeding upon the under-surface of their leaves ; and, on the rue, there are no less than three different species now to be found.

Under all circumstances, the present extremely hot weather is favourable to the development of aphides ; and, therefore, I am afraid we may expect a repetition this year of the injury to the potato plant.

----

### INFLUENCE OF THE VASTATOR ON DIFFERENT KINDS OF POTATOES.

*To the Editor of the 'Farmers' Journal.'*

SIR,—In my treatise on the Potato Plant I have developed the important law of the unequal action of the vastator on different kinds of potatoes. It is singular that so manifest a range of facts should previously have escaped attention; but now let us lose no time to take advantage of its application.

The unequal action of the vastator on different kinds of potato plants must be attributed to two causes—their unequal exposure to the destructive influence of the vastator, and to the unequal capacity of different kinds to resist its deleterious agency.

Potatoes which ripen early run their course before the insect appears in great profusion, and consequently escape: hence all early sets are best adapted for planting, and early planting, to enable them to escape the malady. As the period at which potatoes ripen is well known to agriculturists, I need not call further attention to this subject.

The unequal capacity of different varieties to resist its deleterious agency I find to depend upon the extent which each deviates from its normal type; and the more highly cultivated the plant is, the more prone is it to disease. This is not only true of the potato, but is also true of all other plants attacked by the vastator.

I beg to call attention to the following extracts from my work upon this subject:—

"Every particular kind of potato, however, is not equally prone to disease, or rather, I may say, to carry its individuality or peculiarity into its diseased condition. The supposed original Chelsea potato seems to resist the action of this malady nobly, the disease only attacking it from leaf to leaf, and not affecting so materially the underground stems. I have carefully examined this specimen, in order to observe how it would be attacked, and I found that the large leaves were all destroyed, and that the disease progressed from the large leaves to those somewhat smaller, and so crept on till it progressed to the top. In consequence of this mode of attack, the main shoot and all the lateral shoots were green, healthy, and vigorous, and the plant appeared to a casual observer to be quite healthy; and the large leaves, or those out of sight, being alone destroyed up to October the 16th, the plant was still growing vigorously. At the Horticultural Society's Gardens, on my first visit, Uhde's wild potatoes showed the disease only on the leaflet, and on a subsequent occasion there was also one other leaf curled. In both cases I removed the diseased leaf, and found that they were inhabited by a parasite, which I shall hereafter describe. No two kinds of potatoes show the effects of the disease equally; and it is generally supposed that that potato which ripens in the early period of the year, manifests the malady less than those which ripen later, so that the early shows are tolerable free from it. On examining a field in which many varieties are cultivated, every sort will be found to exhibit the malady in its own way: some varieties will be more diseased than others, and some will die down earlier than others. Some potatoes require more leaf than others, and I have no doubt that those which require an extensive crop of leaves are more prone to the disease than others. At the Horticultural Society's potato-ground, many kinds were found to have the tubers quite healthy, while others were much diseased. The white-eyed red was of the former class; the mouse of the latter. I dare say that it will be found that the more nearly the tuber reverts back to Gerard's old type, the more capable it will be of resisting the disease. The white-eyed red was in some respects similar to the old species in the Chelsea garden. I applied at the Horticultural Society's Gardens for a return of the relative number of good potatoes to bad ones in each sort cultivated by them, but was unable to obtain it, as a similar return was ordered to be printed in their own Transactions."

When I made the application for this return, I thought it a strange coincidence that two individuals should at the same moment have desired the same return, especially as the Society might have rendered the return last year. However, knowing that many funny coincidences do happen, I did not at the time think much about it. However, after I had examined their potato-ground, I found that I incurred no great loss by being debarred from obtaining the above-mentioned return, for I found that the disease had visited them with a comparatively lenient hand this year, and that it did not exhibit itself in its most destructive form.

From the imperfect return which the Horticultural Society could afford, and their unwillingness to afford it, I was induced to write to all parts of the country for information, but yet did not obtain as much information as I could desire.

For this reason I am anxious to procure further information, and particularly beg agriculturists to fill up the return and send it to my residence as early as possible, that further information may be obtained upon this point.

| Kind of Potato. | When planted. | Nature of Soil. | What Manure used. | Total Produce. | Quantity of Good. | Quantity of Bad. | Month in which Disease appeared. |
|---|---|---|---|---|---|---|---|
| | | | | | | | |
| | | | | | | | |

The late frost has diminished, though it has not killed the vastators, and I have found it all round London this week. It exists in nearly every greenhouse, and is killing the verbenas in many situations. Under these circumstances, every fact connected with it should be recorded, and therefore I beg agriculturists to transmit to me accounts of the flights of aphides last year, the present state of the aphides, as well as the return which I have before mentioned. We have now discovered the cause of the disease, and I trust that we may in future prevent it by destroying the vastators.

Dec. 24, 1846.

----

## LETTERS TO A JOURNAL ON THE SAME SUBJECT.

### Mr. Smee on the Aphides vastator.

Sir,—If the late Government commission have recommended the abandonment of the culture of potatoes, it is most unpardonable, but at the present time I have neither leisure nor inclination to wade through their reports. They may with equal good reason recommend the farmer to abandon the carrot, beet, spinach, turnip, parsnip, or even the wheat or Indian corn, as I have shown that the vastator attacks all these, and kills whatever it attacks. We know not whether the vastator will recur again in unwonted numbers, or whether it will altogether disappear. Under such circumstances I most emphatically recommend that the crops should be planted as though no disease were apprehended. With regard to potatoes, choose sound sets, plant early, and select early kinds. The late frost has not destroyed the vastators. I found them on Sunday at Tottenham, on Monday at Fulham, and on Tuesday at Tooting, on the turnip, shepherd's-purse, and mallow.    The green-fly is easily killed by the smoke of tobacco; the vastator, however, will live when the green-fly is destroyed, and thus, in smoking greenhouses, the vastator is left when the green-fly is killed.    At the present time the vastator is to be found in nearly all greenhouses upon verbenas, and it kills them by wet gangrene in the same way that it injures the potato plant.    The vastator is remarkably destructive to the potato and spinach plants, many less being required to kill them than is required to destroy the beet or solani.    I placed twelve potato plants in a greenhouse in October for experiment : the vastator attacked them ; six are now rotten, the other six are dying.    One of the plants perishing from the insect I have sent to the Polytechnic Institution, where every visitor can see it.    Perhaps there never was a series of minute observations made on so large a tract of country as mine, upon this subject.    I made observations over at least 400 square miles round London and Brighton, and received specimens from the midland counties.    I rejoice to find that a knowledge of the insect is rapidly extending itself in all directions.    Any person may find it even now in their own gardens ; and as the spring advances, it will be their duty to endeavour to exterminate it.

Dec. 23, 1846.

---

### REAPPEARANCE OF THE APHIS VASTATOR UPON THE POTATO PLANT.

SIR,—I regret to announce that the *Aphis vastator* reappeared last week upon the potato plant in every district round London.    At present it may be found sparingly upon the under-surface of the leaf, and, though within the last few days it has multiplied twenty-fold, several plants must be examined before it can be detected.    The present hot weather is highly favourable to the rapid multiplication of this pest, which, coupled with its early attack, must lead us to have the worst apprehension for the crops this season.    This creature has already greatly damaged the peach, apricot, and nectarine trees in many localities.    It is now feeding upon the turnip, potato, and other plants.    Allied species are destroying the currant tree, and damaging to such a serious extent the carrot, parsnip, and parsley crops, that they have exhibited in some instances the fatal plague spot noticed in previous years upon the potato plant.    These facts, unfortunately, prove that in all human probability the great plague of aphides will again run their destructive course this year.

June 5, 1847.

P.S.—I shall be obliged for information and specimens of the aphis from all parts of the country.

---

THE POTATO DISEASE—EXTENSIVE DISAPPEARANCE OF APHIDES.

*From the 'Illustrated London News.'*

At various times I have had occasion to call the attention of the public to facts connected with this destructive tribe of insects, and, in the present instance, have to relate other circumstances connected with their natural history which cannot fail to gratify the people. The importance of bringing every fact before the agriculturist as it occurs must be apparent to all; for it is upon a correct knowledge of the habits of these creatures that the farmer must estimate the probable damage when his crops are unfortunately attacked.

During this year the bean aphis has committed most serious damage. It has killed plants in some places to such an extent that not one pod is left; and even over large fields the crop will not nearly yield the seed sown. The insects continued to increase up to a certain point, and then, without reference to the destruction of the plants on which they were located, took wing, and formed an army formidable from their numerical strength, which appeared completely to fill the atmosphere. The entire number assumed the winged state within a few days, and left nothing behind but their cast skins. The winged insects settled upon any palatable food. They fled by thousands upon the beet-root, on which I have observed them feed in a former year. When they alighted, they sucked the juices of the plant in the ordinary manner, and sometimes killed the leaf of the plant, which exhibited dark, black blotches. They, however, were not doomed to remain long in this situation; they speedily died, and have not, in many cases, left a solitary individual to continue the brood. Those which alighted upon the outdoor cucumbers were singularly destructive. They settled upon the under-surface of the leaves in great swarms, and fed upon the plant. Some of the attacked plants died from the injury they sustained; in others the leaf alone was damaged. I have been much interested in watching the destruction of the cucumber: for I have heard that during the last two or three years this plant has gone off in some mysterious manner for which the farmer could not account. In the instances which have come within my observation, every insect has perished, and but a few of the whole plants were destroyed, on account of the short duration of the attack.

The bean aphis also alighted upon scarlet runners, French beans, parsnips, onions, and various other plants and weeds. Groups of large masses of dead winged insects may still be observed, although scarce one live insect exists.

The *Aphis vastator* has also, in those districts which I have examined, become scarce. I do not know what has become of them all, but many have been devoured by ladybirds, some have been killed by ichneumons, others became unhealthy and perished. In proportion as the potato plant is strong and healthy, so does it resist the attack of this parasite. The puncture of the aphis hence is in some instances merely followed by a little black spot; in others by a large black botch; and again, it may be followed by a more or less complete destruction of the entire plant. In every instance where aphides have been feeding, although they have now disappeared, it will be found that the leaves are apt to perish, and the dying potatoes may be frequently observed to be covered with a white down, which in reality is a beautiful appearance of the *Botrytis infectans*. In consequence of these appearances following the attack of the aphis, hasty investigators are sometimes led to the belief that the potato disease occurs without the insect—a delusion now highly prized by those who admire the marvellous, and delight to speculate in aërial, comet, and cholera theories.

The early kinds of potatoes are now, in most instances, ripening to satisfaction, and the golden yellow colour of the foliage demonstrates that the leaf is performing its last functions, and that the tuber is being well filled with starch and other nutritive matters. The late kinds still look well, and scarce any insects now exist in many situations. The agriculturist should not, however, trust too much to the pleasing intelligence, for he should be aware that they may again return between this time and November, and eat down his crop. The large flights of vastators last year occurred between the 7th of September and the end of the month. These remarks are quite independent of some local instances where the disease has committed ravages to a great extent. I have heard of one field which yielded 17 sacks of bad and 32 of good tubers, and doubtless there are many other like cases, but they now form rather the exception than the rule. I have myself nearly 200 kinds of potatoes planted in ground without manure, and I do not think amongst the number that I will find a single diseased tuber.

Carrots and parsnips, which have been infested all the season, are now comparatively free; and the damage has not been so great as to prevent their perfect recovery.

We rejoice also to state that the corn aphis, which was disseminated over every part of the country, even to a few seedling oats growing in a vacant piece of ground opposite the Royal Exchange, is now diminishing, or even, in many localities, has disappeared. Its effect was to injure the produce, and cause black marks to appear upon the ear and stem. It came too late to effect extensive damage in this country. Private letters from Baltimore state that the wheat and potato crops are abundant, and that the former has dropped in price to one-half its highest rate last year.

At the commencement of the season I called attention to the reappearance of the *Aphis vastator*. During the progress of the year I have pointed out the damage which various aphides have committed. Now I have to communicate the singular and welcome fact of their extensive and sudden departure. The past has afforded no indication for the present, nor can the present indicate the future. Before this article is distributed over the country, the aphides may recur; and, though I now write to congratulate the farmer on his present prospects, I must yet caution him to be continually on the watch, so that he may immediately discover if another plague of these all-destroying creatures should visit his crops. By correct information on these points, arrangements can be made beforehand; and cheap food, one of the greatest of all desiderata, may be secured for the people.

FINSBURY CIRCUS,                           ALFRED SMEE.
   Aug. 5, 1847.

No. XV.c.

## RECENT RESEARCHES ON THE POTATO DISEASE.—Royal Horticultural Society, Scientific Committee, April 5th, 1876. Maxwell T. Masters, M.D., F.R.S., in the chair.

Mr. W. G. Smith exhibited a number of new drawings and referred to a recent examination made by him of 360 slides prepared by Mr. Alfred Smee in the first year of the potato murrain, 1845. These slides included slices of diseased potato stems, tubers and leaves, and aphides taken from infected plants. In these tubers and stems, and also within and upon the bodies of the aphides, Mr. Smith had found a large number of the bodies recently referred by him to the secondary condition of the potato fungus.

" During the last fortnight," continued Mr. Smith, " Mr. Alfred Smee has placed in my hands for microscopic examination no fewer than 360 slides having reference to the potato disease. These slides were all prepared by Mr. Smee in the first year of the great potato murrain, viz. 1845, and the preparations include potato leaves, slices of stem and tuber, and aphides taken from diseased potato plants in that year.

" Out of 104 slides illustrative of the structure of the potato plant, twenty-seven distinctly show the oogonia and antheridia, as illustrated by me in the 'Gardeners' Chronicle;' these bodies mostly occur in the stems and tubers of the 1845 potatoes, just where they principally occurred in the Chiswick potatoes last year.

" Of the remaining slides of insects, principally aphides, about one-half show traces of the same bodies. The threads are growing both inside and outside the aphides : sometimes the oogonia are deeply buried in the body, whilst the whole insect is traversed by mycelial threads ; many of the oogonia are inside the legs, sometimes inside the feelers. These oogonia and antheridia are presumedly the same as those I found last year upon and within the diseased Chiswick potatoes, and they are exactly the same as the bodies now to be seen in Mr. Smee's 1845 potato preparations.

" On two special slides of aphides the insects are densely covered externally with a fungus in fruit. So dense is the covering, that very little of the insect's body can be seen. This fruit is almost identical in size and form with the fruit of *Peronospora infestans*, and, like the latter, it shows a marked differentiation of its contents, and apparently produces zoospores. By carefully searching amongst this dense mass of fruit, the oogonia and antheridia above mentioned can also be detected.

" Without wishing to speculate on the meaning of these new facts, it must be confessed that this new association of these fungoid bodies on diseased potatoes and aphides is new and suggestive. As my last year's Chiswick resting-spores are apparently still alive, though latent, I hope to try some experiments with them as soon as they start into life in the early summer."

Mr. Renny considered that the relationship to Pythium was strengthened by Mr. Smee's preparations. In Saprolegnia the antherid was always borne on finer threads than the oogonium.—*From the 'Gardeners' Chronicle,' April 8th, 1876.*

In 1875 it thus appears that Mr. Worthington Smith discovered the secondary form of fruit of the potato fungus in the seed tubers of imported American potatoes growing at Chiswick; and for this discovery the Royal Horticultural Society bestowed upon him their Knightian gold medal. Until that year it would appear that these secondary forms of fruit of the fungus were unknown, although their existence had been previously suspected.

No one challenged Mr. Smith's interpretation of the bodies discovered except Professor De Barry, the French botanist. Professor De Barry stated that he had seen somewhat similar bodies at times within potato plants, but he considered they could not belong to the potato fungus, because he could not make them complete their (fungus) entire life within the potato plant, although he could make them apparently complete it in the decaying bodies of minute insects. This opinion of Professor De Barry was invalidated by some contemporaneous observations made by Dr. Sadebeck, of Berlin, who said he had seen a parasite similar to that of Mr. Smith's and Professor De Barry's growing on a potato plant at Coblentz, and producing a disease in no way to be distinguished from the ordinary murrain of potatoes. The question then presented itself whether the potato fungus could grow on animal substances, like some of the fungi to which it was immediately allied, as the fungus of house-flies, of silk-worms, &c.

As it was the winter season, 1876, when this question arose, Mr. Smith applied to Mr. Smee, who placed his own collection of microscopical slides of aphides and of diseased potatoes, mounted by himself during the potato murrain in 1845–1847, in that gentleman's hands for examination.

Through the kindness of Mr. Worthington Smith, I am enabled to give the following woodcuts of one of the microscopical preparations of Mr. Alfred Smee's own collection, mounted by himself, of the *Aphis vastator* and of a slice of diseased potato. The *Aphis vastator* is here enlarged twenty diameters, and the minute fungus fruits are to be seen inside the insect at A, B, C.

These bodies belonging to the fungus are further enlarged on the margin of the cut to 160 diameters, so that their nature may be better seen. Some of Mr. Smee's aphides are completely filled with the fungus internally, and covered with it externally; and though Mr. Smee did not completely understand the meaning of the fungus (at a time when it had not yet been described), yet it is clear that he saw the fungus on the insect, for some of the slides are scratched with a diamond and marked "fungi." As far as we know, no one but Alfred Smee had detected aphides in this peculiar state of disease, and we believe the condition is unknown even now to most entomologists.

If any further proof had been wanting as to the identity of the bodies found in the potato with those in the aphis, it was supplied by the behaviour of Mr. Smith's secondary form of fruit when (after a whole year's rest) it germinated. Mr. Smith found on germination that the spores grew equally well on vegetable as on animal matter.

It should be here observed that in Mr. Smee's book on the Potato Plant it will be seen that a chapter of that work is devoted to the various kinds of fungi which are to be found on diseased potatoes, and there are several lithographic plates illustrating this subject. On plate 3, fig. 7, is a drawing of a fungoid growth as observed by my father on an *Aphis vastator*. On plate 4, amongst other kinds of fungi, is a parasitic fungus on the leg of the *Aphis vastator*. At page 77 of the same work he writes : "Doubtless the fungi exercise an important influence upon the progress of the disease, although they most assuredly have not the power of producing it. In fact, they never make their appearance until the potato plant has been previously damaged, and until some portion of it is already dead." And again, at page 122 : "There appears to me to be a very close relation between the injury committed by the aphides and the appearance of fungi;

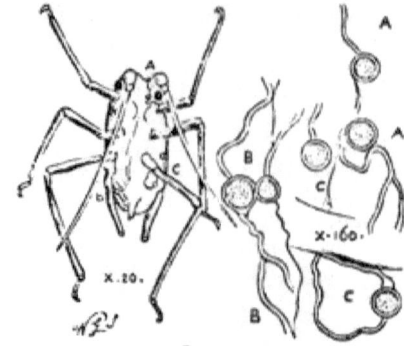

Fig. 14.

Resting-spores of the Potato Fungus within an Aphis at A, B, C, enlarged 20 diameters. The same resting-spores enlarged to 160 diameters on right-hand margin. (From one of Mr. Smee's 1845 preparations.)

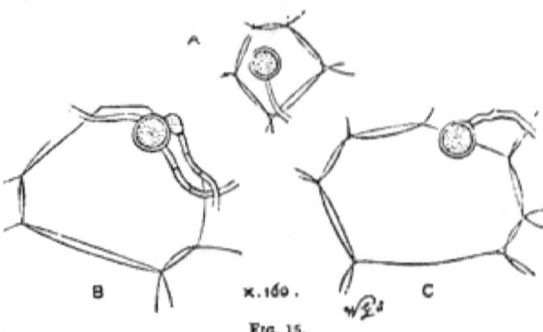

Fig. 15.

Resting-spores of the Potato Fungus within the cellular tissue of Potatoes. A. From the stem. B, C. From the tuber, enlarged 160 diameters. (From one of Mr. Smee's 1845 preparations.)

for in numerous cases where I have observed fungi on the leaf, I have also noticed aphides on the plant.

"It is also a singular fact that there is a word in the Hebrew language which means blight and mildew collectively, meaning thereby aphis and fungus."

In 'Instinct and Reason,' p. 261, Mr. Smee deduced the following law of the ravages of the aphides :—

"1. Aphides feed on living plants.

2. Aphides come first upon healthy plants.

3. Aphides suck the juices of plants after having pierced the cuticle.

4. Aphides, by sucking the sap, impair its qualities.

5. The sap, being injured, no longer performs its proper functions.

6. The injured sap cannot properly nourish the plant.

7. Unnourished or imperfect tissue is apt to die.

8. Partial death, following the attacks of aphides, may be local at the part affected, or remote ; that is to say, at a distance from the attack.

9. The total death of the plant may arise from the death of a part necessary to the whole.

10. Wild plants, or plants in a condition calculated to develop fibre, will resist the attacks of the aphides.

11. Highly cultivated plants, or plants not under circumstances favourable to the formation of fibre, ill resist the attacks of aphides.

12. Plants are most injured by aphides at that period of their growth when they are required to deposit most fibre.

13. Plants having their tissues damaged by aphides are more or less apt to propagate diseased tissue in all their future growths.

14. The damage to the plant hastens the transformation of aphides to the perfect state.

15. The attacks of aphides are almost invariably followed by the growth of fungi."

In 'My Garden,' published in 1872, in the chapter on Fungi, Mr. Smee again puts forwards his theories on the subject of the potato disease, for at page 363 we find these words : "One form of fungus has attracted much attention of late years, as it has been represented to be the cause of the potato disease. From my own observations I believe that an aphis invariably punctures the leaf before the attack of the fungus. It is possible that the punctures of the insect allow the zoospores of the fungus which have ciliæ to penetrate into the interior structure of the leaf, whence the mycelium spreads into every part of the texture of the plant. The fungus appears as a white powder to the eye, but when examined by a microscope the white patch proves to be a forest of little branching stems surmounted by oval bodies. It was called by Berkeley *Botrytis infestans*, and now the genus is named *Peronospora*." A figure of this fungus is then given.

---

## No. XVI.

ELEMENTS OF ELECTRO-BIOLOGY ; or, the Voltaic Mechanism of Man, being a Natural System of Mental Philosophy. By Alfred Smee. Published February 1849. (From ' Chambers's Edinburgh Journal.')

Mr. Smee not only confirms the conclusions of prior investigators; he goes further, and endeavours to account for mental as well as physical phenomena. "The physiological matter," he observes, "required two lines of investigation : the one having reference to the ultimate structure of organic beings ; the other to the actions taking place in them. . . . By the electro-voltaic test, the mechanism of nervous actions has been determined.

. . . . Whilst, however, electricity appears to me to be an important agent for the cure of disease, the cases in which it is especially valuable are comparatively few; and I myself regard the treatment upon general electrotherapeutic laws as more valuable than the immediate action of electricity itself." Thus much premised, it becomes necessary to describe the battery: the author states that "a central parenchyma, a peripheral parenchyma, connected together, and each supplied with bright arterial blood, are necessary for life. It follows that bleeding causes death; that the supply of imperfect blood, such as carbonaceous blood, is insufficient for life. Moreover, a destruction of the central parenchyma, by injuring the brain, or of the peripheral, by destroying the body, instantly prevents the manifestations of the functions of animal life. . . . Now a central apparatus, supplied with a peculiar fluid, a peripheral apparatus similarly supplied, the whole connected together to form one universal total, is the apparatus desired; and such an apparatus we have in a double voltaic battery. If we abstract the proper exciting fluid from either end, or substitute any other fluid, or destroy the structure either at one end or the other, or divide the connecting portions or wires, the effects proper to the apparatus will not be manifested, and the battery will be destroyed."

That animal membranes and fluids may take the place of metallic plates, wires, and acids, is apparent from an experiment suggested by Liebig; a pile was constructed, "consisting of disks of pasteboard moistened with blood, of muscular substance (flesh), and of brain. This arrangement caused a very powerful deflection of the needle of the galvanometer, indicating a current in the direction of the blood to the muscle." On this Mr. Smee observes: "In the muscles we have a nitrogenized material which is acid; in the blood we have a nitrogenized material which is alkaline; and the connecting part or nervous fibres are neutral. . . . . The periphery or body, therefore, consists of the muscular substance, forming one pole; the cutaneous tissues the opposite; the serous fluid, which lubricates the parts, being the electrolyte. The whole forms a voltaic battery, which I shall hereafter consider in minute detail as the Peripheral Battery.

"From the peripheral battery two series of connecting media proceed —the first, the muscular nerves, or nerves supplied to the flesh; the second, the nerves distributed to the cutaneous textures. If we examine the nerve-fibres in recently-killed animals, we find that they consist of fine tubes containing a fluid, and lined with a peculiar species of fat, which may be obtained, from their prolongation into the brain, in large quantities, when the part is soaked in alcohol for a long period. In this structure we have all the conditions necessary to insulation—namely, a fine membranous tube lined with fat on its inner side, and containing a fluid in the centre; and such a structure, as far as electrical properties are concerned, would be analogous to a glass tube containing liquid.

"If we follow the course of the nerves, we find that they are prolonged to the brain, and end in the grey matter, where they again come in contact with a large quantity of blood-vessels. As the two series of nerves are not immediately connected in the brain, it follows, according to the laws of voltaic action, that another battery exists there, which may be termed the central battery. . . . . For the integrity of the circuit, it is essential that the peripheral and central batteries be perfect; that their connection be maintained; and that a proper exciting fluid, or bright arterial blood, be distributed to each part."

Such is Mr. Smee's view of the living battery: we come next to his detail of the mode of action. For this he proposes the term Electro-Aisthenics, or a study of the various organs of sensation; and these are comprised under a new terminology: Opsaisthenics, of sight; Ousaisthenics, of hearing: Gumaisthenics, of taste: Rhinaisthenics, of smell; Cœnaisthenics, of touch: and last, a *sixth* sense, Somaisthenics, or bodily feeling. Blood and nerve being present in a normal condition, the integrity of the various actions is assured. The eye, for example, is stimulated by light, leading to the inference of a photo-voltaic current. By means of various chemical solutions, the author establishes the fact artificially. "Upon exposing," he writes, "the apparatus to intense light, the galvanometer was instantly deflected, showing that the light had set in motion a voltaic current, which I propose to call a photo-voltaic circuit." The eye itself is tested by thrusting a needle through the choroid coat, and another into a neighbouring muscle, and passing the animal experimented on suddenly from darkness into light, when, if carefully conducted, a slight deflection of the galvanometer is the result. With the retina and blood of the choroid coat for the positive pole of the organ of vision, we find the iris and muscles of the eyeball and eyelids proposed for the negative. The phenomena of hearing are accounted for in a somewhat similar way; the poles being the auditory nerve and adjacent muscles. The specific action can only be determined by showing that sound effects a voltaic current; and then how various are its modifications! "The range of sounds appreciated by the human ear consists of about 12½ octaves, and perhaps extends to the 32nd of a note in those endowed with most perfect hearing. From this it follows that the human ear can distinguish about 3200 sounds; and therefore it would require 3200 poles for that purpose." With respect to the organ of taste, Mr. Smee assumes the gustatory nerve as the positive pole; and states that "we may make a voltaic battery in which the circuit shall be determined by savours, in very different methods. For instance, if we place a little persalt of iron, with two platina poles, in a V-shaped tube, and then drop a little infusion of meat into one side, a voltaic circuit will instantly be produced." Next in order comes the sense of smell: and here the author supposes that odorous substances determine a voltaic current, by "facilitating the reduction of the highly-oxygenated blood;" and that the olfactory nerves constitute the positive pole of the battery. He then proceeds to establish a sense of feeling, Cœnaisthenics, as distinct from Somaisthenics, or bodily feeling. The former, he says, "is that feeling by which we derive certain impressions from without, and is never in our understandings confounded with a bodily feeling, or that sense by which we estimate the changes taking place within our own frame." Thus Cœnaisthenics may be excited by heat or cold, or by mechanical or other pressure; and it is possible to imitate this effect by varieties of voltaic apparatus. But it would appear that, in experimenting on the living body, muscular power must be exerted before the galvanometer marks any trace of a current, as will be understood from Mr. Smee's statement. The subject under test was a "black rabbit, into the *masseter* of which," he observes, "I introduced one sewing needle, whilst the second was placed in the subcutaneous cellular tissue. After leaving them for a few minutes, so that they might be in the same state, they were connected with the galvanometer without sensible deflection of the needle. After a few moments, the animal, not liking the treatment, made an attempt to bite my finger, and the deflection of the galvanometer instantly showed the mechanism of volition. I then gave the creature a piece of wood to bite, upon which it used all its power of mastication; and by catching the oscillation of the needle, a very powerful current was exhibited."

We have thus, as clearly as the subject would well admit of, traced an outline of the author's peripheral battery: we now come to the details concerning the central battery. The author maps out the brain into different regions, separated by commissures: to the first, which repeats the impressions conveyed by the sensor, or aisthenic nerves, he assigns the term Phreno-Aisthenics: the second, or that by which combined impressions are retained, is Syndramics: third, the seeing of numerous objects, or hearing of numerous sounds, conveys but one idea of sight or audition; the term for this mechanism is Aisthenic-Noemics: fourth, Syndramic-Noemics, for the ideas derived from combined senses: fifth, Pneuma-Noemics, for the notion of infinity: and lastly, to quote the author's own words, " we have to consider from whence the impulse is sent for the brain to cause action: a study which may be conveniently followed under the term of Noemic-Dynamics. . . . . The details are exceedingly difficult to comprehend in all their minutiæ; and yet I trust, by passing gradually from the simple to the complex, the leading features of this wonderful and intricate apparatus will be developed; and though the exemplification of the structure of a single brain would occupy many acres, I can exhibit examples of the mode of acting in the several departments by ordinary voltaic combinations.

" The requisites of action, blood, and nerve, are found in sufficient abundance in the central battery or brain, as that organ is literally nothing but fibres and blood-vessels. The nervous fibres are so numerous, that no estimate could be given of the myriads of which the brain is composed; in fact, the whole of the white matter of the brain is composed of nerve tubes."

We believe it was Coleridge who once met a metaphysical serving-maid at a tavern in Germany, and was surprised by hearing her express her belief that every thought, idea, or impression received generated in the brain, remained there ever afterwards, each one stored up in a minute cell, and that good or bad memory would consist in the greater or lesser power of re-opening these cells and making use of their contents. If science be competent to determine the point, she was not far from the truth. Mr. Smee states : "When a man receives an impression, it is not evanescent, passing immediately away, but it is retained in the system to regulate future actions. Now, in voltaic constructions, it is not difficult to produce an action which shall influence future motions, and thus exhibit the effects of memory.

" If we take two iron wires, and place them in a solution of argento-cyanide of potassium, and direct a voltaic current through them, silver would be reduced at that wire constituting the negative pole. The two wires would be ever afterwards in different electric relations to each other; one would be positive, the other negative : and thus the effects of memory would be shown, and future actions regulated."

As the nerve-fibres all terminate in the grey matter of the brain, these terminations are taken to be the negative poles. In this way the entire body is repeated in the brain, which organ again is supposed to be double, and yet so constituted, that two impressions made at different parts of the body convey but one idea to the mind. Under the head of Syndramics the author shows that the large size of the brain, with its multiplicity of fibres and vesicles, is necessary for the reception of the endless variety of impressions made upon that organ. When it is remembered that twenty-four changes can be rung on only four bells, we may form some conception of the myriads of changes to be effected in the 2000 or 3000 elements from each organ of sense. Mr. Smee considers that the brain "probably contains room for all the most important, when packed and arranged with the absolute perfection manifested in all the operations of nature."

Without following each step of the investigation, we may state that each portion of the brain, as enumerated above, is severally treated of in a somewhat similar process of reasoning. A few of the conclusions at which the author arrives will serve to show the mode by which he builds up his theory. "The faculty of desiring," he observes, "resolves itself into a tendency to act, and is manifested when the central batteries are in a condition of excitement. Desire is to mental operations similar in all respects to tension in electric arrangements. When the desire is gratified, it ceases for a time. This phenomenon is similar to an exhausted battery in which arrangements exist for replenishing the exciting fluid; as in this case, after a time, the battery would again become active, and exhibit tension."

Again—"I might dilate largely upon the mechanism by which pleasure and pain may be regulated; but it will be sufficient to give a single illustration of the most simple method in which, in the voltaic circuit, a strong impression might stop action. If a very minute piece of metal be placed in a glass of fluid as a positive pole, and a large current be passed through it, the metal would instantly be dissolved, and the circuit could not be completed by that road. What is true of solid poles is true of liquid poles, or intervening fluid; and where repair is constantly necessary, as we know it is in the brain, a strong impression would more than equal the ordinary supply, and thus action, through that combination, would be stopped. The effect upon the brain by a painful impression appears to amount to more than mere exhaustion, as the part seems damaged permanently, and the action through that road does not again readily take place."

Next in order we come to Electro-Psychology, or "properties of the mind, deduced from the voltaic structure of the brain." This portion of the subject involves many important considerations and metaphysical speculations. Mr. Smee finds a process for every faculty, even up to the idea of immortality. "We know," he says, "from the very organization of our bodies, that we are immortal; that God exists; that there is virtue and vice; a heaven and a hell. Man, in every age, in every climate, is compelled, by his very organization, to believe these first principles. . . . Electro-Noemics," he also explains, "should be the basis of jurisprudence. It shows that crime and pain should be associated together at the same time, because a stronger result would attend punishment inflicted the moment the crime was about to commence. Such a course is suitable for the lowest intellects, or persons of the lowest mental capacity. When, however, good principles could be effectively instilled, they would control every action, and prove far more useful.

"Electro-Noemics also show that to produce a strong effect in future actions, a strong impression must be left on the brain. From this cause punishment should be inflicted upon a man in a healthy, vigorous condition, and neither ill-fed nor debased in energy; otherwise the impression would be transient or evanescent, and would not deter the party from the commission of future crime. Electro-Noemics also indicate that slight and proportionate punishment invariably following crime, would have more effect than severer punishment, with less chance of its infliction."

From the foregoing summary of Mr. Smee's book, it appears to contain matter interesting to other classes of readers as well as electricians and physiologists; but we believe that the time is distant when legislators or philanthropists will discuss questions of social economy or politics in an electro-biological point of view. Still, we are willing to accept the work as another contribution towards an inquiry that has long engaged the attention of philosophers: biology, *the science of life*, is a subject of permanent interest; and if a writer do no more than provoke discussion, he may do that which will eventually elicit truth.

We here close our notice of Mr. Smee's book with an enumeration of its further contents—points of the investigation into which we have not thought it necessary to enter. They are—Electro-bio-Dynamics, or the forces produced in the living body; Bio-Electrolysis, or the changes taking place in the human body; Electro-Biology of Cells, or the relation of electricity to growth, nutrition, and circulation; and last, Electro-Therapeutics and Pathology.

---

## No. XVII.

### LECTURE ON ELECTRO-BIOLOGY; OR, THE VOLTAIC MECHANISM OF MAN. Delivered by ALFRED SMEE at the London Institution. ('The Lancet,' April 21st, 1849.)

THE subject of my present lecture is Electro-Biology, which literally means neither more nor less than the relation of electricity to the vital functions. Now, systematic writers divide the vital functions into two great classes — into those of animal life, and into those of organic life.

The functions of animal life will particularly occupy our attention this evening; and for their consideration, we shall have to study the apparatus by which the animal receives impressions from the external world, transmits them to the brain, registers them, combines them, and acts, not only upon the immediate impressions, but also upon those which it has received at former periods.

For the manifestation of the functions of animal life, we require a central parenchyma or brain, a peripheral or body, the two being connected together by a peculiar tissue called "nerve-fibre;" and at both situations a proper supply of bright arterial blood is requisite, for the production of the phenomena of life. If we look to purely physical

contrivances, we find that similar conditions are fulfilled by a double
voltaic circuit.

Z     — — — —     S
S     .... — ....     Z

If we abstract the proper exciting fluid from either end, or substitute
any other fluid, or destroy the structure at one end or the other, or divide
the connecting portions or wires, the effects proper to the apparatus will
not be manifested, and the battery will be destroyed. The analogy between
the mechanism of a double voltaic circuit and that of animal life is
quite complete; for if we pith an animal, an operation which separates the
brain from the body, or remove the blood from the brain or from the
peripheral part, or destroy the structure of either the brain or the periphery, action is stopped, and animal life ceases.

You will at once say, doubtless, that man has no metallic wires, no
plates; and therefore, you may naturally ask, how far does that fact
destroy the analogy which I have given to you? It is not necessary,
however, that the connecting portion should consist of metal; and though
all present are doubtless accustomed to see the electric telegraphic wires
along the course of the railways, yet I have here upon the table an example
of fluid telegraphic conductors, which answer as efficiently for the conducting of the voltaic force, as wires or metals. Those amongst you who
reside at Upper Clapton, may remember some time since to have seen
mysterious wires placed at an elevated situation round the Horse-shoe
Point on the river Lea. At the time these wires were in that situation, I
was experimenting upon the conducting power of liquids, and they were
found to possess that property in an extraordinary degree. If the nerves,
however, carry the voltaic force, they might perhaps be expected to have
within themselves some means of insulation; and from my own microscopical examination of nerve-fibre perfectly fresh, I believe that a layer
of fat exists in the interior of each primitive fibril, which would as efficiently insulate it as the gutta-percha of my tube does these artificial
nerves which are placed on the table.

In this double voltaic apparatus before you, in which the communicating portion consists of gutta-percha tubing, filled with acid and water, a
powerful voltaic current is passing, but one which will yield no indications
of its presence to ordinary voltaic tests. It is no easy matter, gentlemen,
to prove the presence of a voltaic current in a fluid, and for a long period
I did not know how to proceed to render its existence certain. However,
at last I observed, if any metal capable of being oxidized was interposed in
the path of a voltaic circuit, that one portion becomes positive, the other
negative: and that this result is no fanciful chimera, I now show you an
electro-metallurgic precipitating trough, in which a piece of copper is
inserted between the positive and negative plates, and you will at once
perceive that the portion near the negative pole has become acted upon
or positive, the part nearest the positive pole has become negative, and
has metallic copper deposited upon it. From this experiment I saw
that a mode was afforded to me of ascertaining the presence of a voltaic
circuit in any fluid. To give you a practical illustration of the value
of the electro-voltaic test, I have introduced two copper wires into one
of the gutta-percha tubes constituting my artificial nerves, and you will

perceive that the moment I connect them with a galvanometer, deflection ensues. Animal bodies consist solely of membranes and fluids, and therefore, in the order of my investigations, I had to study batteries solely composed of similar materials. This form of voltaic circuit is extremely difficult to investigate, though one is placed upon the table for your inspection.

After I had thoroughly studied the electro-voltaic test, the time arrived to ascertain whether a voltaic current was actually passing during nervous action: for although the analogies which I have detailed were, to my mind, complete, yet analogy would be useless without the corroboration of direct experiment. My first experiment was to introduce two steel needles into a rabbit: the first into the masseter, or muscle which enables the creature to masticate; the second, into the subcutaneous cellular tissue. After two or three minutes, the creature, which was very tame, attempted to bite my finger; the power of volition was sent to the muscle: this acted upon my electro-voltaic test, and you may judge of my inexpressible delight when the deflection of the needle showed to my mind the mechanism of volition. These needles being between the skin and muscle, the course of the voltaic circuit is clearly demonstrated to exist between these two points, and therefore each required a most minute consideration.

Sensations are received by various organs which are destined to be acted upon by certain physical forces, as the eye by light, the ear by sound, the nose by odours, the tongue by savours, or the skin by heat or force.

It is quite certain that if a voltaic circuit is generated in the eye, there must be such contrivances as photo-voltaic circuits; that is, voltaic circuits in which light causes the evolution of electricity. In trying the experiment, I found that there was not only an extensive series of combinations in which the sun's rays determine the generation of electricity, but that in one division light caused a positive voltaic circuit; in the second, a negative voltaic circuit. The table of these circuits will illustrate the manner in which these circuits are formed, by using solutions so arranged that one portion may be screened from the light, and the second may be acted upon powerfully by the sun's rays.

### Negative Photo-Voltaic Circuits.

Mixed solutions of proto-sulphate of iron and nitrate of silver.
,,   ,,   gallic acid and nitrate of silver.
,,   ,,   oxalic acid and chloride of gold.
,,   ,,   ferrocyanate of potash and ammonio-percitrate of iron.
,,   ,,   ferrocyanate of potash and ammonio-pertartrate of iron.
,,   ,,   ferrocyanate of potash and potassio-tartrate of iron.

### Positive Photo-Voltaic Circuits.

Mixed solutions of pernitrate of iron and red ferrocyanate of potash.
,,   ,,   bromine water, phosphorus water, and pernitrate of iron.

These experiments I cannot show you this evening, because I cannot command the sun's rays to shine upon one side of my apparatus; but from what I have stated, you will perceive that it is quite within the range of ordinary physical effects to have voltaic circuits set in action by light.

Having developed photo-voltaic circuits, the eye itself next demands our attention; and we find nerve and blood to be abundantly supplied to that organ. The electro-voltaic test is best applied by the insertion of one needle into the choroid, the second into the muscles of the eyeball, and I found a slight deflection of the galvanometer when a strong light was thrown into the eye, proving that vision was a voltaic phenomenon.

The essential part of the organ of hearing is encased in textures of such extreme hardness, that it will probably be for ever prevented from being the subject of direct experiment. In the cochlea, I believe we may reasonably assume that the pitch of the note is determined; and in the semicircular canals which are placed in the three orthogonal planes of a cube, physiologists are pretty generally agreed that animals learn the direction of sound. Blood and nerve—essentials to voltaic action—are here distributed, and no physical difficulty is presented to the probability of a voltaic circuit being determined by sounds.

The nasal organ is, like the ear and eye, liberally supplied with blood and nerve-fibres. The voltaic circuit is easily demonstrated by the electro-voltaic test; but the animal has an extraordinary repugnance to the operation, and you must be extremely careful not to be deceived by other secretions which are competent to set up the voltaic action. I can very readily show you that it is not at all difficult to form voltaic circuits, in which odours should excite the electric action. The tube which I hold in my hand contains two iron plates, which are separated by a membrane; and on each side pieces of sponge, dipped in very dilute muriatic acid, are arranged. Now, if ammoniacal vapour, which produces the most powerful action on the natural nose, be brought under one side of the diaphragm, you perceive that a very strong action of the needle is immediately produced. The experiment which I have selected is one which shows the result easily, rapidly, and in a very marked manner; but I should not think it a bold assertion to declare, that with a little trouble and patience I could exhibit voltaic effects, although perhaps to a less marked extent, with every other odoriferous body.

When an animal tastes, the matter which contains the savour comes in immediate contact with the tongue, and is there probably absorbed. I need hardly state that the essentials for sensation, blood and nerve, are abundantly supplied to that organ. With respect to physical contrivances analogical with the tongue, it is very easy to show voltaic force excited by savours; and I have here a V-shaped tube, containing a solution of pernitrate of iron, and two platinum poles, which exhibit by themselves no signs of electric action. As soon, however, as I drop a little infusion of meat into one side of the tube, you will instantly perceive that the galvanometer shows signs of action. There is no mystery about the meat, as sugar, or in fact any other savour, would have had a similar property in a greater or less degree. The direct examination of the tongue in the living animal affords unsatisfactory results, inasmuch as secretions in the mouth are very apt to give wrong results—a circumstance which should be very carefully guarded against.

The last organ of sensation to which I have to beg your attention is the skin. Now, by the ordinary sensor nerves, we derive two sets of impressions of somewhat different characters—for instance, we are enabled to judge of impressions upon the body by either heat or force, or what may be termed Cœnaisthenics. We are also enabled to judge of the changes taking place within our own body, which estimation may be more properly called Somaisthenics. By Somaisthenics we are enabled to estimate the slightest muscular motion, and, in fact, I cannot move my finger or my arm to even the slightest extent without having a perfectly distinct idea of the amount of motion produced.

The skin is acted upon by variations of temperature and force: hence we have to inquire how far heat and force can be employed to set in motion the voltaic force. In experimenting upon the variations of temperature, I found a large series of thermo-voltaic circuits, which, curiously enough, are analogical to photo-voltaic circuits, inasmuch as heat, at various times, determines both negative and positive circuits in the same manner as light. I have here a negative thermo-voltaic circuit. The apparatus, as you perceive, consists of a V-tube, containing sulphate of copper. Into each side of the tube a copper wire is placed, and you perceive that the moment I apply the heat of a spirit-lamp to one side the galvanometer is very strongly deflected, the heated side becoming the negative pole.

When force acts upon the skin, I presume the blood-corpuscle is prevented from coming in contact with the termination of the nerve-fibre; and I will beg you to bear this supposition in mind, as in a later part of this lecture I shall demonstrate to you, that if this supposition be correct, a voltaic circuit must be generated. My observations upon heat and force simply indicate that a thermo- or dynamo-voltaic circuit is an ordinary voltaic or physical phenomenon; but that by no means proves that in the living body the mechanism of feeling is voltaic. This, however, is an experiment easily shown, for we have but to introduce our electro-voltaic test into the cutaneous textures, when a powerful deflection of the galvanometer occurs whenever we pinch or otherwise irritate the skin. We thus find that the mechanism of all the sensations is voltaic, and, according to the laws of the voltaic test, the needle nearest the negative pole becomes positive; that nearest the positive pole, negative. From direct experiment I should therefore infer, that the organs of sensation all constitute the positive pole of the peripheral battery. These inferences, however, must always be taken with a proper allowance for the complex character of the voltaic circuits in the body, or rather, I would say, for the complex materials of which the circuit is composed.

Sensations are received by a certain definite number of sensor nerves, which constitute the only means we possess of obtaining a knowledge of the external world. The sensor nerves pass to the brain, and then come in contact with a highly vascular tissue, called the grey matter of the brain; and I invite your attention to the very exquisite injections which I have made of that tissue, by means of the solution of carmine, and which will be exhibited under the microscope in the library after the lecture.

Inasmuch as the sensor nerves come in contact with blood-vessels, it follows from voltaic laws, that a voltaic battery exists in the brain, which is opposed to that in the body, and by which the electro-biological circuit is completed. At this point we leave the regions of direct experiment, and we must deduce the mechanism of the central battery according to voltaic laws on the one hand, and the properties of the mind on the other.

I infer that the sensations are simply repeated in the brain, nerve for nerve, action for action, and this first battery I term the sensation or aisthenic battery; the second pole of this battery is probably connected with the corresponding fibre of the opposite side, by what anatomists call a commissure, and which I have illustrated on the table by a voltaic arrangement.

We have represented to our minds, not only simple sensations, but also combined impressions: thus, whilst I am looking at all the parts of this theatre, one impression—namely, that of a theatre—is brought before my mind. There is no difficulty in obtaining this result by voltaic means; and the mechanism by which I believe it to be accomplished I have termed the syndramic or combination battery. Thus, if we have three primitive nervous fibrils, $A, B, C$, they may be thus combined, $AB$, $AC$, $BC$, $ABC$. The diagram behind me illustrates this mode of combination; and here, upon the table, I have the voltaic arrangement itself, and you cannot fail to observe that these wires, even on this very limited scale, begin to look like the interlacing which we observe in the brain.

If we divide any space into a certain number of squares, and give to each square a certain name or figure, it will be apparent, that by simply giving the names of the squares filled up with black, the word, or name, or symbol, would at once be accurately described. I have divided this piece of card into certain squares, and if I read you a certain combination of numbers, it would appear, at first, to give no definite idea; but if you examine carefully, you will find that this combination of numbers brings out the word LIFE. This word, I find, has been very unfortunately chosen, but in reality I only selected the word in illustration of the principle of combination, because it only consisted of four letters, and because each letter was so formed that it very perfectly filled up square spaces.

Ladies constantly in practice take advantage of this principle in their patterns of worsted work; and it would be possible so to describe a picture, up to the very limit of our powers of sensation, that it might, from the description alone, be repeated in any country, and yet be a perfect facsimile.

I dwell thus long upon the syndramic or combination battery, because, in all probability, it constitutes a very large part of the brain. When we consider the large number of ultimate fibres in each organ of sensation, I do not think that we have reason to suppose every possible combination ensues; and even with regard to ordinary sentient nerves, I think that such a universal combination would be embarrassing to the mind, and that the combination probably would only extend to the nerves of each separate region of the body. It is quite certain that we always know the specific sense by which impressions are learnt—that is to say, that we know whether an idea has been derived from the eye, nose, mouth, or other organ of sensation. This resolves itself into one idea for a vast number of sensations, and is a state which can very easily be imitated by voltaic contrivances. I have upon the table a voltaic arrangement of this character, in which but one action is produced from one or all the combinations which exist in the syndramic battery. In some cases, ideas do not arise alone from action on one sense, but on two or more senses at one time—a combination which I infer to occur in the syndramic-noemic battery; and lastly, it is necessary to assume that all these last combinations of each specific sense are connected together into one total in the pneuma-noemic battery, from the opposed pole of which the dynamic or motor nerves spring.

The situation of this important battery is somewhere in the base of the brain; and I believe that in applying the electro-voltaic test in this situation, I have obtained deflection of the galvanometer. Let me, however, speak with the utmost caution upon this point; for although I have tried the experiment over and over again, the animal is almost invariably destroyed, and in fact by the electro-biological maps * which are suspended upon the wall, you will at once perceive that an action here influences every nerve in the body, and thus may very readily destroy vitality.

Now, what are the qualities of this last battery, which has but one impression for all the sensations of the body? We find that it represents totality, and cannot be limited. It has therefore the properties of infinity, and gives to man his most exalted ideas. The ideas of soul, God, eternity, immortality, are obtainable from this battery, acting in conjunction with the lower batteries which I have already described. I regret exceedingly that the hour allotted for this lecture has now been so far spent, that I am unable fully to consider the properties of the mind deducible from the theoretical structure which I have developed upon voltaic laws; but, under the circumstances, I feel bound to pass on to matters which can be elucidated by direct experiment.

When the voltaic force is carried by the sensor nerves to the brain, it there causes some change of matter, by which polarity is ever after determined. This phenomenon is a physical result of the most ordinary kind; for I have here a solution of argento-cyanide of potassium, with two copper poles, and before the lecture I passed a voltaic circuit from one pole to the second, by which I have effected a change of matter, and silver has been precipitated on one side. You will now see that, immediately I connect the two poles with the galvanometer, a strong deflection will ensue, and, to use a metaphorical phrase, the solution has remembered what I did to it. This experiment, which is but a sample of a class, must only be regarded as analogical, and is only valuable to show that voltaic electricity may produce effects which will ever after be apparent.

In the arrangement of the nerves of the body, every sensor nerve is opposed to every motor nerve, and may excite it to action under certain circumstances. Now before I consider this subject in detail, I may state that the voltaic circuit, when it has the choice of two or more roads, invariably takes the easiest route, to the exclusion of all the rest. Here is an arrangement in which one of my platinized silver batteries is connected with two precipitating troughs, having the same distance to travel in both cases, but one is charged with sulphate of copper, the other with sulphate of zinc; and yet with this trifling difference the entire current has passed through the sulphate of copper, to the exclusion of the sulphate of zinc, because copper was more easily reducible than zinc, and therefore offered a somewhat easier passage to the voltaic force.

Upon examining the arrangement, I find that the experiment has been

---

* Copies of the maps in Mr. Smee's 'Elements of Electro-Biology' and 'The Mind of Man.'

tried under the most trying circumstances, as I observe that the positive pole, in the sulphate of copper, is almost entirely dissolved. Notwithstanding, however, this, the law which I have developed and described in my ' Electro-Metallurgy,' still holds good, though I must confess that I should not have risked the demonstration of this extreme application of the law, which fortunately, by accident, has brought the matter more strikingly under your notice.

From this law, we learn that the voltaic circuit would be completed through the nearest motor nerve, when any sensation was excited, unless obstacles were presented to its passage in that direction, or any circumstances favourable to its passage through any other motor nerve were afforded in some more distant part of the Electro-Biological circuit, when even the furthest motor nerve might be excited to action.

The action of every animal is determined, then, not only by the impression received at the moment, but by every other event which it has registered or remembered from the first moment of its life.

The motor nerves, by which the circuit is completed in the body, are distributed, in man, to the muscles; in other creatures to the electric organs; in others, to light-generating structures. The electric battery of fishes, as it is technically called, is composed of an enormous number of minute cells, supplied with blood-vessels. The nervous force, which I have already shown to be voltaic, acts at right angles to the direction of the cells, and there produces some change of matter which instantly causes a powerful voltaic current.

I have here a glass vessel, containing a solution of ferrocyanate of potash, into the interior of which is placed a porous cell, containing a similar solution; a platinum pole is inserted into both vessels, for the purpose of connection with the galvanometer. Now, if I pass a voltaic current from the outside to the inside ($z\,s$), no change of matter takes place in one part,—the prussiate of potash remains the same; in the other it is converted into the red prussiate. From this change one side becomes strongly positive to the other, and you perceive that so powerful a current has been generated, that the needle completely swings round the instant connection is made with the galvanometer. I have only shown this experiment upon one cell; but it must be manifest to you, that as every cell adds a certain amount of force, it simply requires a number to make a battery as powerful as that of an electric eel. The artificial electric eel I have myself constructed, in a vast variety of ways, which I have not now time to consider.

The muscular substance is ultimately divisible into primitive fibrils, which consist of a sheath, called the sarcolemma, containing, in the interior, a peculiar matter, which, during the act of contraction, becomes wider and shorter; and this contraction is caused by a change of matter, produced by the voltaic force, carried through the motor nerves.

I have here a strong piece of gut to imitate the sarcolemma, and into the interior of this I have placed fluid and pieces of platinized silver. Upon the outer side of this gut is placed a strong piece of amalgamated zinc, so that the moment connection is made between the zinc and silver, gas is evolved, which renders the bladder wider and shorter, and thus moves this bar of wood over a space of three or four feet.

The conditions of the natural muscle and artificial muscle are perfectly analogical. Both possess a power only limited by the strength of the materials. In both cases, the power acts over the short end of the lever, and therefore at a mechanical disadvantage. In both cases it is a great power moving over a small space. I, however, can move my natural muscles much quicker than I can my artificial muscle; but you must please to remember that my organs are not competent to construct a machine having such fine tubes as we find in the ultimate muscular fibrils; and for want of this delicacy of construction we sacrifice the speed and rapidity of action observable in the perfection of Nature's operations.

Anxious to lay before you the leading experiments and deductions of this truly delightful subject, I have delivered this lecture with the utmost possible rapidity, and yet I see around me multitudes of experiments which I fear that I shall have no time to explain, as the hour has already passed. By your applause, I understand that you wish me to proceed; but as some of my audience live at considerable distances, I will only detain you by calling your attention very briefly to a few other points. In the first place, we find that man consists of a double voltaic circuit, and therefore we ought to consider the nature of the changes taking place in that voltaic circuit. Now, there are strong reasons to suppose that hydrogen and carbon act as the positive pole, and become changed in that capacity into water and carbonic acid. It would only require one thirty-second the quantity of these materials to produce any result that it would of zinc: and I can assure you, that many a time have I sought diligently and carefully for a voltaic circuit which should be efficiently excited by carbon or coke as a positive element; and I can promise to the fortunate discoverer of such a combination the delight of being able to supersede the steam-engine, and the pleasure of successfully generating the voltaic light. Then, and not till then, will voltaic batteries be employed to the exclusion of every other means of generating force. Although up to the present time I have not been able to use coke or carbon for a positive pole, I have succeeded in making a variety of circuits, in which substances composed of carbon and hydrogen form powerful voltaic circuits; for instance, sugar and nitric acid, oxalic acid and chloride of gold, ferrocyanate of potash and nitric acid, constitute examples of this class of batteries.

The voltaic circuit in animals is exactly balanced, and does not act without some impression to set in motion the electric current. The arterial or oxygenized corpuscles are admirably adapted for this purpose, and I have here an experiment which will illustrate their functions in a very beautiful manner. The glass vessel which I hold in my hand contains a solution of common salt, and two iron poles are inserted into it. Now in this state everything is balanced, and no voltaic force is exhibited. If I take an artificial corpuscle made of animal membrane, containing a little pernitrate of iron, and bring it in contact with one of the iron poles, a very powerful deflection of the galvanometer ensues, indicating the presence of a current. When, however, one corpuscle is placed against each plate of iron, the effect is again balanced, and no voltaic circuit arises. These experiments well indicate the functions of the blood-corpuscle in the living body; for when one is in contact with each end of the nerve-fibre, no current can take place, but the moment one is removed, or acted upon by heat, light, or other forces, a strong voltaic battery is formed.

I would gladly have occupied your attention with a few remarks upon the relations of electricity to organic or cell-life. By a modification of the aggregation of cells, a plant produces leaves, stalks, flowers, or roots, which every gardener knows is, to a certain extent, as much under human control as digging, raking, or hoeing. During the prevalence of the potato malady, I subjected the plant to every form of electricity, and in every possible manner, over long periods, without obtaining any result.

There is, however, one remarkable circumstance to be noticed with regard to the relation of electricity to cell-life, for I have found that electric currents stop the circulation of the blood, as suddenly as a stop does a watch when put down; and this entire stoppage of the circulation extends not only to the blood-corpuscle, but also to the lymph-corpuscle which creeps so slowly along the side of the vessel.

If we take a review of the functions of animal life, we find that all sensations, the registration of impressions, thought, action, and other phenomena of animal life, are voltaic effects, and solely obedient to physical laws; and to the idea of the performance of these functions we assign the idea of vitality. Life, therefore, is one word used to signify a number of changes. It is no independent reality apart from the matter which exhibits these phenomena. Neither is it an imponderable attached to matter; nor is it an all-pervading ether, or *anima mundi*, as some philosophers would have us suppose. Life, mind, memory, reason, thought, come from organization, are purely physical phenomena, and cease at death.

Man, however, is immortal. Man, at all times and in all regions, has believed in his immortality. Now that which is mortal can have no relation with that which gives to man his immortality. That which is infinite must not be limited; time must not be confounded with eternity, matter with space, the body with the soul, nor material actions with God.

Electro-biology, then, leads us no less to infer, than religion commands us to believe, " that the dead shall be raised incorruptible, and we shall be changed."

---

## No. XVII.A.

### PRINCIPLES OF THE HUMAN MIND DEDUCED FROM PHYSICAL LAWS; being a Sequel to Elements of Electro-Biology. By Alfred Smee, F.R.S.

#### PREFACE.

Some years since, M. Roret, the distinguished French publisher, did me the honour of causing to be made a translation into the French language of my 'Elements of Electro-Metallurgy,' in which it met with as signal a success as the original edition in this country.

As soon as M. Roret received my work on Electro-Biology, he also caused it to be immediately translated, and kindly wrote to me to know whether I desired to make any additions to the English text.

After a careful consideration, I determined to write a short epitome of the Principles of the Human Mind, deduced from Electro-Biology, to form an Appendix to that work.

But, after the remarkable kindness with which the work has been received in this country by my friends and the public, I feel that it would be a want of courtesy, if not an act of ingratitude, to allow further remarks upon the same subject, however unimportant they may be, to appear in a foreign country before they were issued in the English language.

I apprehend that the time is fast approaching, when no other system of mental science will be acknowledged but that which is based upon physical laws and the structure of the brain; and if my researches shall be found hereafter to have contributed to the development of true philosophy, I shall indeed feel more than amply rewarded for the hours of anxious but delightful labour spent in its development.

7. FINSBURY CIRCUS,
    Sept. 18th, 1849.

### Knowledge of the external World.

1. Our ideas of the external world arise, primarily, from an action upon the ultimate nervous fibres of the organs of sensation, by the specific stimulus competent to excite each organ of sensation respectively.

2. Each primitive nervous fibril is called a unit; the repetition of units, *Number*.

3. That which is competent to act upon these nervous fibrils is called *Matter*.

4. Whenever matter undergoes any change which renders it appreciable to our senses, it is said to evince *Force*.

5. The definite combination of nervous fibres excited to action, determines the *character of the idea* presented to the mind, such as form, position, magnitude.

6. Each combination may be expressed by a word or cypher, and forms a definite image. The use of words is called *Language*.

7. The sum total of all the possible combinations of the ultimate nervous fibrils, excited to action, comprises all the possible images which can be represented to the mind.

8. Inasmuch as the possible combination of all the nervous fibrils is immensely numerous, so are the images which may be reflected in the mind immensely numerous.

### Senses.

9. An idea is represented to the mind, when any one or more of the filaments of either specific organ of sensation is excited without reference to the definite image thereby produced.

10. This solitary idea, derived from the filaments of the eye, is termed *Vision*; of the ear, *Hearing*; of the nose, *Smelling*; of the palate, *Tasting*; of the skin, *Feeling*; and probably, from the nerves communicating the changes occurring in our own body, *Personality*.

### Combination of Senses.

11. The perfect knowledge of any object is obtained by impressions received by the sum of the organs of sensation.

12. But as matter may exist without exciting all the organs of sensation at one time, we determine the combination of senses which has concurred to give us the knowledge of any external object.

### Infinity.

13. An idea is represented from the excitement of one or all the nervous fibrils of any organ of sensation indiscriminately. This idea is infinite, inasmuch as it is indivisible, incapable of addition and represents totality.*

### Time.

14. Our knowledge of the external world at any given period is the sum total of the images from all our senses.

15. These images represented to the mind are perpetually changing.

16. When images change, one remains; the other changes perhaps several times before the first changes. The relation of these changes to each other is termed *the time of their occurrence*; that which changes the least frequently is said to be of *the longest duration*.

### Cause.

17. In the change of images, when one specific image never appears without a similar antecedent, and the matter in the external world which gave rise to the first image set in motion the second—the antecedent image is said *to cause* the second image.

18. The mind finds great difficulty in distinguishing between concomitance and cause, because the matter which produces an antecedent image may not set in motion the matter which produced the second image.

### Pleasure and Pain.

19. When images of the external world are produced with a certain intensity, the idea of *Pleasure* is excited; when with a greater intensity, the idea of *Pain*.†

20. The transition from Pleasure to Pain being sudden, not gradual, it follows that the nature of the action on the brain, and consequently of the ideas, is different.

### Memory.

21. An image once formed in the brain produces an indelible impression, and may at any future time recur. This property is called *Memory*.

### Consciousness.

22. When an image is produced by an action upon the external senses, the actions on the organs of sense concur with the actions in the brain; and the image is then a *Reality*.

23. When an image occurs to the mind without a corresponding simultaneous action of the body, it is called a *Thought*.

24. The power to distinguish between a thought and a reality is called *Consciousness*.

---

* Infinity is sometimes confounded with its hyperbolical use in the sense of endless number.

† Every action of our lives is either pleasurable or painful; and thus we perceive how vastly the former state preponderates over the latter.

### Instinctive Ideas.

25. Several ideas must necessarily co-exist, giving rise to compound ideas always existing in the brain: thus personality and infinity give us the idea of the Soul; pleasure and infinity, of Good; pain and infinity, of Evil; cause and infinity, of God; time and infinity, of Eternity; infinity, pleasure and time, of Heaven; infinity, pain and time, of Hell.\*

26. These instinctive ideas are not produced by the immediate action of external influences, but have their origin in the construction of the brain, or organ of thought.

27. Instinctive ideas belong to the higher class of mental images; and there is no reason to suppose that a more simple idea is implanted in the human species. In the lower animals, however, it is apparent that either other images exist, which guide the creatures to perform their operations —as the bird to build the nest, the bee the honeycomb; or that the nervous system is so constructed, that the creature is led to perform specific acts under some definite excitement.

### Reflection.

28. When images already implanted in the brain, which possess many points in common, continually reappear, the party is said to be reflecting.

29. During reflection, the influences of the external world to produce new images are entirely, or to a great part, neglected.

30. By reflection, ideas may be combined so as to form general laws.

31. By reflection, general laws may be applied to specific instances, or images may be analysed into their component parts.

### Judgment.

32. When an idea is represented to the mind, it either accords or discords with other ideas previously received, or with general laws resulting therefrom, or with the moral law. The determination between this concordance or discordance is called *Judgment.*

### Imagination.

33. Man has the power of uniting two or more antecedent images, or the parts of two or more antecedent images. By this power, a totally new image is formed, and hence it is called *Imagination.*

34. Observation is the basis of fancy; and the novelist is fruitful only in proportion as he stores his mind with natural images.

### Action.

35. Man acts by electricity, which is set in motion through the muscular structures, whereby contraction ensues, and parts of the body are moved.

36. Action may be produced by the immediate influence of the

---

\* As these instinctive ideas are simply thoughts, and cannot be proved by our external senses, the mind may be led at times to deny the reality of their existence. Revelation, however, declares their truth, and thus compensates for the natural weakness of man.

external agents upon the body, which give rise to a new image in the brain; and action may also be produced by the recurrence of a former image.

### Specific Action.

37. The mind is one and indivisible; and thus, the particular muscular movement which the electrical force determines is not only regulated by an immediate image, but by every other image which has at any former time been implanted in the brain.

38. Pleasure and pain regulate all actions: hence the particular movement which is determined arises from the pleasurable or painful character of all former images; as animals, as well as human beings, seek those actions which are likely to be pleasurable, and eschew those which are likely to be painful.

39. But the action determined in any particular instance may be painful for the sake of obtaining greater pleasure at future periods; and the idea of obtaining infinite pleasure may allow of the most intense immediate pain.

### Hope and Fear.

40. The idea of future pleasure is called Hope—of future pain, Fear. The government of mankind is conducted by exciting Hope and Fear.

### Desire.

41. When a tendency to act exists, it is called *Desire*; and always exists, more or less, when a being is in good health, and in a state free from fatigue.

### Virtue and Vice.

42. All actions in the higher generalizations would give the idea either of infinite pleasure or of infinite pain. Actions which concur with those which lead to infinite pleasure are called Virtuous; and those which lead to infinite pain are called Vicious.

### Moral Law.

43. The moral law, being infinite, is competent to control all actions. It is therefore important that it should be frequently and strongly impressed upon the human mind.

### Volition.

44. The resultant of the force of an immediate stimulus and of all former ideas implanted in the brain is termed *Volition*.

### Free Agency.

45. A man is born a free agent; but after images are once implanted, he is compelled to act from the ideas existing in his brain. Hence, could we but tell the exact ideas which any human being possessed, it would be practicable to foretell his line of action under any defined circumstance.

---

T

## CERTAIN SPECIFIC IDEAS.

### *Life.*

46. The term Life is assigned to the idea which the mind forms of the capacity of an organized being to perform its functions.

### *Death.*

47. The term Death is assigned to the idea which the mind receives of an organized being incompetent to perform the vital actions.

### *Mind.*

48. The term Mind is assigned to the general idea of any action of the brain, which is a part of the organization of man. An idea is the term assigned to any specific action in the brain.

### *Organization.*

49. Organization is the term assigned to the construction of a being to adapt it to perform certain functions.

### *Future State.*

50. The mind has constantly represented to it the idea of a personality which will exist infinitely.

51. Whilst, however, the idea exists, we have no power to learn the properties of infinity; and hence we cannot define the nature of the state in which we shall live hereafter.

———

### DISEASED STATES OF MIND.

#### *Insane Ideas.*

52. Whenever an idea appears in the brain, which is neither instinctive nor is due to external causes, nor is deduced by the ordinary operation of the brain, it is said to be an *Insane Idea.*

53. When this idea is continuously the same, the party is said to have a *Monomania.*

54. When various images appear and vanish indiscriminately, the state is called *Incoherence;* and when this state is combined with more or less unconsciousness, it is termed *Delirium.*

55. The danger of insane ideas depends upon the *distinctness* with which the idea is impressed upon the brain; for it will determine the party to act in proportion to the power with which it is impressed.

56. To the violent actions arising from strongly implanted diseased ideas, the term MANIA is given; and the violence of the Mania is proportionate to the power of the delusion. To the individual it is an exaltation of pleasure.

57. When, from the delusion, the patient is in continual fear, he is said to be *melancholy;* and it is probably, to the individual, an exaltation of pain.

58. When a fixed insane idea exists in the mind, the party cannot be

said to be partially deluded; for, inasmuch as the mind is one and indivisible, it will control all actions.*

59. A strong moral impression may counteract an insane image, as a party may be kept from doing wrong, by feeling assured that it will lead to present or future inconvenience to himself.

---

### DEFECTIVE STATE OF MIND.
#### Idiotcy.

60. When the structure of the brain is congenitally defective, so that it cannot perform all its normal actions, the party is said to be an idiot.

#### Loss of Memory.

61. Sometimes the power of memory is intermittent, or is totally lost, as after the frequent recurrence of epileptic fits.

#### Fits.

62. Any interval of unconsciousness, except sleep, is called a Fit.

#### Fatuity.

63. When from loss of memory, or want of power in the brain, the functions of reflection or judgment are not perfectly performed, the individual is said to be *fatuous*.

#### Loss of Sensation.

64. Sometimes the power of receiving impressions from the external world is diminished or lost, as in blindness, deafness, &c.

#### Paralysis.

65. When parts of the body do not move by volition, they are said to be paralysed.

#### Senile Imbecility.

66. In old age the brain loses its power to receive new images, to restore bygone impressions, to connect different images, or to apply general laws to specific instances. That which ennobles the man has passed away; the outward form remains, but the inward structure has lost its power to act. Childhood again ensues—not to acquire new ideas, but to forget those before implanted. All that is beautiful or desirable in this world has passed away—the brain has lost its power—the mind ceases—the very existence of the man is unknown to himself, till death gives rise to a new life, and discloses that new and glorious state in which our organization teaches us that man will be immaterial and immortal.

#### Varieties of Races.

67. As individuals differ in their organization, it follows that they differ in their capacity to perform various acts; and we may presume that

---

* As a matter of jurisprudence, it has been held by the Lord Chancellors, in the House of Lords, that the mind cannot be said to be partially deluded, inasmuch as it is one and indivisible.

the mind, being one of the functions of the body, is of varying power in different individuals.

68. The observations which apply to different individuals, apply with greater force to different races.

---

## No. XVIII.

### ON THE PRODUCTION OF CHOLERA BY INSUFFICIENT DRAINAGE. With Remarks on the Hypothesis of an altered Electrical State of the Atmosphere. By Alfred Smee, F.R.S., Surgeon to the Bank of England, &c. (From the 'Lancet,' September 1st, 1849.)

When pestilence passes over the land, and consigns to a premature grave alike the old and the young, it behoves each in his respective department to endeavour to trace out the proximate cause, and strive to discover some antidote to so direful a calamity.

The experience of all the world proves that the lowest districts, the banks of rivers, and natural watercourses are the situations in which the malady chiefly resides. Two physical hypotheses may be framed upon this fact: firstly, that the cholera is caused by a poison which gravitates to those situations; secondly, that in those situations poison is generated.

If, however, cholera be produced by a heavy poison subsiding from the atmosphere to low situations, we should have cholera exhibiting itself in all low districts, and the weight of the air would be absolutely greater in such localities. This fact has not been proved, otherwise the Board of Health could always determine, by weighing the atmosphere, where cholera was likely to appear, and, when existing, when it was likely to depart. The hypothesis of a heavy poison being the cause of cholera is a generalization embracing many facts, but not based upon any direct proof.

In low situations, however, drainage is manifestly more or less imperfect. The effete materials of the human frame are not quickly removed from the sphere of human residences, and thus can act more detrimentally than in higher and drier localities. Nothing is more hurtful to animal life than the effete matter of the same animal, and disease more or less serious is sure to occur when any creature is exposed to the influence of the worn-out materials of its own frame.

Nature has provided that ordinarily the most rapid diffusion of gaseous emanations should take place throughout the atmosphere; and with such force does this diffusion occur, that Professor Graham has beautifully observed, that it would be as easy to stop the mountain torrent as to impede the equable diffusion of different gases.

Every person must have observed that sometimes this diffusion is quicker than at others, and that the same source will sometimes exhale the most pestiferous stench, whilst at others no offensive odour will be discoverable. This difference is clearly attributable to the exhalation passing more rapidly into the atmosphere at one time than another.

Now all cholera cases appear in situations where the victims have been exposed to the exhalations of drains, cesspools, &c., or to the equally hurtful products of the lungs and skin of other individuals. Hence these facts may be expressed hypothetically, by assuming that from some cause the diffusive power of the atmosphere is at the present time below the average; and hence, wherever noxious exhalations exist, there the disease is manifested according to the susceptibility of the unfortunate individuals exposed to their influence.

The non-diffusive hypothesis meets every case with which I am acquainted in this great metropolis; for, from having carefully studied the official facts communicated by the Registrar-General, together with other observations, I have been surprised how constantly cholera has appeared upon the lines of the great sewers.

The Fleet ditch, which is almost a river in the magnitude and length of its course, has furnished abundance of cases, and its immediate neighbourhood many more, from causes which I shall presently detail. This sewer runs its course along the lowest ground between two hills, Ludgate Hill on the one hand, Fleet Street on the other. When the sun shines upon the hills, the air becomes warmer and specifically lighter, and hence, according to immutable physical laws, a circulation of air laden with the hurtful gases is produced in a direction from the river to these streets, and with a magnitude of current directly proportionate to the imperfection of the trappings of the sewers. This life-destroying blast is perceptible to the olfactory organs of the most indiscriminating person.

The cholera does not necessarily follow water, because no case has occurred along the New River, which is a pure, pellucid stream, running at a considerable altitude along the hills, and which therefore does not imbibe the drainage in the neighbourhood. At Highbury Vale a foul ditch runs, and there, I am informed, the malady has occurred. From these facts we learn that water without a sewer is harmless.

The non-diffusive theory, which I submit is competent to account for the fact of cholera, shows that the public have incurred a grave responsibility for not having removed effectually the excrementitious matter from London, as it points out that every death from cholera is a homicide which might by proper management have been prevented.

The most indifferent person must have observed that noxious vapours do not diffuse with equal rapidity at different times, and a question naturally arises, how far electricity may be supposed to influence that state. When particles of matter are electrified similarly, they repel each other; when dissimilarly, they are mutually attracted. As far as gases are concerned, I do not know of any experiments which bear upon the matter; and so far as my own attempts have at present gone, I do not feel at present satisfied with the results. During the prevalence of cholera the electrical state of the atmosphere has been neutral; and when thunderstorms have occurred, the electrical disturbances have only been manifested for a few hours. This neutral state is probably most favourable for the non-diffusion of gases.* It is probable this non-diffusive state does not

---

* Connected with this subject, we must not forget the presence of ozone in the atmosphere. It has the properties of a highly-oxygenated substance, and hence would enter into combination with mephitic bodies. This curious substance is produced whenever electricity is passing through water or aqueous vapour, and is, perhaps, identical with the peroxide of hydrogen.

altogether depend upon electrical conditions, as we have neutral electricity for days together when cholera does not appear.

The absence of diffusive power may not be for all gases equally; and, if subsequent experiment confirm this idea, a cause for each specific epidemic may be ultimately ascertained by the medical practitioner having proper recourse to chemistry and natural philosophy.

Within the last month I have had many inquiries upon the possibility of the disease being due to the direct action of electrical states upon the human frame. Upon this matter I can only say that, having kept small animals under electric tension for weeks together, I never could observe any very appreciable effect; and I do not believe myself that electricity in any form could give rise to cholera. With respect to the statements which have appeared in the papers, of the non-action of an electrical machine, under French auspices, when the cholera raged, I may state that it is contrary to my own experience, and so opposed to physical laws that it partakes rather of the romantic than the real.

With respect to the effect of electricity as a remedial agent for cholera, there are not sufficient physiological reasons for supposing that in any form it can be applied with great success; yet, as a stimulus, Dr. Peacock has employed it usefully, and, by using the intermittent current of the electro-magnetic or magneto-electric machine, the asthenic and dynamic pole of the great peripheral battery may be excited to action, and, according to the experiments which I have elsewhere described, the entire capillary system of the surface and extremities of the body would be stimulated, and the blood thereby drawn off from the interior. There would be no difficulty in keeping a cholera patient under electrical tension, by simply placing the legs of the bed on blocks of glass, and connecting the bed with the conductor of an electric machine; but, upon physiological grounds, I do not apprehend that much benefit would arise in so severe a disease as cholera.

I invite the attention of our profession to the non-diffusive theory, for its universality or its incorrectness can only be proved by a multitude of observers. At present, it appears to me to express the greatest number of facts, and to be the most useful for practical application, as it declares that cholera may be avoided by pure air, proper ventilation, and perfect drainage.

The practical man is never contented without inquiring into the best mode of action. It is clear that in a few days we cannot alter our gigantic sewage works, and therefore the best preventive which can be adopted is to cause the flow of such a great abundance of clear water that the poison may be retained in the sewers. Clear water contains oxygen to combine with the noxious products, and it is found that, up to a certain state, water takes from the atmosphere, gases to which it has an affinity, instead of yielding them to it, to spread abroad the poison.

The supply of water in London must in a great measure be procured from the New River, though thousands of tons might probably be thrown into the sewers by employing the waste labour of workhouses and prisons to pump water from such wells as already exist.

## No. XIX.

ON BINOCULAR PERSPECTIVE. From the Second Edition of ALFRED SMEE'S book, 'The Eye in Health and Disease,' and from other notes, &c. 1854.

" IN the last edition of this book, I stated that we know that it is impossible for any painter to delineate a picture in the manner in which we see it with both eyes, because two eyes give us a view of three sides of a cube, and he can paint but two. I conceive it possible, that for objects at moderate distances, painters may, in some cases, take a certain liberty with perspective and depict the two perspectives; but it certainly cannot be attempted with near objects.

" Notwithstanding the assertion of the impossibility of delineating a picture as seen with two eyes, which was the correct opinion of the time, certain abstract considerations, with which I need not trouble my readers, induced me to believe that such a delineation was more practicable than at first sight was supposed; and after much thought and studious experiment, I trust that I am enabled to submit the laws by which painters may represent, to a great extent, objects as seen with both eyes, and consequently in all their natural beauty.

" In studying the phenomena of binocular perspective, it must be remembered that the two eyes, being placed at two inches and a half apart, give a different perspective view; and, as in nature the eyes are directed to the same point, it follows that the same part of the same object must be the same point of sight for the two perspectives.

" The picture in a binocular perspective drawing really consists of two drawings overlapping each other, the point of sight in both being the same. By this overlapping, lights and shades, tones and the effect of breadth, are produced, such as the eyes really observe in nature.

" The following may be regarded as the leading rules or laws of binocular perspective, which may be useful to the painter as a guide in the production of the drawing, or as a test for the detection of error when it has been made. Much judgment and skill are no doubt requisite for the painter so to construct his picture that the effect of solidity may be suggested to the mind rather than hardly delineated; and, as far as I can judge, from the observation of paintings of some of our great artists, they have, as an effort of genius, really depicted objects as seen with two eyes."

For example, he found that " Paul Veronese most skilfully obtains the effect of solidity by the suggestion of a line more or less broken to conceal his artifice, outside the limbs of the figures which he has represented." My father never entered a picture-gallery without testing the pictures by his laws of binocular perspective; and when he was at Rome in 1868, he made some interesting notes of the pictures in the Vatican, in which he found that the great masters produced in somewhat different manners the principles of binocular perspective, although the laws for the same were unknown to them. Thus, in Baracci's pictures, there is "an indefiniteness of edge;" in Guido's there is " a gradation of tint—an undefined half-tone;" in Correggio's, "the edge is double;" in Paul Veronese's, "the second line is half pencilled in;" in Andrea Sacchi's, "half-tone outside edge;" in Bartolomeo's, "hairy edge;" in Caravaggio's, "shade over line, colour;" in Perugino's, "hard outline;" in Guercino's, "indeterminate outline," &c.

My father was greatly interested in this celebrated collection of pictures in the Vatican, and spent considerable time over them. Unfortunately the above notes, with the sketches attached to them, were consigned for care in the writing-case of my travelling bag, and have remained there forgotten for several years. Lately, in thinking over events in my dear father's life, the remembrance of his visit to the Vatican and of these notes suddenly flashed across my mind. Had he lived, he would probably have again brought forward his theories on Binocular Perspective, with these notes fully set forth as illustrations.

He gives eleven rules or laws on Binocular Perspective :—

"1. The point of sight appears the same to both eyes as to one.

"2. Small objects of less width than the distance between the pupils of the eyes, when placed in a plane before the point of sight, are increased in width and rendered either wholly or in part transparent, according to their distance from the eyes.

"3. Large objects, in a plane before the point of sight, are increased in width, and their lateral edges become transparent and allow objects to be seen through them.

"4. Objects or parts of objects on either side the point of sight are increased in width, and the edges become transparent.

"5. Objects in a plane, behind the point of sight, are seen in two places, but indistinctly, because they are out of focus, and because their images fall upon the internal surface of the retina at a greater or less distance from the point of distinct vision.

"6. Solid bodies or parts of solid bodies, appearing transparent, modify the tints of objects seen through them.

"7. Bodies of a light colour throw a light veil over objects seen behind them. Bodies of a darker colour throw a dark veil.

"8. Colours of different character, as yellow and blue, when superimposed according to the preceding law, produce a tint different from either, and yet not the colour which would arise from their admixture.

"9. In cases where objects or parts of objects are widened and rendered transparent, the breadth of the distinct or solid part is narrower than when viewed by one eye alone.

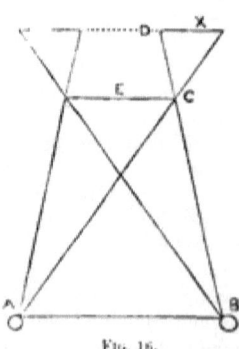

Fig. 16.

"10. Small objects placed some distance before the point of sight and near the eyes appear in two places, but one impression is generally neglected.

"11. Parts of objects becoming transparent have frequently much light reflected from them, and where the image is seen in two places sometimes the light is only reflected from one image.

"The annexed figure will serve to give an illustration of the interpenetration of objects when seen by two eyes, and will also explain the geometrical law on which it is founded. It will be seen that by two eyes we are enabled to see a greater amount of the back object than would be discernible by one eye alone. This amount may be called X, and the quantity denoted varies directly as the base AB, and the line CD, and inversely as the line BC. By similar triangles $AB:BC::X:DC$; therefore $X = \dfrac{AB \times DC}{BC}$ an equation which gives the value of X in every position.

"In studying these principles nothing has more astonished me than the fact of the colours which overlap to the two eyes not giving the compound colour, which would result if they were mixed and seen by one eye. In all those parts of a picture where colours overlap, much skill will have to be exercised by the painter, as the appearance in nature is that of a film or coloured gauze overlapping other colours, and the result is not the ordinary compound colour.

"One of the few artists who have seen Turner paint, stated to me that in painting the near objects he lightly touched with his brush and then placed his finger over it, whereby he produced a semi-transparent streak instead of a line. This streak enabled the more distant objects to be seen behind it, and thus the conditions of binocular perspective were in part fulfilled.

"Another curious phenomenon connected with binocular perspective is observable in the case of a landscape viewed through a window, for in that instance the vertical bars become either wholly or partially transparent, and the objects behind them are seen with a shade over them. The horizontal bars retain their solidity and obscure all the parts they shade. This phenomenon occurs when the head remains in its ordinary position; but when the head is turned so that the eyes are one above the other, the horizontal bars become transparent, and the vertical bars retain their solidity. It is requisite for the observance of these effects that a distant object should be the point of sight, and not the window bar.

"According to the laws which have been detailed, we observe that objects behind the point of sight are seen in two places, although indistinctly, from being out of focus, and from being seen at the lateral part of the retina. From these facts it is apparent that a painter should depict the objects in the background of a neutral or tertiary tint and very indistinct. In nature the object directly viewed is alone seen in perfection, and he that would carefully study nature should contrive that his principal subject should be the brightest in colour and most distinct in detail, when it will stand forth in all its beauty.

"The outline effects of binocular perspective may be readily obtained by placing two candles at 2½ inches apart, from flame to flame, and examining the shadows which are produced upon a white screen. It will then be seen that objects near the screen will have a light shade at each lateral border. Small objects will, at a greater distance, appear double; and the double images being superimposed, a body different from either will be produced. A finger held horizontally across the flames will have the end prolonged by its shadow, but it will be observed that no change takes place at the upper and lower edges. By this experiment only the outline effect is produced; but I cannot too highly recommend to the painter to shut himself up with two candles and study these effects.

"As a rule, the image of an object in two places is not appreciated entirely, because one object falling upon the margin of the retina is scarcely visible. These considerations curiously bring before our mind the fact, that even the apparent imperfections in the construction of the parts of our body are necessary for the highest integrity of their functions.

"It occurred to me that, if the laws of binocular perspective were correct, pictures might be obtained by photography which should represent the appearances observed with both eyes. The conditions required for binocular sun-pictures are similar to those required for binocular drawings or paintings. As it is requisite that there should be one point of sight for the two perspective drawings, considerable nicety is required in the production of binocular photographs, as the slightest deviation from correctness produces doubleness or great distortion. To obtain a binocular picture of any body, the camera must be employed to take half the impression, and then it must be moved in the arc of a circle of which the distance from the camera to the point of sight is the radius, for about 2½ inches, when a second picture is taken, and the two impressions, conjointly, form one binocular picture.

"There are many ways by which this result may be obtained. A spot may be placed in the ground glass, on which the point of sight should be made exactly to fall; the camera may then be moved 2½ inches and adjusted till the point of sight falls again upon the same spot on the ground glass, when, if the camera has been moved in a true horizontal plane, the effect of the double picture will be perfect.

"For obtaining this motion in the true arc of a circle, Mr. Hensman, the engineer to the Bank of England, recommended me to adopt a carriage with two movable axles, with wheels of which the front pair is a little smaller than the back pair. The idea of the construction is, that the carriage should revolve on two cones which run round a circle, and the diameter of the circle is determined by the distance between the larger and smaller wheels and the convergence of the axles. In practice, on a surface adjusted by spirit-levels, it answers well, and probably may be found useful in some cases. At Messrs. Horne and Thornthwaite's photographic room, an apparatus has been fixed, which allows the motion of the camera to be made perfectly horizontal in the arc of a definite circle. From experiments which we have made, I rather give the preference to pictures made with the camera in continual motion,' backwards and forwards, for 2½ inches, as the picture is, in this case, even more beautiful than if the two images were superimposed. This experiment is very remarkable, for who would have thought formerly, that a picture could possibly have been made with a camera in continual motion? Nevertheless, we accomplish it every day with ease, and the character of the likeness is wonderfully improved by it.

"Whenever a solid body is depicted in binocular perspective, a suitable background should be arranged behind it to exhibit the interpenetration. If this be not considered, the picture has an increased width with double edges, and does not exhibit that glorious delicacy of shading which Nature gives to objects seen with both eyes. In all cases of binocular perspective we must be careful not to imitate Nature by endeavouring to depict an excessive range of distances. In practice, the eye can only focus objects within a certain range: hence in pictures we still take Nature as our guide when we only depict a moderate range.

"It is not easy to predict the extent or the importance of this mode of drawing, because an extensive experience is required before artists can judge of these matters. From the best consideration which I can give to the subject, I am inclined to believe that, with regard to paintings, it will reduce to rule the methods intuitively practised by our great and honoured masters; and, with respect to photographs, it may be possibly found to supply the desideratum so long required of delineating a delicately-shaded picture, instead of, as at present, a hard perspective drawing.

" In viewing these binocular representations, the best effect is produced by examining them with one eye when they are tolerably close; or, if two eyes be employed, by viewing the representation at such a distance that we are not enabled to detect the flatness of the picture, and thus discover the cheat. How far we may take liberties with the distance between the two sights, for the camera, will be a subject of future investigation under various circumstances.

" The light falling upon the edges of bodies obliquely is reflected to a considerable extent. This effect must be carefully noted by the painter, as this phenomenon much increases the appearance of the rotundity of bodies. In this case the light is the colour of the source from which it arises. Sometimes it is white light; in the evening it is red.

" In the cases of bodies in a plane either before or behind the point of sight, which from their size and position are seen in two places at once, the impression of one is generally neglected. In these instances it does not follow that the light reflected from one image should be reflected from the other, because, from the position of the eyes, the position may not be congenial for reflection in both cases. The effect of light is extremely difficult for the painter to represent, because white or yellow paint is a very poor substitute for the glorious light of day.

" The investigations which I have conducted upon binocular perspective have afforded instructive and interesting views of the mental image which results from the combined physical pictures of both eyes. To represent this mental image so that it may be visible at one glance, has been a work with me of much thought; and its practical application has been a deduction from my electro-biological speculations."

## XX.

ON EDUCATION. LETTER OF ALFRED SMEE ADDRESSED TO THE COMMITTEE OF INDUSTRIAL INSTRUCTION IN 1853.

I have very carefully considered the various questions transmitted by the Committee of Industrial Instruction, and beg to submit the following remarks in reference to the matter.

1. It appears to me in the highest degree desirable that the endowed grammar schools should teach subjects more congenial with the spirit and requirements of the present time. Having been educated at St. Paul's School, I can confidently state that many important branches of knowledge now neglected could be taught in addition to the mere routine of Latin and Greek. Childhood is that time of life which is most suited to receive knowledge by the medium of the senses, and hence an exclusive application to grammar, Latin and Greek, does not comport with the natural aptitudes of the individual at that period. To meet this important defect, it would be desirable to add to the present usual course of study the elements of Arithmetic, Chemistry, Physics, and Natural History.

Up to twelve years of age, I believe that subjects of instruction should, as far as possible, be brought tangibly before the child; for every object which is impressed upon the mind, and every property of which it is made cognizant, remains till the latest period of life, and may give rise hereafter to important results. Simple facts brought tangibly before the senses may be regarded as units of knowledge, and I must submit that such units should especially be regarded in any scheme of sound education for early childhood. After twelve, the mind well stored with units may be taught to combine and arrange them, and at that period the best and soundest theories should be the subject of education.

I much fear that those who seek to improve the endowed grammar schools will be met with the usual cry of "No room for such subjects here." To those who employ this old and hackneyed phrase, I will reply that it is impossible to confine a child's attention to Latin and Greek for more than half the period that he is usually employed at school, and that such additional subjects would be an agreeable diversion for his mind, would command his attention, and render his scholastic studies far more agreeable to him.

A child not only likes to derive knowledge by the medium of his senses, but he is also fond of doing some work for himself. This desire should, as far as possible, be gratified; and a child may practise drawing, be taught to make pieces of mechanism, and even conduct some of the more simple chemical processes.

The number of masters even at our first grammar schools is extremely insufficient. In some cases a single master has the charge of as many as forty boys, a number far too many to insure a satisfactory tuition; and thus the addition of masters for other subjects could not fail to be extremely beneficial.

The introduction of additional studies into the endowed grammar schools would probably require not only the force of public opinion, but even would demand a legislative enactment, so far are the managers wedded to bygone practices and antiquated customs.

2. With respect to the Mechanics' and Literary Institutions as now constituted, they seem rather to be places of amusement than institutions for study. If we take for example the London Institution, which is noted for its wealth and its means for instruction, we find that at the present time not one single educational course is provided. Its laboratory is tenantless and useless, and, with the exception of an evening lecture twice a week during the winter months, its magnificent theatre is unused.

It appears to me that all these institutions should have professors to direct regular educational courses adapted to the young, and occasionally that special evenings should be set apart for the illustration of new discoveries and principles, in order that those engaged in business may be fully made acquainted with all the scientific novelties of the day. The improvement of these institutions in many cases depends upon the managers; in too many instances the managers regard the post as an honour to be coveted, for a certain rank which it is supposed to bestow on account of their sitting in a more prominent seat, and by placing amusement before instruction they forget the real educational objects for which such institutions are destined: but there appears to me to be no valid reason why regular systematic instruction should not be supplied at the Mechanics' and Literary Institutions.

3. The same class of boys are sent to the grammar schools as to the proprietary schools: hence their requirements demand a similar education. For instance, an education which is good for King's College would be good for St. Paul's, Westminster, or Merchant Taylors', as the boys in each case belong to the middle class of society.

Different classes of society manifestly require, in many respects, a very different education; nevertheless, amongst all classes, there are many points in common. A knowledge of the properties of numbers and of physical forces is as useful to the poor as to the rich. The master who orders the steam-engine to be manufactured should understand its several parts and the power which it is likely to possess. The engineer who designs the steam-engine must of necessity be fully acquainted with its principles and properties. The man who works the steam-engine should equally understand the principles upon which it is constructed; and the mechanic who makes the engine would be the more trustworthy servant if he possessed the intelligence to comprehend the nature of his work and were fully aware of the purposes for which each part was destined.

A knowledge of the properties of matter and of physical forces should be taught to every child, irrespective of station or future occupation. It cannot fail to be useful in every grade of life, should be regarded as the foundation of secular knowledge, and taught at every school.

In this country, the people, as a mass, seem to be greatly destitute of an acute appreciation of colour and form. To acquire a knowledge of this character, Nature must be studied. The beautiful flower, the elegant plant, or the symmetrical proportions of animated life must be observed, and their appearance fixed upon the mind at an early period of life.

The appreciation of beauty is as suitable for those in a lower as for those in a higher station of society: yet the difficulties presented to the observation of Nature in the environs of a large metropolis are far beyond what might have been anticipated.

Many a time I have seen troops of police scouring the woods in the vicinity of London to prevent an invasion of property by an entomologist catching an insect, or a flower-seeker gathering a primrose.

At every school there can be no reason for the omission of botanical and natural history rambles under the surveillance of competent persons. At medical schools it is the practice of the professor to take such rambles, and the day is much enjoyed by the pupils. Independently of the pleasure derivable from such rambles, which cannot fail to endear the master to the pupil, the mind would be thereby led not to despise the beautiful because it is common; and would be trained to admire and to study the form and colouring of Nature, the only reliable guide for the artist or designer.

Even with respect to works of art, the mass of the people have the greatest difficulty in obtaining copies of approved examples, or of viewing approved devices; and consequently their education on this score is extremely defective, and their taste extensively vitiated. When I first prosecuted my electro-metallurgic researches, I thought that some system might be adopted to enable the public to obtain copies of the beautiful coins or medals of antiquity; but I found that although the cabinets and museums were freely open to me, yet they were practically closed to the working man. I have on several occasions been employed on the part of the Crown to give evidence against false coiners, who might have earned a large remuneration if they had had subjects upon which they might have exercised the same amount of skill. In matters of art, description is but a poor apology for the reality, and therefore copies or models should be placed in every school.

Great mischief appears to arise from an inaccurate use of words and language. Frequently a sufficiently definite meaning is not attached to the word, as the mind is not sufficiently trained to regard the object signified. At grammar schools the pupil is always treating of words instead of things, and from want of definite ideas the pupil is much more exposed to the influence of quibbles. I believe that half the discussion and difference of political and religious opinion depends upon an imperfect appreciation of the meaning of words, depending upon their being so much used without relation to the things signified, and in this respect we frequently observe a deficiency in the education of the clergy.

A great defect of the schools for all classes of children in this country is their exclusive attention to the mere book information of man, to the neglect of the real knowledge obtainable by the study of Nature.

My professional duties have given me ample opportunities to observe different classes of society. I need hardly make any remark upon that degraded class whom we occasionally see, and who scarcely know their name, age, and abode, or in fact possess much more intelligence than an animal. Amongst mechanics we frequently observe a strong desire to obtain knowledge as far as possible, but they have slender means for learning the *rationale* or theory of the means which they employ in their respective trades. They read to a certain extent, but they can only afford to purchase the cheaper books of the day; and amongst my dispensary patients I frequently observe signs of moderate intellectual culture, which doubtless would have been further developed had they only the advantage of better means for improving themselves.

Amongst the middle classes I have frequently been astonished at observing, not only that there is a total absence of books of any kind, but also that there are no indications of any pursuit of knowledge of any kind whatsoever; and frequently, in answer to my interrogatories, I have discovered that they have no occupation whatsoever besides that of their monotonous business. The good effect of a variation of study is well manifested amongst the gentlemen employed in the Bank of England; for almost all who have obtained the higher posts are distinguished for their general knowledge, and amongst them may be found historians, musicians, painters, botanists, floriculturists, mechanicians, political economists, microscopists, entomologists, numismatists, and in fact students of many other branches of knowledge. With those who have no occupation I have often enforced additional studies as a healthy exercise to the mind.

The middle classes in many cases are deficient to a great extent in the appreciation of general principles, and thus when called upon to govern, even to a slight extent, are often much perplexed by not having been trained to control their action by fixed and immutable laws, and are bewildered by a conflict between feeling and principle.

The upper class follow the bent of their inclination with respect to their occupation and pursuits, and I have known persons in their private capacities alternate the most manual labour with the most intellectual studies. In respect of intellectual culture by the study of Nature and Art upon the highest philosophical principle, they are frequently greatly in advance of those in a less exalted state.

To remedy the defects observed amongst different classes, an example must be afforded by extensive changes in the system of education pursued at the endowed schools; for though it is impossible to overrate the high tone of feeling and valuable traditional rules for the guidance of conduct which pervade these noble establishments, yet we cannot forget that the scholastic learning there followed belongs to a bygone age, which, though well suited to that period, yet is not adapted to the present state of human knowledge.

4. Enterprise in this country is always competent to adapt the supply to the demand, and therefore I myself am inclined to question the necessity of issuing cheap books, maps, models, diagrams, or apparatus. At the same time there appears to be a great want of well-arranged devices of this character, so designed that they can be made readily and cheaply. On this account I believe that it would be a great desideratum to employ the highest talent to write books or make patterns from which manufacturers might construct their models. In all probability private printers and private manufacturers would make from a pattern more cheaply than could be effected in Government or other central workshops. The cost of the copyrights of educational works, or of models, is of very little moment, as any expense could be afforded for so great a national object.

5. It appears to me that great care must be taken in issuing general rules for education, for fear that an undue preponderance be given to particular directions of study. It is manifestly important that all classes should be instructed not only by words, but through the medium of their senses. After a general preliminary education great care should be taken that every department of knowledge be carried to its fullest extent by different persons, and that no superiority or bias be given to one science over another. There is always a fear in a central governing council that one party may get a preponderance, when sore mischief may be caused; but, with a due regard to abstract and practical knowledge of all kinds, plans of education may be very conveniently set forth for general guidance.

6, 7, 8. The question of prizes must be regarded as one of extreme difficulty and delicacy. No doubt the substantial prizes awarded exclusively to successful cultivators of classical learning do positive injury to the advance of human knowledge, and, in my opinion, a decided preponderance of substantial prizes should be bestowed upon the successful prosecutors of real learning over that of the dead languages. When we take into consideration that our forefathers bestowed their prizes on the students of the dead languages at a time when they were a key to every form of useful knowledge, should we not regard their intention by diverting some part from their comparatively useless purpose to the furtherance of the various branches of human knowledge for which they were doubtless instituted, and which ever must fill a full page in the annals of the world?

Whenever prizes are given the student should be taught to estimate knowledge for knowledge itself, to prosecute science for science itself, and on no account to regard the prize as the end to be attained. Upon the whole, I am myself adverse to the liberal use of prizes, for we find that even the philosophers of the Royal Society are apt to display considerable weakness in the disposition of the royal medals.

An excessive stimulus to competition appears to me calculated to urge men always in some way to try to vie with their neighbours, and ill-feeling is produced by continual attempts to have some slight advantage or superior rank. From boyhood it will be desirable that knowledge should be cultivated for a more noble end. The infant should be taught that knowledge itself is above all considerations of wealth or station; that it should be valued for its own intrinsic worth and for its positive power of conferring happiness upon the possessor, independently of any accidental adjuncts as wealth, position, or power, which may or may not be its accompaniments. The infant should be taught that knowledge itself confers upon the individual an inexhaustible source of pleasure which will remain through every vicissitude of life.

I perceive another reason for employing prizes very cautiously. To obtain a prize the pupil is led to give up his own mode of thought and substitute that of his examiners. In any extensive system the minds of the pupils are led to esteem knowledge for the opinion the world has of it, instead of being encouraged to follow and practise that more severe frame of mind which judges of knowledge by knowledge, tests theories by facts, and gives that moral courage which enables the man to put forward and maintain his well-considered opinions against those of all the world besides. For this reason I fear that an extensive central system of prizes might retard knowledge, and produce one general public opinion and a universal mediocrity.

The answers given in competing for a prize are not of necessity a test of the opinions of the writer. The sceptic may give answers inferring his belief, and lately the medical profession was greatly scandalised by a gentleman answering all the questions upon the treatment of disease, by describing the most approved medical practice, whereas within a few hours he announced himself as a subscriber to the absurdities of Hahnemann.

I can speak from experience that those who work for prizes not only seek a knowledge of the subject, but make a practice of ascertaining the modes of thought of the examiners, and a competitor sometimes obtains success by confining his studies to those parts of the subject which he considered would probably be selected for examination.

In the medical profession it is notorious that the questions likely to be asked at the public examinations are narrowed into a small compass, so that whilst a student makes himself acquainted with his profession he also frequently considers it necessary to make himself acquainted with the knowledge and peculiarities of his examiners.

If, however, prizes are not carried to great excess, I believe that they are useful. I am, however, inclined to believe that far greater benefits may arise from affixing a certain designation to a certain standard of knowledge, as I have observed that the designation of M.A. and of F.R.S. are esteemed by the public as indications of a certain standard of knowledge.

Substantial prizes, as fellowships, scholarships, and annuities, I should greatly prefer to honorary prizes, as being better adapted to promote the desired end. Being of intrinsic value, they would in most cases be free from the objections which appear to be attached to purely honorary distinctions.

## No. XXI.

AN INTRODUCTORY DISCOURSE on the Objects and Advantages of Educational Lectures, in connection with the London Institution. With a Diagram showing the Faculties of the Human Mind at different Periods of Life. Delivered by Alfred Smee, Esq., F.R.S., on Saturday, October 14th, 1854, on commencing the season of Educational Lectures.

Young Ladies and Young Gentlemen,

The proprietors of the London Institution, which was founded by the munificence of the merchants and bankers of London for the promotion of literature and science, have resolved to give up this theatre to your use upon two afternoons in each week; in order that you may advantageously partake of the inestimable benefits of instruction from well-qualified teachers, and perfectly enjoy the delightful pleasure which arises out of the knowledge of natural science.

I have been requested by my fellow-managers to address you this first afternoon *on the general use and value of those scientific subjects* which will be hereafter more particularly considered by the eminent lecturers who have been engaged to instruct you; and I must also ask you to give me your careful attention, and to think of nothing but that which I am saying, whilst I detail what *you can learn* and what *you cannot learn* by coming here and listening with your best attention to the different lectures as they are delivered.

You are not all of the same age; and you will observe that these lectures will not be attended by the young only, but occasionally even by such as are advanced in years, and sometimes by those who are still in the prime of life. I shall endeavour to show you the parts of the different subjects which will most interest and most instruct my different hearers; for rest assured that each of us, from the time we leave the cradle till we recline in the arm-chair of extreme old age, has different powers, different capabilities, and different duties to perform. At no period of life can any neglect be allowed, without that neglect producing a corresponding injury at every subsequent period; and a loss of time and opportunity *now*, will be attended by a loss of honourable position and of happiness *hereafter*.

Now, my young friends, at your age you have all your senses acute in the highest degree. Nothing can escape your bright sharp eyes, if rightly used. Your ears, also, are endowed with the highest faculty of hearing, and your tender skin with feeling. In these respects you will have great advantages over the older part of the audience. Here you excel; and it is your duty to take full advantage of the acuteness of your senses. Sharp, however, as your eyes are, you will find that to appreciate *all* the beauties of nature, you will want much additional and artificial assistance. You will first require the aid of the microscope to help you, since for seeing the lovely down upon the butterfly's wing, covering and protecting the wing-case, like the slates on a house, it is absolutely necessary; and you will find that when you have strained your eyes to the utmost upon a drop of water, and yet have seen nothing, the microscope will reveal to you thousands on thousands of living beings, enjoying their

U

life, and, even in their inconceivable minuteness, completely fulfilling the object for which the Creator of the universe in His wisdom designed them.

By the kindness of Mr. Thornthwaite, I am enabled to show you an elegant microscope which he has devised for the purpose of exhibiting microscopic objects to a number of persons at the same time. For illuminating the specimens, he uses a spirit-lamp, which is fed by oxygen gas from a tube instead of atmospheric air. This intense flame renders a piece of lime incandescent; and, by means of a microscope constructed like a magic lantern, a magnified representation is shown upon a white screen. By it you are enabled to see the curious structure of the foot which is given to the spider for arranging the threads of his web : by it a thin slice of common wood is shown to be built up of cells aggregated together ; a drop of blood is found to contain the most curious organized bodies, called corpuscules; and a section of hard bone exhibits a structure rivalling the most beautiful carpet. In every object in nature a perfection is contained which requires the aid of the microscope to reveal, for after unaided vision has exhausted its powers of appreciation, a new world is brought to light at every increase of magnifying power.

As you require the microscope to reveal the hidden treasures of terrestrial bodies, so the telescope must be used to show you the wonders of the heavens. Saturn, to the naked eye, looks but an ordinary star; but I have here a drawing of the glorious form which it assumes when seen by the assistance of the telescope constructed by Mr. De La Rue, one of the managers of this institution.

In your intercourse with each other, you will find that you are not all equally endowed with the same powers of perception by the senses. Those who are more highly favoured should bestow a kind consideration upon those who are less blessed. You have nothing to lose by aiding each other to acquire knowledge, but everything to gain by promoting and exercising this social kindness.

Your period of life philosophers may call the AISTHENIC, for now your senses are in the highest perfection. They will never grow better, though they will gradually and imperceptibly become worse, till extreme old age may terminate "this strange eventful history," and you may be left

"Sans teeth, sans eyes, sans taste, sans everything !"

You have all seen the little child reposing upon its mother's lap, admiring its fingers, as it moves them, with delight and astonishment. This is one of the first acts of observation; but you are no longer children, and your desire for new objects has increased with your age ; and you now excel in the power which you have to observe different objects with intelligence, and to fix their images in your minds for ever. Some of you who are yet young are not so quick of perception as those who are older ; yet the period of youth *is* the period for obtaining lasting impressions. Although you have the power of vision, you scarcely can tell how many things you may have seen, which you have never noticed. How many of you know that a bee has four wings, or that a common fly has but two? And I will dare venture to assert that many of you have never noticed that a beetle has six legs; but yet you all have seen bees, and flies, and beetles hundreds and hundreds of times.

Fig. 17.

Faculties of the Human Mind at different Periods of Life.

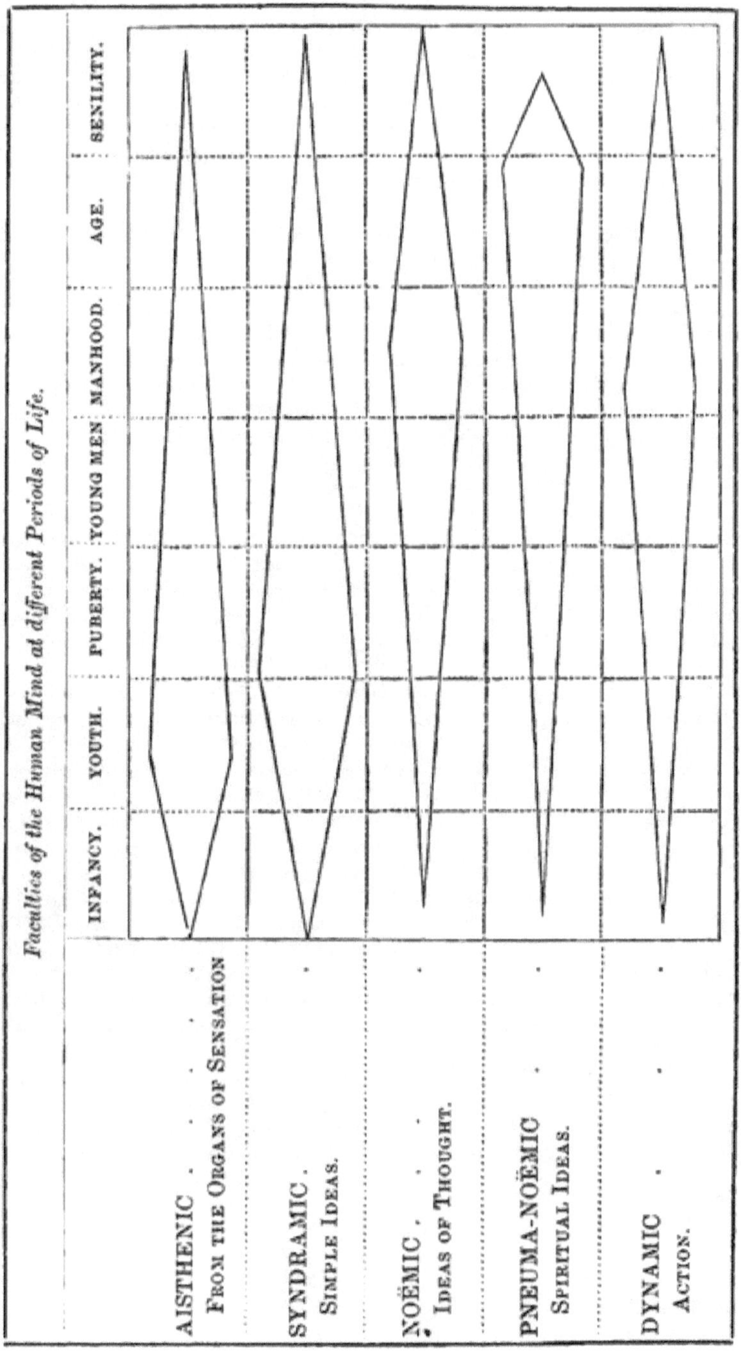

The advantage of the knowledge of objects, and the proper name to be assigned to each, is very great. At these lectures you will find that a large number of objects, embracing also a very great variety, will be shown to you. Excellent and accurate drawings will likewise be exhibited, so that you may be led to form a correct idea of the appearance of those different objects which are presented to your notice. I must here tell you of some instances where persons have not known objects when they have seen them, in order that you may judge for yourselves as to the use which it may be to you to come here and pay attention to these lectures which the proprietors have so liberally provided for you. A working man went to the gold diggings and found a beautiful stone. He showed it to his companions, who thought it a most valuable diamond and offered him at once £200 for it. Being determined not to make a bad bargain, he refused this sum, brought it to England and offered it for sale, when to his horror and dismay he was told that it was really not a diamond, but only a crystal of quartz, and scarcely worth half-a-crown.

In making you acquainted with the knowledge of objects, the London Institution will be of much use to you; nevertheless we have not the collections here which exist in our national museums; and whilst I ask you to attend diligently these educational lectures, I still also beg of you not to neglect frequent visits to the British Museum, to Kew Gardens, to the Zoological Society, and to the Crystal Palace; in each of which you will see fresh objects every time you go, although your visits may be very frequently repeated; for you will discover it to be an equally curious and interesting truth, that the oftener you go and the more attentively you look, the more you will find to observe and admire.

The power of observing increases with its exercise. One boy takes his walk, and sees nothing; another takes the same walk, and sees many things. The observant youth has bestowed his attention upon everything around him; but the other has passed heedlessly by the most interesting objects. In youth attention is the faculty of the mind which ought to be the most carefully cultivated and practised; and I hope that no one will come to these lectures who will not *try* to attend, and in fact who will not try diligently to attend to all which is passing.

I am well aware that the youngest of you may sometimes find it difficult to fix your attention. The best plan, however, is to bring with you a pencil and a note-book, and put down the principal points which the lecturer mentions. Whenever your thoughts wander remember the word " ATTENTION." Let " attention " be your watchword; and then the lectures which you are about to hear will be a source of pleasure *now*, and perhaps of profit for all future time.

The managers of the London Institution will spare no expense and no trouble to render these lectures interesting and instructive to you. The more you desire, the more are they prepared to give you, as it was the only wish of the great merchants who founded this noble institution, that it should, like the sun, send forth its light upon all who desire to partake of its genial influence.

It is, however, not only the observation of simple objects which is important, but the *changes* which each object undergoes must be carefully noted. We see the egg of an insect hatched into a caterpillar; the caterpillar grow till it spins its web, and turns into a chrysalis; and the chrysalis finally lose its case and become the beautiful butterfly. This forms a palpable series of changes, the order of which your memory is not likely to alter; but changes continually occur in all bodies, and these changes you must be very careful to note in the order in which they occur.

In chemistry the transmutations of matter under various circumstances are of the most extraordinary character. The beautiful pigment called Prussian-blue is but a change of offensive animal matter, potash and iron. Some of our scents and flavours also, as the oil of pine-apple and the oil of the delicious ribstone pippin, are the products of chemical changes from fusel oil, a most offensive product in the distillation of spirit. In acquiring a knowledge of these changes, the educational lectures at the London Institution will be of great service to you. We have a laboratory with all necessary materials, and every form of apparatus is at our command, which may be required to illustrate the different subjects. A lecture would frequently cost a large sum of money, were not the apparatus at hand, or could it not be easily borrowed. It is for this reason that ordinary schools cannot undertake the teaching of these subjects: and were I to tell you of the labour and expense required for some of the lectures which have been delivered within these walls, you would be especially thankful for the privilege which you possess of being enabled to attend these demonstrations.

The knowledge which here will be brought before you will be of the utmost value in future life. Each fact may be regarded as a unit of knowledge; and those who acquire the most will have a great advantage over their fellows. I show you a piece of gossan, a peculiar sort of stone which guides the miner to the detection of copper ore, and large fortunes have been made by a knowledge of the peculiarities of the stone. This is a simple mineralogical fact, but I might illustrate similar facts in every department of science.

It is not, however, a mere question of utility, but there is the highest gratification also to be found in a careful observance of Nature, and the study of Nature's laws. A touching anecdote was told me by Mr. Spence, the distinguished author of the work on Entomology, which I commend to the notice of you all. At the Model Prison a person was confined in a dismal cell, with windows which did not allow him ever to see the sky. When he took exercise, he paced a few square yards in the same spot day by day. His only amusement under this terrible sentence was minutely to notice every little weed which grew upon it. He saw these sprout from seed, increase in growth, bud, flower, and seed again. Now, when I tell you that the plants so observed were simply the shepherd's-purse, the groundsel, and a few more weeds, you will see how great is *your* advantage, when you consider the multitude of plants which clothe the earth, the countless swarms of insects which fly in the air, the fish, the birds, the animals, the changes of the seasons, and even the works of men's hands which are open to your observation in freedom. In fact everything which is contained upon the earth and even in the firmament of heaven, the sun, the moon, the planets, the comets, the stars, the nebulæ, will afford you objects for observation, study, and delight, if you will only regard them with intelligence and attention. There is in fact no end to the acquisition of natural knowledge: for if you could know all which others have discovered, it would be but as a drop of water to the ocean. The study of

Nature and Nature's laws forms an inexhaustible source of pleasure; and the longest life will not suffice to exhaust a fountain which can never be dried up.

I regret to state that I have heard persons declare, that they have been present at nearly every lecture delivered by the eminent men who have honoured this institution by their discourses during a period of many years, without deriving any advantage from them. Let such a fearful statement weigh heavily on your minds; for if you come to our lectures as those persons have done, without paying a proper attention to the subjects explained, you will, like them, derive no benefit. Others who have attended to the lectures, have acknowledged that they owe their present position and power to a careful attention to the great truths which have been taught within these walls. It is, therefore, better for you to hear a few lectures attentively, than hundreds with that carelessness and inattention which allow no permanent effect to be produced upon the mind.

If we carefully consider the evils arising from an absence of knowledge, we shall soon perceive what lamentable consequences must be the result. Two or three years ago, many persons were poisoned by belladonna-berries sold about the streets; and I remember a man to have been bitten by a viper as he carried the creature about, supposing it to have been only a harmless snake. This year we read that in Italy, during the visitation of the dreadful scourge which passed over the earth, the people believed that the doctors were the cause of it, and drove them from the city when they most needed their aid. At another place they supposed the doctors had poisoned the water, and compelled them to drink to prove their innocence. Curiously enough also, five hundred years ago, by a similar lamentable ignorance, a fatal epidemic of the period, called the black death, was ascribed to poison cast into the wells by the Jews; and hundreds of poor wretches were cruelly tormented and barbarously put to death, for a malady which was entirely owing to a visitation of God.

Do not think to put off the time for attention to surrounding objects to "a more convenient season," and wait till you are older before you begin to observe. If you do so, you are not only losing precious time, which never can return, but your faculties of appreciation will rather diminish than increase. Although the faculties of observation last as long as the senses last, yet in advancing years new objects do not make such vivid impressions as they do in early life. The faculty of deriving simple ideas from Nature, I have called from reasons which I need not explain, the SYNDRAMIC FACULTY: a faculty which increases from childhood to adolescence, and decreases from puberty to old age. It is your time now to observe, and if you neglect it deficiency of information and inferiority to those around you must inevitably be your lot.

It is, however, not only necessary to obtain facts, but the facts must by thought and reflection be brought before the mind, and so combined and arranged together, that they may constitute principles. In this way we derive our ideas of force and power, and obtain a notion of heat, light, and electricity, and all the various qualities and properties of matter.

Thus, if I throw a piece of potassium into water, it combines with the oxygen, one element of the water, and forms potash; or I may remove one element by a piece of zinc, or a piece of iron. When we find from a vast number of facts that we can join simple bodies together, separate compound bodies in their elements, and convert two bodies into a third, we then obtain one idea of chemical affinity.

It is not my province to show how we obtain the ideas of all the physical forces, or the relations of one to another: that will be the duty of your different teachers. This part of the subject is confessedly difficult, and will require your fullest attention and reflection. As youthful persons, however, you can have but a faint glimmer of those great and glorious principles which hereafter you will more fully perceive.

This high mental faculty is termed the NOËMIC FACULTY, which is almost entirely absent in early childhood, then increases to manhood, and declines again with advancing years. For the exercise of it, you must well employ your time whilst young in the collection of observations for reflection. Without facts you can have no thought, without thought you can have no principles; and it is upon the correctness of your principles that your success in after-life will most materially depend.

We have remarkable instances of the power of a knowledge of principles over the mind of those who are ignorant. Sir Harry Smith, when he conquered the Africans, desired to show them his superior power. He ordered a baggage-waggon to be placed at a distance, to which he had connected wires communicating with a battery. When the Africans had assembled, he told them at his command the waggon would blow up. They marvelled. He spoke the word; they saw nothing. The circuit was secretly completed, and the waggon was shivered to atoms. Some voyagers, taking advantage of an eclipse, the occurrence of which was predicted by calculation, have stated that they so frightened the Indians, that they obtained from them whatever was desired; and though I entirely and utterly disapprove of this mode of proceeding, it nevertheless equally illustrates the power which is conferred by an intimate knowledge of the great principles of science.

By thought and reflection we are likewise enabled to form right judgments in general; and when two assertions, apparently different, are brought before our minds, we can select that which is the true one. Last year the merchants of London were startled by the large amount of gold stated to exist in certain English rocks. Some of my friends were interested in a particular mine, which by the mechanical process yielded large quantities of gold; but by chemical processes, only such an amount of the metal was found as was insufficient to cover the expenses of extraction. After much careful thought, therefore, we judged it most prudent to trust to the chemical processes, but many persons trusted to the mechanical processes and lost thereby various sums of money; and in one case I heard that a single individual lost as much as £4000 by this error of judgment.

With all our care we shall not always judge rightly, or, judging rightly, we shall come to wrong conclusions, because we shall sometimes act upon *wrong facts.* We should therefore have much compassion upon those who are proved to have formed erroneous judgments; although true *facts and principles* will always in the long run prevent mankind from believing the plausible statements of quacks, pretenders, and schemers. We cannot judge rightly by our own unaided reason, for without a proper set of facts and principles no judgment can be made; and we only deceive ourselves if we call our thought a judgment without proper data. Nevertheless, the tendency of man to judge with insufficient data is so great, that more than half the errors of mankind may be traced to this source alone.

Before you are called into action, also, your mind must be stored with facts and principles properly to guide your designs. The child knows but little, and does scarcely anything; the boy has more facts, and therefore effects more; but the man is in the plenitude of his power till age weakens him, and lessens his capability. The faculty of action is called the DYNAMIC FACULTY; and to judge of what you may be called upon to do, consider what has been done since the period when I was but a youth. Since that time the railway system has been devised; and then consider the tunnels, the cuttings, the embankments, the bridges, and the many elaborate contrivances necessary to be devised before this great revolution in locomotion could be effected. During the same period, also, the electric telegraph has been invented; and now intelligence is conveyed so rapidly that events are daily transmitted over extensive regions of the globe, and frequently a knowledge of events is received at one part of the globe at an earlier period by the clock than that at which they actually happen.

Again, the application of electro-metallurgy to the arts has led to great improvements, and most extensive alterations in our processes. Moreover, in the course of the same period, the Thames Tunnel has been constructed under the river Thames; and also the Britannia Bridge, which crosses over an arm of the sea. The formation of a palace of iron and glass is another example of an extraordinary effort of human intellect. It is impossible for you to tell what may be effected in a similar number of future years; and if you desire to take part in the rapid course of human improvement, your mind must have been stored beforehand with those units of knowledge which I have already described.

As youths you are neither expected, nor are you competent, to carry out any great work; but certain things you can do for yourselves, and you can thus bring your knowledge into play within reasonable limits. You do not require expensive materials for many processes. A few little glasses and a retort will enable you to make analyses, and even to manufacture many substances. In these employments you will find great amusement in the long evenings of winter, as well as in the dreary wet weather which sometimes occurs in the Christmas holidays.

At this Institution, during these holidays in the present year, Mr. Malone has arranged to receive a limited number of young persons and to give them laboratory instruction; and those who take advantage of his teaching, will thus be enabled to conduct many chemical processes for themselves in the laboratory of this building.

Accurate original research often requires costly apparatus; but to carry out that which is known, the simplest contrivances will suffice. I am tempted here to show you a little electrical apparatus which I once set up on the spur of the moment. We had a beautiful garden in one of the London suburbs, and we received information that whilst the family were at dinner a systematic robbery of the fruit was carried on. After pondering over the matter, I got some wire, and connected it at one end with a battery and at the other with a cup of mercury; and with another wire I connected again the mercury to the other pole of the battery, enclosing in the circuit a magnet, the keeper of which was attached to the alarum of a Dutch clock. I then stretched a delicate piece of thread across the garden,

tying one end to the copper wire and the other to the trunk of a tree.   All
being ready, I went in to dinner, and the alarum speedily rang.   The thief
had moved the thread and pulled the wire out of the mercury.     I ran out
and caught the boy, who declared that he would never come again if we
only would let him go this once.   All such little devices you may contrive,
and they have a good influence in encouraging the habit of spontaneous
invention.

Chemical and mechanical occupations are more especially for the
young gentlemen, but the young ladies may have their share of occupation.
They will find that their botanical studies may be much improved by
studying the growth of plants.   Those who live in the country, may
cultivate their flowers with more ease; but even those who live in the
middle of London are not altogether precluded from this pursuit by the
difficulties of their situation.   Many plants may be grown under glass in
great perfection, as Ward has taught us.   Here is a specimen of the rarest
of English ferns (called the Tunbridge fern), which grows and fructifies
in Finsbury Circus as well as in any part of Great Britain.   I myself love
to see plants grow in this manner, and I have generally lilacs in blossom at
Christmas; and with a little trouble and protection you also may have
many choice plants even in the centre of London.   To such of you as may
at once like to commence the cultivation of plants by this process, I have
brought some Lycopodiums, which I will distribute after the lecture, and
which you can readily grow under glass.

To cultivate plants with success, it is quite necessary that you should
attend to certain circumstances.   As horticultural weapons you must
employ and regulate the heat and cold, the light and darkness, and the
damp and dryness of the soil and atmosphere.   By properly managing
these natural powers, success will attend your efforts, and you will be
delighted to see the fronds of ferns unfurl themselves, and many a choice
flower will gladden your eyes with delight and fill the room with odoriferous
perfume.   However much the sun may be obscured from your room, still
some forms of vegetable life will be put forth; and though by comparison
the rose or lily may superlatively excel chickweed or groundsel, yet there
is no plant, however insignificant, however common, which has not its own
peculiar beauties and charms, and which would not be esteemed as a
marvel of design if others more beautiful were absent from the comparison.

In the study of natural history young people may bring many objects
of the greatest interest under their notice.   Here is a pet toad, which has
lived under my roof many years.   It was the smallest toad I ever saw,
when I caught him in the woods where the Crystal Palace now stands.
He has done me much good service, by eating the insects which damaged
my plants; and you see that he has now grown to reasonable proportions.
It is a matter of much interest to see this creature feed.   When he
perceives an insect like a cockroach, he sits perfectly motionless, till, by
directing both eyes upon the creature, it exactly ascertains the distance,
when in an instant it darts out its head with an inconceivable rapidity
and swallows its prey.   Now every creature, if attentively examined, will
be found to have its peculiar mode of feeding; and really a large volume
might be written on this subject alone, full of the most curious
information.

Look at these beautiful Guernsey lizards, which astonish us by their rapid and graceful movements, and which we have opportunities of observing by keeping them in my glazed plant-cases. Even fish may be brought within the range of this kind of observation. Here is a very great favourite of my family, a little fish from the Thames, called a Pope, who has banished his natural shyness. The moment he sees us he comes up to the top of the water to receive his accustomed food. By watching animated beings, we find that everything possessing life has its own proper interest; for everything is beautiful. Even that which at first appears ugly and deformed on a more intimate acquaintance is found to be perfectly adapted to its end, and endowed with the highest interest.

The young ladies and young gentlemen who this day attend in our theatre, have all of them their own different and particular objects to attain; and should therefore make their knowledge subservient to a different end. You are all of you the sons and daughters of persons holding a good position in society. As for the youths, some of you will be blessed with independence, and live upon the fruits of your own estates. To you botany will be invaluable, for enabling you rightly to manage your woods and fields. Mineralogy and geology will also be extremely useful, to guide you to the knowledge of the qualities of various soils and of the mineral products of the land. Others of you may be destined to be merchants, and send your ships over every quarter of the globe. To all of you a knowledge of the sciences will be an invaluable acquisition. Some again will become engineers; others will be manufacturers; and some will enter into the medical, legal, or clerical professions: but in every path of life which any of you are likely to follow, the subjects which will be taught at these lectures will certainly come into every-day use.

· The duties of the young ladies will hereafter be not less important, though, perhaps, less stirring than those of the young gentlemen. Your knowledge of chemistry will enable you to conduct your households with economy. In the sick-room, the knowledge of the laws of life will enable you to comfort the afflicted; and your knowledge of Nature and Nature's works will render each of you a fitting mistress for your respective households, suitable teachers of children, and worthy companions for the intellectual man.

In your study of Nature you cannot but be deeply impressed with the beauty of the objects which you must observe. You will find the most marvellous design in the favourite theme of philosophical speculation for more than 2000 years. Shakespeare's immortal "Seven Ages" is a fitting monument to an unrivalled genius; but in the Transactions of the Society of Antiquaries for 1853 are many very interesting examples of the manner in which the division of the life of man was anciently regarded. Of these the following is a very remarkable composition. The original was written in Hebrew 900 years ago; and is especially curious from the states of man at his different ages being compared in their characteristics to those of various animals.

" At the age of *One Year* he resembles a King on a Daïs, whom every one kisses and adores.

" At the age of *Two or Three* he resembles a Pig, routing in dirt.

" At the age of *Ten* he capers about like a Goat.

" At *Twenty*, a Neighing-horse, he attires himself, and looks out for a wife.

" After being married, he is like an Ass (that is, burthened).

" Having got children, he must find food for them; and is therefore as impudent as a Dog.

" Grown old, he gets like a Monkey,—but (this is) only the ignorant man: whereas of the wise man Scripture says, 'King David was old' (1 Kings i. 2). Old, but still a king." *

In the remarks which I have made this day, I would wish you clearly to understand that I do not expect all of you are to become professed chemists, naturalists, or botanists; nor in fact necessarily professors of any other branch of natural knowledge. I have particularly desired to call your attention to the value of natural knowledge to all classes of society. You should esteem natural knowledge as indispensable to every gentleman; and I feel sure that all the points which I have reviewed for your consideration should not be neglected by anyone aspiring to the title of an educated Englishman.

I doubt not that there are very few of you who would not greatly prefer these lectures to your ordinary school exercises. You must not, however, neglect the tediousness of books for the pleasures of lectures. Follow the study of languages, arithmetic, and of mathematics at school as the most valuable aids to the understanding of natural knowledge; and prosecute natural science as a guide for the conduct of your own affairs. The study of Nature confers on you pleasure, honour, power, the means of procuring wealth, of benefiting your fellow-creatures, and leads you to the contemplation of the Source of All Good.

The London Institution has given you great opportunities of instruction; and if my discourse should determine any of you rightly to take advantage of the benefits now offered, the words of my heartfelt appeal to study Nature with earnestness and attention, will be engraven on your minds to the latest day of your lives; and you will rejoice that you have been this day present at the London Institution.

---

## No. XXII.

### ON THE NEW BANK OF ENGLAND NOTE, AND THE SUBSTITUTION OF SURFACE-PRINTING FROM ELECTROTYPES FOR COPPER-PLATE PRINTING. By ALFRED SMEE, F.R.S., Surgeon to the Bank of England. 1854.

I FEEL some delicacy in appearing before the Society of Arts upon a matter of so much importance to the commercial community as the printing of the Bank of England notes; nevertheless, from the part which I have played in this matter, I trust the members of the Society will not think that I am exceeding my duty in bringing the matter before them.

In the month of November 1851, I had the honour of presenting a report to Mr. Hankey, the Governor of the Bank of England at that

---

* 'Archæologia,' vol. xxxv. 1853, p. 171.

period, that from facts and observations which had come under my notice, I believed that the time had arrived when surface-printing from electrotypes could be advantageously employed for Bank of England notes, and that they could be both printed and numbered by ordinary printing-presses, with considerable saving of expense and increased identity of appearance. In presenting this report I further stated that many difficulties presented themselves, and, therefore, I would suggest that a trial be permitted upon the cheque, and, when the production of this was brought to perfection, we might carry on our processes upon the bank-note, with such extended experience as the printing of the cheque might afford.

Heretofore the notes and cheques of the Bank of England had invariably been printed from copper and steel plates, in which the lines were engraved or cut into the metal. Into these hollows the printers rubbed the ink, which, in process of printing, was transferred from the plate to the paper. In surface-printing the reverse state of things exists, as the design, instead of being cut in the plate, is left in relief, and the ink being applied to the eminences by means of the rollers, is transferred in the press to the paper to form the impression.

For plate-printing, a single cut with a graver forms a groove which holds the ink. For surface-printing a line must be cut on both sides, and equally finished on both sides. This materially increases the difficulty of engraving, yet the difficulty simply resolves itself into one of labour, skill, and expense.

Having an original design, the means of multiplication must be perfect; and here, although I foresaw many difficulties, yet my electro-metallurgical experience indicated that the perfection which the Bank required, and the mercantile community demanded, might be obtained. With a sufficiently excellent original and ample power of duplication, the very important question which had necessarily to be solved was the capacity of the surface press to give such a print as would serve our purpose.

In plate-printing the paper is pressed into the grooves or design, and there is no tendency of the ink to spread, but in surface-printing there is a liability for the paper to be pressed round the edge of the letters, or, from the pressure applied, for the ink to be spread over the margin, when an extended print would be produced from the original design. I foresaw that the success of surface-printing for bank purposes must depend upon the power of the press to yield rapidly, perfect impressions. In this matter my experience was in a great measure founded upon the observation of the impressions of the 'Illustrated London News,' and periodicals of similar character, when I observed that even with their rapid production, under the most unfavourable circumstances, at times we obtained, either entirely or partially, perfectly sharp impressions, without any appreciable lateral extension of the ink. From this I concluded that it was only necessary to study the conditions necessary to have a clear impression, and in this matter surface-printing would rival plate-printing, and besides give us all the advantages which are pre-eminently the characteristics of typography.

In accordance with this report, Mr. Hankey at once directed the experiments to be commenced, and subsequently allowed me to act with Mr. Hensman, the engineer, and Mr. Coe, the superintendent of printing; and though each of us had our separate departments in which our individual labour and knowledge was most useful, we consulted together on every matter, and by our mutual exertions, acting together to one end for the benefit of the Bank, we have been enabled to overcome every difficulty, and to bring the process into practical operation for all the manifold varieties of cheques and notes which the Bank of England requires for its purposes. Independently of the original idea, which was exclusively my own, the responsibility of settling the various processes for carrying out the system devolved equally upon Mr. Hensman, Mr. Coe, and myself, but upon Mr. Hensman and Mr. Coe falls the labour of conducting the operations.

The original form or pattern of the various notes and cheques which have been adopted, was accomplished and settled under the direction of Mr. Hankey and the Court of Directors, before any of us commenced our labours, and, though the particular manner in which the note was designed added very materially to our difficulties, it was an imperative condition with the Bank that we should in no way deviate from that design; but we were compelled to reproduce it exactly as designed, a condition which has been so rigorously adhered to, that in only one case has any deviation been made. In that instance the lines have simply been allowed to be somewhat more open than in the original design, as it was found that even in the original plate the work had been made so fine that the successful printing could not be insured for large quantities.

When we found that we were bound to copy implicitly designs specially adapted to plate-printing, we almost despaired of success, for in all other instances where surface-printing has been adopted, the design has been suited to the nature of the printing. This difficulty, however, only served as an incentive to further exertion, though I must confess that as we proceeded, step by step, we were by no means certain that we should not be compelled to abandon some part of our original design. With the exception of these stringent conditions, we were permitted to conduct our operations entirely in our own way; and to the kind consideration of Mr. Hankey, the late Governor, and Mr. Hubbard and Mr. Weguelin, the present Governor and Deputy-Governor of the Bank of England, our success must in a great measure be ascribed.

The cutting of the original design is necessarily the basis of future operation. The whole of the written part of the note was originally cut by Mr. Beckett, the engraver to the establishment, but the Britannia was designed by Mr. Maclise, and engraved by Robinson. This engraving was the basis of our operations. After various experiments, the cutting of the Britannia in a manner suitable for easy duplication was executed on a steel die, by that veteran engraver Mr. Thompson, whose artistic feeling is fully recognized by the public. The other parts of the notes and cheques were in a great measure cut by Mr. Skirving, in some cases upon pieces of brass, in others on plates of copper, about ½ an inch in thickness. In no case is the original ever employed for printing, but is simply used to make moulds, so that, throwing out of consideration accidental mechanical or chemical injuries, they will retain their integrity for any length of time without change, and will enable any number of duplicates to be made therefrom. From our inquiries, we have reason to think that there are very few persons who have attained sufficient perfection to execute this class of work in the manner which the Bank requires, but the finished manner in which Mr. Skirving has executed his part of the work has met with the highest approbation. It is the province of supply, however, always to be equal to the demand, and therefore, if surface-cutting increases, we have no right to suppose there will be dearth of labour or talent in that department of art.

For the duplication of the original designs, we have recourse to the power afforded to us by the processes of electro-metallurgy. For the purposes of the Bank of England, we have had recourse to the various forms of battery apparatus described by myself in the 'Philosophical Magazine' for June 1840, and subsequently in my 'Elements of Electro-Metallurgy.' We employ, as a source of power, the platinized silver voltaic battery, which many of the members of this Society may remember was brought under their notice some years ago. It was devised when I was a student of medicine at King's College, and resided in my father's house in the Bank of England. With friends entirely devoted to other than scientific pursuits, I was placed in an awkward position by the discovery of the principles on which it was founded. I brought it here unknown to any member, and after a long investigation a gold medal was awarded for its invention. For fourteen years it has stood the test of experience : and when we see that by its agency the plates of the maps of the Ordnance Survey have for years been deposited; when we see at the present time that by it the types of the Bank of England notes and cheques are formed; and lastly, when amongst other purposes we find that it daily transmits the power from the Observatory at Greenwich to indicate the correct time in London, I trust the Society, in consideration of its applica-tion to these truly national objects, will not consider that their medal has been altogether bestowed in vain.

At the Bank we employ large batteries, in vessels holding several gallons of the acid charge. The platinized silver plate is of fair thickness, and the zincs are so arranged that they can be readily changed. The purer we can obtain thick-rolled zinc, the more economically can we con-duct our process, for then we are not subjected to the inevitable loss which arises if tin, a very frequent impurity, is present. We are careful, for the sake of economy, very thoroughly to amalgamate the zinc; in fact, we prefer to repeat the process once or twice, that no local action may exist.

For charging the battery we use dilute sulphuric acid, and generally mix the fluids in the proportion of one-eighth acid to seven-eighths water. It is convenient to adjust the mixture to a specific gravity of 1130, which gives a strength suitable for battery purposes. A battery charged with this liquid will last in action nearly three weeks before it is completely exhausted; but practically, after it has done efficient duty from 7 to 14 days, it has become feeble, it exhibits the natural decay of old age, and we generally respite it from further work and substitute a new charge, to resuscitate its former life and vigour. When the battery is thoroughly exhausted, the solution has a specific gravity of 1360, and contains 144 grains of zinc for every 1000 grains of bulk, if evaporation and conden-sation have been compensated for by the daily addition of sufficient water to make up the original bulk.

To ascertain the changes which are occurring in the battery we commonly employ an hydrometer; but I have specially constructed an instrument which I call a battery-meter. The point corresponding to specific gravity 1130 is called unity, and the interval between that part and 1360 is divided into 144 parts. By this division every degree represents one grain of zinc dissolved in 1000 grains of bulk of the fluid. The opposite side of the scale, between the same parts, is divided into 60 parts, each of which is, for every 1000 grains of bulk in the fluid, about $\frac{1}{1000}$ of an inch in the thickness for every superficial inch of surface, upon which the copper is reduced in the precipitating trough. In this division a little allowance has been made for some local action of the zinc. By this instrument we really weigh the zinc which has entered into combination with the oxygen of the water in which it is subsequently dissolved. By the attraction between the zinc and the element of the water the power is produced wherewith the plates of the bank-notes are made, and this attraction differs not in kind from the attraction between the coals and air in the act of combustion which gives us the power in the steam-engine. In the electro-metallurgic battery, however, is perhaps observable the first instance of the estimation of the primary change of matter, to determine the amount of work actually performed. In the steam-engine the coals burnt will not necessarily give us a satisfactory clue to the work done ; and even in the animal, the most perfect of all machines, the food the soldier eats will not indicate the number of miles traversed, or of the enemy killed.

In an application of the battery-meter we have an illustration of a law which governs all physical phenomena. Without a change of matter we can have no physical force ; and all physical force is referable to a corresponding change of matter. In our electro-metallurgic apparatus we obtain an effect equal to the original change of matter within a very trifling percentage, a result which must be regarded as a glorious triumph of human improvement. If by the use of the battery-meter these great laws are popularized, and lead to a more universal reference of effect to cause, it will amply repay any little trouble which has been bestowed upon it.

To contain the battery with its charge, we generally employ the best salt-glazed stoneware. Strange as it may seem, no form of earthenware permanently resists the attacks of the metallic saline solution. They pass into the innermost texture of the material, and, even with vessels for holding writing ink, disintegration eventually ensues. Upon the whole, earthenware is preferable to glass, because it is less brittle, and I trust that the mention of the subject may lead some member of the Society to produce a cheap material, as impermeable as glass, and as durable as pottery.

At the Bank of England we generally find it convenient to employ parallelopiped-shaped vessels. Those made of mahogany and lined with gutta-percha are convenient and economical. For most of our purposes, we use the vertical trough, because the subject can be readily inserted and removed for inspection. For rapid deposition we employ the horizontal trough, in which the subject is placed at the bottom, and the copper pole above. In the use of this apparatus some refined chemical laws are involved. In the first place, sulphate of copper possesses a low diffusive power, and is carried, by virtue of that property, so slowly through the fluid, that if we relied upon it failure would surely attend our labour. Secondly, the saturated solution of sulphate of copper formed at the positive pole is so heavy that it descends from the place of its formation, like a cataract, to the bottom of the vessel. Lastly, the part of the solution deprived of its copper becomes so light that it rapidly rises to the top. For all rapid deposition we seek to form our new salt at the top of the apparatus, that it may descend to the place where it is required, and the light fluid may rise to mix with the denser portion. Practically, the vertical trough is suitable for the purposes of the Bank; but however important may be the requirements of this corporation, the laws of nature are paramount, and will not vary to suit its convenience.

Up to the present time the best standard salt for the reduction of copper by electro-metallurgy, is the sulphate, and, with the occasional exception of the nitrate, is invariably employed. We always have a neutral trough containing a simple solution, three parts saturated. For general purposes we use a saturated solution diluted with dilute sulphuric acid of battery strength, to the extent of from one-half to one-third of the bulk. We are careful to use recrystallized sulphate of copper, distilled sulphuric acid, and distilled water, as all impurities are hurtful. For our positive pole of copper it is very desirable to get good metal, and probably the sheathing of the innumerable Russian vessels we intend to capture will best serve our purpose, as the Russian copper is proverbially pure and free from tin.

If we regard the precipitating trough, we can but regard it as a very curious and wonderful chemical laboratory, in which two processes are being conducted at the same time, and in precisely equivalent proportions. In it we have the best of all chemical factories for the production of sulphate of copper by the combination of the plate of copper with the acid of the salt, and in it we may perceive the most perfect of all foundries wherein the metal is cast upon the mould atom by atom, with a skill which rather shows the perfection of nature than the deficiencies of the operations of man.

As a general rule we employ a single battery with one trough. Where we desire rapid action, we employ a compound battery of two cells in series, but this entails a double cost of battery power. In a great many cases, where time is of no object, we employ a compound trough with a single battery—that is to say, we arrange two troughs in series with one battery—a contrivance whereby we use our battery power twice over, and obtain two equivalents of copper, one in each trough, and consequently at half the cost. This form of apparatus is no trouble to manage. We have placed it in one of the iron safes for which the Bank is so famous, and wires are carried through the wall to supply the electric power. Here, unseen, and without labour or attention, the process goes on by night and by day, on Sundays and holidays; and when the deposit has acquired sufficient thickness, the mould is taken out and the deposit removed.

The deposited metal is of excellent quality, and a part of one of the Britannias, when carefully weighed, was found to have a specific gravity of 8·85. To ascertain the ductibility of the metal, I sent one of the scraps to Messrs. Horne and Thornthwaite, and one pound of metal was found to be capable of being drawn into three and a half miles of wire.

The authorities of the Bank are justly jealous of fire, and therefore we have not been able to keep our rooms or solutions at an elevated temperature, which is very desirable for many purposes. It is far better that we should be put to inconvenience, and our processes retarded, than that one single document should be jeopardized by our operations.

After having procured suitable originals, with proper means of duplication, the next process which we have to consider is that of obtaining perfect moulds. Where the original is of wood, gutta-percha is generally employed, but it is necessary that the mould should be used as soon as made, as it will shrink gradually till it is no longer fit for the purposes required. When gutta-percha is employed it is blackleaded, by the process described by Murray, who was rewarded by a medal from the Society of Arts. It is placed in the solution, and the copper grows over it. All blacklead is not equally good, and when it has remained in the air for some time we find it advisable either to heat the blacklead or use a little bisulphuret of carbon, or other volatile fluid, to drive off the adherent air.

Occasionally, when we have metal originals, and are pressed for time, we employ cliché moulds, but we never employ them when they can be avoided. The Britannia, I have already stated, is engraved on steel, and moulds are made from it by striking it upon pure soft lead, fixed upon brass plates, by which process very perfect moulds are secured.

For all our other originals, when we desire perfection, we rely upon electro-moulds, and electro-moulds alone. For this purpose the original is placed in the precipitating trough, and a thick electro-mould deposited. There is very little risk of adhesion, and very little difficulty, with moderate care, in obtaining a perfect mould. I need hardly mention that it would be a serious matter to place the original on the wrong side, for great would be the horror of the operator, on peeping into the trough, to see its costly original to have wasted away, instead of receiving the deposited metal.

When the electro-mould is sufficiently thick, a wire is soldered to it: it is waxed on the back and sides, and used for the deposition of the duplicate. In the use of the electro-mould there is much risk of adhesion, which requires skill to prevent. Sometimes we employ the film of air which I have already described in my 'Electro-Metallurgy;' sometimes we employ with good success the vapour arising from sulphuret of ammonia, a process which has been specially devised for the purposes of the Bank. In both these cases the moulds are inserted into the solution in a dry state, and little bubbles of air are apt to adhere, and be carried down into the solution, to the great detriment of our electro-cast. Upon pondering over this inconvenience, I thought it would be desirable to have a process whereby the mould could be inserted in a wet state. After some thought and many experiments, it occurred to me that we might use the layer of metal in the infinitely divided state in which it is employed in my battery. With care many metals in that state will answer, but I give the preference to platina. When the process is carefully performed, I have seen the most perfect success attend the platinizing process. Nevertheless, commonly enough, without care, we find that there is a liability for little adhered drops of water to be carried down, which in the electro process have been covered with metal, and the casts show slight indents, which are fatal to success. Upon the whole I regard this process as an addition to our knowledge, and it is particularly applicable to deeply-cut wavy line work.

The casts of the Britannia are generally deposited so thick in the compound trough that they can be turned down to the required form and size. Other subjects are generally backed with solder, and turned to their proper thickness. In cases where the lines are very thin, and at the same

X

time deeply cut, the metal must be aggregated very carefully, otherwise the metal grows on each side of the holder of the mould, and a slit is left down the centre of the metal. In some cases this would be a fatal inconvenience, and, where it is indispensable to avoid it, we use a feeble battery power, with a stronger solution of sulphate of copper in the precipitating trough.

All depositions in electro-moulds require for the highest perfection the utmost care. It would be tedious to the Society to dwell upon all the little points which require attention. Nevertheless, with proper care, no mode of duplication has ever been devised which is attended with similar identity. In all our electro-casts, whenever the most trifling air-bubble is found, it is thrown out directly, as the few halfpence required as the cost of the deposit of a small quantity of copper is nothing as compared with the supply of perfect notes to the public.

Although circumstances have led me to study more especially electro-metallurgic operations, yet it is important that electricity should take its proper place, and not be pressed into our service on every occasion, whether it be suitable or not. In the bank-note it was a matter of debate whether in some parts the steel die and punch should not be used, but for various reasons it was decided to use a steel original, with lead moulds, for electro-casts. There are some cases, however, in which the punch-and-die system, or even the transfer system of Perkins, might be advantageously applied in the typographical art.

The electro-casts, when ready for printing, are mounted on solid brass blocks, and many tools had to be constructed for this purpose. In this detail there is involved the difference between making and manufacturing, the formation of one article and the production of an infinite number. By this system of tools, if any part of a forme is damaged, another piece is immediately inserted. The same screw-holes in the plate and the same screws are used for the new piece; and, by every portion being made to one gauge, an exactness is given to the system which it would have been impossible to have obtained by leaving such details to the caprice or judgment of the workmen. By this system every part of the note is maintained in exactly the same relative position, and thus identity in the form of the note is absolutely secured. At the Bank a large stock of electrotype plates are always ready to be mounted at a moment's notice, and if one happens to be accidentally damaged, another is ready for insertion in precisely the same place as that which preceded it. The electro-copper is so durable that there is scarcely any limit to its wear, and at the 'Times' newspaper one cast is said to have printed nearly 20,000,000, and yet not to have been completely worn out. The limit to the duration of electro-casts for the purposes of the bank-note has yet to be discovered, as above a million have been printed with no perceptible effect. This duration alone is a matter of considerable importance, as by it a constant identity is more particularly insured.

There is, perhaps, no part of the process of the manufacture of the note of more importance, and more replete with curious interest, than the production of the paper, by Mr. Portal, on which it is printed. The mill is situated in Hampshire, on the river Test, and this beautiful stream supplies the water to drive the machinery necessary for the production of the paper.

The motive power of the mill is obtained from a turbine, an horizontal water-wheel, new to this country, but much used in Belgium and France. It is applicable to places where the fall is either slight or great. It is reckoned that by this contrivance from 70 to 75 per cent. of the whole force is obtained, while the vertical breast wheel, which would have been required for this situation, would not have afforded more than from 60 to 65 per cent. of the initial power. In using this turbine the quiet state of the water below the mill is not a little remarkable, for instead of the bubble and boil, it is as smooth as at the mill-head.

The new bank-note has a new water-mark, and the design which has been adopted is attributed to Mrs. Wyndham Portal, who suggested the form of water-mark which has been approved. These alterations in the water-mark constitute an important part of the new note, and the tinting is effected by means of Smith and Brewer's patent—an invention which is considered as a valuable addition to the mechanical appliances of paper-making, and was rewarded by a medal at the Great Exhibition of 1851. They have carried out their contrivances in the Bank. The essential part of this process is the use of steel-faced dies, which are engraved with the desired pattern, after which they are hardened, by being heated in leather charcoal, and then suddenly plunged in water. These dies are used with copper or tin forces in a stamping machine, to give an impression upon plates of sheet brass, and these plates when embossed are filed on the back to the requisite proportions, to allow the moisture of the pulp of the paper to pass through the apertures. The different pieces of brass, when struck, filed, and put together at the paper-mill, by Mr. Brewer, form the mould for the paper, and are so arranged that each mould is designed for two pair of notes.

In practice, great advantages attend the use of this patent. In the first place, identity in the water-mark of the paper is secured, a matter of no small importance when the subject of bank-notes is considered, and moreover it is specially adapted to give gradations of tints, lights, and shades, which, for the first time, has been introduced into the paper of the Bank of England notes.

If we contrast this elegant and simple method of mould-making with that previously adopted, the difference is sufficiently striking. In a pair of five-pound notes prepared by the old process there are 8 carved borders, 32 figures, 168 large waves, and 240 letters, which have all to be separately secured by the finest wire to the waved surface. There are 1056 wires, 67,584 twists, and the same repetition where the stout wires are introduced to support the under-surface. Therefore with the backing, laying, large waves, figures, letters, and borders, before a pair of moulds are completed there are some hundreds of thousands of stitches, most of which are avoided by the new patent. Moreover, by this multitudinous stitching and sewing the parts were never placed precisely in the same place, and the water-mark was consequently never identical. In this process we may detect principles which are not only valuable to the Bank, but to all public establishments having important documents on paper, as it affords to the public one more test whereby they may readily discover the deceptions of dishonest men.

For the preparation of the paper, cuttings are selected from the finest pieces of linen of the purest and whitest colour. These are carefully dusted, placed in the machine, and reduced to pulp. This pulp is passed through the finest strainer to the vat at which the paper-makers stand. To insure as far as possible identity even in the paper, Mr. Portal has put up machinery constructed by Mr. Donkin, in which all the improvements and adaptations heretofore adopted by machine paper are brought into operation for bank-note papers. The mould is dipped by hand into the vat of pulp, and a sufficient quantity taken up to make the note. This, as soon as the water is drawn off, is passed to a man, who puts it on a blanket, which slowly moves at a regular pace, and brings a new part into play for each mould of four notes as they are made. After the notes are placed in the blanket, they are carried under successive rollers till the water is squeezed out, and the pulp acquires consistency. This part of the process has performed the duties of the flannel and powerful press of the old system. The paper then, instead of being removed by a boy, as in the old process, is carried by machinery to the next part of the machine, where it is dried by passing over warm cylinders. This part of the machine answers to the old drying-room. When dry, it is spontaneously carried to the sizing apparatus, where it is sized with the whitest and purest size, when it is finally dried in the last compartment of the machine by passing over heated cylinders. By all those processes which have been in use in those machines which make paper by the mile, paper made by the hand mould is dried, sized, and dried again in the short space of half-an-hour, instead of requiring an interval of many days, as in the old process.

Mr. Portal, however, does not so much look to the rapidity as he seeks identity, for in all cases the pulp, being subjected to precisely similar conditions, may be expected to afford precisely similar results.

When the paper is dried, it is moderately glazed to give a smooth surface for printing. Formerly the paper used invariably to be wetted previous to printing, and a pretty-looking apparatus existed in the Bank for wetting the paper, by excluding the air from a receiver with an air-pump, and then allowing the water to rise and wet the paper. This wetting, however, damaged and weakened the paper, and hence it was very desirable to take advantage of the power of surface-printing to be applied to dry glazed papers. The smoothness is given by placing the sheets of paper between plates of copper, and subjecting them to a pressure sufficient on the one hand to give a fine and true surface, and yet not sufficient on the other to damage the water-mark.

When the paper is rolled, it is carefully inspected, and every damaged sheet thrown out, for if any little speck remains it is liable to injure the electrotype in the subsequent printing; and, after one inspection, the paper is re-inspected by two of the sharpest-eyed of the sharp-eyed inspectors of the mill. The paper is then inspected as to its gauge, as occasionally a sheet shrinks considerably in its manufacture. The paper is again inspected to see that every sheet is placed with its face uppermost, after which it is counted and packed up ready to be sent to Mr. Marshall, the chief cashier of the Bank.

These numerous processes of inspection are performed by females, and they generally belong to families who have been engaged in the manufacture of bank-note paper for 150 years. Each inspector is seated in a green box, opposite to a north light; but the ladies who have honoured the Society with their presence this evening will probably think that the inspectors are subjected to some torture when I state that rigid silence is expected in the room they sit in, and the whole number of females daily perform their allotted duties without gossip of any description.

The strength of the paper made in the manner above described is very great when we consider the nature of the water-mark, which is calculated to render it weaker than it would otherwise be. To be sure that no change is being made in the materials, its strength is actually tested by a simple machine; and a sheet of note-paper, although so thin, will always bear a weight of fifty pounds, and sometimes as much as seventy-five pounds, before it breaks.

The printing-ink for the bank-note is also a matter which has received attention. The properties of ink, when carefully prepared, are very curious and require considerable judgment to adjust them to particular papers. To Mr. Winstone, the printing ink manufacturer, has been entrusted the preparation and adaptation of the ink for the note, as it required somewhat careful treatment for the peculiar arrangement of the blacks and lights in the note. The black colouring material is made by burning coal-tar naphtha, and collecting the smoke in large rooms. This smoke or lamp-black is placed in a retort, and heated to a high temperature, to drive off all volatile matters, when the ink becomes consolidated and improved in colour. This is subsequently ground with a suitable varnish to a proper consistence to rest firmly on the delicate lines of the Britannia, without spreading to produce a rugged edge, and yet completely fill the black patches of the letters of the designation. In the bank-note it is also expected that the ink should dry sufficiently to allow handling immediately after being printed, a property which Mr. Winstone's chemical knowledge has enabled him to produce. To my mind, whatever may have been the results heretofore attained, the typographical art for rapid production has much to be improved by the adjustment of the distributive machines to the ink, and the ink to the distributive machinery. For the peculiar viscidity and tenacity of the ink, the weight of roller and rate of motion should be adapted to the character of the ink. At present no laws have been deduced upon this matter, but extended experiments upon perfect work will, perhaps, eventually give us a knowledge of the relation which ought to exist between roller and ink.

In my original proposition to the Governor of the Bank, I suggested that, in the first instance, the hand-press should be employed, because by it the pressman could more perfectly manage the ink, and have everything requisite for the adaptation of the typographical system to the bank-notes before the selection of a printing machine was made. The authorities of the Bank, however, determined, at the instance of Mr. Hensman and Mr. Coe, at once to attempt the use of the machine, and these gentlemen made an investigation of nearly every printing machine in use before the kind of machine to be employed was selected. It was found that the machines in greatest repute by the best printers were not sufficiently perfect for the Bank, inasmuch as the type did not always fall in the same place in regard to the tympan, a circumstance which interfered with the overlaying, so necessary to fine work, and in no case was the inking apparatus sufficiently good for this class of work.

For the cheques they considered that the double platten was the best machine which was in active operation at that time. For that reason a machine by Hopkinson and Cope was adopted, and the cheques were printed by it, as also some of the notes.

For the other bank-note a new platten has been specially constructed by Messrs. Napier and Son, with contrivances for both the tables and the inking rollers to traverse, by which means an effect is produced equivalent to rolling with a single hand-roller twenty different times. In this machine a plan of great value is employed, as the form of every note is made to one gauge, and every denomination has its separate tympan and over-laying. By these means, when a note-plate is once made ready for press with its overlaying, it is always ready at a moment's notice without further preparation for taking impressions. This appears to be a contri-vance which has added additional power to the system which, under the circumstances, well meets the requirements of the Bank.

Counting machines are appended to each end of the machine, that no impression can be taken without being registered; and when 100 impres-sions are printed, a bell strikes to call attention to the fact. In Napier's machines 3,000 notes are printed per hour, and two boys are required to feed with paper, and two to take off the printed notes.

After the note is printed, as a part of the system, it was proposed that it should be numbered and dated at the ordinary machines, instead of the Bramah's machine heretofore employed. These machines are also double, requiring two boys to feed and two to take off. By this working the note is completed, and handed over to the cashier to be examined and counted. By this part of the system, the note is decidedly superior to that of the old; the printing by the new process being very much improved as a mere question of printing.

Curiously enough, the numbering apparatus originally invented by Bramah has been adapted, with the necessary modification, for the Napier's gripper machine, with an improved inking apparatus.

When the forme is arranged in the printing machines, the first act of the printer is to obtain a perfectly level impression, equal in tint at every part, which is accomplished by filing the back of the blocks wherever he finds any elevation exists. This may be called a general picture, which possesses the general appearance, but without the lights and shades which give beauty and excellence to the impression. When the general picture is obtained to the parties' satisfaction, four impressions are taken upon thin paper, and, according to the gradations of tint required, the impression is cut away, so that in one place no thickness exists; in others one, two, three, or all the thicknesses remain. For the darkest portion the four thicknesses are left, for the lighter none are allowed, and for the inter-mediate tints two or three thicknesses are left. The whole are then pasted together and placed over the electrotypes, and, by the contrivance of the overlaying, those parts which are desired to be darkest get the heaviest pinch, those parts required to be of a lighter tint are the least heavily pressed, and in this way the impression is in a great measure brought to perfection

Upon the trial of this overlaying little alterations are made, to bring it to the utmost uniformity. In this part of the process much depends upon the skill of the superintendent of the printing department, who has the final examination, and when he is satisfied the printing is allowed to commence.

The time has long since passed away when scientific men would think of attempting to devise an inimitable note. A note to be inimitable must be made with a skill superior to the power of imitation of all men. The doctrine of inimitability should be buried with that of the philosopher's stone and the elixir of life; nevertheless, certain properties are demanded by the mercantile community, whereby a man may readily determine a good note. In this matter constancy of appearance is of paramount importance, and in this particular the new surface note stands pre-eminent. The vignette is printed in every impression line for line invariably the same. The same expression of face is constantly maintained; the same number of lines in one impression is visible in the second, and, however many thousands of notes may be issued, not the slightest possible variation within certain limits can exist. Moreover, the note is printed with a similar ink, and the same tone of colour preserved, that the public may be familiarised with a constant standard, and a uniform appearance will be marked in their mind.

Probably many of the members may recollect that the Society of Arts many years ago very warmly entered into the question of inimitable notes, and a very interesting little volume was issued by them on the subject. Some of these proposals were remarkable from the intricacy of their designs, but so far as the protection of the Bank is concerned no such intricacy is required, as the Bank is never at a loss to detect a forged impression, be it executed ever so skilfully, and the system pursued by the Bank is so perfect that no forged note has ever escaped eventual detection.

The doctrine even of difficult imitation is one which must be studied by physiological principles, and must be considered in reference to the faculties of the eye and the properties of the mind. By actual measurement I have ascertained that the eye can see perfectly over a range of $2° 18'$, which for twelve inches' distance would represent a space of half an inch diameter. However, it has been ascertained by other philosophers that an impression on the eye lasts for the one-tenth of a second, wherefore it follows, to look over very carefully every part of a note, no less a time than a third of a minute would be consumed, and probably in practice three times as much would be required. As nearly 30,000 notes are daily presented for examination, it follows that one gentleman must be employed 166 hours to inspect every single portion thoroughly. Practically, however, the work is perfectly performed by nineteen inspectors, and therefore they cannot enter into a minute and elaborate examination of every part of every note, but only judge by the general appearance of all manifestly good notes; and a careful examination of any one where there may be *primâ facie* grounds for suspicion.

From such causes it is found by long experience, that any extraordinary complexity is not only useless, but delusive and dangerous, from leading the mind into details which cannot be successfully appreciated. The labour and exhaustion produced by minute inspection of any very fine work for any length of time is shown by experience to be great, and, though to the psychological surgeon it presents many features of intense interest, yet the limits of this paper forbid me to enter into its consideration.

In speaking of identity, there is also another property of the eye to be considered; for although there can be hardly any such thing as absolute identity or likeness between any two objects, yet any objects which do not differ more than four seconds will appear alike to unaided vision, though with the microscope great differences may be discernible. Whenever, then, throughout this paper I speak of identity, I refer to the identity observable by the unaided sight; and after all it is but a rough comparative identity, a mere vision of identity when examined in a philosophical point of view. As far as the public is concerned, nothing can exceed the value of a uniform appearance; this the new note affords in the highest degree. Day after day, and year after year, the character of the paper will not vary. The same signature of " M. Marshall " which appears in the paper of one note will be repeated in the next. The same wave lines, the same rough edges on three sides, the same shadows in the water-mark will be brought continually before the sight. The Britannia will have the same expression of countenance, and will be repeated line for line, and dot for dot, for millions of impressions unchanged and apparently unchangeable. The very weight of the paper does not vary above two or three grains, unless damaged by wear, and the colour of the ink will be maintained as far as possible. As the stone is worn by water constantly dropping, so will the mind be impressed with one uniform appearance. With these constant appearances, the public should become familiar; and really in a country like this, where the circulation of notes is so large, and the Bank has taken such pains to secure identity, he that does not make himself acquainted with the appearance of a genuine bank-note does not deserve to be its possessor.

To attempt to construct an unforgable or inimitable note would be a mere delusion and snare. The public should know that everything which has been made can be copied; and without due care, whether they are numismatists, and look after Daries and Queen Anne's farthings, or antiquarians, and collect old Bibles or ancient manuscripts; whether they seek to buy gold-dust or sell precious stones; whether they transact their business by bills, notes, cheques, or coins, they are in all cases liable to fraud and deception, and ever will be liable so long as evil remains in the world.

Bank-notes are perhaps as little or less liable to be falsified than most other human inventions, in consequence of the certainty of the eventual detection of the fraud, and the great risk of punishment from the care and vigilance employed to trace out delinquents.

All questions of fraud are amenable to certain principles, which, on this occasion, it is not my province to consider. Whatever knowledge may have been obtained upon this subject has been obtained at the Bank, and may be regarded as the property of the Bank, which I have neither the liberty to communicate, nor am I granted permission to discuss. At the desire of the Bank, many experiments have been conducted upon chemical means of multiplication. Without entering into details, I am led to adopt a principle for the prevention of chemical changes; namely, to put the paper in the same chemical relation as the ink which we desire to protect, and in this way we obtain security against change in both writing ink and printing ink. In these experiments new fields for investigation were found, but it is not in my power in this paper to enter into their consideration.

As far as the Bank is concerned, the new system has insured increased excellence with diminished expense, but probably its adoption by the Bank will lead to a far more important use in the arts. Since the printing of the cheques, the Government have adopted surface-printing for the receipt stamps, and more recently for their new bill stamps. For extensive production and uniformity of expression, surface-printing stands pre-eminently as the master. Although the daily production of the 'Times' and the weekly production of the 'Illustrated London News' may justly be termed the typographical wonders of the world, yet the care bestowed upon the note to render its unlimited duplication perfect, has a tendency to materially influence the printing art in this department in a beneficial manner.

One application of surface-printing, although disconnected with bank-notes, I cannot pass over in silence, as I think the Society of Arts should recommend the adaptation of surface-printing to the Ordnance Maps; and though I am fully sensible of the difficulties which would attach to this new system, and fully estimate the perfection of these plates, nevertheless I feel persuaded that all difficulties may be surmounted, and every Englishman may be in a position to have a correct map of the land of his fathers, at a price not exceeding that of an ordinary newspaper.

In regarding the future operations of the Bank, I cannot but think that the results which have been described are the first step of the commencement, and not the end, of those improvements which will take place in the production of bank-notes. If the use of the steam-press exceeded my own propositions, yet in many respects the result has fallen short of my anticipations. Considering the great importance of a uniform note of a certain standard of perfection, it was necessary to take the most prudent course; nevertheless I cannot bring my mind to suppose that the processes can possibly stop where they are. In the first place, the original cutting of certain parts of the note will be far more highly finished than it is at present when increased skill is brought to bear upon it. With regard to the printing, hereafter, probably four, and possibly six or eight, will be printed, and subsequently numbered, at a single operation.

We are all too apt to think that art will stop at our point, and not progress, but it is the property of invention ever to move forward. The point at which we have arrived must be the step from which future improvements must spring, and, proceeding step by step, the highest possible excellence will doubtless eventually be secured.

There are certain characteristics which are common to the whole class of Bank of England notes which should be known to all the world. In the first place, every note has three of the natural edges of the paper, and one cut edge. In the centre of every note is a water-mark composed of waved lines, and the words "Bank of England" are inserted in the substance of the paper at the upper and lower portion, with a facsimile of the autograph of Matthew Marshall, the esteemed chief cashier of the corporation. The Britannia is printed on notes of all denominations, and all notes have the words "I promise to pay the bearer on demand."

The entire class of bank-notes include twelve genera, as each of the eleven branch establishments issues notes with the town upon it, as Manchester, Liverpool, Birmingham, Leeds, Newcastle, Leicester, Bristol, Portsmouth, Plymouth, Hull, Swansea; and these, with London, form twelve establishments issuing notes.

Each genus comprises several species, as notes are of several designations. Thus, in London nine notes are issued,—£5, £10, £20, £50, £100, £200, £300, £500, and £1,000 notes. In every branch, notes are issued up to £100; and at the two important commercial towns of Liverpool and Manchester, notes of £500 are issued in addition. In every genus of note the denomination up to £50 is placed in the water-mark in letters, and twice in shaded figures.

Every species of note is made up of innumerable individuals, each of which has an individuality as distinct and determinate for a bank-note as the individuality which characterises every human being, and also characteristics as marked in the eyes of the Bank, to distinguish one from another, and no more likely to be mistaken than our chairman is likely to be mistaken by you for our secretary, even when you are not so perfectly familiar with their likenesses. This individuality is given by a number and date being added to the denomination. The number is of no use alone, the date is of no use alone, but the number, date, and denomination together conjointly mark the specific individual; and any person having these particulars can learn at the Bank to whom the note was issued, and when it was issued, the date of its return to the Bank, and the person to whom money was paid for it, with many other matters of its pedigree and family history, which are only objects of interest to its mother, the Old Lady of Threadneedle Street.

It is not generally known to the public that there are two letters preceding the numbers on every note, and which, with the number, tells the whole story of the note. Therefore, if the public will but take down the letters and numbers, they can learn every other particular on applying to the Bank.

To give an idea of the extent of our operations, I find, in casting them up, that there are sixty-six kinds of bank-notes, and about fifty varieties of cheques, which had to be prepared. Besides these, there are twenty-five kinds of bank-bills, issued from eleven different places, independently of sixty day-bills, and various matters which would not be interesting to the meeting, further than to show that the Bank has not merely adopted surface-printing to a bank-note, but to all similar documents of a similar character which they require.

Had time permitted, it would have been interesting in this paper to have considered the progress of typography, and traced, step by step, the successive improvements which have taken place before it could have been adapted to Bank of England notes. In such an investigation we must commence with Tung-Tsou, A.D. 924, who appears to be its first inventor. From the works of the Chinese and Japanese we should pass to the Biblica Pauperum; the illustrated Bible of the period, printed by blocks, between 1420 and 1470. Then we should consider the movable types of Caxton, and works printed by this benefactor of the human race. Upon examination of the choicest specimens of Faust, Schoeffer, and Caxton, Shoensperger, and other great printers, we find that even at the beginning of this century, when Baskerville, Didot, Bensley, and Bodini, produced their finer specimens, surface-printing, as at all adapted to the present form of the Bank of England note, was only in its earliest infancy.

If we examine forms of notes printed by typography, we shall observe that the note of the Bank of France and the Belgian note are so produced, but in these cases the character of the note is adapted to the style of printing, and even there the number printed is so small as to appear insignificant when compared with the number issued by the Bank of England. At the former establishment about 300 impressions are printed every day; at the latter, nearly 30,000 are produced, as 9,000,000 notes are issued per annum, representing nearly £300,000,000 of money.

I remember, when a boy, the waggon-loads of machinery which were carted away from the Bank, which had been used for the production of the four millions of one-pound notes, which had been printed and never issued. Of these I cannot learn that one exists as printed for circulation, and the character is so different, that it throws but little light upon the application of typography to the present note. The same observations which apply to the suppressed one-pound note apply equally to the paper-duty stamp, which is familiar to every stationer.

When we consider the great difficulties which the peculiar water-mark of the bank-note paper has entailed, it never could have succeeded had we not applied a very much improved inking apparatus, assisted by the excellent composition rollers of Messrs. Harrild, the whole being materially helped by a totally novel method of preparing the forme for the press. As far as my examinations have gone, the typography of our cheapest periodicals far surpasses in sharpness of impression the very choicest efforts of preceding ages.

The theory on which my report was founded was deduced from a multitude of facts, and the result has proved that inductive reasoning has not deserted us when brought into practical operation.

The examination of typography has strikingly shown that invention is rather due to the period than to the man; and as those who have gone before have taken advantage of the inventions of our predecessors, and again we in turn have received the benefit of their labours, so our successors will use our experience as a stepping-stone to attain their results.

If we examine the note through its different stages, we cannot help being struck with astonishment at the care which has been taken to protect the public from imposition. In the manufacture of the paper every sheet must be accounted for, and the Legislature has wisely provided that no person, under the pain of transportation, may manufacture, sell, or expose for sale, paper with the words " Bank of England " in its substance, or any curve bar lines, or any denomination in writing. When it is received in the Bank, it is again counted and arranged by a decimal system, under the care of the treasurer, before it is stowed away. When issued to the printer, the same number must be handed over to the treasurer; and when it receives its final imprint and is converted into the representative of money, it is received by the cashier, who again examines and counts the number. These perfect notes are deposited in a place of security till life is given to them, by being carried as a credit into the Bank books. When it passes into the hands of the public, it is amenable to laws which are known to the authorities of the Bank. Each denomination has a different average duration of life, like individuals in different cities, and some are never heard of again, like people who go to foreign lands, and their fate ever remains unknown. When the note returns to the Bank, after inspection, it dies, never to be resuscitated. The signature is torn off, the denominations are punched out, and it becomes a piece of waste paper. The registry of its death is taken by a system devised by my brother, Mr. William Smee. This system, which is remarkable for its simplicity and rapidity of execution, has been in use with great success for many years, and those who are partial to the details of scientific book-keeping will discover many devices of interest, but which it is foreign to the purposes of my paper to consider in detail. After the death of the note is registered, it is then deposited in the vaults for reference for ten years, when it is burnt. The object for retaining the notes for so long a period is exclusively for the accommodation of the public; for although such a course entails a very considerable cost to the Bank, yet the value of the information which is daily being supplied from this cause, shows the importance of it to the monetary community. It is not an easy matter to utterly destroy so large a number of notes as those which are issued by the Bank. Experiments have been tried to reduce them again to pulp, but they have never altogether succeeded, and no plan answers so well as their destruction by fire. A large iron cage is built in the middle of the yard, including a light brick furnace pierced with holes. In this cage the notes are placed and burnt by sackfuls at a time, and nothing is left but a little white ash. Formerly the paper was coloured with smalt, and this was left at the bottom of the furnace as a curious blue mass. The same care which is taken in the manufacture of the paper, and in its transition through its various stages, is maintained to its final destruction, so that from the linen pulp to the cinder, no person can become possessed of a single sheet without committing a felony, immediately liable to detection. As the final result of the changes bank-notes undergo, I am enabled to show you a piece of the blue ash, a portion of the white ash, and a curious mass resembling peat, which arose from the conversion of a number of bank-notes into a peculiar substance from years of exposure to wet and pressure.

In bringing this paper to a conclusion, I am fully sensible of its defects, and regret that so important a subject should have been treated in a much less efficient manner than the members of the Society have a right to expect. The original intention was simply to have described surface-printing from electrotype for the purposes of the notes and cheques of the Bank of England; and if a wider scope has been given to these remarks, I trust that they have not been found tedious to the members of the Society, nor have been altogether uninteresting to the mercantile community. If hereafter the adoption of this system of Bank of England notes shall have been found to be beneficial to the arts, I shall feel amply rewarded for the anxious thought and labour which I have bestowed upon it—a feeling which is equally experienced by Mr. Hensman and Mr. Coe, who have, from the first, made every exertion to bring the system into successful operation.

## No. XXIII.

## THE MONOGENESIS OF PHYSICAL FORCES. A LECTURE DELIVERED AT THE LONDON INSTITUTION, FEBRUARY 18TH, 1857. By ALFRED SMEE.

IN our intercourse with Nature and natural phenomena, we, each of us, according to the peculiarity of our minds, view the same phenomena in a somewhat different manner; some of us perceive more vividly by our organs of sensation, whilst others with less powers of perception store up facts more accurately. Some generalize simple facts into extensive laws, whilst it is permitted to a few to compare and bring into relation numerous generalizations at first sight apparently distinct. From this diversity in the powers of the human mind, I have always strongly felt that society is benefited by each person unfolding the impressions which his own mind receives, as by that means all are made acquainted with the various aspects from which external nature may be viewed.

This evening it will be my endeavour to carry out the suggestion, that this year the soirée lectures should be undertaken by amateurs, and chiefly by the managers of your Institution. I have chosen for my theme the 'Production of Physical Forces,' and this lecture will be a cursory glance of that view of natural phenomena which I published in the year 1843, in a work entitled 'The Sources of Physical Science,' and which constitutes one of that series of metaphysical works which I have made it the business of my life to develop from Nature. Some of these views you have done me the honour on former occasions to allow me to unfold in this room; and from the kind manner in which you received those speculations, I venture to hope that you will neither be surprised nor offended in my submitting this view of Nature, especially as I have myself practically applied it for a period of fourteen years in the ordinary transactions of life, and I trust not altogether without some advantage to the public.

We live in a material world, but we can neither make nor destroy matter. However many times matter may be combined or acted upon by matter, it remains the same in amount; and even when it is so changed that it possesses no vestige of its former state, yet it is neither increased nor diminished.

When our great poet in his lofty flight says—

> " Imperious Cæsar, dead and turned to clay,
> Might stop a hole to keep the wind away ; "

the change is not more wonderful than the daily transmutations in our manufactories, where offensive offal is converted into beautiful pigments for the dresses of our fairest daughters, and noxious residues are changed into exquisite flavours for sweetmeats.

In every case in which we observe matter, we notice that it possesses a power whereby two portions are drawn together or mutually attracted. From this we deduce a law, "That whatever attracts is matter, and whatever cannot attract is not matter." To my mind, attraction is an inherent

property of matter, which it has possessed as long as matter has existed,
and will possess till matter ceases to exist, by the fiat of an IMMATERIAL
POWER.

We know not how far matter is divisible, because we can readily
separate it into particles far below what our senses can appreciate; nevertheless, it is convenient to assume that matter is divisible into definite
particles which can no longer be divided, and hence called atoms. We
know not, moreover, how many kinds of matter there are, or whether there
is more than one kind. It by no means follows because we cannot decompose the so-called sixty elements that they are separate bodies. We must
remember that it is possible, as every element has a different combining
number, that each may be only a number of atoms attracted together so
firmly as to resist our powers of separation. These considerations are
entirely within the boundary of speculation, and not at present of fact;
yet this view meets all the known facts of the case, and when two theories,
equally expressing all the circumstances, are offered for our consideration,
it is more consistent with natural science to choose that which involves
the fewest hypotheses. One of the most subtle divisions of solid matter is
to be found in the black pulverulent state of metals, such as employed for
my form of battery. It has been supposed that all matter is black when
extensively divided, because the particles are too small to reflect light; but
the form of the black particles is unknown to us, because the highest
powers of the microscope are insufficient to render them visible to the eye.
At the last Bakerian lecture Professor Faraday made known methods for
dividing gold to an extreme amount. He precipitates the metal from its
solution by bi-sulphuret of carbon, and obtains a ruby-coloured liquid, in
which metallic gold is so minute that the particles are invisible by any
microscopic power. This distinguished philosopher satisfied himself that
the ruby glass owes its colour to gold in a metallic state in an infinite
division, and by adding gelatine to the ruby solution he obtained a ruby
jelly precisely similar.

Ultimate particles of matter are aggregated or attracted into masses,
of which we may observe many varieties. Look at ice: how different is its
appearance at different times; and in our electro-metallurgic deposits,
where we build up our objects atom by atom, we obtain many very different
kinds of aggregation. The copper electrotype from which the Bank of
England note is printed, is so excellent, that a portion I tried was found
capable of being drawn into three and a half miles of wire, whilst under
certain circumstances copper deposited breaks with a conchoidal fracture
with the greatest ease.

We are ignorant whether there is any difference in the mode of attraction between the ultimate particles of solid, fluid, and gaseous particles;
but having regard to the entire range of physical knowledge, we may
assume that the particles are most firmly attracted in the solid, and more
in the fluid than the gaseous state, as by different amounts of attraction we
obtain the difference between the solid and gaseous states. I have specu-
lated whether one atom might not by itself have boundless expanse, and
fill the firmament—a limitation of extent being due to the attraction
between two or more atoms of matter.

Masses of matter aggregated together still have the power of attracting each other into one uniform mass, by adhesion, as when two pieces of

lead or glass are brought into contact they mutually adhere, and sometimes greatly to the manufacturer's discomfort.

Liquids and solids in contact have a power of mutual attraction, as in
capillary attraction.

Gases and liquids have also this power of attraction, as in the case of
muriatic acid gas and water.

I will now show you a very beautiful experiment, proving that attraction is existent between gases and solids. Some years ago I discovered
that coke or charcoal might have so much hydrogen firmly attracted to it,
that when plunged into solutions of gold, silver, or copper, an extensive
deposition of metal takes place, and I have found that it would retain the
gas for many days.

Attraction is also exerted between gaseous bodies, according to the
law of diffusion so elegantly developed by Graham; and even carbonic acid
(a very heavy gas) passes into the atmospheric air.

Lastly, liquids attract each other by a law very similar to that of the
diffusion of gases.

Hitherto we have considered the attraction of particles of matter in
indefinite quantities, or of the attraction of masses already aggregated;
but particles of two or more different kinds of matter may be attracted to
produce a totally new substance, having none of the properties of former
particles: thus chlorine and sodium form common salt; oxygen and
hydrogen, water.

Attracted matter, either in masses or in the most attenuated particles,
attracts other masses at any distance, and by this power of gravity everything in the universe is kept in position; to this power the sun, the moon,
the earth, the stars in the firmament, and every substance in the world,
owes its position.

In the cases of attraction already described the power appears to be
exercised promiscuously, but there are cases in which attraction is exerted
in definite directions. Crystals are masses of attracted matter of this
character, as their particles are attracted unequally in different directions.
In consequence of this they yield to mechanical force in some directions,
not in others; they expand unequally by heat, they are acted upon
unequally by magnetism, and they have very curious properties in relation
to light. Not only in crystalline bodies do we observe that attraction is
exercised in a definite direction, but we observe a direction in the power
of attraction during the magnetic state. A bar of iron, when it suddenly
assumes this state, appears to have its former attractions altered, for under
favourable circumstances it will sound a distinct musical note. When a
magnetic body attracts another body capable of assuming the magnetic
state, the second substance also evinces a similar direction in the exercise
of the power of attraction. From these views we deduce that the idea of
magnetism is derived from certain kinds of matter, under certain circumstances, evincing the power of attraction in a definite direction.

We have considered the mode in which attraction acts to unite
particles of matter, and thus construct the various objects of which the
material universe is composed. Now let us pause to consider the earth at
rest. The quiet which gives the loveliness to evening, and soothes the
mind after the business of the day, forms but a dim shadow of that awful
quiet which would exist were attracted matter not capable of being acted

upon, when there would be neither heat to cheer, light to gladden, sound to enliven, nor motion to excite.

Nature, however, abhors quiet, and delights in action. In every case where attraction is exerted, it can be destroyed by a new attraction; and thus, whilst attracted matter exhibits cohesion, composition, and position, so a new attraction can cause disintegration, decomposition, and motion. Hence we deduce the law, "that a new attraction can destroy a former attraction."

For a study of the effect of a new attraction acting upon attracted matter, the voltaic battery stands forth pre-eminently as an instrument well calculated to exemplify the phenomenon. For a voltaic circuit it is essential to have a fluid compound built up of two atoms only: this compound is decomposed by any matter either in a solid, fluid, or gaseous state capable of setting up a powerful attraction between itself and one element of the compound: this is the positive pole. The second element is evolved at the negative pole, and the two points may be connected together by matter extending for miles and miles; a fact on which depend the electric clock and telegraph. In a single battery there is but one point at which the new attraction is excited. In the compound battery there are as many points as there are cells in the series. A single voltaic battery may act through a series of similar troughs, provided that in these secondary troughs the tendency to destroy the former attraction is nearly equal to the tendency to maintain it. I place before you an example, in which one battery is reducing gold, silver, copper, tin, lead, iron, zinc, in separate cells, having solutions of the positive poles of those metals. In this case, one grain of zinc in the battery reduces $6\frac{1}{4}$ grains of gold, $3\frac{1}{4}$ of silver, $3\frac{1}{4}$ lead, $1\frac{7}{16}$ tin, 1 copper, $\frac{7}{16}$ of a grain iron, these being the relative weight of one atom of each of these metals.

By the voltaic battery, especially if we employ the platinized silver battery, as is now almost invariably used for heavy work, we obtain results equivalent to the original attraction within a very trifling percentage, a result which must be regarded as a glorious triumph of human skill. On account of this perfection of result I have been enabled to construct an instrument which I call a battery-meter, in which every degree shows that a grain of zinc has entered into combination and become sulphate of zinc. By this we can tell the amount and thickness of metal reduced in our precipitating trough. This instrument is the first instance in which man has estimated work done by the primary attraction or source of power. In the steam-engine the coals burnt do not point out so accurately the result obtained; and I have elsewhere observed that even in the animal, the most perfect of all machines, the food the soldier eats will not of necessity indicate the number of miles traversed, or of the enemy killed.

This instrument was designed for the Bank of England. You are all doubtless aware, that upon my proposition the entire system of printing the Bank of England notes has been changed, and that they are now printed from the surface: a change which has contributed so much to give identity to the note. The original dies are cut in copper, steel, or brass; from these, moulds are made, which again are electrotyped to make the cast for printing. The battery-meter, placed in the battery, shows us the thickness of our deposited metal in the trough; and though our practised eye enables us to dispense with extraneous aids, I can but think this little instrument is a very beautiful practical application of profound physical laws.

The cause of all voltaic phenomena is referable to a new attraction, and when this is opposed by obstacles tension is manifested. Tension, to use a figurative expression, is "a desire for action ungratified;" and thus, as soon as the tension is increased, or the obstacles are diminished, action results, and disintegration, decomposition, or motion occurs.

It was from the long-continued and close study of the voltaic battery, requisite to enable me to write my treatise on ' Electro-Metallurgy,' that I was led, step by step, to develop the system of physical philosophy upon which this lecture is based. I could, therefore, tarry and dwell upon this beautiful instrument, did I not remember that on this evening it will be my endeavour to compress into one lecture a slight sketch of the entire range of physical phenomena.

Passing from the study of the action of a new attraction upon binary fluid compounds, we may next, with advantage, consider its effect upon solid substances, or substances under the attraction of aggregation, and the electrical machine is well adapted for this purpose. In this case, force is applied to a solid body, whereby tension far exceeding that which is readily obtainable by a voltaic battery is manifested. Whenever the electrical machine is excited by any force, the origin of that force is due to some new attraction, and hence the new attraction is the primary cause of the electrical tension; and when this is increased sufficiently, or the obstacles decreased, action ensues by a destruction of attractions, such as disintegration, decomposition, or motion, and is frequently accompanied by light, heat, and sound.

From the above views, the mind is led to suppose that electricity is not an immaterial essence, imponderable, or spirit attached to matter, to which the effects are due; but that the phenomena of electricity are entirely owing to the action of a new attraction upon matter aggregated or composed by former attractions.

By frictional electricity we can trace how repulsion is a phenomenon of attraction, and not an inherent power of matter; as by electricity we can readily suspend some of the numerous forces by which any body is held in position, when it moves in the resultant of the others. Two balls suspended close together, when similarly electrified, appear to repel each other; but in reality they are attracted to surrounding objects.

Carry the reasoning one step further, we find that which we term a positive or negative electrical phenomenon is due to the direction in which the new attraction acts, and this direction is analogous to the polarity of the magnet or the condition of the electrolyte in the voltaic battery.

Passing from the known to the unknown, we may glance at the thunder-cloud, the awful grandeur of which must for ever appal the human mind. From the dense black masses of clouds which usually accompany this grand natural phenomenon, we have seldom an opportunity of observing that which is taking place; yet on one occasion, on Forest Hill, I saw that which probably is the cause of the electric action. It was a damp day in June, and there had been much rain previously (the entire sky being covered as it were with misty clouds, through which the sun was seen in an obscured form). Suddenly, without warning or the slightest apparent reason, clouds aggregated above our heads so rapidly, that

Y

within five minutes we were in comparative darkness, when the most terrific flashes of lightning occurred, accompanied with peals of thunder. This was followed almost simultaneously by enormous hailstones, so thick that we could scarcely see a few yards before us. We had great difficulty in proceeding to the nearest house, which was scarcely a hundred yards, and it was only after incessant ringing, that one of the inmates ventured out to open the gate to give us shelter.

In this case there was manifestly an instantaneous and rapid development of new attractions in the aggregation of aqueous vapour into large hailstones, and I believe that aggregation of vapour acting upon the attracted matter of the clouds is the true source of the electric development.

The sublime phenomenon of the thunder-cloud I have watched as it plays over the ocean's bed; I have been in the midst of it at the top of the mountain, I have seen it hovering over the lake, and heard the thunder reverberate from shore to shore of the castle-bearing hills of the Rhine, yet it is worthy of mention that in no place has it been so grand as in this Circus during the stillness of night. Here we have a multiple echo, and when the cloud is overhead, the crash is reverberated from side to side with a majesty unequalled by any other natural phenomenon, and which well marks the power which is acting during the electric discharge.

The capacity to produce action is called force, and, whenever a new attraction is set up, force results. Force differs from tension in being able to do that which tension is prevented, by a resistance, from accomplishing. Any kind of attraction gives rise to force. The attraction of gravitation, capillary attraction, the attraction of aggregation, or of chemical affinity, will produce force.

When a new attraction is exerted, the force emanating therefrom may be propagated through aëriform bodies, when it is termed pneumatic force; through fluid bodies, when it is called hydrostatic force; through solid bodies, when it is called mechanical force.

I have heard it stated that whenever force is generated it is never annihilated. To such an extraordinary proposition my system not only gives an unqualified denial, but points out the manner in which force comes to an end. However long it may endure, however many bodies it may pass through, its final action is to destroy some pre-existing attraction, and either disintegrate, decompose, or move previously attracted matter.

The resistance of matter under attraction to a new attraction leads to the production of various phenomena. Under certain circumstances, that which we call heat is evinced. For heat, it is necessary that a resistance to the new attraction should be afforded by the pre-existing attraction. In the voltaic circuit, if any part is contracted heat is manifested, and in this way water may be boiled, or platinum (one of the most infusible of substances) may be made to fuse like wax. Mechanical force causes heat, when applied to solid bodies; and whenever attraction acts with sufficient energy upon attracted matter, heat results. Where we require intense heat we must employ an intense new attraction on an intense aggregation, and hence every practical man uses light or strong coke according to the intensity of heat he requires. Whilst heat exists, the new attraction is merely attempting to destroy other attractions, and the force may be transferred to any other body: by conduction, that is, through bodies in contact; or by radiation, that is, to bodies at a distance. In every case where heat ceases, either the new attraction ceases to exert itself, or the former attraction is destroyed, and disintegration, decomposition, or motion is the result.

Some difficulty is presented to our knowledge of the actions and reactions which constitute heat, but, upon the whole, I am inclined to think that heat is best described as that action of matter which from a distance influences the nerves of sensation in the skin, or, in other words, heat is that which is felt from a distance by the skin.

There is another range of actions and reactions which are not appreciated by the skin, but are alone seen by the eye. This range is termed light, and by the prism we are enabled at once to distinguish that which is seen by the eye, or light, from that which is not seen by the eye. Chemistry indicates that there are actions both more refrangible than the violet ray on the one hand, and less refrangible than the red on the other. For the production of light the new attractions must be of the most powerful kind, so that they may act with great intensity upon matter attracted, and it is preferable to be in a solid state. The inflammation of hydrogen gives little or no light: add solid matter, and a beautiful light is the result. Hydro-carbons give us the most convenient light when they are burnt with such energy that the solid matter is first deposited to be acted upon by the new attraction, and subsequently burnt that it may yield no smoke; if all is burnt at once, so that no solid matter remains in the flame, light will not be produced. An illuminated body may communicate the force which is seeking to act upon the solid matter to other bodies, and finally decomposition, disintegration, or some destruction of attraction takes place.

As the skin feels heat, the eye sees light; so, by the ear, are we made acquainted with the actions and reactions constituting sound. The vibrations constituting sound have been accurately measured by philosophers; and though different people differ in the power of appreciating the higher and lower notes, it may be generally stated that all vibrations from 8 in a second to 24,000 are appreciated by the ear, and are consequently sound.

Sound, like light and heat, requires attracted matter: this is acted upon by a new attraction, and in the conflict between the old and new attractions vibrations ensue; whilst the vibration continues, the force may be propagated to other matter which may also take on vibrations.

I have always thought that odours constituted a further range of actions and reactions. I am the more confirmed in that view, the more I watch those animals, as the bloodhound, which have the nerves of the nose highly developed. Upon this matter, however, we are much in the same position as the man born blind, who can only receive his ideas of light through the medium of the eyes of others, for man has literally only a rudimentary nose, if it be compared with that of other animals.

A theory is not to be a mere mental creation, but a law or principle to guide our actions and bring forth fruit. The law which I have developed is so pre-eminently of practical application, that every human action may be regulated by it. When we desire to obtain any result, we begin by generating new attractions. For this purpose we select substances having the lowest equivalent, because the least weight would answer our purpose ; hydrogen and carbon have the lowest equivalent, and coal being an hydro-carbon, is that matter which is pre-eminently adapted to combine with oxygen, the more especially as the product of the new attraction is readily dissipated. If we compare zinc with coals, we find that it has an equiva-lent eight times higher, and its energy of combustion with oxygen is perhaps not more than one-third that of carbon : moreover, the cost of zinc is forty times dearer than coals ; consequently, as a source of power, zinc would be 960 times dearer than coals.

Our theory thus indicates why we select coals for light, heat, motion, and chemical changes, instead of zinc ; and this difference of cost prevents the voltaic battery, the most perfect human device, from universal application.

In animals the hydrogen and carbon in the food they consume is the source of power, and the horse without hay and oats is as powerless as the steam-engine without coals or the battery without zinc.

Starting with the new attraction of hydrogen and carbon, with oxygen as a source of power, we must take care so to apply it upon attracted matter, that we may produce, according to our necessity, heat, light, motion or electricity ; for it would not be difficult, in fact it constantly happens in practice, for one variety of force to be produced when another is desired, and whatever is thus improperly generated is wasted.

In physics and physiology, in mechanics and medicine, facts, no less than theory, declare that no effect occurs without material cause, that no initial change takes place without equivalent result, and in all cases there is but one source ; in fact a complete " Monogenesis of all Physical Forces."

In consequence of the " Monogetic Origin of Physical Forces," each possesses within itself the power of a new attraction, which, according to the amount of the initial change, can produce an equivalent or relational amount of any other force. Electricity may produce light, heat or motion. Motion may produce heat, light, electricity ; light may produce electricity ; motion, heat ; heat may produce motion, electricity, light ; and so we may ring the changes of the convertibility of physical forces *ad infinitum*.

Whenever a new attraction acts upon matter under attraction, the attraction already existing seeks to maintain itself, and in consequence of this resistance time is occupied, and according to the energy of the change, so is the time diminished or increased.

I know no part of physical science which presents more important matter for consideration than the phenomenon of time : for let us suppose that a change of matter could take place without time ; the coals in our grates would be consumed instantly—if our house caught light, the whole would momentarily vanish—if we set in motion any body, it would arrive at its destination quicker than thought, and be dashed to pieces. Chemistry supplies us with substances, the particles of which are held together so slightly, that upon the slightest application of force they are separated : iodide of nitrogen, for instance, separates upon the slightest agitation into its component parts. The safety of the proper use of gun-powder depends upon its progressive action, which is slow as compared with iodide of nitrogen, or with some varieties of gun-cotton.

Man derives the idea of time from the resistance to change : if the total changes constituting an event are performed with energy, but little time is occupied; if the resistance to change is great, considerable time is evinced. The sum total of all time is the representation of all the events which have happened from the commencement of matter to the present moment; and the number of revolutions of the earth round the sun, or of the earth upon its axis, are generally the events which are counted as our measure of time.

From the nature of time, one preceded all subsequent events; namely, the first rushing together or attraction of particles of matter, which gave to every object its composition, form, and position. We must look for the cause of this primary attraction to a source extrinsic from matter, as it could not have caused itself to take on that power. From this consideration the mind is led to contemplate an "IMMATERIAL POWER," to confer this property on matter. This argument is independent and altogether different from the argument of design, but this is not the proper place to enter into this consideration, which I now leave to your own meditations, or refer you to the seventh chapter of my 'Sources of Physics,' for its further development.

Every event from which we derive our ideas of time has a beginning, the generation of a new attraction; and an end, the destruction of a former attraction; and as events have followed since matter existed, and will continue till matter shall cease, time began with matter and will terminate when matter shall cease, and "The great globe, yea, all which it inhabit, shall dissolve." From these views we find that time can have none,—no, not even the feeblest quality of eternity; and that however exaggeratedly it may be increased, time never becomes eternity. Time is a mere repetition of events, each having a beginning and an end. Eternity is not made up of events, and has, therefore, no beginning and no end.

I have now completed, as far as the limited time will permit, a short sketch of the views of the "Monogenesis of Physical Forces," which my study of Nature and natural phenomena has forced my mind to adopt. This doctrine has the merit of discarding the notions of æthers, essences, imponderables, or a plurality of forces being attached to matter, and places such vague assumptions rather amongst the mental creations of the philosopher than amongst the realities of Nature.

I am free to confess that this combination of physical facts and known laws into one consistent doctrine was a matter of intense study and profound thought; but should it fortunately have the same power on your minds, to render physical science of easy application, as it has had upon mine, you will pardon me for occupying your attention whilst I have endeavoured to teach, that attraction acting on attracted matter is the source of all force, and that, therefore, every physical force has a monogenetic origin, and when generated a truly equivalent power.

## THE ECLIPSE OF THE SUN. 1858.

*To the Editor of the 'Morning Chronicle.'*

SIR,—I am afraid that your correspondent may think he has good cause to accuse me of want of courtesy in not having supplied to him an account of the experiments on the light of the eclipse, but the observations exceeded 150, and at the moment I could not compress them into a form suitable for your paper, or I should have had great pleasure in giving the details at once. The great interest which naturally, however, belongs to this grand natural phenomenon, induces me to send a short account of some observations made at Blisworth upon the darkness which marked the progress of the obscuration, in the hopes that it may not be unacceptable to many of your readers. It has occurred to me that my "abstract photometer" might do good service; for whether the weather was fine, or whether it was cloudy, yet it was calculated to give us an insight into the extent to which the sun's light might be veiled from the surface of the earth.

The photometer consists of a wedge of neutral tint coloured glass, cemented by Canada balsam to a similar wedge of colourless glass, and the

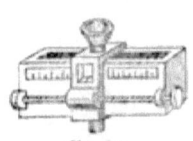

FIG. 14.
Smee's Photometer.

solid which results from the junction of the two prisms is divided into degrees, each of which is equal to the capacity of the one-hundredth of an inch of pure bromine, so that the short account now given may be compared by future philosophers with the results of subsequent eclipses hundreds or thousands of years hence, if they do but know the length of our English inch. Armed with this instrument, I proceeded to Blisworth, where I found a field conveniently located, which had been secured by some of my friends, and where chronometers and all other instruments for accurate research had been provided. I determined to take three sets of observations: the first, of the light of the horizon, at a spot where a tree cut sharply the line to the south; the second, of the light of the ground at our feet; and the third, the light of the sky overhead: and I anticipated that I should be able to test by the vigorous proof of scientific truth the wonderful stories which are told of eclipses, which appeared to my mind as the results of overheated imaginations, or of stories fit for an appendix to the curious Travels of Baron Munchausen.

In the morning, at half-past eight, the sky showed a light which was veiled at 17:* but at the commencement of the eclipse the clouds were so dense that the horizon was obscured at 14·15. From this time till 12h. 53', the light continually diminished to 11. The next observation was taken at 1h. 2', when it stood at nearly 14, from which it rose to 15 at 2h. 16', at the termination of the observations. I need not here allude to the rises and falls of light as the clouds became thinner or denser, as it is sufficient to notice that the horizon lost light continually from the beginning to the total, and gained from the total to the termination.

---

\* This and the following numbers refer to the degrees of the photometer.

The illumination of the ground presented far more interesting and important variations. At the commencement of the eclipse the illuminating power was 11; it varied with the depths of the clouds, but gradually receded to 8·5 at 12h. 53′. At 12h. 55′ it dropped to 8·3; at 12h. 58′ it reached 8; at 12h. 59′ it was as low as 7·25. This was about the minimum of light and maximum of darkness, when suddenly, in little more than a minute afterwards, the earth became illuminated, and two or three seconds after 1 o'clock the light rose to 10, and continued to rise with the variations of the clouds till 2h. 15′, when it stood at 12·5. This illumination of the earth was a wonderful natural phenomenon: the country people called out, " It's all over!" and to see the ground brightly lighted whilst the sky remained in great darkness was a surprising, and to me an unexpected, appearance.

The sky was observed as near the zenith as convenient: at the commencement it was equal to 14·25; from this it gradually, with variations according to cloud, diminished to 11·75 at 12h. 50′, and then rapidly dropped till 1 o'clock, when it stood at the lowest amount, 9·25. At 1h. 2′ it rose to 12·5, many seconds later than the rise of the illumination of the earth, so that the earth, brightly illuminated for some seconds, remained with a dark canopy overhead, and this peculiarity appears to give a marked character to the darkness of an eclipse which differs from other obscurations.

From these observations it is apparent that a great diminution of light gradually occurs from the commencement to the totality, at which point it very rapidly further declines; after the totality it almost suddenly rises, and in fact so rapidly as to appear like a scene at a theatre suddenly illuminated, from which time the light increased to the end of the eclipse.

To the wondermongers who put all the birds to roost, I may state that the lark sang in the air at 12h. 47′; that other birds flew about and chirped to 12h. 50′; that larks rose in full song as late as 12h. 52′, and remained in full song to 12h. 55′, at which time the cocks were heard to crow; even the birds in the hedges whistled at 12h. 58′, and, in fact, continued their songs and flights from the beginning to the end of the eclipse: and if there was an interval in their proceedings, it could not have been for more than three minutes. The sun became visible at 1h. 0′ 21″, and again at intervals till 1h. 57′, when the light of its disc amounted to 18·25.

The barometer did not sensibly vary. I ascertained that the difference between the dry and wet bulbs lessened at the time of the greatest cold from about 3° to 1½°.

Although these results are by no means so perfect as could be desired, yet they are of considerable interest, and I trust they will lead on a future occasion to such observations that the variations of light and darkness may be accurately detailed.

　　　　　　　　　　　　　　　I am, Sir, your obedient servant,
7, FINSBURY CIRCUS,　　　　　　　　　　ALFRED SMEE.
　　March 16.

## No. XXV.

## ON THE WATER SUPPLY OF THE METROPOLIS.

### EXTRACTS from LETTERS to the 'Times' and 'Standard.'
### by ALFRED SMEE.

THE deep springs which supply our rivers round London flow from the chalk, which absorbs the rain which falls upon it and retains it like a sponge, and the great chalk hills which surround London are Nature's storehouses for water, which yield a steady supply, influenced by the total rain which falls over a period of several weeks, but uninfluenced by any sudden showers. The Lea, the New River, the Colne, the Wandle, the Grays water springs, and other streams, have their source in the chalk, and it is our duty to take the water at its source, before it is contaminated with sewage. Moreover, the rivers round London are full of weeds, which grow with great rapidity in hot weather, but which die and rot at the beginning of September, and this decaying matter is then supplied to London at a period of the year when epidemics are most rife, and when its presence is most dangerous.

By taking spring water as it pours from the earth, and stowing it in dark reservoirs, vegetation cannot occur, and the water can be supplied in its purest condition.

Although the cause of the choleraic impairment of water is unknown, the pernicious influence of cesspools near surface wells is now thoroughly recognized, and, possibly, the choleraic poison can run through the earth as a fungus can extend for a considerable distance, &c.

While London cries for a further supply of water, it is not generally known that there exists at Grays in Essex a series of fissures, or underground rivers, which pour their water into the Thames, and the yield of which is estimated at upwards of 10,000,000 gallons a day. Some of this water is used for the supply of Brentwood, and Romford will be supplied in two or three weeks, but the remainder is absolutely wasted, notwithstanding that it is destitute entirely of organic matter, and is of a quality declared by the Government commissioners as the best which is obtainable for the metropolitan supply . . . .

---

AGAINST DRINKING WATER CONTAINING ORGANIC MATTER. Speech delivered by ALFRED SMEE at the Civil Engineers', May 21st, 1867.

MR. SMEE denied that a small quantity of organic matter in water was immaterial. A small quantity of small-pox matter would infect a large number of persons, and a less quantity of scarlet fever poison was required to propagate that disease. There were many other poisons communicated by means so subtle that the material agency by which the poison was carried from one person to another had never been discovered, whilst there was distinct evidence that it was so carried. When the great cholera epidemic struck the neighbourhood of Golden Square, Dr. Snow visited every house that was attacked, and in each instance traced the mortality to the use of the water from the pump in Broad Street. He thereupon went to the vestry, declaring that the remedy against cholera in that district was to chain up the pump. When the authorities heard of the simple means he recommended, they were inclined to treat the suggestion with ridicule, but they argued it could do no harm if it did no good, and when they chained the pump-handle the mortality decreased.

It had been alleged that cows and farm-horses preferred to drink water contaminated by sewage, and he would state, of his own knowledge, that if those animals had the choice of clear water and foul water, they would leave the pure water for the latter. For instance, the water which flowed through Croydon had been habitually taken by some cows. These were attacked with the rinderpest, whilst those around the district did not suffer from it. Nevertheless, it was not only cows, but mankind who in many cases preferred this particular class of water. Churchyard pumps were resorted to in preference to others; there was something in the taste of the water, probably from the salt it contained, that excited the palate and induced people to drink it in preference to pure water. On the last epidemic visitation of cholera, he recommended the authorities to take off the handle of the pump over the old Roman well in the Bank of England. That well, which was a celebrated one, was derived originally from the gravel; but now there was reason to believe it was supplied from leakages beneath the urinals. It appeared that, when the handle was taken off, some of the people of distinction in the locality begged that they might not be deprived of that water, as it was the only drinking water they enjoyed. He had no hesitation in saying that, where tainted water was supplied to the public, it was a matter of great moment; and that whenever an epidemic appeared, the community must be cautious to do all they could to avoid the use of it.

The next part of the question was the character of the organic matter. This, if like the white of eggs, or a basin of soup, was harmless; but let the soup or white of eggs get into a putrefactive state, and the operation, like the leaven of bread, would communicate its taint far and wide. It was matter in the act of change, and it set up change in contiguous organic matter. The damage done to individuals of every species by the excreta of the same species, was generally recognized by the medical profession; and the doctrine of the harmlessness of changing organic matter was universally regarded as a medical heresy.

Now, what did Boards of Health frequently do? He would rather call them in many cases Boards of Death. The Croydon Board of Health formerly took the water which naturally flowed into the stream, passed it through the town and the water-closets, and then poured it in at the top of the river Wandle, to poison every person living upon its banks. At one period of an epidemic he thought it his duty to call the attention of the Privy Council to the circumstance, when the inhabitants were warned not to drink the water of the river Wandle. It was only by a series of bills in Chancery that the residents succeeded in suppressing that nuisance; and it was observed that the Croydon authorities found the greatest difficulty in getting rid of the putrefying animal matter upon the land. He could give a recipe how to test imperfectly-purified water. It might be clear and bright and pleasant; but put it into a bottle upon the mantelpiece in a warm room, and in two or three days, notwithstanding the filtering process had removed suspended matter, it would begin to change, and give unmistakable evidence to the olfactory nerves of the presence of putrefying organic matter. Everything tended to show that animal matter in a state of decomposition was to be feared. In seasons of epidemic it was impossible to pass the excreta of one town to another in rivers without great danger of propagating disease; and for that reason water ought never to be taken from such a source. Now, if it was matter in a state of change which was injurious, there came the consideration whether the sewage was presented as a totally changed matter in river waters; in other words, whether the sewage assumed a totally different form. Suppose sewage was put upon the ground and absorbed by vegetables, such as cabbages, or was absorbed by weeds in rivers, it was no longer sewage: but notwithstanding, there were several cases on record which showed that it was not perfectly safe to manure gardens by pumping sewage: under these circumstances, as the plants grew up they would quickly decompose after being cut for use, and would not be as wholesome for food as those manured with sweet and fresh fertilizing matter. But if organic matter assumed another form, it was really a new substance and harmless. The question of changed matter was brought forward every month by the Registrar-General and fallaciously estimated as pre-existing sewage, which had caused some persons to be misled as to the wholesomeness of perfectly unobjectionable waters. The matter must be utterly changed before it could safely be used, and that change could be effected on the strata of the earth by long-continued contact with mould and air. There was reason to believe it was so with chalk. Wherever the water percolated through chalk strata it was deprived of organic matter,—perfectly deprived of that changing organic matter to which he had referred as being noxious, and which was converted into nitrites and nitrates. No doubt animal charcoal could do a good deal artificially; but while a great and perfect filter-bed existed in Nature, he held it was right and proper to get for a large town, especially for London, such an amount of water perfectly filtered by Nature as to extract all organic matter from the water, whether in the original or the changing state. In that way alone could wholesome water, wanting no artificial filtration whatever, be supplied to the community.

———

LETTER of ALFRED SMEE read at a meeting of Medical Men convened to consider the Paper read by the late Dr. Letheby, 'On the Methods of estimating Nitrogenous Matters in Potable Waters, and on the Value of the expression "Previous Sewage Contamination," as used by the Registrar-General in his Monthly Reports of the Metropolitan Waters.'

DEAR SIR,—I regret that recent indisposition will prevent me from accepting the invitation to be present this evening at the reading of Dr. Letheby's paper.

The doctrine of " Pre-existing Sewage " has for some time occupied my attention, because as now understood it is one of the most dangerous fallacies of the day.

The question resolves itself into two parts:—1st. The question of pre-existing sewage contamination, as inferred from matters containing nitrogen in organic matters in the act of change, or undergoing oxidation. 2nd. The question of pre-existing sewage contamination, as inferred from the presence of nitrates which are assumed to have arisen from the final oxidation of organic matters.

On the first part of the subject I have a little to comment, because all organic matters in the act of change are bad, though doubtless sewage is materially worse than other forms of changing organic matters. The dangerous part of the doctrine is, the inference of pre-existing sewage from the presence of nitrates.

As a matter of fact nitrates may be present without any pre-existing organic matter, and every flash of lightning causes the union of the elements of the air, and the production of nitrates without any previous sewage contamination.

The originators of the doctrine of pre-existing sewage say that at any rate the presence of nitrates shows the possibility of antecedent sewage contamination.

The fallacy of the doctrine consists in assuming a possibility as a probability, and acting upon it as a reality, which in practice in this metropolis may be followed by the most disastrous consequences.

A very considerable quantity of water is supplied to London from the overflow of water from the great chalk hills which act as a perpetual storehouse.

The water from the chalk deposits, both in this country and abroad, contains a very appreciable quantity of nitrates, which does not vary in any very important manner.

Chalk water by running over water weeds loses its nitrates and greatly stimulates their growth, and especially it may be noted that the best watercresses are grown in water which has lately emanated from the depths of the chalk formation.

In consequence of this result, the metropolitan waters contain more nitrates the less they have been exposed to the contaminating influence of rivers.

The New River Company is mischievously returned by the authorities as supplying more pre-existing sewage to its customers, in proportion to the quantity of water which the company pumps from its deep springs and the less it supplies from the river. In this way, the purer the water which it supplies to its consumers, the more pre-existing sewage is officially returned by the authorities.

The origin of the nitrates in chalk waters has not been satisfactorily discovered. I myself have made many investigations on the subject, and the day before my recent indisposition believed that I had obtained a clue to the solution of the mystery, which demands full inquiry. I have considered the question under four heads:—1st. Do the nitrates come from the nitrogen and oxygen of the atmosphere? 2nd. Are the nitrates fossil products of the animals which formed the chalk deposits? 3rd. Are the nitrates the products of animal matter superimposed upon the chalk?

4th. Are the nitrates the products of animal matter on the surface of the ground washed down by rain into the chalk?

I have heard of cases of persons being deterred in times of cholera epidemics from drinking pure spring water because of the tons of pre-existing sewage with which that water was said to be contaminated, and in place thereof have taken the surface-water, springs indeed with perhaps less nitrates, but possibly with cholera poison in an active state.

It would be desirable if the medical officers of health would unite in remonstrating with the authorities against the fallacy of the doctrine of Pre-existing Sewage and the danger of promulgating such crude theories amongst the populace. It is calculated in the highest degree to suppress truth and promote error, and the officers of health should be fully prepared to deal with the fallacy before another cholera epidemic arises and victims are sacrificed to the influences of crude and undigested theories.

I have the honour to be, dear Sir,

7, FINSBURY CIRCUS,                              Your obedient servant,
    April 16th, 1869.                                        ALFRED SMEE.

---

No. XXVI.

## THE PRIVATE AND SECRET BURIAL-GROUND OF THE ORATORY. REJOINDER TO THE MANIFESTO OF DR. DALGAIRNS, PRINCIPAL OF THE ORATORY. BY ALFRED SMEE. 1863.

THE Oratory has at length spoken, by its Principal, Dr. Dalgairns, and it is my purpose to examine critically every word he has written upon the private and secret burial-ground of the Oratory.

Dr. Dalgairns declares the burial-ground to be private, but says that it is untrue and inaccurate to call it secret. Surely that is secret which is most carefully kept from everybody's knowledge. The Incumbent of the parish never heard of it, nor the tax-collector of the district, nor the next door neighbour, nor the adjoining proprietor; nor has it ever been gazetted, nor its locality fixed in any public document; and though I have No. 134 Parliamentary Paper before me, together with an accurate map of their grounds, I cannot tell, nor can anybody tell from these, where the licensed burial-ground really is.

It is not only secret, but the most secret burial-ground which has been made known to the public.

Dr. Dalgairns says that the proper protection of the dead ought to be secured and regulated by public legislation. In this we both agree, and I trust that the Government will bring this private and secret burial-ground under the protection of an Act similar to that which governs all the public burial-grounds of this kingdom.

Dr. Dalgairns says that the burial-ground is in the centre of a small property, but the persons buried are not buried in the centre, but on one side of the ground. So here further confusion as to position exists. The Inspector of Burial-grounds says the burial-ground is stiff clay, without water at eight feet. My relative was buried in sand, with water at five feet. Another mystification of identity. This conflict of evidence makes us wonder whether Dr. Dalgairns has not mistaken the place licensed. But why waste our time over words? Let the plan and licence be published and gazetted, when it will be open to all the world, and no longer remain secret. Dr. Dalgairns can cause the secrecy to cease when he desires; at present the burial-ground is still secret.

Dr. Dalgairns confirms my statement that the burial-ground has no boundary walls and no public access; that it is impossible to go thither without permission to cross the private grounds of the Oratorians. Is it right to expose the relations of those buried there to the influence of the priests, when we see that Wells, my relative, and Dr. Faber left all their possessions to another of their body? I ask public access and boundary walls, and surely, sooner or later, my request will be granted.

Now something more serious has to be answered. Dr. Dalgairns says, "It is untrue that we keep no register of burials." Show the register, Dr. Dalgairns, and prove when the register was written. I am in a position to substantiate upon oath that every inquiry by letter or personally has been rejected. Personal application has been answered by "I do not know." Letters have not been answered at all. This is a matter deserving of the fullest parliamentary inquiry. A register—and cannot be seen; a register—and Dr. Dalgairns to judge who is to see it.

Surely this is the grossest violation of the spirit of the burial laws which has ever come before the public.

Dr. Dalgairns may endeavour to keep the register secret, but surely the Legislature will compel him to make it public.

Dr. Dalgairns seeks to explain the change of names on tombstones. He states that my family knew my relative by the name of William. This is true. William was his name, and we all addressed him by the name of William till the day of his death.

He described himself by the name of William in his will, and is known to the outer world by the name of William.

The Oratorians, however, knew him only by the name of Anthony, and on his tombstone he is called William Anthony, so that positively we have one person going by three different names. What can be more damnatory to secret burial-grounds and secret registers? How is the money to be traced in Chancery, and by the Chancellor of the Exchequer when he looks after the succession duty, which will be pretty large by-and-by? The great lawyers in the House of Commons may solve this question; for what is affirmed of William will be denied by those who only know Anthony; and what is affirmed of William Anthony, will be denied of William, and also of Anthony.

William was my brother-in-law, Anthony was the Oratorian, and William Anthony was buried at Sydenham. There will be no possible method of describing my brother-in-law hereafter but by calling him William, sometimes called Anthony, sometimes called William Anthony.

Who could possibly imagine that Frederick Fortescue, the Oratorian, was the same person as Albanus, the gentleman buried?

Where property exists, names should be distinct.

Dr. Dalgairns says that the wishes of the dead should be respected. Does Dr. Dalgairns not know that my relative had no wish, had no will of his own,—had passed his will and wish over absolutely and entirely to Dr. Faber? Is it not so expressed in his so-called will when he states that he desires to be buried where the Superior shall direct?

My relative met Dr. Faber at the Bishop's house at Birmingham, where he was kept, and I was not permitted to have access to him. Faber there persuaded him of the necessity of implicit obedience, and desired him to quit his family and former friends for ever.

I begged and implored him in vain to renounce the obedience to Faber, and have a living mind for himself.

Only one answer was given,—that I did not understand, and could not comprehend, Christian obedience; and that he was bound implicitly to follow out Dr. Faber's instructions for his salvation.

How can Dr. Dalgairns, then, talk of the will or wish of my relative, or of Dr. Wells? They had parted with their will or wish, and it was Faber's will or wish which regulated everything; and he did so decide their wish and will, that he got their property by the so-called wills.

I asked Father Rowe if there was a will. He replied that he did not know. As this seemed to me impossible, I pressed the question again, when he said that Father Stanton, who was acting for Father Faber, knew these things. On again pressing the question, he said he would go and ask. He did go. He returned, and after a short time Father Knox entered, and said he was executor, and he would undertake the funeral.

Now Father Rowe's name appears as a witness to the will, and to this day I cannot tell whether his name has been forged, whether he did know there was a will, or whether he was under the influence of religious obedience, and dared not answer without the leave of the Superior.

I and my son attended my relative's funeral, and received great courtesy and much valuable information, which I now acknowledge publicly with thanks; and I now write publicly what I also wrote privately on my return from the funeral :—

"7, Finsbury Circus.

"DEAR SIR.—I have to return you and the other members of the Oratory my most grateful acknowledgments, as well as that of Mrs. Smee, for the manner in which William Hutchison has been treated during his severe affliction; and have no hesitation in stating that, to the best of my belief, as far as his bodily ailments have been concerned, everything under the circumstances has been done which kindness and humanity could suggest, and that he has invariably received that attention which might have been expected from gentlemen and Christians. But to the spiritual intimidation under which he has been kept by certain persons from the moment he entered the Bishop's house at Birmingham, I consider his premature death has been due; and I believe that this spiritual control is not only opposed to Christian principles, but is contrary to the law of the land, and for this I hold all implicated responsible.

"I remain, dear Sir,

"REV. FATHER KNOX,                    "Yours respectfully,
"The Oratory, Brompton.                    "ALFRED SMEE."

Dr. Dalgairns says "we are unbound by vow." Dr. Dalgairns, how do you belong to the Order of St. Philip Neri and make no vow? Why, Dr. Dalgairns, did you put on the black cloak to look like monks if you were not monks? And why did you pull it off again when the Queen's proclamation forbidding monastic gowns came out, if it was not a monastic emblem?

I have always understood that the Oratorians were the Jesuits of Jesuits; that where the Jesuits could not get in the Oratorians did. And surely you of the Oratory, who have got so much money together, have not falsified your character for high intellect, political intrigue, and the hold you obtain over your followers to get their money.

Dr. Dalgairns quotes Father Faber's relatives. I fear that they have suffered most acutely for his conduct; and when they have seen family after family separated, and seen the members of these families, over whose mind he had the singular power of exercising so complete a control, estranged from brother and sister, they may well be expected to have been horrified.

This powerful control of one mind over another seems inexplicable, though it is true. The separation from family and loss of property is too bad for complaint; and how can the widow or orphan complain when I scarce dare complain?

It is not worthy of the members of St. Philip Neri to deny they are monks, that they belong to an order and do not belong to an order, as it suits their purpose. Dr. Dalgairns says they can leave without dispensation or permission, either from the Superior or any other ecclesiastical authority whatever. This does not correspond with that implicit obedience which Faber exacted. And when Dalgairns says that "the obedience which we pay to the rule of the Superior has no place here," it is in entire variance with the action and statements of my relative. He told me that obedience to his Superior was absolutely necessary to salvation. I have urged this matter over and over again, with the same result.

My relative's life and death was an example of the doctrine of implicit obedience. When Faber ordered him to leave his family and friends, he did so! When he told him to make his will, he did so, and in Faber's favour.

Now, as a matter of fact, from the moment my relative came in contact with Dr. Faber, he acted most implicitly as he was directed. My relative on many occasions pointed to the value of this implicit obedience, as by that they were enabled to embarrass the Ministry and Parliament. In fact, so great and necessary is implicit obedience, in the opinion of the Oratorian votaries, that it is respected as far more important than truth. Truth, he has argued, is doubtless a great virtue, more important, however, for mercantile circles than for religious circles. In fact, truth is very well, but faith is higher; but highest of all is Christian obedience.

My relative has declared to me that the community could dare the Government and Parliament to interfere with them; that they could cause a riot when they liked; and triumphantly pointed to the Hyde Park riots in illustration. He always represented that the Ministry were afraid of them, because the members acted together, and, by throwing their weight in on even-balanced questions, could decide the issue. This was always pointed out as the aim and effect of religious houses, and the obedience they enforced.

Are the counsels of this great country to be embarrassed by the Oratory? Are Whigs and Tories—each honestly fighting for their opinions—to be controlled by a score of the monks of St. Philip Neri, who out-Jesuit the Jesuits? A new party must be made up of Whigs and Tories who can honestly submit questions for discussion without the interference of the congregation of the Oratory, acting obediently to their priests. Liberty requires that the Government of this country should be freed from such coercion by the abolition of the Oratory.

My relative, under this notion of Christian obedience, was not in any way the master of either his capital, his income, or any of his actions.

As an important fact, Faber got my relative's money. Faber got Wells's money; and Faber, again, has left his money to another priest.

Dr. Dalgairns says that we (N.B.—Who?) are justly fond of liberty. Then abolish the Oratory, which prevents liberty; abolish all wills where liberty of action is prevented under religious terror. It is for the sake of insuring liberty of conscience and action that monastic houses should be abolished. In future give persons the liberty to make wills for themselves, not for their priests; and I know that I am carrying out the will and wish of my relative's un-Fabered mind when I expose Faber's iniquitous control.

It is true that I do not exactly know what my relative's fortune was; I believe it was upwards of ———, and that I understated it before, to be within the truth.

I understand that the executors propose to swear the personalty under ———, but how are they going to deal with his share of the Oratory estate? It is of no use to attempt to suppress this question; sooner or later it must be answered, as it is contrary to the policy of the State to allow the fortunes of families to be absorbed by confraternities: if the acquisitions of the Oratory continue at the same rate, they will soon reach an enormous amount.

The statement made of the excellence of my brother-in-law I am too happy to confirm. He was one of the most truly good men I ever knew. From conscience, and conscience alone, he became a Roman Catholic. From a conscientious belief in the necessity of implicit obedience, he gave up his family, to whom he was intensely attached. From an anxious attempt to do good he sacrificed his life by devotion, and a continual conflict, which was manifestly going on between Christian obedience and family affection. Whilst he was so good, Dr. Dalgairns, why did your community have everlasting punishment as the effect of non-obedience to the cruel order to separate himself?

Dr. Dalgairns rejoices over my disappointment at not getting my relative's money. Disappointment! Dr. Dalgairns. Do you give me credit for such imbecility as not to have known that the moment my relative met Faber he would be denuded of every farthing? I wrote to him, when Faber denied me access to him at Birmingham, to that effect; and I have told him in his lifetime that when they had run through his money I would receive him at my house; for he was so high-minded and truthful that we fully believed that some day he would leave Faber in disgust.

Religious influence is slow and subtle, but sure; for what will a religious man not do to save his soul?

It is true he was writing a book up to the day of his death. For the sake of the honour of the human mind in this century, it should be known that the book, which treats of some fifty special interpositions of the Almighty, was written when the unfortunate sufferer was dying of disease of the brain.

The end is a clue to the melancholy story. Here was the brain active and showing the utmost partial intelligence, gradually being destroyed; and the same incapacity to judge of the truth of hopping houses, and other concocted miracles, made him incapable to judge of the truth of Faber's pretension to rule his mind.

Where there is organic disease of the brain, the mind may be active and capable in a high degree of exercising some functions, and yet be damaged and incapable of performing other functions.

My relative was capable of doing great things, but incapable of resisting the unnatural influence which Faber exerted.

Dalgairns asserts that I want to introduce the principles of foreign legislation. Certainly I do, as far as religious houses are concerned. Many minds seem incapable, as a matter of fact, of resisting the combined action of priests. In foreign Catholic countries they have had more experience of priestly mode of action to secure the property of their members. I believe myself that the Oratory is the most dangerous form of Catholic confraternity. These houses have been suppressed before, and doubtless will be again; and therefore the simple question is, are the monastic houses in England now of sufficient importance to be abolished? That is a matter for the Legislature to decide.

Dr. Dalgairns argues that an heir-at-law has no right, but every person in a family has a natural expectancy over the fortune of every other member. He had this natural right to his sister's property, and his sister had a natural right to her brother's.

These religious houses disturb the natural right, and not only are they destructive by an absorption of the property, but also from the loss of the influence and mutual assistance which takes place by intermarriages.

Dr. Dalgairns says that he left a small reminder to his oldest and most intimate friend, meaning Dr. Faber. Perhaps the world will estimate Dr. Faber as his deadliest foe; but why did he leave his property before to the Duke of Norfolk, and why did not Dr. Faber leave the money to his own family, who are known to have paid his college expenses, and are supposed to have supported him at the time immediately preceding his hold over my relative?

I will tell Dr. Dalgairns why. The whole transaction is a sham: and the will found within the walls of the Oratory, leaving the money to the head of the Oratory, with witnesses members of the Oratory, and the executor another member of the Oratory, is for their common benefit; that they are all co-partners; and consequently that Dr. Dalgairns himself is benefited by this legacy.

The fortune which my relative possessed when Faber obtained his mental rule, was not saved or collected by himself, but by his father and uncle, for the general good of his family. Nothing can tend more to prevent persons from saving money, if the successor, to save his soul, must give it to his confessor, as my relative did.

It is folly to argue that my relative could do as he pleased with his money. He could not. He was bound by a spell. He had been cajoled into believing that hell was his perpetual doom, if he did not obey Faber.

I asked my relative if I should be damned, as I was the keeper of my own mind. He replied that I did not know the necessity of obedience: he did. He was bound to act from his knowledge of this necessity to salvation; but that God, of His mercy, might pity my ignorance of it, though, if once I realized that necessity to my mind, I should imperil my soul if I did not yield.

Dr. Dalgairns says it is implied that the secret burial-ground would be used in cases of murder. This is an ingenious phantom he has raised simply that he may knock it down. Such a thought never occurred to me; but, as he has raised the question, is it desirable as a matter of prudence to let any confraternity have a secret and private burial-ground?

Now, when Dalgairns disdains to notice the allegation as to scheming monks without visible means of living, I tell him he cannot answer it, for it is true, in substance and fact, that Father Faber had not one farthing when he secured my relative, and that he was even supposed to be living upon the charity of his family at that moment. He had no cheque-books at that time; he had no banking account that Dr. Dalgairns could examine. If there be one redeeming point of that man who subverted natural affection, it was that he for conscience sake left a good church preferment and became a pauper. But an ambitious man made no bad exchange when he secured the formation of the Oratory, and was constituted its head.

Again, when Dr. Dalgairns asks how he can disprove that the house of the Oratory is so constructed to favour the concealment of men of position, I reply, Show the plan, when everybody will see that it is a house within a house, and admirably adapted for concealment.

I have frequently had the greatest difficulty even to know how my relative was, when by long silence his sister feared illness.

Dr. Dalgairns alludes to my assertion that I am prepared to offer myself for election to Parliament, that I may ask the Secretary for information which he stated he would only give to Parliament—if I cannot get it by other means. But Dr. Dalgairns must see that I am bent upon action, not upon trashy words and arguments. Private and secret burial-grounds must cease; religious obedience must be controlled; and I am prepared to offer myself, at any convenient opportunity, to support measures to prevent priests of any denomination obtaining money from those over whom they hold control under the fear of eternal damnation.

It is perfectly true I am well off, if not to spend my income is to be well off.

Were I otherwise situated than I am, how could I dare brook the denunciation of a confraternity with such great power as the Oratorians, who pride themselves on managing the Legislature of this great kingdom?

There was always the most intimate affection between my brother-in-law and myself, and up to the latest day of his life he took great interest in watching everything I was doing, and frequently knew more what appeared in the papers with reference to myself than I did. I heap no obloquy upon my relative; I place it on the head of Faber.

My relative was one of the kindest and best men I ever knew, and I must confess it was a great consolation to me to have been permitted to see him the last few weeks of his life—for which I give the Oratorians my best thanks.

The same intimate cordiality seemed to exist as formerly during these visits.

But why? He told me that Faber was dying, and he ceased to see him; and upon Faber's head and memory the obloquy of separating him from his family rests; and I assert, not only did Faber separate him, but the public have a right to know how many others he has separated from their families, and to what extent the same practices are now prevailing.

The Oratorians, present and future, will have the money. I regard all as co-partners, and doubtless a full inquiry will lead to an important change in the law of this country. Secret and private burial-grounds should be rendered public; authorized burial registers should be kept; and paupers under the veil of religion should lose the power of getting the money of those whom they persuade must be obedient to secure their salvation.

Therefore it is not a matter of wonder that others have not complained; it is only extraordinary that I can bring my mind to expose this terrible faculty which Faber possessed.

Faber did not use the unnatural faculty for nothing; he had no property when he met my relative at the Bishop's house; and how many families whose money he has obtained, and was in process of obtaining at the time of his death, may never be clearly known.

Now, Dr. Dalgairns, I have but one more word; you insinuate insult in your concluding paragraph, and will perhaps carry it into the House of Commons by members under your control. If you deceive yourself, you will not deceive the world, as to our present position. I give you and your colleagues credit for courtesy and kindness of manner, and have not a word to say against you or them personally, and, as far as my limited acquaintance is concerned, I should esteem them. This question is not a question of religion, and now I have no comment to make upon the form of religion which you follow. I am acting in my capacity as a civilian, and not as a partisan for any one special form of religion; and I ask all Roman Catholics, Protestants, and Dissenters to join in considering calmly the question, before the entire country is roused to indignation. Retract in time, Dr. Dalgairns, if you wish justice. My complaint against you, Dr. Dalgairns—not personally, but as the head of the Oratory—is:

1. That you have a private and secret burial-ground, without public access or boundary walls, which has no public register of burials, and where the names on the tombstones are changed.
2. That this private and secret burial-ground, and the means of concealment you have in your houses, are used to obtain money from converts under religious intimidation.
3. That one of your body did cause my relative, under the fear of eternal damnation, to appropriate upwards of £40,000 to purposes dictated by your Superior.

I quote one case to illustrate the general principle, and for that I ask that your Order of St. Philip Neri may be banished from this country, and the control of the burial-ground may be assimilated to the general law of the land.

There are clauses in the Roman Catholic Relief Act of 1829,—by which Act members of that Church were admitted to Parliament and to various offices in the State,—which are intended to provide for the suppression of Jesuit and other monastic establishments in this country. My sad experience has brought me to the conviction that the intention of these clauses ought to be carried out for the protection of families in this country, and in defence of the freedom to which every inhabitant of this country is entitled, but which the members of these establishments abuse and invade, unless legal enactments are adopted and enforced which can restrain the tyrannical and covetous practices of these orders.

---

### APPENDIX.

*Correspondence with Sir George Grey in citation of Parliamentary Paper No. 134.*

March 30th. 1864.

Sir,—May I venture to take the liberty to ask whether the private and secret burial-ground of the Oratory at Sydenham is an exceptional case, or whether any other licences have been granted to confraternities of Roman Catholics, or of any other religious creed, for the use of a burial-ground where no register is kept, and where the names on the tombstones are falsified?

Roman Catholics are more interested in this inquiry than other denominations, because their families are more exposed to be victimised by the Oratorians; and even the late Duke of Norfolk, who applied for the licence, and who, before the money was left to Dr. Faber, had the entire fortune of my relative left to his Grace, doubtless for the purposes of the Oratory, will suffer, as the Oratorians, whose schemes he assisted, have persuaded his Grace's daughter to enter a nunnery in Paris.

These private and secret burial-grounds are of much importance to the Oratory, as they lead to the inference of an entire separation and estrangement of the members from their families, an intimate union between themselves, and consequently the possession of the money for their common purposes.

The Rev. Father Knox, the executor to the will of my relative, obligingly told me, in answer to my inquiries, that the Oratory estate paid no legacy or succession duty; that they passed it from one to another. In confirmation of this, I found that the will of Frederick Fortescue Wells, whose name is changed on the tombstone to Albanus Wells, and whose money Dr. Faber also got, was proved under £300; and we have Dr. Dalgairns' authority (the present head of the Oratory) for stating that the will of my relative will be sworn under £5000, and thus the large possessions which the Oratory has already acquired will be ignored. Under these circumstances, the changed names on the tombstones, as destroying means of identification, is of importance to the Oratory, and its prevention a matter of consequence to the State, as some future Chancellor of the Exchequer may claim the duty years hence.

I venture most respectfully to solicit that you will grant me the fullest particulars, as no person can tell how many families have been injured by Dr. Faber and his colleagues. When the Oratorians get the money, they abuse the family they deprive, to stifle complaint; and fear deters many men and most women from brooking the insult of an organization so powerful as to include the names of Faber, of Dalgairns, and the other priests of the Oratory, assisted by Bowyer and lawyers of high rank, and who have newspapers under their control to vilify the families of those whom the Oratorians deprive.

April 4th, 1864.

Sir,—I am most anxiously awaiting your answer to my request to know if there are any other private and secret burial-grounds besides that at Sydenham, so that the public may be informed upon the matter before it comes before the House of Commons. Since that letter, I have carefully perused the papers which you have presented to Parliament upon the private and secret burial-ground of the Oratory belonging to the Order of St. Philip Neri, and I most respectfully urge that they do not contain that information which the relatives of those there buried are entitled to have.

1. The position of the burial-ground of 500 square yards in the garden is not given. The definition of the precise spot allotted as a burial-ground is the more important, as the Government inspector has stated that it is on the part of the ground constituted of stiff clay, and without water at eight feet from the surface: whereas at the spot where my relation was buried the ground was sand or sandy clay, with water at five feet. Dr. Dalgairns states that it is the centre of the ground, whereas it is on one side. This discrepancy might be immediately used by Oratorians, keen in the use of words, should any dispute as to position arise.

2. The ownership of the land is not given. The estate at Sydenham belonged to the family of the Bowdens, and is mixed up in a complicated trust, whereas it is provided that, should the trust be illegal, the property shall vest in its former owners; a provision showing that the skilled barristers who have been consulted have been perfectly well aware of the provision of the Catholic Relief Act,—fear themselves that they could not evade the law, so that years hence this land may fall into different hands, and the graves of the dead may be desecrated.

The terms of their licence are not given. The necessity of a correct public burial-register is paramount, and at present all access to a register has been denied. I most respectfully urge for your consideration that I, as husband of the next-of-kin and heir-at-law of a person there buried, ought to possess this information, and therefore I trust that you, as Conservator of the burial-grounds of this country, will kindly furnish me with these facts.

Whitehall,<br>April 5th, 1864.

Sir,—I am directed by Secretary Sir George Grey to acknowledge the receipt of your letters of the 30th and 4th, and to inform you that although several licences have at various times been given for the opening of a burial-ground for the exclusive use of the members of a particular religious community, he has not the means of informing you whether a register is kept of the interments in such burial-grounds, or whether the names, if any, on the tombstones are falsified, as these matters do not come within the scope of the power vested in the Secretary of State by the Acts which regulate the burial of the dead.

I am, Sir, your obedient servant,<br>H. A. Bruce.

*Petition of* ALFRED SMEE, *Fellow of the Royal Society, of No. 7,*
*Finsbury Circus, in the City of London,*

Sheweth.

That on the 16th of July, 1863, your Petitioner attended the funeral
of a relative in a private garden attached to a house called St. Mary's at
Sydenham, in Kent, belonging to the members of the Order of St. Philip
Neri, now located at a building called the Oratory at Brompton, in the
county of Middlesex.

That your Petitioner was informed by the Rev. William Knox, one of
the members of the Order, that this garden had a licence, which was procured by representations made to the Secretary of State by his Grace the
late Duke of Norfolk, whose family was in close association with the
members of the Order, and assisted them in their various schemes.

That your Petitioner has seen his Grace, the present heir to the
dukedom of Norfolk, with his Grace's brother, assisting in ecclesiastical
garments in the public performance of services on the 16th July, 1863, at
the Catholic chapel at the Oratory at Brompton, in conjunction with the
priests of the Oratory, and also subsequently on the same day at the
garden of the house called St. Mary's at Sydenham.

That young men of position and wealth are concealed from their
friends by the members of the Order, that they may be converted from
their faith, and that their property may be obtained for the maintenance
of the Order.

That the existence of the burial-ground at St. Mary's at Sydenham
was unknown to the clergy of the parish of Sydenham, to the neighbouring landowners, and to the tax-collector; and your Petitioner has been
informed that the Ordnance surveyors were ignorant of its existence.

That the part of the garden used as a burial-ground has no boundary
walls and no public access.

That the persons there buried are described on tombstones by names
falsified by the addition of a second Christian name, so that the names on
the tombstones do not correspond with the names known to the families,
or with names as used by themselves in their wills, whereby the means of
identification are destroyed.

That no register of burials is kept; and up to this moment your
Petitioner has not been able, after many applications, to obtain a certificate of the burial of your Petitioner's relative.

That the house at the Oratory at Brompton is so constructed as to
afford means of concealment.

Your Petitioner therefore humbly prays that your honourable House
may institute an inquiry into the facts alleged, to ascertain whether it
may not be desirable that legislative enactments should be framed to
compel the owners of the burial-ground at St. Mary's at Sydenham to
erect boundary walls, to afford public access, and to keep a public register
of persons there buried, as required under the general Burial Act in force
in this country; also to institute an inquiry whether it may not be desirable that enactments should be framed for the more effectual protection of
families from the concealment of individuals in the houses of these confraternities or religious societies, and from the combined action of the
members of the Order to deprive the heirs-at-law of the fortunes of their

converts and members; and, lastly, to institute an inquiry whether laws in other countries to protect families and heirs-at-law from the combined actions of the members of confraternities and members of religious societies may not be beneficially followed in the construction of enactments to restrain members of the Order of St. Philip Neri, or other monastic orders, from absorbing the property of those whom they convert, or induce to become members of such orders.

---

## No. XXVII.

### PRACTICAL REMEDY FOR EXTORTION AND INTIMIDATION PRACTISED BY THE AID OF THE SUPERIOR LAW COURTS.

*(Pamphlet.* ANON.)

THE continual increase of extortion and intimidation through the medium of the superior Law Courts is now attracting great attention, not only among the mercantile and professional classes of the community, but also among the higher class of solicitors, who are greatly scandalised by the extent of this demoralizing practice.

In the innumerable methods by which the superior Law Courts contribute to this end, there are always similar circumstances—a needy client, an artful lawyer, and a man with money to be attacked.

The lawyer declares that he is the mere agent, and although the cause may be bad, yet his client is a great rascal, and orders him to proceed; and therefore, to avoid solicitors' and counsel's fees, and the expenses, he had better compromise and pay at once, as the cheapest thing which can be done.

The sum total extorted annually from persons of respectability, and which goes into the pockets of the lawyers, in the aggregate is very large.

As far as possible, the actual mode is a charge damaging to reputation, and calculated to raise a question and prejudice in the public mind : such as, firstly, a charge of wrong professional advice; secondly, a charge of infringing the patent law; thirdly, a charge of fraud, which is chiefly directed against those engaged with public companies; fourthly, a charge of *ultra vires*, where there is a trust; fifthly, a demand for money with only partial information ; and, sixthly, the extortion is effected by keeping possession of a house or other property.

As a matter of experience, most men will make sacrifices to prevent charges, as denials and explanations will not prevent those in a similar line of business from stating that such a charge was made; and hence these cases are usually compromised, by the payment of the bill of costs, and perhaps some small sum to the client in addition.

The remedy for all this is very simple. The extortion cannot be effected without the lawyer : then let him be responsible for the transaction, and if fraud is charged improperly, or an untrue attack is made, let him and his client conjointly be liable for damages.

In our present social state, there is no greater damage that a man can receive than a false attack in law or Chancery. The immense expense of lawyers, counsel, and witnesses—the harass of mind and damage to reputation—are excessive; and yet there is no remedy against such severe injury. The man attacked must lose. He can never get more than a portion of his costs, and yet at this moment no remedy is provided.

Wherever we turn, these cases of injury and gross injustice crowd upon our view; and though they can never be got at in their exact detail, by a variation of names, circumstances, and place, a few specimens of extortion may be safely glanced at for the purpose of considering the general phase of the subject.

Mr. Bolus, a medical practitioner, sends in his bill of £20 to Mr. Crafty, who apparently was a respectable tradesman. The answer was, "You maltreated me; I shall try an action against you, unless you give me £1000." Terrified and alarmed, Mr. Bolus consulted a London surgeon, who begged him to resist the claim, as he treated the case very skilfully. A writ was served; the case was carried to the eve of trial; the trial was countermanded. The medical man was harassed for months by the charge, when suddenly Mr. Crafty becomes a bankrupt without assets. If the lawyer, who had done rightly to effect a compromise, had been liable, this attempted extortion could not have been perpetrated.

Mr. Faith consulted Mr. Quack upon a secret malady. Mr. Quack sent in a bill of £700, carried the case to London, at great cost, to the eve of trial, when it was abandoned, and it was discovered that Mr. Quack had evaporated to America. Surely the lawyer here was as bad as Mr. Quack. Several in London live by this method.

Great cruelties are practised under the Patent Laws. In a village the greater part of the people made a respectable but slender living by turning black buttons into white by a chemical process. One fine morning, whilst their operations proceeded peaceably and quietly, a writ was served upon each by Mr. Whiting, a patentee of a similar process. What was to be done? The whole village was in consternation. They thought they were all ruined. In this dilemma they sent one of their body to London to consult a scientific man who had written the book they consulted upon turning black buttons into white. This gentleman was interested in their case, and told them that they did not infringe the patent, but that they must put in an appearance to the writ. With difficulty they got together £5, which they took to a solicitor, when no further proceedings were taken. Here were men harassed for months by the bold manœuvre of Whiting, which would unquestionably have succeeded but for the kind gratuitous advice of the scientific man.

In the same way the pioneers of photography were greatly harassed by Mr. Sunshine, who claimed to be the original inventor and patentee of sun-portraits. Now Mr. Sunshine was a wealthy man, and had great possessions in Moonland, and was very ambitious of a baronetcy, which he is supposed to have lost from his practice. Why should he not have been made to pay for the great injury he inflicted upon the poor photographers?

Public companies are peculiarly exposed to this kind of fraud. The directors, or some of them, in the Waste Land Regeneration Company received a polite note from Messrs. Catchem and Squeezem, asking them to call, as they have something very particular to communicate, having been consulted by the Rev. Dr. Blackleg. That having failed, a clerk was sent with a long bill, stating his employers take a great deal of interest in the company and do not wish to do it any harm, but the reverend doctor has some shares in it by virtue of some assumed services; and as he is largely in debt, wants the company to buy his shares immediately, so that he may pay some of the more pressing of his debts. He stated that the reverend doctor had written a frightful charge of fraud, which they will be compelled to file, and if they do file they must advertise according to law. As friends and well-wishers of the company, his employers, Messrs. Catchem and Squeezem, advise an immediate payment to the reverend doctor, who must have money. Any attempt to wind up the company must injure it, and cost besides a great deal of money. In truth, if the company gains, the reverend doctor has no money wherewith to pay the costs; and besides, the doctor is a desperate character, having misapplied money of the Society for the Promotion of the use of Coloured Trousers, and embezzled money given to him to pay the bills of the Young Hottentots' Improvement School.

A safe remedy would be to make Catchem and Squeezem, as well as the pious doctor, responsible to every person he sought to damage by endeavouring to extort money by the aid of the Court of Chancery.

In this case their number is legion, for all who hold the improved land—all the shareholders, all the surveyors, engineers, clerks, and work-people—may be damaged by the injury the society received from this charge. In the end the shareholders desired a compromise, and the Rev. Dr. Blackleg got some hundreds of pounds to stop the case going further than the advertisement, but that itself did great damage to its financial credit.

As another example of the same kind, the Rev. Mr. Snowdon is a great buyer of shares to sell again at the Stock Exchange. When he makes money, he does so; when he cannot, he charges false statements. The cases are generally compromised, to prevent scandal, and this man alone has extorted money from many companies.

When companies are in difficulties some lawyers advertise for clients, and guarantee them against costs, for which they allow them to harass the directors; and the more respectable and more numerous they are, the better the game—the better for the lawyers. Messrs. Thief and Robber live entirely in this way, and by charging fraud against every person, however remotely connected with the company, are sure to find some who dare not resist their extortion. The real plaintiff is not allowed to have any voice in the matter. Now, surely Thief and Robber are the real plaintiffs, and ought to be held responsible for the false charge and liable for damages and costs to their victims.

Winding-up companies are invariably attended by an accountant and a lawyer. Mr. Accurate, the accountant, has got large estates that way; and Mr. Virtuous made a fortune by the winding up of the Celestial Bank, to the great damage of the poor shareholders and depositors.

Another form of extortion is practised by making a claim and not giving particulars. Mr. Hardup has a claim against Mr. Easy, who is liable. "Granted," says Mr. Easy, "but tell me what your claim is and how it was incurred." "Find out yourself," says Hardup. "I simply tell you I have a claim." "I cannot," says Easy; "I do not know where to get the information." "Then here is a writ," says Hardup, "and expenses begin this day." The case is carried up to trial, and stopped; and this is repeated till Easy has much more than he ought to pay extorted from him to stop the continual expense of getting up the defence.

It is contrary to public policy that the lawyers should be able to institute actions for their own benefit. In every case where they have a pauper client, he is entirely in their hands. In the celebrated case of "Box *versus* Cox," where Box took two suits of clothes from home, and put one on the edge of a precipice, and walked off in the other, Box appeared to be dead. Box's brother, who was in league with Box, claimed under a policy from the Pay-in-every-case Assurance Company. Everybody saw through the trick. The judge, jury, and public were astonished at it. But Box's brother could not stop, because then his own lawyer, Mr. Gammonem, would have made him bankrupt for his costs; and if he did go on, he was told he might have a sympathising jury, who would patronise the individual against the company, and save him from expenses. Surely, Mr. Gammonem ought to be liable for the costs, as his interest in the office was much larger than that of his client. Box's barristers are said not to be paid to this day, and the Pay-in-every case Assurance Company have lost hundreds in law costs.

Not only needy lawyers who are in league with roguish plaintiffs, but needy counsel are sometimes in similar collusions; for in hardly any extortion case is the fee paid before trial. If the plaintiff wins, the counsel gets paid; if he loses, the plaintiff is bankrupt, and the lawyer regrets the absence of funds.

How can it satisfy the public to hear fervid eloquence by a briefless barrister, when Mrs. Briefless and the little ones at home are dependent for their dinner upon the result of the case? When a barrister deliberately goes into court and makes an attack to secure his fee, he is equally guilty of extortion as the lawyer or plaintiff, and all ought to be equally liable to the defendant for his costs and for the damage he causes.

It is not only on the plaintiff's side that extortion is practised. There is a class of cases, especially with respect to the letting of houses, where a false defence is used as a means of extortion. This is so frequent, that hardly any person who has had to do with house property has not been victimised. In this case, a needy man gets into possession, pays no rent, does damage to the property, and will not go till he has extorted money, which is done by a false defence instituted by a low attorney.

It is, perhaps, quite unnecessary to burden this sketch with fuller illustrations of extortion and intimidation, for even respectable solicitors know that they themselves sometimes have money extorted from them.

The principle of the remedy for extortion and intimidation is plain. Make all participators responsible and liable for the damage which they seek to commit.

Firstly. Where fraud is charged, or complaint made, or occupation of property kept without adequate cause, let the plaintiff be liable for the damage.

Secondly. Where the plaintiff has not the means to incur the liability, let the lawyer and barrister who propagate these false charges be liable for the damage.

Thirdly. Where plaintiff, lawyer, and barrister are paupers together, and seek to extort money, let the defendant have the power of requiring security for costs and damages before the charges are either published, advertised, or come before a public court.

The application of Courts of Law and Equity for the purposes of extortion and intimidation has a highly demoralizing effect upon society. The respectable community shrink with horror from the scene of a Law or Chancery Court. Stop extortion and intimidation in the name of law and equity, by making lawyers and barristers responsible when getting the wages of extortion and intimidation, and the Law Courts of this country will again command the affection of all friends of order.

July 1st, 1863.

*Postscript.*—The cases given in this pamphlet, although so like the truth that many readers may think they know the particulars to which they refer, are nevertheless, as a matter of course, pure creations of the imagination, and have no relation to any person, place, or real circumstance. If any reader should think the cap fits, and should apply any of the fanciful creations to himself or friends, the thought comes from a guilty conscience; let him wear the cap, and be thankful he has not got that measure of justice to which he is so rightly entitled.

---

## No. XXVIII.

## THE PUPPET PARLIAMENT OF EARL RUSSELL, K.G.

### (*A Political Skit.* ANON.)

EARL RUSSELL has postponed his doctrine of Final Reform to a more convenient season. His partisans could not bear to change their Reform Club into an auction mart for the sale of constituencies, and so the building stands as a nest for illiberal demagogues, for the denunciators of all governing authority, and for partisans of every form of spurious religion, or of no religion at all.

Earl Russell's bill is not final; it is not even the penultimate. It is to be followed by a series of little bills, which are designed to make Members of Parliament the abject tools of the populace, and destroy their personal individuality, so that at last they may be the mechanical puppets of the people.

When Earl Russell perfects his Parliament, flesh and blood will not be required, humanity must be dispensed with, or an independent mind might show its transcendent power, and for one moment resist the crying desire of an illiterate mob.

The ultimate perfection of Earl Russell's Reform will be the completion of his suppression of mind and reason, by the substitution of mechanical puppets for rational thinking beings.

Each seat in the House of Commons, instead of being occupied by a living soul responsible to God for acts and thoughts, will be filled by a graven wooden idol, fitted with machinery for saying Aye and Nay, and worked by electric wires from the several counties and boroughs having the privilege, and obligation of returning members to Parliament.

Of these wooden-headed Puppets the majority will, like speaking dolls, simply say, Aye and Nay; but others will require more elaborate cries, which the genius of Wheatstone will doubtless be able to supply.

The Brightian Puppet will speak when pulled by its constituents: "Down with—Down with—Down with—All formalities—Court Breeches—The Throne—The House of Lords—The Church—The Army—The Navy—Everybody!"

By ingenious machinery the ejaculations will be uttered at intervals, by indifferently coupling together the phrases. In this manner everything will be said that brainless demagogues now say, and Dr. Percy can utilize the steam-engine now used to cool the heated heads and calm the excited hearts of the present Members, to make the popular Puppet roar and roar again.

Other representative images will be made to shout "Sing, sing!" when moved by the Papistical Manning wire, and the condensed steam from the engine will pour forth tears from the eyes of another image when Oratorian priests are reviled for their girl and boy concealing propensities.

"No State Church, no Church Rates!" the Binney wire will move. "No gallows!" the murderer's puppet will cry. Burglers and garrotters will make their puppet shout, "No flogging!" With these and a few other words, howled by wooden images, the Puppet Parliament would be so complete that no one could fail to recognize it as the present House of Commons one stage further Darwinially developed towards the Russellian perfection.

The Puppets of Parliament will have no responsibility, as men have, but will be obedient to the persons who set them up. A puppet has no conscience; has no belief in moral law, and dispenses with all religion, or even the notion of a God. Glorious news for those reformers who seek to annihilate the Church, and to destroy an obedience to the One over-governing Power!

Over the doorway of the Puppet House of Commons will be written in letters of brass, "The mob is God;" and in the House itself a suitable cartoon will be painted, depicting the triumph of Russell over Mind and Religion.

It is strange that Gladstone, in his advocacy of a puppet Parliament, should denounce the votes of dockyard labourers, and declare that dockyard representatives should be protected from the influence of dockyard labourers. Gladstone views with horror the possibility of Phinn, Otway, Martin, or Kinglake standing, cap in hand, at the dockyard gates, to beg and pray for dockyard votes, when the men are skilled enough to know that the term Liberal Reformer is that which is used for an illiberal paymaster. When the candidates earnestly implore, the men are wont to sneer; and if rumours are well founded, it is a costly proceeding for the country whenever the so-called Liberal Government causes the men to vote against any candidate opposed to Reform Club tyranny. Why this inconsistency? Tell us, we pray thee. For why shall you give all other classes their puppets, and refuse them to dockyard labourers?

Gladstone, you are now upon your trial! It is for you to decide whether you will attain to one of the highest pinnacles in the temple of Fame by joining the great party of Lawmakers, or sink into insignificance by becoming a Ministerial Puppet to the people's Parliamentary Puppets. Gladstone! you are qualified by nature to be a great Lawgiver and teacher of the people, and you are not adapted to be a mere tool and Puppet. Use, then, your high mental power to govern your words, and let not mere words, resounding from the ignorant and designing, govern your mind. *Vox populi, vox Dei* may be your damnation: *vox Dei* the One over-governing Principle of Truth, your salvation!

There is a great issue to be tried. Are Members of Parliament to be Puppets or lawgivers? Are they to be passive instruments, to act and vote according to the requests of the noisy section of their constituencies; or are they to be the initiative, thoughtful leaders of the people? It is ten thousand times easier to be a Puppet than a Lawgiver. Every fool glories in being a Puppet of the people, and will rejoice to support Earl Russell's Puppet Reform; but every wise man seeks rather to reform Earl Russell, and be a Lawgiver and teacher to the multitude.

The Derby Lawgiver solicits votes on a pledge to do his duty to his constituents, his country, and to his God. The Russellian Reform-Club-Puppet solicits votes on a pledge to follow blindly the wishes of his constituents, not caring for his country, nor fearing his God.

A Derby Lawgiver is an adviser to the people, and brings the knowledge of the whole to bear upon the study of the part. The Russellian Puppet deals with fragmentary notions, and does not understand that a one-idead man, not one whit less dangerous in action, is next akin in mental intellect to a monomaniac, who is impelled by one single ever-recurring thought.

The Reform Bill of Earl Russell is the intermediate link between the present state of things and his final Puppet development. For the moment, he desires to sweep away legislators and substitute one-idead members to be elected from one-idead voters. Every conceivable speciality of occupation is to be represented, from the maker of Bright's odious Court breeches to the parliamentary place-selling agents of the Reform Club, to the total exclusion of any consideration of the general welfare of the country.

A preponderance of Puppet power is to be given to the smaller class of shopkeepers, who work not, but rob the poor and cheat each other. It is imperatively necessary for them to have Puppets for under-skilled legislators; how long would they sell adulterated beer and bad bread, to impair the muscle and sinews of our skilled mechanics? Little shopkeepers have ever feared legislative interference, and so Earl Russell panders to their iniquity, to keep his feeble Government in power. A legislator would control their doings; they now control the Legislature.

The Puppet Parliament must reflect its actions back to the people themselves, and workmen will hereafter expect masters to be their Puppets. Doctors even now wonder whether my Lord Russell will graciously issue a proclamation ordering men hereafter to live without their brain, which co-ordinates and regulates the movements of each individual limb.

A good lawgiver, on the contrary, makes a good constituent. The man who appreciates honest and earnest thought in those above him will bestow thought upon the affairs of those below him. Every person is second to some other person on some question; so a good lawgiver has a continuous beneficial influence upon the entire community.

A great battle is at hand. The Puppets have made a deadly attack upon the lawmakers. Russell conflicts Derby; but who will be their soldiers? Whigs and Tories now consult together against the common enemy of intellect. Conservatives and Reformers confusedly jostle together, despite their former differences. All, regardless of former opinions, are disposed to join their talent for the common protection of mind and thought. Two new divisions in political circles separate themselves in battle array. Brainless, mob-idolatrous demagogues will fight under Russell. Thoughtful, studious lawgivers will join the ranks of Derby.

Already the common-sense and intellect of England cries for the people to abandon Earl Russell's Puppet, which hears not, sees not, understands not, thinks not, but acts simply as an uninformed mob may cause it to move. In place of a senseless idol, the good and great respect the human mind in its natural purity of intellectual truthfulness, and trust that after hearing, seeing, remembering, understanding, judging, comparing the present with the past, it will create laws and ordinances for the people to follow for their welfare and happiness.

Shall the people elect an intelligent Lawgiver, or manufacture a senseless Puppet?

Shall Russell carry out the behests of the mob, or shall Derby legislate for the nation?

---

## No. XXIX.

## THE FINAL REFORM BILL OF EARL RUSSELL, K.G.

### (*A Political Skit.* ANON.)

A FINAL Reform is now demanded from the Legislature by forcible, far-seeing men who know the worth of importunity.

Speeches are more telling than thought, and one pseudo-political orator is more attractive to a Minister bent upon retaining power than ten thousand quiet, thoughtful men who simply follow their business and advance the wealth and commerce of the country.

Politicians have spoken—a final Reform is requested; so who can be more ready than the present Ministry, under the leadership of Earl

Russell, to gratify the wish that the wealth and talent of the country should be entirely deprived of all influence in the country?

Palmerston is no more! Final Reform is therefore attempted, for there is no one now in the Government to support order and prevent anarchy.

Agitators agree that the franchise should be extended to every one who is not independent, and to whom the sale of a vote is an object. To extend the franchise to £6 householders would not be final, for other agitators would put in a claim for £5, and afterwards to £4, £3, £2, and £1. After this, why should not the non-householders have a vote? for money would be as useful to them as it is to the householder; and, following out the same idea. when all men have the suffrage, it would be demanded for women and children, who would have as much right to receive remuneration for their votes as men have.

Earl Russell knows well that money has kept his Ministry in power; nobody knows better than the ministerial whip how many thousands the last election cost, and who can so well tell as those who were in the thick of the fight how the tens and hundreds of thousands were divided amongst the electors? Had not every borough its price, which could be ascertained from the agent to the Reform Club, and the names of the voters in each borough who got their £2, £5, £10, and £20? for their vote is registered in heaven, even if the register on earth cannot be found to be produced before a parliamentary inquiry.

Money is the clue to final Reform. Every borough has a price, increasing or diminishing, according to the doctrine of supply and demand. Afford a fair market to parliamentary representation, and final Reform is accomplished; that is, if you give credence to my Lord Russell.

The Bill, the whole Bill, and nothing but the Bill, is comprised in the grand idea—SELL THE PLACES IN PARLIAMENT BY AUCTION, to the highest bidder, and divide the money amongst the voters.

Final Reform has the rare and singular merit of extinguishing Reform. Reform being no more, leaves the Reform Club a house without a purpose, and the house can then be sold for a parliamentary auction mart.

Perched in a rostrum in the central hall, Earl Russell might be entrusted with the office of auctioneer, and thrilling will be the effect when Leeds, Chester, and South Lancashire, on the next election, are knocked down to the happy aspirants to political power.

If the Reform Club be sold to the State, how excited will be the feelings of many of its members when the conveyance is effected! How many, for the first time, will have the extreme gratification of finding themselves possessed of some portion of this earth's wealth!

The auction final Reform will doubtless bring out the financial tact of Gladstone. Has he not already made the State a trader in Assurance? And has he not shown skill in making his poor Post-office protégés perform their duties for nothing? With such rare expedients, shall not the Ministry be able to command money for a parliamentary majority? If sorely pressed, could Gladstone not make the post-office a vehicle for the sale of milk? and how great would be the profit if the work can be done without further pay for rent, labour, and risk. Even if that field be insufficient, his fertile mind could create money by causing the post-office to take charge of umbrellas, or good soled boots, to protect the heads and keep dry the heels of old gentlemen and ladies who want to shield themselves from the slightest moisture.

There is reason to expect that Sir George Bowyer, and the money-getting, heir-spoliating Oratorian priests, would accept final Reform, as they could command thereby more votes in the House. If the Oratory is as earnest in fortune-getting as it has been of old, surely with the pleasures of Heaven and benediction, and the pains of hell and damnation, ten heirs and heiresses can be caught every year. Now, a single fifty-thousand-pound heir or heiress could allow the Oratorians to buy many boroughs; and if they could only bag their Duke, one year's ducal income would suffice to purchase more than one county franchise.

Besides the Oratorians, the nigger Baptists would delight in an Auction Reform, for when the black men desire to massacre the white men, they could by obtaining a preponderance of votes make the extermination of the whites legal. When the black men of Jamaica howled under their punishment for murder and rapine, did not Earl Russell supersede their punisher? Gordon has been hanged, so Earl Russell has lost an opportunity of placing him with Bright in the Ministry. Both Gordon and Bright had equal merit in stirring up the evil passions of mankind. If Bright makes most noise, Gordon produced the greatest effect, and both are equally entitled to sympathy and reward.

Generally, all special religious enthusiasts would welcome the final Reform Bill. Double extra High Church, double diminished Low Church, and every form of cant and hypocrisy, would crown Earl Russell for giving them an opportunity of obtaining an ascendency, which they would not fail to do, if only pastors could find flocks foolish enough to sacrifice their fortunes to support fantastic notions.

Not only special religionists, but certain parts of the monetary interest, will hail an Auction Reform with delight. Does not the Stock Exchange derive millions from new companies every year? Nobody can see any difference between the Stock Exchange and the gambling hells of the lesser princes of Germany, although every person, in fairness, admits that the German hells are, at least, superintended by the police, whilst the Stock Exchange is not. As there is a current belief in a parliamentary interference with the peculiar mode in which the Stock Exchange gets money from the public, a tithe of their gains would command many parliamentary seats to protect their acquisitions.

Again, the lawyers about the Reform Club who sigh for place may be expected vehemently to support Earl Russell, as in future they may calculate with accuracy whether it is worth their while to invest a definite sum for an expected income. How many briefless barristers at the Reform Club have bribed electors to secure a seat and obtain a judgeship, and yet remain Mr. Briefless still? How many poor fellows wander helplessly over the Reform Club who might, by an Auction Reform, get by chance a borough cheap, and show their competence for employment by a servile ministerial support?

Everybody cannot be pleased, and we may expect Bright to dissent from final Reform, as it would cause his occupation as a democratic agitator to be gone. Could he, however, not be recompensed with a seat in the Ministry? would it be discordant for the noise-maker to sit beside the noise-user? If Bright creates desire, Russell gratifies it. Let them sit side by side, models for future ages to avoid.

Any skilled lawgiver admitted into Parliament would be a curse to Bright. Without a mob, what is he? With logic he is abroad. Ignorance and folly is his gain; knowledge and ability his loss. Partially true, universally false, he is a god to those who don't work, can't work, and won't work. Education would for ever blast this idolatrous belief, and so he clings to the untaught and undisciplined masses. He and Earl Russell agree in abhorring a comprehensive mind which leads, and in holding to the servile mind which implicitly obeys. Both eschew Nature, which has ordained that some men should be tall and others short, some should invent and others be the mechanicians. Both tamper to a universal mediocrity, where no ray of intellectual superiority enlightens. Is not their character shown by their companions? And do not both partake of the mediocrity they worship?

All must admit that there is one large class, hated by Bright and despised by Russell, who consider finality in human legislation impossible, and think that the vote of an elector should be the vote of Intellect, Intelligence, Independence, and Integrity, and who would despise the sale of a franchise by auction, and equally deplore the purchase of individual voters by any Reform Club agency. That class believe that Providence has wisely ordained that many must be ruled, few can be rulers. Bright ignores Providence by subverting natural order and seeking to make the governed governors. Russell follows; and, driven on by a power he is unable to restrain, he goads on that power that he may remain a moving instrument of an ignorant multitude. The true governor leads, and would not be driven without horror and humiliation. Russell must be the tool of the disaffected, or he would be nothing.

A higher principle over-governing a subordinate; a universal law overriding a subsidiary; a comprehensive mind overruling a contracted; the whole over-regulating a part, are doctrines for Bright to damn, and for Russell to agree with Bright. Bright, however, can never accede to the peerdom of Russell while he remains a commoner, nor can Bright let Russell lead whilst he only follows. Bright as a democratic orator and hater of superiority is great in the way that lovers of order abhor. For Bright to retain his greatness he must deal with littleness, and therefore the auction final Reform would not quite suit Bright, as it might enable Parliament possibly to have members as great to Bright as Bright is to the imbecile inmates of Earlswood Asylum.

There are four great diseases before Parliament this year :—1. The rinderpest, or death of cattle; 2. The cholera pest, or death of mankind—both bodily diseases, to be treated after an exact study of Nature's works: 3. The Nigger pest—white murder by blacks; 4. The Fenian pest—the annihilation of social order and religion: both mental epidemics, to be treated after an earnest study of God's moral laws.

Who shall legislate upon these serious maladies? Shall they who have bought their parliamentary seats by money, and tampered to the follies of their age? Or shall they who represent independent, thoughtful voters, and who have studied Nature's works and followed moral laws?

2 A

## No. XXX.

## LOCKED-UP MONEY.

*From the 'Standard,' June 6, 1866.*

Sir,—Permit me to call your attention to a practical remedy for the great inconvenience which the public now suffer from large sums of money being locked up in monetary companies now under liquidation. At the present time persons are distressed, not so much from having lost some of their money, as from having been suddenly deprived of the use of all their available cash, although, perhaps, only for a time. On Saturday nights masters cannot pay their workpeople, and even private individuals are placed in an awkward position from their inability to command a single shilling. This difficulty might be easily met by the liquidator granting to the creditor, on his releasing his debt, a certificate of indebtedness, payable to bearer, or, where the sum is large, a number of certificates representing the total amount. These certificates would doubtless be immediately marketable at a price, and also available as a security. Debtors to the estates, and shareholders having calls to pay, would be glad to purchase these certificates to extinguish their liabilities, and thus the company would gradually liquidate itself. Perhaps an order in Chancery would suffice to carry out this recommendation, or, failing that, a short Act of Parliament might be obtained to enforce it.

(Signed)        ALFRED SMEE.

### PROPOSED FORM OF CERTIFICATE.

*Overend, Gurney, and Co. in liquidation.*

This is to certify that Messrs. Overend, Gurney, & Co. (Limited), in liquidation, is indebted to bearer £100.

(Signed)                    , *Liquidator.*

*From the 'Standard,' June 12, 1866.*

Sir,—In my letter recommending that certificates of indebtedness to bearer should be immediately issued by liquidators of the banks and companies, where so many companies are now locked up, I omitted to point out that the certificate would not place the holder ultimately in a better position than the other creditors, as the bearer would receive the same dividends under the bankruptcy.

The advantage of issuing certificates of indebtedness to bearer would consist in the grant of a document to the creditor, which might be readily rendered marketable.

The highest judicial authority has called my attention to the fact that this scheme requires the sanction of Parliament, but surely Parliament will not withhold an Act which must prove a blessing to many, and can inflict an injury on none.

These certificates of indebtedness would doubtless, as soon as issued, bear a price in the market, according to the estimate of the amount which the estate will realize, and the time in which that realization will be effected.

The indebtedness of the Agra Bank, the Bank of London, or the Consolidated Bank, would probably command an immediate price of 50 or 60 per cent., whilst that of other companies would not sell for more than 20 or 30 per cent.

I hear in all directions that this scheme may save hundreds of respectable persons who have deposits now locked up in the Agra and other large banking establishments, so that the question is one which demands attention and immediate action.

(Signed)  ALFRED SMEE.

*From the ' Morning Advertiser,' June 12, 1866.*

SIR,—My proposal to issue certificates of indebtedness to bearer for money locked up in companies under liquidation appears to meet with general approval, and it needs but parliamentary action to save creditors now suffering from an inability to meet present requirements.

These certificates would be useful under the three states which liquidating companies present: firstly, when there are assets sufficient to meet eventually the liabilities; secondly, when the assets are ultimately sufficient by making calls upon the shareholders; and thirdly, when the assets are insufficient even after exhausting the subscribed capital.

When the assets equal the debts, the certificates would not only be marketable instruments, but debtors could terminate their obligations by purchasing them and paying them in as cash to the liquidator.

For every £100 thus paid in £200 of transactions would be settled, and thus the company would rapidly liquidate itself.

It must be borne in mind that with liquidating banks debtors are often great sufferers, from being suddenly compelled to pay an amount for which, under any fair probability, time would be allowed.

When calls upon shareholders are required, the certificate holders would not only obtain a portion of their debt much sooner, and thus in many cases be saved from ruin; but the shareholders, by paying money down, would lose a less amount, and in some cases be themselves saved from ruin.

When the total assets of the company are insufficient, a difficulty apparently presents itself, but even here the certificates would be of utility, as they might be used in payment of calls and debts, by which the extent of the transactions would be narrowed every day; and should the certificates be ultimately found to be worth only 10s. instead of £1, the parties paying the certificates as cash would be called upon to pay the difference.

Certificates of indebtedness might properly be called notes of liquidation, and like bank-notes every one issued should be numbered, to confer an individuality upon it, registered, and finally cancelled. A fee of 5s. for stamping and registration would surely not be grudged, from the benefit which would be conferred on all parties subject to the present terrible process of liquidation, where creditors and debtors are alike sacrificed for the benefit of accountants and lawyers.

(Signed)  ALFRED SMEE.

*From the 'Morning Advertiser,' June* 18, 1866.

Sir,—The money-locked-up public heard on Friday, with dismay, the Right Hon. the President of the Board of Trade declare in the House of Commons that Her Majesty's Government did not, as at present advised, intend to apply for an Act to enable liquidators to issue certificates of indebtedness.

It appears that a singular misapprehension exists as to the nature of the document proposed to be issued, as the sum indebted to the estate is evidently confounded with the sum which will ultimately be paid.

A certificate of indebtedness would be a certificate of the sum which a bankrupt's estate is liable to pay to the creditor. This differs widely from a certificate for actual payment. The one can be given at once, the other can only be ascertained at the termination of the liquidation; and the certificates of indebtedness are equally applicable, whether the estate ultimately pays 20s. or only one farthing in the pound.

Again, some persons have erroneously considered that an Act for the issue of these certificates has been proposed as an exceptional case to meet the failure of certain banks and discount houses; and because exceptional legislation is bad, they reject the scheme.

My proposition, however, is not particular, but universal, and instead of applying to one firm applies to every case of bankruptcy and liquidation; for if the stoppage of the Agra Bank has involved its thousands, the failure of smaller firms has involved their tens, and the tens are as worthy of legislative care as the thousands.

Sufferers cowed by misfortune have not the energy and courage to be outspoken: but justice, no less than charity, demands that a scheme which promises so much good to so many innocent persons, and which may prevent so much wide-spread misery, should be considered either by a Government commission or by a parliamentary committee, that no misconception or misapprehension may prevent, if beneficial, its immediate adoption.            (Signed)    Alfred Smee.

*From the Money Article of 'The Times,' July* 16, 1866.

The following note relates to a point that might much mitigate the suffering daily experienced in all parts of the kingdom from the recent panic :—

"London, July 14.

"Sir,—Sufferers from locked-up money earnestly hope that the session will not pass away without a short Act being obtained to enable the liquidators of insolvent companies to issue certificates of indebtedness to bearer.

" Had this Act been obtained earlier, much needless misery would have been avoided; but even now it would enable persons to raise funds who are at the present time in the greatest embarrassment, simply because they have money locked up, which will be ultimately paid, but upon which they can obtain no advance, because they have no documents upon which they can borrow.

" It is now admitted by great lawyers, and most persons conversant with monetary transactions, that certificates of indebtedness to bearer, signed by a liquidator, would command their utmost value to shareholders having to pay calls, and to debtors of the estate, and that they could always be negotiated at a fair market price as a matter of business.

"I have the honour to be, your obedient servant,

"LOCKED-UP."

[A monetary crisis in this country may unhappily arise, when it may be considered expedient to carry out the above suggestions of Alfred Smee.]

---

## No. XXXI.

### ANONYMOUS LETTERS ON THE MANNER IN WHICH COMPANIES IN LIQUIDATION WERE BEING CONDUCTED AFTER THE INSOLVENCY OF OVEREND, GURNEY, & CO.

SIR,—Who would now be a director? is a question you may well ask in the 'Times,' in these days of prosecution at the Mansion House and persecution by the Court of Chancery.

Gentlemen who are now directors are timid to act, for they cannot tell whether ten years hence some needy lawyer and briefless barrister, at the instance of a penniless shareholder, may not impeach his action when all the facts and reasons are forgotten. But the public suffer from this incompetency of the Court of Chancery, or imbecility of the law. At the present moment there are numerous undertakings of great importance, and which are urgently required, which, although they have received the sanction of Parliament, cannot be executed because they cannot raise money, on account of the distrust which exists.

If these works were carried out, the distress which now exists would be averted, employment would be given to numerous workmen, and money would be circulated in England instead of going abroad to benefit foreign States.

It is high time to inquire into the manner in which distrust is created and families are ruined by the costly proceedings in Chancery, which bring all legitimate enterprises into disrepute. From the date of the last panic matters have gone continually from bad to worse, and at the present time it is far more difficult to carry out a legitimate English enterprise than it was a week after Black Friday.*

The Government owe it to the country to frustrate the lawyers and liquidators who are causing this distrust, and make them either settle up their accounts of liquidating companies forthwith, or be discharged from their office ; and if the Court of Chancery is too imbecile to deal with the question, the Government should constitute a court of practical mercantile men who can deal with the difficulty in a plain, sensible manner. Hoping that the 'Times' will never let the matter rest till Parliament interferes with these causes of distrust and restores confidence,

I remain, Sir, yours obediently,

TRUST.

---

* The Friday after the failure of Overend, Gurney, and Co., in March 1866. So many failures took place on that day that it was termed by the mercantile community Black Friday.

SIR,—The observations made in the City article of the 'Times,' on the hardship attending the delay in the distribution of the assets of shareholders of banks with unlimited liability, apply with tenfold force to the estates of shareholders of unlimited companies in liquidation.

Insolvent companies are nominally wound up by the Court of Chancery, but practically by accountants and lawyers, whose special object it is to incur costs and procrastinate the liquidation. Some companies have already been years in liquidation, and will remain so for years to come, during which time no estate of a deceased shareholder can be divided.

It is worthy of consideration whether the benefits of unlimited liability to creditors are not more than counterbalanced by the hardships inflicted on the shareholders. By the Joint Stock Companies Act, any pre-existing company was permitted either to register as a limited or unlimited company; but the Registrar holds, rightly or wrongly, that a company, then having made its choice, is ever after prohibited from changing its character.

At the time when the Joint Stock Act was passed, the doctrine of limited liability was novel, and shareholders of successful companies were afraid to adopt it; but could the companies again be permitted to have the choice, there are probably but few in this country which would not assume a limited character, which, after all, is the only rational plan for the conduct of a public company.

(Signed)   LIMITED LIABILITY.

January 21, 1873.

SIR,—Experience fully confirms the observations in the City article of the 'Times,' that there are high-minded accountants who do their duty by the liquidation of companies; nevertheless, there is a certain class of lawyers who promote excessive litigation for the costs which they continue to obtain.

If any member of Parliament will move for the time occupied and the costs incurred in the liquidation of unlimited companies, to say nothing of the further cost which the contributories themselves are compelled to pay, there will be such an amount of hardship and wrong-doing revealed that, doubtless, some well-considered legislative enactment would be passed.

In limited companies there is less temptation to incur these improper costs, as there is only a certain amount of money to be spent, and the creditors, as far as they can, take care that this undue waste does not occur.

January 29, 1873.                        (Signed)   SHAREHOLDER.

----

## No. XXXII.

## ON THE UNSEAWORTHINESS OF SHIPS SENT TO SEA.

SIR,—The shareholders of marine companies express great satisfaction at the 'Insurance Times' having noticed the scandalous frauds which within the last few years have been perpetrated on the shareholders of marine companies. I have the pleasure to inform your readers that a plan has been devised for detecting the most flagrant delinquents, and that some gentlemen who have suffered from these frauds will speedily take action in the matter. It is intended to move for a return of every marine claim made upon every company in liquidation, stating the person who brought the insurance to the office, the nature of the assurance, the sum paid for the assurance, and the amount ultimately claimed. This interesting little document will disclose the most frightful state of facts, and will lead to the most vigorous legislation next session.

(Signed)    MARINE SHAREHOLDER.

SIR,—I am a loser by marine insurance, having made an investment in a marine company now in liquidation. From inquiries I made I find that the insurance of ships is not like any other business, carried on by the directors personally, but devolves upon the underwriter entirely. The underwriter becomes the sole responsible director, and settles what risks are to be taken and at what price, and all the shareholders are absolutely at his mercy ; for no matter how able or high-principled the directors may be, they virtually have no power whatever in the matter. If I had known this before, I never would have become a shareholder ; and I think your paper would do good service if you would give the names of the underwriters of every defunct company, as a warning to future investors. There are strange reports afloat about underwriters and their doings of late.

Manchester.                                    (Signed)    X. Z.

SIR,—I have been much upon the river Thames and had frequent opportunities of conversing with the sailors. They say that frequently when they are hired they find from the general cut of a ship that it is intended to be lost. It is impossible to leave her, as by the law, if they do not go, they would be liable to be sent to prison ; a matter which they complain of as a very great hardship. Sometimes when a ship is doomed to be lost, they find at the last moment that a sufficient assurance cannot be effected upon her ; and then a telegram is sent to be very careful of the ship, as she is not sufficiently insured. The sailors do not appear at all to relish the risking of their lives for the owner of the ship to get the insurance money, and they say that something ought to be done for their protection, and that forthwith.

(Signed)    CRUISER.

SIR,—In the discussion which the 'Insurance Times' has raised upon marine insurance the question of property has alone at present been considered. Now I do not care one jot for the property question, but I have a very decided opinion upon the sacrifice of life which the present destruction of ships produces. The sacrifice of the lives of our seamen is needless ; and by the manner in which marine assurance is now practised, the loss of a ship is too often a great benefit to the shipowner in a pecuniary sense, although attended with a great loss of life to our brave sailors. Under any circumstances, such strong legislative enactments should be provided as to protect the lives of men who are too much at the mercy of the shipowners, for all experience shows that those who profit by ship destruction care nothing for the loss of human life.

(Signed)    YACHTSMAN.

Sir.—I trust I may be excused the liberty of asking for a small portion of valuable space to write a few words upon marine insurance. Unfortunately I was a clerk in a winding-up marine insurance office, and thus had ample opportunities of observing how the black-legs who effected the assurances proceeded in their nefarious practices. Before they brought any business to the office I always observed that those who intended to rob the company were very minute in their inquiries as to the amount of un-called capital. When quite satisfied upon that point, they began to honour the company with their confidence. At first they brought two or three unexceptionable risks, amongst which they introduced one a little doubtful, so that all might be taken together. Then by degrees they gradually slipped into the office their peculiar assurances of ships to go to the bottom—cargo, sailors, and all. When this business was at the height, it was curious to observe how broker Mr. A. was jealous of broker Mr. B., and would go away if he spied him in the office doing his little bits of iniquity. Each man greatly preferred to see the underwriter alone and be closeted with him unseen; and as soon as he had done his business, there was always a desire to slide away from the office as quick as possible. I knew them all, and hated the sight of them; and only wondered how the under-writer could be talked over by these villains. The directors came every day to sign the policies to which their underwriter had committed them, and vainly imagined that they were only transacting first-class business. They had no more control over the risks which were taken than I had as a junior clerk. After a little time claims began to come in. The same men used to come and say, " I have got a little claim, which I should take as a personal favour if you would settle at once. I will leave you the pro-test, and will call again to-morrow, when I have several good risks for you." I read many of these protests in sheer amazement. The captain used to say that in latitude so and so, longitude so and so, a wind sprung up, which gradually increased. He then ordered the pumps to be sounded, and found there was some water. After a few hours' pumping he tried again, and found more water. He then saw it was no use pumping any more, so he told the men to get the boat ready, which they lowered. Then the wind began to blow a good deal harder, and he told the men that to save their lives they must get into the boat. They rowed about three or four hours to know what became of the ship, when at some precise minute to some hour the ship went down head foremost in very deep water. He saw it was no use remaining, so he told the men to row ashore, as the wind was blowing a hurricane. And the protest finished by protesting against the winds and waves, and he ever would protest against the winds and waves; and the whole of this precious document is verified by the British consul at the port where the crew landed.

Lots of ships are never heard of when over-insured; and bullion, which nobody ever saw before it was put on board, always went down in such very deep water that the directors had no chance of getting it up again. After a few of these eligible risks the customers began again to inquire into the stability of the office, and make their own personal inquiries whether each shareholder could pay his subscribed quota. As soon as they put on the company as many risks as they thought it could bear, they began to withdraw, and speak in very virtuous indignation because the company was not at once wound up, and at last they were most particular to endeavour to get one of their clique to be liquidator. The consequence of this was that their claims were all admitted, and the poor shareholders squeezed to their uttermost farthing, and abused by those who robbed them. My heart quite ached for the poor shareholders, who were so cruelly cheated. Apologizing for so long a letter, I am,

Camberwell.                     (Signed)     MARINE CLERK.

SIR,—Your correspondent in the last week's number of the 'Insurance Times' protests against the word "gang" as applied to those who defraud marine insurance offices. The whole tenour of the letters to your paper clearly demonstrates that there is an extensive organization, widely scattered, who derive their wealth from these practices. The word "gang," however, is so generally applied to convicts that it is hardly applicable to a set of men not convicted. For exactness of language I would suggest the use of the word "sea-thug" for all those who obtain improperly money from underwriters and marine insurances. From this appropriate term we should derive the verb "to sea-thug," and the abstract principle "sea-thuggery." Hereafter they may be described as Liverpool sea-thugs, London sea-thugs, Glasgow sea-thugs, Lloyds' sea-thugs, *et signa sunt similia.*

St. Pancras.                    (Signed)     WORD FANCIER.

SIR,—Mr. Plimsoll has done good service to the State by having called the attention of Parliament to the unnecessary yearly destruction of the lives of more than 500 brave sailors.

In his admirable speech, however, Mr. Plimsoll did not fully realize to his own mind the important manner in which all the evidence shows that marine insurance has led to this excessive mortality.

Insurances are effected beyond the value of the thing assured. The loss of the object assured is thus an event to be desired, because it produces a pecuniary gain. The desire for the event leads to its occurrence. Ships and goods are desired to be lost. Ships are consequently wrecked, and therefore the poor sailors perish.

Marine insurance leads directly to the following results :—

1. Ships are scuttled.
2. Ships are burnt.
3. Ships are run ashore.
4. Ships are deserted.
5. Ships are sailed unsound.
6. Ships are imperfectly stored.
7. Ships are shortly manned.
8. The freight is uncared for.
9. Valueless articles are substituted for valuable freight.

Whenever any of these events happens a claim arises. Insurers are defrauded, and the lamentable consequences to underwriters, shareholders of marine companies, and to *bonâ fide* assurers, so graphically depicted by the correspondents of the 'Insurance Times,' are brought to pass.

The first object in a civilized country is the preservation of life, and the second the protection of property; hence the temptation to fraud which marine assurance offers, by the destruction of property and consequent loss of life, should be restrained by legislative enactments.

There are reasons to suppose that ships doomed to destruction, together with their cargoes, are frequently assured to many times their value.

No insurance ought to be permitted beyond three-quarters of the value of the object assured, so that the owner may have a direct interest in the preservation of the thing assured.

Any enactment should provide against the probability of the payment of a claim beyond the intrinsic value of the object assured. This might be done by the public registration of every claim paid.

With regard to the past, perhaps it would be more magnanimous to let bygones be bygones; but if it be thought advisable to make an example to deter others, then it is manifest that the archives of all the winding-up marine companies would supply ample materials for a wholesale punishment of the worst offenders.

The exposures which have already taken place in the 'Insurance Times' are reported already to have made the stoutest hearts of the delinquents to quake, but Parliament next session will take care that marine insurance shall no longer lead to the death of sailors and the destruction of ships.

Westminster.　　　　　　　　　　　(Signed)　　　　JUDEX.

SIR.—There is a phase of marine insurance which has not as yet been noticed by any of your correspondents, and that is the bearing which the electric telegraph has upon the results of marine insurance. In former times every marine risk offered was a fair insurance risk, as the result was unknown. Now, however, the electric telegraph extends so far, and communicates its intelligence so rapidly, that persons are able to effect insurances after the event has happened. As a matter of fact it is possible now to hear of a loss of a vessel in America, and assure the vessel, if lost in Europe, by the clock time before it was lost. To assure a contingent event after the event has happened is no insurance at all, but direct, downright robbery, and yet it has been known that ships have been chartered to convey the intelligence of the loss of a vessel to the nearest electric telegraph station, from which a telegram has been sent directing assurances to be effected upon a lost vessel. Neither insurance offices nor underwriters can stand against claims arising in this manner, and the only wonder is that this class of cheating has not been described before.

(Signed)　　　R. Y.

— — — — —

## No. XXXIII.

## ANONYMOUS LETTERS ON CHANCERY REFORM.

### CHANCERY LIQUIDATIONS.

Remarkable stories are current amongst the members of the Bar, of the power which some liquidators claim to possess as officers of the Court of Chancery, and more wonderful facts are narrated of the means by which some of these appointments have been obtained.

In some liquidations every legal quibble is raised. Acts done for the common good are misrepresented. Bygone transactions are questioned. Fraud is freely imputed. Agreements acted upon for years are repudiated. Every possible proceeding in law or equity is taken to make costs; and the very costs themselves are sometimes the subject of arrangement between the liquidators and the lawyers.

Terrified contributories submit to any extortion. Even security for money is exacted from their families or connections by the threat of breaking up their homes. Some, maddened by a sense of persecution, become insane. Some commit suicide, stupefied by despair. Some perish from disease, caused by protracted anxiety. Some go abroad to die in other lands; and others become reckless, declaring that there is neither justice nor mercy for a contributory.

Some liquidations have existed for years, and will continue for years to come. Other liquidations have paid no dividend to this day. The expenses of some liquidations have eaten up nearly the entire estate. Nevertheless, all this is done under the pretence of the sanction of the High Court of Parliament.

The Chancery judges have shown themselves to be as helpless as creditors are to restrain the power which liquidators have assumed; but what the Court cannot do, Parliament must.

## Shall Life Assurance Companies change their domiciles to avoid the meddling interference of Government, and the pernicious jurisdiction of the Court of Chancery?

Fellow Policy-holders, — The dangers to which we are exposed demand immediate action, as our property is continually in peril. Unprincipled persons are always seeking to destroy the credit of the various offices in which we are assured. Some desire to ingratiate themselves with the Board of Trade to become its referee. Some hope to gain the inordinate fortunes which liquidators obtain. Needy lawyers are always on the alert to destroy a company, that they may bring actions and Chancery suits against the unhappy contributories; and it is even alleged that black mail is often sought to be extorted from directors, under threat of attacking the company, or the presentation and advertising of a winding-up petition.

Judges in Chancery have given evidence that they are powerless to prevent these iniquities, although they must be held, by the public, responsible for them. Chancery courts open up questions settled years before, and thus tend to demoralize the community by teaching them repudiation. Persons first seek, by the aid of a meddling Government, to lower the credit of the company; then, as soon as its credit is impaired, it becomes food for the harpies of Chancery, who get enormous incomes, and realize large fortunes, by the ruin of innocent men. The legal profession, besides, talk of a scandal which no man dare tackle. Any attempt to cleanse the Augean stable must be a vain mockery: nothing less than the abolition of the Courts of Chancery can suffice. The judges should be called upon to frame laws, that men may know the law and obey it: and the judges should no longer exercise their individual will by the interpretation of the motives and equities of transactions, years after their occurrence, upon the garbled statements of counsel and lawyers, who stir up strife to live upon the contention. Men of fortune and position now fear to undertake the duties of director, and yet for the conduct of Life Assurance we want men as upright as the judges themselves.

England is the only country in Europe subject to the caprice of Chancery. All other nations view it with the intensest horror. Here one honourable judge praises an act done under difficult circumstances, whilst another equally honourable judge, upon the same facts and upon the arguments of the same counsel, declares the same act to be fraudulent, and condemns the innocent victim in ruinous costs. Unprincipled lawyers employ unscrupulous counsel, supposed to have private influence, and to have the faculty of using strong language where the profits of a liquidation are at stake; and there have been scenes in court as to facts, so great is the voracity of the vultures, when they see a prospect of a carcase to devour. Some liquidations have taken years when they might have been settled in months, but for Chancery. Contributories have been ruined; and what the creditors should have had, the lawyers, liquidators, and counsel got.

If Chancery cannot be abolished, and all its terrible demoralizing machinery swept away, Life Policy-holders should require that their companies be removed to some other kingdom, out of the jurisdiction of the English Chancery, and away from the pernicious meddling of the English Government officials.

TRIPLE POLICY-HOLDER.

### JUDGES AND THEIR FAMILY RELATIVES.

The propriety of barristers practising in courts of law presided over by their relatives now demands consideration, as the matter requires immediate action.

The legal profession condemn the practice, as the public never can respect decisions given under such circumstances.

Rightly or wrongly, suitors anticipate defeat if a relative of the judge is employed on the opposite side.

On account of this prevalent idea, crafty solicitors seek to retain the relation, whereby injustice is inflicted on other members of the Bar, and dissatisfaction caused to the public.

When suitors hear a relative of the judge make an unfounded statement, or use strong language, they fear that their cause will be lost, and when lost they believe the decision to be unjust.

It is agreed on all hands that a relation of a judge must, in future, be prohibited from acting before him.

This rule may press heavily upon some barristers, but the time has come when public opinion demands that barristers should not practise before judges who are their family relatives.

## CHANCERY REFORM.

The present session of Parliament is passing away; but the infirmities of the Courts of Chancery remain.

Our estimable Lord Chancellor, anxious to do good, has done much harm, by seeking to change the Court of Final Appeal, which has ever commanded the confidence of the Bar, whilst he has neglected to reform the Courts of Equity, in which the scandals occur that are so justly the subject of universal complaint.

The will of the Equity judge is absolute law, and great fear is inspired when the opposing lawyer leads to the supposition that he has private access to the judge.

As the Equity judge is all-powerful, he must be held responsible for the shortcomings of his chief clerks, for the misdeeds of his liquidators, and for the cost-makings of the lawyers practising in his court.

The Bar have a right to complain when they are not permitted to speak upon briefs which have been prepared with anxious care and enormous cost; suitors will complain when the judge refuses his attention to hear the arguments: and both the Bar and the public marvel when the judge sleeps during the statement of the case, and only wakes to give judgment upon that of which he knows nothing.

The public will no longer tolerate the fortunes of a suitor to be imperilled by the dictum of one man, subservient as it may be to prejudice, to influence, to infirmity, or to temper. A twinge of the gout, a fit of sleep, or an indiscretion in the diet of a judge, may make or mar the happiness of a family for ever.

It is cruel mockery in many cases to suggest an appeal. The costs are ruinous, and the deposit of the money at issue in most cases impracticable. To appeal is to be hung first, to be tried afterwards.

It is the duty of the Bar to ensure justice, and they now declare that it is necessary for that object that every court should be presided over by two judges, who, on failure of concurring in a decision, should call in a third. Every judge should retain the vigour of youth to appreciate the facts, and possess the maturity of age to adjudicate upon them; all others should retire from the bench.

## THE SLEEPING JUDGE.

The Equity Bar has for some years past been placed in a painful position by one of their esteemed judges being unable to keep awake on the bench.

Sooner or later the feebleness of age will overtake us all, but sound sleep on the bench must be regarded as incompatible with judicial functions.

Suitors are frantic when they find that their case has never been heard. The Bar do their best to make the judge hear, for when he awakes, to their horror he decides upon a different state of facts, from only having heard a part of the case.

A growing discontent and distrust of the decisions of the Chancery judges is observable amongst the public, as they allege that it is natural that the infirmity of age should rest upon the vigour of youth; and this has been increased by the injudicious, and doubtless false, boastings of certain low class lawyers.

The Bar unite in considering that the time has come when the judge who daily cannot refrain from sleeping on the bench should rest on his former well-earned laurels, when everyone will heartily wish him a long and happy life to enjoy that to which we may all fairly aspire—*otium cum dignitate*.

### CHANCERY REFORM.

The highest expectations are entertained by the Chancery Bar of the reforms anticipated to be made by the learned and earnest mind now presiding over our Courts of Equity; but much may be done before his great scheme of reform can be perfected and brought into operation.

Any judge who, from peculiarity of habit or infirmity of age, sleeps on the bench during the argument, should gracefully retire, and two judges should preside over each of the lower courts, to satisfy suitors that partiality for any particular advocate does not exist.

The scandal of the present combination of liquidator and lawyer has arisen from modern legislation, and is one of the worst features of Chancery administrations. Needy accountants and wit-making lawyers now get a higher remuneration than the Vice-chancellors themselves, by using the funds of the creditors to harass contributories for their own gain, and matters which might be settled in five minutes now frequently occupy as many years.

Unfortunately but few of our present Equity judges have been behind the scenes to know the working of this machinery, which has caused so much dissatisfaction; but they must perceive that a restriction of the discretionary powers of liquidators is now absolutely necessary.

By careful regulations a court of appeal may be rendered less necessary, and confidence in the administration in the Court of Chancery restored.

---

### No. XXXIV.

A GOSSIP ABOUT GARDENING.   A Lecture delivered *impromptu*, December 4, 1871.   By ALFRED SMEE, F.R.S.

ABOUT two thousand years ago, the great poet Horace said that the height of his ambition was to have a garden with a crystal stream running through it, and also a small wood.

That also is my case, and my wish, as I suppose his was, has been gratified; and on this occasion I will shortly give you an account of the philosophy by which we conduct our garden, and of some of the more remarkable plants which are grown therein.

All plants, as you know, are organized beings which require certain forces for their development. In the first place, it is absolutely necessary that they have a sufficient supply of the light of the sun. Light is one of the most important physical agents which we use. Some plants require the full light of the sun,—for instance, the cucumber as grown in our frames; others require it more subdued,—for instance, the ferns which grow in the caves. Then again, we are obliged to shield some of our plants from the light, such as the orchids; and lastly, we have to grow some in dark caves, as in the case of some fungi, and other of the lower plants which require almost a total exclusion of light. Now with regard to light, we place our plants which require little light on a North aspect, and those which require much light on a South aspect, but we must also shade our houses. One of the best plans for shading is to make use of coloured glass, which filters out many of the rays. This plan is adopted in the Royal Gardens at Kew, where it seems to answer very well. At Paris they have series of pantile laths placed side by side, leaving a little gap between them; and lastly we cut off the light from many of our plants by putting a linen shade over our houses. Now, unless you regulate the light, you may give up all idea of cultivation. It is no use to try without it, for you cannot succeed.

Well then, besides light, every plant requires a certain amount of heat, and unless it has this it will not grow. It will be in vain for you to try to grow the sugar-cane in this climate; it would be in vain for you to try to grow the geranium in Jamaica: for the sugar-cane would not have enough heat here, and the geranium would have too much heat in Jamaica, so that in either case the plant would be destroyed. You must know, then, the right temperature at which the plant will grow. If you employ more heat than what is required, as is usual in this country, your plant will die. When I was at Florence, a botanist told me that he could not grow Alpine plants there, the climate was too hot. With regard to heat a very curious thing must be noticed, and that is, that heat must be applied at certain intervals. Heat and light must be applied to every plant, so that the plant rests and then grows, and then rests again. Rest is as necessary to a plant as it is to man, and many of our plants are not able to be successfully grown because we are not able to give them their precise intervals of rest and growth as in their native spots. The Alpine plants in the summer are exposed to the full heat of the sun, but in winter they are kept warm by a thick covering of snow.

Now, not only do we have these considerations of light and heat, but a certain condition of the atmosphere is absolutely necessary to vegetation; there must be a certain amount of moisture in the air. It must be dry at the right time, it must be wet at the right time; and unless you are acquainted with the proper time to apply moisture and to withhold it, your garden will be a failure. Take the delicate vine: it sprouts in spring and requires the air to be moist. If you expose it to a dry atmosphere, you injure the tissues of the plant; but if you carry on your moisture above a certain point, the plant will keep on growing and be injured. During the period when the leaves are sprouting a damp atmosphere is necessary; as it forms its berries the atmosphere is gradually dried, and when the fruit attains perfection you give all the air and light you can, and a much drier atmosphere than you had before.

Now we all know that electricity is an important agent in nature. Some years ago some extraordinary ideas were put forward as to the effects of electricity upon plants. So far as we know, at the present moment, all we can say is, that we know not at all what effect electrical force has upon plants, either upon their growth or maturation. Experiments were tried by placing wires over plants in the hope that electricity might be excited, but they were all useless. I have myself kept plants under considerable tension in a room in a house, but I could see no effect whatever, and I may fairly say that we have not the remotest notion of the way in which electricity will affect a plant. But we see what electricity will do in the violent discharge which takes place in a thunderstorm : if a tree is struck, the lightning goes down it just under the bark, and then jumps to the ground where it is wet or damp, so that the bark of the tree is peeled off, and this is one of the common effects of an electric discharge on a growing tree. I have the figure of a tree which was struck in the grounds of a friend of mine. It stood in a field where some hurdles were placed, and the electric discharge could be traced from the tree to a point where these hurdles entered the ground. This may be taken as the effect of lightning upon a tree. Those stories which we hear of trees dying because struck by lightning are merely fables; and as far as I have seen, in many instances the effect which is produced is that the bark is thrown off and torn and loosened all round the tree. With regard to the immediate effects produced by electricity on the growth of plants, nothing is known, and in my opinion it has no important effect on vegetation at all.

But having a knowledge of these forces and even using them aright, the plant will not grow unless put in proper earth. A peach in a pot will never bear fruit unless you have hammered down the earth about its roots as hard as you can, and one great expense in growing these plants is that a great many pots are broken by the force which has to be applied in thus hammering the earth. The mallet is used so that the roots come in contact with the earth, and then the plant will do well.

Now the camellia, treated in the same way, will surely die, for the roots of the camellia require a more porous earth, and the distribution of the material among them should be light and peaty. I may mention that in Florence, where the camellia was first introduced into Europe from Japan by a monk of the name of Camella, they grow their plants in rotten chestnut wood, and in that only. I was very much struck with this, and in one garden the gardener said, " Yes, when I receive plants from your country, I shake off all the stuff you put them in and change the soil." I have tried camellias in various soils. If you put them in loam, it will kill them. I have tried them in rotten wood and tan, and find them to grow admirably well. This shows the necessity for a particular sort of soil to the growth of a plant. It must have certain ingredients, and these ought to be sought for in the analysis of the ashes of the plant. Our knowledge on this point is in a most imperfect state, but we may say that almost and perhaps all plants require a certain amount of phosphates and a certain amount of potash. These are essential. There are other particular materials in specific plants. The grasses require a large amount of flint in their composition. Other plants require other definite salts, but potash and lime seem to be required by all, and it would be as impossible to grow them without these bodies as it would be to grow them without light and heat.

Now this brings us to another point; how are plants nourished? They are nourished from certain constituents of the atmosphere. A certain amount of carbonic acid exists in the air, and it is from that that the fibre of a plant is made. With regard to the nitrogenous materials found in the composition of plants, they take it from the ammonia and nitrates in the soil.

Under all these conditions you will succeed; without all these conditions you can never be a successful horticulturist.

We know how to grow our plants; now what plants are we to grow, and how are we to obtain them? In the first place we obtain them from seeds. But what do we obtain from seeds? A plant of a like species to that from which the seed came. Of a like species, but likely to vary somewhat. There are certain limits to variation, but those limits of variation are marked. Take the wild crab, which is so acrid that you cannot eat it: compare that with the ribstone pippin. There is a wide difference between them, but within the limit of variation. Take a wild pear, compare that with the delicious pear of the present day, and the variation is enormous, yet it is within the limit of variation, and horticulturists have never found that one species transforms itself into another. I may say from experience that I have never seen anything which could indicate to my mind that one species of plant could be converted into another, and I do not believe that there is any conversion of one into another, but simply that each species, by itself, exhibits varieties which differ greatly sometimes, but are always within the limit of variation, the progeny being only varieties of the same species, and not being different species. This I believe to be the sum and substance of all that is true of what is familiarly known as Darwinism.

Well, we have then from our seed a plant with a certain likeness to the preceding plant, but which has this difference, that members raised from the seeds of the same plant exhibit certain peculiarities. We, therefore, want to propagate any good variety that turns up; how do we proceed to propagate an improved variety? Without knowing how to do this we could not get on, and it is a matter of fundamental importance. We want commonly to grow that which is improved; how then shall we propagate that improved variety which is turned up by accident or by high cultivation? In the first place, a convenient mode of propagating a plant is by layering it. This is done by putting a part of the plant under the ground, when it will take root and will be part of the original plant with roots of its own, and you can cut it off and it then grows as an independent plant, and that propagation of the original plant may take place to any extent. Sometimes we want to propagate in a more remarkable manner, and then we put part of one plant on part of another. This operation is grafting. I cut off a shoot of one plant and put the shoot of another in its place, then I have the last variety growing upon a stock of the first. It may be a saddle graft, where a notch is cut in one part to fit the other; or it may be a whipped graft, where the two cut parts are side by side, or a hole may be cut in the one and the other thrust into it. But there is one condition on which only you can be successful: you must bring the new wood of the one against the new wood of the other. By this process we multiply any trees that we like upon another stock.

Then we propagate the same individual by the division of bulbs or by dividing the roots, as in the Amaryllis tribe. You see then that when we want to cultivate the same variety as we had before, we must not resort to the seed, which may give us a plant with some slight difference from the parent plant, and it is only by a special mode of propagation that we can make any particular variety continue to produce the same variety year by

2 B

year. That is a very important point. In the propagation of our fungi the same thing occurs; the fungi have very small spores, which answer to the seeds of other plants. They start, throw out minute threads, and give rise to a new plant. If we come across a particularly good mushroom, it is no use to try and propagate it by the spores. This must be done by the mycelium, which consists of minute threads which traverse the ground in which the mushroom grows, and which is commonly known as mushroom spawn. By this we can propagate any particular variety. So that the modes of propagation of plants are, the propagation of different varieties by seeds, and the propagation of any specific variety by cuttings, grafting, division of roots, budding, by spores, and by many other ways.

Having noticed those great points upon which we must base our operations in order to ensure successful horticulture, I should like in imagination to take you round my garden, and say a few words about the plants which grow in it.

I will first say a few words about the vegetables. They are not the most interesting perhaps, though you all know how important they are. You know it has been said that more people have perished from want of vegetable food than have ever perished in battle, and probably at the present time there are as many lives saved by taking vegetable food to sea as ever were lost by sending ships to sea. With this before us we have to consider what vegetables we should grow. To my mind, the king of all vegetables is the watercress. To have it at its best it must be grown in a very pure stream of water, which ought to come from the depths of the earth at the temperature of those depths, say 52° F., and then ought to run over a clean pebbly bed. To start, you take a handful of watercresses and put a stone upon them, then another and so on until you have covered the space on which you want them to grow; and then, if you pick them fresh from the brook, they are one of the most wholesome vegetables which the country can afford. But you often see them grown upon the verge of sewage beds, and then consequences may arise from eating them which are almost too serious for me to contemplate. You have heard of the terrors of the tapeworm; you know that it may consist of two or three hundred joints, and that each of these may contain about 30,000 ova. If you consider that these are common in the sewage beds and that they are so distributed to the watercress plant, and if you consider that they are thus taken into the animal economy, you may judge the danger there is in using watercresses, and the necessity for preventing their sale under those circumstances. When they are sold in the neighbourhood of large towns, the danger is much greater than those who eat them are aware of. We cannot all get perfectly pure and fresh watercresses, but I can. My crystal brook comes to my aid. But we cannot all have this crystal brook.

Now mustard is always at hand. We buy mustard, but we get rape seed. These two are very much alike, and there are very few who can tell the difference. But there is a total difference in their quality, and what we pay for we ought to have. But those who sell, think they ought to sell us the cheapest article at the dearest rate.

But I will not detain you with the salading plants, I will not take you through the various herbs, except that I will say one word upon one of them. I have a plant of absinthe, not to use myself or to give my friends, but to point to as a dangerous plant. Absinthe is now drunk enormously in Paris. From four to six o'clock in the afternoon, everyone is drinking this absinthe, and I have consulted my brother medical practitioners of France, who say that many brain diseases and epileptic fits are produced by taking this pernicious herb. Therefore, if you have it, have it to show persons that they may not introduce it into this country.

I will pass from vegetables to fruit trees. I like fruit, and I find that most of my visitors do not object to it also. Let us begin with the apple. We all liked apples as children, and not only do children like them, but the geese, and not only geese but the fowls, and not only the fowls but horses, and not only horses but the oxen; and I know this because my bull got out and ate up a whole tree of apples, tree and all. Now the varieties of apples are mere varieties of the wild crab. They are all within the limit of the variation we may obtain of any one plant, and they are not new species. But these varieties are very numerous: I have more than three hundred kinds. I believe there are one or two thousand varieties which are not recorded. Many varieties are obtained by horticultural processes. Now, with good management, we ought to have an apple for every day in the year. You begin with a little apple which ripens in July. You go on step by step until you have apples ripening at Christmas. You go on again until March, and then you still have apples, for there are some which do not become ripe until March, and we finish off with the French crab in June, which is not only in perfection then, but will last over a second year; and so by a little careful adjustment we may have not only culinary, but also eating apples all the year round. About thirty to forty kinds are amply sufficient for this purpose.

Then we come to the pear; but pears are either very fine or very bad, and we must make a much more careful selection. If we begin by the end of July with a small early pear, and go on from one to another, we can have fruit well into the winter. That delicious pear the "Marie Louise," I may say in parenthesis, was raised by Van Mons, a Dutchman. There is an enormous number of different varieties, and in selecting a variety you have to go over an extensive range to find one truly fine pear.

Now we go to work in a particular manner with pears to obtain quick produce. "He who grows pears grows for his heirs," is an old saying. Virgil says, "Plant pears, and thy posterity shall gather the fruit." But we know how to get them much sooner. We must proceed in a true horticultural manner for this purpose. We cut the shoot of a pear-tree true off and plant it upon a quince. By grafting it in this way we render the pear-tree fertile, and then in a year or two we get fruit which we might have had to wait twenty years for if the tree had been grown in the ordinary way. It is to be observed that the quince stock should be cut off close to the ground, not under the ground, or else the pear will throw out roots and you will be no better off than if you had planted the pear-tree.

Having planted our pear-trees, we must train them in a particular way. We so arrange that the quince stock comes exactly level with the ground, then all the upper part is the pear-tree, and this must be trained in a certain manner to allow the light and warmth to come upon the fruit. We cut the branches into the form of a pyramid, as near as may be, to look like a Jack-in-the-green. Every branch is exposed to the sun and light, and upon every branch, there we get the pears.

2 B 2

We pass from the pears to the plums, which are secondary; and from those to the grape-vines, which I have already told you how to manage; and I pass from those to the nut-trees, where you must notice the two blossoms, from one of which the catkins, the male part of the flower, come out early in January and February. Then a little red flower comes out, and that is the female part of the flower, so that it is divided into two parts, and this is a very interesting thing to observe. The first time in February you have the opportunity, examine that pretty little flower, for very few have ever noticed it.

The time runs on, and when one gets into a favourite subject one may go on a much longer time than I could speak to you, or you would care to hear me.

For the flowers and plants I must tell you what I grow. I am a lover of ferns. Fern roots do not like to be soddened in water and do not like to be dry: now you must find the happy medium. They should be never dry, ever moist, and yet neither too dry nor too moist. The best way to manage that is to plant them upon a bank. And what happens? There is always moisture draining through the earth, and the wet is always running away from the roots, and if you plant them in that way you will have as luxuriant specimens as are to be seen anywhere. Now ferns you know as a rule like a little shade, not too much, however. There are some which will bear the full blaze of the sun. The *Osmunda regalis* and the beautiful feathery fern bear well the light of the sun; but next in order we come to those delicate ferns which will not bear so much light, and these we must put in another situation. I have never succeeded in growing the fern of Tunbridge Wells without shelter. It is a most delicate fern, and is altogether a most charming plant. But the way I can manage, with most perfect success, is to bury in the ground a little square box, put in the fern, and then put a piece of glass over it: that is sufficient to protect it from the wind and to keep up a continual moisture, and it never gets materially frozen; and so, many of these tender ferns may be grown to perfection. I have grown in this way that wonderful fern which was discovered by Captain Cook in New Zealand, the *Todea superba*, so you will see what may be done by a simple protection of glass. Sometimes we adopt other plans: we make a little pocket for the plant by putting two or three stones round it in a little hole, and so it has the advantage of full light and air and yet is protected. There are many exotic ferns, however, which will grow out of doors as well as the English ferns, but we carry their outward growth to a greater extent by housing some of the delicate ones in the winter and putting them out of doors in the summer. In this way the large tree-ferns will grow, and show their forms remarkably well. In this way many ferns from other parts of the world will grow successfully. This is what we cannot do altogether out of doors; we have to shelter them in a house, and there, by a judicious arrangement, we can obtain that creation of the poet's idea, perpetual summer. To go into my house in winter when all there is beautiful and green, and then to come out and regard the snow and ice and naked trees, is an effect which is as remarkable as it is beautiful.

I do not altogether neglect the gaudy flowers which are known as florists' flowers, where geraniums are selected as monstrosities and where many other plants are grown in the same way; but though these are showy they are not to be classed with the lovely Alpine flowers which decorate the mountains in the Apennines and Pyrenees. I have many hundred species of these. They can be grown with perfect ease on one condition, that you allow no gardener to dig amongst them, and that you leave them carefully alone as soon as they are established. I know of no greater pleasure than to select your flower on the mountain and bring it home to plant in your garden, and then to see them as reminiscences of the beautiful scenes you have before seen. My Alpinery is a very delightful place to me. I always go there to see what flower is out: the last was the Lily of the field of the Bible, the plant to which were applied those celebrated words which I will not now venture to repeat. That is an Amaryllis. In the sandy places where it grows, it comes up and makes a display of bright flowers. Then there are the Saxifrages, and the grass of Parnassus, which was thought so beautiful as to be dedicated to the Muses. It may be found in Whitby in quantities. Then there is another plant in the Alpinery which I must notice, the *Linnæa borealis*. It is the smallest of all the honeysuckles, and that great naturalist chose it as a type of himself, because it had so lowly an origin. He obtained permission from the king to use it in his coat-of-arms. It is a very scarce plant, and I can hardly describe the pleasure I have found in seeing it in a wood in Aberdeenshire. I brought a large block with the earth on in triumph home with me, and there it grows. We are not restricted to foreign plants; our very woods and fields are beautiful with flowers. There is no more beautiful plant than the marsh marigold; to see it growing in spring is a sight not to be forgotten. Its perfection of form renders it a plant which is one of the beauties of our streams. The purple loosestrife which grows by the banks of the Thames renders them a perfect flower garden. When we find the wild digitalis, the wild violet, the wild honeysuckle, and many other plants, we may say that there is a beautiful flower garden in our woods. I was never more struck than when I saw some drawings of some wild flowers; I found that we had put aside for our garden-flowers, others which had higher claims. The time has nearly run out, but am I not to speak of my orchids, my bees, and my flies? Am I not to speak of the man orchid, which looks as though a little man were dangling from the flower? This is to be found within a few miles of London. The curious fly orchid is not far off, and must not be forgotten. The remarkable dancing girl orchid which we have in our houses is worthy of notice; every flower, by a little exercise of imagination, is converted into a dancing girl. There is another remarkable one which is called the dove orchid, and when you look into the flower of this you see a perfect figure of a dove. It is looked upon with considerable superstition by the Spaniards in Central America where it grows. I cannot describe the many beauties we grow, and it would take much longer to describe the plants we might grow. A garden must ever be a source of great pleasure to a man; it helps him over his troubles, soothes his nervous system, and carries his mind from the beautiful things which grow there to the Author and Designer of them all.

No. XXXV.

## SPEECHES DELIVERED AT ROCHESTER BY ALFRED SMEE.

### 1. SPEECH AT A COMPLIMENTARY DINNER TO ALFRED SMEE, DECEMBER 19TH, 1868.

MR. SMEE, who on rising was received with loud cheering, said:—Mr. Chairman, my Lord, and Gentlemen,—It is with a great deal of diffidence that I rise to express the thanks which I feel for the honour you have done me this day, in asking me to come amongst you, after the defeat we have experienced at the late election. We have unmistakably had a great defeat in Rochester—a defeat which we did not expect. The moment I entered the city I received numerous promises of support; those promises came rolling in day by day till 10 o'clock each night: they amounted at last to 1,024 on the day before the nomination. After the nomination, at which, as you know, we gained the show of hands, that same evening no more promises came, but promises began to fall off; withdrawals began to be made, which showed the city must be under the power of certain persons in it. (Sensation.) And on the next day these 1,024 promises degenerated into 702 performances. (Shame.) Accustomed as I am to numbers, I sat ticking off the votes at the Guildhall as they came in, and I soon saw that there was something wrong. I sent word to my committee, "Why don't the voters come up?" No answer came. I wrote again, "Tell me, why don't the voters come up?" A slip of paper then came with £ s. d. upon it. (Sensation.) I understood at once the meaning. Now there must be some very potential reason which prevented 1,024 promises from realizing more than 702 votes. In the first place, I think many good Conservatives were victims to despair. I found they worshipped success, and the moment they saw we were not at the head of the poll they stayed at home and did not vote. (Shame.) With this despair it is very difficult to deal; and I can only call your attention to the wife of that great man on whom our gracious Queen has bestowed a high honour. In the difficulties and disappointments of her husband, she supported, she comforted him, and all, even from the Queen on her throne, recognized what she did. (Hear, hear.) I will commend the victims of despair to the ladies of Rochester, and I am quite sure, as no "faint heart ever won fair lady," the ladies of Rochester will never let a man become a coward because his cause does not happen to win. (Cheers.) Mr. Smee then proceeded to quote the words of Sir Robert Peel, in the debate of 1833, in which he argued that if property of 300 years' possession was not secure to any establishment, little hope could be given of the safety of private property. Lord Palmerston had also expressed a belief that the Church and State establishment was essential to the constitution of every civilized country. (Cheers.) Lord Castlereagh and Mr. Canning were of opinion that the union of Church and State and the maintenance of the Irish Church were necessary for the well-being of the empire. Could we, in the face of all this great mass of opinions before us, proceed to vote step by step for the disintegration of Church and State? (No, no.) We had no need of apologizing to Mr. Martin for having voted in the Conservative cause, even if we had known we should not have been successful. (Hear, hear.) But despair was not the only cause of the defeat. There was a question which would be tried by numerous petitions, viz. the one day's pay. This was a very difficult question; the one day's pay in some circumstances might, he thought, be allowed and paid. He was advised that it should not be done in Rochester in this election, and it was not done; and to that trifle he attributed a great deficiency in the votes. Numbers of men, again, were compelled to vote as their masters wished, and not as they themselves thought proper. He believed, if every voter had been free to vote as he thought proper, three-fourths at least would have voted for the Conservative cause and not for the Liberals. (Cheers.) The parliamentary representation of the country had no doubt been considerably changed in the present Parliament. For some years past the middle classes had principally been represented in Parliament, but now the working men were the largest body amongst the electors. But in this city the men had been compelled to vote as he had said, immediately against their own principles. They had to vote in support of a party amongst whom was one man— Bright—whose principles they all knew, viz. that he wished to get the greatest amount of labour for the smallest amount of pay; and, again, to receive the greatest amount of money for the smallest amount of the necessaries of life. (Hear, hear.) Mr. Bright said that all dockyards were useless, and it might come to pass that Chatham dockyard might be done away with, in order that Mr. Bright might get the work put to tender amongst his favourites in the North, and then the inhabitants of this place would be left without anything but poverty and starvation. (Hear, hear.) Now, it had been seriously impressed upon him to petition against this return for the city of Rochester. He might have done so on safe grounds. But he did not wish to disturb the peace of the city, and it would have raised much ill feeling; and he felt that the working of the Act would be sufficiently proved by the fifty-four petitions which had been sent up: by those the law would be sufficiently demonstrated. And he would leave those masters who had not allowed their men to vote according to their own wishes to be racked and tormented by their consciences. (Hear, hear.) Those masters would be in constant fear that their men would not be doing that justice which they would otherwise have expected, and by that fear they would be tormented morning, noon, and night. (Hear, hear.) Now he believed that the doctrines he had had the pleasure of bringing before the city on many occasions would have their due weight. The doctrines would spread and grow, and finally they would overthrow the whole bulwark of Radicalism in the city. (Cheers.)

Now what had they to look forward to, and what had they to fear? As Conservatives they had a large majority against any other body of men holding contrary principles; but when they brought against the Conservatives all the eccentricities of character and opinion which the kingdom contained, they found themselves in a minority. Who were the Liberals? That body was composed of people professing opposite kinds of religion, who joined together for a time to overthrow one of the principles of the Constitution. (Hear, hear.) There was a confusion which ran through the whole country. This was demonstrated by the fact that they could not walk in the streets of London without being in fear of the garrotter; they could not sit in their houses without being in fear of the burglar. This was caused by the laws not being made to fit one another; the laws should be made upon one basis. In America they saw the same state of confusion exist. At last it caused that country to divide into two parts, and war ensued; and many lives and millions of money that war cost. It was caused simply by the want of principles. Nothing could be done by fits and starts; we must progress step by step from that which is good to that which is better if ever we were to reach that height of perfection which could be obtained under any human system. But the Conservatives must prepare for their work by organization. (Cheers.) They must have over them lieutenants of tens, captains of hundreds. and commanders of thousands, by whom they must be led to the poll. They ought to be so organized that at the next election the city could be canvassed in one night. (Cheers.) They must also have unity amongst themselves. (Hear, hear.) There must be one Conservative Association, and they must follow it, and then their cause would succeed at the next election. (Cheers.) And having been victorious in Rochester. step by step they would carry the Conservative cause throughout the empire. He thanked them again for the honour they had done him. Whatever he might be in future, and no one could tell whether he would be their member, or would ever remain the adopted but non-elected candidate for this city. he should ever be grateful for the kind reception which had been granted him here. (Cheers.) And as long as he lived. he should always remember the very kind manner in which they had greeted him that evening. (Loud cheers.)

---

## 2. Speech delivered on the occasion of the Presentation of Plate at the Corn Exchange, April 2nd, 1874.

Mr. Smee rose to return thanks, being received with tremendous applause. He said: Mr. Chairman, proposer, and seconder, I must confess it is not a new era of my life to receive a testimonial; for although I believe it has not been due to my merits but to the kindness of my friends, I have, either for services rendered or for fancied services rendered, received during my life more than I either could have deserved or desired. (Applause.) I am proud to say that I have many most valuable tokens that have been given to me. Then why should I accept this token from you, and think it far more agreeable than any one that I have received before? It is upon this principle, that whilst families, whilst single people, have thought it necessary to give me testimonials before, this is the first time in my life that I ever had a testimonial with a list of names spreading across this room, and numbering hundreds of persons. (Applause.) For why have you given me this testimonial? (A voice: Because you deserved it.) It is not for my merits, because there are many persons much more meritorious than I am (No, no) to whom you might have given this testimonial better than to me. But I know it is upon the truth of those principles that I have taken up and those principles which I have discoursed upon in the city of Rochester. (Applause.) I came here and said that I was an advocate for Conservative progress. Mind you, what was done in a room in this city has been adopted by the Prime Minister of this country. (Applause.) It commends itself to all your attention, for I pointed out to you that by wise laws the working men of this country might be benefited with respect to the land upon which they dwell, in the houses in which they live, in the food which they eat, in the liquors they require to drink. In fact every social problem of life demanded careful legislation and improvement with the knowledge of the age, and I stood before you as a firm and warm advocate of Conservative progress. (Applause.) There are two parties in this country; one the Conservatives, another who style themselves Liberals. We don't; we call them the Radical party. (Applause.) What are the Conservatives but the great national party of this country? (Applause.) They stand or go forward from time to time, venerating the Constitution and fully supporting the Church; and the principles upon which they rely will endure and must endure from generation to generation. (Applause.) The Conservative party is a substantial party. It is a party that has principles for its foundation. It has unity of purpose; and although of late years it has been somewhat repressed by a combination against it, it has now come forward triumphantly to maintain its proud position. (Applause.) And I am delighted to see the success it has met in every part of this country, and more especially the great rise which has taken place in the opinions of this city. (Applause.) We find the Conservatives are distinguished by fixed principles, by civilization, and by their love of order. Now let us see what distinguishes the Liberals: false theories and barbarism. (Applause.) Amongst the Liberals there are no two persons holding the same doctrines; every one has a fancy doctrine of his own. We find a combination of conflicting, erratic theories on religion, on science, on politics, on health, and upon medicine. Every one calls himself a Liberal; every one dislikes every other one of his class; but all join with the one common purpose of opposing and of voting against the Conservatives. (Hear, hear.) That does not constitute a party in itself. The union of dissimilar principles cannot make a distinct and definite idea to work upon. We have to contend with all the conflicting ideas of all mankind, but we rely upon truth, and truth comes out victorious under every possible form of fair inquiry. (Applause.) You see that the Liberals, or rather the Radicals, are like the bundle of sticks—every one dissimilar, but, joined together, forming a grand aggregation of strength. Hitherto we, who are regarded as the "heart of oak," have been unable to resist the "bundle of sticks" while tied together. But the time has come when we must adopt their idea. We must be like a bundle of sticks, move together, and then there is no power on earth which can repress the Conservative progressionists. (Applause.) Now that is the weak part of this city. If Conservative progress is to maintain its way, if the constitutional institutions of this country are to maintain their own, one and all, of all classes, must combine, must unite and go together to the poll, and then victory is before them. (Applause.) If once it is to be presumed that the working men are entirely to lead, they will fail; if the rich are to consider that they are to lead, they will fail: but if the rich and poor, if high and low and every grade of life, loving truth above all things, will unite together, then their strength will be such that no power can resist it. (Applause.) That is not my opinion alone. I have received this day from Mr. Gorst, who, you know, is intimately connected with managing election affairs throughout this country, a letter in which he says, "My dear sir, I am very glad to hear that an effort is about to be made in the city of Rochester for the re-organization of the Conservative party. Our success at the late general election was largely due to the existence in most counties and boroughs in England of Conservative associations which represented all classes of society. Elections cannot be won by the isolated efforts of a few persons, however able and influential they may be; what is required is a combined effort on the part of all who are attached to the Crown and the Constitution, and who desire the freedom of the people. The Conservatives of Rochester may rely on our sympathy and assistance in their attempt to constitute a united and powerful party in Rochester." For the first time since the last election, which we lost from various causes, you have constituted yourselves into committees to carry that out. You have only to thoroughly organize those committees, and success is yours. A gentleman has favoured us this evening with his presence—my friend Mr. Trego, Chairman of the Conservative organization at Tottenham (applause)—and he will tell you presently, if you call upon him, what success attended his efforts in Tottenham, how hundreds voted at the last election in comparison with tens who voted before; and as he won the victory in Middlesex, so you may win Rochester by a thorough combination. (Applause.) Do not let us neglect to follow the Liberals in whatever may be good; and they in this city have done much to show what organization can do. They have got a house for the purpose in which they "keep dark," in which they attend to the registration and to the votes, and they by that organization have obtained the advantage for many an election. (Hear, hear.) But the working men of this city are powerful indeed, for they constitute the majority; they have only to be true to themselves, and true to each other, and the member they desire will be placed at the head of the poll. (Applause.) I look upon this letter as a pledge that they in London will render every aid in their power if you do your duty in looking after each other, and securing the vote of every man who is upon the register. (Applause.) Now, the power of Conservatism over the country cannot be too highly estimated. It is a matter of high principle; it is a matter of principle which influences every action of our lives. We begin by combining religion as a part of our government, feeling that it ought to be carried on on just the same principles which we carry into every action of our lives. (Hear, hear.) The working man is essentially Conservative; by nature he must be so. (Applause.) I will illustrate that by one simple instance. I have alluded on other occasions to that machine which is contrived over in Strood by Mr. Aveling—with its piston to go quick and its wheels to go slow—which can be seen in the streets of London continually. Now, supposing you were to act contrary to principle—to screw down the safety valve—it would be blown into ten thousand pieces. Or supposing there was some little damage and the engine would not go at all, you would not think of trusting it to any man to repair who did not understand the principles upon which it was made. Yet this country has trusted the most recondite principles of government, the most recondite principles of action, to men of all sorts of varying ideas, and who had no principle upon any subject whatever. (Applause.) Now let me take a glance at the growth of the doctrine of Conservative progress since I first entered into your city. When I first addressed you in the King's Head rooms opposite, I was astonished at the multitude of my audience. We had to take precautions that no accident should happen to the house from the number of persons who were present. That was followed by the meeting when we applied for and were refused the room in which we now stand. They said, "What do we want with principles of Church and State, of religion and government? We are beyond all that. The days have passed for anything like propriety in that way. We'll not even allow you the use of this room." And we were refused, by the Radicals of that time, even this room in which I might address you. (Hear, hear.) When I came the second time, I found that you were much more deeply interested in the principles I had put forward than you were on the first occasion. The Radicals were violent; the Radicals were excited, and the whole city was placarded with announcements that in this room a meeting was to be held to denounce the principles put forward at the King's Head by "the stranger who had come down from London." Who resisted this but the working men of Rochester? (Applause.) Who said that no man should—as was intended—pass a resolution against me unless I was heard first? (Applause.) You would not permit in this room one word to be said till I was heard, and I was sent for; and when I was sent for, the voice of the meeting called out that as I was to be attacked I should be heard first. (Hear, hear.) Hour went on after hour, and not one word was spoken. Here we stood in dumb show, when your respected and estimable member said across the table, "Since, we have got all the people in here; how shall we get them out again?" (Laughter.) I said, "I am ready to stop here all night. I have entered into the fight and I assuredly will go through it. (Applause.) But if you wish to disperse this meeting, I'll disperse it in two minutes." "How?" he said. "Take hold of my arm, and we'll walk straight out." We did walk out, and there was an end of that meeting. (Applause.) That time you rallied round me and gave me the show of hands at the Guildhall, but still that was no use against the strong combination of all the odds and ends of fancy sections who came against me and won the election. When I look to those events and look to this proud occasion, when I am to receive a testimonial not from one but from hundreds of my fellow-countrymen, I have reason indeed to be proud of the doctrine of Conservative progress, and to thank you most cordially for being here to-night in the hall which has been granted in the kindest manner by your mayor. (Applause, and a voice "Three cheers for Mr. Edwards.") Now, our position at the present time is confessedly difficult. You have got in this city in particular a large mass of earnest Radicals who are joined one and all against your doctrines and to oppose your principles. That alone would require a great effort on your part to overcome. You have also to recollect that the Radicals have been a long time in power. Place has fallen to their lot, and consequently we may say of those who have had place that they may be expected to exhibit gratitude. With regard to that gratitude I must say I felt a little astounded when the question of the separation of Church and State was on, that some of those who lived by the Church did not support that Church in the manner which might have been expected. (Hear, hear.) Probably they relied upon the doctrine of gratitude to Gladstone, who had put them in their situations; but I cannot but think that gratitude to God, who had given them this Church, should have had a greater effect upon their minds than gratitude to a patron who had put them in place. (Applause.) But, contrariwise, I was also astonished by the manner in which those who heartily felt that religion and state should be united, expressed their feelings. One of your clergy at Strood, being confined by disease, was carried across by two men to the poll, there to record his vote for Church and State. (Applause.) I have given you some of your difficulties, but now comes the difficulty of that *vis inertiæ* which many in your city have been afflicted with. (Hear, hear.) Working men know what this *inertia* is; if they have a block of stone, they know how difficult it is to set it in motion. They know how difficult it is to move a steam-engine in the first instance, but once set going it rolls on. Now some hundreds of persons who call themselves Conservatives in this city had this *inertia*, that they could not roll out of their arm-chairs on the day of the poll and cross perhaps one hundred yards to record their votes. (Hear, hear.) That is the difficulty you have to cope with by argument and by persuasion; but in counting your forces you must say that everyone who is not with you heart and soul is against you. (Hear, hear.) You must count them against you, for it is a very dangerous thing to rely upon the vote of a man who will not rise out of his chair simply to deliver it. (Hear, hear.)

Now, gentlemen, these are great difficulties, but there is a greater still—a difficulty which it is customary not even to whisper from one person to another—that the person who dared to do it should close his ears that they might hardly hear what he had to say. And yet I think it is desirable that the whole case should be put before you; for I never will appear as a candidate for this city without being thoroughly above-board and telling you all the circumstances of the case. (Applause). The question to which I have to call your attention may be called the money question of an election. Now you know as well as I do that the working men have thought it right to ask for a day's pay if they lose a day's work in going to the poll. To give that day's pay is an act of illegality which renders the donor liable to serious consequences, the receiver to equally serious penalties, and might forfeit the franchise of the borough itself. Now I have taken this thing most carefully into my consideration, and I advised at the last election that you should throw up this day's pay at once for your vote, and show that you will be free men, and that you will esteem the privilege of electing any person you like to Parliament, independently of any small monetary consideration. (Applause.) Now what does a day's pay amount to? A day's pay for the city of Rochester, for those who are likely to take it and think they are fairly entitled to it, would amount to about 7s. 6d. per man; and that will not amount in the whole to above £100 or £150—a sum too insignificant for a candidate to think worthy his attention when he has to pay for the printing, advertising, the parliamentary fees, and the many other things which are connected necessarily with a powerful contest. This £100 or £150, I say, is immaterial to the candidate except that by giving it the election may be lost afterwards and the borough may be disfranchised. But what do you think is the price asked for this borough in the London markets? The price is £2000 a candidate, or £4000 for the two. (Shame.) Now, are you ever likely to get that money? In the annals of the city has it ever been divided among the people? (No, no.) I say not. Then who has received it, and where has it gone to? (Hear, hear.) Now this is a very serious question indeed, for you may depend upon it, if there is any man in this city who looks forward to receive his £100, and if when a candidate comes down to the borough and offers himself he does not come down with that money, it will be that he is not quite the proper man for the place. (Laughter and hear, hear.) Now I will tell you plainly that that insinuation has been put forward in Rochester, and it is your duty to find out who is looking forward for that money and who has put forward that insinuation. (Hear, hear.) It has been insinuated that the people who asked me down here wanted my money. Who asked me down here? Messrs. Watson, father and son. I declare upon my honour that I have never paid them one shilling, I never have promised them one shilling, I never intended to give them one shilling. (Applause.) Moreover, they have given me good and safe counsel in every part of this election, and advised me not to waste my money amongst prodigals who would not be benefited by it, but to trust entirely to your probity and sense of right to return that candidate whom you may think fit. (Applause.) Now I am speaking very perspicuously upon this point, because it is on this a great deal will turn in future elections. If you wish me—after giving me this magnificent testimonial—to retire to London, I shall retain that ever afterwards as a sense of your kindness and as a proof that the doctrines I have spoken have affected properly your minds; but I say emphatically I will not come here to be a party to giving £2000 for myself, or £4000 for two candidates to be distributed amongst I don't know who. (Applause.) The moment it was announced I had set my foot into Rochester it was communicated to me through a friend that your late lamented member, Sir William Bodkin, wished me to call upon him at the Sessions House in Clerkenwell. I did call there, and the burden of his song was, "Beware!" "Beware of whom?" I said. "Of what I can't tell you." I named every person up the High-street of any pretensions. "I can't tell you, but I sent for you and beg you to beware." Not only that, but I have seen other persons connected with this city and they have told me also to beware. I have had I cannot tell you how many letters from parties I have been associated with in relations of business telling me to "Beware." But what am I to beware of? (A laugh.) I have spent nothing here but what the law imposes upon me according to the contract I made with you at the King's Head before the last election; and instead of being fleeced as it was represented, I am almost ashamed to say I fleece you by taking this magnificent testimonial. (No, no, and laughter.) I will say but little more, but if you wish me to come forward it must be upon that basis. I am prepared to fight with you as long as you are prepared to fight (applause); but I am not prepared to pay this money, and upon this it will greatly turn, although nobody, as I have said before, could ever tell me who received it. (A voice: We don't want pay.) Now I again, for the last time, thank you from the very bottom of my heart for the very kind manner in which you have made this presentation to me; and I tell you fairly that the moment it was presented to me it passed partly out of my hands, because my son and myself have made a compact to devote our time, whether literary, whether politically, or whether professionally, to our mutual benefit, and therefore this present goes at once not only to myself but to my son after me. (Applause.) It has already become half his property, and I feel confident he will transmit it to his sons and grandsons to show in how very kind a manner the people of Rochester received me. (Applause.) You nobly supported Church and State. May that State, by good government and the administration of fair laws, contribute to your perpetual comfort here; and may the Church lead to your eternal happiness hereafter. (Loud cheers followed the conclusion of Mr. Smee's speech, and a call for "One for the son" was warmly responded to.)

### No. XXXVI.A.

## CORRESPONDENCE ON MILK, TYPHOID FEVER, AND SEWAGE. By ALFRED SMEE.

THE following observations on Milk, Typhoid Fever, and Sewage, some of which appeared in the columns of the 'Times' newspaper, and all in those of the 'Standard,' have been reprinted in consequence of the intense interest they have excited.

Sewage-grounds, as now conducted, are a failure. They do not disinfect the sewage. They are dangerous to health. They are not adapted for healthy vegetation, and the produce, under certain circumstances, is unfit for either the food of man or beast.

The Houses of Parliament have been deceived by exaggerated statements to pass Acts which have proved an injury to the community.

So-called skilled witnesses and dilettante counsellors, to the great annoyance of professional men and to the disgrace of science, have made declarations before parliamentary committees where, with ordinary intelligence, they could not have been ignorant of their falsity.

As a consequence, serious evils have arisen by the formation of pestilential sewage-grounds, which now imperatively demand steps to be taken for their entire abolition where possible; and where their abolition is impracticable, then for their regulation and inspection by competent authorities, that the town-councillors of one district may not poison the air and pollute the wells of the territory of their neighbours.

7, FINSBURY CIRCUS,                           A. SMEE.
     Sept. 11th, 1873.

SIR,—In reference to your leading article in this day's 'Standard,' I beg to forward a copy of a letter which I have this day sent to Mr. Simon, the distinguished Officer of Health to the Privy Council.

### LETTER TO JOHN SIMON, ESQ., F.R.S., D.C.L., PRIVY COUNCIL OFFICE.

I am in a position to explain the occurrence of typhoid fever from the use of milk. We keep a small herd of cows, from which my house in London is supplied with milk, cream, and butter. What is not required for our own use is sent to the members of the families of the men employed at my garden, and when there is any surplus the neighbours purchase it.

During the spring my son directed, without my knowledge, that the cows should be fed with a small proportion of sewage grass, when, without knowing the reason, the butter was so offensive we could not bear it on the table; the other members of the family were loud in their complaints, and the neighbours for a long time came for no more butter.

Upon inquiry, I heard of the feed of sewage grass, which was immediately ordered to be discontinued, when the milk, cream, and butter resumed their former excellence.

This seemed to me too seriously important to pass unnoticed, so I desired my son again to repeat the experiment suddenly, without any notice, when the same results again occurred. Cows like the sewage grass, and the milk is slightly increased in quantity by its use. The milk has a slightly rancid odour when about twenty-four hours old, and has this quality a day or two after the cows are fed with the grass. The butter becomes bad about a day or two after it is made, and no care in its preparation can avert its rancidity.

I have long known that the use of putrid manures affects the quality of vegetables, and have called special attention to the fact in the book of ' My Garden.' I did not, however, know till lately that the putrid matter could be taken by animals and communicated in the dangerous putrefactive state by the milk to other animals. If you would like to verify the experiment, a cow shall be placed at your disposal for the purpose, but I have reason to suspect that the fact, which has a bearing upon many social problems, is thoroughly well known to our dairy proprietors.

August 15.

It is currently suggested that in cases where typhoid fever has occurred near sewage farms the milk has been directly adulterated with sewage.

I can hardly myself entertain so horrible an idea, but if the suspicion has been entertained, why was not a coroner's inquest held upon those who died, and why was no attempt made to bring the supposed adulterators to justice ?

As my letter has opened the whole subject of sewage irrigation, and made the public alive to the importance of the subject, I will take the liberty of answering all correspondents in a few days, but much information has been supplied to me which, for obvious reasons, I dare not write.

August 19.

In the first week in July I visited a friend in Harley Street, the centre of the present epidemic of typhoid fever, when a fine cat was shown to me which would not touch London milk, though in the country it drank milk as freely as other cats do.

It was suggested that I should send to puss a can of milk from my garden as I received it for my own use. This was done, and the following answer was received on July 8:—" The milk was immediately submitted to Fluff's judgment, and he, after a most careful inspection, appeared to be of the opinion that it was excellent, and he, after once having fairly tasted it, drank every drop I gave him. It certainly is a very curious circumstance, and shows pretty plainly to me (as you suggested) that the London milkman supplies something besides water with his milk."

Assuming the milk to have been the sole cause of the present epidemic, how much pain and how many deaths might have been averted if the sagacity of the cat had been rightly understood ! I have been asked how putrefactive milk can be determined. I reply, " From the creatures thy instructions take." Follow the example of the cat, and get evidence of the act of putrefaction by the nose. Keep the milk for twenty-four hours in a moderately warm place, when the bad odour will demonstrate the evil.

Not only milk, but water contaminated by putrefactive compounds, will after twenty-four hours discover its death-producing qualities. Good water will travel all over the world without change, but if it contains the elements of putrescence it will not keep twenty-four hours without the odour being apparent.

Both men who attend to my son's cows state that they can detect no difference in new milk produced from grass grown upon land irrigated with town sewage till after some hours have elapsed: and I have ascertained that the milk from sewage farms is regularly consumed in some of our large towns too soon for its source to be detected, and, perhaps, too soon for it to be actually hurtful.

August 18.

The time has arrived for grouping the valuable information which the milk controversy has elicited. My observations were limited by the word "putrid," and the facts appear to turn upon the right use of the word. A putrid state of decomposition as is observed in town sewage is very different from the ammoniacal state which is observed in stables, and which the gardener uses in his hotbeds, and which should always be employed for the culture of first-class vegetables.

In answer to various inquiries, our cows are of the Alderney, Brittany, and short-horn breeds, and are usually fed on fields on the lower tertiary bed of sand, immediately above the chalk, or upon a drift bed of flints, which in bygone days have been washed out of the chalk. In the first case my son gave the cows two rods of grass from the Croydon sewage fields, fresh cut, which was about a full barrowful to each cow per day, as a part of their usual food, when the putrid state of the milk and butter became apparent. He tried the experiment without my knowledge, having a full belief in the benefits which would accrue, as at that time he did not share my opinion of the hurtful qualities of sewage grass. That, and the subsequent experiment, admit neither of qualification nor explanation.

*　　　　*　　　　*　　　　*　　　　*　　　　*

The proprietor of a large dairy, who supplies several of our largest institutions in London, informs me that he had the Edmonton sewage farm, but was obliged to abandon it, as the milk was unsaleable. Letters confirming my view, or rather in most cases going beyond my statement, have been received from Mr. Bardwell, of Great Queen Street, Westminster; also from Mr. Hollis, of Eastbourne, who states that when fresh night soil was applied to a meadow the butter afterwards had the flavour of night soil, and was utterly unfit for use. A letter has been received from the celebrated private inquiry office of Field the detective, stating that in America the same thing is noticed. Mr. Butt writes that in all towns and villages of India the buffaloes eat putrid matters, the consequence being that the milk has a most offensive smell, and all Europeans like to have their own cows and keep them tied up.

At Beddington School, when supplied with sewage milk, 60 cases of typhoid fever occurred, and three deaths, No. 243, No. 249, and one other. It has been endeavoured by the sewage promoters to account for the disaster upon the plea that the milk was directly adulterated by sewage; but no inquest was held, neither was any man prosecuted. Dr. MacCormack, the medical officer of Lambeth, states that an attack of fever occurred from the Croydon sewage milk; and a clergyman from Scotland informs me that a cow-keeper neglecting to give his cows fresh water, they drank sewage. After partaking of the milk he had that evening diarrhœa. All observers agree that cows will drink sewage freely, and eat vegetables or other substances in a putrid state.

Both my men agree that milk from sewage grass must stand a certain time before it shows signs of putridity, and that they themselves would not hesitate to use sewage grass if the milk is used at once. The milk from the cows of the Croydon sewage farm goes to Croydon and is there consumed. It is alleged that it is sold at 1s. a gallon, and sold again to the Croydon workhouse at 10d. . . . .

I have before me certificates of the deaths which occurred from fever in the houses near the Croydon sewage-grounds, which I give in detail :—

### No.                    1868.

73. Typhoid fever, 19 days; congestion of brain.
95. Typhoid fever, 16 days; congestion of brain.

### 1869.

243. Enteric fever; ulceration of bowels.
249. Enteric fever.
250. Fever.
286. Peritonitis; pleuropneumonia.
336. Scarlatina maligna, 14 days.
350. Gastritis, 4 days.
359. Scarlet fever, 9 days.
375. Scarlet fever; convulsions.

### 1870.

376. Scarlet fever; convulsions.
395. Diphtheria; inflammation of chest, 1 week.
436. Malignant scarlet fever, 5 days.
485. Scarlatina, 7 days; effusion of brain, 48 hours.
489. Scarlatina, 14 days; albuminuria, 5 days.
490. Scarlatina, 5 weeks; albuminuria, 14 days.
498. Scarlatina, 18 days; albuminuria.
22. Scarlatina, 19 days.
65. Scarlatina, 11 days; diphtheria, 5 days.

As about 20 cases of illness occur for every one of death, it follows that immediately surrounding the sewage-ground not less than 380 cases occurred between the 21st May, 1868, and the 4th August, 1870, the period over which I had certificates beside me.

Town sewage-grounds are really in some cases pestilential marshes, where putrid matter is taken from the courts and alleys of the towns and carried before the drawing-room windows of suburban houses.

During the discussion the effect of the solid matter deposited upon the stems of the grass has very properly been considered, though I restricted my remarks to the effect of putrid sewage on the juices of the plant.

At any moment some malignant form of fever may break out on ill-managed sewage farms, as similar fevers have originated at Marseilles from a neglect of the laws of health.

All vegetables are affected by putrid sewage. Asparagus is rendered particularly offensive. The whole cabbage tribe are easily rendered particularly offensive, and even the delicious strawberry becomes disgusting when watered with putrid manures.

Stock fed upon sewage farms, if mismanaged, suffer materially, and in the public interest should have stringent Government supervision before they are admitted to be sold for human food. Information upon this point was directly refused in August 1869, but a Government commission with full powers may obtain valuable information.

Credible and disinterested witnesses have written to me privately and to the newspapers stating that they have used sewage grass, and yet their milk and butter are excellent. In each of these cases the sewage is small. It passes directly to the land, which is large in area in relation to the amount of liquid, and it has not time to become putrid. Dr. Symes, of the County Asylum, Dorchester, says cabbages grown on their ground irrigated by sewage are good, and no fault is found with the milk and butter. Dr. Phillips, of the Devon County Asylum, says that the milk and butter produced from their sewage-ground are excellent. Mr. Hales, of the South Metropolitan Schools, states that the use of milk provided from their sewage grass has been innocuous.

After this evidence I must admit that fresh sewage under certain circumstances may be safely applied over a large surface of land without injury, and have so advised since this controversy. Nevertheless I should myself prefer to keep milch cows from sewage altogether.

Under all the facts of the case we are bound to admit that town sewage irrigation as now practised is a failure, and dangerous to health. At present there appears to be no plan which can be absolutely recommended, but the question of sewage must be practically dealt with. If we look the difficulty fairly in the face, we may rely that the intellect of man will surely provide a remedy, and preserve for the community healthy milk and wholesome meat.

August 22.

Typhoid fever is known to be propagated either by animal or vegetable matter in decomposition, or by both together. Of the exact nature of typhoid poison nobody knows. No person has ever isolated the poison. No one has ever seen it. No one knows how typhoid fever originates, but all medical men trace it to putrid matters, and it is known particularly to be transmissible from person to person by sewage. I have seen this terrible disease at Naples and Florence, and had the misfortune to treat it in those cities, and in both those places I had conference with the municipal authorities for its prevention, and was authorized by capitalists to offer a million and a half of money to lessen the mischief by adequate water supply and drainage. It is not known, when a number of persons are exposed to typhoid poison, why some are affected and some escape, nor is it known, either with typhoid fever or with cholera, why apparently the same conditions do not at all times produce the same results. The human mind is now in a curious state of embarrassment upon the question. The sewage irrigators are irrational in their arguments. They form conclusions without premises, and they reason as though logic was the art of wrong reasoning.

Medical men abhor putrid sewage, even in isolated patches, as the focus of disease, from the poisonous effluvia which it exhales. Sewage irrigators take a number of isolated putrid sewage foci, and describe the vast resultant pestilential sewage swamp, the emanations from which are concentrated and overpowering, as a sanitary panacea. When the absurdity is demonstrated, they retreat under the charge of mismanagement; but sewage farms, as they are now laid out, cannot be managed other than to be an offensive and dangerous hotbed of disease, liable to be active at any moment. When disease is charged against them, the sewage irrigators falsely reason thus—sewage irrigation is good, *ergo* some other cause for disease must exist. Chemists have wisely pointed out the danger of putrefying matter in water, even in small quantities. They have carried their doctrine to such an extent that a grain or two of nitre in a gallon of water condemns that water for town use, on the ground that possibly nitre may have come from the nitrogen of previous sewage contamination, although at the moment utterly changed to chemical salts. The sewage irrigators cover the ground with putrid matter, poison wholesale the wells of the district, let some of the sewage pass unchanged into the rivers, to be drunk unawares by the neighbouring villagers. The so-called sanitary guardians relieve a town at the expense of the suburbs. All this is done at an enormous cost to the ratepayers on the ground of danger to health; but the aggregation of danger to the suburban residents is called innocuous irrigation. Sewage logic is as bad as sewage irrigation—one focus of disease is dangerous, a thousand foci aggregated together are innocuous. Milk is known to be a conveyer of typhoid poison. Sewage on a single farm is rightly condemned, but an aggregation of a hundred farms with sewage to constitute a sewage farm is considered by the sewage theorists free from harm.

When cows feed on farms where sewage is, or feed on a sewage farm, the labourers, it is alleged, make the quantity of milk for sale increased in volume by directly adding sewage to the milk; but no proprietor has ever been made by custodians of sewage farms to punish those guilty of such a horrible crime. Cows drink sewage—in fact, its saline character makes them prefer it; and whether it be sewage on a farm or the sewage of a sewage farm, the milk, after the cow has drunk the sewage, becomes contaminated, is capable of putrescence, and therefore forms putrescible matter, in which typhoid poison may revel. Plants which grow on farms which have recent putrid sewage, take up into their composition and juices the manurial matters. These remain unchanged for some time in the plant, and during that period make the plant liable to putrescence and to be poisonous to man and injurious to animals. The power which plants possess of changing matters which they imbibe is not always equal. It differs with the states of atmosphere and with the seasons. Heat and cold modify this power. Light, darkness, or the quality of the light, or even the hygrometric state of the air, influences the result, so that at every period the same class of plants must of necessity have a variation in its power of assimilating sewage. How putrid sewage, when absorbed, is converted into plant-structures, is not known, as botanists generally believe that animal matters are converted into ammonia or nitrates before they undergo their changes into vegetable tissues. When cows eat plants containing unchanged manurial products, the milk is tainted. It putrefies, and the putrescent milk may be as liable to communicate typhoid poison as the putrescent water was before it was taken into the plant.

In the case of the recent epidemic, the sewage on the farm was either added directly to the milk, which I hesitated to believe, or the cows

2 c 2

obtained the poison by drinking the sewage or by eating plants which had previously absorbed the sewage. As long as good milk is a necessity to a town, let us have no putrid sewage on a dairy farm. Let not the cows drink sewage or eat putrid sewage grass.

A farm with sewage on it, and a sewage farm, must be held to be pestilential, death-producing swamps, until the sewage is disinfected. Nature should be followed, and manurial matters in the putrid state should be changed to mineral matters before they are absorbed by the plants which feed upon them. Theoretically earth disinfects the sewage. In practice, as now managed, part of the sewage never gets into the earth to be disinfected, as the whole is spread over the waterlogged ground, where it exhales its pestilential gases. Cows, whilst it is so spread over the field, drink some; blades of grass attach to themselves solid particles, and plants take up other particles in their juices. Notwithstanding this absurd deviation from the ways of nature, sewage farmers, engineers, speculators, and others living by the promotion of sewage farms, recommend sewage farms, as now conducted, as the source of all sanitary good. All men know that if we do not return to the ground that which we take from the ground the earth will not restore to us its usual crops. Sewage-farm speculators assume that they alone know this great fact, and are always demonstrating it to draw off attention from the infraction of the laws of Nature. If they return sewage to the land, they care not in what state they apply it, and either do not know, or pretend not to know, the danger they incur. The gardener who makes up his hotbed sweetens his manure by fermentation, when ammonia is produced. The rootlets of his cucumbers and melons run in the manurial mass, and sweet and wholesome produce is obtained.

The gardener also uses liquid manure with care and caution in certain stages of the growth of a plant. He particularly abstains from giving the ripening strawberry such manure, as he knows that his fruit would be corrupted. The sewage irrigators, regardless of consequences, use putrid manure at such a period that the plants are dangerous to animals. They do not know, or they care not for the fact, that vegetable dyes, as madder, will permeate an animal and colour its bones, which demonstrates to all physiologists how animals are affected by the food they eat. Much more may be said upon the effect of sewage vegetation on cows and sheep used afterwards for human food, which must be considered at a convenient season. Sewage promoters say that they can conduct their farms with safety to the community. Take them at their word, and if any complaints fairly arise from mismanagement, let the delinquent be fined £100 a day for every day a sewage farm is mismanaged. Sewage farmers who sell sewage directly put into the milk, or sewage transmitted through the cow to the milk, or transmitted through vegetables imbued with sewage to the cow, and from the cow by the milk to man, would be rather astonished if they were found legally liable for their acts as railroad companies are liable for preventable accidents. A verdict of £10,000 against a town council for the death of a father of a family, in consequence of poisoned milk sent from a dairy farm with sewage upon it, or a badly-managed sewage-ground, will do more than any argument to rectify it. Town councillors, as a whole, have neither intellect to comprehend, intelligence to perceive, nor public spirit to undertake an expense necessary to deal with sewage as a whole to ensure safety to their neighbours, whilst they protect the inhabitants of their towns.

August 30.

The interest in the milk typhoid question does not abate, judging from the amount of correspondence I receive. This morning the medical officer of one of our largest establishments informs me that he has known parsley to take up the flavour of gas-tar so as to be useless, which is a remarkable instance of the absorption of matter by growing plants. With respect to the remarks of Mr. Holland, we are driven to the alternative that either the typhoid poison originated in the milk or the milk was a convenient pabulum for the typhoid poison to be absorbed in, as nobody now doubts that milk has been an extensive conveyer of the typhoid virus. The facts relating to typhoid in all countries must be considered; and whether in England, or in the hotbeds of the disease in Rome, Florence, and Naples, sewage stands prominently forth as the source whence the poison acts on the human system. Probably it has fallen to my duty to examine the personal history of more cases in most countries of Europe than any other person, and the large number of cases of fever which are recorded in cities on the Continent, where sanitary regulations are confessedly imperfect, is very striking. The act of putrescence is the common concomitant of typhoid poison, and my observations prove that milk, under certain circumstances, is putrescible. It is undeniable that putrescible milk has been supplied where typhoid fever has originated. Does the typhoid poison pass through the cow to the milk? This is a question which our imperfect knowledge of the nature of the poison forbids us to answer. Then comes the question —Is the typhoid poison absorbed by the milk from the atmosphere after it has passed from the cow, and then, if it is so absorbed, does it come from the solid particles of the atmosphere, or does it come from matter in a gaseous state? Some philosophers have considered that the particles of dust which dance in the sunbeam are molecules of disease and death, but no proof has ever been afforded, and I believe that a large majority of the medical profession do not acquiesce in that doctrine. With respect to what is contained in the atmosphere in a purely gaseous state, an elaborate series of experiments has been made at various stations in London, in some of the more important hospitals, and at my experimental garden, and the result has been that not only can the odour of flowers be reduced from the atmosphere, but that large and variable quantities of nitrogenous materials are contained in the atmosphere. Practically it is immaterial whether putrescible milk originates or absorbs typhoid poison. We know that milk under certain circumstances communicates typhoid poison, and it is our bounden duty to make such provision that our large towns are supplied with good and wholesome milk. Medical men generally agree to treat typhoid fever with milk, and it is horrible to contemplate that they have sought to cure the disease by administering additional doses of typhoid poison. The public must reject all milk which is readily putrescible, and refuse milk from all sewage farms which are in the mismanaged state which partisans directly state that they are at present. Mr. Holland most properly asks why putrescible manure spread over the land differs from sewage. The answer is, that there is no perceptible difference. Sewage, however, is applied to the grass immediately before it is used, and contains the products of fever cases. In the former case, however, it is applied long before the grass is eaten by the cow. A field where cows continually pasture yields grass which produces milk of bad quality.

It is satisfactory to find that the sewage milk typhoid controversy has thoroughly aroused the country to the importance of the subject, and it is likely thoroughly to discomfort those who have of late years inflicted so much damage to sanitary science by their absence of knowledge and want of skill.

September 3.

My observations upon the milk question have in some cases been misunderstood, in others they have been mis-stated; but the broad fact that recent sewage on grass affects milk is recognized and being acted upon throughout England, as all prudent persons now discard milk which has any proximity to sewage. I took the most active part in turning the sewage out of rivers. I prepared the evidence upon which the sewage was turned out of the river Wandle, as it runs through my experimental garden, by procuring a series of perpetual injunctions in Chancery, when it was diverted from the land; and now the sewage farms are so mismanaged that I have again to take active steps to remedy this evil, which is as bad or worse than when it was turned into the river. I earnestly warned the Government in the former instance to avert the danger which threatened the inhabitants from their drinking the polluted Wandle water, when persons were sent round to inform the residents; and I now publicly, most earnestly warn the Government as to the mode in which these sewage farms are conducted. In the former instance the same universal denial of facts, the same attempt at ridicule, the same personal invectives, the same false arguments, were used by those who had an interest in the river pollution as have been attempted to be used on the present occasion by those who have an interest in the pollution of the land. By patience and perseverance I carried my point. I turned the sewage from the river which runs through my garden, and the proceedings served as a precedent for preventing the pollution of all the other rivers in England. By similar patience and perseverance I trust on the present occasion to compel those who are reckless of the comfort, the health, and the lives of residents near sewage-grounds, to compel them to adopt such a system as may not be a nuisance to their neighbours. Town councillors have to learn this one great fact—that sewage taken from their own parish and distributed to their neighbours is no more a sanitary mode of dealing with the question than if a housemaid of one house throws all the offal over the wall into her neighbour's premises; yet so does Croydon to Beddington, and Enfield to Edmonton. It is not only typhoid fever which is propagated by sewage-grounds, scarlet fever seems to be distributed wholesale by it; and what can be expected when highly contagious epithelial cells are sown broadcast over the land? We have not had a great epidemic of cholera since sewage farms have been at work, but I look with fear and trembling on what the consequences may be if sewage irrigation is not improved before the next visitation, which now threatens. I hope, whatever mistakes may have been committed, that the Dairy Reform Company will ensure the future confidence of the public by giving the most minute particulars to those qualified to judge of the matter, that every drop of fluid sent out by them should be traced to its origin, that scientific men may know how the typhoid poison infected the milk, as much damage has ensued to the company by the defiant tone assumed by one of its directors, who was a great promoter of sewage farms, and who might have shown becoming humility when so great a disaster occurred in a company immediately under his control.

September 8.

Now that public attention is directed to the sewage-grounds, advantage must be taken of the opportunity to remedy their evils. The difficulty in a proper application of sewage is the amount of water with which it is mixed. From Croydon a river of sewage runs, which at its origin turns a turbine wheel to work a Latham's machine for the separation of stones, bottles, and other solid matters. The first attempt to utilize sewage in the metropolis was made many years ago at Fulham, where a pumping engine was erected. The company was most anxious to supply experimentally the important market garden belonging to Messrs. Fitch, and I was empowered, for the sake of experience, to offer sewage free of charge, and the company even undertook to lay pipes over their garden. A serious conference took place between the landowner, the three partners, and myself, of some hours' duration, when they pointed out the immense importance for healthy vegetation that the water should be got from the grounds; and, after a most earnest and careful discussion, they declined the offer. Thirty years' experience has added but little to the valuable knowledge of these first-class cultivators. Our first object should be to relieve our towns of that which is detrimental to health; the second, to use the material profitably, if we can; but health must not be sacrificed for gain, nor disease incurred for the prevention of loss. The serious nature of this particular case is that the evils of sewage occur at one spot, and the distribution of the poison takes place at another, far distant; so the connection between the source of the evil and the resultant mischief is difficult and in many cases impossible to be traced. It is now of paramount importance to the multitude that sewage shall be under stringent enactments and searching Government supervision; and, on now leaving the controversy, everybody must admit the time has been well spent if it leads to a supply of good milk to the people, and a better mode of rendering sewage innocuous to our cities.

In reference to your able article of last Saturday, may I be permitted to observe that my remarks have been misunderstood by a few persons and mis-stated by others?

I have assumed as a generally-accepted fact that typhoid fever is intimately associated with putrescible matter, although the exact nature of the poison, as you so powerfully put it, is unknown. Upon this assumption I pointed out that if a cow ate sewage, or drank sewage, or ate sewage vegetable produce, that the milk became putrescible, and, according to all analogous experience, a competent vehicle for typhoid poison.

I have never passed an opinion as to how the poison actually got into the milk during the late epidemic. Whether it was directly added by polluted water, as many eminent authorities are inclined to believe; whether it was absorbed on the farm of the Dairy Reform Company, as some are inclined to suppose; whether the poison was taken by the cow and passed through to the milk; or whether the milk self generated the poison—the public have not as yet sufficient evidence to form an opinion, and it is deeply to be regretted that no inquest has been held to unravel the mystery on oath.

My observations have been restricted to the fact that vegetables take matter into their juices which renders them putrescible, and that a cow eating plants in that state produces milk which is putrescible, and consequently well adapted as a nidus for typhoid poison.

Sept. 15.

The statement of Mr. Morgan in his letter to the 'Standard' with respect to my opinion on sewage is liable to be misunderstood.

I am of opinion: 1. That sewage-grounds, as hitherto used, are the most dangerous nuisances which have ever been devised, creating vast perpetual swamps calculated to spread disease, or even to engender new forms of disease. 2. That the herbage grown upon sewage-grounds, under improper culture, is unfit for milch cows, as it sometimes infects the milk and is injurious to cattle, as it causes disease. 3. That putrid sewage is liable to be absorbed by growing plants, rendering them putrescible under some circumstances, and unfit for the food of man or animals. 4. That sewage irrigation cannot be employed as a commercial success, and, where cleansing by terrestrial filtration is necessary, towns must consider that they have a nuisance to abate upon the best terms they can.

Since these opinions have been extensively promulgated, sewage irrigators have not been so rampant, and sewage farms have been conducted with somewhat more respect to the laws of Nature, and vegetables and herbage have been allowed sufficient time to change the raw sewage before they are consumed by animals and man. Notwithstanding this partial improvement, I have reason to believe that tons of the wholesome watercress, so desirable for large towns, are sold in London, although grown under circumstances in which the stalks are liable to be besmeared with fæcal matter. I have, therefore, in no way altered my opinion that sewage grounds require official supervision and control, to protect the public against the crude theories and malpractices of the sewage irrigators. Mr. Morgan is unquestionably following the right course, and doing good service to sanitary science, by his experiments to precipitate the sewage principles and obtain their manurial properties, and finally cleansing the water through an oxidizing terrestrial medium; but whether his is the best precipitating process which can be adopted on a large scale, further experience is still required.

October 14.

————'s letter is a fair specimen of the tone adopted by the Croydon Board of Health when complaints are made, and by these general defiant denials ———— has done more to throw discredit over properly-conducted sewage irrigation than any man living. It is true that I took a prominent part in preventing the pollution of the Wandle by the Croydon sewage, which has had an important effect in preventing the pollution of other rivers. It is true that I stopped the lime process and other chemical precipitating processes; and it is also true that I recommended that the sewage when withdrawn from the river should be placed on the land. All these results were obtained by the powers of the High Court of Chancery, and not by the good sense and neighbourly feeling of the Croydon Sewage Board. Every statement was met with as flat a denial as ——— gives to the complaint of the great nuisance which has been created; but truth upon oath prevailed, as it will again, if necessity demands. On the occasion when a cartload of trout was destroyed in the river and proceedings were pending, the Board relaxed their usual arrogance, and they asked the favour of my friendly advice, which was readily given, and the costs of Chancery proceedings were saved to the ratepayers. If Nature is interrogated in sincerity and truth, we shall assuredly find a satisfactory solution of the difficulty. The investigations of the phenomena which are presented in sewage-grounds is confessedly difficult. Perhaps there are not ten men in Europe, and of these not two in England, who are competent to unravel the physico-physiological problems of a sewage farm; and therefore, whilst I am quite prepared to give ——— credit for a desire to the proper conduct of his sewage-grounds, I would ask him to consider how far he has the requisite knowledge to dogmatize on the subject. Whilst ——— eulogizes the manner in which the sewage-grounds are conducted, where are the sanitary engineers to approve it, though any one of them could rid them of much of their abomination?

——— has avoided the question as to how many tons of water-cresses have been sent from the sewage-grounds during the last six months. ——— denies that badly-conducted sewage-grounds cause disease in cattle. I affirm it. It becomes then a matter of credibility of statement. My affirmations in the former cases were accepted by the Court of Chancery; those of his party were discredited, and a decree was obtained. The same exactness and truthfulness which carried the causes before will carry them again, if the disease in cattle should ever occur under circumstances when oaths can be administered. Perhaps ———, from his habit of using universal denials, is not aware that his letter of the 20th is little short of an accusation of fraud. Does not this come with a bad grace from a party who have suffered from repeated judgments, to which they have submitted? I have neither interest in nor favouritism to any particular sewage process, though inventors have generally submitted them for my inspection, and I believe that no person wishes to interfere with sewage farms if they are properly conducted, but every one desires to aid the cause when they are conducted in the spirit of earnestness and truth.

October 22.

SEWAGE, SEWAGE PRODUCE, AND DISEASE.  Paper read
before the Health Section of the Social Science Congress, held at
Norwich, October 3rd, 1873, by ALFRED SMEE.

ONE of the most serious problems of the day connected with medical
social science is the question of the effect of sewage-grounds, as now
conducted, on the public health.

The present system is to collect sewage by drains arising from each
house in a town.  These are joined together, first, according to streets,
then according to districts, till the whole forms one vast and continuous
stream, which flows by night and by day, differing somewhat in amount
according to the hour of the day, till it reaches its outfall.

From this point the great stream is again subdivided over a territory
of varying extent, when the sewage is supposed to be disinfected by the
land, and the quasi-purified water is again collected into a channel, which
has its outpourings in one of the rivers of the district.

During the whole course, sewage is a dangerous nuisance, tends to
many deaths, and more cases of illness, which by skill and prudence, acting
with due regard to the rules of social science, may be averted.

In the first part of its course, the sewage is in a state of fermentation,
decomposing and disintegrating the solid matters to such an extent that
pieces of paper, which all photographers know may be kept in water for
days and weeks, are torn to shreds, and at the outfall nothing but discoloured water with slimy particles are to be seen.

During this fermenting process, the so-called sewer gases are exhaled,
faint and sickening in odour, and unmistakably, according to the experience of all medical men, the cause of typhoid fever and other diseases.

A preventable cause of these maladies is to be found in the successful
dissipation of the sewage gases.  If pent up in the sewers, as they are
reported to be at the West-end of London, they find their way into the
houses and poison the inhabitants.  The whole doctrine and practice of
ventilation ought to be regarded in this part of the subject to dissipate or
alter the poison.  I have known cases of typhoid fever at the top of a hill,
from the drain forming a flue, acting as certainly as the tall chimney used
by the manufacturer, to carry the sewer poison directly into the rooms of
the dwelling-house.

In the city of London ventilating openings are placed in the centre of
the streets, and it is rather grotesque to see openings on either side of a
narrow lane trapped, while in the centre, about two feet distant, a ventilating shaft is left open.  Upon the whole, this ludicrous plan is better
than that adopted at the West-end of London, where these openings are
either wanting or much less frequent.  The distribution of sewage gases
still requires study and experiment to render them innocuous to the public.
I should myself recommend the trial of small shafts from the sewers to the
tops of the houses from the house drains.  The engineer to the city of
London has, however, presented a most important exhaustive report upon
this subject, demonstrating all the dangers and difficulties, but candidly
confessing that he is unable to settle the questions which have arisen.

At the outfall of the town, if of any magnitude, a river of sewage exists, carrying down stones, brickbats, bottles, sticks, and other solid rubbish. As may be expected, the stench is equal to the increased volume of the sewage. About thirty gallons per day may be reckoned roughly for every inhabitant of a town, and at Croydon the magnitude of the sewage river is sufficient to work a turbine wheel, a form of hydraulic apparatus used in France, but very seldom in this country. Of the few employed, it may be mentioned that one is used for the manufacture of the paper used for the Bank of England notes. The amount of sewage yielded by a town may be understood when it is stated that the sewage of Croydon for one day would cover an acre 15 feet deep, and for the year 5475 feet deep.

The sewage river exhaling its pestiferous gases ought to be protected in any well-devised scheme; but it is a curious fact that the moment sewage is removed from a town it appears to cease to be an object of thought and attention to the authorities of the town.

The usual practice is, for the councillors of a town to carry their sewage to the boundary of the land under their control, and then pass it to the land in the district of their neighbours, when economy and not efficiency guides their actions.

In any part of a medical social science scheme for dealing with sewage, every district should dispose of its own sewage; thus Croydon should not purify itself by poisoning Beddington, nor Enfield by poisoning Edmonton.

As an example of the utter recklessness of the council of a town to the inhabitants of another district, it was alleged, upon many strong affidavits, that Croydon had so purified its water that it was fit to enter the Wandle for the inhabitants of the next parish to drink! I mildly replied, upon affidavit, "that I was not aware of any process which could turn sewage into a good potable water." The Croydon irrigators adhered to their statement, and were not a little surprised and disconcerted when I rejoined that their statement disposed of all difficulties, for they had only continuously to pump back the transformed sewage into their own water tanks when the law proceedings would be terminated, a test of the perfection of their process which Croydon never for one moment contemplated.

As a fundamental principle of a medical social treatment of sewage, one person ought not to be relieved at the expense of a second.

The river of sewage freed from large matters is next conducted by various channels to the land, as, theoretically, earth is capable of assimilating to itself the manurial particles, and of separating the water.

Now comes into play the overwhelming difficulties which are afforded by the small quantity of solid sewage which exists in proportion to the enormous quantity of water.

About a quarter of a century ago a company was formed by an enthusiastic sewage irrigator, and a pumping engine was erected at Fulham. Within a mile of the pumping engine one of the principal gardens which supplied Covent Garden exists, and the company requested me to offer to lay down suitable pipes and supply sewage gratuitously, as an experiment. I visited Messrs. Fitch with the landowner for the purpose of offering this supposed boon; and, after a long discussion, each of the partners pointed out the necessity to get the water off the land if successful culture was desired, and they declined the offer.

Those experienced cultivators at once hit the blot of successful sewage application, for the problem still remains, how to separate the water from the sewage in solution.

Practically, it is not now done. The sewage is passed over the land, which for a short time absorbs the water, but the sewage continues to run by night and day, the land becomes water-logged, and refuses to take more. It becomes inactive, and putrescible water runs over the land to the neighbouring brook, there to poison those who have recourse to it for drinking purposes.

It is pretended, by the Croydon Local Board, that about 150 feet of sewage in depth is filtered by every square foot of ground per annum, which amounts to about seven times the natural rainfall of the district; an amount which is so preposterous that, with the feeblest intelligence, the councillors ought to know it is practically impossible.

When the land is water-logged, the earth is not aërated, and what soaks through passes to the springs of the district, and renders them poisonous. Wells near the Sewage Farm of Croydon cannot be used, being thoroughly poisoned by the pestilential sewage.

It is not a disposal of the sewage question for the inhabitants of a town to turn the sewage into the wells of the next village; and this is a question in social science which requires a vigorous treatment.

As the sewage is supplied over a large area, all good water supply ceases. The cattle are compelled to drink sewage, and the men, under the great pressure of thirst, seek the cleanest water they can find, although, if taken near the farm, it is poisonously contaminated with putrescible matter.

As a matter of medical social science the wells of a district should never be allowed to be poisoned, if possible; and, if impossible, without an adequate supply of pure and wholesome water being afforded.

When the land is water-logged, the sewage passes over the surface, when, instead of the pestilential effluvia being restricted to a channel a few feet wide, it is spread over acres of surface, where the utmost possible amount of sewage poison is communicated to the atmosphere.

What a perversion of medical social science it is for the doctors of a town to protest against the exhalation from a few square feet of exposed sewage, and yet to regard as immaterial the effluvium of hundreds of acres of sewage marsh.

But the sewage, as it runs over the earth, is now generally caused to run through rye-grass, because the irrigators say that grass has a cleansing effect. They are true to this extent, that the grass acts as a sort of brush to the sewage, and the pestiferous slime adheres to the blades of the grass, to be carried elsewhere, to be eaten by cattle. When the sewage grass is made into hay, this slime is still adherent; and, if it be steeped in water, the infusion is acted upon by the sewage ferment, and sometimes putrefies with disgusting effluvia.

Sewage irrigation cannot be said to be practised according to the rules of social science until the irrigation is so conducted that the earth does not become water-logged, and until the grass is not besmeared with all the poisonous materials which sewage contains.

If the sewage-ground remains wet, vegetation is crippled, and it is quite remarkable to observe how the roots of trees rot and how the trees are blown over in the sewage-ground when the ground is water-logged. Rose-trees, &c., are shown, in the committees of the Houses of Parliament, as samples of sewage culture, which could not have existed on water-logged sewage-grounds as now ordinarily conducted.

It has been stated that there is at the present time no town sewage ground which does not exhale its detestable stench, and which does not leave all the slush on the surface or on the grass. It is a curious fact that, when the slush is left on the surface of the ground, it still exhales, after the earth is dry, the faint, nauseous odour of sewage; and I have walked over sewage fields in the depth of winter, when even intense frost has not prevented the faint and sickening exhalation from dry ground.

When the earth is dried after sewage irrigation, vegetation is prodigious, oats attain incredible growth of straw, monster cabbages are raised, extraordinarily-sized onions may be grown, but then, without particular care, their juices are impaired, and their texture is so imperfect that they have a tendency to rot.

It is necessary for the perfection of the vegetable tissue that the sewage should be commingled with the earth and changed in its nature before it is absorbed by the plant. Asparagus watered with putrid manure is most offensive, even after having been cooked. The strawberry, if watered too late with liquid manure, becomes disgusting; and it has been noticed that cabbages become bad, and cauliflowers nauseous, if grown in undecomposed foul manures.

Sewage produce is grown at one spot and transferred to another; so it is almost impossible to trace its baneful effects. Cartloads of watercresses are sold in London, where some sewage (for they will not grow in pure sewage) runs directly over them, so that their stalks are smeared with the excrete of typhoid fever cases, with the epithelial scales of scarlet fever, and with the ova of entozoon. And what may not happen, if we are again afflicted with the scourge of cholera, if persons eat vegetables besmeared with cholera virus? Sewage produce not only contains within it, but has disposed upon its surface, the germs of all contagious diseases, and who can tell how many isolated cases of disease may have happened from this source? for who can tell whence their food has come? and who can tell where sewage produce goes?

The followers of social medical science should take steps that persons may not be poisoned unawares, and, when the mother goes to market to provide the necessary fresh vegetables for her offspring, that she should not buy at great cost a scarlet fever, a typhoid fever, a diarrhœa, or a cholera. One town produces the poison, another, perhaps far distant, is affected by it; and as the peer, as well as the poor man, in the great metropolis, has to depend upon the public markets for his vegetable supplies, competent authorities ought to take care that wholesome food, and not contagious poison, is sold to the public.

To the influence of sewage food upon cows I have lately called the attention of the public. It seems to be worse at one season than at another. When the experiment was tried in the spring, the milk became putrescible, and so did the butter. Both were so bad that they could not be used. Here again the difficulty arises as to how the wholesome milk can be distinguished from the putrescible. As far as I as yet know, the best plan is to place aside some of the milk in a warm place, when, in a few hours, if it contains any putrescible matter, it will show itself by an offensive odour, and the amount in the milk may be determined by the amount of the odour and the length of time over which it is exhaled. Experiments are still proceeding on this matter.

Many attacks of typhoid fever have been traced to milk; and as it is no small difficulty, from the nature of the case, to trace an attack of typhoid fever to milk, we may assume that there have been ten attacks from that cause for every one that has been detected.

When milk has been the vehicle of typhoid poison, the following causes have been assumed :—

1. Foul water, containing typhoid poison, had been added to the milk.

2. The milk had absorbed the typhoid poison from the air.

3. The cow had been in a diseased state.

4. The cow had drunk sewage.

5. The cow had eaten sewage deposited on the outside of the grass.

6. The cow had eaten grass the juices of which have been affected.

In the last cases the milk becomes putrescible, and, according to all known science, capable of either producing or conveying the poison.

In the recent epidemic at Marylebone, the source of the typhoid was traced to milk supplied by the Reform Dairy Company, and there the clue appears to be lost; and much more information is required, under all the circumstances of the case, before any one is warranted in forming a decided opinion.

The Reform Dairy Company, however, had, some years ago, a contract with the Metropolitan Sewage Company for the supply of milk from the sewage farm at Barking.

The Reform Dairy Company complained that the milk would not keep, but turned sour and stank.

By direction of the Reform Dairy Company the Metropolitan Sewage Company added to the milk at various times sulphate of soda, silicate of soda, phosphate of soda, and sulphide of sodium, to prevent the milk from going bad; nevertheless, the Reform Dairy Company alleged that the milk still continued to be very bad, and in the spring of 1869 the Reform Dairy Company claimed a considerable sum of money for damages on account of loss of customers from the bad milk, and proceedings at law were taken by the Reform Dairy Company to recover the same.

The Reform Dairy Company attributed the mischief to the bad water the cows drank; and the water of one well was reported by an analyst "as unfit for man or beast."

Since the action, the Reform Dairy Company were so impressed with the danger of putrescible milk from sewage-grounds, that they determined to have no more sewage milk. . . . .

It appears that two epidemics of typhoid fever have appeared in establishments whilst supplied with milk from the Croydon Sewage Farm, one at Beddington Schools, by the Wandle, where about sixty were attacked, and three died; one at the Clerks' schools, where one child and one governess died. The second case was communicated to me by the Secretary lately, and was not known to me before. In these two cases it has been stated that there were unfavourable conditions in the houses, beside the supply of milk.

The use of bad milk affects the rich as well as the poor; and the twenty deaths and the 200 attacks of fever which occurred lately from poisoned milk distributed in Marylebone occurred amongst those in a good position in society.

Milk is of such paramount importance to a metropolitan community, that it should be an object of solicitude to the medical social inquirer that it should be given to the public free from poisonous taint.

All medical men treat typhoid and other fevers by milk, and what can be more contrary to scientific principles than to supply a fever case with putrescible milk? Hence the most stringent rules should be adopted to keep milk from the dangerous proximity to sewage; so that the cupidity of man should not cause it to be added to the milk, nor the thirst of the cow for it to be drunk, and thus to be passed on to the milk. Every household knows that when the nurse is injudicious in diet the baby cries, and cowfeeders are fully aware that when cows eat wormwood the milk is bitter, and when they partake of garlic it is highly tasted.

The effect of sewage food on the health of cattle and sheep is well known to be deleterious. It has lately been stated by Mr. Scott that the cows of Edinburgh, where they are fed upon sewage grass, have so high a mortality, that the Cattle Insurance Company refused to renew the insurance; and I have the authority of the late auditor of the company for stating that the enormous claims paid by the company for the Edinburgh cows insured by them, and which died, ruined the company, and the refusal to renew the insurance came too late.

An intelligent man who worked upon a sewage farm informed me that many of the sheep on the farm, as anybody might reasonably have expected, became, to use his own word, "rotten." The rot in sheep is due to an entozoon called a fluke, which in the human being becomes an hydatid, and whilst sheep had the rot and were passing the ova of hydatids, the water was flowing to watercresses, from whence this terrible malady (which is estimated to kill 400 persons annually) might conveniently be conveyed by its host to the interior of man.

In 1869 a great epidemic broke out on the sewage-grounds of Croydon amongst the cattle, about which there were strange reports. To clear up the mystery, the following questions were sent to the Croydon Board, who declined to answer them :—

1. How many cattle existed on the sewage-ground before the epidemic appeared?

2. Had cattle been introduced from any other locality? if so, how many, and from whence?

3. On what day did murrain appear on the irrigation-ground?

4. How many cattle have been attacked in all since that day?

5. Have any cattle since that day been killed? and, if so, how many?

6. If sold, to whom were the carcases consigned?

7. Were the carcases used for human food? and, if so, who inspected them, to see that they were fit to be eaten?

8. Have any cattle been sold other than for human food? if so, were the purchasers informed that murrain existed in the sewage-grounds, that the contagion might not be propagated?

9. What are the number of cattle now on the sewage-grounds?

\*        \*        \*        \*        \*        \*

It is reported that twenty cattle died last winter on the sewage-grounds of Croydon, and that four horses died this summer, so that it is both heartless and cruel for Boards of Health to sell sewage grass as a healthy produce.

In this case, again, the cattle are fed at one place, sold to a butcher at a second, and distributed for food to a third, and the person who eats them does not know that he is eating sewage-fed cattle, nor can any person tell where the sewage cattle are sent.

When illness arises from the use of bad meat, how is the poor person to trace it, when the local so-called Boards of Health will not assist, but resist the application for information in a contemptuous way?

I once asked a clerk, who was troubled with tapeworm, why he bought second-rate meat, which might have been grown on a sewage farm. He replied that he had a large family, and could not afford to pay more. "Then," I rejoined, "why do you not thoroughly cook it, to destroy any germs of disease?" "If I do so," was the ready answer, "the meat would so waste that there would not be enough to go round." The tapeworm in the man and the wasting of the meat showed the diseased state of the food consumed; but the councillors of one town do not eat the diseased meat— it ultimately finds its way to other towns, and the poor man obtains no protection. In this case it is hardly to be expected that either a Bishop or a Chancellor will suffer from disease or tapeworm as a sacrifice for the good of the people, because they obtain good meat, and it is left to the middle-class clerk to suffer from the cupidity of the sewage irrigators.

Labourers and navvies cannot perform their labour without good meat, and they contrive, when in full work, to get the best beef, and leave it to those above them, with limited incomes, to eat that which is inferior.

If social science is here to step in to protect the people, it must act at the source of the mischief, where the cattle become diseased, and stop the supply thence to the cities.

The sewage-grounds, after long-continued irrigation, become converted into pestilential swamps, which snipes and wild ducks visit in winter, and which exhale the most disgusting effluvium. The stench varies with the weather. In a bright, windy day, it is comparatively little apparent, but in a close evening it is most disgusting.

Why such a state of things, contrary to social scientific principles, should not always give rise to cholera, typhoid and scarlet fever, no medical man can tell. But when these diseases have a tendency to appear, then the action of the sewage poison intensifies the maladies. And upon these grounds social science ought to interfere and compel the sewage irrigators to conduct their operations without causing these poisonous exhalations.

Whether it is possible on a large scale, by under-draining or otherwise, to thoroughly purify the water, remains to be proved; but when we see a large sewage-ground, as that of Croydon, left undrained, the probability of any improvement seems hopeless.

It may be possible, by a thin distribution of sewage—say not more than two feet in depth per annum, in favourable porous soils—to dispose of sewage, that it may all be taken into the earth. There is no doubt that such an absorption might be effected in some uplands in the vicinity of Croydon; but as there are 4,000,000 gallons per day to be disposed of, no less than 2,700 acres would be required to take the water. The amount is so large that the mind does not realize it, for who can form any conception of 1,460 million gallons of sewage, which is the sum per annum of the sewage of Croydon upon the chairman's statement of its amount at 4,000,000 gallons a day, though I should have thought that it would not have averaged above half that amount?

After the sewage soaks through the land, the water is collected again into another main stream. If the whole has filtered through the earth, the fluid is clear; but, notwithstanding its brightness, it is frequently found to be putrescible, when it ought not to be allowed to pass to the neighbouring brook. In practice, the irrigator is often neglectful; and I have seen an acre or more transformed into a small sewage lake, from whence the sewage has run unchanged into the river, to act as a poison to the inhabitants who live lower down the stream.

It is not safe to trust our senses to discover a small quantity of sewage in a large quantity of water. On the occasion of the last visitation of cholera, I was aware of a well the water of which was poisoned. I urged the immediate removal of the pump handle, but loud were the remonstrances of some of our most eminent bankers, who were thus deprived of their usual water for luncheon. The water was proved to have been derived from the worst of all possible sources; but the presence of saline matters in water is as attractive to human beings as it is to cattle.

It is perfectly manifest that sewage irrigation as now practised is a failure, commercially as well as practically, for the disposal of sewage, as sewage farms are continually to let. It therefore becomes a question for social science to endeavour to devise, if practicable, some more perfect system for the disposal of sewage. On a small scale this has been effected by the earth closet; but this has never been adapted to a town, and its practical use on a large scale presents many difficulties and dangers.

If no better plan than irrigation can be discovered, then social science must determine whether any mode can be adopted to destroy the sewage matter before it goes upon the ground. The Lime process, the Salts of Iron process, the A. B. C. process, Anderson's precipitating process (as used by the General Sewage and Manure Company), Scott's process, and others too numerous to mention, are in this direction. If any plan for the thorough destruction of the poisonous character of sewage can be discovered, great good will be effected. Some of these processes have been highly extolled; but further experience is required before the universal adoption of any such plan can be recommended.

The influence of carbolic acid in determining the mode of putrefaction is very remarkable. It is stated that it has been applied with success to sewage; but a more extended experience is required before it can at present be recommended on a large scale. The influence of animal charcoal, peat charcoal, and cinders, has also to be considered and made the subject of further experiment; but hitherto they have not been reported to be successful, and every process appears to fail to get rid of the urea.

Unquestionably difficulties present themselves in dealing with the sewage question. Financial companies are said to have large sums of money invested upon a false estimate of the high money value of sewage. The Mapplin Sand speculation influences the matter; complicated private interests are interfered with; and some landowners get as much as £10 an acre to permit sewage to be used on their land. The mode in which the subject is handled by committees of both Houses of Parliament, where so-called skilled witnesses have made the most ignorant and exaggerated statements of the money value of sewage and the perfection of irrigation, has interfered seriously with the scientific solution of the question. Notwithstanding all these difficulties, medical social science has only steadily to point out the ill effects of sewage irrigation, when we may confidently predict that ultimately the sewage irrigators will be compelled to respect the health of the general community as well as that of their own town, that the public may be protected against a vitiated atmosphere, poisoned water, water-logged soil, sewage-tainted vegetables, putrescible milk, and diseased meat.

It is curious with regard to all sewage questions, that the facts are cross-stated. Whilst independent and disinterested observers see the great evils attendant upon the system as now practised, others, who are interested either in the promotion of sewage irrigation or continuing it, speak of the results in the most superlative manner. . . . . The dissentients are fully entitled to ask that all sewage produce should be labelled as such. If the produce is as good as the sewage irrigators declare, such a course must enhance its price; but if it is as indifferent as impartial observers state, then those who do not like it will not have it thrust upon them by stealth.

The problem of the day is, how to deal with sewage in our inland towns, as vast sums of money have been already spent. The treatment of the subject requires great prudence and moderation, for it is clear, where millions of gallons of water have to be dealt with, that the fluid must ultimately go by some river or channel to the sea, or be distributed over so large a surface that it can be absorbed by the earth, a case which can but rarely happen. If a due supply of water for ordinary cleanliness be employed, the resultant discharge of water from large towns must always be enormous. I submit that the only safe plan, under the circumstances, is to confess our ignorance, and to set to work experimentally to decide the question at issue. First, let us try to keep the sewage proper within a more reasonable compass and separate from the enormous bulk of water with which it is mixed. Secondly, let us endeavour to destroy the poisonous character of the sewage, and get it into a state adapted for vegetation. Thirdly, let us endeavour to cleanse the water by precipitation, and then by filtration through so large an area of land that a pestilential marsh is not created.

When all these things are effected, and the public health secured, it will be time to consider the economical bearing of the problem; but life and health ought to be considered before any question of wealth and gain.

It is folly to trust the management of sewage to town councils, constituted as they usually are, especially whilst we are ignorant of the best plan to be pursued. The only practical method is for the country to place the sewage from one or two of our large towns under trained persons, accustomed to original investigation and to the interrogation of nature, to work out experimentally the matter, that the country may know upon what principles, under varying circumstances, the distribution of sewage may be rendered innocuous, when, from the circumstances of the case, it cannot be carried to the wide ocean, which, with our present knowledge, is the safest plan that can be followed.

## No. XXXVI.c.

## PROPOSED HEADS OF LEGISLATION FOR THE REGULATION OF SEWAGE-GROUNDS. Paper read before the Society of Arts, Dec. 1, 1875, by ALFRED SMEE.

THE extension of the water-closet system in our towns during the last quarter of a century has been attended with great convenience to the inhabitants of individual towns, but the consequences have entailed corresponding injury on the general public. The quantity of water required for the water-closet system amounts to about thirty gallons per head a day, which for a town of reasonable magnitude causes a river of sewage to run from the town, which has to be disposed of.

At first the sewage was carried to the nearest stream in such quantities that every river in England was converted into a huge sewer, and the Thames itself on one occasion was black from the putridity of the sewage matters discharged into its waters.

The pollution of rivers was of so serious an extent that a Rivers Pollution Commission was instituted, and steps were taken to prevent our rivers from being destroyed and contaminated by the sewage of our towns.

To remove sewage from the rivers it was determined to apply it to the earth, and at first the most exaggerated notions were entertained by high authorities as to its value as a manurial agent, and theorists indicated that by its use so much vegetation would be grown, and so large an amount of meat produced, that every one in this land who scarcely tasted animal food once a week would have a daily and ample supply.

Unfortunately, however, such fallacious hopes have been long dissipated. Sewage irrigation has been found, as a general rule, to be a troublesome, an expensive, and an unsatisfactory process. Wherever practicable, it is preferable to carry it to the wide ocean, there to be oxidized by the winds and waves; and only when that is impossible from the distance to be traversed, are sewage-grounds, with the present state of our knowledge, to be adopted.

There are situations where the water-closet system is employed, in which it is necessary to purify the sewage, and in these cases the question of the conduct of irrigation-grounds has to be considered.

The theory of returning to the earth, by sewage, that which is taken from the earth by food, commands our respect and attention. But the sewage is diluted with so much water that it cannot be practically returned to the earth in a suitable state for plants. Up to this moment it has not been satisfactorily separated from the fluid so as to be economically applicable in a dry state, and the enormous bulk of the liquid prevents its being economically employed in the fluid state.

In considering the qualities of sewage, the large quantity of inorganic poisonous matter which is cast into sewers deserves notice. Cyanide of potassium and the refuse of all the photographic establishments, various metallic poisons from the electro-chemical works, the fluid residue of various manufactories, disinfecting solutions, &c., are passed into the sewage.

Sewage has had so poisonous an effect on the river Thames that where fish formerly abounded none are now to be found. Within my memory flounders were caught in abundance between London and Southwark bridges. At Erith abundance of fish used to be caught, but now it appears that the river there is void of fish. Lamperns are now only taken by hundreds where thousands were formerly caught, and eels are gradually disappearing.

Sewage-grounds are to be employed solely for the purpose of sanitary protection. All questions of cost must be subordinate to sanitary science. Sewage-grounds should never be employed except in the absence of better methods of disposing of the sewage, and when used should be regarded as a necessity, to be placed under the most stringent regulations, to protect the health of those exposed to their influence, and to protect damage to property which may arise from their vicinity.

The idea of profit from sewage-grounds is fortunately now exploded. The real object is to get rid of the sewage at the least possible cost, and by the least objectionable method, and if judiciously used the value of the produce may tend to diminish the expense of the abatement of the nuisance, and that is all which is possible to be effected. In some cases a subvention from the town may be necessary to get rid of the sewage.

Sufficient experience has been afforded of the properties of sewage-grounds to enable us to settle the chief points which are required to be enforced for their proper conduct, and it is manifestly desirable to obtain a legislative enactment that they may be so controlled that they may inflict a minimum injury on the health of the adjacent inhabitants, and the least possible depreciation of the value of the neighbouring property.

If sanitary science be true, then is the principle on which sewage-grounds have been hitherto conducted false; and if the principle of the present conduct of sewage-grounds be true, then is all known sanitary science false.

The usual plan which is adopted for the location of a sewage-ground is to select a spot in a district away from the town to be cleansed, so that in fact the nuisance is simply transferred from one district to a second which has no voice in the management, and the residents of which are powerless to help themselves against the encroachment. Thus Croydon cleanses itself, but pollutes Beddington. Croydon has no interest but to save expense to itself, whilst Beddington has to suffer from the parishioners of Croydon.

This manifest injustice might be remedied by requiring a majority of the ratepayers of any other parish to concur in the establishment of a sewage-ground within its district. Should a sewage-ground be formed in any neighbouring parish without such leave, a fine might be inflicted of £100 a day. The fine may appear large, but the irrigators having to deal with the funds of the ratepayers would take no heed of small sums, unless, indeed, it was enacted that the persons violating the order should pay the amount of the fine from their own pockets, when probably a much smaller fine would be adequate. At present the sewage is no more disposed of by carrying it from one district to another than if the housemaid of one house were to throw the refuse over the wall of her master's house into the garden of the adjoining house.

When a sewage-ground is proposed to be located, the scheme should, in the interest of all concerned, be approved by an independent public officer. The nature of the ground to be irrigated is of importance, for it is necessary for successful irrigation that the sewage should pass completely into the ground. Any place which is waterlogged is not suitable; and even at the Croydon sewage-ground water lies on an average within two or three feet from the surface of all parts of the sewage farm. Again, care should be taken that in the choice of a situation underground channels capable of directly conveying the sewage to distant parts should be avoided; for example, chalk strata have cracks probably of miles in length, having an uneven character. The cracks or fissures vary in width from a hair's breadth to a width of nine or ten inches, and if sewage were turned into one of these fissures it might reappear some miles off. The question of these fissures, which exist all round London, opens up very serious considerations, as the water is liable to contamination from cesspools. The importance of the subject has attracted the attention of engineers, and may possibly be the subject of a paper at some future period. The employment of a sewage-ground without the approval of a public officer should be forbidden under a penalty of at least £50 a day.

At the present time parts of the sewage-ground actually employed for irrigation frequently abut on the property of neighbouring proprietors, which is greatly damaged. It is also frequently abutting on the highway. I have heard it given in evidence before a committee of the House of Lords that a sewage-ground was so near suburban villas, that the inmates played at croquet upon the very verge of the pestilential marsh so created, a state of things which should be rigidly prevented. At Beddington, I have often seen the irrigation carried to the very verge of the high road, or beside the property of neighbouring landowners. Now not less than 200 yards should intervene between the part irrigated and any highway or adjoining property, under a penalty of not less than £10 a day. The interval of 200 yards is by no means sufficient under all circumstances to fully protect the public from the abominable stench and pestiferous effluvia of sewage-grounds, though it would afford very substantial relief from the emanations whenever the atmosphere possessed an average state of diffusive power. In calm "muggy" evenings the distance will be manifestly insufficient, and therefore should be increased wherever practicable. The nuisance committed by the emanations of a sewage-ground varies every day, and at every hour of the day, with the atmosphere. In a clear bright day, with wind and a rapid motion of the air upwards, it is reduced to a minimum. In evening and morning with slight haze and stillness it is increased to a maximum.

At the time I was writing the work 'My Garden,' I was examining historical remains on the sewage-grounds. I was there one evening (when only one irrigation had taken place); the ground had dried, and the grass-seed was sown, and yet the stench at sundown was so intolerable that we were glad to leave the place. I have also been at the sewage-grounds during frost, and even then the exhalations were most offensive and disagreeable.

The fact is, that unless the sewage is defecated before irrigation, a layer of fæcal matter is deposited on the surface of that part of the ground which has no crops upon it; and if there are crops, the fæcal matter is deposited upon the plants growing upon it. For this reason sewage irrigation cannot be practised without creating a nuisance, except by the previous removal of the solid matter, and the precipitation of the greater part of the dissolved parts of the animal matter.

As defecation is a necessity, the penalty for neglect should certainly be not less than £50 a day. It would not be desirable to compel sewage to be defecated by any particular process, because some experience is required as to which, in the long run, under all circumstances and at all times, shall have the preference. The processes of precipitation by lime, by alum, by sulphate of alumina, by phosphate of alumina, by alum, blood, and clay, are in good repute, for their powers of precipitation, but not for the expense which they entail. General Scott has invented a remarkable and very original mode of dealing with the sludge. He converts it into cement to be used in building, and the similarity of the mud with that on the Medway, ordinarily employed for the manufacture of cement, is remarkable. Doubtless this process would never entirely cover the cost of the purification of sewage, though it may tend, in a great degree, to lessen the expense.

There is no question but that sewage may be rendered perfectly bright and clear by precipitation, even when coloured, as at Leeds, with dye matters, but then it mostly contains some animal matter in solution, which has to be afterwards removed. Most praiseworthy attempts have been made to render this precipitate of real agricultural value. The sludge ought to contain all the manurial properties, but probably it is altered, for farmers will hardly carry it away at one shilling a ton. Some inventors have sought to add to it elements which may increase its value; but although some of those products are claimed to have a value of from £3 to £4 a ton, experience does not warrant us in saying that any one process, up to this time, is a substantial commercial success. It is a curious fact that the sludge of a charcoal process has the remarkable power of oxidizing organic matter, from the animal charcoal which it contains, and if an animal be placed in it the flesh will be entirely destroyed without smell. If ever one process be found which shall yield a precipitate of universally acknowledged value, the difficulties of the sewage question will in a great measure be overcome. The question is not yet quite satisfactorily determined which process, taking into consideration the value of the resulting product, is attended with least expense. The sewage water when defecated and precipitated should pass into the ground, and not over the ground; for when it passes over the ground, as I have myself often seen, it passes off as sewage with all its concurrent evils.

The fine for the impropriety of neglecting to cause the water to pass into the ground might well be fixed at £10 a day, as the result would greatly depend upon the irrigation being conducted in a proper and suitable manner.

It not unfrequently happens that the sewage, when allowed improperly to run over the ground, is not retained in the sewage-ground, but passes to the territory of neighbouring proprietors. This is a serious injury to them, for whilst the proprietor of the sewage-ground obtains as much as £12 an acre for permitting the abomination on his land, otherwise not worth £3 an acre, the adjacent owner is subjected to all the evils and inconvenience without any compensation whatever. A penalty for such a violation of the rights of property might be fixed at £20 for every day when such an injury is inflicted. I have myself seen the places where sewage has overflown the beautiful park of Beddington for fifty or sixty yards from the neighbouring sewage-ground.

The general conduct of the sewage-ground from the commencement of the process to its termination requires the most careful supervision. The great artery passing from the town is usually covered up within their own district, but the moment it passes from their district it is no more an object of solicitude to the ratepayers of the town, but is frequently left open to pollute the air of the neighbouring villages.

Sanitary science enjoins the most vigilant care of sewers in the district, but the moment the district is crossed, sanitary science is disregarded as though it were unimportant.

What the Boards of Health of towns do not do with a good grace they should be compelled to do under fine, and it would not be unreasonable to subject them to a fine of £25 a day if they permit their main or sewage arteries to be exposed within 100 yards of a highway or of any private property. At the present time it not unfrequently happens that no precaution is taken against the sewage, whether not defecated or defecated, from passing on to vegetables used for food in a raw state. For instance, at the fever-stricken town of Croydon, there are no special precautions taken to avoid the excreta of a typhoid case from passing to watercresses, and hence fæcal matter may be served back to themselves, or on the tables of the unsuspecting aristocracy of London, within forty-eight hours from its passage from a patient about to die of the disease.

Watercresses act as a scrubbing-brush to the sewage, and remove all the solid flocculi from the water which adhere to the stalks.

Typhoid fæcal matter is absolutely poisonous in the sanitary district, but how many persons take it into the stomach after it has passed their own immediate district the so-called sanitary authorities appear to be perfectly indifferent.

To prevent this horrible, disgusting, and dangerous outrage on the community, a penalty of at least £100 a day should be inflicted on any person growing, or permitting to be grown, salad of any kind upon a sewage-ground, and the public ought to be further protected against the cupidity of Boards of Health who would imperil the lives of communities for a small extra gain, by imposing a penalty of £5 on any person knowingly selling salads from sewage-grounds, and this penalty should be imposed for every offence committed. There is no reason whatever why unsuspecting persons should be exposed to this loathsome and dangerous risk, and the fullest protection ought to be offered to the public against it. Salad may be defined, for the purpose of such protection, to be any plant ordinarily used by man in an uncooked state.

As it may be regarded as an undoubted fact that vegetables take up foul sewage matters, and it requires considerable time before they are changed in the tissues of the plant, no vegetable ought to be used for human food, even in the cooked state, until suitable time is allowed for the assimilation and changing of the sewage matter in the substance of the plant. The time would necessarily vary with the time of year, the temperature, the active state of the plant, the amount of light, and various other conditions, but probably an interval of two months would afford a reasonable protection after defecated sewage had been applied to the growing plant. The penalty for infraction of the law might be fixed at

£20 for every offence, and any other person knowingly selling such produce might in like manner be subject to a penalty of £5 for every offence. It is known in France that when vineyards are irrigated by sewage the quality of the wine is impaired and not restored for years.

It cannot be a proper thing for cattle to be fed on food which in its relation to sewage is under circumstances unfit for the food of man. At the present moment we are not thoroughly acquainted with the action of the typhoid fever poison, the cholera poison, or the erysipelas poison on cattle, and until we have such knowledge we should act on the side of prudence. We know the communicability of disease from one kind of animal to another. We know that the milk of cows suffering from the foot-and-mouth disease is highly fatal to pigs, and so we ought to protect cattle by reasonable care from either eating or drinking the excreta of diseases of mankind of a contagious character.

Much grass is sold from sewage farms. Of the state of that grass one member of a Board of Health has favoured us with an account.

Probably a penalty of £5 for every offence of the sale or employment of vegetables for cattle, other than milch cows, less than one month after the application of sewage, would be an adequate protection to the community.

But everybody knows that the milk of all animals is affected by what the mother eats, and therefore it is much more important that milch cows should be further protected than cattle: hence a higher penalty may be inflicted in these cases, and a longer time after irrigation demanded. The real time actually required after irrigation must necessarily depend upon the temperature, the light, the power of assimilation by the plant, as has already been pointed out ; yet, in a practical way, an interval of six weeks may be taken as a necessary time which ought to elapse after irrigation, and this might be enforced by a penalty of £10 for every offence.

The buyers of the sewage grass, in the state which has been described, are mostly poor men, of little experience and less knowledge. They believe that they are buying cheaply and safely, relying upon the honour of a Board of Health as to the quality ; but whether the sale of such stuff as wholesome grass does not in point of law really amount to a fraud, I must leave to be decided by the legal advisers of Boards of Health.

We have experimented upon it with cows, but used alone it seemed to be insufficient for the support of life, and it had to be discontinued to prevent its killing the animal by diarrhœa and wasting. The milk from cows fed from such grass I have ascertained, by numerous experiments, to be liable to become putrid, while butter made from such milk goes rapidly rancid, and I have found the casein is frequently altered in quality, and sometimes will actually dialyse. An elaborate account of our investigations upon this head occurs in my son's book, 'On Milk in Health and Disease,' and so it is unnecessary to consider the matter further in this paper.

No infant or invalid should ever be fed on milk from cows fed with sewage grass. It is of such great importance to the public to insure the sale of a pure wholesome milk, that they should abstain from buying milk of any dairyman who is known to purchase sewage grass. As long as Boards of Health can sell sewage grass, their cupidity will prevent them from knowing that sewage grass is immature grass, plus fæcal matter.

If the addition of fæcal matter to grass and hay be right for cattle to eat, as irrigators pretend, then have all former agriculturists been at fault, as they ought to have added fæcal matter to the food wherewith they fed their cows and heifers.

Either agricultural science is true, and irrigation science is false; or, irrigation science true, and agricultural science false.

I have suggested to the engineer of the Leeds works that the final oxidation of animal matter in effluent sewage water may possibly be effected in the water instead of exposing it on the land. For this purpose I have ventured to recommend tentatively that it be run through ponds full of *anacharis*, which is a rapid grower and gross feeder, and evolves much oxygen. I have also suggested that beds of reeds might be tried for the same object. By experiment it has been ascertained at my garden that the growth of *anacharis* is enormously promoted by sewage, and the water is much purified thereby, but how far it may be advantageously employed on a large scale experience can alone decide.

The water, after it has passed over the sewage-grounds, of necessity must pass to the nearest river, except in such cases where the ground absorbs the whole, or where there are underground cracks by which it can be carried away. At a late meeting of the medical officers of health, one of the District Board of Croydon pointed out that persons drank the effluent water, and spoke of it with such apparent delight that but for our natural understanding it might have been supposed that effluent sewage was a good and proper beverage. I have heard other persons descant upon the merits of effluent sewage for the beverage of the inhabitants of neighbouring villages, but never for their own use. Now a more disgusting insanitary idea cannot be imagined; and if the directors of sewage farm towns have not the good feeling to prevent so filthy a use of sewage by their neighbours, they surely should be compelled by law to pay the penalty of their want of decency.

Those who are likely to drink sewage water are travellers, tramps, and others, who do not know what it is, and if they contracted disease thereby would carry it away to distant places. On this account the entire community is interested in preventing its use unawares. Sewage irrigators, in the height of their enthusiasm for their subject, have been heard to declare that persons have preferred their effluent sewage to the well waters of the district.

The best protection might be afforded by enacting that every stream conveying effluent water from any sewage-ground should have a notice-board affixed at every point where it abuts upon a highway, or on property belonging to other owners until it enters a river, and that the notice should be placed in legible letters:—" Town Sewage, Effluent Stream, Dangerous for Use." The penalty for any neglect should not be less than £50 a day, as the danger is so great and the remedy so simple. With such a notice-board our sense of propriety could never again be offended by innocent persons drinking the water which has passed within a few hours from the water-closets of sewage towns.

In all sewage farms the water in the district irrigated, or even in the neighbourhood, is more or less poisoned, according to the circumstances of the case, and it is only reasonable that those who poison should afford an antidote to the poison. Before a sewage-ground is allowed to pollute the springs, pure and good water should be supplied. On the sewage-ground itself pure water should surely be at hand at stations within 250 yards of each other at a minimum, and it would be no great hardship to place such a number of stand-pipes. The penalty for such an obvious neglect of sanitary principles might be £20 a day.

There is reason to suspect that milk on sewage farms has been directly adulterated with sewage, which unfortunately is very difficult to detect, and permits more to be added with impunity than when pure water is used; but at any rate, when employed on sewage farms, cattle should at least have wholesome water for beverage. Wherever the wells in the neighbourhood of sewage-grounds are poisoned by sewage, a similar penalty might be enforced for neglect to supply pure water for the wants of man and beast.

Sanitary science forbids the use of well-water contaminated with sewage, but sanitary administrators take no heed of communicating sewage to the wells of their neighbours, as they appear to think that sanitary science is unimportant when any expense to themselves is incurred. Shallow wells, for instance, near the Croydon irrigation-grounds, are unfit for use.

Sewage towns have always been very jealous of giving information, because it may lead to expense, but Boards of Health ought not to be allowed to shelter themselves under a suppression of facts. It was only at a late meeting of the medical officers of health, to which I was politely invited, that all present went away, at 10 o'clock on Saturday night, firmly impressed that Croydon was perfectly healthy and free from all fever. We were all astonished, but delighted, for many of us considered that Croydon was in great peril of serious epidemic diseases. Judge my surprise, however, when the first person who came before me on Monday morning at the Bank of England informed me that his child had typhoid fever. My informant stated that he knew of other cases, and of some deaths, and subsequently that his wife and servant had died. These were followed on the following Wednesday by the declaration by the Registrar-General of five cases of death from fever from Croydon, and the following week of another five cases. On further inquiry from the inhabitants of Croydon, I found that cases of fever were interspersed all over the town, that a great epidemic was raging in it, so that at the very time that a member of the Council Board was giving information to the medical officers of health of this great metropolis, the excreta of numerous fever cases were being distributed over the sewage-grounds, and no precautions were being taken that fever fæcal matter was not served with salad upon the tables of the inhabitants of London, Croydon, and the neighbouring villages, and no means were taken to prevent innocent persons from drinking the effluent water which, according to the information of persons whom I employ to watch the conduct of the sewage-grounds, was to some extent running direct from the water-closets of Croydon to the affected stream. The public have a right, after such facts, to possess accurate knowledge. At Florence, the rate of death from fever I have myself seen to be posted weekly at the door of the Registrar to warn the inhabitants, and what can be done at Florence can be done at any farm sewage town; then, is it not desirable that the Legislature shall enforce it to be done, under a penalty for every omission of £20, and that any person wilfully concealing a death from zymotic disease, or giving knowingly any false information to deceive the Registrar, shall be subject to a penalty of £5 for every offence?

It is perfectly plain that a certain member of the Croydon Board was not even aware that a terrible epidemic of typhoid fever was raging in his district. He wrote thus on the 15th of May:—"Instead of the farm of Beddington being a dangerous swamp, a pestilential swamp, a pestiferous marsh as some persons have stated, no offensive odour can be detected, and the neighbourhood is not injuriously affected by miasma, neither has the farm been the means of introducing disease and death into the district, as its introduction has been coincident with a less death-rate and a clean bill of health, and in particular no death from fever had occurred during the whole of last year." Now, if any person living in this lamentably fever-stricken town never heard of the epidemic, how are the public to know that every one of their families was exposed to disease and death? How urgently is it required that the members of Boards of Health, instead of giving imperfect information to the public through the newspapers and societies, should have the means of knowing the truth that they may not propagate error.

Ninety-one persons have perished from typhoid at Croydon since this erroneous information has been given to the public. How far might a right knowledge of the facts have saved valuable lives and permanent injury to the constitutions of those who have been attacked by disease? how far might the injury to property have been averted by persons leaving Croydon or abstaining from taking houses there? how far might the panic at this terrible epidemic have been prevented? This it is hardly possible to state. Truth alone can restore confidence; for, in spite of any amount of newspaper letters to the contrary, Croydon will be regarded justly with suspicion for a long time to come.

In our consideration of sewage-grounds we should remember that there are two distinct modes of fermentation of excretal matter; one the ammoniacal, the other the putrid. The ammoniacal fermentation is used by the gardener in his hotbeds, and it produces warmth and a genial atmosphere particularly favourable to the early and perfect growth of all plants. The putrid fermentation is to be noticed in sewage, which causes large leafy vegetation with delayed perfection, and so horticultural flowers have leaf with little or no flower when watered with sewage. Crops grown under sewage irrigation are always late, and consequently of much less value in the market.

In the present state of our knowledge sewage-grounds should be avoided where practicable, but when they are absolutely necessary, (1) the sewage-ground should be located by a public officer under the Privy Council; (2) the sewage-ground should appertain to its own district, and on no account be placed in any other parish without leave of the majority of the inhabitants; (3) irrigation should not be conducted within 200 yards of any highway or private property; (4) the sewage should be carried to the grounds in covered ways, (5) and then defecated; (6) the fluid should then be passed through the earth; (7) in some cases it would pass through the earth to unknown districts, and in others it would pass off as a stream; (8) it ought not to run over the neighbouring private property, (9) but be retained within 200 yards of adjacent lands; (10) the effluent stream should be labelled, to show what it is; (11) the sewage should not be applied to any salad; and (12) no herbage should be sold or used less than one month after irrigation has ceased: (13) nor should herbage be used for milch cows less than six weeks after the cessation of the irrigation; (14) no vegetables should be sold for human food within two months of irrigation; (15) good and wholesome water should be supplied to the sewage-grounds, (16) and to any district where the wells are poisoned by the sewage; (17) in all towns having sewage-grounds the Registrar of deaths should post every week at his office the number of deaths from zymotic diseases, and, where practicable, the number of persons attacked, particularising the name of the disease.

When all this is done, still the miasmatic, marsh-like influence of a sewage-ground remains as a perpetual irremediable evil. If these conditions are requisite for the reasonably safe conduct of sewage-grounds, then where is there a sewage-ground which has attended to any one of them, and has not conducted its operations regardless of injury to adjoining property, but solely as a saving of cost to its own district? Surely legislation is urgently needed; and unless all known sanitary science is ignored, sewage irrigators should be compelled to act under recognized universal sanitary laws.

The penalties which have been recommended have been only those which would commend themselves to the minds of any impartial person to protect the public against the misdirection of sewage-grounds. They are so obviously important as to require no comment. From my experience of these local Boards of Health every statement is met with a flat denial, and I should not be surprised to hear the necessity for such legislative enactments denied. If there are local Boards of Health, however, who deny the premisses upon which the necessity for penalties is concluded, they need not fear the consequences. The penalties would not apply to themselves, and they would conduct their self-esteemed perfect processes without fear of molestation. To those who assume that their operations are perfect I would say, Help the public to make those who do not conduct their operations properly change their bad course.

The great sewage irrigation farm of Croydon is near my experimental garden, and I have therefore had the fullest opportunities of noticing its disgusting career. If the proposed penalties were enacted, the Board of Health would have fallen heavily under the lash. For instance—

1. Sewage is carried in a parish away from their land without leave of the inhabitants: they would incur a penalty of  ..  ..  ..  ..  £50 a day.
2. They constantly irrigate within 200 yards of other property or highways  ..  ..  ..  10 „
3. Sewage is not defecated ..  ..  ..  ..  ..  50 „
4. Sewage often runs over the ground, and is not filtered through the ground..  ..  ..  10 „
5. Sewage runs over other property ..  ..  ..  20 „
6. Great sewer artery is not covered near highway ..  ..  ..  ..  ..  ..  ..  25 „
7. Sewage is used for the growth of salad to an enormous extent ..  ..  ..  ..  ..  ..  100 „

8. Cooking vegetables sold for human food within two months of irrigation (no information).

9. Sale of vegetables for cattle less than one month after irrigation .. .. .. .. .. £10 a day.

10. Employment of vegetables for milch cows within six weeks of irrigation .. .. .. 10 „

11. Effluent water not protected .. .. .. .. 25 „

12. No good water supplied to sewage farm .. 10 „

13. No good water supplied where wells are poisoned .. .. .. .. .. .. .. .. 10 „

14. No list of zymotic diseases posted at door of Registrar's office .. .. .. .. .. .. 20 „

Total  .. £350 a day.

For the purpose of observing how far the principles which are inculcated in this paper are carried out abroad, I visited last week the sewage-ground of Paris, which is situated in the district left by a bend of the Seine, between Asnières and St. Denis. About one-twelfth part of the sewage of Paris was distributed over the ground. It was pumped by an engine over a bridge of the Seine to a small reservoir, from which it flowed in a channel, to be subdivided into lesser channels to be distributed over the soil. The principal canal was, curiously enough, carried by the high road to St. Denis, so that travellers were exposed to its pestilential emanations, which had the most awful stench, and which, under the proposed regulations, would have exposed the authorities to a fine of £10 a day. The position of the ground itself is not approved by the neighbourhood, for which a fine of £50 a day would have been incurred. No good water was supplied to the irrigation-ground, which would have rendered the authorities liable to a fine of £10 a day, nor was good water supplied to parts where the wells were poisoned, for which they would have been liable to a fine of £10 a day. The sewage was not defecated, which would have rendered them liable to a fine of £50 a day.

Salad, as lettuce, endive, and it is stated celery, was grown upon the place, for which a fine of £100 a day would have been incurred. I could not ascertain that any precautions were taken to prevent cabbages and other vegetables being used immediately after irrigation, though asparagus was grown, which becomes most offensive when recently treated with putrid sewage. There was no visible stream, so that the recommendatory precautions against its improper use were not required, but the great sewage artery was not covered, which would render them liable to a fine of £25 a day. Upon the whole, it is difficult to imagine how the French people could possibly violate the laws of health, of physiology, and of physical science, as they have done in the conduct of their sewage; and what may be the results, if twelve times the amount be conducted and concentrated on one spot, may be difficult to be prognosticated. The state of the case has been well set out in a petition to the Government from the inhabitants of the neighbourhood. The petition was signed by 414 persons residing in the district, and was presented to the National Assembly.

" The petitioners do not deny that the irrigation as hitherto practised has conferred upon the sewage-grounds a fertility which they did not formerly possess, and which has created some excellent kitchen gardens; but they beg to observe that the irrigation-grounds have been selected amongst those best adapted for the purpose. The irrigation-grounds on the 1st October, 1874, only comprised 113 hectares, and even then they have only been subjected to the application of 50,000 cubic metres per annum.

" The petitioners are, therefore, not astonished to find that amongst the cultivators of Gennevilliers there are some who are satisfied with the irrigation and ask for the continuation, and even for the extension, of it. However, the petitioners do not believe that their approval will be continued, for can the grounds continue for ever, and without rest, to imbibe 50,000 metres for each hectare for every year putrescent waters which deposit on the surface their offensive and putrid mud, and permeate the ground with a liquid loaded with organic matters and deleterious gas ?

" The petitioners question the future because the absorption of 50,000 metres per hectare is impossible, and is recognized as being exorbitant, as was proved by experience in Lombardy and in England, and so far imperfectly at Gennevilliers, that a great number of cultivators have declared that they would not use a mode of irrigation which they consider as inconvenient, unhealthy, and prejudicial to their cultivation.

" The sewage after having penetrated the superficial layers of the soil is but incompletely purified, and does not return to the river, as is wrongfully asserted in the report of the technical commission to the Minister of Public Works. The sewage water joins the subsoil water which percolates from the Seine, and is added to it, so that since 1872 the level has been raised two metres. In this case the subsoil water has overflowed the wells and corrupted the water. They have overflowed the cellars, which they have rendered wet and unhealthy; they have filled the vaults and the quarries where they are exposed to view, and exhale the noxious effluvia, and the marsh fever heretofore unknown in this country has taken possession of it.

" If such results are already manifested by an irrigation which has only had an existence of three years, and which is limited in extent to 113 hectares, what would the result be if that irrigation were extended to 2000 hectares, with an amount of sewage amounting to 100,000,000 of cubic metres per annum ?

" The irrigation-grounds would become an immense marsh, from which the pestilential emanations would evaporate, and not only affect Gennevilliers, Asnières, Colombes, and the other districts around, but would penetrate to Paris itself."

The land upon which the irrigation is carried on is naturally barren, and a contrary petition was presented by some cultivators who benefited by the practice.

It is proper to notice that on a visit to the engineer, he distinctly stated to me that he did not subscribe to the notion that the level of the subsoil water had been raised two metres, but it appears to me that if the sewage flows on to the land more rapidly than it can penetrate through it, then the level of the subsoil must be raised.

The creation of so large a pestilential swamp must be a source of serious injury, and, according to all known science, may in the future lead to the fructification and distribution of some serious epidemic. Sewage nuisances may exist for years without generating typhoid fever and cholera, but where the diseases exist they intensify their power to the destruction of the neighbouring people. At Paris the amount of vegetation is increased by the sewage being used over a deep bed of sand, and so the cultivators are anxious for the profit; but the use of such vegetation after recent irrigation, with the prevalence of the typhoid which now exists in Paris, may well make all persons fear who value wholesome food as a preservative of health.

The whole tenor of these observations is to assimilate sewage-grounds and sewage produce to the ordinary state of cultivated land and agricultural produce. If any of these precautions are omitted, then secondary protections would be required—for example, against tapeworm and diseased meat. There are strong reasons in the past for requiring, under very heavy penalties, that the buyers of sewage-fed cattle should have their names registered in a book open to the inspection of the public.

Under the system of penalties, which is the very minimum adequate to preserve the public health, the Board of Health of Croydon would sometimes have incurred a payment of £350 a day. If this scale of penalties is not found sufficient to restrain the above described reckless career of those who conduct the sewage farms of this country, then the Legislature might make the penalties personal upon the members of the Boards of Health. It is not to be tolerated that those appointed to protect the health of one district should be permitted to impair the health of the neighbouring district. The effect of sewage-grounds, as hitherto conducted, has been as bad morally on the minds of the people as it has been physically on their bodies. Largely exaggerated statements have been made by their supporters. Facts are suppressed, or not fairly given. General denials are made to all complaints. The most insolent observations are made to those who point out their dangers. Knowledge is arrogantly assumed where ignorance abounds; the promotion of sewage-grounds is made a source of revenue at the public damage. Being an independent observer of the mad career which the conductors of the sewage-ground are following, I have placed this paper before the Society to indicate the scientific principles which should guide their safe conduct, and also to serve as a public protest against sewage-grounds as now conducted, that should, in the future, some terrible calamity occur from their abuse, blame may rest upon the heads of those who recklessly abjure all known sanitary science.

---

The discussion that ensued was adjourned, and at a subsequent meeting (Jan. 19th, 1876) Mr. Smee said his paper was intended to be a belligerent one, in order to evoke discussion. He was not an enemy to sewage irrigation, and the whole point of his paper was to show that sewage farms must and ought to be properly and fairly conducted. Referring to the letter received from Mr. Hope, he said he considered it ought to be printed in letters of gold, for in that letter the greater part of the sewage questions were dealt with in a practical, philosophical, and almost perfect manner. Time was the very essence of the thing, because if animal matter were taken into the stalk of a plant it required a certain time before it was assimilated, and that point was now conceded by those who knew anything of the subject. Mr. Hope had not mentioned whether

he would defecate it; but if he would, he should consider the labour
bestowed upon the preparation of the paper had been well spent. Next,
General Scott stated that all the evidence given before the Parliamentary
Committee showed that sewage must be defecated before it was put upon
the land; and if that principle were admitted, the sewage question was
almost settled. That was why he thought there ought to be a penalty on
its non-adoption. Of course there was the difficulty and expense, which
often stood in the way; and he had no doubt that if Mr. Latham could have
his own way, and were not hampered by the penny-wise and pound-foolish
principle, which he had himself condemned, he would soon have things in
proper shape. It has been said that he (Mr. Smee) had given no principles
on which the question should be dealt with; but the fact was, it depended
on the principles of heat, cold, moisture, dryness, vegetable and animal
physiology,—in short, on all the principles of nature. As to the fines of £350
a day being too heavy, that was but a small sum compared to the penalty
of £10,000 to which they were liable for a breach of the injunction
granted by the Court of Chancery against allowing any of the sewage to
flow into the river Wandle to the injury of neighbouring owners, and
three such injunctions were granted against the Croydon Local Board.
There was a specimen on the table of a trout, one of a cartload which had
been killed by the poisonous matter turned into the stream, and which he
had assisted the Local Board authorities to trace to the gas-works, and
showed them how to get rid of it. This showed he had no ill-feeling
against them when they were willing to act properly. It has been asked,
why were they not prosecuted? Perhaps it was not known how near they
had been to prosecution several times. He was not a public prosecutor, or
they would have been in his clutches long ago. With regard to the denial
of the statement that there had been an epidemic of typhoid fever, he
must say he never heard a more astounding statement. He held in his
hand the printed report stating the mortality, and no reference, even in a
note, to the fact of the epidemic, although it must have been known before
it was issued. An eminent medical man wrote as follows :—" In February
three cases of typhoid appeared in the district. Two of these cases were
imported, and I was aware of their presence. By the end of April
more than 200 cases were known to have occurred." That was signed
" Alfred Carpenter, M.D.," and by the end of June he reported 34 killed
and 400 arrested. Then it was said that for ten years up to that time
Croydon had been perfectly free from typhoid fever, but this he (Mr. Smee)
could show not to be the case by reference to the returns. With regard
to the penalty he suggested for not making proper returns of the cause
of death, he considered that absolutely necessary for the security of the
people. On one occasion, having reason to believe that cases of fever had
occurred, he inquired of the undertaker where the deaths were registered,
and found it was at Sutton; but on sending to obtain the information he
was told he would have to pay a fee of 2s. 6d. for every certificate, and
thus it would have cost him £40 to get the information he wanted. That
showed that the system required alteration. A gentleman then present
told him that a friend of his came from Australia, and looking upon
Croydon as a healthy place took lodgings there, took the fever, and was
now in his grave. With regard to the sewage being diluted, he referred
to the enormous quantity of water involved, which no one but an engineer

would have any idea of. One million gallons represented a height of 1,340 feet on an acre, or upwards of 4,000 feet for three millions, and dividing that over 400 acres it represented 120 inches per annum, which was so excessive that it must convert the land into a swamp. None of the Local Boards could see it in that light, but the birds soon found it out, as was proved by the quantity of snipe which visited it in the winter. If further proof were needed, he might mention that on the previous Saturday some thirty or more boys and girls were skating and sliding on the piece of ground where it was said the water was drained away in the most satisfactory manner. Again, it was said there was no putrid sewage at Croydon ; but every medical man knew that the poison of typhoid fever was far more effective in its fresh state, and he stated that the sewage passed over the land within ten hours, so that in less than a day the fæcal matter was in full bloom on the watercresses, tons and tons of which were grown and sent to London. On the table were two vessels filled, one with watercresses, and the other with grass, over which filthy sewage had been poured, and it would be seen that the water which flowed through was tolerably clear, showing that the feculent matter was arrested by the leaves and stalks of the vegetation, which was eaten, in one case by human beings, and in the other by animals. Then it was said that no one had suffered from the sewage farm, but extracts from the register would show the cause of death in the instances referred to. (See p. 385.) He had also obtained from Dr. Farr, at Somerset House, the following figures as to the deaths at Carshalton, and it was there you must look for the effects, not in Croydon itself :—

### Deaths at Carshalton.

|  | Deaths. | Scarlet Fever. | Fever. | Whooping Cough. |
|---|---|---|---|---|
| September quarter, 1875 ............ | 71 ...... | 11 ...... | 0 ...... | 4 |
| December 　　,, 　　,,　 ............ | 60 ...... | 8 ...... | 1 ...... | 1 |

### Croydon Sub-district.

|  |  | Zymotic. |
|---|---|---|
| June, 1875 ................................................ | 369 ............ | 60 |
| September, 1875 ......................................... | 359 ............ | 69 |

Mr. —— had reproduced statistics which he had shown to be fallacious on more than one occasion already, and in order that the matter might be properly understood he had obtained from an eminent actuary the following tables, the meaning of which would be explained by the correspondence :—

"7, Finsbury Circus, London, E.C.,
January 3rd, 1876.

"MY DEAR SIR,—It is a matter of public interest to know the rate of mortality which may be expected per thousand in the town of Croydon, where during the past year a great epidemic by typhoid fever has raged.

"If adequate materials exist for the calculation of an authoritative statement of the numbers at each age and of both sexes, I should be greatly obliged if you would calculate the expected number for me. It appears to me that they should be calculated on the results of the mortality of Surrey, that is to say, of the population of Extra-Metropolitan Surrey, which from its large amount will give satisfactory results; and I further think that we should make the comparative calculations for the same year that the ages were determined, as the only method which can give reliable results.

"Are there reliable data upon which similar calculations may be made with regard to Beddington parish, as it is of much public importance that a minute calculation should be made to compare the expected with the real results?

"I have the honour to be, my dear Sir,

"Yours very faithfully,

"ALFRED SMEE.

"F. A. CURTIS, Esq., F.I.A., Actuary to the
Gresham Life Assurance Society."

"The Gresham Life Assurance Society.
37, Old Jewry, E.C.
London, January 14th, 1876.

"MY DEAR SIR,—Adequate materials exist in the Census Report for 1871, and in the Registrar-General's Annual Report for the same year, to calculate the mortality which might be expected amongst the population of Croydon based on the mortality which occurred amongst the population of Extra-Metropolitan Surrey.

"I have the pleasure to enclose the result of the calculations, made for every year up to five years of age, for every five years up to twenty-five years of age, and subsequently for every ten years of age; but as the population of Croydon is included in the population returns of the Census with reference to Extra-Metropolitan Surrey, I have deemed it necessary for the purpose of a rigorous comparison to subtract from the population of Extra-Metropolitan Surrey the numbers of persons living and dying in the district of Croydon, by which it is shown that 56 more deaths at all ages occurred at Croydon in 1871 than might be expected from the mortality of Extra-Metropolitan Surrey. I have also calculated the mean mortality per thousand; the results will be seen in the accompanying tables.

"It is to be remarked that the mortality of the first years of infancy is greatly in excess at Croydon over that in the Surrey district.

"I am not aware that any materials exist for estimating the mortality in Beddington parish, as the Census reports do not distinguish the population of that locality from the population of Extra-Metropolitan Surrey, and the deaths are not given separately by the Registrar-General.

"It is proper to observe that as the deaths in Croydon town are conjoined with those of surrounding districts, it is probable that, if the returns of its suburban districts were subtracted from the returns under the head of 'Croydon,' so as to reduce the figures to those of the town proper, the deaths in Croydon would appear in still greater excess.

*" Comparative Mortality of Croydon and Extra-Metropolitan Surrey (with and without Croydon).*

## " MALES.

| Ages. | Croydon Deaths. | | | Actual Deaths per 1000. | | |
|---|---|---|---|---|---|---|
| | Actual. | Estimated on Surrey Mortality. | | Croydon. | Surrey. | |
| | | With Croydon. | Without Croydon. | | With Croydon. | Without Croydon. |
| 0 | 231 | 195 | 184 | 188·0 | 158·6 | 149·7 |
| 1 | 52 | 44 | 42 | 48·2 | 40·9 | 38·7 |
| 2 | 14 | 20 | 22 | 11·9 | 17·3 | 19·1 |
| 3 | 15 | 13 | 13 | 14·0 | 12·4 | 11·9 |
| 4 | 15 | 13 | 12 | 14·0 | 12·0 | 11·4 |
| 5— 9 | 26 | 30 | 31 | 5·3 | 6·0 | 6·2 |
| 10—14 | 13 | 17 | 18 | 3·1 | 3·9 | 4·2 |
| 15—24 | 39 | 37 | 37 | 6·4 | 6·1 | 6·1 |
| 25—34 | 56 | 60 | 61 | 9·8 | 10·5 | 10·6 |
| 35—44 | 60 | 64 | 65 | 13·8 | 14·8 | 15·0 |
| 45—54 | 51 | 56 | 57 | 16·5 | 18·1 | 18·6 |
| 55—64 | 61 | 59 | 59 | 33·4 | 32·4 | 32·2 |
| 65—74 | 50 | 59 | 61 | 48·8 | 57·5 | 59·5 |
| 75—84 | 56 | 56 | 56 | 151·8 | 151·9 | 152·0 |
| 85—94 | 13 | 13 | 14 | 282·6 | 292·0 | 294·1 |
| 95 | .. | .. | .. | .. | .. | .. |
| | 752 | 736 | 732 | 20·2 | 19·6 | 19·5 |

## " FEMALES.

| Ages. | Croydon Deaths. | | | Actual Deaths per 1000. | | |
|---|---|---|---|---|---|---|
| | Actual. | Estimated on Surrey Mortality. | | Croydon. | Surrey. | |
| | | With Croydon. | Without Croydon. | | With Croydon. | Without Croydon. |
| 0 | 202 | 148 | 131 | 163·3 | 119·3 | 105·5 |
| 1 | 45 | 38 | 36 | 40·8 | 34·3 | 32·3 |
| 2 | 22 | 20 | 20 | 18·9 | 17·4 | 16·9 |
| 3 | 21 | 13 | 11 | 18·7 | 11·6 | 9·4 |
| 4 | 20 | 13 | 11 | 18·9 | 12·1 | 10·1 |
| 5— 9 | 26 | 31 | 32 | 5·2 | 6·2 | 6·5 |
| 10—14 | 24 | 20 | 19 | 5·2 | 4·4 | 4·1 |
| 15—24 | 42 | 46 | 48 | 4·3 | 4·7 | 4·9 |
| 25—34 | 51 | 55 | 56 | 6·4 | 6·9 | 7·1 |
| 35—44 | 38 | 57 | 64 | 6·9 | 10·4 | 11·6 |
| 45—54 | 41 | 51 | 54 | 11·3 | 14·1 | 14·9 |
| 55—64 | 78 | 62 | 58 | 32·1 | 25·7 | 23·8 |
| 65—74 | 65 | 77 | 81 | 46·4 | 55·1 | 57·6 |
| 75—84 | 63 | 69 | 71 | 127·3 | 139·7 | 143·0 |
| 85—94 | 23 | 23 | 23 | 359·4 | 366·3 | 364·6 |
| 95 | .. | 1 | 1 | .. | 625·0 | 714·3 |
| | 761 | 724 | 716 | 16·3 | 16·4 | 16·4 |

"MALES AND FEMALES.

| Ages. | Croydon Deaths. | | | Actual Deaths per 1000. | | |
|---|---|---|---|---|---|---|
| | Actual. | Estimated on Surrey Mortality. | | Croydon. | Surrey. | |
| | | With Croydon. | Without Croydon. | | With Croydon. | Without Croydon. |
| 0 | 433 | 343 | 315 | 175·6 | 139·1 | 127·7 |
| 1 | 97 | 82 | 78 | 44·4 | 37·6 | 35·5 |
| 2 | 36 | 41 | 42 | 15·4 | 17·4 | 18·0 |
| 3 | 36 | 26 | 23 | 16·4 | 12·0 | 10·6 |
| 4 | 35 | 26 | 23 | 16·4 | 12·1 | 10·7 |
| 5— 9 | 52 | 61 | 64 | 5·2 | 6·1 | 6·4 |
| 10—14 | 37 | 36 | 36 | 4·2 | 4·1 | 4·1 |
| 15—24 | 81 | 86 | 87 | 5·1 | 5·4 | 5·5 |
| 25—34 | 107 | 117 | 120 | 7·8 | 8·6 | 8·8 |
| 35—44 | 98 | 123 | 131 | 10·0 | 12·5 | 13·3 |
| 45—54 | 92 | 107 | 112 | 13·7 | 16·0 | 16·7 |
| 55—64 | 139 | 123 | 119 | 32·7 | 28·9 | 27·9 |
| 65—74 | 115 | 136 | 142 | 47·4 | 56·2 | 58·5 |
| 75—84 | 119 | 125 | 127 | 137·7 | 145·2 | 147·1 |
| 85—94 | 36 | 37 | 37 | 327·3 | 333·3 | 334·7 |
| 95 | .. | 1 | 1 | .. | 777·8 | 875·0 |
| | 1,513 | 1,470 | 1,457 | 18·0 | 18·0 | 17·9 |

"Comparison of Deaths from various causes in Croydon, and in Extra-Metropolitan Surrey (excluding Croydon).

| Causes of Death. | Actual Deaths. | | | Estimated Deaths for Croydon based on Extra-Metropolitan Surrey, excluding Croydon. | Difference of Croydon Actual Deaths on Estimated Deaths. | |
|---|---|---|---|---|---|---|
| | Extra-Metropolitan Surrey. | Croydon. | Extra-Metropolitan Surrey, excluding Croydon. | | + | — |
| Small-pox | 184 | 81 | 103 | 31 | 50 | .. |
| Measles | 83 | 27 | 56 | 17 | 10 | .. |
| Scarlet fever | 220 | 41 | 179 | 53 | .. | 12 |
| Diphtheria | 37 | 5 | 32 | 10 | .. | 5 |
| Whooping cough | 86 | 41 | 45 | 13 | 28 | .. |
| Typhus fever | 13 | .. | 13 | 4 | .. | 4 |
| Enteric or typhoid fever | 119 | 30 | 89 | 27 | 3 | .. |
| Simple continued fever | 33 | 5 | 28 | 8 | .. | 3 |
| Erysipelas | 46 | 4 | 42 | 13 | .. | 9 |
| Metria or puerperal fever | 18 | 5 | 13 | 4 | 1 | .. |
| Childbirth | 34 | 12 | 22 | 7 | 5 | .. |
| Influenza | 7 | .. | 7 | 2 | .. | 2 |
| Dysentery | 13 | 4 | 9 | 3 | 1 | .. |
| Diarrhœa | 311 | 88 | 223 | 66 | 22 | .. |
| Cholera | 4 | 1 | 3 | 1 | .. | .. |
| Phthisis or consumption | 757 | 159 | 598 | 178 | .. | 19 |
| Diseases of respiratory organs | 956 | 219 | 737 | 220 | .. | 1 |
| Violence | 186 | 36 | 150 | 45 | .. | 9 |
| Inquests | 323 | 48 | 275 | 82 | .. | 34 |

"The population in the district of Croydon is very nearly three-tenths of the population of Extra-Metropolitan Surrey, exclusive of that of Croydon. Therefore, the deaths returned in Extra-Metropolitan Surrey, after deducting the deaths returned for the Croydon district, would be the basis for the estimates of death that should occur in the population of Croydon, upon the assumption of an equal rate of mortality. I subjoin a nosological table of mortality.

"Believe me to be, my dear Sir, yours faithfully,

"F. A. CURTIS.

"ALFRED SMEE, Esq., F.R.S.,
　　"7, Finsbury Circus, E.C."

When Mr. —— spoke of the Female Orphan Asylum, he conveyed the idea that no injury had been caused to its inmates, but the fact was, they had had sixty cases of fever and three deaths; and though he could not say these were caused by the milk, because he had not investigated the cases, it was a curious fact that the more milk the patients drank the worse they became, and on one occasion a tadpole was found in it. A specimen of hay had been produced, but he had no hesitation in saying that it was not a fair sample, because on passing his fingers over it he found no sewage excreta adhering to it, as he had done when he had taken a sample from the stack himself. With regard to the roots, he acknowledged that if the ground were properly turned over, roots might be found fit for use, though not so good as those treated in the ordinary way. He had seen the sewage overflow into Beddington Park, even since he read the paper, and had got the park-keeper to measure the distance, 19 poles; in fact, a deep drain was now being made to prevent it. No one had really opposed his proposals except Mr. Addy, who said that if they were adopted sewage farms could not be carried on; but if they could not, without encroaching on their neighbours' rights, the sooner they were stopped, in his opinion, the better. He said it would be very inconvenient; and in the same way some people thought it inconvenient that they were not permitted to pick other persons' pockets. He had as much right to be protected against injury from sewage as against petty theft, which was of much less real importance; and, no doubt, he could protect himself by Chancery proceedings, but they were difficult and expensive. Mr. Botly spoke of the violets grown at Aldershot; he could only say that if they were grown under sewage irrigation, the officers must have presented to their ladies much which they never bargained for; but the mystery was cleared up by a succeeding speaker, who said that the sewage went on the farm two days a week, and the remaining five through a pipe direct into the watercourse. If that statement were confirmed, the sooner all such farms were put under stringent regulations and regular inspection the better. The following table would show the difference between the pure water from the Croydon wells and the effluent sewage from the farms:—

*Croydon Well.*

| | |
|---|---|
| Common salt | 2·00 |
| Nitrogen oxide | 0·018 |
| Ammonia | 0·003 |
| Organic matter | 0·001 |

*Effluent Sewage every quarter of an hour.*

| | |
|---|---|
| Salt | 3·400 |
| Nitrogen | 0·419 |
| Ammonia | 0·032 |
| Organic matter | 0·144 |

*Sewage towns, Norwood and Beddington.*

Organic carbon
and nitrogen.

| | |
|---|---|
| Minimum | 0·114 per gallon. |
| Maximum | 1·786    „ |
| Average | 0·821    „ |

The Royal Commissioners said, " We unhesitatingly condemn the whole of them as dangerous and totally unfit for drinking." Average Thames water was much better than this, only containing an average of ·021 organic carbon and nitrogen, whilst rain-water contained ·084. The effluent system at Croydon was an abomination; the effluents were very difficult to trace, but he had reason to believe that not being protected by notice-boards persons might drink of the water unwittingly. In conclusion, he hoped the discussion, which had been taken up with such earnestness by so many leading engineers, and which would be read very widely, would not be wasted, but that before long the sewage question would be settled in a more satisfactory way than it was at present, especially at Croydon.

LONDON: PRINTED BY WILLIAM CLOWES AND SONS, STAMFORD STREET
AND CHARING CROSS.

www.ingramcontent.com/pod-product-compliance
Lightning Source LLC
Chambersburg PA
CBHW030939110726
47900CB00004B/1057